EILEEN MUELLER

DRAGON STRIKE

RIDERS OF FIRE

BOOK FOUR

PROLOGUE

The moon slunk out from behind dark clouds, scattering a broken shaft of silver on the waves crashing against the shore. Bruno held tight to the raft carrying his son and dead wife, kicking through the cursed water to angle it toward the moonlight—although it was hardly a welcoming beacon guiding him home. He tested the depth, his boot barely scraping sand. Fangs and bleeding teeth, it was too deep to gain a foothold. And his legs were so numb it was a miracle he could even feel the ocean floor. He kicked the raft closer to land, so weak his efforts were as pathetic as a littling's.

His foot struck the ocean floor. And again. He slid off the raft, staggered, and shoved it on the inflowing tide. But as the tide ebbed, dragging the raft out, he stumbled and it hit him, knocking him under the flimsy platform, the ocean's claws dragging his wife and son back out to sea.

Bruno thrashed, rolled out from under the raft. He swam alongside it and clutched at his son, shaking him awake. "Simeon, help," he croaked, throat raw and parched.

His son's bleary eyes fluttered and closed again. Gods, no. Not so close to land, only to lose him too.

A wave crested, splashing Simeon's face. He stirred.

Bruno shook Simeon again. "We're here. Help."

Simeon grunted and slid into the water. They kicked until they were waist-deep. Leaning their backs against the raft holding Fleur, they pushed until they drove the nose of the rickety raft into the sand above the tide's reach. The front of the raft splintered. Fleur's arm flopped onto the sand.

Bruno collapsed, panting, on the damp grit. Simeon fell down beside him. Pale foam hissed around their ankles.

They were home.

§

Bruno woke in darkness, wracked with shivers, and clambered to his feet. He helped Simeon up the beach to a clump of towering grass with long fluffy stalks. Here, Simeon would be more sheltered from the wind.

He trudged back to the raft, its end bobbing on lapping wavelets, and hoisted Fleur into his arms. Her face was pale in the moonlight, her beautiful lips now leached, and her glassy eyes empty. Bruno's throat grew tight. Fleur had survived rust vipers, deadly scorpions and the cursed endless orange sand of the Wastelands, only to die at sea a day from Dragons' Realm. He and Simeon had watched her slip away right before their eyes. All he'd been able to do was keep kicking toward land.

That stinkin' Roberto and the Queen's Rider had sealed Fleur's fate by banishing them. He'd bide his time, get strong again, and hunt them down.

He laid Fleur in the grass next to Simeon. His son was moaning, shivering. Unless Bruno was quick, he'd be burying both members of his family. Hopefully there was a village nearby where he could find food and water. Two days ago he'd given their last precious sips to Fleur. It hadn't been enough to save her.

"Back soon, Son."

So dizzy he could hardly stand, Bruno grabbed a stick of driftwood, and, leaning on it, limped along the coast toward a lone twinkling light. He had to stop regularly to catch his breath.

Soon he reached a road and some isolated houses. Fishing nets drying on lines glimmered like webs in the moonlight. Boats bobbed on the waves, moored to sturdy posts by thick ropes, their furled sails as pale as Fleur's face. How he'd love to take one of those ropes, tie it around Roberto's scrawny neck and choke the life out of him. No, that would be much too quick. He'd make the shrotty Master of Mental Faculties suffer. Or Zens would. Bruno grimaced. That'd be an unpleasant end, tortured at the hands of the Commander. But he'd never do that. Bruno relished the job too much to let anyone else make Roberto scream as they peeled his skin off his pretty face.

The light he'd seen was a torch burning in a sconce on a large outbuilding on the outskirts of a township. It was the dead of night, and no one was around. Bruno edged toward the building. Warmth radiated from its open double doors. A giant horseshoe hung over the lintel. What luck. A smithy, with the forge still glowing.

Bruno crept inside.

He shambled over to the orange embers on the forge, holding out his numb hands. Around the forge were stacks of tools, horseshoes, and weapons in racks. At the other end of the building were a huge metal tub and several washboards. A line hung over them, strung with drying clothes. The blacksmith's wife obviously ran a laundry from here, using the heat to speed the drying.

Bruno limped over, discarded his sodden, tattered clothing and pulled on a fresh shirt and breeches, tying the waist with a short length of rope. After nothing but desert rations and water for weeks, he was skinnier than the handle on the smithy's bellows. He huddled by the fire for a moment, but he knew he had to hurry. Every moment he lingered could cost Simeon his life. Besides, he wanted to bury Fleur before morning—before any nosy snoops started asking difficult questions. The last thing he needed was an overzealous dragon rider shipping him and Simeon back to the Wastelands.

Bruno found an empty sack in a corner with Naobian Salt stamped on it. Was he outside the Naobian township? That'd be a stroke of luck. Naobia was the main port and largest city in the south. They could've run ashore near any of the tiny villages that dotted the Naobian coast. Or hit a patch of wilderness and been stranded.

He shoved a spare set of clothes, spade, knife and dagger into the sack. Then he scooped some coals into a small metal bucket, darted out of the smithy and tucked his new possessions under a hedge. He added a horse blanket from a neighbor's fence to his stash.

A few houses closer to town, he plucked some oranges from a branch hanging over a wall and stuffed them in his pockets. His nose led him to a smokehouse, so he sneaked inside and stole a few fish and snatched a waterskin from a hook on the door. He slurped the water greedily down his raw throat until his belly was distended.

The next moment, he was retching behind a bush over someone's low garden wall.

Inside the house, a dog barked. A candle flickered behind curtains, and a woman called, "Who's there?"

Bruno ducked behind the wall and crawled away, nearly losing one of the oranges from his pocket. When he was out of sight, he scurried along the road and retrieved his loot. With the sack and blanket slung across his back, cradling the coal bucket against him for warmth, he hurried back to Simeon, this time, sipping cautiously from the waterskin.

It was still dark when he shook Simeon awake. They needed to be quick or someone would catch them burying Fleur.

Simeon dressed in dry clothes and drank a little water while Bruno peeled an orange and passed it to him. His son bit into it, groaning at the tang of the sweet, tart flesh. "Oh, that's good." Leaning back on his elbows, he took another bite. "Never thought I'd be grateful for oranges again." His eyes were sunken and his cheeks gaunt.

Not as bad as Fleur's. Bruno averted his eyes from her. "True." He nodded. They'd survived the Wastelands by stumbling upon a seaside oasis. They'd eaten only dates and oranges for three days before gathering up supplies and making a raft out of palm trunks bound with fronds.

Bruno piled up some dry sticks and fluffy grass, tipped some coals onto them, and blew to spark the embers into flame.

"Wait here, Son." He took the spade and headed farther inland to the high bluffs that overlooked Naobia. Then he started digging a grave for his wife.

A tear slid down Bruno's face—the first he'd cried for Fleur. Until now, he'd been too dehydrated for tears.

§

Unocco stretched his wings and took off over the basin at Dragons' Hold. In the dim starlight, the snow-tipped fangs of Dragon's Teeth pierced the sky above him, hemming him in. A fierce ache was building in his chest. Had been for days. Restless energy danced inside him. He wanted to soar, to fly until he dropped.

"Are you out roaming the night again?" Ajeurina mind-melded. *"You can't be hungry. You fed a few hours ago."*

Unocco glanced down at the southern caverns where Ajeurina would be huddled on the ledge. It was too dark to see her, but he could imagine her beautiful jade scales. She'd be curled in the back corner, her tail up over her haunch, leaving space for him to nestle against her, should he choose to join her.

But his aching chest wouldn't be soothed by sleeping, even next to his mate. He soared higher and higher, climbing the side of Heaven's Peak, his wingbeats setting snow tumbling down the mountainside.

"Watch out, you'll start an avalanche." She hesitated. *"You're missing Bruno, aren't you?"*

The pang in his chest grew. There it was—his pain laid bare. *"Of course not,"* Unocco lied. *"Why would I miss a rider who implanted me with an evil crystal?"*

He snorted, hoping to convince Ajeurina that he didn't care about losing his rider—that there was no aching hole inside him.

"Imprinting with another rider will help you. The pain of Fleur's betrayal was almost too much to bear." Ajeurina's sorrow cascaded over him, deepening the hurt in his breast. Then she sent a new feeling, a keen excitement that quivered at the edge of his mind. *"Meeting Lovina healed my heart. Please, Unocco, give another rider a chance. There are many fine candidates who need a steady, loyal dragon like you."*

Ajeurina was right. He was steady and loyal. And although Bruno had mistreated him in the last few years, Unocco had fond memories of when Bruno was younger. Sure, he'd been tough, a rebel at heart, but Unocco had tamed him, harnessed that wild energy inside him. They'd fought valiantly together. Been the closest of friends.

Even when Zens had turned them.

But surely, now that Bruno had been banished with his family to the Wastelands … surely now, he'd had a change of heart.

Unocco wheeled in midair over the top of the mountain, the scar under his wing where Zens had implanted that awful crystal twinging. Thankfully, the terrible dark shadows and whispering voices in his mind were gone. He owed Marlies for extracting that shrotty crystal.

And yes—now that his mind was his own and he could think clearly—he missed Bruno. But what if his rider were dead? Or alive but still corrupted by Zens, still fighting the queen and the realm?

Unocco had tamed Bruno's wild tendencies before. He could do it again—if his rider still lived.

Before he gave himself to another rider, he had to know if Bruno was alive and could be saved. Unocco turned south toward the Wastelands. The savage pain in his breast eased.

Without another word to Ajeurina, he soared into the night.

§

Three days in Naobia, a few sleights of hand at the market, and some stealthy late night excursions had provided Bruno and Simeon with adequate supplies—and some luxuries. High on a bluff above the beach, Bruno lowered the far-seers and wriggled back on his belly to join Simeon. "I was right. It was them I saw yesterday," he said. "The Queen's Rider and Roberto are down there, dancing on the sand without a care in the world."

"So that sharding, arrogant shrot-heap got the girl," Simeon snarled. "I should've taken her when I had the chance."

Bruno sniggered. "A fine thing that would be: your seed in the belly of the Queen's Rider." He scratched the scraggly beard he'd grown since he'd been banished to the Wastelands. "Good idea, Son. Let's arrange that. We'll bide our time, strike when their dragons are gone. When you've taken your fill of the girl, she'll make good shark fodder."

Simeon grinned, eyes glinting.

Good. That had put a bit of color into his son's cheeks. Gods knew they both needed something after that awful orange hell, the tragic raft trip and burying poor Fleur in a shallow grave. Someone had to pay for her death. Why not Roberto and that snivelly girl?

Naobia

Ezaara and Roberto strolled through the Naobian marketplace, his sun-warmed arm around her waist. The market teemed with life, its vibrant colors clamoring for her attention. The scent of lilies and orchids battled with the mouth-watering aroma of roasted pecans and peach pastries. Exquisite fabric cascaded over stalls. Hawkers cried over the crowd's babble and littlings' laughter. Bright strings of glass beads, spices in tiny pots, wolves carved from honeyed wood, pretty glass vases—there was so much to see.

People here dressed differently, too. In Lush Valley and Dragons' Hold garments were functional, except for at ceremonies. Naobian clothing was beautiful. The crowd seethed with orange Robandi Desert garb, embroidered traditional costumes and bright billowing robes. And their jewelry. Ezaara had never seen so much finery in one place.

"What are these?" she asked, pointing to some earrings on a jeweler's stand.

Roberto leaned in, smiling. "Jewel beetles. Littlings find their brightly-colored shells in nearby caves and sell them to jewelers. When we were small, Adelina and I collected them with Pa to earn coin." A shadow flitted across his face.

Whenever Roberto mentioned his father, Amato, pain flickered in his eyes. He'd said some scars ran far too deep for forgiveness.

Ezaara squeezed his hand. Gods, she'd do anything to erase that pain. To make his ebony eyes light up. Despite recent troubles at Dragons' Hold, these few short days on their hand-fasting holiday had been blissful.

He brushed her hair with his lips, sliding his arm up to her shoulders. She leaned into him, his warmth seeping through her.

"Look." Ezaara picked up an earring. The beetle's shell was luminous turquoise, crisscrossed with tiny silver veins. No wonder the jewelers coveted them. "It's not just their stunning colors," she murmured. "It's the way the shells wink in the sunlight that's pretty." She set the earring down, admiring a necklace of amber shells.

"The jade ones are my favorite," Roberto said. "They remind me of Naobia's verdant hills. When I was living in Death Valley, I tried to remember those hills every day." The muscles in his jaw rippled.

No matter where they went or what they did, shadows dogged their pasts. Ezaara shuddered. "By the First Egg, I hope we never end up back there."

"Today we'll make new memories." He smiled. "Why don't you look around while I organize a picnic? I'll meet you by the sea dragon fountain in an hour."

Ezaara knew the one. They'd passed it on their walk here. Guarding one of the myriad entrances to the marketplace, it was a writhing tangle of long-bodied serpents with water cascading out of their crystal maws. "A whole hour? Are you baking the food yourself?"

He laughed, the rumble in his chest pleasant against her shoulder. "No, I'm just fetching you a little surprise." He squeezed her hand, dark eyes dancing. "When our dragons come back, we'll go to Crystal Lake, where Adelina and I used to swim. "

Their dragons, Zaarusha and Erob, were flying along the coast to stretch their wings and feed on fish.

"Sounds lovely."

Roberto kissed Ezaara, really kissed her, right on the lips in the middle of the marketplace. She blushed, remembering the bed they now shared. "A picnic sounds perfect."

"See you soon." His cheeky grin made him years younger.

Ezaara's gaze lingered on Roberto's strong back as he made his way through the crowd past a mage lighting sticks that shot colored stars into the stark-blue sky. *"Those are pretty,"* she mind-melded. *"I'd heard of Naobian fire-sticks, but never seen one."*

Littlings gathered gleefully, hands up for sticks as the mage pocketed their coppers. He waved them into a side alley so they wouldn't fire their stars at market goers.

"I'll buy a couple to take with us," Roberto melded. He passed the mage a few coppers and tucked the fire-sticks in his rucksack.

Next to the mage's stand was an herbalist with bunches of herbs hanging from ropes above her stall. Vials, jars and pouches spilled over the elderly woman's rickety stand. Ezaara needed to check if the herbalist had any of the valuable remedies that Ma was running short of at Dragons' Hold.

"See you soon." A rush of warmth enveloped Ezaara with Roberto's thoughts. He waved, walked past a green guard sitting atop a jade dragon, and disappeared down a street on the far side of the marketplace.

How had she ever lived without him or Zaarusha? She was so full of sunshine, she wanted to burst out of her skin. And it wasn't just the climate in Naobia. Her past was a pale reflection of her vibrant life now.

Ezaara pushed her way through the crowd, side-stepping a boy leading a goat, and making her way past cloth decorated with dragons. There was blue, embroidered with gold and green dragons chasing each other; and black with bronze, silver and red swooping dragons. Her breath caught. The black cloth was the same as Old Bill had shown her in the marketplace the day she'd imprinted with Zaarusha in Lush Valley. That scrap had been contraband in the backward valley where her parents had hidden their family. When she'd seen it, she hadn't even known if dragons were real.

More fabric, studded with dragons, spilled over the stall: dragons blasting fire; soaring; dragonets with fledgling wings; even dragons sleeping. They were exquisitely detailed. She feasted on the sight, her hand reaching for her coin pouch. Hang on, she was Ezaara, Queen's Rider, and Ma was master healer. She had a duty to the realm. Maybe later, after she'd purchased vital healing supplies. With a lingering glance, she pushed her way forward to the herb stand.

Ezaara scanned the remedies cluttering the stall but there was no piaua juice. Drumming her fingers on the table, she waited while the white-haired woman measured powder into a vial for a boy and pressed it into his hands, refusing payment. "Wish your Ma a speedy recovery," she said with a strong Naobian accent.

At last she turned to Ezaara. "How can I help?" she asked.

"I'm looking for piaua juice. Do you have any?"

The herbalist's shrewd dark eyes flicked over Ezaara. "No, our last tree speaker died three months ago. What little juice we have is with the healer, not for sale." Ma was a tree speaker, too, one of the privileged few who could harvest juice from the mighty piaua trees.

Most of the other herbs and powders at the market looked familiar, but there were some Ezaara had never seen. "What's that?" Ezaara asked, pointing to a jar of ocher powder.

"Eases aching bones and pains," the old woman answered.

"And this?" Ezaara held up a jar of tiny black granules.

"A strengthening tonic for expecting mothers." The crone flashed a gap-ridden grin. "You'll be needing that. I hear you're on your hand-fasting holiday with our Master Roberto, curse his rotten father." Her gaze drifted to Ezaara's belly and she cackled gleefully.

Oh gods, the woman knew who she was. Might have even seen her kissing Roberto. How mortifying. "Ah, no, thank you."

"Perhaps a contraceptive tonic then." Her voice rose with glee. People were staring at Ezaara now. The crone gave vulgar wink. "Having lots of fun?" she crowed.

A woman behind Ezaara tittered. A couple of men guffawed.

"You must be," the herbalist continued. "It's far too hot here to wear much at night." She thrust the tonic at Ezaara, the blood-red liquid sloshing in its bottle.

"I don't need a tonic, thank you." Cheeks hideously hot, Ezaara stalked through the crowd, chin high, the crone's laughter chasing her.

A ragged boy pulled at her sleeve. "I heard what she said, I did."

Speechless, Ezaara stared at the littling.

"I mean about piaua juice. She's wrong, she is. I know where you can buy some. Come." He pointed to a narrow winding alley, shrouded in shadow.

She wasn't falling for that. "I'm fine thank you." She pressed a copper into his hands. "Here, buy something nice to eat."

The littling pocketed her copper, but kept tugging her sleeve. "Come with me. Get some piaua juice. Finest quality, I promise."

Ezaara snorted. Piaua juice didn't have various grades. "No, thank you. Now, be on your way."

But the boy didn't let go. She couldn't really pull her sword on the littling, could she? Not as the Queen's Rider, here in the middle of a marketplace.

"I got piaua, I do." He gave her a practiced winsome grin, the little scam artist. "Come with me."

"Excuse me," said a cloaked man wearing an orange Robandi headdress that covered most of his face. His accent was Northern, similar to hers. He addressed the littling, "There are only two suppliers of piaua in Naobia, young rascal, and you're not one of them. Unless you want to feel the point of my sword, I suggest you leave this visitor to our fair town alone."

Eyes wide, the boy dropped her sleeve and fled.

"Thank you," Ezaara said.

"My pleasure." The man smiled, the skin around his eyes creasing. Although his skin was tan, it wasn't as dark as a true Robandi's—not Robandi or Naobian, then, but someone who'd lived here for a while and adjusted to the local customs.

A littling ran past, sparks shooting from her magic stick as she darted for the alley.

The man strode off.

Ezaara followed him. "Um, excuse me, but you said there were two sources of piaua here in Naobia."

He turned. "Yes, the healer has some, and I have a limited supply in my store."

"Can I buy some?" Ma was so terribly short.

He tilted his head. "I'm afraid it's not for sale." He stalked through the crowd.

This might be her only chance. Ezaara ran after him. "I have coin. We need piaua at Dragons' Hold."

"Dragons' Hold?" He turned and scanned her face with narrowed eyes. "Maybe I'd better fetch you some, then."

Ezaara hesitated, poised on a knife's edge. She probably shouldn't stray too far from the marketplace, but she and Ma had saved enough lives with piaua juice to know it was essential. She might not have this chance again. "I'll come with you," she said.

With a brief nod, the man spun, cloak swirling, and strode through the alley. It was an odd combination, the Northern cloak to keep out the cold and the Robandi headdress against the heat. She shrugged. She'd lived most of her life in Lush Valley and had a lot to learn about customs and traditions, so who was she to question his garb?

Fire-sticks fizzed and popped as bursts of gold and green stars shot above the man's head through the dim alley. He waved a hand, clearing a path through the littlings. Ezaara tagged along behind him, staring at the pretty display of mage fire, the gleeful littlings shrieking and oohing.

They turned a corner into a shady alley, leaving the littlings behind. A beggar called out. Ezaara threw him a coin and he shoved it into a tattered pocket. A brawny man was towering over a scrawny lad in a doorway, ice in his eyes. They stilled, not finishing their conversation until Ezaara had passed. Sounds of a scuffle came from the mouth of a narrow adjoining alley. Ezaara hurried to walk level with the man, her hand hovering near her sword.

Although the man's mouth was covered with the desert headdress, his eyes crinkled in a smile. "Just in here." He gestured to an alley barely wide enough for two horses to walk astride. Beyond the shadows, a shaft of sunlight lit up a stone wall, a dead end. Good, there wasn't far to go now. She'd be back to the market in no time. She stepped into the alley.

A figure leaped from the shadows, slamming her back into a wall. A flash of blond hair. The slash of a white toothy smile. Simeon—his skin was darker, cheeks gaunt and hair bleached by the sun, but it was him. He clenched her throat.

Ezaara gurgled.

He rammed her head against the stone with a crack.

Skull throbbing, Ezaara cried out, but her yell was cut off as the man in the headdress shoved bitter-tasting berries into her mouth.

A blade pricked her throat. "Chew," Simeon barked.

Ezaara spat the berries in his face.

Purple juice and berry skin splattered Simeon's nose and cheek. A memory flashed to mind of Ma setting farmer Orsin's leg, back in Lush Valley. He'd thrashed so much she'd given him purple swakberries to make his muscles go slack. Her tongue tingled. Her lower lip was going numb. Gods, no, they were swakberries.

Ezaara spat again and drove her knee toward Simeon's groin. But Simeon twisted away, letting go of her.

"Rough her up, Son," the man goaded. "Have a little fun."

Bruno—Simeon's father. He'd lured her here, disguised in his headdress and cloak. Probably bribed the boy, too, that gut-swiving scum. She kicked out, her foot striking Bruno's thigh.

Bruno punched her in the belly, winding her. Ezaara gasped and drew her sword.

Simeon slammed his body into hers.

She fell, Simeon's body pinning her to the ground. Her sword clattered across the cobbles.

"Quick, father, more berries," he hissed.

The two men were bigger and stronger than her, so she had to use her head. She wouldn't open her mouth. Couldn't let herself be rendered useless by swakberries.

"So, you snooty little cow, I've finally got you where I want you." Simeon leered, yanking her hair.

Her eyes smarted. Still, she clenched her teeth.

Simeon snarled. His knife pricked her throat. "Open your shrotty little mouth."

Blood trickled down her neck and around the back of her riders' garb. He pinched her nose. She couldn't breathe. Her lungs burned. She thrashed her legs and head, trying to buck Simeon off. She grew dizzy. Tried to twist her head away. Still, he squeezed her nostrils shut.

Laughing, Bruno knelt on the cobbles beside her. "Thought you'd get the better of us, did you?" He wrenched her mouth open with his dirty hands.

Ezaara gasped a quick breath and tried to clench her teeth again, but Bruno shoved a foul-tasting finger in her mouth. She bit him. Hard.

Bruno yelped and backhanded her face. "I'll fix you!" He rose, narrowing his eyes. "Actually, Son, I'll show you how to quieten the feisty ones without laying a finger on 'em." He stalked off.

Cheek stinging, Ezaara thrust her knee up and tried to roll over, but she couldn't dislodge Simeon.

"Stupid girl. You could've had me instead of that son of a traitor. But no, even though both my parents are masters, I wasn't good enough for you."

Ezaara spat in his face. "Dragon-swiving s-scum." That idiot Simeon had tried to poison her at Dragons' Hold. He was the traitor, not Roberto.

Bruno dragged a pale, shaking littling girl into the alley. The fire-stick in her white-knuckled grip sputtered a lone gold star, then died. Bruno palmed a blade from his sleeve like a street fighter, and held it to the girl's throat. "Eat the berries, Ezaara, or the littling dies."

He wouldn't, would he?

She wouldn't put it past him. He and his wife, Fleur, had murdered dragon masters, drugged their own dragons, and teamed with tharuks to enslave the people of Dragons' Realm.

"Need some convincing?" Bruno pressed the knife, making the girl cry as it pierced her delicate skin. Droplets of blood ran down his blade.

Ezaara opened her mouth.

Simeon shoved berries between her lips and clamped her jaw shut, holding it with his hands.

Bruno threatened the girl. "I'm letting you go, but if you say a word, I'll hunt you down and kill you."

"Y-yes." Without a backward glance, she ran off.

Ezaara didn't blame her.

"Chew, stupid cow. Chew," Simeon snarled.

She didn't. But the berry skins dissolved anyway, tingling on her tongue. The pulp slid down her throat, making it burn. Heat spread through her like wildfire, setting her limbs ablaze.

"That's how you get the spirited ones to cooperate." Bruno smirked. "Now hurry, Son. Test her."

Simeon raised a dagger above his head, the blade angled toward her heart. He smiled, teeth glinting. And thrust down.

The dagger plunged toward her. Ezaara raised her arm but it flopped clum-sily against his. She pushed with her legs, but her thighs spasmed and twitched, her legs sprawling at strange angles.

Simeon held the dagger over her, laughing. "Yes, you're woozier than a drun-ken pirate." He pulled her to her feet. "Let's see you walk."

She swayed and staggered, careening into the wall. Grateful for the stone, she leaned against it.

"Ha, look at you now, fancy Queen's Rider," Simeon jeered.

Ezaara snatched at her hip but her sword still lay on the cobbles, too far to reach. Her fingers were clumsy, awkward. The two men laughed at her as she fumbled with both hands to pull her dagger from its sheath and held it in front of her. Her arms convulsed. The dagger swayed and bucked, as if it had a mind of its own.

Knife out, Simeon lunged. Ezaara swung to deflect it, but missed his blade completely, the motion pulling her off balance.

Bruno grinned. "Be quick, those berries won't last long."

He was right. Farmer Orsin had barely held still long enough for Ma to straighten the bone and Ezaara to hastily splint it. If she could hold Simeon off for long enough, she'd soon have control of her limbs again. And what did Bruno mean by *be quick*?

"W-what do y-you want?" Her tongue was thick and fuzzy, wouldn't form words. Flame it, her blade was so heavy, her arms so weak. Her jaw grew slack and her knees faltered. She slid down the wall and slumped on the cobbles.

"Father, drag her over here where I can see her pretty face." Simeon laughed, stalking into a patch of sun at the alley's end. "I want to see *everything* Roberto's seen."

"That's my boy. You take after your father."

Ice slithered into Ezaara's veins. Simeon had tried to force himself on her once, but she and Gret had fought him off. But now, no one knew where she was. She tried to lift her arm, but it flopped around like a dying fish. Bruno dragged her by the legs, her head thudding a tattoo over every cobble. She could barely move her arms. The only thing she could use was her mind.

Maybe she could distract them. "S-so S-Simeon, clever y-you survived the Wastelands. H-how?"

Oh gods, she was a fool. She still had her *mind*! Desperately, she flung out her consciousness, trying to mind-meld, *"Roberto!"*

No answer. Were their dragons close enough to hear her? *"Zaarusha, Erob, help!"*

Bruno dumped her in a pile at Simeon's feet.

The sun glared high above the buildings, casting Simeon's face in shadow. "Revenge made me survive—the thought of doing *this* to you." Simeon toed her thigh with his boot.

Gods, no. *"Zaarusha. Roberto."* Nothing. Roberto must also be too far away to hear. And she'd left Anakisha's crystal necklace—the dream-catcher that helped them meld over distance—on her bedside table in the cottage.

Simeon crouched, his face coming into view in the sun. "So pretty." He flicked his tongue over his lips like a viper.

"Roberto?" By the flaming dragon gods, where was he?

"I'll guard the mouth of the alley while you enjoy yourself," Bruno said. "Be quick. And rough."

"Shuddup, Pa, I'll do this my way," Simeon snapped.

Bruno shoved a finger in Simeon's face. "Remember, your ma died because of that shrotty cow. The sooner you're done and we cast her in the sea, the better." He strode to the alley's mouth, boots echoing on stone.

Running a finger down her cheek, Simeon crooned. "This won't take long Ezaara. You'll be ready for me now that Roberto's already had you."

A shiver of revulsion rippled down Ezaara's spine.

§

Roberto put down his teacup and rose to go. "Thank you."

Warlin's grin was a flash of white in his bushy beard. "It was the least we could do for you after all these years," he said, the tan wrinkles around his warm eyes half hidden by his wild black hair.

Anastia, the best seamstress in the whole of Naobia, reached out to squeeze Roberto's hand, her embroidered sleeve brushing his wrist. "It's good to see you, Roberto. Bring Ezaara by if her outfit needs adjusting."

"Everything will probably fit fine, but I'd like to pop by with her." Warlin and Anastia were the closest thing he had to family—apart from his sister, Adelina. "I'm sure Ezaara would love to meet you."

So much excellent food stowed in his rucksack, not to mention the fine new ceremonial riders' garb he'd ordered for Ezaara. He'd wanted nothing but the finest for Ezaara and had ordered the garments when he'd flown down to organize their hand-fasting holiday. She'd refused payment—for the food and the clothing. He hadn't expected that.

"You know you're welcome any time. Our hearth is yours and Adelina's. Give our love to your sister." Anastia's dark eyes glimmered. "We miss her."

Anastia and Warlin's daughter had been kidnapped by his father and given to tharuks as a slave. When Roberto's parents died, Adelina had lived with them for a few moons, and they'd loved her as their own.

"I'd better go, or Ezaara will be wondering where I am." He embraced them and walked out the door, through their garden, their farewells hanging on the air. Closing their garden gate, he entered the piazza and sat on the wide lip of the sea dragon fountain, trailing his fingers in the water while he waited for Ezaara. Carved from opaline crystal, the sea dragons glimmered in the sunlight, rainbows rippling through their scaled bodies, and sparkling water cascading from their maws.

After his long catch-up with Anastia and Warlin, he'd expected Ezaara to arrive before him. Where was she? Was she all right? He huffed his breath out, trying to shake off the uneasiness creeping over him. It was nothing, only the memory of Amato's treachery that was making him uncomfortable.

The feeling didn't ease. *"Ezaara."*

No answer. She was easily within melding distance. Was she distracted? *"Erob, any idea what's up?"*

No answer. Erob must still be out of range.

Roberto inhaled, trying to ease the tension in his shoulders. For the Egg's sake, they were on their hand-fasting holiday. He'd wanted to show Ezaara Naobia, share his homeland with her. Wanted to relax in the sun and leave the stressful politics of Dragons' Hold behind them. So far it had been beautiful. There was no need for his past to get him down.

He rolled his shoulders and waited, watching the sunlight cast pretty colors over the shimmering dragons.

§

Simeon ran his shrotty finger over Ezaara's cheek.

"Help! Green guards, help," Ezaara melded. *"Your Queen's Rider needs you!"*

"What is it, my Queen's Rider?" a dragon replied.

"An evil man has me. I'm paralyzed." Ezaara showed him her location, Simeon's ugly sneer as his finger traced down her throat, sliding across the bloody skin at her collar bone. *"Please, help. Tell Zaarusha and Master Roberto."*

"Right away," the dragon replied.

"So pretty, and all mine." Simeon's eyes glinted. "A shame we had to rough you up a little, but at least Pa didn't mar your face." He wiped her blood on his breeches as his eyes slid down her chest.

Her mouth grew dry. She had to keep him talking until help arrived, stop him from—

"I-it was brave of y-you to cross the ocean. H-how did y-you do it?" Gods, if only she could speak coherently. Her tongue was thick and clumsy.

"Help's coming," the dragon called. *"We're having difficulty determining which alley you're in."*

Ezaara showed the green her walk from the square. Simeon stalked around her prone body, gloating.

"We built a raft from palm trunks," Simeon said. "Luckily there wasn't a storm. We're the only survivors from the Wastelands. We outwitted the likes of you, while you danced around on the sand with your pretty-boy lover, not a care in the world." His gloat twisted into a snarl. "You and that rotten Roberto sent my mother to her death. But now, it's my turn to exact revenge."

He knelt again, tracing his dagger along her ribs. The blade pricked through her clothing.

Ezaara attempted to hit him, but her arm only twitched. The berries had taken full hold now. She could only lie here. *"How soon will you be here?"*

"Not long now," the dragon answered. *"Hold on."*

Hold on to what? She couldn't even grip anything. Her sword still lay abandoned on the cobbles. She was useless.

No, she was the Queen's Rider. She rode Zaarusha, the most powerful dragon in the realm. She would not submit to Simeon. Help was on its way. She had to keep him talking. Distract him.

"You know S-simeon, I always appreciated your k-kindness when I f-first arrived at D-dragons' Hold." Kindness that had been an ulterior motive to poisoning her. "You w-won m-my heart. I really l-liked you." She'd been gullible and impressionable and had no idea of the depth of his treachery.

"Good," he sneered. "That'll make this easier for you." He twirled his blade in his hands, then sheathed it.

Although the conversation had taken a bad turn, at least he'd sheathed his knife.

"Simeon, you fool, take the wench." Bruno called from the mouth of the alley. "Those berries won't last forever."

"Sure, Father," Simeon called. He muttered under his breath, "Mind your own shrotty business, old man. She's mine and I'll take her how I want." He fumbled with the fastenings on her jerkin. "Let's see what Roberto finds so attractive about you." He laughed. "Let's see if you scream."

ZENS' WEAPON

Maazini perched high on Heaven's Peak, his talons scrabbling through snow to grip a giant boulder, as dawn broke over the horizon, setting his orange scales ablaze, and bathing the snow in liquid gold. Tomaaz hunkered down over the saddle. Since they'd been flying patrol with the blue guard, dawn had become his favorite time.

Behind him in the saddle, Jael huffed on his hands. "Breathtaking, isn't it? If I'd known it was going to be this cold, I would've worn two pairs of gloves."

"It's such a stunning view," Tomaaz replied, gazing over the icy plateau, the deep chasm running through it, and the snow-strewn trees beyond. "It's hard to believe there are tharuks spilling blood down there somewhere."

"Technically, we're not sure there's been bloodshed this morning. We haven't had word yet," Jael replied. "Although I imagine word will come soon enough."

"I hate to break up the chitchat, but Seppi's asked us to do a sweep above Great Spanglewood Forest," Maazini mind-melded with Tomaaz, unfurling his wings.

"Have the blue guards or Septimor seen any tharuks?" Tomaaz asked. The leader of the blue guards, Seppi, coordinated patrol and relayed messages to Maazini via Septimor, his dragon.

"Not this morning. This is just a precaution." Maazini glided off the peak, the sunlight glimmering like molten fire on his scales.

Jael's arms tightened around Tomaaz's waist. "You could have given me some warning."

Tomaaz laughed. He'd forgotten again. "Where would be the fun in that?"

"Glad to know my discomfort brings you pleasure," Jael answered, not loosening his grip.

Tomaaz grinned, squinting against the wind. He and Jael had been fighting tharuks together the past five days since Commander Zen's man-made beasts had rampaged through Great Spanglewood Forest, Jael shooting mage fire from his fingertips whilst Tomaaz loosed arrows. So far, things had gone remarkably smoothly: none of the bloodthirsty creatures had breached Dragons' Hold; Tomaaz's cloak hadn't caught fire once; and Jael hadn't received a single arrow scratch—far better than many of the other mage and rider combinations had fared. They were now nearly as good as Kierion and Fenni. Nearly, but not quite.

Maazini swooped over the snow-dusted forest, the breeze from his wings loosening white powder from the tips of the tallest strongwood trees.

"A little higher, Maazini," Tomaaz melded. *"Tharuks could be hiding in those trees. I don't want to be taken by surprise."*

Maazini adjusted his altitude, beating his wings to soar above the forest. *"The only place I like to see tharuks is at the end of a lick of flame."*

Tomaaz patted his neck. After being captive in Zens' slave camp, neither of them had any affection for those brutal beasts. "You comfortable back there?" he asked Jael.

"Of course," Jael answered. "I've never said otherwise, have I?"

Several years older than Tomaaz, Jael was tough all right. Tomaaz had seen him kill a horde of tharuks with just the mage flame that sprang from his hands. But the cold? That was another thing altogether—Jael was from Naobia where the weather was warm all year. Tomaaz had quickly discovered that snow wasn't Jael's thing.

Far to the south and north, blue dragons and their riders were smudges against the snowy terrain. Great Spanglewood Forest was several days' flight wide. Luckily, Seppi only wanted them to check the outer perimeter of the patrol route—the end of the forest closest to Dragons' Hold.

They zigzagged over the trees, all three of them keeping their eyes peeled for signs of tharuks or skirmishes. The only sound was the muted flap of Maazini's wings.

"Look," Jael gasped.

Tomaaz's eyes flicked above the expanse of Spanglewood.

A dark smudge rose above the trees, clearly visible against the snow. It was a cloud. Yes, a small cloud was hovering above the distant trees.

Maazini's senses sharpened.

"Perhaps it's smoke," Jael whispered.

"I'm not sure," said Tomaaz. "Pretty strange smoke just to float there." And an odd shape for a cloud, too. *"Maazini, let's get closer."*

Maazini shot over the snowy forest.

The cloud was a strange shape. Almost as if it had a tail and wings…

Jael gasped behind him.

Tomaaz gulped. The cloud had talons and wings.

A dark dragon rose above the forest, rushing to meet them. It's body was black as night; its eyes emitted a strange golden light. It beat its tattered wings, talons outstretched.

Tomaaz had never seen a black dragon at Dragons' Hold. *"Maazini, that dragon must be lost,"* Tomaaz said. *"Look, tharuks have shredded his wingtips. Perhaps he's lost his rider. Can you mind-meld with him and find out what's going on?"*

Tomaaz stayed melded with Maazini so Maazini could share the dragon's reply.

The dark dragon flew closer, now, and an ear-splitting screech ripped through Tomaaz's mind. He clapped his hands over his ears and grimaced in pain. By the dragon gods, what was that?

"He's hurting." Maazini's words scraped in Tomaaz's mind like a file along bone.

Tomaaz shuddered. *"The poor thing. Can we help him?"*

Maazini opened his mind again. The relentless scream ripped through Tomaaz's dragon. Maazini bucked, clawing at his head with his talons. *"I can't. I can't help him. He's in too much pain. It's overwhelming me."* Maazini's wings faltered.

Tomaaz's stomach rushed into his throat as they lost height.

Jael gripped his waist with a vengeance.

The black dragon bore down on them. Yellow light streamed from its eyes, bathing Maazini's wingtip in its glow.

Maazini's pain ripped through Tomaaz's skull, making every bone in his body rattle. He gritted his teeth and hung on. His mind was frying. Rasping screeches ricocheted through his head. Panting, he threw his arms around Maazini's neck, and broke mind-meld. *"Maazini, break mind-meld,"* Tomaaz yelled.

His dragon thrashed. They dropped toward the trees, the outstretched branches like a sea of lances below them.

Gods, they only had moments before they'd be speared. Moments before Maazini's stomach would be impaled upon those points and his guts strewn across the forest.

"Maazini! Maazini!" Tomaaz yelled, slapping his dragon's neck. *"Maazini, listen to me! Fly east. Break away."*

Whether it was his slaps or his yelling, Tomaaz didn't know, but Maazini belched a volley of flame, skewed east, and ascended.

The dark dragon followed them, flapping its tattered wings. Opening its maw, it let out an unearthly, high-pitched screech, the sound of a tortured creature.

"Your turn," Tomaaz shouted over his shoulder.

Turning in the saddle, Jael flung out his hands, shooting bolts of green mage fire at the beast.

The creature's tattered wings burst into flame, and it plummeted into the trees, still screeching.

"Maazini, are you all right?" Tomaaz rubbed Maazini's neck scales, trying to soothe him, but Maazini clawed at his head with his talons, refusing to mind-meld.

§

"No one's ever taken me out for breakfast on my name day before." Adelina looked up at Kierion through her long dark lashes.

Kierion smiled and helped her into Riona's saddle. "I'm full of exciting new ideas."

Adelina laughed. "I know. That's why you're always getting into trouble."

"Totally unfair." He pretended to look mortally wounded, but she was so cute and perky, even at the crack of dawn, that Kierion had to chuckle. He swung into the saddle behind her.

Dragon's claws, she was petite. She barely reached his chest. He lifted his hands, unsure where to place them, then dropped them onto his thighs. He inhaled the jasmine scent of her hair as she turned back to him.

Grinning, she took his hands and placed them around her waist. "Roberto always holds me so I don't fall off. Better safe than sorry."

Kierion nodded, his mouth suddenly dry. His hands spanned her entire waist.

Riona mind-melded. *"You've been looking forward to this all week. It's supposed to be fun."*

He laughed. *"You cheeky fire-snorter!"* Trust his dragon to pick up on his feelings. *"Let's head to the clearing by the lake."*

"Now, which clearing would that be?" she huffed, although they'd been there an hour ago, while it was still dark. A happy rumble echoed through her belly. *"It's the perfect spot for fishing."* She tensed her haunches and sprang off the ledge, the gold highlights in her purple wings catching the early morning sun.

Adelina leaned back against Kierion's chest. His bones nearly melted. This trip was already going better than he'd expected. Gods, he'd dreamed of holding

Adelina in his arms for moons, always afraid she was too young—until Roberto and Ezaara's hand-fasting ceremony, when she'd mentioned that today was her sixteenth name day.

This morning, she'd insisted on letting Linaia sleep. Perhaps Adelina wanted to ride Riona with him—or was he reading too much into things?

"She asked you to share her special day with her. I don't know why you're so nervous," Riona said. *"Human mating rituals are so awkward."*

Heat rushed into Kierion's cheeks. *"Stop it, you naughty dragon. I'm not mating her."* His face felt as ruddy as a boy's in front of a blazing hearth. Thank the First Egg, Adelina wasn't looking at him.

Gazing over the basin, Adelina sighed. "I love this time of the morning. It's so peaceful."

There were a few lone dragons about—blue guards on perimeter patrol—flitting above the peaks of Dragon's Teeth, the fierce ring of mountains that protected Dragons' Hold. More blue guards would be further afield, scanning Great Spanglewood Forest and the territories for tharuk attacks.

"It is quiet." Kierion's breath steamed in the chilly air. "A lovely morning for breakfast outdoors."

With Commander Zens' tharuk troops marching through Dragons' Realm, there was no guarantee that the day would stay peaceful, so they'd decided to steal the early morning to celebrate. Her brother, Roberto, was Adelina's only family, but he was in Naobia with Ezaara on their hand-fasting holiday. Kierion had been glad to step in to help her feel special.

They glided over the lake, the water flashing silver as the sun peeked over Dragon's Teeth, glinting off the snow.

"Look, Kierion." Adelina pointed out some herons at the water's edge. "White herons are good luck. And on my name day. It's going to be a great year for me."

The dragon gods knew she needed a good year. From what Kierion had heard, her littling years hadn't been a ball of pranks and laughs like his. She'd grown up too young, the daughter of one of the realm's worst traitors. The breeze riffled its fingers through her hair, carrying that sweet jasmine scent toward him. Her hair looked so soft and inviting. Kierion released his breath slowly, resisting the urge to bend and kiss her head.

"Are you sure this isn't a mating ritual?" Riona asked. *"You're sending mating signals."*

"*Stop it.*" Kierion tamped down his emotions. Foolish of him, really, to feel like this. He had no idea whether Adelina was interested in him. He'd see what the day would bring. There was no way he'd destroy their friendship for the sake of a kiss or two. Adelina meant too much to him for that.

They landed in a grassy clearing near the lake.

Kierion slid out of the saddle and Adelina jumped down after him.

He toed the snow with his boot. "Uh, I got you some gifts for your name day."

"That's kind of you." She looked up at him expectantly.

Would she think he was crazy? "I, ah, hid them. You have to find them." It'd seemed like fun at the time. He shrugged. "If you don't want to look, I can—"

Adelina grinned. "I should have realized you'd do something funny like this." She held up a hand. "Don't worry. It's a great idea. I'm always up for fun." Adelina crunched through the snow to the strongwood trees.

Kierion tagged along. "Did you know that in Horseshoe Bend, they say exercising under strongwood trees increases your strength?"

"Really?" Adelina frowned. "Do you believe that?"

"Not sure," Kierion said truthfully. "I've heard it from a few people. Apparently, there are a burly blacksmith and woodcutter there who swear by it. But me? I'm not sure what to believe, so I keep an open mind."

"Well, if it were true, Master Lars would have everybody out training under strongwood trees."

He chuckled. "I'm sure he would."

Adelina bent down and searched around the base of a strongwood. "Am I warm?"

"Not yet. In fact, you're icy cold."

"Well, if you'd give me a little hint about how big my gift is, I might know where to look…" She raised an eyebrow, smiling at him, then scanned the trees above.

Dragon's claws, he was in deep. Just that smile warmed his belly. "No way. That's half the fun." He winked.

Adelina rolled her eyes and wandered among the trees at the edge of the clearing, peeking behind trunks, and kicking loose snow aside. "What is it? Would it get ruined in the snow?"

"You won't know until you find it."

She stamped and folded her arms. "Don't I get breakfast either?"

He shifted from foot to foot. Was she really getting impatient? Or just teasing?

She smiled, eyes dancing, and ran to the lake's edge, snow squeaking under her boots.

Claws! Two of her little boot prints could fit into one of the galumphing great craters his boots created.

Gazing out across the lake, she said, "Give me a clue, Kierion." A cool breeze rippled the water. Adelina rubbed her arms.

From here, the hiding spot was so obvious—if you knew where it was. "You're warm now."

"Actually, I'm freezing." She scanned the dead reeds at the edge of the lake, and huffed on her gloved hands.

"Really? And I thought you were toasty warm."

With cry of glee, she bent back the dead reeds and pulled out a small cauldron with a rope securing its lid. "This is heavy. What's in it?" she huffed, carrying it back into the clearing.

"Riona, now please," Kierion melded.

Riona blew a warm breath over a hump set back from the lake. The snow melted to reveal a wooden bench with wood tucked underneath it. Kierion pulled a blanket from his dragon's saddle bag and dried the seat off, then folded another blanket onto the bench. "Now you can sit down while I prepare your name-day breakfast." Kierion pulled the wood out from under the bench and piled it on the snow. Riona set it alight, and soon a fire was blazing.

"Thank you." Adelina sat down, placing her cauldron on the bench. "You're very inventive, aren't you?"

"What do you mean?" he asked.

"Well, I've never noticed this bench here before. And that wood was so conveniently tucked underneath it. You must've been up half the night organizing this."

She'd seen right through him. He spluttered. "I-I, ah…"

"Mind you, someone who can organize the blade thrusters to steal all the hold's arrows and hide them up a mountain could easily organize something as fun as this."

Fun? So she was enjoying herself, thank the Egg. "I'm never going to live that down, am I?"

"Afraid not." She gestured at the cauldron. "Can I open it?"

EILEEN MUELLER

Kierion sat on the bench next to her and pulled the cauldron onto his lap. "Sure." With a flourish, he untied the rope.

Adelina lifted the lid and pulled out a gift he'd wrapped in sky-blue tissue. Her dark eyes grew wide. "It's a gift. It's really a gift. I thought you were joking."

He swallowed. Would she like it? Suddenly Kierion was lost for words.

Adelina opened the paper. "Oh." It was more of an inhalation than a word. She shook out the gold fabric, making the scarlet dragons on it dance. "Oh, Kierion, it's beautiful." Her black eyes glimmered with tears.

Words still escaped him.

She clasped his hand. "That's so thoughtful, so sweet. Such a pretty scarf."

"It matches the dress you wore to your brother's hand-fasting." The dress she'd looked so ravishing in. He'd had to conquer the urge to fight every man who'd danced with her. "And the paper represents Linaia with her blue scales."

She swiped at her eyes. "No one's ever given me anything this lovely. I mean, brothers don't count, do they?"

He snorted. "Hardly." Kierion reached into the cauldron and pulled out a tiny companion parcel. "Don't lose this."

When she opened the little box inside, silent tears slid from her eyes. "You noticed my ears have holes? But I haven't worn earrings since..." Her smile dropped and her eyes looked hollow and desolate.

"Since when?" he asked gently.

"Since my mother's funeral."

Oh claws. "I'm sorry. I—"

"You weren't to know." She fiddled with the little gold dragons in the box. "You know my father killed her, don't you?"

Kierion's heart lurched, leaving his stomach hollow. He shook his head and said nothing. How did you answer that?

"He pushed her off his dragon. It took her a few moons to die. Roberto and I cared for her. I was still a littling... When she died, Roberto left me with good friends and disappeared for a few moons. I felt all alone." She turned the earrings over, rubbing the dragons' wings. "I buried my earrings with my mother." She glanced up and smiled through her tears. "Thank you for these. They'll remind me of her."

Kierion passed her a kerchief. He'd had a sheltered life in Montanara, nothing like hers.

"You know, my father died that same day. His dragon Matotoi was so ashamed his rider had pushed his wife off his back he plunged into Crystal Lake, killing himself and my father."

So that was how she'd lost her parents. What ugly shattered littling years she'd had. No wonder her brother Roberto was so tough. Who would've thought that beneath her bubbly smiling exterior Adelina held such dark secrets?

Kierion placed a tentative arm around her shoulders, and she leaned into him. He waited until she'd stopped crying. "How about some breakfast?"

"First…" Adelina sat up and put the earrings in her ears. The golden dragons swung from her ears as she tilted her head. "How do they look?" Her dark eyes were huge, her smile, hesitant.

"Beautiful." Gods, he didn't care about the earrings, although they suited her tanned skin and dark hair. It was Adelina. She took his breath away.

Her lips quirked up into a smile. "How about that breakfast?"

Kierion reached into the cauldron. "Have you ever had wizard porridge?"

She wrinkled her nose. "What's that?"

"It's savory, with herbs and cheese. Fenni and Jael showed me how to make it a while ago. I guarantee it's tasty."

Kierion filled the cauldron from the lake, then bustled around the fire, adding ingredients from Riona's saddlebags.

Adelina helped him, stirring the porridge with a ladle as Kierion sliced cheese and mushrooms into it. "You know," she said, "my father wasn't always bad. When I was a tiny littling, he was the leader of the green guards in Naobia. I wanted to be like him when I grew up. Sadly, everything changed after Zens took him captive."

Kierion sprinkled salt and herbs into the mix.

Sorrow shadowed Adelina's face. "He used to beat me and Ma. I was so small. One day, Roberto came inside and saw it. From then on, he never let me out of his sight. And if Pa was on the rampage, my brother would hide me in the barn, the wardrobe, or even take me far away to Crystal Lake so we could swim and be happy."

"You were lucky to have a brother like that."

She looked up at him, her eyes damp again. Her voice was hoarse. "Though it never stopped me from hearing Pa beat Roberto in my stead."

Suddenly, Kierion was glad Adelina's father was dead because if he were alive, he'd rip that shrotty man's throat out. He looked her directly in the eye. "If you want me to toss those dragon earrings to the bottom of the lake so you never have to think about any of this again, I'll gladly do it. I never meant to give you something painful."

Her eyes widened. "Oh no, Kierion, it's not your gift. Because Roberto went home to Naobia, I've been thinking about my family all week." She gave him a tremulous smile. "The earrings are lovely." Her fingers drifted to the scarf at her neck. "And apart from my grandmother's keepsake, I've never had anything this beautiful before. Thank you."

Kierion went to the saddlebags to get the bowls but found only mugs. "I was going to save them for tea, afterward, but do you mind eating out of these?"

She shrugged. "We could eat straight from the cauldron and still have tea after."

So they sat on the bench, the cauldron between them, and feasted on wizard porridge.

When the cauldron was empty, Adelina licked off her spoon. "This is grand. I never dreamed mages ate so well."

Kierion scrubbed the cauldron out with lake weed at the river's edge, his fingers numb in the chilly water. "I've always thought it would be better if wizard porridge was magic and could make me fly, but every time I've eaten it, my feet stay on the ground."

Adelina laughed at his bad joke. At least she was smiling.

"Lucky we get to fly dragons instead." She tilted her head. "Thank you for cheering me up today. I've been missing my brother."

"If he's your only family, it'd be strange him being hand-fasted now." Kierion put the cauldron of water back on the fire.

Adelina shrugged. "I've gained a sister."

A dragon's bellow ripped through the air. Birds squawked, flapping out of the trees.

Adelina cringed. "What was that?"

"Riona?"

"A dragon in pain," Riona answered.

"Linaia says Septimor's hurt." Adelina sprang to her feet.

"Riona says so, too. Come on, there's no time to lose." Kierion emptied the cauldron over the fire. Steam billowed into the cold air. He threw everything into saddlebags and they leaped into the saddle. Riona's great haunches bunched as she thrust them into the air, her muscles rippling and her wings beating the air.

They shot above the forest as another bellow sliced the sky.

Kierion twisted in the saddle.

It was Septimor, all right—bucking and writhing in the sky, his talons thrashing at his head. Seppi was hunched low in the saddle, arms around Septimor's neck.

"Fly, Riona. Fly," Kierion urged. *"Do you know what's wrong?"*

A flurry of colored wings emerged from the Southern caverns signaling a horde of dragons flying out to meet Septimor and Seppi.

Riona projected a babble of alarmed dragons' voices into Kierion's head. *"I'm surprised you can think with that din."*

Abruptly, the dragons' voices ceased. *"I can't,"* Riona replied, *"and no, no one has been able to mind-meld with him properly. All they hear is this."*

A scream of terror shattered Kierion's thoughts, making his head pound. He let go of Adelina's waist and gripped his head. *"Stop. Stop it."*

"That's the only thing we can hear from Septimor," Riona replied.

Dragons were escorting Septimor toward the infirmary ledge. Riona swooped down. Septimor's enormous blue body slumped onto the ledge, his wings flopping uselessly at his sides. He writhed, still clawing at his head.

Riders ran to help Seppi dismount. His riders' garb was drenched in blood from the abdomen down.

"By the holy dragon gods," Adelina gasped. "They were on a routine patrol. What could've happened?"

SIMEON'S REVENGE

Roberto tried melding with Ezaara again. *"Ezaara, are you running late? Distracted at the jewelry stall? Where are you?"* Nothing, again.

A green guard was shooting over the rooftops, emerald wings catching the sun. For a moment, it reminded him of his littling years when Amato had been their leader. Why was that green dragon swooping so low? Couldn't the beast and rider see they'd collide with a house if they didn't change course?

Hang on, the green was spiraling down to meet him.

Oh gods, something was wrong. Roberto leaped to his feet, running.

The green banked steeply and landed in the piazza with a thud. "Master Roberto," called the green guard, "the Queen's Rider's in danger."

Fear lanced through Roberto. Chest tight, he scrambled into the saddle behind the rider. "What's wrong? Where is she?"

"Some men have her in an alley. A green guard is rushing to her aid."

"Is she hurt?" Ezaara was good with a sword. Hopefully she could fight her way out of that alley. *"Erob. Ezaara."* Oh, claws, why had he insisted on this rutting picnic? Ezaara was more important than fancy clothes, more important than anything. *"Ezaara!"* Still no answer.

"I don't know," the guard said, the dragon flapping her wings and springing skyward.

The green guard must've found out by Ezaara melding with it. He laid his hand on the dragon's hide, behind the saddle. *"Please show me what happened to Ezaara."*

A man leering over her, sunlight streaming between narrow buildings, casting his face in shadow. The man moved. Roberto gasped. It was Simeon. Back from the Wastelands. Something was wrong with Ezaara, she wasn't fighting him, just lying there. *Simeon knelt and ran his finger down her throat, spreading something warm and sticky.* Blood. Oh gods, what had Simeon done?

"Hurry," Roberto urged the dragon, *"please hurry."*

§

"Help. Now!" Ezaara's plea was answered by the swish of wings overhead. Simeon was so engrossed with undoing her jerkin that he didn't notice the shadow flitting across the alley.

But Bruno did. Without a word to his son, he raced away.

"I'm paralyzed. They've drugged me. Help."

"The alley's too narrow. I can't get in." the dragon replied.

Simeon rubbed his filthy fingers over the skin beneath Ezaara's collarbone. "So soft," he crooned as if he were her lover.

Sweat beaded on Ezaara's forehead. She forced a smile, anything to distract him.

Wingbeats stirred Simeon's hair. A lick of flame shot between the buildings. Simeon spun, drawing his sword, and ducked the flame.

Talons clattered on the shingled roof as a dragon landed. A moment later an arrow zipped between the buildings at Simeon.

He deflected it with his sword.

Ezaara tried to wriggle her fingers. They responded. Thank the Egg, the berries were wearing off. Her sword was still too far away, but if she let Simeon think she was helpless, perhaps she could grab it. She flexed her toes in her boots. Good, they were working too. Her legs spasmed, control returning to her muscles.

Simeon dragged Ezaara to her feet. He stood behind her, pulled her against his torso, and held a dagger to her throat. "One more move, rider, and I'll slit her throat."

The green dragon roared, flame gusting above the buildings, but the rider froze.

She slumped heavily on Simeon as he hauled her toward the alley mouth— toward her sword.

"Lie, belly down, on that rooftop," Simeon yelled at the rider.

The rider lay on the verdigris copper shingles. The dragon stalked, scraping the shingles with her talons.

Simeon's grip didn't slacken as he pulled Ezaara along the alley, blade at her throat. She stayed slumped, every nerve tingling with awareness. Seven paces to her sword.

Six.

Five paces. She shared her plan with the dragon.

It settled, watching from the rooftop. *"If anything goes wrong, I'm not holding back. You're our first Queen's Rider in eighteen years. I won't have you harmed."*

Four paces.

"Ezaara!"

By the dragon gods! *"Roberto."* Three paces. She didn't dare look up.

"Hold on, I'm nearly there."

Two paces.

"Wait," Simeon said. "Something's up. How did that dragon know to come here? And why is he peaceful now? You're melding with it, you dirty little snipe."

It was now or never. Ezaara stomped on Simeon's foot and drove her elbow into his ribs.

Not brilliant, but enough to loosen his grip.

She drove her head up under his chin. His head snapped back. She bent and grabbed her sword, spinning to face him.

Simeon rushed her.

Ezaara parried Simeon's low swipe, then blocked another downward strike. Metal clashed against metal, ringing through the alley.

Behind Simeon, another green guard landed on a roof. Riders nocked their bows, arrows trained on the fight.

"Our archers can't shoot because they might hit you," melded the green she'd been conversing with. *"Try to get free of him."*

Simeon jabbed the point of his sword at her throat, and she knocked it away, his sword scraping along her blade up to its guard. But her muscles, still fuzzy after the berries, were tiring fast. Gradually, he drove her backward. Her foot struck a wall. He had her cornered.

"I'm tired of messing around," Simeon snarled. "If I can't have you, Roberto won't either. He thrust his blade past Ezaara's guard, toward her heart.

§

"Do you have a rope?" Roberto barked at the rider.

"Back left saddlebag," the guard replied, hunching low as they swooped over alleys and rooftops so Roberto could see.

Roberto pulled the rope out of the saddle bag and stowed his rucksack inside. He tied the rope around his waist then fastened it to the dragon's saddle strap. Not the best place, but hopefully it would do. He pressed his hand on the dragon's side. *"How soon until we're there?"*

"A few dozen wingbeats," the green replied.

"Ezaara," Roberto tried melding again. *"Are you all right?"*

He caught snatches of movement, a sense of panic.

"*Hold on, I'm nearly there.*"

"*Roberto,*" Erob's call was strong. His dragon's urgency rushed through him. He glanced back to a flash of blue wings and the glint of sun on multi-colored scales far behind him. Erob and Zaarusha were coming but they'd be too late.

As long as he wasn't.

A cold sweat broke out on Roberto's neck. "*Faster,*" he urged the dragon. "*Faster. We must save the Queen's Rider.*"

The verdigris copper roofs of Naobia flashed by below. Ahead, green guards were poised on rooftops above a narrow alley. Roberto placed a hand on the dragon's hide.

"*Don't land,*" he said. "*Swoop as low as possible. I'll be going in.*" He tugged the rope around his waist. It held fast. He yanked the end on the saddle strap— firm too.

The other green dragons scattered to make space as Roberto's green swooped toward the short alley. Roberto peered down. The sunny patch where he'd seen Ezaara was empty. His stomach lurched. By the dragon gods, where was she?

"*Along there,*" said the dragon.

Roberto squinted. There, ahead in the shadows, was Ezaara, clashing swords with Simeon. She was valiantly parrying his blows, but he had her up against a wall. It was only a matter of heartbeats.

Roberto melded. "*I'm going in now. Brace for impact.*" Removing his hand from the dragon's hide, he flung his leg over the saddle and, feet first, slipped off the dragon's side.

Roberto fell through the air, his stomach shooting into his throat as the rope spooled out. He clenched his teeth, absorbing the jolt of the rope. The dragon faltered with the impact, then leveled out again.

So far, Simeon hadn't noticed him. Perfect. If only the dragon would fly a little higher. He wished he could mind-meld with her. As if she'd sensed his thoughts, the dragon lifted. Roberto pulled his feet to his chest as he swept along the alley.

Ahead, Simeon batted Ezaara's blade aside and drove his sword toward her heart.

The dragon sped. Roberto thrust his feet out, slamming Simeon's shoulder and knocking him to the cobbles.

"*Ezaara, run!*"

A wave of her relief washed over him. She bolted down the alley toward its mouth, just behind Roberto still swinging from the rope.

"Follow us," he melded, hoping the dragon would lead them somewhere safe. They turned the corner, a flurry of wingbeats and the clatter of arrows echoing behind them as the green guards sprang into action.

CRYSTAL LAKE

Roberto swung through the alleys, suspended on the rope from the dragon's saddle strap. The green slowed as she negotiated the corners, the buildings' stone faces looming and receding with each swing of the rope. Ezaara pounded the cobbles behind them, the dragon slowing her pace to make sure she could keep up.

Blood was smeared on her throat and her jerkin was disheveled.

"Are you hurt?" Roberto asked her.

"Not badly, just shaken up. Oh, gods, it was awful."

Her exhaustion hit him, making him want to cradle her in his arms and shut out the world. Gods, this was horrible. Their love was so new, so tender…

He caught snatches of her chaotic thoughts: Simeon's face leering; his ugly gaze ogling her body; Bruno's harsh threats; the paralysis that had consumed her, made her helpless; her sense of powerlessness; her horror.

Icy fury swept through Roberto. If he caught those two, he'd personally gut them. He tried to shelter Ezaara from his rage, and only send her loving thoughts, but his anger leaked through the wall he tried to build around it.

She needed love and protection, not a man bent on vengeance and violence. He reigned his emotions in. *"So those conniving shrot heaps survived the Wastelands. We should've planned for that. Should've known someone else would."*

"We couldn't have known. The only way we survived was by having Ithsar help us escape."

The alley they were in opened into the deserted piazza with the sea dragon fountain. It sickened Roberto to think he'd been sitting here while Simeon… His rage boiled over again.

The green dragon descended, lowering the rope until Roberto's boots slapped the cobbles. Before he could untie the rope, Ezaara rushed into his arms.

He held her, murmuring into her hair, "It's all right. You're safe now. We'll catch them and bring them to justice."

Gods, if anything had happened to her, anything…

How had Ezaara wormed her way so deep into his soul that just the thought of losing her left him adrift? After his father's betrayal and abuse, he'd protected himself, built an impenetrable wall around his emotions for years, letting only Erob and Adelina in.

Until Ezaara. This beautiful woman, trembling in his arms.

Oh gods, why had he left her alone? "I'm sorry, Ezaara. I should've stayed with you." Roberto shook his head and held her tight. He kissed her forehead. "You're bleeding."

"It's just a scratch."

"Let's get you cleaned up." He untied the rope from around his waist. The dragon flew over and settled next to the fountain. His arm around her, Roberto led Ezaara to the water spray and cleaned up the blood on her neck.

She was right: it was only a scratch, but it had bled a lot.

Ezaara gave him a wan smile. "Necks and faces bleed easily because of all the blood vessels. It's not too bad." She passed him some salve from her healing pouch.

"No," he said, "Pass me the piaua. I don't want you wearing Simeon's scars." He'd do anything to erase the harm done to her—emotional and physical.

She fumbled in her pouch and passed him the vial. "There's not much left. Use only a drop, Roberto. Ma doesn't have much at the hold."

She wasn't putting up a fight, which showed how much she wanted to be rid of it, too. Roberto applied the juice gently. "Anywhere else?"

"M-my head." She gingerly touched the back of her hair.

"Let me see." He parted her blonde tresses. There was a bloody welt on the back of her head.

Wind ruffled Roberto's hair as Erob descended into the piazza, Zaarusha on his tail, and landed on the far side of the fountain. Ezaara rushed around to Zaarusha, flinging her arms around the queen's neck. From their body language, Roberto knew they were mind-melding, but he couldn't hear what they were saying—very odd.

He tried to mind-meld with Ezaara. *"Are you—?"* No luck again.

"Erob?" Again, nothing.

Roberto strolled around the fountain to his dragon and scratched the warm scales on his nose.

"This morning must've been terrible for Ezaara," Erob said.

"It was. She's very shaken. Thank the Egg, she's all right." He hesitated. *"We can meld again, now. I couldn't hear you before."*

"That'll be the opaline. When it's between us, the crystal blocks mind-melding." Erob snorted. *"As beautiful as that fountain is, it's a poor imitation of real sea dragons."*

Now that they were melded, Ezaara's memories shot through Roberto as she shared them with Zaarusha: Bruno dragging her by her legs across the cobbles…

Anger, deadly and icy, surged through his veins. He would not be merciful when he faced Bruno and Simeon. They'd already killed Master Shari and Master Jaevin. And Fleur had fouled the healing of many at Dragons' Hold.

Erob's blue-scaled tail twitched, scraping the cobbles. *"Watch out, Roberto,"* he warned, *"or hate will grow like a canker in your blood."*

Perhaps it already had.

§

Erob spiraled down on a grassy slope near a stunning blue lake. Zaarusha followed, thudding down beside him. Despite Simeon's ugly grimace flashing through her mind and her tight breath during her flight here, Ezaara was determined to put the morning's incidents behind her and enjoy their picnic. She slid off Zaarusha onto the grass and walked around to her snout.

The queen butted her hand. A cozy, warm sensation washed over Ezaara. *"The least I can do is comfort you. I'm sorry I was so far away."*

She flung her arms around Queen Zaarusha's huge scaly neck, pressing her cheek against her dragon's sun-warmed hide. *"You can't be everywhere—and you can't hover over me."*

"I can't lose you." Zaarusha huffed warm air over her back.

Ezaara stepped back and scratched her snout.

Behind them, Erob settled on the grass, wrapping his tail around his body and tucking his head under his wing.

Roberto pulled a blanket out of one of Erob's saddlebags and spread it out on the lush grass.

Ezaara sat on it, hugging her knees, staring at the expanse of blue crystalline water. It was easy to see how Crystal Lake had got its name. Nestled among grassy hills dotted with trees, a short flight from the Naobian township, it lay in a secluded spot, sheltered from the sea breeze. Nearby, a stream burbled its way down a hill, ferns—taller than a man—lining its banks. Doves cooed in the trees, and small birds twittered in the sunlight.

Roberto came over and sat beside her, placing a gentle arm around her shoulders. She didn't realize she was shaking until his warmth enveloped her.

He drew her against him, and she curled up, the thrum of his heartbeat against her cheek. His voice rumbled through his chest. "Adelina and I used to swim here when we were young. It was a sanctuary, a haven for us. Sometimes we'd wake up early and get our chores done so we could slip off when my father wasn't looking. We'd play here for hours in our safe place." He gazed down at her, his dark eyes inviting her to make this her safe place too.

"I can't let Simeon get the better of me. I want to enjoy today."

He stroked her cheek. "Good," he murmured softly, pulling his rucksack closer. "You must be famished."

Eating was the last thing Ezaara felt like doing, nausea still roiling in her belly. Refusing to let Simeon and Bruno win, she nodded.

Roberto raised an eyebrow, obviously not taken in by her nod, and pulled a jar from the rucksack. He held it up. Sunlight hit liquid honey, turning it to burnished gold. A lazy grin spread across Roberto's face and lit his eyes. "That first night when you hurt your ankle, your hair in the candlelight reminded me of sunlight on honey."

The tightness in her chest eased. "That's sweet of you."

"Sweet?" He cocked his eyebrow at her again. "Was that meant to be a pun?"

"It was meant to be romantic," she mock-punched his arm.

He laughed. "I've been called many things, but never sweet."

Ezaara couldn't help laughing, too. "Sweet wouldn't be the word most people would use to describe you." He'd been so tough and arrogant, even cold, when she'd met him.

He grinned and set the honey down, reached into the rucksack again and drew out a heart-shaped cherry tart.

She inhaled the fruity aroma. "Oh, Roberto." He was always doing such kind things for her. "Remember the walking stick you carved for me?"

"You know, I think I loved you, right back then," he said, "although I was fighting to deny it." Setting the tart on the blanket, he leaned in and brushed his lips against hers.

He'd always been surprisingly gentle with her. Except when training her—then he'd been the toughest taskmaster she'd ever faced.

Next, he produced a loaf of fresh bread, a round of herb cheese and some fat, juicy apricots.

Ezaara's mouth watered.

With a rustle, Roberto passed her a package wrapped in fine, green tissue paper and tied with a gold ribbon.

Another gift? He'd been showering her with keepsakes since they'd arrived, one little surprise after another. "For me?"

He gestured at the hills around them. "Who else? I love you, Ezaara. I want you to remember it every day."

How could she forget? They'd spent many intimate hours in their giant four-poster bed over the last few days. Her cheeks warmed. "Thank you." She untied the ribbon. It felt like fabric. Ezaara peeled back the paper and gasped.

She was holding light-blue fabric covered with dragons in many hues. She tugged the fabric free, and shook it out. There were two pieces—a tunic and breeches.

"Fine ceremonial wear for a Queen's Rider," Roberto said. "Do you like it?"

"Like it? I love it. I was admiring similar cloth in the marketplace this morning, but it was only half as beautiful." This morning she hadn't thought it was possible to find prettier cloth, but this was exquisite.

This morning, before Simeon had attacked her. Her eyes filled with tears, and she dropped the tunic and breeches into her lap. "Oh, Roberto."

"You're safe here." He held her until her tears stopped, gently stroking her back.

She sniffed and picked up the tunic again. "These dragons are much more detailed than the ones in the market." She stood up, angling the garment to see properly. "Look, their scales flash in the sun like real dragons' do, and their eyes look so realistic, as if they're watching us. You can almost feel them overhead." Ezaara involuntarily glanced up into the cloudless, steel-blue sky.

"This one's Zaarusha," Roberto said, pointing to a multi-hued dragon on the front of the tunic. "And that dark blue one's Erob.

"There's Maazini, Handel and Liesar." Their orange, bronze and silver scales winked in the sun.

"I had it woven especially for you," he said.

Her mouth formed an *o*, but no sound came out. He'd done *all that* for her?

"These are all made by a couple who are old friends of our family. Anastia sewed the tunic and breeches and embroidered them especially for you. She also makes great bread and the best cherry tarts in Naobia, and Warlin makes cheese and tends bees. Come on, let's eat." Roberto sliced her a heel of bread and placed a wedge of herb cheese on it. "I'd like you to meet them." He gauged her. "But maybe not today."

Ezaara bit through the crunchy crust into the soft bread and groaned in pleasure. "This is delicious." Her nausea was gone.

He plied her with another slice of bread, drizzled with honey.

The cherry tart and apricots were even better—sweet and satisfying.

After they'd eaten, Roberto lay back in the sun and Ezaara nestled against his side. Soon, her eyes drooped and she dozed off.

When Ezaara awoke, she was hot and sticky from the relentless sun.

Roberto stirred and sat up. "Do you feel like a swim?" he asked tentatively.

Yesterday, they'd gone skinny-dipping in the sea in the middle of the night, but after what had happened this morning, Ezaara wasn't so sure… She glanced around.

"You could leave your undergarments on if you feel more comfortable," he suggested.

That was a great compromise. She wouldn't let her experience with Simeon beat her, but she could be careful. Her breath shuddered out of her. "Good idea."

Roberto helped her undo the fastenings on her jerkin and hung it on a tree. He produced a shirt for her to swim in. "Here, wear this, just in case someone turns up."

He helped her into it. That felt a little better.

Roberto undressed, leaving his own undergarments on too. Probably just to make her feel comfortable. He kissed her forehead. Then he spun and dashed off to the lake yelling, "Last one in is a stinky dragonet!"

Ezaara laughed and raced after him. He really did know how to make her feel great.

The strong muscles in his back rippled as he dove from a knoll, making a perfect arc into the water. Ezaara hesitated, not from fear, but to watch the sheer beauty of his tan, lean figure cutting through the clear blue water, casting a rippling shadow on the pale sand. Fish flitted between sparse clumps of lake weed, their scales silver, tinged with orange or gold. It was peaceful here—beautiful. This could easily become one of her favorite spots in the realm.

Roberto burst out of the water, shaking the hair out of his eyes, sending a spray of silver droplets cascading around him. He grinned. "Jump in. The water's great."

She and Tomaaz had grown up spending half of their lives in the river near home. Ezaara dove off the knoll and swam through the cool, pristine water. Oh, it was good to wash away the morning's events. The sun played on the surface, refracting into ripples of silver light that danced across the smooth sand. She popped above the surface, smiling at Roberto.

He looked so free and happy, years younger. This was one of those rare moments they'd treasure when they returned to Dragons' Hold to wage war against Zens.

Ezaara dove down again, aiming for the sandy lake bottom. She'd never seen sand that pearly-white. Or the pretty crystals that sparkled in the pale sand, catching the light. Down she swam, kicking strongly. Oh gods, it felt good to be in the water. She stretched her hand out, trying to touch the sand, but it was farther away than it looked. She kicked again, pressure building in her ears, hand still outstretched. The water was so clear it was deceptively deep. With a final kick, her fingers brushed the sand. Picking up a crystal, she turned, kicking off the bottom of the lake and shooting back up toward the surface. She couldn't resist tickling Roberto's feet on the way up. She burst out of the water, spraying crystalline drops. "Look."

"Opaline crystals," he said. "That's how the lake got its name. The sea dragon fountain in town is made of this stuff."

Ezaara dropped it back in the lake, watching it sink to the bottom.

"Race you to the other side." Roberto kicked off on his back, waiting for her to join him. "There's something I'd like to show you."

Another surprise? Ezaara lay on her back, kicking along beside him.

He held out his hand, and she took it.

"This is how I'd like to live," he said. "None of that other tough stuff. Just you and me, enjoying ourselves in the sun, flying our dragons and exploring the realm."

"Maybe one day."

"These days we have together, we'll take them, Ezaara, and make them ours. No one can steal them from us. No matter what happens, they'll be ours forever."

"What about that race?" she asked. Ezaara flipped onto her stomach and plowed through the water toward the other side of the lake, Roberto at her side.

When they were three-quarters of the way across the lake, Roberto led her to a towering boulder jutting out of the water. They ascended the boulder on hand-carved steps and lay on the top, overlooking the lake. Water lapped at the edges of the rock—their tiny island amid the expanse of blue. A hawk flew overhead. The smooth sun-baked stone warmed Ezaara's back.

"You know what?" Roberto rolled over and kissed her collar bone. "Even in my shrotty old shirt, you're beautiful," he said, the sun turning his dark eyes into molten fire.

Then he was kissing her, his water-cooled lips igniting flames deep in her core. Ezaara pulled him closer, the hard planes of his chest meeting hers. Their *sathir*—the life energy that bound them—danced around them, her multi-hues swirling with his silver-threaded midnight blue.

Were they truly alone? Somehow after this morning... She pushed him away, glancing around.

"It's all right," he melded. *"I understand."* He gave her a reassuring smile. "We have our whole lives together. Come on, let me show you the special hideout that Adelina and I found." He rose and extended his hand, his tan figure limned in light against the vibrant sky.

"You're beautiful too." Ezaara stood and kissed him again. *"After this morning, I just need a little time."*

"It's natural. You've been through a shock." He gestured to the stairs. *"Come on, you'll love this."*

Ezaara didn't take the stairs. She dove off the boulder into the clear turquoise-blue water.

In a heartbeat, Roberto was swimming beside her.

This was how life should be: spontaneous, happy, free. They'd seldom had the chance to enjoy each other. Until a week ago, they hadn't even been allowed to admit their love.

He swam to a bank near a rocky outcrop. A huge willow grew upon the rock, its gnarled roots wending over stone into the lush earth beyond, and its fronds draping into the water. They swam under the curtain of fronds, the light an eerie green.

"Adelina and I call this tree Old King Willow," Roberto said. "It's been here since we were tiny."

"It's a great hiding spot." Ezaara flicked her wet hair out of her eyes.

"Oh, we're not there yet. We have to dive to get to my hidey hole. What I'm about to show you is stunning. I haven't been here since Pa died. I'm not sure if anyone else knows about it." Roberto took her hand. "Hold on and I'll show you the way. Don't be alarmed if we swim through some lake weed. It's harmless."

She nodded and took a deep breath.

Roberto tugged her down into the water by the edge of a rock face. The green light cast by the Old King Willow's leaves made the water murkier. He kicked, guiding her downward, one hand still holding hers and the other skimming the rock face. Suddenly his hand disappeared into gloom—an enormous gaping cavern in the rock face. Roberto swam inside, motioning her to follow.

Ezaara grabbed the jagged roof of the cave, and pulled herself inside. It was so huge and dark, she couldn't see the bottom. Tendrils of lake weed brushed against her legs, body and arms as she swam. *"I'm glad you warned me."*

"We've a way to go, so conserve your breath." Roberto shot upward.

It wasn't a cave, but a wide tunnel. Ezaara kicked up, swimming beside him through a sea of waving lake weed. It brushed her face. Something cold slithered against her leg and she kicked out.

"Probably just a fish." Roberto melded.

"Or an eel." Her lungs were burning now. *"Much farther?"*

"Nearly there. Just a few more kicks." He tugged her upward and they burst out of the water, gasping for air.

Above them was a dark starry sky. Roberto trod water next to her, pale starlight illuminating his smiling face.

"Stars?"

He chuckled softly, still breathing hard. "Glowworms."

"Glowworms?" She kept her limbs moving, keeping herself afloat as she stared at the pale blue lights winking down at her. They looked like stars. "What are glowworms?"

"Little creatures that light up the dark," he whispered, water splashing as he wrapped an arm around her shoulder. "If we're too loud, they'll go out."

That there were such creatures… little beings of starlight for dark places… Ezaara shook her head. *"I love their light. They're amazing. Let's mind-meld instead of talking, so we don't scare them into putting their lights out."*

"We can watch them from the rock." Roberto gestured at a wide ledge running along the far wall of the enormous cavern.

They swam over, knees soon bumping the sides, and climbed out to catch their breath. Ezaara wrung out the ends of her shirt, and they leaned against the rock wall, watching the twinkling glowworms.

Roberto crossed his legs, his foot bumping a stone which clattered across the ledge. The glowworms winked out, shrouding the cavern in darkness. *"Don't worry, they'll turn their lights back on soon."*

"It's not that dark. See? There's a glimmer at the back of the cave, as if there's light around a corner."

"There is," he replied. *"There's a shaft to the surface back there, but it's too far up to climb. Want to see it?"*

"Sure."

"We'll go slow, so we don't stumble in the dark." He took her hand.

As they stood, the glowworms lit up again, a few at a time, until Ezaara could see better. *"That was sweet of them."*

"All part of the service." He bowed.

They made their way toward the back of the cavern, which turned into a spacious area.

"*Wow, it opens right out.*" Ezaara's home in Lush Valley would fit in here three times over.

This part of the cavern didn't have any glowworms, but was illuminated by a shaft of pale light filtering down from the rock ceiling. Dust motes stirred in a gentle breeze.

"*It goes quite a way in,*" Roberto melded. "*Want to take a look?*"

"*Sure.*" Ezaara blinked. Beyond the light, something stirred in the shadows. Ezaara's skin prickled. "*What's that?*"

"*What?*" Roberto tensed.

"*There.*" Ezaara pointed.

A snort echoed off the cavern walls. Something large and pale shifted, looming in the blackness, scratching stone.

§

The sound of talons skittering on stone made Roberto's neck hair rise. "A dragon," he murmured, dread trailing its clammy fingers down his spine. "It's a dragon."

The beast moved toward the light, pale wings drooping, its protruding ribs showing through the saggy skin hanging from its sides. The creature gazed at them, then slunk back into the dark, and nuzzled at a bundle on the floor.

"*It needs help.*" Ezaara tugged Roberto forward, but his legs were like blocks of wood, unmoving.

Solid. Bolted to the stone.

A dragon, here in Crystal Lake.

A voice croaked. Someone shifted in the dark, feet slapping against stone.

And a rider.

Ice pooled in Roberto's belly. No, it couldn't be.

"*Roberto?*"

He blocked Ezaara, wouldn't let her in. Gods, this was their hand-fasting holiday. And now…

The dragon gusted flame, lighting up the darkness. A man—a skeleton with hanging flesh and bulging eyes—was walking toward him. Wisps of long gray hair framed his gaunt face. Eyes wide, the man held up a trembling, bony finger and croaked again.

Roberto stared. No, impossible. It couldn't be.

"Roberto?" Ezaara squeezed his hand, gazing up at him.

He swallowed, as chaos broke loose inside him.

DEATH VALLEY

Zens stalked back and forth in front of the huge tank that lined the wall of his den. He gestured at Tharuk 000 to flick the switch. Methimium-powered light bathed the body parts floating in his preservative solution. It always helped to have reminders of his conquests in front of him. The furry tharuk hands and the slaves' ears, fingers and toes crystallized his thoughts and helped ease the throbbing in his head.

"Our troops must capture Master Giddi. He holds the key to the world gates." He scratched the stubble on his head and spun to 000. "Our experiments are too weak. Too fragile. We must create a stronger breed. Let's inspect the young mages again. It's time we milked everything they have."

Tharuk 000, tusks gleaming yellow in the methimium's glow, held the door to Zens' underground cavern open. "Commander, the latest batch of mages seems hardier. They're ready for testing."

"Very well, we'll take a look." Zens strode through the door into the maze of tunnels, 000 trailing him. Tharuks working in the tunnels bowed as he passed. It was only proper that they showed deference to their creator—he curled his lip—just as the mages soon would.

They exited the tunnels and marched across Death Valley's arid dusty terrain, past slave crews, the crack of tharuk whips echoing off the valley's desolate mountain slopes. The latrine gang shuffled past, their eyes locked on the ground, jaws hanging slack. They barely needed guards, the numlock in their rations was so high.

000 gazed at the charred hillside looming above them.

"Focus, 000. We can't let that last battle beat us. We will shape the destiny of Dragons' Realm and defeat those stupid men who sit on those stinking lizards." He licked his lips, ignoring the reminder of their defeat. "The new weapons we're developing will conquer them all. And when we're ready, we'll char their littlings in their beds and incinerate every mage in Dragons' Realm. Except Master Giddi. Him, I need alive."

"Commander, that blackened hill reminds me how much I hate those riders, and all the ways I can torture them when I get my claws on them." 000 replied, dark saliva dribbling off his tusks onto his furry chest.

Zens chuckled as they entered the tunnel system on the far side of the valley. They marched past a mining crew of human slaves, driven by tharuks. The slaves' drab, expressionless faces were covered in yellow methimium dust. Good, more crystals for his work.

A littling girl tripped and fell, and a tall male slave stumbled over to help her. Zens glared at them. The man writhed on the ground, screaming, as Zens fried his mind, killing the nerves. As his gaze slipped to the girl, she spasmed then lay still without uttering a sound.

"Clear the bodies," Zens snapped. "Put their ears in my tank."

657 snapped alert. "Yes, Commander." He signaled for two grunts to cut off the ears and take the bodies to the human flesh heap.

Zens grinned as blood from the slaves' severed ears splattered the stone.

As the tharuk underlings dragged the bodies away, Zens turned back to 000. "Don't worry, 000, we'll have our chance at revenge. Soon, dragon riders across the realm will be begging for mercy."

000 chuckled as they took the spiral access way deep into the bowels of the mines. Zens trudged downward, his mind churning. How could he increase the quality of the specimens?

The automatic stone-covered aluminum sliding doors hissed to admit them to the laboratory.

Zens ignored the two young mages—male and female—strapped to the examination beds in the anteroom. He stalked through to the lab where methimium-powered lights cast a yellow sheen over enormous glass vats in rows throughout the room. Tharuks busily tended the creatures growing within them. Dark masses of wing undulated gently in clear fluid, the odd talon, sinewy neck or fangs pressed against the glass sides.

Zens strode through the lab, under the left archway, and into the next chamber. 000 followed him in and barked a command at the tharuks tending smaller vats along the back wall.

The furry, tusked beasts swung about, their beady red eyes focused on Zens. They saluted, fists on chests. "Commander," they barked in unison, their guttural voices rumbling off the stone walls.

Which only increased Zens' headache. "Troop leader," he said.

Tharuk 873 stepped forward.

"They tell me your latest batch of experiments is ready for testing. If these specimens aren't hardy enough, the heads of your entire troop will roll."

"We start testing now."

Zens nodded. 873 had nerves of steel. There was nothing like the threat of carnage to keep tharuks in order. "We need more, faster. Double your production by tomorrow. 000, organize it."

Triple pointed at the troop of tharuks and clicked its fingers. "Follow me." They exited to the anteroom.

Zens lingered. "873, show me your best specimen."

"This one." 873 pointed at the closest vat.

Zens peered inside. The specimen appeared to be perfectly formed—four human limbs, the face a perfect replica of the girl on the bed. Even the blonde hair would fool anyone. What was causing his new humans' inherent weakness?

He melded with 873. *"Send me this specimen through with some testing material."* Grinding his teeth, he stormed through the main lab, following whimpers of terror to the anteroom.

The young male mage was whimpering more than the girl, who lay there in shock, hardly moving, only the occasional moan escaping her lips as the tharuks sliced deep into her thigh tissue.

000 and 873's highly trained team were driving needles into the male mage's spine and more into his hip bones. Keeping them conscious for the process was half the fun.

"Strap down his skull," Zens snapped. "Harvest the cells from his brain."

000 mind-melded with him. *"That might kill the mage."*

"He's strong enough," Zens replied. "And if he's not, we'll catch another, and another—until my army is indestructible."

As the mage's screams of pain filled the chamber, Zens' headache eased and he smiled.

873 marched the blonde mage they'd created into the room, hair still dripping from the vat. 924 dragged a littling slave into the antechamber, a boy whose lank red hair hung over his eyes.

Zens prowled around the clone, admiring the muscle tone in her limbs. He projected an image into the clone's mind: the female mage firing flame from her hands.

The clone raised her hands, fingers splayed, and shot a burst of flame at the antechamber's sliding door. A patch of the metal was stained black. Smoke and the stench of burned chemicals drifted though the antechamber.

924 knew the drill, placing the boy in a fireproof chamber in the corner.

"Not bad, but can you create enough flame to kill?" Zens goaded, sending the clone another vision.

The clone spun and flung her hands at the boy. He didn't stand a chance. Green flame licked up the shreds of his pathetic clothing and his skin caught. Too numlocked to react, he stood there, eyes vacant and jaw slack.

"More. Show me what you have." Zens pulsed power into the clone's head.

Torrents of flame speared from her fingers and whipped around the boy, engulfing him until he was a pillar of fire.

Zens waved the clone to stop. She stood with her hands at her sides awaiting his next command. He strode over and held out his hands, warming them over the burning child.

Wounded

Marlies heard thuds and shouting from the ledge outside the infirmary. Dragons were landing.

"Wounded incoming," she called to her husband, Hans. She put down her herbal tea and grabbed her cloak.

Hans clutched her arm, restraining her. "Marlies, pace yourself. You're looking tired." His green eyes were full of concern.

She was always tired nowadays. More so with every patient she treated. And every wound inflicted on her people by Commanders Zens and his tharuk armies. "I'm fine."

"You're far from fine and you know it." Hans donned his cloak too, and rushed out with her to the infirmary ledge.

Dragons landed. Riders clambered down into the snow and rushed to a dragon hauling a bloodied man from his saddle. They stumbled toward her, carrying him. His hands were gripping his abdomen, holding a gaping wound together. Marlies gasped. It was Seppi. The riders swept inside with them, taking Seppi to a bed. His face was blanched like an almond, teeth gritted in pain.

Riders propped his legs up as he hunched at the head of the bed.

Something had sliced through every layer of his clothing, spilling his guts. Glimpses of pale white and green showed through his bloodied fingers and bulged from the edges of the wound.

Hans, lips pressed into a grim line, brought piaua juice and clean herb over to Marlies. He passed a cup of water to a rider milling around nearby. "Ask Handel to heat this. My dragon knows exactly how warm." He gestured to another. "Fetch a needle and squirrel-gut twine from that drawer. Quick now, your leader needs you."

Seppi had been the leader of the blue guards ever since Marlies had come to Dragons' Hold. She'd patched him up more times than she could remember, but he'd never looked this bad.

Need anything else? Hans melded.

Marlies shook her head as she crumbled the clean herb into the warm water. "Seppi, this is going to hurt like hellfire."

He nodded. Wheezed. None of his usual banter.

Agonized grunts escaped from his clenched jaw as Marlies cleansed the wound. "Hans, get Leah. I need her steady hands before he bleeds out." Hans dispatched a rider to fetch her trainee healer.

It was an odd wound. A clean slice. The flesh was cut to the same depth right across his belly. And there was no dirt at all. She set her clean herb aside. Luckily the intestines and stomach appeared to be intact. "Who, or what, did this?" she asked.

Seppi's eyes were glazed. He didn't answer. One of the riders spoke up, "He was muttering about a dragon cutting him when we pulled him off Septimor."

A dragon? It couldn't have been. The wound would be ragged and dirty from its talons. Perhaps a very sharp blade. No, not with that precision while a man was on dragonback. "And how's Septimor? Is he injured too?"

"Rocco is with him. He has slight wing damage, and my dragon says something keeps screaming in Septimor's mind. Apart from that, he doesn't seem to be injured."

"My needle please, Hans," she barked. "And, Henry, bathe his gut with water so nothing dries out."

The rider stepped up with a wet cloth as she took the threaded needle from Hans. "Bring a candle please, I need more light. The rest of you, give us some space please, and make sure Septimor is all right."

Leah rushed to Marlies' side, her hair tied back in a scruffy tail. "You need me to hold the wound?"

Marlies nodded. "Thanks."

Seppi clenched his flesh, refusing to let go. Hans helped pry his fingers open. Leah grabbed the edges of the wound, tugging them together, and nimbly tucking his peeking gut back in. For the hundredth time since the girl had become her trainee a few short weeks ago, Marlies thanked the dragon gods that Leah had such steady hands and an instinct for healing.

Awash in blood, patches of Seppi's fatty layer gleamed white in the candlelight, as Marlies sutured the deepest layers of tissue together in Seppi's gut.

"Sorry, Seppi, here comes the hellfire. Hans, hold him down." He obliged, and she dribbled piaua juice over the tissue, watching it knit over before her eyes.

Seppi winced, groaning.

Piaua burned as it healed. Unpleasant, but lifesaving.

"That's the lining that holds the viscera in," she told Leah. "And these are the muscles that strengthen the stomach wall." She stitched the fibrous red meat that held Seppi's stomach together.

He moaned, his eyes rolling back in his head, and slumped on the bed.

"Maybe we should've given him woozy weed to knock him out," Leah murmured.

Voice tight, Marlies replied, "We couldn't. With a stomach injury, he couldn't digest it. And if there was a leak in his gut..."

Marlies held the slim vial of green fluid up to the candlelight. There was hardly any piaua juice left, and she still had to sew the layer that protected Seppi's muscle, and then his skin. "Hans, could you please get me more piaua juice?"

Hans retreated to her supply alcove.

"Marlies, you know there's only one more vial, don't you?" Hans melded. *"Those recent tharuk skirmishes in Spanglewood exhausted most of your supplies."*

"I'm well aware, but I can't let Seppi bleed out here on this bed. When all this is done, I'll nip back to Lush Valley and get some more."

Hans frowned as he returned with the precious vial in hand. *"I don't want you off on adventures again. I nearly lost you last time."*

He didn't have to say she hadn't been the same since Death Valley. She felt it every day.

The doors to the ledge flew open, and Kierion and Adelina rushed into the infirmary, washed their hands, and came over to the bed. "How can we help?" Kierion asked.

Leah answered. "You could collect some clean cloths from the alcove. Adelina, get Handel to heat some more clean herb in a large bowl of water. We don't want to infect Seppi when we're cleaning all the blood away."

Not that it would matter once his wound was healed with piaua and safely closed over, but Marlies didn't say anything, glad Leah was using her initiative.

"Sure," said Kierion. Whirling on his heel as Hans passed Leah the piaua, Kierion's elbow knocked Hans' hand.

The slim glass vial flew into the air, spinning, the juice glinting in the candle light. Marlies dropped her needle and snatched at empty air. Hans lunged. Kierion gasped and launched himself at the vial. He and Hans collided, his fingertips barely brushing the glass. The vial shattered on the stone, the precious piaua splattering and now contaminated with dirt.

Adelina gasped.

"I'll get you another one." Kierion raced toward the alcove.

"It's too late," Hans said. "That was the last one."

"Oh." Kierion's blue-gray eyes widened, then darted to Seppi. "Will he be all right? He'll make it, won't he?"

Shards. Shrotty bleeding shards.

"The lad feels bad enough," Hans melded, fists bunched at his sides. *"We can't rub salt in his wound."*

As the precious life-giving juice soaked into the stone, Marlies glanced at the few remaining drops in her nearly empty vial and smiled brightly. "Of course, Kierion. He'll be fine. Now, why don't you go and help Adelina get that warm water?"

As Kierion's slumped figure disappeared outside with Adelina, Leah leaned in and whispered, "If we can't seal the wound, what will happen if Seppi gets an infection?"

Marlies picked up her needle and tugged a stitch closed. It wasn't just Seppi she was worried about, although that was worry enough. She'd grown so used to using piaua, she'd come to rely on it. What would happen when the next tharuk battle came and wounded riders poured into the infirmary? How many would die from blood loss or infection then?

She had to get to Lush Valley to retrieve more juice. To hang with how sick and exhausted she was. The sooner she left, the better.

§

He was such a clumsy idiot. Kierion shook his head, still seeing the piaua vial shattering on stone, the precious juice—those drops that could've healed so many people's wounds—wasted. He passed Marlies the cloths she'd requested, then trudged out to the infirmary ledge with Adelina.

She squeezed his hand and disappeared under the overhang where Handel was resting.

Fenni was sitting on Riona's foreleg, leaning against her warm hide, his long legs crossed at the ankles.

Someone must've dropped him off here. Trust Fenni to find him right now after he'd just made such a blunder.

"That was quick. How's Seppi doing?" Fenni asked.

"Marlies is looking after him." There had to be something he could do, something, to make things right again. He'd give anything to fix what he'd broken. "Let's get on with training." He swung into the saddle and Fenni climbed up behind him. "Bye, Adelina."

She nodded, cradling a cup of clean herb.

"Kierion, you're unsettled. Why?" Trust Riona to notice.

Kierion didn't answer, turning to Fenni instead. "Let's shoot some targets."

Riona swooped over the target range. Fenni shot bolts of green mage fire from his hands. The flames sizzled through the air, hitting every target, extinguishing the moment they touched the boards, leaving a smoking black mark.

Kierion shot arrow after arrow.

"You're getting better," Fenni said. "You nearly hit all of them this time."

"Huh!" Kierion elbowed him in the ribs, and then nocked another arrow. Riona swooped and he loosed it. The arrow gave a satisfying thwack. "That was a bullseye."

Fenni laughed. "Riona helped by swooping."

"As she should. She's my dragon."

Riona snorted.

"All right, all right," Kierion replied. *"I'm* your *rider. I know no one owns a dragon."*

"Don't forget it."

Although Fenni couldn't understand their mind-melding, he laughed harder, guessing what Riona's snort had meant.

Kierion loosed another arrow, hitting the next target. He wasn't an arrow flinger. His skill was with a blade, but that was less useful on dragonback. He had no choice but to learn archery. His next arrow went wide.

No matter how many arrows he fired, though, the fragments of glass glistening green with piaua juice were still bright in his mind. Kierion sighed, his shoulders slumping.

"Hey, why are you so glum?" asked Fenni. "Was it the news of that dark dragon? Or seeing Seppi?"

"No, it's not the dark dragon, although that's bad enough. I messed up badly today. I smashed the last vial of piaua juice. Now, Seppi's wound isn't healed. If it wasn't for me, he'd be back in the saddle, fighting fit."

Fenni sucked his breath through his teeth in a hiss. "Oh, that's bad."

"I know. I'm not a tree speaker, so I can't get more juice, but there's got to be something I can do to fix it. Something I could do to make up for it."

"Don't worry," said Fenni. "We'll think of something. We've always gotten you out of every scrape before."

He was right. In all the long years they'd known each other, Fenni had often helped him out of trouble. Only recently, he'd saved his hide from tharuk tusks—yet again.

"What's that?" Fenni called, pointing toward the western summits of Dragon's Teeth. An orange smudge crested the mountains.

"Looks like Maazini." Kierion melded with Riona, *"Is that Maazini flying erratically over those peaks?"*

Riona replied, *"Yes, it's Maazini. His mind is tortured with the screams of a dark dragon."*

They sped toward the orange dragon, who was swooping, thrashing his claws.

Images cascaded through Kierion's mind. His ears rang with tortured screams. His head pounded, fit to split. A dark beast loomed in his mind, with roiling flame spouting from its maw. The black dragon, wings licking with green mage flame, plunged down into Great Spanglewood Forest. Even though they were only Maazini's memories passed via Riona, the scent of burning wings made Kierion's stomach roil. Gods, how awful.

"Riona, can you try and soothe him?"

"Of course. I am already. It's helping." Riona headed out toward the clearing by the lake where they'd breakfasted that morning. *"I've asked them to land so we can talk."*

Had it only been an hour or two since he'd been thinking of nothing but Adelina? So much had happened since then. He'd ruined the hold's most precious healing supply, and they'd discovered a new threat looming over Dragons' Realm.

Fenni's hands tightened around Kierion's waist as Riona descended.

Below them, Maazini landed, furling his wings, his feet crunching in the snow. He sunk to his haunches, obviously exhausted. Tomaaz was hunched over him, arms around his neck, crooning to Maazini.

Kierion's heart lurched. Gods, Tomaaz had only just rescued Maazini from Death Valley and Commander Zens' enslavement. What Commander Zens had wanted with the dragon, Kierion didn't know. Speculation was rife at Dragons' Hold. Perhaps the Council of the Twelve Dragon Masters knew something…

Riona landed with a grunt in the clearing. Kierion slipped off her back and strode over to Tomaaz. "What can we do to help?"

Tomaaz, lying against Maazini's orange scales, turned his head. "He's all right. He's settling now. At least that horrible screaming has stopped. It was like my head was on fire, burning with pain. It must've been worse for him."

Kierion patted Maazini's neck. "Poor boy."

Tomaaz shook his head. "The dark dragon had strange yellow beams that shot from its eyes—like the sun's rays."

Kierion had never heard of anything like it. "Seppi and Septimor were attacked too."

Maazini growled.

"I don't think there's anything that can fight that beast." Tomaaz's face was haggard. "With flames like that, and a mind that drives any dragon or rider crazy, what can we do?" Tomaaz barked a harsh laugh. "Attack it from behind while it's not looking?"

Kierion pursed his lips. Actually, that might not be a bad idea.

"Kierion, what are you thinking now?" Riona's tone was full of warning. She flicked her tail, showering him with a flurry of snow.

Kierion just stared at her tail.

Patting Maazini's foreleg, he said, "Take care of yourselves today. It'd pay to report to Lars. I have some urgent training."

Kierion leaped into the saddle, but this time, behind Fenni. "Fenni, strap yourself in. Riona, please let Linaia and Adelina know we need them, urgently."

"Why am I up front?" Fenni shook his head, groaning. "I know that look. You have another crazy idea, haven't you?"

If it could help, maybe it wasn't that crazy.

SECRETS

"Roberto," Ezaara melded. "Roberto, don't shut me out. Not now, when you need me."

Roberto had to. He couldn't let her into his mind to see the turmoil: fists on young skin; boots in the ribs; blood on his sister's face; his mother, broken in a heap on the ground.

Bile rose in Roberto's throat. He swallowed it. "You." His voice was a harsh whisper echoing through the cavern.

The monster before him raised another trembling hand. "Son?" Amato croaked.

"You forfeited the right to be my father." Beside Roberto, Ezaara cringed at the harshness in his voice. Gods, oh gods. He'd thought his father was dead. The Naobian Council had searched the lake and never found any sign of Matotoi or Amato.

Ezaara elbowed him in the ribs.

He blocked her out, keeping himself safe behind the wall he'd erected. The wall she'd broken through just moons ago, with her honesty, naivety and beauty.

"You used to look like her," croaked the skeletal man, shuffling forward. "Like your mother. But now…" He faltered and stopped just beyond the shaft of daylight, staring at Roberto. "But now… now you look like me."

Ice shot through Roberto's veins. "*You?*" Roberto sneered. "I am not like *you.*"

There it was: his deepest fear laid bare.

After the terrible things Zens had made him do, he'd spent years proving to the world—and himself—that he wasn't his father. Roberto wanted to lash out and strike Amato—to drive his sword through his father's throat. Oh gods, he didn't even have a weapon with him. Did wanting one make him as much of a monster as his father? His hands shook. Cool pebbles of sweat broke out on his forehead.

"You need me now, more than ever," Ezaara hissed in Roberto's ear. "You can't be the only strong one, always there for me. Let me be here for you, now." She grabbed Roberto's hand and squeezed it. Hard.

Reluctantly, he let down his walls.

"So, this is the monster that ruined your family."

He swallowed, his mind too numb to reply.

"I believe you're Amato." Ezaara's word echoed off the cavern's stone walls.

The dragon, Matotoi—now only a pale faded version of the healthy green he'd once been—nudged Amato's back. A quick bob of the head was the only sign Roberto's father gave that he'd heard Ezaara. His eyes didn't leave Roberto's face. The hunger in his gaze set Roberto's cheek twitching. His father looked desperate, a starving, destitute man outside a bakery window.

Ezaara tried again. "How long have you been here?"

"Don't know," Pa croaked, eyes still on Roberto. "How long has it been, my boy, since I killed your mother?"

Roberto broke his silence. "I'm not your boy."

"Son." Amato sprang, his wiry legs propelling him across the shaft of sunlight. Dropping to his knees, he grasped Roberto's arm with clammy hands. "Please, Son. Please. It was Zens' fault. He made me do it."

"You killed her, all right. She suffered long moons in living torture before she died. But you did her a favor shoving her off your dragon—it was better than living another day with you."

"He drove me to everything. With his methimium crystal, he turned me. It wasn't in my nature. None of it was." Amato sobbed. "Please, you have to believe me."

Roberto raised an eyebrow, appraising the worm that had robbed him of his innocence, given him into slavery and corrupted him. It had been a long hard crawl back to decency. "I have to do nothing of the sort." He shook Amato off his arm.

"Out of the goodness of your heart, I beg you, please take me with you." Amato's words croaked out between sobs.

"Goodness? You think there's goodness in my heart? After the way you treated me?" There was goodness in his heart, but not for Amato. The only thing he had left for his father was a black rotten canker that was rising up his gorge and threatening to choke him. And it was getting worse by the heartbeat. Roberto tugged Ezaara's hand. "Come on, let's go." He turned his back on Amato.

"Please," Amato called. "You're my only hope. I can't hold my breath long enough to swim out any more. Please, let a rope down through the hole and pull me out of this miserable hell."

"Roberto, look," Ezaara melded.

"No. That louse ruined my life." Roberto pulled Ezaara back through the chamber the way they'd come.

"Take me with you." Amato's plaintive cry echoed off the cavern walls.

Roberto strode toward the lake, dragging Ezaara with him. He had to get out of here, get that man out of his head.

"*Roberto! You're squeezing my hand so hard you're hurting me.*"

"Oh, sorry." He released her hand but kept walking. He had to get out of here before he exploded. Before he went back to pummel that frail wretch. Before he did something that he'd forever hate himself for.

Matotoi keened, his wail making goosebumps ripple down Roberto's back.

"*Oh, Roberto! This is awful,*" Ezaara melded.

"*He's awful. He killed my mother and beat my littling sister black and blue. You know that.*"

"*No, I meant this.*" Ezaara shared her memory of Amato stepping into the sunlight, stretching his arm high toward the hole in the cavern's rocky ceiling. "Please, let a rope down through the shaft…" his father said. A puckered scar ran across his father's back under his shoulder blade. "*That. That scar's what I mean.*"

"*I don't care if he's got old injuries or whether he's been hurt. He killed villagers in Naobia. He betrayed us to—*"

Ezaara shared another memory. It was Roberto, lying on her bed, unconscious. Marlies made a deep incision into the skin under his shoulder blade. He felt tears on Ezaara's cheeks, tasted their salt as she squeezed the edges of the wound. A fat yellow crystal slithered out onto his back. "*What if your father had a crystal from Zens, just like you did?*" she asked. "*What did he call it, methimium?*"

By the holy dragon gods, no.

Even though he'd loved her, Roberto had come close to killing Ezaara, goaded by the dark shadows and whispering voices in his mind. His feet became leaden and he slumped against the slick stone wall.

When Ezaara and Marlies had drugged him and removed his implant, he'd wondered whether Amato had been driven to his actions through Zens' yellow crystals.

He folded his arms, staring down at Ezaara's earnest face, illuminated by the pale light of the glowworms. Nearby, the lake lapped at the rock, beckoning him to escape from this nightmare. "*I don't care. He still did what he did*"

Ezaara folded her arms. Thrust her chin out. *"And I don't care. You did what you did."*

"I felt terrible about what I did. My father's a monster with no conscience."

"We can't change the past, but we can change the future." She stalked off, away from the entrance, deeper into the cavern.

"Hey, where are you going?"

"If you leave your father here and he dies, that bitter hate inside you will grow until it consumes you. We're starting our life's journey together. I don't want to live with a man who'll end up hating himself."

"I don't hate myself. I hate him."

"It's the same thing, Roberto." Ezaara's quiet footsteps were drowned out by Roberto's thudding heart.

§

Ezaara sighed as the Naobian coast came into view. Thank the Egg, they were nearly at their holiday cottage. Roberto had been silent and tense the entire trip back from Crystal Lake. What had been a short trip there had turned into an extended nightmare on the return flight. Matotoi, a pale skeletal thing, had needed a light scarf across his eyes—it'd been so long since he'd flown in daylight. Or flown anywhere. His wings were weak, so they'd had to land regularly to give him enough rest between short bursts of flight.

And although Ezaara had offered to take Amato on Zaarusha to spare Roberto the pain of traveling with his father, Roberto had insisted the danger of him attacking her was too great. So Amato's scrawny form was hunched in front of Roberto, his arms flung around Erob's neck. His eyes were closed, and there was a trace of a smile on his face.

"Is he asleep?" she asked.

"No. He says sun's too strong for his eyes."

"Poor man."

"Don't poor man him again, Ezaara. He was a terrible tyrant."

She understood. She really did. Agony laced Roberto's words. His memories still roiled inside him. Blood. Pain. Beatings. Amato had enjoyed inflicting pain, reveled in it.

But the gibbering man she'd seen in the cave had not been the same Amato as the one in Roberto's memories, just as Roberto was not the same as when he'd been drugged to train with Commander Zens. They both had blood on their hands. Roberto had redeemed himself. Amato had not. But that didn't mean that he couldn't. If Roberto had left Amato in that cave today, he wouldn't have forgiven himself. Zaarusha banked, heading over the verdigris copper-shingled roofs of Naobia, toward their little cottage by the shore. The faint tang of smoke hung in the air. The Queen landed on the beach, a flurry of sand swirling in the draft from her wingbeats. *"Stop fretting, Ezaara. Roberto will be all right. It'll take time, but he'll get there."*

Roberto's stormy eyes flashed and his jaw was clenched as Erob landed near them.

"I hope so."

Ezaara slid out of the saddle, gathered her belongings from the saddlebags, and trudged up the beach to the cottage. Better to give father and son some space. She didn't need to watch out for Roberto. Amato was in no shape to attack, and Roberto could defend himself.

Tough grasses and hardy beach daisies peppered the path through the yard. At the threshold of the cottage, she paused. The door was slightly ajar. Had Roberto forgotten to lock it?

No, *she'd* locked the door. She remembered turning the key. Cautiously, Ezaara pushed the door open.

Holy dragon gods.

Food was mashed across the walls. The comfy sofa had been slashed and stuffing strewn over the floor. Drawers were overturned, and crockery smashed.

Heart pounding, Ezaara dropped her belongings on the doorstep, and drew her sword. She tiptoed through the living room, over the debris and pushed the bedroom door open.

The curtains around the fourposter bed had been ripped down. The bedding was shredded and her clothing flung about the room. The bedside table was still standing, but the top was empty.

No. Anakisha's teardrop-shaped crystal necklace, the dream-catcher, was gone. And so was Anakisha's ring—the key to the realm gates.

"It's only me." Light footsteps echoed on the floorboards as Roberto checked the rest of the cottage. *"No one's here."*

"The ring, Roberto…"

"Gods, not the ring, too," he said, coming through the doorway and enveloping her his arms. *"We'll find it. We'll hunt down whoever stole it."*

It was too much. After everything that'd happened today—Simeon, Amato, and now, this. "Why?"

"Because you're Queen's Rider."

"Can't we ever have peace? Time for us?" Her breath shuddered out of her.

His warmth wrapped around her, his *sathir* enveloping her completely. Roberto's only answer was a sigh.

Hours later, after they'd salvaged whatever wasn't broken and burned and disposed of the rest, Ezaara and Roberto went outside to Amato, asleep under Matotoi's wing. The moon lit a trail of shimmering silver on the sea.

"Erob and I caught them some fish." Zaarusha was settled on her haunches nearby, watching them. *"You've had a tough day."*

Erob dropped to the sand. *"Would a short flight in the moonlight help?"*

"I'll guard the prisoners." Zaarusha snarled. *"I'm not letting them get away. Even though they're broken, Amato and Matotoi must still be tried at Dragons' Hold for Amato's crimes. Take some time to recover."*

Roberto turned to Ezaara. "Just a short flight?".

Ezaara nodded and clambered up into Erob's saddle. With Roberto's warmth at her back and his arms around her, they ascended into the night to the swish of Erob's wingbeats and the muted hiss of the tide washing against the sand.

Roberto's voice rumbled through his chest, against her back. "It's amazing to think that all that sand was made from those rocky cliffs. That the water beating relentlessly against those cliffs has worn them down into something as minuscule as sand. You know, Ezaara, when I was a littling and things were hard, I'd come to this beach and remind myself that I wasn't sand. I refused to let my father beat me down into sand." His arms tightened around her waist. "We're young. Strong. We can let the sea rage at our feet without crumbling into sand. Together, we can do this."

"Together, yes." Because by now, alone, she'd be falling apart. She leaned back into him.

Roberto lifted her hair and kissed the side of her neck. "Together," he murmured.

Ezaara sighed, gazing at the white-tipped tide below.

Erob flew along the beach, riding the warm thermal currents.

When they landed near the cottage an hour later, a green guard was awaiting them. "I've come to check that you're all right, my honored Queen's Rider."

"I was shaken, but I'm fine, thank you."

The guard raised a questioning eyebrow at Roberto.

"The Queen's Rider can speak for herself." Roberto said tersely, his eyes darting to Matotoi. Amato was peeking out from under his wing. "*I don't want anyone recognizing Amato. Not yet. Not until we've figured out what we're doing with him,"* he melded.

"Did you capture Bruno and Simeon?" As Ezaara said Simeon's name, his lewd glances and threats loomed in her head.

They guard grimaced. "I'm sorry, they got away."

An ugly chill crawled over her skin.

"They what?" Roberto snapped, dark eyes flashing. He stepped up to the guard, jaw clenched and voice icy. "There were green guards at the scene. Several of them."

"Bruno raced through the littlings, scattering their fire-sticks, deliberately setting a corner of the market alight. We were busy fighting fires and rescuing folk. Your attackers slipped through the alleyways and were lost."

Suddenly, everything made sense to Ezaara. "You might have lost them, but they weren't lost. They came here and ransacked our cottage. Come with me," she said, leading the guard to their rented cottage. *"Get Amato out of the way so he's not recognized."* She opened the door. "There was food and smashed crockery everywhere. They shredded our bedding and the curtains. And they've stolen two of Anakisha's precious heirlooms, which we need to fight this war against Commander Zens. If they fall into Zens' hands, the consequences could be dire."

If Zens got his hands on that ring, he'd have the ability to travel anywhere instantaneously. Even to Dragons' Hold. But she kept that quiet. There was no point in informing the entire green guard troop about the ring's purpose.

"I apologize that this has happened to you in Naobia."

"Bruno and Simeon could strike anywhere. Whatever happens, we need to track them down and retrieve those heirlooms. Bruno is thin and wiry with brown hair and—"

"There's no need. Queen Zaarusha has shared her memory of them with my dragon. I know what they look like—a ring and necklace, right? I'll get someone to bring you more food and bedding. I'm sorry you've had to go through this on your hand-fasting holiday, my honored Queen's Rider." He thumped his right fist on his heart and left.

When the green guard had gone, Roberto came inside.

"Where's Amato?" Ezaara asked.

Roberto screwed his nose up. "On the latrine. Apparently those apricots we gave him had quite an effect after he'd only eaten fish and lake weed for years."

He slumped into an armchair, his head in his hands. "What are we going to do with him, Ezaara?"

She walked over and sat on the arm of the chair, stroking his dark hair. "He needs to be heard and tried. The question is whether his trial should be here or at Dragons' Hold."

"We're supposed to be back tomorrow evening. We'll never make it without the rings. Even with a healthy dragon, it's a three-day flight. With Matotoi, it'll take a week. Maybe we could leave his dragon here."

"No!" The strength of her reaction surprised her. "I know. I've been mulling it over. Leave Amato here or take him? His crimes were against Naobia and the realm. I think he needs to come back to Dragons' Hold, but I just can't find a way of getting him there fast." He sighed and stood. "I just thank the Egg that you were with me. I might have gutted him on the spot."

"I'm glad you were there for me today, too."

"I'm kicking myself for leaving you alone. If that louse had—"

"No." She placed a finger on his lips. "Don't let him intrude here."

There was a knock at the door. Ezaara opened it to the herbalist from the marketplace. "I've come to bring you bedding and food," the old lady said, eyes raking over them both. She held a large basket of goods.

"And to gather fodder for her gossip," Ezaara added to Roberto.

He chuckled and kissed the old lady on the cheek. "Nice of you to help us, Martha. I've an errand to attend to." He melded with Ezaara. *"Let me know when she's gone. She's the last one I want to see Amato."*

"Is that you, Martha?" Amato's voice croaked from behind the herbalist.

"Too late."

Amato stepped into the light spilling from the door.

Martha spun. Dropped her basket. Apples rolled across the path, bouncing across Amato's bare feet.

"By the roaring dragon gods," Martha whispered. "You!"

"I can explain." Amato combed his matted beard with his fingers. "I—"

"No one could ever explain your atrocities, Amato," she snapped. "My friends and neighbors were killed, thanks to you. You—you poisonous viper!"

She thrust the quilts into Ezaara's arms, the food into Roberto's, and snatched up her basket. She stormed past Amato. "I hope you don't live through the night," she hissed, spitting on him.

Amato's shoulders caved as he gibbered to himself, "Zens made me do it. Zens. He made do it, he did."

Roberto glanced at Ezaara. *"So much for keeping his presence secret. The whole of Naobia will know by morning."* He strode inside and plonked the food on the table. Then he manhandled Amato into the house, shoved him onto the couch, and flung a quilt on him. He walked over and locked the door. "You're sleeping here. No leaving—or I will hunt you down and gut you."

"Matotoi. I must have Matotoi. Sleep by Matotoi." Amato answered, crawling over and clawing at the door.

"He can watch you through the window... now that the curtains are torn off. Get on the couch, so we can get some sleep."

A few moments later, Matotoi appeared outside one window and Erob outside another.

Amato curled up in a tight ball on the couch and drifted into a fitful sleep.

Roberto frowned. *"He could wake any time and slit our throats in our sleep."*

From outside the window, Erob melded, *"Zaarusha and I will keep watch."*

Ezaara picked up one of Martha's quilts. *"You both need your strength for flying."*

"Excuse me, Ezaara," Erob melded, *"but Zaarusha and I have done nothing but rest and eat since we got here, while you two have been, um ... expending energy."*

Ezaara's cheeks grew hotter than the Robandi desert.

Roberto huffed. "Lucky we did. We won't have much chance for that anymore with my father around."

STRATEGY

The snap of Lars' gavel on the granite table echoed through the council chamber, making Tomaaz and Maazini twitch.

"Easy boy," Tomaaz melded.

At least his dragon's mental agony had ceased. The only wound Maazini had received from the encounter with the dark dragon over Spanglewood Forest was a hole on the edge of his wing. They hadn't been caught by an arrow or sword, and it didn't appear to be a burn hole, so Tomaaz couldn't figure out what had caused it. He'd slapped some healing salve on it to soothe his dragon before they'd been summoned to this council meeting.

Masters Tonio, Derek and Alyssa broke off a quiet discussion in the corner and took their seats—Tonio and Alyssa on either side of Master Aidan, who was nursing a mug of peppermint tea; and Derek next to Hendrick on the opposite side of the horseshoe-shaped council table.

Lars cleared his throat and stood, his imposing figure towering over the remaining dragon masters and master mages seated at the table. With Ezaara and Roberto gone, Ma and Pa in the infirmary and Shari and Jaevin dead, there were easily enough seats for the master mages, including Jael, at Tomaaz's side next to Giddi and Starrus.

The masters' dragons sat along the rear wall of the cavern behind their riders, talons scratching stone as they settled onto their haunches.

"A dark dragon prowling Great Spanglewood Forest has attacked two of our dragons and riders," Lars said. "This isn't a dragon we've seen before. This creature hasn't come from the brown guards over the far ranges in the north, or from the red guards posted near the northern Terramites. In fact, we don't know where it's from, or who has sired it. Roberto said he'd seen Zens growing black creatures that could've been dragons when he was captive in Death Valley. We suspect it's one of Commander Zens' creations."

The council chamber erupted in a chorus of strident outbursts. Masters gesticulated. Hendrik thumped the table. Crouched at the back of the council chamber on their haunches, the masters' dragons scratched their talons on the stone floor. Chips skittered across rock. Lars' dragon Singlar thrashed his tail against the wall with a boom that silenced the babble.

"*Thank the Egg for that,*" Maazini said. "*That racket was making my head ache again.*"

"*Are you feeling better now?*" Tomaaz asked.

Maazini rumbled in assent, but the mind-frying screech they'd both heard had rattled him.

"Seppi is lying gravely injured in the infirmary," Lars continued, "hence Marlies' absence. With the leader of the blue guards incapacitated, I call upon Tomaaz, who was also attacked, to report."

Tomaaz rose to his feet. "We were on a routine patrol when a dark dragon rose from the trees and flamed us. Strange yellow beams came from its eyes, but the worst thing was its mind scream. It rattled my skull like a thunderstorm in my head." In the corner, Maazini whimpered. "It was worse for Maazini. He was clawing at his head, yowling. It took some distance and a while before he could calm himself again."

"A mind scream?" Lars asked. "Is this some awful weapon that these dragons used against you? Are you sure it wasn't trying to meld?"

Tomaaz shrugged. "I don't know. I've never felt anything like it. But it definitely felt like an attack, not an attempt to meld."

Lars turned to Tonio. "In all your experience as spymaster, have you ever come across this?"

Tonio's dark brows furrowed. "I can't say I have." He steepled his hands, resting his chin on his fingertips. "It was screaming in Maazini's mind? And yours?"

"Because I was melded with Maazini, it was agonizing. It drove everything else out of my head. When I broke meld, the screaming was quieter, but still there."

"Hmm, an effective weapon," Tonio said. "What was the effect on your dragon?"

"Maazini was thrashing and bucking, clawing at his head. I've never seen him so distressed."

Tonio arched an eyebrow, as if Tomaaz's short experience with dragons didn't count for much.

True. He'd only melded with Maazini short moons ago.

Battle Master Aidan spoke up, "There's other news from Montanara: one of the blue guards reported a fracas among the tharuks. More of them are infiltrating the city each day. We need eyes and ears on the ground there to keep us informed of what's happening. A troop of dragons would be good too, if we can spare them."

Tonio sighed, running a weary hand through his hair. "We need eyes and ears everywhere. Zens is producing tharuks at such a rapid rate our forces are stretched thin as it is."

Aidan shoved his mug across the table. "We could do with an extra few hundred dragons, but we can't breed them that fast. It takes time to grow a dragon to maturity and its useful state."

An answering chorus of snorts came from the dragons along the back wall.

"With all due respect." Aidan inclined his head toward them.

The heavy double doors to the council chamber opened, and Ma walked in with Pa hovering by her side, his hand on her back.

"Gods, Maazini," Tomaaz melded, *"when did Ma get those dark shadows under her eyes? She's so thin."*

"She's looked like that since I first met her in Death Valley," Maazini replied.

Surely not. Why hadn't he noticed? Had he been so busy he'd missed what was happening with his family? He nodded to himself. Yes, after a six-week stint in Death Valley, he'd been out on patrol every day and spending his spare moments with Lovina. The only time he'd visited his family's cavern was to sleep.

Ma took her seat at the council table between Master Hendrick and Roberto's empty one, and Pa slid into his chair next to Master Lars.

Master Giddi nodded at them. "Greetings, Marlies, Hans."

"How's Seppi?" asked Lars.

Ma cleared her throat. "Not well." Deep lines bordered her mouth and eyes, lines that hadn't been there when they'd lived in Lush Valley a few short moons ago. And she was pale. Yes, they all were—it was winter—but not like her.

"Maazini," Tomaaz melded, *"Can you please ask Liesar if Ma is sick?"*

"Of course."

Ma continued speaking, "...there's a gash across his middle but I can't figure out what made it. Seppi swears yellow beams of light shot from the dragon's eyes and cut him open, but surely that's impossible. Yet the cut was so clean, it couldn't have been made by claws or teeth."

Tonio's eyebrows shot up. "Yellow beams?"

"Yes, that's what he said, but he's fevered, so it might be delirium." Ma shook her head. "The worst thing is that we've run out of piaua juice."

"By the dragon gods, how?" Lars thundered.

Ma turned to Lars. "It was an accident. Someone knocked the last vial and it spilled on the floor."

Tomaaz's hip had been shattered only weeks before, and Ma had repaired the bone with the miraculous juice and some compounds she'd had on hand then closed the wound. Without piaua, he would have bled out or remained a cripple. What would happen to the wounded riders returning from battle to be healed by his mother? A hollow ache opened in his belly. Half of his friends would be dead without piaua juice.

Tonio leaned over the table, stabbing a finger at Ma. His voice was quiet. "It was Kierion, wasn't it, Marlies?"

Everyone froze, awaiting Ma's answer. You could've heard a dragon scale drop.

The doors creaked open. Kierion stood in the doorway, his eyes sweeping the council room and the silent masters. "Oh, I've interrupted something, haven't I?" He backed out of the chamber, tugging the door closed.

Tonio called, "Kierion, please come in. I have an opportunity you may be interested in."

Kierion entered, his eyes darting toward the spymaster and away again. He stood, shoulders back and chest thrust out. "Yes, sir?"

The spymaster pushed his chair out from the table and stalked toward Kierion. "You're from Montanara, aren't you?"

Kierion replied with a terse nod.

Tomaaz stared at Kierion. What was going on? He was usually so full of life and exuberance. Now, he was as tense as a battle-ready dragon.

"So you'd be familiar with the city?" Tonio said sternly. "The streets and alleys? And know many Montanarians?"

Kerion nodded again, his wary eyes flitting around the room. "Yes, sir."

"It seems we have a disturbance in Montanara. You might be the right man to figure out what's going on."

Kierion opened his mouth as if to protest, but Tonio shot him a meaningful glance. Kierion nodded. "Yes, sir. I'm your man."

Tomaaz shifted in his chair. What had just passed between those two?

Kierion continued, "Actually, Master Lars and honored council members, I came here to tell you about an exciting development in training. Fenni and I have a new tactic that could help in battle."

Derek, the training master, raised an eyebrow. "And you've brought this to the council now because...?"

Kierion studied the floor then raised his eyes to meet Derek's. "Because I feel terrible about breaking the last vial of piaua."

Gasps rippled through the room.

"Hasn't Marlies told you?"

Ma hadn't confirmed anything. If only Kierion had kept his mouth shut.

"Yes, Master Tonio," Kierion continued, "I'll go to Montanara, but first, let me show you this technique we've mastered."

Lars spoke up, "What about Gret, the Montanarian swordmaster's daughter? Surely she could go to Montanara if there's something to be uncovered?"

"We could send a whole troop of dragons and riders in," Tonio said, "but that's more likely to spark a battle than prevent one. If Kierion and Gret can casually infiltrate the city and find out what's going on, we may have a chance of nipping any conflict in the bud before it escalates into an all-out battle."

It sounded reasonable. But during battle, everything went haywire despite the best plans. Before tharuks had attacked Lush Valley, Tomaaz had never even seen them, but his boots were soon grimy with their dark sticky blood.

"Then it's decided," Lars said. "Tonio, please inform Gret that she's traveling to Montanara tomorrow night with Kierion. After this meeting adjourns, Kierion will show us what he and Fenni have developed. Kierion, Fenni can accompany you to Montanara so you can perfect your training techniques there while you ferret out whatever's going on. It won't harm you to have a little mage power at your side. If you find any valuable information, get Riona to mind-meld with the closest blue guards to keep us informed."

Master Starrus, leader of the Wizard Council, flung a hand toward Master Giddi, the dragon mage. "You know, none of this would have happened if it wasn't for you. If you'd controlled your rutting lust for that trumped-up student of yours, Commander Zens and his tharuks wouldn't be in Dragons' Realm."

The blood drained from Master Giddi's face.

Starrus stood, face splotched red. "Years ago, I watched you strut around, flashing your power about like a littling with a new toy. Young and impressionable, Mazyka fell for you. And you were stupid enough to act on it. Thinking of your loins, not the safety of the realm, you took her to your bed and shared every last magical secret with her—despite her power—even though you were leader of the Wizard Council and should've known better." Bitterness laced his words. "And when Mazyka wanted to open a world gate, I warned you, but no, no, you knew better."

Giddi had gone deathly still. Too still, like a viper about to strike.

"She had her way with you," Starrus continued, stabbing a finger at Giddi. "She used you and broke our realm forever." Spittle flew from Starrus' mouth, spraying his snowy beard. "As long as I'm the head of the Wizard Council, I'll never ever forgive you."

Giddi's eyes tracked Starrus' every movement, but the most powerful mage in the realm said nothing.

The two mages stared at each other, tension crackling between their locked eyes.

The hum of magic made Tomaaz's scalp prickle.

"Well, thanks for the history lesson, but we need to get on with strategy," Lars said dryly.

Nervous chuckles rippled around the room.

"History?" Master Giddi snapped. "I hardly say his account has historical accuracy." Giddi barked a brittle laugh, but didn't break his glare at Starrus', staring at him until the leader dropped his eyes to his hands—as if they held the secrets to saving the realm.

Lars smacked his gavel on the table. "Now, to the next matter. How will we replenish the piaua juice? As the only tree speaker among us, Marlies must inform us."

Ma rose to her feet, gripping the tabletop. "The closest piaua tree is in Great Spanglewood Forest near Master Giddi's cabin; however, when tharuks rampaged through Spanglewood, they destroyed that source. I propose that I visit the piaua tree in Lush Valley and take Leah with me to train her as the next tree speaker for Dragons' Hold."

"No!" Pa's retort shot across the room, echoing on the stone, leaving the masters stunned and Master Alyssa open-mouthed.

Lars raised an eyebrow. "That's rather strong sentiment from you, Hans."

"Marlies hasn't been herself since Death Valley," Pa replied. "She's unwell, exhausted, and hasn't recovered yet. I beg you keep her here. Please, for her own good."

Lars scratched his blond beard, the rasp grating on Tomaaz's ears.

Oh, gods, even Pa knew.

Tomaaz felt terrible because he hadn't noticed.

Lars addressed Ma, "Marlies, the future of the realm weighs heavily upon us. What are our chances of healing our wounded without piaua juice?"

Ma's hand shook as she tucked her dark hair behind her ear. "Our chances are greatly reduced. Without being able to instantly heal riders' wounds, the risk of infection is high. We'll face more amputations, fevers, and we will lose many, perhaps up to a third or half of our wounded. I personally don't want to risk losing that many of my friends."

Pa's voice was hoarse. "Even at the risk of us losing you?"

"I told you, I'm fine, Hans. I'll pack my things, prepare Leah, and leave tomorrow." Ma sat again, landing heavily on her chair.

Her legs had been about to give out. She hardly had strength to stand. No, this couldn't be happening to Ma. She'd been so vibrant and full of life. Stricken, Tomaaz's eyes met Pa's.

Pa gave him a grim nod, his green eyes heavy.

"That's settled then." Lars tapped his gavel on the granite. "We'll adjourn to watch Kierion and Fenni from the ledge."

Tomaaz and Pa hung back, waiting silently for Ma, while everyone else filed out, sensing their need to be alone as a family.

"Does Ezaara know how sick you are, Ma?" Tomaaz asked, taking her cool hand in his.

Ma forced a cheery smile. "She knows I'm tired."

Tomaaz squeezed her hand. "This is not just tired, is it, Ma? You're ill. You haven't recovered, and you may not."

Tears glimmered silver in Ma's eyes. "I have to do what's best for the realm. I destroyed so much, years ago. Now I have to—"

Hans stood abruptly. "Now you're going to destroy yourself to try and pay Zaarusha back?" He paced the floor behind the empty chairs, his boots drumming an angry tattoo into the rock. "No one is expecting you to do this. You can't."

Ma stared at Pa in that way of hers, her turquoise eyes piercing his bright green ones—until he looked away.

Finally she spoke, "I'm leaving tomorrow morning at dawn."

TRAINING

A cool trickle of sweat slithered down Kierion's back. Behind him, all the masters and master mages of the realm were gathered. Hopefully he could prove himself. And clear his name. Surely they'd be impressed by his latest trick?

Fenni waited in Riona's saddle, eyeing the masters as Kierion approached and climbed into the saddle behind him. Fenni whispered, "I hope this doesn't muck things up even more."

Kierion pasted a grin on his face, turned to the assembled throng and spoke with confidence he didn't feel. "This new trick could be vital in battle. Tomaaz has told us of the formidable dark dragon who injured Seppi and frazzled Maazini's nerves. It attacked using mental assault, fire, and strange rays from its eyes. One of the best ways to outwit this type of dragon may be to sneak up on it from the rear."

The stony-faced gazes of the dragon masters did nothing to bolster his confidence.

Lars said dryly, "Let's see what new tactics you've come up with this time."

Master Jerrick, next to him, nodded.

"*Well, here goes.*" Kierion melded with Riona.

She unfurled her wings, took a running leap and tensed her haunches, soaring off the ledge. Kierion's usual thrill at being airborne was replaced with a rash of chilly goosebumps across his back. They'd only practiced an hour. What if things went wrong and he plunged to his death?

From a nearby ledge, Linaia sprang into the air, racing toward Riona, gusting fire.

"*Steady, girl.*" Kierion melded. He slipped off the saddle and slithered backward, careful to slide around her spinal ridges and not impale himself. Yikes, if he messed this up in battle, he'd ruin his chances of ever having littlings. Soon he was at the base of Riona's back. She flew behind Linaia. The trees and snowy clearing beckoned below, teasing him, promising sure death should he slip and lose his grasp. Hands slicked with sweat, Kierion wormed his way down her tail. "*Am I too heavy?*"

"No," replied Riona. *"Slide down a little farther."*

Kierion scooted over two more of her tiny tail spines and hooked his legs around her tail to hold on. Beaded with sweat, his scalp and forehead prickled in the cool breeze. *"Now, Riona, or I'm going to lose my nerve."*

"You had plenty of nerve while we were practicing," she replied.

"I know. But I'm surprised you can even carry me with the council glaring down at us. I'm sure I must be half a dragon-weight heavier than usual."

She gave a dragonly chuckle and edged closer to Linaia.

Linaia blasted flame at an imaginary enemy, just as they'd practiced. Riona swept down behind her and flicked her tail launching Kierion through the air.

Snow and a blur of trees flew past beneath him. Gods, was he going to fall short? He flailed his arms and wheeled his legs.

He had to keep calm, stay focused. He slammed into Linaia's sky-blue scales, grabbed one of her spinal ridges and hoisted himself up onto her back. Kierion drew his sword, and held it at Adelina's throat. "Surrender and call off your dragon," he crowed.

Singlar, Lars' dragon, gave a mighty roar that sent a chunk of loose snow ricocheting down the mountainside.

"We're wanted urgently back up on the ledge," Riona melded.

Kierion leaned forward to Adelina. "Are you all right?"

"Of course I am," she said. "But I don't like the way the masters are looking at you."

Oh well, he'd tried. He had nothing else to offer. Only his daring, his head for heights and his crazy ideas. Kierion sighed, using the opportunity to slip his arms around Adelina's waist while Linaia took them back to the ledge. That was the other thing: how was he going to get to know her better if he was stationed in Montanara? They landed on the ledge alongside Riona and Fenni.

Lars' expression could have melted the icy peaks of Dragon's Teeth. Kierion dismounted and stood, knees trembling, before the council. Adelina and Fenni came to stand on either side of him.

Master Jerrick was shaking his head, Master Derek was frowning, and Master Tonio had his eyes narrowed, scrutinizing him. The spymaster's gaze made Kierion feel like he was wearing clothes of glass—naked, vulnerable.

He glanced to Master Lars. But there was no sympathy there. His face was a thundercloud.

"Kierion," the leader of the council said, "you're wasting your time. And ours. Any dragon worth its talons would have blasted you from the sky before you got close enough to land on its back. Dragons don't fly steady in battle. They swoop and turn and whirl. That party trick of yours will never be useful. Your high jinks are nothing but fancy acrobatics, designed to show off your dexterity and foolishness. They have no application in battle."

Although he felt as if the weight of Dragons' Realm had settled upon him, Kierion refused to bow his shoulders or slump. They had a new enemy to confront. They needed new tactics, and if this wasn't the one, he'd find another. He'd ruined the hold's last piaua supply. There had to be something he could do to fix things. "In all fairness, sir, I've only had an hour's practice. We haven't had a chance to gauge how we'd implement this in battle."

Adelina squeezed his hand.

"Do you think I want my riders falling to their deaths because of some harebrained scheme? Not only have you spilled our last drops of precious piaua, but you've also wasted our time. I expect more of you. Much more." Lars shook his head and turned away. "This meeting is adjourned."

The sky was filled with churning wings as masters clambered upon their dragons and took to the sky. Only Master Giddi—the dragon mage—and Master Tonio remained behind.

"I can wait," said Master Giddi wandering to the far end of the ledge with Adelina and Fenni to give Tonio time to speak to Kierion privately.

Kierion knew what Tonio wanted.

"I'm glad to see you remembered our deal," the Naobian spymaster said, rubbing his hands together.

How could Kierion forget? Master Tonio had caught him sneaking off to consort with mages in Great Spanglewood Forest when dealing with mages had been expressly forbidden. He hadn't reported Kierion but had warned him he'd demand a favor in repayment. Being stationed in Montanara wasn't what he'd imagined, but then again he hadn't really imagined anything. The spymaster was too full of surprises. Kierion nodded.

"Good. Get packed and be ready to leave immediately."

Kierion swallowed. "Yes, sir."

As Tonio stalked off, Master Giddi approached. Riona shifted impatiently, the snow squeaking under her weight.

Adelina turned to Kierion and Fenni. "What now?"

Kierion shrugged. "I don't know."

Mirth in his eyes, Master Giddi chuckled. "Well, that was quite a feat, young Kierion. I wonder what you'll have up your sleeve next?"

Kierion kicked a lump of snow off the edge and gazed out over the forest and the lake, shining silver in the sun. Some great day this had turned out to be.

§

Giddi stretched a kink out of his back, watching the mages and trainee riders. A red dragon zipped through the main cavern, Nadira leaning low over the dragon's spinal ridges as she threw a knife at a target. Tylishia, the mage behind her, flung her hands up and shot a firebolt at the cavern wall.

Master Giddi nodded in approval at the dark scar on the stone. As the dragon swooped, he called, "Good shot, Tylishia. Next time, lean out a little farther or you're going to singe Nadira's hair."

A titter ran through the gathered riders and mages perched upon dragons behind him. Slowly, Master Giddi turned. One glare, and they were quiet. He flicked a hand, and the next dragon, a green, took off from the stage. This time, the rider used a bow, loosing an arrow. Once again, the mage didn't lean out far enough.

"Really lean out of your saddle, Arturo. The moment you feel you're going to fall is when you've got it right."

The next pair mastered it. They passed overhead to cheers echoing through the cavern.

Giddi nodded to himself. Yes, after years of separation, dragon riders and mages were finally bonding again. Despite his impatience, it had been a scant week since wizards had retreated from Spanglewood Forest to Dragons' Hold. The forest had been swarming with tharuks seeking vengeance for the damage Kierion and Fenni had wreaked when they'd rescued Ezaara and Adelina from Death Valley. Dragon Riders had had no choice but to take all the mages in.

No, it wasn't the way it'd been in his heyday.

Master Starrus, leader of the Wizard Council, strode into the cavern. The students stiffened, eyes flitting and terse whispers rustling against stone like crisp autumn leaves. Starrus swaggered to the stage and stood next to Giddi, smiling condescendingly. "Morning, Giddi, how are my trainees doing today?"

His? As if he ever put time into training them. Giddi kept a cool exterior, fighting the urge to grind his teeth. Every day that Starrus crowed over him was a day too long, but it'd been that way since he'd stepped down and given his reign to the lesser wizard. He'd had his reasons. Good ones.

Giddi raised himself on his toes, craning to see past the dragons and trainees. Now, where were Kierion and young Fenni? Come to think of it,

Master Jael was missing with Tomaaz, too. He refrained from shaking his head. Those four had been riding together longer than the other riders and mages, although only by a couple of scant weeks. They'd already experienced battle, fighting tharuks in Great Spanglewood Forest—working together although riders dealing with mages had been forbidden. Master Jael, from Naobia, was levelheaded and experienced enough to keep them out of trouble—hopefully. Kierion's exuberance was difficult to contain.

Oh, Giddi missed his days of riding dragons. He melded with a brown. *"Are you ready?"*

"I am," the brown replied. *"But this mage won't sit still in the saddle."*

"Give her time, she'll settle. She's a good student."

The brown leaped into the air and both rider and mage executed perfect shots, the mage leaning right over to clear the rider's shoulders. Finally, someone was listening.

Starrus yelled, "That is exactly how you don't fight." He spun to address the gathered trainees. "Young mages, don't lean so far, or you may fall off. A little mage flame won't hurt a rider."

There it was: Starrus was the epitome of everything stupid, often making decisions that went against common sense. These mages would not fall. Their innate sense of timing and their ability to sense their environment and understand *sathir*—the ebb and flow of energy—would prevent that. But as usual, Starrus was like a mother hen, clucking around, not allowing any of them to explore their power, to train the autonomy and the senses they'd need to survive in battle.

Shaking his head, Giddi silently departed.

§

Tonio paced at the front of the small training cavern, addressing Kierion, Fenni and Gret. They sat in chairs, listening as the spymaster drove home every point, his blunt finger spearing toward them.

"And you, Kierion." There was that finger again. "Learn not to be so impulsive. Granted, your impulsiveness has led to some good changes here at Dragons' Hold, but it could have easily gone the other way. If you have any bright ideas, consult with me first."

Well, that would be a little hard with Master Tonio back here at Dragons' Hold and Kierion in Montanara.

The finger stabbed toward Gret, who flicked a long blonde braid over her shoulder as Tonio addressed her. "As the Montanarian swordmaster's daughter, you'll be recognized. You'll need to maintain the facade that you're visiting family to lend support to your father."

Gret shrugged. "Excuse me, Master Tonio, but it's not as if my father needs support."

"You're all too young and arrogant." He shook his head. "We're a step ahead of you. I've sent messenger birds to Montanara. Your father is currently circulating the news that he needs another assistant to help train more warriors. You now have the perfect excuse for a family visit. Anything else?"

Kierion would have shriveled under that glare, but Gret just answered, "Excellent, Master Tonio."

"Your dragons will leave you in Great Spanglewood Forest and patrol the area for tharuks. Once you arrive, you'll be *visiting family* for a few weeks. Kierion, your father needs your help on the farm."

"Thanks for organizing that, sir." Kierion stifled the urge to groan. He'd tried to get out of farm work for half his life—and now that he was a dragon rider, he was heading back to it.

"You'll leave your riders' garb in your dragons' saddlebags and wear Montanarian clothing. Master Hendrick has clothing and supplies for your trip."

Tonio strode to a desk with a map laid on it. "Tharuk numbers are swelling in Spanglewood Forest. They also seem to be staying here, here and here." He jabbed his finger at the stables on the west side of town, the Brothers' Arms tavern, and another stable south of town. "As you can see, they've formed a crude perimeter at the city's main entry and exit points, and are using Nightshade Alley to connect with the seedier side of Montanarian life. So far, we have no idea what they're planning."

His keen eyes pierced Kierion. "Kierion, when you get there, I want you to contact Danion, head of my dragon corps operation in Montanara. Whatever you do, don't act without speaking to him. Via the blue guards' mind-melding with each other, we have a chain of command that reaches all the way back here to Dragons' Hold."

So that was how dragon corps spies kept in touch with one another and obtained Tonio's sanction on their activities.

"Sir, does this mind-melding network extend across the whole of Dragons' Realm?"

Tonio huffed. "You only need to know what's necessary to complete your given task."

Heat flowed to his cheeks. Kierion wished he wouldn't blush so easily.

As if he could read his mind, Tonio said, "If you keep blushing like a strawberry, it'll give you away every time you lie. No good when you're eyes and ears for dragon corps."

"That won't be an issue. I never blush when I lie."

That penetrating gaze again. "And you lie often?"

Kierion coughed.

Tonio swept right on. "Tomorrow morning, you'll undertake mind-blocking lessons with Master Giddi in case you come up against tharuk mind-benders or that dark dragon. You'll leave late tomorrow, arriving in Montanara under the cover of darkness." He nodded at them. "Get to the Brothers' Arms as soon as you can to meet Danion. He'll give you further directions so you can get to work. The code to give Danion when you meet him is black pepper. Repeat it now."

"Black pepper," Kierion, Gret and Fenni chorused.

"At least you've got that right." Tonio stalked forward, thrust his face into Kierion's and jabbed a finger into his chest. "Just for a change, don't do anything stupid."

PRECIOUS TIME

Leah entered the infirmary and approached Marlies, grinning. "I have the piaua juice vials, all clean and ready to go." She held out a small wooden box containing row upon row of slim vials nestled in sheep wool.

Marlies pulled one out and held it up to the light. The girl had done a good job. An eager trainee, Leah was keen for any opportunity to learn new skills. She nodded. "Excellent. Pop them in Liesar's saddlebags and then get ready." She turned back to Seppi, who was thrashing on the bed.

Adelina sponged his forehead. Mara hovered nearby with a brew of feverweed.

"Good, sponging will help keep him cool. His fever should come down by nightfall unless he has an infection. If it doesn't break in two hours, give him more feverweed. If you're really worried, ask Ezaara for help. She'll be back from her hand-fasting holiday tonight."

Seppi's wound wasn't looking promising, but Ezaara would be here to tend him in a few hours. A twinge of guilt hit Marlies. Now wasn't the best time to look for piaua juice, days away in Lush Valley. But there was never going to be a good time. She was exhausted, bone weary and worn out. Battle could come at any moment. They needed the juice as fast as possible.

As she rose, Seppi turned over, clutching her hand. His eyes became focused. "Marlies, the dark dragon seared me with its eyes, yellow rays slicing through my belly."

He'd been babbling like this all morning, making no sense at all. She squeezed his hand. "I'm sure it did, Seppi. Rest now, and you'll recover more quickly." If his wound didn't get infected. It was too early to tell whether this fever was due to infection or just the pain he was in.

"You don't believe me, do you?" Seppi's eyes were lucid, his gaze steady. "Yellow fire shot from that dragon's eyes. Like sunbeams. But everywhere it touched, it burned and sliced."

She squeezed his hand again and turned to Leah who was coming back from the infirmary ledge.

"I'll be back in a moment, Master Marlies," Leah said, ducking out the door.

They had to go now. It was three days' flight to Lush Valley, then they'd spend a day there, harvesting, and have to fly straight back. Living in Lush Valley with direct access to the piaua tree had spoiled her. She'd grown sloppy, relying far too heavily on the restorative juice. She'd taken it for granted for years.

Seppi gripped her hand again, his voice low and urgent. "If you don't believe me, check Septimor's wings. Everywhere those light beams hit, there were holes in his wings that left him howling and screaming in pain."

Marlies paused, turning back to Seppi. Rocco had healed Septimor's wings and mentioned those wounds, wondering what had caused them. Seppi was experienced, had been the leader of the blue guards for more than twenty years. Perhaps it wasn't just fever speaking. "Thank you for letting me know, Seppi. I hope you're on your feet and back in the saddle flying Septimor when I return."

She nodded to Mara and Adelina. "Be sure to let Ezaara know if you have any concerns tonight." She hugged the girls. "Thank you for filling in for me and Leah."

As she turned, a figure stirred in a chair in the shadows of the infirmary. *"Surely you weren't going to leave without saying goodbye,"* Hans mind-melded as he unfolded his legs and stood. *"Marlies, you've hardly slept in days. You're exhausted. Please, rest for a few days before you go."*

"Hans, we need to face reality. I know you've been trying to deny it."

"Just because you're exhausted doesn't mean something's wrong with you. I've told you that before. If you take things slowly, you'll recover."

Gods, she could throw her arms around him. If only it were true. Aware of the girls' eyes upon her, Marlies didn't dare speak aloud. *"Hans, I'm the master healer. I'm not afraid to diagnose myself. I knew the risks when I took piaua berries in Death Valley. Those berries would've killed me if Tomaaz had found me a few hours later. But he saved me. And if it wasn't for the berries, I'd be dead at Commander Zens' hands, so they served their purpose. But the damage has been done. Piaua berries have long-lasting effects. I may not have realized how far-reaching the effects would be, but I feel them now. My time is coming."*

Leah entered the room wearing her thick winter cloak and tall boots. The young girl nodded at Hans.

Behind them, Marlies heard Leah bustling the girls out to the ledge to say goodbye to her and Liesar. Mature beyond her years, the girl knew Marlies and Hans needed time.

Hans approached Marlies, his eyes glimmering. *"But a few short moons ago, when you left Lush Valley, you were in the prime of your strength."*

"Not anymore," she murmured, keeping her voice gentle. It broke her heart to see him aching like this. Broke her own heart to acknowledge the truth that she'd been hiding these last few weeks.

"How could your health fade so quickly?" he croaked between sobs.

"That's why I have to train Leah while I can. She's a true tree speaker, Hans. She's gifted in healing."

He enfolded her in his arms. How she wished she could stay in his warm embrace, safe and comforted. But it wasn't reality. War was looming. A battle could erupt at any moment, and wounded riders and mages would flood Dragons' Hold.

"Marlies, I haven't told you. I didn't want to tell you because I didn't want you to go." Hans' sigh ricocheted through his chest against her breast. "This dark dragon that plagued Seppi and Tomaaz... there are more, Marlies. Swarms are coming. I saw them in a dream last night. They could overrun us."

A shiver snaked down her spine.

He kissed her brow. "We're going to need all the piaua juice we can get. May the dragon gods speed you and keep you both safe. Whatever you do, don't get caught."

Marlies' throat was raw and swollen. *"Fleur corrupted healing at Dragons' Hold. We don't know how many people she murdered with her poisons. Now, there are no healers left here, except me and Ezaara."*

He nodded and held her tighter.

"Ezaara has other responsibilities, Hans. She can't be Queen's Rider and the only healer at Dragons' Hold. I have to train Leah while I can."

"I know," he whispered against her hair, his breath soft and warm.

"And what about you, Hans?" she asked. *"Anything could happen to you. Bruno corrupted prophecy as much as Fleur corrupted healing. What are you doing to train your successor?"*

Before Hans could answer, Marlies bent and shouldered her rucksack.

"I nearly lost you last time." Hans' bright green eyes shimmered.

"And I nearly lost you," Marlies melded, stroking Hans' stubbled chin. *"I love you, Hans. I always will."*

Her heart aching, she walked outside into the snow to Leah and Liesar.

§

Taliesin sat at a corner table, took a spoonful of soup and closed his eyes. Tuning out the hubbub in the mess cavern, he savored the taste of sweet potato and lemongrass.

"Mind if I sit here?"

He snapped his eyes open. His cousin, Sofia, was standing on the other side of the table, holding a bowl of soup, watching him.

Taliesin gestured with a spoon to the seat opposite him. "Sure," he said, taking another spoonful.

She sat down, sighing. "The same soup again."

He didn't care whether he ate the same thing all year. Any food was better than the rock-hard bread and weevil gruel the tharuks had fed him in Death Valley.

"Taliesin, um..." Sofia stared at him.

An awkward space stretched between them. Taliesin hadn't seen much of Sofia since her trial for attempting to kill the Queen's Rider, but she was the only family he'd talked to in years. His parents and siblings had been murdered in Death Valley.

Sofia ate her soup and took a few bites of bread, her eyes scanning his face.

He didn't mind not speaking—he hadn't spoken for weeks when he'd first come to Dragons' Hold. In fact, having numlock as a slave in Death Valley had meant he'd been incapable of coherent thought or much speech for years.

Sofia's mouth quirked up in a smile. "You know, I wondered for years what had happened to you..."

Taliesin shrugged. It would have been strange for her to have a whole family go missing, but that was no reason for Sofia to attack the Queen's Rider.

She stared at him. "I, um...."

"What is it, Sofia?" he asked.

A tear slid from her eye. "I'm, um, sorry."

That, he hadn't expected.

She reached a hand across the table. It had been so long since he'd been with his family... He reached out, placed his hand near hers. She grasped it. "Taliesin, I'm so glad you're alive."

His eyes pricked.

She squeezed his hand tightly. "It's all right, Taliesin. We're family. You can be yourself with me."

Anger swelled inside him. "I don't know if I want to be your family, Sofia. Tomaaz's family has taken care of me, and you tried to kill his sister. I don't know if I want family who try to kill the people I love."

Sofia gripped his hand tighter. Her mouth drooped. Her soup forgotten.

Taliesin disentangled his hand, pushed his soup bowl away, and left the mess cavern.

§

Hans paced the length of his sleeping cavern, turned, and paced back. Turned again… He couldn't go on like this all morning—it had already been hours since Marlies had gone, but her words were still pounding through his head. *"The damage has been done. Piaua berries have long-lasting effects… I feel them now. My time is coming."*

She couldn't be dying. No, he refused to believe it. Lars wouldn't have sent her off if he thought she was unwell. She must be tired. That trip to Death Valley had taken everything out of her.

Nagging doubt persisted, eating away at his mind.

Gods, how could he face life without her? They'd been together twenty years—longer. And with the ability to mind-meld, a talent only three other couples and their dragons had ever achieved, her death would rip apart his soul. He ran his hands through his unruly curls.

Someone rapped at the door. Thank the Egg for the distraction.

Hans opened the door to Lars standing there, face grave. "Can I please come inside?"

Hans showed him in. "Would you like a cup of tea?"

"No, I'll make this quick and to the point." Lars closed the door and placed a hand on Hans' shoulder. "Hans, I'm concerned about Marlies. She doesn't look well, and you're looking tired too. Bruno and Fleur made such a mess of healing and prophecy." He took a deep breath. "I hate to mention this, but we need a contingency plan in case something happens to either of you. And soon. I'd like you and Marlies to train your successors."

Marlies' words rang in Hans' head. *"And what about you, Hans? Anything could happen to you. Bruno corrupted prophecy as much as Fleur corrupted healing. What are you doing to train your successor?"*

Hans swallowed. Nodded. "Of course, Lars."

§

A whimper woke Hans. He sat up, cocking his head. There it was again, a terrified yelp coming from Tomaaz's sleeping cavern. He swung his legs out of bed and rushed into the room. Taliesin was thrashing in his sleep. He often had terrible dreams of the treatment he'd suffered at tharuks' hands in Death Valley, but this was different: he was clutching his head.

Hans shook him awake and sat on his bed, pulling the boy into his arms. "Taliesin, what is it?" He stroked sweat-sodden hair off the lad's forehead.

Taliesin stared up at him with those deep, lake-blue eyes and shuddered. "It was awful. Screaming in my head. Everything was dark. Hundreds of flapping wings."

The dark dragons. It had to be. Hans had dreamed of them only yesterday.

Someone knocked at the door. Had Tomaaz finished patrol? No, he wouldn't knock. Who could be visiting at this hour? "Come in," Hans called.

Lovina padded into the bedroom in her nightdress with a riders' jerkin thrown over it. "He's been dreaming, too, hasn't he?"

Hans nodded. "So have I."

Lovina's eyes were grave. "Hordes of dark dragons, Hans, the ones Tomaaz fought. I've been dreaming of them for the past two nights. Huge, leathery wings blotting out the sun. And screams, as if someone was torturing a thousand beasts." She shuddered, rubbing her temples. "Even after the dreams have finished, I can't get them out of my head."

This was it—his teaching moment. Hans had started training these two gifted young ones weeks ago. Now they had no time left. "It could be a prophecy, or a dream, brought on by what we've been hearing." He rocked Taliesin gently. "How would we tell the difference?"

Lovina's brow crinkled. "If more than one of us with the gift dreams something, that's a sign."

"Anything else? Hans asked.

Taliesin pursed his lips. "The light looks different in those dreams," he said. "It's clear, with golden edges."

This boy would never cease to amaze him. Hans had been trying to explain to Marlies for years how his visions were different than normal dreams, but he'd never being able to put his finger on it. Now here was a young boy, barely escaped the torture of Death Valley, who'd nailed it. Sure, he was Anakisha's descendant, so he probably had prophecy in his blood, but still… Hans couldn't help grinning.

He ruffled the boy's hair. "Well done, Taliesin." He winked. "That's exactly how it is."

"It is indeed. You're so clever." Lovina leaned in and gave Taliesin a quick hug. "I'm glad Tomaaz rescued you."

"So am I." Taliesin clambered off Hans' lap onto the bed. He grinned. "I love my new family."

Hans grinned back. Among these terrible times, there were pockets of joy, things to celebrate. "And I'm glad to have you both as part of my family. Let's put on a brew."

Handel mind-melded. *"Those young ones awake again?"*

Chuckling, Hans stood and reached into a drawer to grab some woolen socks for Taliesin. Lovina helped the boy pull them on.

"That they are," he replied. Hans could feel his dragon's mind whirling. *"What is it?"*

"I've been dreaming of dark dragons, screaming, blotting out the horizon with their wings, burning fields and villages. Searing the skin off our people. Is this what has plagued these young ones?"

Hans sighed, running a hand through his hair. *"Yes. These are dark times."*

"Enjoy this quiet moment while you can, Hans," Handel replied. *"We haven't seen the worst of this yet."*

DISCOVERY

"**I** told you, Son. You were too slow. You should've taken that girl when you had the chance." Pa whirled, his boots scraping stone. "But no, instead of listening to me, you had to play with her, a cat with a mouse." His father's eyes cut through him. "I've trained you to be a wolf, not a pussy cat."

The blow came out of nowhere; Bruno struck Simeon's cheek snapping his head around to face the cavern wall.

Simeon's eyes smarted. He clenched his jaw, staring at stone, refusing to face his father.

Pa yanked his hair, pulling his face around. His stinking breath wafted over Simeon as he thrust his face close. "Hear me?" he growled. "Next time, pump your seed in that girl, then we're gone." Pa let go of his hair and paced the stone floor again. "I know what I'm talking about, Son. I have experience. I'll teach you the best way to take an unwilling woman."

But Simeon didn't want to take the Queen's Rider and run. He wanted her, the whole deal, all right, but he wanted to take his time. Make her pay. He suppressed a smile. When it was time, he'd do it his way. Not Pa's.

"Hear me, Son? Next time you do what I say."

"Sure, Pa. I'll be quick." He wasn't talking about Ezaara. At his side, hidden from Pa's view, Simeon ran a finger along his blade.

§

Unocco's wings were tiring and he was hungry. The Naobian sun warmed him as he soared on a tailwind over Crystal Lake. Ahead was a forest and the caves where Naobians fossicked for dead jewel beetles. He could rest in a cavern there before he attempted the flight over the Naobian Sea to the Wastelands—not that he'd ever stoop to eating the brightly-colored bugs or their larvae. No, a young goat would do fine for him.

"Bruno, can you hear me?" He'd been casting his mind out, asking the same question for days—without an answer. But he had to try.

He was thirsty too. That water below was so clear, his reflection flapped back at him. *"Bruno, can you hear me?"*

Maybe Ajeurina was right. Maybe he should turn around and head back to Dragons' Hold. Just the thought made his chest ache and the hollowness inside him deepen. No, not without Bruno.

"Unocco?"

He was imagining things. Must be the heat. Or the hunger. He'd have to eat soon.

"Unocco, did you call me? It's Bruno. How are you, boy?"

Unocco's heart thrummed. *"You're alive."*

"Very much so. I've missed you." The warmth in Bruno's voice made Unocco's chest lighten. *"I'm terribly sorry I mistreated you. I was under Zens' influence. It was awful. I tried to fight it, but he was too strong."*

His poor valiant rider. *"How do I know you won't do it again?"*

Genuine sorrow washed over Uncoco as his rider replied, *"I promise I'll take care of you. I feel so terrible about what I did. I'd do anything to make it up to you."*

"If I talk to the council, will you come back to Dragons' Hold and be my rider?" Dared Unocco hope? It was too much. He teetered on the edge of a precipice, barely breathing.

"For you, Unocco, I'd do anything."

Joy streamed through Unocco, banishing the pain in his chest, his hunger and tiredness. He soared higher into the sky on the warm breeze, above the shining lake below. *"Where can I find you?"* He'd go anywhere for his rider, do anything.

"I'm waiting in the jewel beetle caves."

"I'll be there in no time at all." After years of pain and Zens' dark whisperings, he and Bruno would finally be free.

§

"Hurry, Son, put more water into that cauldron." Bruno threw a dead branch on the fire and watched the flames lick greedily at the wood.

Simeon unfolded his legs and pushed off the cavern floor to stand. He strolled past the tidy hearth and cooking equipment as if he hadn't a care in the world.

"You want to ride on dragonback across the realm?" Bruno asked icily. "Or would you prefer to walk? Because that's what you'll be doing if you don't get that swayweed tea ready."

Simeon rolled his eyes. "It's not as if we have a dragon we can turn. None of the greens were keen for a new rider."

"I've just spoken with Unocco, you idiot. He's on his way." Hah, that made the boy run. Bruno fished one of the pouches of swayweed he'd nicked from the herbalist at the market out of his pocket.

Simeon dragged the cauldron over and shoved it on the fire, sending a spray of sparks over Bruno's boots. "This isn't going to work, father." He smirked, as he emptied their waterskins. "He's going to smell the swayweed and know you're turning him again."

Bruno jumped up, grabbed Simeon by the neck of his jerkin and pulled him close. Spittle flying into his son's face, he snarled. "That's why I have soppleberry to disguise the taste, you numb skull. The stupid beast will think he's drinking our leftover tea." He poured the entire pouch of swayweed powder into the cauldron and threw in a liberal handful of soppleberries. "Now get stirring, if you value your hide. We have a dragon to snare."

Naobian Justice

Roberto struggled to his feet. "I won't. I won't do it." His breath rasped, chest aching. "I won't hurt people just because you want me to."

Zens gestured at a man in riders' garb, chained to the wall. "Are you sure, Roberto? I'd hate to force you. Just lay your hands on this dragon rider's head and use your new skills. A little pain will make him talk."

"No!"

"Very well." Zens' silken voice caressed his mind. Roberto shuddered as Zens' eyes took on a feral gleam. "You leave me no choice." Zens turned to a massive tharuk with a broken tusk. "Tharuk 000, bring in the others."

"Yes, beloved master." 000's eyes gleamed and dark saliva dribbled off his tusks, splattering on the floor.

Moments later, he was back with four littlings. Pitifully thin and hollow-eyed, they were about four to six years old. Littlings—slaving for Zens. The eldest had a festering lash mark on her cheek. Their faces were slack and expressionless—they were victims of numlock, wasted and broken.

What were they doing here? Did Zens want him to test them too? Well, he wouldn't.

"Place your hands upon that man's temples, Roberto. Extract the information."

"No."

"If you don't, I'll kill this girl." Zens gestured to the blank-faced littling with the lash mark.

It was an empty threat to bully him into submission. Roberto lunged for Zens' knife. "I'd rather kill myself than help you."

Tharuk 000 leaped between them and grabbed Roberto, tossing him against the stone wall. His shoulder throbbed.

"First, the girl. We'll see if he cooperates afterward." Although Zens was mind-melding with 000, his voice slithered into Roberto's skull, battering him from the inside. "Remember, Roberto, this was your choice. Now, she'll die, and it's your fault."

That's why the littlings were here. They were hostages, to get him to cooperate. "No! Don't! I'll do anything you—"

000 raked his claws across the girl's throat. For a moment, her eyes flew wide. Blood welled along the gash, then spurted down her neck. Her mouth went slack and her head lolled to the side, eyes dead.

Roberto awoke to shattering glass. He was back in Naobia. Back in the present. Gods, half asleep, he'd thought he was still with Zens.

"Slave monger."

"Murderer."

Another smash sounded.

Beside him, Ezaara sat bolt upright in bed. "What's going on?"

"We'll kill you, you shrotty traitor." In an instant, he realized. "They're after Amato. Get your shoes. There's broken glass." They scrambled out of bed and yanked on their boots.

Ezaara melded, *"For a moment, you thought it was you, didn't you? You thought they were after you?"*

Roberto brushed aside her question and raced into the lounge as a stone flew through the jagged window, crashed onto a table, and skidded off the edge to the floor. He heard a roar and saw a plume of dragon fire shoot into the air outside the window. Erob and Zaarusha pounced into action, driving back the crowd that had assembled outside the cottage. A cabbage flew through the window.

Roberto ducked.

It hit the table, smashing a vase, spraying water and flowers everywhere.

His boots crunching through broken glass, Roberto ran for the door and flung it open. A rotten tomato hit him in the face.

Wiping off his cheek, he faced an angry crowd: farmers wielding pitchforks; fishermen waving diving spears; and villagers bearing knives, swords, rocks and rotten vegetables. A pumpkin sailed through the air, smashing against some roses trailing up a latticework on the side of the cottage. Splinters of wood and tattered petals exploded onto the ground.

"It's Amato! He's come to kill us," someone cried.

This was getting way out of hand. Roberto drew his sword and held it high. "I am Roberto, son of Amato. As a master on the Council of the Twelve Dragon Masters, I ask for your listening ears."

Murmurs spread through the crowd as people whispered his name and pointed.

"He looks just like Amato to me," a farmer yelled, inciting more angry comments.

"Amato killed my cousin," a plump woman holding a rotten gourd shouted.

"And my wife and daughter!" a red-faced, middle-aged farmer hollered. "He gave them all to Zens, who murdered them in cold blood."

"Kill him. Kill him. Kill him," the crowd chanted

Erob roared. The rabble huddled closer together, backing away from the ferocious blue dragon.

Suddenly, Ezaara strode past Roberto and stood next to Zaarusha at the back of the crowd. Zaarusha nuzzled her shoulder. Ezaara scratched Zaarusha's forehead.

"It's the Queen's Rider," shrieked a farm girl with a basket of tomatoes over her arm.

Murmurs spread throughout the crowd.

The girl yelled again, "Look, the new Queen's Rider."

Ezaara held up her bare hand, and they quieted. "Indeed, Amato is here," she said, her clear voice silencing the assembled throng. "We found him yesterday, by accident. Years ago, when his dragon, Matotoi, realized the extent of Amato's treachery, he plunged into Crystal Lake, trying to kill them both. But they didn't die. Instead, Matotoi dragged Amato into an underwater cavern where they've survived by eating fish and lake weed these past six years."

The red-faced farmer waved his fist in the air. "Amato survived. My family didn't. He deserves to die. I'll help him on his way."

"I understand how you feel," Ezaara said. "As does Queen Zaarusha." A rumble from the Dragon Queen filled the air, making the hairs on Roberto's arms rise. "We're taking Amato back to Dragons' Hold to be tried by the Council of the Twelve Dragon Masters. However, we are aware of your grievances. If you would like them recorded, I am happy to do so personally this very morning and bring your testimonies to Dragons' Hold. Please, form a line, and I'll be with you in a moment." She gestured at her nightdress. Thankfully, because Amato was in the cottage, she was wearing one. "Just give me a moment to get changed."

More people were drifting into the yard, by the moment. The hubbub grew as people explained what was going on and argued among themselves.

Roberto escorted Ezaara into the house, his hand at her waist. *"You were amazing. How did you know what to say?"*

Ezaara shrugged. *"I don't want Amato killed. And these people need to be heard and understood. This way we can collect their evidence for his trial."*

"But he's already been tried in Naobia. He was tried for his crimes and found guilty, posthumously—we thought."

"But now that he's alive, Zaarusha insists he be tried at Dragons' Hold."

"That I do," the Dragon Queen interjected.

Amato was sitting on the couch, his knees tucked to his chest, body trembling. "Don't let them get me," he croaked, burying his face in his knees and wrapping his arms around his head.

Pathetic creature. His father was hardly a man anymore, just some gibbering idiot.

Roberto shook his head. It would be easier to leave his father to the wolves outside and fly away pretending they'd never found him. Easier not to ever face him again. Easier—but he couldn't do it, not with Ezaara and Zaarusha insisting they take him to Dragons' Hold. Not when he'd pledged allegiance to his queen.

So much for their hand-fasting holiday in Naobia—another thing Amato had ruined. Roberto sighed. It was only fair that these people have justice. Only fair that their grievances be heard again. No matter how many times they mentioned their dead, the pain of Amato's actions would never diminish.

§

There were so many people milling outside the cottage that Ezaara couldn't get changed without being noticed through the windows. In the end, Roberto sheltered her with his cloak while she pulled on her riders' garb.

"Here you are." He thrust a pastry and a couple of plums at her. She scarfed them down quickly in between lacing her boots.

Roberto wiped the remnants of the shattered vase and strewn flowers off the small table, and carried the table and a chair outside. He retrieved some paper, a quill and some ink from a drawer in the kitchen. "You ready?" he asked.

She nodded and they stepped outside together.

Ezaara faced the line of Naobians—so long it snaked all the way around the cottage and onto the road. She'd felt a twinge of sympathy for Amato, but she shouldn't have if he'd wronged this many people.

Roberto stood at her side as she seated herself at the table and arranged her paper and ink.

"I'd like you to go first," she melded, slipping into Roberto's mind, sensing the disgust and raging anger his father's presence had awoken. His hurt ran deep, deep enough to destroy him.

"Me?"

"Yes, you. And I'd like you to tell all the people assembled here what it was like to live with your father." Was she pushing him too far?

Roberto's face closed over, that impenetrable wall springing up around his mind, blocking her out. His jaw clenched, muscle rippling along bone.

"If you don't want—"

"I'll do it." His voice was hard.

He was steel, forged in the fire and crucible of pain Amato had inflicted upon him.

His throat bobbed as he stood in front of the line of his fellow Naobians. "Some of you know me. I'm shocked that my father is alive. I thought I'd buried him forever." Despite the warm sun beating down on them, the frost in Roberto's voice made Ezaara shiver. "He committed many crimes, but today I bear witness to the crimes he committed against me and my family." Roberto's fists clenched at his sides, his body taut. "After my father was captured by Zens and then released, I grew up, sheltering my sister from his beatings, taking them for myself. Our nights were broken with splintering wood, splattered blood, and my mother's whimpers."

A soft sob reached Ezaara's ears. Casually, she turned toward the house. Amato was peeking out the shattered window, unnoticed by the crowd, who were riveted by Roberto's account.

Roberto's lips twisted. "He lured Naobians into traps where they were captured by tharuks and taken as slaves to Death Valley. I was one of them. Taken by my own father, my mind warped to become a vicious tool in Zens' hands."

Gasps rippled down the line as Ezaara scratched the quill across the paper.

Roberto nodded. "Yes, I might have stayed that way, were it not for Erob, my dragon."

Erob padded over and nudged Roberto's chest with his head.

Roberto patted his scaly neck. "At Dragons' Hold, our master healer discovered crystals called methimium that Zens implants under people's skin to control their behavior. They're effective. Deadly. And perhaps, in light of these crystals, I could forgive my father for his crimes against me. But not for killing my mother. Not for killing your loved ones. For that I cannot forgive him." Roberto's chest heaved.

The Naobians watched him in silence. Ezaara dipped her quill in the ink bottle.

"I would gladly hang him myself, but it's not my job to kill a man without a trial. My mother..." Roberto swallowed again, wetness glistening on his tanned cheek. "My mother wouldn't have wanted me to hate Amato. I've failed her because I do hate him, which is why I cannot judge him myself." Roberto spat on the ground. "Turn him over to the council. Let them have him. Let justice be done at last."

Tears glinted on Amato's wrinkled cheeks, in his tangled beard. Before anyone else saw him, he scurried away from the jagged glass at the window.

The ruddy-faced farmer was next in line. "My whole family, gone. A wife and three littlings, taken as slaves."

A young woman was after him. "Pa, Ma and my sister Suzie tried to fight the tharuks after Amato led them into a trap at the riverbank, but they didn't survive. They were gutted and left for dead."

"It's going to be a long morning," Roberto melded.

Ezaara glanced up from her paper. More people were joining them. The queue stretched half a dragonlength down the road. *"I suggest you go inside and tend to your father."*

"Him? He survived six years without me... in that cave. I'm sure he'll be fine for a few hours." There was a hardness to Roberto's words that made her shoulders twitch.

But she didn't blame him. She scratched her quill against the parchment as she made the list of the people Amato had led to destruction.

§

Hearing his father's crimes enumerated was like reliving Roberto's own litany of nightmares. Amato's murders weighed heavily on Roberto's shoulders. No, he would not cower as if the crimes were his own. He straightened his back, gazed directly at the line of bereaved waiting to give testimony. He'd paid his dues. Being forced by Zens to torture people's minds and drive them crazy with anguish had been punishment enough.

"I lost my only son," a young woman in a bonnet said. Her voice was hollow. Dark circles rung her eyes. "Amato led my boy to pick blackberries on the riverbank, but tharuks were hiding in the underbrush. The only thing left were tufts of tharuk fur on his little wooden pail half-filled with berries. He was eight summers—" she sobbed, shaking her head, and couldn't continue.

A deep voice yelled from the back of the line. "Get out of my way." A burly man wearing a baker's apron strode from the road, pushing his way through the people with huge muscled arms. "Where's Amato?" Whipping a knife from his belt, he ran at the cottage. "I'll kill that murderer."

Roberto raced toward the door. He drew his sword. The big man swung at him, and he parried the blow.

"You good-for-nothing son of a murderer. I should gut you as well," the man growled, slamming Roberto's blade with his.

Erob roared and spurted a gust of warning flame. People screamed. The line scattered. Folk huddled near the trees by the roadside. Roberto's sword clashed against the big baker's blade. The knife spun out of the man's hand, flipping through the air.

The man jerked another knife from the back of his belt and flung it.

Roberto ducked. It thudded into the door. Gods! He lunged, grabbed the baker's shirt, and thrust his blade at the man's thick throat.

Through gritted teeth, Roberto ground out, "I hate my father as much as you do. More. I deny you the privilege of killing him. It's mine." His chest rose and fell, his breath coming in gasps. "But he'll be tried at Dragons' Hold. Queen Zaarusha has willed it."

The man snarled, "Just make sure when you kill him, you do it right."

"Oh, I will," said Roberto. "Don't worry, I will this time."

SEPPI

delina wrung her cloth out and wiped Seppi's forehead. Within moments, the cloth was warm. Mara passed her another damp cloth. She dabbed his neck and shoulders.

Seppi rocked his head back and forward, moaning, "Black dragon. Yellow, yellow eyes... burning..." He groaned, then was still.

Adelina wiped his brow again. Still so hot. He'd had a high fever for more than a day. She lifted the bandage to peek at the wound on his stomach. It was red and puffy, stitches pulling his skin taut.

Seppi moaned again. "Water."

Mara poured water from a pitcher into a cup and passed it to Adelina, who tilted Seppi's head up and held the cup to his cracked lips. Cheeks hot, Seppi sipped.

Mara was wide-eyed. "Will he be all right?"

It was pointless asking. He wasn't all right, and they wouldn't know more until his fever broke. If it broke at all. Adelina pasted a cheery smile on her face—a smile she'd honed for years. "Mara, I'm sure things will be fine. Why don't you fetch Seppi's family?"

The girl swallowed and left the infirmary.

Moments later, there was a knock at the door, and Kierion walked in hastily, his long legs eating the stone floor as he powered toward her. His step faltered, his eyes darting over Seppi. "He's not going to make it, is he?"

Adelina bit her lip and kept sponging Seppi's forehead.

"You look fit to drop." Kierion stepped over to Marlies' workbench, dropped soppleberries into two cups of water, and took them out to Linaia on the ledge. Moments later, he was back with steaming tea. He passed Adelina a cup. "Have a break and let me take over for a while." He ran a hand through his hair. "After all, it's my fault. Without me, he would've been back in the saddle."

Adelina laid her hand on his arm, gazing up at him. Riders teased Kierion about his pretty eyes—ocean-gray flecked with blue—but right now, they were troubled. "Supplies were desperately low already, Kierion. You can't take full responsibility. We would've run out of piaua with the next influx of wounded riders."

"Thanks. I needed that." He tilted his head, flashing a smile. "Did you know you're really pretty?"

"I, ah—" Adelina's cheeks heated. Well, that was unexpected.

He winked and took the cloth out of her hands. "Now, drink your tea and relax while I look after Seppi."

She could think of nothing more relaxing than watching Kierion, so she sat at the foot of Seppi's bed and propped her feet up on a chair.

"He's burning up." Kierion wrung a fresh cloth out. "Do you think snow melt would cool him down?"

She shrugged. "Maybe."

Kierion took another bowl out to the ledge. He soon returned with an icicle, swirling it in the bowl until it melted in the water.

"Let me try." Adelina set aside her tea and dipped a cloth in the water. "Oh, it's freezing. Hopefully it helps." As Kierion laid the cold cloth on Seppi's head, Adelina sent a silent prayer up to the dragon gods. *Please, please heal Seppi. And help Kierion not to feel so guilty.* She took a long sip of soppleberry. "So, you're going to Montanara."

"I am." He shrugged. "It was Tonio's idea."

"Tonio?" Adelina hadn't intended her voice to sound so sharp. "What's it got to do with him?"

"Remember when we were sneaking out to train with Fenni in Great Spanglewood Forest back when consorting with mages was forbidden?"

Adelina nodded. She remembered it all too well. After being attacked by tharuks and injured badly, how could she forget? They'd both been hurt. And it was here in the infirmary she'd first seen Kierion's tanned chest. Her cheeks heated again. "Yes, I remember it well." Too well. The sight had stolen her breath.

"Well, Antonika spotted me and Riona sneaking out one morning. Of course she told the spymaster. When Tonio confronted me, I thought I'd be in for another six weeks' kitchen duty, but instead, he told me I owed him a favor." Kierion shrugged again. "I guess this is it. Montanara is my home town. I want to help Montanarians beat tharuks, so I'm his man."

It was Adelina's turn to raise an eyebrow. "Will he give you spy training?"

"He already has. I have to hang out in a tavern in Nightshade Alley."

"Nightshade Alley?"

He grimaced. "The home of the Nightshaders."

"Sounds dangerous." Would he be all right? "What do you make of those dark dragons?" she asked.

Kierion shrugged, tilting his head again. That stubborn lock of blond hair tumbled across his forehead. "Don't know. I've never encountered one. Master Giddi has trained us in mind blocking, though. Just in case."

Adelina smiled. "Mind blocking isn't too hard when you get used to it."

He laughed. "I should've expected that from the master of mental faculties' sister." Kierion leaned in, staring at her. "Have you ever mind-melded with anyone?"

"Only with dragons." Adelina sucked in her cheeks. "But guess what?" She couldn't risk patients hearing, so she scooted her chair over to Kierion's and leaned in to whisper a secret.

§

The scent of jasmine enveloped Kierion. He inhaled deeply. Adelina's breath tickled his cheek as she whispered, "Roberto and Ezaara can mind-meld."

Kierion nearly fell off his chair. "What? I mean, I asked, but I didn't think…"

Adelina nodded at him. "Neither of them has admitted it. They often look at each other intensely, the way we look when we're melding with dragons. Sometimes they leave the room, having made some decision without ever discussing it with me. It's odd, knowing people sitting next to you are having a silent conversation of their own." Her shoulder touched his.

She was such a gorgeous wee thing. Kierion wanted to scoop her off her chair into his lap and kiss her. Just the thought made his cheeks burn.

§

Adelina stood up and felt Seppi's forehead. "Still too hot."

"Should we open the infirmary doors to cool the place down?" Kierion asked.

Adelina gestured at a man in the far corner. "We can't. That man has a cold in his chest and has to be kept warm. I've given Seppi feverweed tea, sponged him—we've tried everything. If only Marlies were here."

"What about Ezaara. Is she back yet?"

Adelina's stomach twisted. Why weren't her brother and Ezaara home yet? What could have happened to delay them on their hand-fasting holiday? She kept her voice bright. "No, she and Roberto aren't back yet."

Seppi's body started shaking, his limbs twitching and spasming.

"What's wrong with him?" Kierion asked.

"He's got the rigors. His fever's too high. We have to get his temperature down immediately."

"Shall we take him out to the ledge? It's cold out there."

Would the cold harm Seppi or help him? Adelina had no idea, but either way, they had to do something. Numbly, she nodded.

Kierion flung the bowl and cloth aside and cradled Seppi in his arms, careful not to wrench his stitches. They rushed outside, their boots crunching through the snow. It was freezing. Kierion stood there, shoulders bowed, holding Seppi against his chest. "Sorry, Seppi," he muttered. "I'm sorry I was so clumsy."

Seppi opened his eyes and raised his hand to Kierion's cheek. "Thank you, my boy. You have a good heart." His eyes slid closed, his chest spasmed. Then he was still.

Thank the First Egg, his rigors had stopped. "Kierion, your idea worked. Now, we'd better—"

"Seppi?" Kierion bowed his head over Seppi's face. "Adelina, come check."

Adelina gazed up at Kierion's panic-stricken eyes. She placed her fingers to Seppi's throat. No pulse. "He's gone." She placed her hand on his chest. No movement. "Oh, gods," she sobbed, "what have we done?"

§

Kierion stared at Seppi's face, his closed eyes, slack face. One moment, Seppi had been there, touching Kierion's face, speaking. The next, he was gone. Gods, one breath was the difference between life and death. For the hundredth time that week, Kierion cursed his overeagerness. His impulsive nature was always getting him into trouble. What had driven him to do such a stupid thing? He thought he'd learned his lesson when Adelina had been injured by tharuks, but no, he always leaped, again and again, without thinking.

His chest constricted, making it hard to breathe. He stood in the snow, numbness stealing through his body.

There was a gentle touch on his arm. Adelina. He'd forgotten she was still here. "I'm sorry," she said, her dark eyes lined with tears.

"So am I," he whispered hoarsely.

She placed a hand at the small of his back and leaned in against him. "Come on, let's get him inside."

Kierion would have gladly stood out here all night in the snow if it would help Seppi.

Had the cold killed him?

Would Seppi have survived if he hadn't intervened? The lump in Kierion's throat was like a chunk of ice. He couldn't swallow. Nodding, he let Adelina guide him inside and laid Seppi on his sweat-drenched bed.

"Kierion, can you help me?" Adelina's huge dark eyes were pleading. Her hands were shaking.

He got it. He understood. It was one thing to see riders bleed out in battle, but to hold someone as they died…

Oh gods, was this reminding her of her mother's death at her father's hands? He forced some strength into his voice. "Yes, of course, what would you like me to do?"

She cleared her throat. "His family are on their way. Perhaps it'd be a good idea to move him to a fresh bed."

"Sure."

Adelina flipped back the bedding on the next bed. He carried Seppi over and laid him on the fresh white sheets.

She produced a new shirt and riders' jerkin. "His family left these in case he needed them." She choked on her words.

Kierion placed an arm around her shoulders. He couldn't help it, he hugged her. He'd been such a fool, lamenting his stupidity. He'd forgotten about her, how she must be feeling, having a patient die under her care.

§

That night, Kierion tossed and turned, hardly able to sleep. It'd been the middle of the night when he'd finally stumbled to bed, avoiding Seppi's family at the infirmary. Even a long flight and a run along the edge of the lake hadn't helped ease the heaviness in his chest and his stinging eyes. He flung back his covers, rolled out of bed and shoved his clothes and boots on. There was only one place to go this late. He trudged down the stone tunnels toward the mess cavern, his footfalls echoing hollowly against the stone walls like an angry heartbeat.

A heartbeat that Seppi no longer had.

He swiped his cheeks with the back of his hand, dashing away the stubborn tears that'd leaked from his eyes. Flame it, flame it, flame it! There was nothing he could do, nothing he could fix. Everything he'd touched was broken. And now Seppi was gone.

"Not everything," melded Riona from outside on their ledge. *"I'm not broken. You also helped Ezaara save Zaarusha from poison. You've helped train mages and bridge the long-standing gulf between mages and riders. You'll be a valuable asset in this war."*

"Thank you." Swallowing hard, Kierion took a few deep breaths and entered the deserted mess cavern. A cauldron of soup simmered on the hearth, a welcome snack for riders on patrol.

After barely eating all day, he was famished. He ladled himself a cup of soup, took a handful of bread rolls and sat in a corner in the dark. Rumors had already been running rife through the hold since Seppi had died. Riona had heard dragons mentioning his name as riders' whispers echoed down the tunnels.

He sighed. He'd have to avoid everyone until he went to Montanara. Hopefully it would blow over soon enough. Not the memory of Seppi, though. He deserved to be remembered.

Famished, he plunged his bread into his soup. It was sawdust in his mouth. It was no use, he'd have to face the other riders sooner or later.

The door to the mess cavern creaked open. Kierion ducked deeper into the shadows, hunching over his soup.

It was Adelina, with tear-stained cheeks and red-rimmed eyes.

She helped herself to a bowl of soup and sat at a table on the other side of the mess cavern. She stirred her spoon around and around in her bowl then dabbed at her eyes with a handkerchief.

Here he was again, forgetting about her, buried in his own mess of feelings. Maybe she needed time alone...

No, he couldn't sit here watching her sob. Kierion unfolded his legs from under the table and strode over to Adelina, plonking his cup and bread rolls on her table.

"Mind if I join you?" he asked softly. Gods, his hands were shaking, his heart perched on a precipice, ready to tumble off at a moment's notice.

Adelina dropped her spoon. "Oh, I, just, just..." she gasped.

"Do you need to talk?" he asked.

"It's just that..."

He sat and covered her tiny hand with his large, clumsy one. "Are you remembering your mother?"

She nodded, tears rolling down her cheeks.

"And my father," she said.

Adelina was always bright and cheery. After all she'd been through, he should have known she was hiding dark feelings.

"The worst thing is, I don't know if..." She broke off, gazing at him, her dark eyes pools of tears.

"What is it?" He wanted to help, not mess up.

She dried her eyes and tucked her handkerchief away. "I don't really want to talk about it."

"Are you sure?"

"Absolutely." She gave a short sharp nod.

What had changed? A moment ago, she'd looked so open.

She stared at the stone wall, silent.

He squeezed her hand. "Sometimes it really does help to talk, Adelina."

She didn't reply. She tugged her hand away from his and took a sip of soup.

"Are you really sure?" he asked.

Adelina's spoon slammed into her bowl with a clunk, spraying soup over the table. "Flame you, Kierion. The worst thing is I don't know if we killed Seppi by taking him out into the snow." Her chair rasped as she stood, glared at him, then stalked out of the mess cavern.

§

Adelina pounded down the corridor toward her cavern, boots striking stone. Heart thundering.

Kierion was right. Seeing Seppi lying dead in his arms had awakened her memories of Ma's death—and more. It had roused all the sleeping horrors from her past: her father's raging storms behind the kitchen door; the thud of Ma's body hitting the wall, of Pa's boots kicking Ma's belly; blood streaming down Roberto's face; Ma crying bloodied tears the day Pa had gouged her eye; the pain of her father beating her with his fists; her screaming as Roberto intervened...

And worse. The awful day Roberto had disappeared, taken by tharuks. But it hadn't been tharuks. Her father had given her brother to the enemy.

Commander Zens had broken something inside Roberto. Not the way he'd broken her father. Roberto hadn't become nasty. No, but he'd become distrustful. Distant. Closed. And his awful screams of terror in the night. His sobs through the bedroom walls...

She shuddered.

And even worse. One day Roberto had come home with Ma cradled in his arms because she could no longer walk. The slow moons of them nursing Ma, hoping for recovery, but knowing in their hearts that her time was near.

The only relief—thank the First Egg—was that Pa had died.

When Ma had spasmed in pain then finally drifted into endless slumber, Adelina's dam of grief had burst.

And so had Roberto's. He'd snapped. Disappeared again.

During all Pa's years of horror, Roberto had held everything together. He'd been Adelina's mainstay. The big brother she could lean on. Then he was gone. Her entire family, gone.

Adelina had thrashed and churned, sucked into a sea of sadness. Waves of sorrow had crashed over her, threatening to drown her.

And tonight, Kierion's heartbreak, holding Seppi exactly how Roberto had held Ma, the tears on his cheeks and desolation in his eyes... She'd seen her brother all over again.

Her trusty smile and bright demeanor—the fortification she'd built up for years—had crumbled.

Memories bashed at Adelina's head, trying to take root, to engulf her, suffocate her. She reached her cavern and thrust open her door, wood smacking stone, then slammed it shut. Adelina leaned her back against the solid wood and slid down the door onto the floor, sobbing.

WEASELS

"Matotoi's tired," said Amato, slumped over Erob's neck in front of Roberto as they flew north toward Dragons' Hold. "He needs to rest his wings."

They were only an hour's flight from Naobia. Roberto rolled his shoulders. After dealing with people incensed with Amato all of the previous day and most of this one, he was exhausted, too. He melded with Erob, *"We'll need to land soon."*

"Matotoi has already told me," Erob replied. *"What about that meadow?"*

"As good a spot as any."

"There's no point in traveling much farther tonight," Erob said. *"We'll only tire him more. Hopefully, after a rest, he'll do better tomorrow. Perhaps we could stay in our old cave?"*

"The jewel beetle cave? Good idea, it's close by." Roberto sighed. They would've been back at the hold last night instantaneously with Anakisha's rings—if Bruno hadn't taken Ezaara's ring, and he and Ezaara hadn't found Amato. Hopefully, nothing dire had happened while they were gone. Perhaps he should nip back to the hold with his ring and check…

No, he didn't want to leave Ezaara, not on their hand-fasting holiday. Not with his father.

Once they'd landed, Roberto helped his father off Erob and strode into the bushes to relieve himself, keeping a wary eye on Amato.

His father sat near Ezaara, his back to Roberto, while she unpacked food onto a blanket. The old man's voice was a murmur on the breeze. What was he up to? Roberto finished up and hurried back.

Amato was holding a bunch of bluebells out to Ezaara. "My respected, honored Queen's Rider, you know, when Roberto was young, he used to love these flowers."

That shrotty weasel. Roberto ground his teeth. Amato was worming his way into Ezaara's confidence by chatting about Roberto's littling years—the very years he'd destroyed. Roberto gritted his teeth as he stomped back toward them. There was no way he was going to let his walls down around this man.

He melded with Ezaara, *"Don't trust him. He's trying to impress you, show you what a loving father he was. But I've shown you what he did to me."* Roberto shuddered. This man had poisoned his past.

"I know, Roberto. You don't have to remind me." There was an irritated edge to Ezaara's voice.

Did she think his father had changed? Did she believe he could redeem himself?

Roberto snatched the flowers from his father, dropped them to the grass, and ground them under his boot. "From hiding in Zens lair, to lurking in caves, and now, smelling flowers." He spat on the ground at his father's feet. "Keep your distance from the Queen's Rider. It's my job to protect her. And I won't hesitate if I need to." His hand drifted to his sword hilt. He shot daggers at his father with his eyes.

"Cheese?" Ezaara asked, ignoring Roberto and slicing a piece off a round of goat cheese. She held it out to Amato on the point of her knife.

"No, thanks. Too rich for me," Amato said, helping himself to some dried fish Ezaara had laid out on a cloth.

How could his father think that just because Roberto had found him, things could be back to normal? Even before he'd disappeared, things hadn't been a normal for years. From the age of eight, Roberto had sheltered his terrified sister behind the kitchen door as his father beat his mother. Did that old fool think he could come back from that?

"Roberto, give him a chance."

"He never gave me one. Never gave my mother one. Or my sister." Roberto couldn't keep the bitterness from his thoughts. He knew he should be trying, but he didn't want to. Every time he saw Amato's wizened, stooped figure and his bony ribs poking through his shirt, he knew he should feel sympathy. But how could he feel sympathy for the monster who'd destroyed his life, turned him over to the enemy, and made him a pawn in a game of war?

And killed his mother.

"Roberto?"

"Enough, Ezaara." He snapped mind-meld, wishing he could stalk off into the rolling meadows, but he couldn't. He'd never leave Ezaara alone with that traitor. Amato was far too dangerous.

§

Erob landed high on a cliff where the jewel beetles bred, just out of Naobia. Memories flooded Roberto: collecting dead beetles to sell at the markets with Pa and Adelina when he was littling, and later, sleeping here for moons, high above the forest, the sea glinting in the distance. He'd wanted to bring Ezaara here—but not with his father.

Matotoi thudded down to the ledge beside them panting, wings drooping. Amato stirred. Roberto looked up, ignoring his questioning glance.

Zaarusha rode a thermal, spiraling high above the cliff.

"Wow, this place is beautiful," Ezaara mind-melded.

"It is," Roberto said. *"Did you know I lived here for a few moons after my father's trial? I left Adelina at Warlin and Anastia's house, and fled."*

"It's such a picturesque, peaceful area, Roberto. Despite the difficulties we've had here, I love Naobia. And I love the sea. I can see why you call it home."

"Ezaara, anywhere you are is my home now." It was true. He'd settle in the vicious Robandi desert with her—if that was what she wanted. *"And you're beautiful too."*

Her laughter drifted down the hillside, freeing the tightness in his chest. *"Which cave was yours?"* Zaarusha dove, plunging down to land on the ledge. She dipped her head under her wing to preen her scales. Ezaara slid out of the saddle and raced over to Roberto, flinging her arms around him. The moment would have been perfect, except—

"Roberto," croaked Amato, "a fine young woman you found yourself. Reminds me of Lucia."

Releasing Ezaara, Roberto spun. "How dare you mention her name. You murdered her." He stabbed a finger at Amato's face. "The only reason you're alive is because Zaarusha wants you to be tried. Don't forget it."

Roberto strode into a large cavern where there was room enough for all of them, the others following. There were still rudimentary cooking utensils and grains in jars along the wall where he'd left them. Some of his firewood had been used. The fire pit was still warm. *"Someone's been here recently."*

"I saw fresh dragon dung on the top of the cliff," Erob mind-melded.

Roberto shrugged. *"Probably a green guard on patrol."*

Erob huffed over the hearth, setting the wood alight, and then curled up in his customary spot.

Amato cowered in a corner next to Matotoi. As he should. It was an insult to think he could waltz back into Roberto's life.

Ezaara stared at Roberto. *"You're very harsh on him."*

"As he was on me, Ezaara."

She came over to him and placed her hands on his shoulders. He leaned down, touching foreheads with her. Their breath mingled as she melded, *"That's in the past. Now, Roberto, I know he's killed people."* She patted the bulging pocket in her jerkin with her notes from the victim's testimonies, the list of grievances against Amato. *"You may not have long with him. I'd hate you to regret your actions when he's gone. Please find a tiny space in your heart for forgiveness."*

§

Roberto awoke in the middle of the night to scratches echoing on stone. Footfalls. He sat bolt upright. Ezaara stirred next to him and rubbed her eyes. There it was again. Someone was creeping into the cave.

"Roberto, wake up," Erob warned. *"Intruders."*

Quietly rising to his feet, Roberto pulled on his boots and slung his weapon belt around his hips. He drew his knife. And tiptoed toward the ledge.

A blaze of Erob's fire lit up the mouth of the cavern, outlining a man in the gloom. A knife hissed through the air, just missing Roberto's head and clanging off the stone wall.

Shielding his eyes from the light, Roberto flung his knife. It bounced off a stone jutting from the cavern wall and clattered to the ground.

An arrow thudded into the stone. "Let me at the Queen's Rider. I have unfinished business."

Roberto knew that voice—Simeon.

He drew his sword.

Another gust of Erob's flame lit up the darkness.

Simeon was crouched at the cave mouth, dagger in hand. He leaped at Roberto.

Roberto parried with his sword, sending Simeon's knife spinning through the air to skitter along the ledge. "The next thing flying along that ledge will be you, Simeon. Get out of here." Roberto lunged for him.

His hair ruffled as an arrow flew past him from behind, narrowly missing Simeon's chest.

Simeon raced out of the cavern.

Zaarusha roared, sending a lick of flame after him, illuminating a beige dragon perched on the lip of the ledge, a rider atop his back.

By the flaming infernos of hell, it was Unocco and Bruno. Roberto yelled, racing for the ledge.

Simeon leaped into the saddle behind his father, and they winged off into the darkness. Zaarusha tensed her haunches and sprang after Unocco, blasting flame at his tail.

Roberto spun to thank Ezaara for her arrow.

Amato was facing the cavern mouth, another arrow nocked.

Ezaara shrugged and splayed her hands, her face in shock. Seeing Simeon again had rattled her. She'd always seemed unbreakable, strong. He rushed over, and cradled her in his arms. He should have known it hadn't been Ezaara who'd fired the arrow because she wouldn't have missed—her aim was too good.

Amato had tried to save him.

FAREWELL

Giddi stood on the edge of the crowd as Lars placed Seppi's body on a blanket on the snow-covered bank of the lake. Snow clouds overhead made the lake's surface murky and the air chilly. Four dragons gathered around Seppi: Seppi's valiant blue dragon, Septimor, Handel, Liesar and Antonika. The dragons picked up the ropes extending from the corners of the blanket and ascended, their wingbeats ruffling the onlookers' hair.

Gasps broke out as the underside of the blanket revealed a fierce battle scene—Seppi with his sword held high riding Septimor, charging over masses of tharuks, flame spurting from Septimor's maw. The artist had used a vibrant palette, a testament to Seppi's fierce courage.

Giddi blinked, his throat choking. Seppi had been at Dragons' Hold when Giddi had first been appointed head of the Wizard Council. The blue rider had overseen the training of hundreds of riders. Giddi shook his head. Such needless slaughter of a good man. For more than twenty years, Giddi had been watching friends fall at the hands of Zens' vile creations. Zens wouldn't stop at this latest abomination he'd unleashed on the realm—the dark dragon that had murdered Seppi. What other horrors was the commander planning?

Murmurs of appreciation rippled through the crowd as Lars spoke of Seppi, his valiant deeds, the esteem Dragons' Hold had for him.

The four dragons flew high above the lake, Seppi suspended between them on the blanket. Septimor roared, and the dragons let go of their ropes.

Seppi's body plunged through the chilly, gray sky toward the lake. Septimor dove, a torrent of fire erupting from his maw. Seppi's body burst into flames. He was a pillar of fire streaking through the air. Septimor flew down with him, burning his beloved rider. When there was nothing but ash, Septimor ascended, roaring his grief across the basin of Dragons' Hold, his cries shattering against the peaks of Dragon's Teeth.

Seppi's dark ashes speckled the water, rippled and dissolved from sight.

Giddi shook his head. It shouldn't be like this, that every time someone passed through the veil to fly with the spirits of departed dragons, this fierce, aching grief haunted him. Grief for dead riders, but also for Mazyka and what they'd lost. Grief for the damage that he and she had done to Dragons' Realm. Grief for the needless suffering of riders like Seppi, who didn't deserve to die.

At the edge of the crowd, young Kierion swiped at his eye. The poor lad looked tormented, no doubt riddled with guilt at destroying the piaua that could have saved Seppi. But it wasn't Kierion's fault Seppi was dead. No, that responsibility lay firmly with Zens. The commander needed to be destroyed.

Septimor was racing toward Fire Crag, the northernmost and highest mountain in the ring of Dragon's Teeth.

Giddi stretched out his mind. *"Septimor, I understand."*

The anguish ripping through the dragon flooded Giddi senses. His knees buckled. All the dragons of the hold roared, their mighty bellows reverberating through Giddi's bones. They took to the air, swooping in a circle around the lake.

Eventually, dragons and riders drifted back to their duties. Giddi stayed, feet numb in the snow. *"I'm here when you're ready, Septimor."*

A low rumble in his mind was the dragon's only reply.

Giddi understood grief. And also the need for silence and solace.

People drifted past. Soon, Kierion came, Fenni at his side. Master Giddi jerked his head, raising his eyebrows at Kierion.

Kierion came to Giddi's side, waiting.

With a wave of his hand, Giddi dismissed Fenni. *"He'll be with you in due course."*

Fenni replied with a barely perceptible nod and strode off.

"I thought you'd be in Montanara," Giddi said.

"I stayed to say farewell to Seppi." Kierion's voice was tight.

There was a blue flash on Heaven's Peak. A roar carried faintly on the breeze.

"A dragon's grief is a terrible, beautiful thing," Giddi murmured.

Kierion opened his mouth, then snapped his jaw shut and shoved his hands deep in his pockets.

Giddi placed an arm over the young man's shoulders. "Commander Zens' dark dragon killed Seppi." He stared directly into Kierion's eyes, glazed with unshed tears. "You can let this destroy you, Kierion, or you can grow from it. We have a realm out there, pristine and beautiful, full of noble people who deserve the best. You can spiral into destruction, blaming yourself, or you can hone yourself into a weapon upon your dragon's back and destroy the evil breaking our realm."

Kierion swiped his eye with his hand and thrust his chin up. "Thank you, Master Giddi."

§

Adelina saw Kierion standing with Master Giddi. More than anything, she wanted to tell him how awful she'd been and bridge the gulf she'd created.

But with Giddi standing right next to him, and Gret at her side, she could hardly stride up to him and apologize.

Gret tapped her shoulder. "Did you hear me?"

"Sorry?"

"I said, you didn't hear me, did you?

Adelina glanced back at Kierion, but he hadn't even seen her.

"Come on, it's cold," Gret grumbled. "Let's go inside. I need to pack my saddlebags for Montanara." Gret swept her along with the crowd into the main cavern.

She'd talk to Kierion soon. She had to. Gods, her temper could lose her a friend—or more.

Adelina went back to work at the infirmary.

By the time she finished, she was exhausted and it was late, so she went straight to her cavern to bed.

The next morning in the mess cavern, Gret's seat was empty.

When Adelina arrived at the infirmary, her friend was still nowhere to be found. "Where's Gret?" she asked Mara.

Mara frowned. "Didn't you know? Gret, Kierion and Fenni left for Montanara last night."

Adelina's heart lurched. Gret had left without saying goodbye.

Even worse, so had Kierion.

§

Hans woke, beaded in sweat, heart pounding. Thank the First Egg, it had only been a dream. He'd seen Marlies standing in the Lush Valley's square, surrounded by wounded people and steaming entrails of dark dragons. Ezaara and Roberto had been with her too. He rose from bed, padded through to the living area and poured a glass of water from the waterskin.

The water was cold, refreshing on Hans' parched throat. Had this latest vision already occurred? Or was it a prophecy goading him to action?

Behind him, a door creaked. Taliesin entered the room, his footfalls soft.

"Bad dreams too?" Hans' asked, knowing the answer before he voiced the question.

Taliesin nodded, taking the glass from Hans and cradling it in his hands. "I saw dead dragons in a square. Marlies was there too. Tharuks were killing people." The lad shivered.

Grim news, indeed. Hans was itching for action, sick of being cooped up here at the hold.

Lars wanted him to train this boy in the gift of prophecy. To do that, the lad had to see prophecy in action. There was no point staying here in the hold, awaiting news. It was time this boy cut his teeth in battle.

He jerked his chin at Taliesin. "Come on, Taliesin, let's grab our weapons, riders' garb and winter cloaks. We're going to Lush Valley."

§

Lovina adjusted her weight on the bed and picked up her charcoal, tilting her head to gaze at Tomaaz. She added some shadow to her sketch, under his left cheekbone. "Have you seen Unocco lately?"

"No, not lately. Why?" Tomaaz shifted on his chair.

"Don't do that, you'll ruin my drawing."

He shifted back. "Not that we should be drawing when there's so much to do."

"Tomaaz, it's late. You were on patrol at the crack of dawn." She smudged the shadow with her finger tip. "And apart from Seppi's funeral, you haven't taken a break from patrol all day. You need time to rest."

"And sitting still like a statue is resting?" He laughed. "You just want to sketch."

"Wouldn't you, with such a good-looking subject?" She raised an eyebrow, her face warming.

He grinned and winked. "You're really blossoming, you know that? Such a change." He cocked his head. "Why were you asking about Unocco?"

"Ajeurina's worried." Lovina set her parchment and charcoal on her bed, and patted the quilt. Tomaaz came over and sat next to her. "The night before the dark dragon attacked, Unocco was pining after Bruno."

"I guess that's to be expected." He took her hand, threading his fingers through hers. "The bond between dragon and rider runs deep, even if Bruno treated him badly."

Lovina swatted his arm. "I know that."

"So, you're worried he's lonely?"

"No, Tomaaz. It's more urgent than that. Unocco hasn't been seen for days. He may have gone after Bruno. I think I should tell Lars. Will you come with me?"

He leaned in and kissed her hair, his comforting warmth seeping into her side. How had she lived before him? Her life had been so bleak.

"You're remembering, aren't you?" He kissed her cheek, his breath fanning her lips. "It's all right, the old memories will fade as we make new ones. Lots of them."

Hand in hand, they walked along the stone tunnels to Lars' cavern and told him what Ajeurina suspected.

Lars scratched his blond beard. "Thank you for bringing this before me, Lovina. However, I doubt that a dragon that has been maliciously implanted with a crystal would be that eager to meet with his ex-rider."

"But that's the thing, Lars. My information comes from Ajeurina." Lovina stood straight, her chin high, grateful for Tomaaz's warm hand on the small of her back. "Ajeurina's agitated. She believes Unocco has gone to the Wastelands to look for Bruno."

"That's preposterous." Lars paced before his hearth. "Why would Unocco do that? We all know there's barely a chance of surviving the Wastelands."

"Ajeurina disagrees. She heard Unocco thinking about how Ezaara and Roberto had survived."

"That was different," said Lars. "They had help from the desert assassin."

"Exactly," said Lovina. "If Unocco helps Bruno, then perhaps he'll survive too."

THE NIGHTSHADERS

Kitted out as travelers with rucksacks on their backs and a range of weapons—both visible and concealed—Kierion, Fenni and Gret made their way through the edge of Great Spanglewood Forest.

"My father's farm is only half an hour's walk from here," Kierion whispered. "But we'll need to move fast. I don't want to be caught out at night by a passing tharuk."

Gret glanced around quickly before answering, "Are you sure your family won't mind us staying the night?"

"Of course not." He chuckled softly. "My brothers and sisters will probably think you're my girlfriend."

Fenni cleared his throat. "They'd better not."

That elicited a quiet laugh from Gret. "I've got no chance with Kierion," she said. "Everyone knows he only has eyes for Adelina."

"True." Fenni chuckled. "She's got you wrapped around her finger, my friend."

It felt like a knife between the ribs. Fenni and Gret didn't know Adelina hadn't spoken to him since the other night. He faked a casual grin. "Do you blame me? She's cute."

Gret rolled her eyes. "We're not here to discuss your love life, Kierion."

"Or the lack of yours," he quipped, jabbing her in the ribs with his elbow and rolling his eyes at Fenni.

Twigs cracked in the forest behind them. There was a muffled snort.

Gret stiffened and froze, eyes wide. "What was that?" she whispered.

Kierion cocked his head. Footfalls. He held up his hands in a T—*tharuk tracker*—the code Tonio had shown them.

Fenni jerked his head forward. The three of them broke into a stealthy jog, slipping through the trees.

§

The fug of beer and stale breath in the Brothers' Arms made Kierion's eyes water. He nursed his ale, strolling past the tharuks sitting at the bar, keeping his ears pricked. The tavern's patrons were a motley crew: scarred, tattooed, and as rough as guts. Thank the dragon gods, they were inside the Brothers' Arms, and not outside in Nightshade Alley.

"Zens said five come tomorrow," an ugly tharuk with a jagged tusk said, slamming its beer down on the bar.

A tiny wiry brute answered. "How many next day?"

Jagged Tusk shrugged. "Don't know. Ask Zens yourself." It let out a threatening guffaw.

"Should be fun. Bloodletting my favorite." Wiry gestured to the barkeep with a furry, clawed hand. "More ale."

The woman hastily complied.

Five were coming tomorrow. Whatever the *five* might be. Kierion loitered, sipping his beer. Bitter stuff. He'd never liked it, but it fit the part he was playing tonight. The beasts shoved their snouts into their tankards. There was no point hanging around these grunts any longer.

Over in the far corner—past crowded tables full of patrons playing nukils, having drinking races and laughing raucously—another group of tharuks were deep in conversation—if you could call tharuks' short broken sentences conversation.

Kierion edged through the throng of colorful characters from the shadier side of Montanarian life. He feigned casual interest in the goings-on around him, cheered when everyone else at a table did, and flicked his gaze over a game of cards as if he was looking for an easy mark. He brushed past a table of especially formidable thugs and thieves, probably members of the Nightshader street crew. Flames, Tonio and his dragon corps spies picked their bars, all right. He pressed on toward the tharuks, trying to remain unnoticed.

Sitting between him and the tharuks' table was a tough with crude stitches on his cheek and dragon tattoos covering his arms, surrounded by rough burly men at a table that bore worse scars than the ugly gash on the man's cheek. He had a pile of nukils before him. Silver ones. The type Kierion had never been able to afford. This guy was making good money doing something, and Kierion bet his undergarments it wasn't brewing soppleberry tea. The tough's eyes swept Kierion from head to foot as he tried to squeeze past them, noting the sword and knife at his belt, the extra blades up his sleeves and—hey, this guy was good—he'd even spotted the blade hidden in his boot.

Kierion prayed he wouldn't have to use them.

The tough thumped his hand on the scarred table. "Deal me in," he said. "And my friend here, who wants to play too." He jutted his chin at Kierion and smiled, his black-toothed grin as friendly as a hungry, antsy dragon's. "Sit down." A command, not an invitation.

One of the tough's cronies nudged a chair at Kierion with his boot.

He obliged, nodding in greeting.

"Dragon got your tongue?" Tough snapped.

The dragon had his whole flaming throat. Kierion was out of his depth. The tough knew it too. He'd best play along. No one came into this bar with as many weapons as he was carrying without looking for trouble. He should've concealed them better. He'd thought he had.

If he ran, that was it—no chance of returning. If he could prove himself, he might get to come back. Or end up dead in Nightshade Alley.

Oh well, he was in over his head. Might as well try to swim.

Kierion swaggered to the proffered chair and sank into it. "Evening gentlemen." He grinned and sat, propping his foot on his knee. He took a slug of ale that nearly made him splutter, and then banged his glass on the table. What had his mother called it? His insufferable cockiness. Hopefully it wouldn't get him killed tonight. "Thanks for inviting me. What are we playing for?"

The tough's eyes glinted. His men sniggered.

Oh flames, he was so dead. Eight of them looked like they'd give a dragon a run for its money in a brawl, the ninth would look good doing it—a pretty boy who caught a tharuk's falling tankard and slugged back the dregs in a neat move that had the others cheering.

The tough slid five nukils over the table at Kierion. "You any good?"

"I've played once or twice." Kierion raised an eyebrow. No point telling them he knew all the best ways to cheat at nukils.

"We play for coin," the tough said in a tone not to be disputed.

Each of his men threw a silver into a pile in the middle of the table. The tough nodded, a mental tally flitting across his face, as if he hadn't already provided his men with the coins so they could pull in new suckers.

Kierion shrugged.

The tough leaned in, face close. "Anyone with weapons that good had coin to buy them."

Except dragon riders who got them as part of their training. "Correct, but now I've no coin left." He pouted. Let them think he was green, eager.

"Then I suggest you put up your sword."

"Good idea." Kierion beamed.

"Hand it over."

"When we're done and tally the money, I'll put it on the table. It's too big, it'll just get in the way."

The tough gauged him for a moment, then nodded. "Sounds fair." His smile was all teeth and holes, mostly holes.

But this game wasn't fair—the moment Kierion picked up the nukils, he could feel they were weighted.

The tavern door flew open. Heads around the table turned as a cloaked figure swaggered inside, his hood hanging so low only a pale chin showed beneath it.

One of the tough's minions leaned in, whispering to his crew leader, "Another easy mark, Captain."

The tough grinned like a shark about to begin feasting. "Every newcomer has to play at my table," he bellowed.

It was only a few moments before the cloaked stranger, no sword or knife at his hip, sat at the table with his tankard. Only a fool would wear no weapons in here. The stranger flicked back the hood of his cloak, revealing a familiar face, blond hair and keen green eyes. Curling his lip in a sneer, Fenni said, "Deal me in."

Clever of him to strategically take a seat close to the tharuks so he could listen in.

Kierion scowled, sliding his meanest gaze over Fenni. "New around here?" he asked.

Fenni held his gaze. "Maybe."

The tough leaned forward, guffawing—a sound that crept down Kierion's back like fingernails scratching bark—and slid five nukils across the table to Fenni. "We were just starting. Five rounds, winner takes all. Why don't you go first?"

Fenni tossed in a silver and threw his nukils, catching them all on the back of his hand.

One of the men whistled. "Full hand."

Fenni slammed the nukils down again.

That was the easy part. The game would get progressively harder.

Nukils clattered around the table as each man took his throw. The tough folded his arms, leaned back in his chair and observed, eyes glinting with promised menace.

A few full hands resulted, and a few dropped nukils. Kierion gauged each player's skill, pretending to sip his beer. When his turn came, he deliberately fumbled, letting two nukils slide off his hand onto the table. He'd learned the hard way, years ago, that it didn't pay to show your skill too early, especially in a bar like this.

He scrunched his face in a frown, glowered at Fenni and folded his arms. Only a fool or a crew leader would dare fold his arms here. Most men had their hands on their rapidly emptying glasses or near their swords—just in case.

The tough watched, eyes flitting to Kierion's weapons again, evaluating his every move—and Fenni's.

A roar ripped through the bar. Everyone turned as Jagged Tusk slashed a man's neck with its claws. Blood sprayed on the onlookers. The man slumped to the floor.

Everyone turned back to their beer and kept drinking.

Dragons' claws—a man killed, just like that. Kierion restrained himself from rushing over. It was too late to save him. With a chunk that size ripped out of his throat, he would've been dead when he hit the floor.

Fenni raised an eyebrow. "Unlucky." He threw his nukils, catching five again, this time flipping them high off the back off his hand and snapping them into his fist with a satisfying clink. He leaned back, took a hard pull on his tankard and sighed. "Next."

Claws, Fenni would have to watch it, or he'd soon be drunk. The last thing Kierion wanted was to babysit a drunken mage.

Kierion feigned a casual glance around the bar. "So, dragon riders don't drink here?"

Across the table, Fenni snorted. "Now, why would we want those shrotty riders to drink with us?" Another sip. He slammed his tank down and leveled a challenging stare at Kierion.

"I was curious. That's all," Kierion answered.

So far so good. Despite his weapons, this street crew had taken him for an arrogant fool and Fenni for an unarmed threat, playing right into their hands.

"We make short work of the dragon riders in Nightshade Alley," the tough said. "Your turn." He gestured at Kierion, as if he knew he was holding back.

§

Fenni stretched his arms and locked his fingers behind his head, exposing his ribs to a possible knife plunge, the ultimate gesture of someone in control of a situation. From the moment he'd walked in the door, he'd realized the leader of the Nightshaders knew he was a mage. Fenni didn't know how, but they said some people could sense magic as a hum—like a swarm of bees hovering about their senses. Maybe this scarred, black-toothed leader was one of those people.

He leaned back, straining to hear the tharuks at the table behind him. "Everything ready for tomorrow," a tharuk grunted. Its slurping drowned out the nukils clattering at its own table. That brute must have its snout deep in his tankard.

"After tomorrow?" asked another tharuk with a reedy voice.

Snuffling. "Then more come here. And every day after, more."

"Hey! What you do? That my beer." The tharuks began arguing among themselves.

More were coming, but more what? Tharuk troops, probably. Fenni refrained from scratching his chin, keeping his eyes on the game.

Only two more men until it was his turn. Kierion messed up his turn—again. Growing up, Fenni and Kierion had been the best nukil players in their neighborhood, but Kierion was acting as if he was a rookie tonight. Fenni could barely wait until Kierion started cleaning up.

A tharuk at the bar snarled, and another lowered its tusks, as if to charge. A roar from a third, larger beast brought them both back into line. Thank the Egg, he'd convinced Gret not to come to this horrible place with them.

As if on cue, Gret opened the door and walked into the tavern. For the sake of the First Egg, had she no brain in her stubborn skull?

§

The noise in the tavern faded away. Fenni's heart stilled. What was Gret doing here? The Brothers' Arms was no place for a woman—especially one as beautiful as her. Wolves looked up from their beers, eyes glinting, licking their lips as they watched her hips sway toward the bar.

Fenni fought not to clench his fists, trying to remain nonchalant and casual as he pretended to watch the game of nukils move around the table. The Nightshader crew leader leaned in. "Pretty, isn't she?"

Fenni feigned a yawn and turned to him. "Aren't they all?"

If any of these thugs learned how much Gret meant to him, they'd use her as a weapon against him. He picked up the nukils, threw through them high in the air and made them clack against each other as he caught them one by one.

Kierion's eyes roved the tavern and finally landed on Gret. He gave Fenni a wicked grin. "What do you say, shall we invite the pretty girl over?"

"It's all the same to me." Gods, it wasn't all the same to him. Dressed in tight breeches, a red jerkin and dark cloak, Gret was gorgeous. Her long blonde braids gleamed gold in the light of the tallow lanterns. She smiled at the barkeep, flashing her pretty white teeth, and asked for a cider. An instant later, a tankard was in her hand.

A man near the bar reached out to grab her. She batted his hand away, spinning and striding between the crowded tables, holding her cider.

The hum of magic zapped underneath Fenni's skin. He clamped down on it, not wanting to show his hand.

The crew leader's head snapped to him, and his nostrils flared as if he could scent Fenni's raw power. Eyes narrowed, he barked at one of his men, "Invite the girl to play. This should get interesting."

A handsome thug leaped up and strode confidently over to Gret as she made her way through the crowded tables. He was a flashy type, wearing breeches so tight Fenni was surprised he hadn't castrated himself. He bowed with an extravagant flourish, his dark curls catching the lamp light. His eyes flashed, his gaze roving over Gret's face, chest and long legs. Lingering. Appraising her. "Please, my lady, we invite you to join a game of nukils at our table." He took Gret's free hand and kissed it, his lips lingering longer than any decent man's would.

To Fenni's surprise, instead of swatting the man away or calling him out, Gret giggled, her cheeks turning the same shade as her vibrant red cloak.

Fenni hooked his foot around his chair leg, straining against it until the wood creaked, to stop himself from kicking the louse's shins.

"Quite a beauty, isn't she?" Asked the crew leader. "Fancy her?"

Fenni feigned a yawn. "I have a woman already," he lied. "But I do appreciate beauty."

"Maybe you'd appreciate beauty more if she were in your bed tonight?"

Although he liked Gret—a lot—he'd never dared picture her like that. Just the thought made Fenni's insides warm. He shrugged the comment off, clacking the nukils in his hand.

The slimy, hand-kissing toad led Gret to their table, but instead of offering her a chair, he patted his lap.

For a moment, Gret's eyes flashed in panic, but then she perched gingerly on the end of his knee. He guffawed and laid a hand on her hip. "Deal her in."

Fenni could sear that hand from its wrist in a heartbeat, leaving nothing but a charred stump. He reined his simmering magic in.

Gret flipped a silver into the center of the table.

The toad's teeth flashed, eyes gleaming. "No need for coin, little lady. The winner gets you to warm his bed. And it just so happens that I am the undisputed champion."

Fenni's head pounded. Under the table, sparks flitted from his fingers.

The toad snatched up Gret's coin and flipped it high into the air toward her.

By the time she caught it, her dagger was at the toad's throat. "I decide who'll warm my bed. No one else. Now get me a chair and get your hands off me so I can join the game and drink my cider in peace."

The toad nodded, the promise of violence sparking in his eyes and dragged over a chair from an adjacent table. Gret holstered her knife.

The scarred crew leader tossed back his head, roaring with laughter. "I like her spirit. Ever considered joining the Nightshader crew?"

Gret took a long slow sip of her cider, regarding the leader over her glass with her warm brown eyes. "How about a game of nukils, first?"

The men around the table snorted, grinned and chuckled. The handsome toad pulled his chair closer to Gret's, close enough to slide a dagger between her ribs while no one was looking.

Gret flashed him a cool smile. "Thank you for inviting me to join the game."

"You're welcome," the toad replied, his eyes lingering far too long on Gret's full red lips.

It was all Fenni could do to not flip the table, blast that toad with the full brunt of his mage flame and burn him to ash.

A seat over from Gret, Kierion met his gaze, sending a silent warning: *not now.*

A GAMBLE

By the end of the first round, Kierion's sword was on the table. By the end of the second round, his dagger was too.

Fenni was in the lead, his score even with that of the flashy man who'd invited Gret to play. Gret was scoring somewhere in the middle of the bunch, and Kierion was lagging way behind everyone, just as planned.

With each round, more beers were bought, and the pile of coins, weapons and possessions grew taller. Gradually, their large table drew the attention of most of the patrons in the Brothers' Arms. Despite several casual questions, Kierion was no closer to finding out where Danion was, whether anyone had seen him lately, and what was going on. He could only hope that Fenni, seated closest to the tharuks, had overheard something useful. Although, since Gret had entered the tavern, he doubted Fenni had noticed much except her and the vile thug flirting with her.

The head tough grinned at Kierion. "A shame you paid so much for those fancy weapons when you won't get to keep them."

Kierion summoned up a cocky grin, gripping and un-gripping his fists on the table where the tough could see them. "Game's not over yet, but I need a quick latrine trip. Back soon. "

"Not slipping out on us, are you?" the tough's brow furrowed.

Kierion grinned as he stood. "Now, why would I do that? I need to win my sword back."

The tough gestured, and two men trailed Kierion outside to the latrine at the back of the tavern. Once inside the outhouse, Kierion made the appropriate noises, while whipping a hot pepper from his pocket. He munched it down, eyes watering. When they returned to their table, he took a long swig of beer to disguise the pepper on his breath. Soon, his forehead broke out in a sweat. He fumbled his next turn, letting the nukils scatter over the table.

The men laughed at his clumsiness.

Kierion mopped his forehead with a kerchief. "I'll get it right, soon. Just wait." He gave a forced grin, more of a painful grimace than a smile.

Fenni flipped all the nukils, double bounced them and caught them in a clatter. "What's in your beer?" he asked. "Woozy weed?"

Kierion bared his teeth in another smile. "I'll up you all. Double it. The winner of this round takes all."

The tough sneered, "The fool wants to lose more. How about wagering the other dagger in your boot, pretty boy?"

"Pretty boy?" Kierion burst out laughing and looked pointedly at the man who'd fetched Gret. He didn't need to say a thing. The whole table started laughing. Except the pretty boy, who glowered at him.

"Get on with round three," Fenni snapped. "I don't have all night. I have somewhere to be."

The tough raised an eyebrow and grinned, as if none of them would be going anywhere soon.

Kierion gulped, a drop of sweat rolling into his eye. This time, when the nukils came his way, he executed a triple snap perfectly, pretending to look surprised as the nukils clacked into his hand. He spluttered and grinned.

"Fluke," Fenni said, shooting him a cutting glance.

"Nice move." Gret said, eyes shining with admiration. From behind her back, the flashy man glowered, cleaning his thumbnail with his teeth.

Nukils cracked and clattered as the other men took their turns. Flashy did a double snap, to maintain his lead, but then Fenni's triple flip put him in front.

Flickering lamp light winked off the coins and weapons piled on the battered table.

Kierion needed respect from these men in order to work with them and gain information, but he didn't want to end up dead in a gutter along Nightshade Alley. In his next turn, he performed a sideways snatch and rumbling roll. He let himself roar like a dragonet with new horns, earning a glower from Fenni.

"I suppose you think you're a dragon's prime catch," Flashy snapped, "but try and beat this." He attempted a triple roll, but fumbled it and the nukils scattered across the table and clattered onto the floor. He swore and plucked them off the floorboards amid raucous laughter.

Dragon's claws, from the looks Kierion was getting from Flashy, he'd be lucky to get out of this alive.

§

With a quick succession of triple rolls and flying snatches so stunning they made Fenni's head whirl, Kierion won the game. An angry uproar erupted from the remaining players.

Fenni had to get Gret out of here quickly. He stood, roughly shoving his chair over, sparks dripping from his fingers. "As I said, *I have somewhere to be.*" As he stalked past Gret, he stopped—as if she was an afterthought—and asked, "Care to join me?" He kept his face bored, impassive, raising a cool eyebrow at her.

She tilted her head at him. "Don't mind if I do."

Before anyone could object, they were striding from the tavern, Fenni's arm possessively around Gret's slim shoulders. He tucked her tightly against his side, wondering if he was doing the right thing, leaving Kierion alone. But he had to get Gret out before the whole bar turned to mayhem.

Two Nightshaders slipped out the bar door behind them, as silent as shadows, trailing them along the alley.

"We're being followed," he whispered to Gret. "We have to put up a good act."

Gret's only reply was a fake drunken giggle. She tugged him over to the side of a building, and leaned back against it provocatively, one boot against the wall with her knee up, arching her back so her breasts were raised to the sky. "Kiss me," she whispered, eyes flitting over his shoulder.

By the flaming dragon gods, he'd wished for nothing else since he'd first met her in the stone corridors of Dragons' Hold. But not like this. Not with some thugs watching nearby. Not as a ruse to prove their disguises.

She gave a low soft laugh, then whispered, "Hurry up. They're watching."

Fenni placed a hand on the timber above her, letting sparks flit from his fingertips, and leaned in, gripping her waist.

Their breath mingled.

"Come on," she purred. "Let your flames roar."

Although it was likely she'd only said that for the benefit of the onlookers, a crackle of energy rushed through Fenni. Flames licked from his fingertips, leaving charred marks on the timbers of the building wall. Blood pounded through his veins. He leaned down. In the flickering light from his flames, her brown eyes were wide, lips parted.

Maybe, just to keep up appearances…

He bent his head and brushed his mouth against her lips.

Once.

Twice.

Molten heat seared from his lips to his core. But it was her gasp, the sharp intake of breath against his lips that made something inside him unravel.

Gret reached up and twisted his hair in her fingers, pulling his face closer. Arching toward him.

Oh, Gods. Fenni, against all wisdom, closed his eyes and kissed her.

§

Gret had never kissed a man before. Never wanted to. But from the moment she'd first met golden-haired Fenni, green sparks dripping from his fingertips, something deep inside her had woken and whispered, "He's the one." She'd yearned to know how his kiss would taste. Yearned to run her hands through his soft hair and touch the planes of his face until she knew them by heart.

When he'd suggested she stay at home, away from the danger at the Brothers' Arms, it'd rankled. Her father, proud of her swordsmanship and keen to help the realm, had encouraged her to go along. So she'd dressed to kill. The tavern had been packed with tharuks, thugs and Nightshaders. She hadn't anticipated the reactions of those men, leering at her, making her feel unclean. Then Fenni's familiar face across the room had anchored her.

But when that handsome Nightshader had kissed her hand and invited her to play nukils, an impish desire had seized her, and she'd played along to see Fenni's reaction. Until the scummy thug had gone too far. Oh, she'd been a fool. She could've landed herself in dire strife tonight if Fenni hadn't whisked her out the door.

Fenni claimed her mouth, heat searing through her body as his soft, soft lips moved against hers. His hand slipped from the wall above her head to her waist and he pulled her against him.

A jolt went through her. She opened her eyes and gazed at him in wonder.

Over his shoulder, something metallic flashed in the lantern light.

Gret shoved Fenni aside. Snatched her sword from her scabbard. And lunged. She deflected the blade aimed at Fenni's back. The thug's dagger clattered on the cobbles.

A crackle of Fenni's mage fire cast the handsome thug's face in a green glow. "So," he sneered, "our lady can fight."

Beside him, the other thugs chortled. "Let's see what else she can do," one called out.

"Hands off," the handsome one snarled, retrieving his knife. "She's mine."

HUNTING DARK DRAGONS

Jael gripped Tomaaz's waist as Maazini flew over the peaks of Dragon's Teeth and swooped down toward Great Spanglewood Forest. The snow muffled everything except the muted swish of the blue guards' wings on either side of them. For the past five days, Jael and Tomaaz and the blue guard patrol had been hunting for dark dragons over Great Spanglewood Forest. There'd been no sign of the beast that had fought them and killed Seppi.

As the blue guards fanned out over the forest, Jael scanned the trees and horizon for any traces of the beast. The eerie quiet of the forest made the hair prickle on his neck. Was it just the blanket of snow muting the sounds? Or was the forest stiller than usual?

He tapped Tomaaz's shoulder. "Anyone hear anything yet?"

"Don't worry, I'll let you know as soon as I have news. Lars only wants us melding in emergencies so the dark dragon can't access our minds."

"Makes sense," Jael replied. "That beast was near Mage Gate. Should we look there?"

"Good idea," Tomaaz answered.

Maazini soared toward Mage Gate, the orange membrane on his wings a stark contrast to the snowy forest below.

"Maazini, let's skim the trees," Tomaaz said aloud.

Leaning out, Jael scouted the forest to the right of Maazini while Tomaaz checked the left.

"What's that down there? That dark shadow?" Jael pointed past Tomaaz at a dark smudge among the trees.

So close to Mage Gate. Did Zens realize the potential of this area? He must know it was where the world gate had been closed. Jael had only been a littling when it'd happened, but the stories had been told for years around Naobian hearths. Stories about Mazyka, her tempestuous quest for power, and how Master Giddi had been forced by dragon riders to lock out hundreds of mages, including his own wife, from Dragons' Realm to prevent Zens from bringing more tharuks in.

Not that it had mattered in his opinion. Zens had made more tharuks here anyhow.

"Maazini, can we take a better look?" Tomaaz asked.

Maazini wheeled around and flew back.

"Down there," Jael pointed. "Underneath that strongwood cluster."

Maazini swept down and landed by the riverbank. Flaring his nostrils, the dragon stalked the dark mass in the shadowy trees, Tomaaz still on his back, his bow drawn. Without melding, Tomaaz wouldn't know what his dragon scented. Jael leaned around Tomaaz, hands at the ready.

Rays shot from the shadow, melting two holes in the snow at Maazini's feet, illuminating the black dragon staring at them with shining yellow eyes.

Snarling, Maazini leaped back, then sniffed again.

"By the First Egg," Tomaaz cursed.

The dark beast scrabbled its talons in the snow and raised itself off its haunches, only to stumble a few steps and crash to the snow, neck sagging. It flapped snow from its wings, revealing tattered, burned edges—the scent of singed flesh wafting from them. Jael wrinkled his nose.

"It's another dark dragon," Tomaaz whispered. "Much older than the one we saw a few days ago."

"I don't think so," Jael replied. "That's exactly where I singed the beast's wings."

"It can't be. There's no way. This beast is far too old. Look, it can hardly move."

The dark dragon raised its head and coughed, a pathetic gust of flame spurting from its maw. The wrinkled, sagging skin on its neck wobbled, shedding dark scales, like flecks of ash, onto the snow.

"Maazini, do you want to risk mind-melding with it?" Tomaaz asked.

Jael placed his hand on Maazini's hide, so he could hear through Tomaaz's dragon.

A faint phantom scream echoed in Maazini's mind. Even though it was quiet, it shot through Jael's head like lightning.

Tomaaz shook his head. "That beast's in pain. Its dying. We should put it out of its misery."

Jael snorted. "You're showing compassion now? After that thing fried Maazini's mind and slit Seppi's gut?"

"If it's the same one, it's only a shadow of what it was. We need to kill it anyway. I'd rather kill it out of compassion, than vengeance."

"Very well. I'll give it a funeral pyre, but I need a better vantage point than perching behind you like a littling craning its neck to see fire-sticks. Jael slid off Maazini and stood in front of the huge orange dragon. Not too far, just in case it was faking its feebleness.

He stretched his hands out, feeling the hum of the *sathir* inside him. Bright-green fire roiled at his fingertips. He pulled it into a fireball and bounced it between his hands, pouring in *sathir* until the molten ball was as big as his chest and blistering hot.

The dark dragon bucked to stand and staggered toward him, snarling. Its yellow rays seared a path through the snow as it picked up speed. It was surprisingly fast.

A screech shot into Jael's mind. A wave of pain ricocheted inside his skull. He dropped his fireball to the snow, and it fizzed out. He clutched his temples, staggering. Oh, gods, the beast was lurching toward him. Jael dodged its yellow rays. They brushed the hem of his cloak, leaving smoking holes. The tortured scream of pain was going to split his head asunder.

"Look out!" An arrow zipped past him from behind and pierced the beast's side. The wound only amplified the scream in Jael's head.

Jael yanked his hands from his temples, flung them out, and blasted the beast with a crackling plume of mage flame. The creature's hide caught fire. Green flames licked over its chest, up its neck and along its back and wings. It howled and twisted in a ball of flame. Then it slumped to the snow in a blazing heap.

At last, the scream in Jael's head stopped. Panting, he stumbled to Maazini and clambered back into the saddle. They took to the sky, chased by the stink of burned dragon flesh and black, billowing smoke.

§

Maazini ascended through the smoke of the burning dragon. The stench of burnt flesh clung to Jael's nostrils. Dark shadows flitted among smoke and haze. How much smoke could one dragon create? It went on and on, a stinking pall across the forest.

But something was off. The air crackled with tension. Jael leaned forward. "Can you feel it?"

Tomaaz nodded. "My neck's prickling. Something's hunting us."

Out of the roiling smoke, two burning embers appeared, golden glowing eyes searing through the black. Beams sprang from them, slicing through the smoke and hitting Jael's cloak.

Before his eyes, the fabric was sheared in half, the smoking remnants fluttering away on the wind.

Maazini roared, flapping his wings and sped up through the smoke into clear sky. Jael hung on to Tomaaz with one arm, flinging mage fire at the cloud-cloaked dark dragon behind them.

He missed.

The beast bellowed, opening its maw, exposing rows of sharp fangs. Fire belched from its jaws at Maazini's tail.

Maazini snarled and thrashed at his head with his talons. He whirled, trying to escape the dark dragon's flame. Its yellow rays shot out and scored the scales on Maazini's tail.

Jael twisted in the saddle and flung more mage fire, but Maazini's bucking threw off his aim. Every bolt went wide. His head was pounding again. Hooking his hand through a saddle strap, he leaned back and turned, aiming his other hand at the beast. By the holy dragon gods, someone was riding it!

As they surged upward, the last trails of smoke cleared from around the dark dragon.

Velrama—one of the mages who'd been kidnapped by tharuks—was perched upon the evil beast, her blonde hair whipping in the wind. The last time he'd seen her was when she'd melted a hole in her ice wall for him and Fenni to walk through.

Jael hesitated, not wanting to hurt the less-experienced mage, but the hesitation cost him. The rays from the dragon's eyes shot forth, searing Maazini's hind leg.

Maazini bellowed in pain, pivoting in midair to face the dark dragon.

Velrama laughed, flinging her mage fire at Jael.

Velrama was under Zens' control—she had to be. Jael had no choice. He countered with a wall of flame that sucked the magic out of Velrama's blast and consumed it. His head throbbed as Maazini charged toward the dark beast, talons out and fire blazing. The mighty orange dragon roared, his sides rumbling under Jael's legs.

The dark beast snarled in reply.

Roaring flames split the sky as two blue dragons swept up from below and drove back the dark dragon with bursts of fire.

EILEEN MUELLER

The blue guards chased the beast as Maazini swerved away whimpering.

"My dragon's hurt," Tomaaz said. "Let's get out of here."

"Good idea," Jael replied as Maazini headed back to the safety of Dragons' Hold.

Jael's hands trembled. Velrama wasn't evil. If they'd been in the wrong place at the wrong time, it could have been he or Fenni who'd been riding the dark dragon.

He fumed over his hesitation to blast her. It had hurt Maazini. What had he expected? He'd heard that Zens implanted crystals in people to control them. It made sense. Velrama and Sorcha, who'd been kidnapped with her, were now riding Zens' dark dragons.

Jael snorted. What were two mages and a few dark dragons against many mages and disciplined riders?

A tendril of doubt gnawed at the back of Jael's mind. Those beams from the dark dragons' eyes were formidable. What if Zens had something else up his sleeve?

FLASHY

lthough he'd used the pepper to induce fake sweat and fool the other players into thinking he was stressed, Kierion was really sweating now. Nightshaders shoved to their feet, knocking their chairs loudly to the floor. Their faces contorted into ugly, snarling grimaces.

Kierion smiled and plucked his weapons from the table. "I don't need any coin, really," he said, "just my weapons. Though, I'd love to play with you again sometime." He sketched a bow.

The head tough's mouth dropped open, as astounded as a dragon who'd laid chickens.

Kierion spun and strode quickly across the tavern, leaving the crew to fight over the spoils. As he pushed the door open, a blade hit the wood a hand's breadth above his fingers, quivering.

The tavern fell silent as he plucked it out of the wood and turned to face the Nightshader crew. Their blades were drawn, eyes pinned him.

One false move…

With a casual flick of his wrist, Kierion sent the knife spinning over the tavern-goers heads and into the scarred table, right next to the loot pile. "Enjoy your spoils gentlemen." He bolted out the door.

The clash of metal echoed through Nightshade Alley. A blast of mage fire lit up the gloom. Drawing his sword, Kierion ran.

In the next blast, he saw Gret fighting two men, another four attacking Fenni.

Kierion flew into the fray, sword spinning. He knocked a knife from the hand of one of the thugs fighting Gret, and then whirled to help Fenni.

The flashy, handsome thug was giving Fenni a run for his coin, ducking his flames, and lunging in to strike when the others distracted him. If he could lure the thug away, perhaps Fenni could fight off the others.

Kierion raced up behind Flashy and jabbed him in the ribs with the tip of his sword. "Scared to fight me, one on one?" He danced back, farther down the alley, into the gloom.

"You!" Flashy chased him.

Kierion ran, not too fast or Flashy might turn back to Fenni. Then he spun and lunged at Flashy as the thug tried not to slam into him. But Flashy twisted and Kierion's blade sailed past his gut, missing by a hair's breadth. Kierion jumped back and they faced each other, panting.

Flashy attacked with a series of fast moves. Kierion parried every one of them, and lunged to strike the thug. But Flashy blocked swiftly and drove Kierion back.

Ah, it was good to be moving, fighting, after being stuck in that stinking tavern all night. Dragon's claws! They'd learned nothing tonight. No news of Danion. No idea what the tharuks were up to tomorrow. And he'd landed them all in trouble. Great spy he was.

He lunged again, but Flashy ducked under his blade and spun to attack. Kierion knew that move—he'd learned it at Dragons' Hold from Master Jaevin before the sword master had been murdered. He moved to block, but Flashy feinted, spun, then lunged again—another dragon rider technique. Kierion barely parried it. By the flaming dragon gods, he'd never have guessed. "You're a dragon rider, aren't you?"

Flashy snarled, "What makes you think that?"

Kierion ignored his answer—he could tell—and lunged again. Why hadn't he seen it earlier? "Why are you running with the Nightshader crew?"

"Why are you still alive?" Flashy snapped, beating Kierion's blade aside. "Most nosy shrot-huffers don't live to your age. Who in the Egg's name do you think you are?"

Flashy thrust again. Kierion beat his blade down and pressed his weight on it, keeping it down.

"I'm just a courier," Kierion huffed, straining to keep their swords locked. "I have some black pepper for a guy named Danion."

Flashy faltered, brow creased. "What?" He leaped forward, swung his blade around, knocking Kierion's blade aside and driving him up against a wall, his sword tip at Kierion's throat. "What did you say?" he hissed.

"I have some black pepper for Danion." Kierion swallowed, hoping Master Tonio's code-word or the rider's name hadn't jeopardized his life.

Flashy glanced down the alley, toward the luminous-green flare of Fenni's mage fire, and whispered, "Come with me."

§

Thank the flaming First Egg, Kierion had turned up and led away that pretty thug who'd been ogling her all night. He'd been a tricky opponent, their best fighter. At least now, with only five to oppose them, she and Fenni might have a fighting chance. She thrust her sword, ripped through a man's cloak and scored his jerkin. Flames, it didn't slow him down at all. She lunged again, shredding his cloak as he spun away. The heat of the mage flame at her back was unnerving, even though she usually liked the crackle of magic—alive and full of possibility. She spun, slashing a thug's leg. He howled and crashed to the cobbles. Panting, Gret parried the blade of the huge man who stepped over him.

From the shadows, a deep voice said, "Drop your sword or your friend dies. You, with the mage flame, put it out."

The luminous green glow died. Tiny flares zipped from Fenni's fingertips, mage lights shooting into the gloom and illuminating the handsome Night-shader—who was holding Kierion at swordpoint.

Kierion was pale, eyes wide. A trickle of blood ran down his throat.

"I said drop the sword."

Gret did nothing of the sort. Instead, she sheathed it and held her hands out in front of her where he could see them. Fenni stepped to her side, his arm around her, the scent of mage fire clinging to him.

The Nightshaders closed in, surrounding Gret and Fenni.

"Brutus, bring the girl here at knife point."

There was nothing charming about the handsome man now. Gret wanted to shred his pretty face.

Two men grabbed Fenni, who lashed and kicked, sending sparks flying into their faces.

The huge Nightshader, Brutus, wrenched Gret's arm up her back and shoved his blade under her chin. If she moved, her blood would gush over the cobbles.

"Mind you don't scratch her," the pretty thug said. "I don't like my women marred." He laughed, a deep throaty sound that grated down her spine.

"Young mage, hold your fire or your friends die."

Two thugs held their knives at Fenni's ribs. He winced.

"You lot, over there, hold this whelp fast."

Another thug gripped Kierion, and the pretty one let go of him. He took the knife from Brutus, the pressure never easing off Gret's throat, and kept her arm pinned firmly up her back.

"It was mighty suspicious, three of you turning up tonight," he purred. "But don't worry, with a little *persuasion*, this beauty will soon explain everything," His breath brushed Gret's ear, making her shudder. "If you two want to see her alive again, get out of here. When I've had my fill, she'll be back here at dawn, waiting for you." He sneered at Fenni, laughing in his face. "Then we'll see if you still want her."

Fenni's eyes were wide. Hands trembling. Gret sensed his coiled power, waiting to erupt.

He subtly moved one of his fingers, but a thug pressed his knife harder into his side. "Want your guts on the ground, now, lover boy?"

"No, Fenni." Gret's voice cracked. She swallowed. Gods, what would happen to her? Her legs shook like a sapling in a storm. It wasn't hard to tell what the man wanted, but this way, they'd all live, at least for now. "It's for the best, do what he says."

Sparks dripped from Fenni's hands. He glared at the man holding her, but didn't make a move.

The thugs released her friends. Kierion yanked Fenni's arm. "Come on, Fenni."

Fenni gazed at her as the Nightshader dragged her in the other direction.

The other four Nightshaders guffawed into the hollow dark, the injured man groaning in the snow-strewn gutter.

"Hurry up," Flashy barked at Gret.

He pulled her down a narrow, twisting alley. A rat scarpered across her foot, making her wince—although rats were the least of her worries. Cold prickles broke out over her skin as he led her down alley after winding alley. When she was thoroughly lost, he lowered the knife from her throat to her ribs.

"Open that door." He gestured at a narrow wooden door half hidden in the gloom of an alcove.

Her hand twitched toward her sword.

"Nothing stupid. We don't want you to die here in this little alley. You'd like to live when I've finished with you, wouldn't you?" His laugh echoed through her bones, rattling her pounding heart.

§

Fenni caught one last glimpse of Gret's pale stoic face. Her beautiful face. What had he done? He should've whisked her off to safety, not been cocky about his own power. He should have known that although he was a mage, his friends were not—enemies could always get to him through them. He should have burned the handsome face right off the thug's neck. Now, the arrogant thug would—

"You're not thinking of following them are you?" a dangerously soft voice crooned in the dark.

Fenni snapped his gaze to the Nightshaders. Four were advancing, blades flashing.

"Come on!" Kierion snapped. "Gret saved our lives. Let's get out of here." Kierion bolted up the alley toward the street.

With one last glance at the alley, Fenni threw up a wall of flame and ran hard on Kierion's heels.

The Nightshaders ran after them.

They were running away from Gret. Running like cowards.

Gret was braver than him. He wasn't even trying to save her. Flames leaped from his fingers. He whirled. "I'm going back for her."

"No!" Kierion grabbed him by the collar and slammed him against a wall. He whipped his blade up to Fenni's throat.

What in the dragon gods' name?

"Don't argue," Kierion said. "Now is not the time."

"How can you be so callous? How can you just let them take Gret?"

"We had no choice. Our skins or her virtue?"

What a choice—the virtue of the woman he loved or his life and the life of his best friend. Flame Kierion. To hell with Kierion. He should've let him die—and run with Gret instead.

Actually, there hadn't been a choice. The slimy thug had made it for them.

Footsteps hammered down the alley.

"Hurry or they'll find out." Kierion broken into a run, counting the side streets under his breath, and ducked into an alley.

Fenni stumbled along behind him, hands numb and feet as heavy as stone. Find out what?

Ahead, Kierion was still counting. He paused at another side street, frantically gesturing. "Quick," he whispered. "Down here."

§

The pretty thug dragged Gret up steep dingy stairs. On each landing, eyes stared through peepholes in doors. Gret panted up the steps. Her hands were slick with sweat. A single candle spluttered on the third landing. The moment he let go, she'd grab her sword. The cur kicked open a door and shoved her inside. "Strip off and get on the bed," he yelled, and kicked the door shut.

The creep leaned against the door and gave her what he must've thought was a winsome smile. The candle on the bedside table in the shabby little room made his teeth gleam.

Gret fumbled with the top button of her jerkin, stalling.

"It's all right," he whispered. "You don't have to take off your clothes." He darted to the window and peeked out a chink in the curtain. "Your friends will be here soon."

Hands still clammy, Gret let go the button. "W-what?" Were the other thugs bringing Kierion and Fenni to watch this man ravage her?

The fool had turned his back on her to look out the window. Stealthily, she grasped the pommel of her sword and drew it from its scabbard.

Before she could take a breath, he whirled, knives in his hands.

"I should introduce myself. I'm Danion, Tonio's dragon corps man here on the ground in Montanara."

"What?" She gripped her sword—although she had no chance against his throwing knives in such close quarters. If she could roll...

He chuckled. "You said that already. I'm sorry. Forgive me for giving you a fright. If I hadn't put on such a good act, the Nightshaders would've gutted your friends and dragged you off down the alley." He shrugged and tucked his knives back into their sheaths at his belt. "Better me than them."

"You sharding idiot!" Gret sheathed her sword. "You scared the living daylights out of me."

Danion glanced out of the curtains again. "Here come your friends."

Sure enough, stairs creaked outside the room, the soft thud of boots heralding someone's approach.

Danion cracked the door open and quickly ushered Fenni and Kierion inside.

Fenni rushed over to Gret, grasping her face in his hot hands and gazed into her eyes. "Are you all right?"

She shuddered, breath hissing out of her. "Yes, I'm all right."

He pulled her into his arms, warmth surging over her.

Danion shook his thick curls. He nodded at Gret. "My apologies again. This is a risky game we're in."

Fenni released Gret, stood legs apart, hands at the ready, as if he was in a mage duel. He glared at Danion, eyes simmering with rage.

"It's all right, Fenni," Gret said.

Danion ignored him. "Now, let's get down to business."

LUSH VALLEY

The Western Grande Alps lay before Marlies, Liesar and Leah, glistening in the sun like peaks of beaten egg white. Beyond those alps was Western Settlement, where Marlies had recently stayed at Nick's inn. In a few hours they'd be at Lush Valley—her home while she and Hans had raised the twins.

"What's the next one?" Leah asked.

"Huh? Oh." She'd been drilling Leah on herbal remedies until they'd seen the breathtaking alps. "Tell me the remedy for dragon's bane?"

"Rubaka leaves, ground into a fine green powder."

"Excellent." Marlies pulled some slim green leaves from her healer's pouch and passed them back to Leah.

"I think that's woozy weed," the girl said.

"And how would you administer it?" Marlies asked.

"I'd steep the leaves in hot water to make a tea and feed it to someone who needed sleep."

Not bad for a trainee healer. "What else could you use it for?"

"I saw you give woozy weed to Sofia when you cut that crystal from her shoulder."

Marlies chuckled. "Your memory serves you well. Once, a friend of mine in Western Settlement slipped woozy weed into some tharuks' beer so I could escape from his inn." Marlies turned to wink at Leah. "There are many applications for a good remedy."

Leah laughed.

Uneasy, Marlies forced a laugh too. What would they find when they reached Lush Valley? Hopefully, the settlement would be peaceful.

"Pass me another," Leah called, handing back the woozy weed to Marlies.

Marlies tucked it back in her pouch and passed her some pointed juicy leaves.

Her reply was instantaneous. "That's koromiko, good for belly gripes. Too easy. Give me a hard one."

Marlies tucked the koromiko back in her pouch. "I'm afraid you've identified every herb and remedy I have with me. We'll need to find some more." If she was to train this girl to replace her as master healer at Dragons' Hold, she needed to impart her knowledge now, before it was too late.

She kicked herself. She'd never been this macabre before, never brooded over death or illness. She'd always been fit and healthy. Perhaps she was over dramatizing her exhaustion.

She shook her head. No, she'd seen similar tiredness in people with the wasting sickness—especially her best friend Alena who'd died when Marlies was young and still living in Montanara.

Liesar soared over the Western Grande Alps, Marlies' heart skipping a beat. It was home—well, for the past eighteen years it had been.

Something was moving down between the snowy peaks. By the First Egg, a steady stream of tharuks were making their way over the Western pass.

"I can smell them from here," Liesar melded. *"Those stinking monsters leave an offensive reek, a stain on our landscape."*

"I can't smell them, but I agree we'd be better off without them."

The excitement she'd felt dissipated. Blue guards had been stationed here to keep the beasts at bay. Had something failed? *"Press on, Liesar. Hurry to Lush Valley Settlement."*

They swooped down the eastern side of the mountain range. Western Settlement was a black smudge on the snow. Dirty piles of rubble and charred ruins were all that was left. She hoped Nick escaped in time. Had she brought this upon him by staying at his inn when she'd fled Lush Valley? She swallowed. The cost of war was too high. Too many innocent people were slaughtered. The cost of her own actions was the lives of innocent people.

Leah's grip on her waist tightened. The girl asked, "What was here?"

"That was Western Settlement."

Leah's hands clutched the fabric of Marlies' jerkin. "And Lush Valley Settlement?"

Marlies gazed across the meadows and out over the forest. Her breath gusted out of her. There was no smoke above Lush Valley Settlement. "We'll be there in a couple of hours, but first, let's take a look and see if there's anyone we can help here."

Liesar furled her wings, swooping down to the ruined township. At the foot of the Western Grande Alps, on the outskirts of town was Nick's inn. Marlies wrinkled her nose. The stench of rot hung over charred buildings, wagons, scorched grass and strewn dead horses, villagers and tharuks.

They swooped across the settlement. Not a live soul was to be seen. "There are no embers, no smoke. This happened quite some time ago," Marlies said, throat tight with grief.

The silver dragon angled her neck, nostrils flaring. *"Dragons set this town alight, but I don't recognize their scent."* She glanced from side to side. *"They're long gone now."*

"Then let's get to Lush Valley. There is no time to waste." Gods, hopefully she wasn't too late.

§

Liesar rose into the sky, and winged across the forest.

"Tell me more," Leah asked, her voice shaky.

Marlies had forgotten. Leah had lost her parents when tharuks had attacked her village. She squeezed the girl's hand, tugging it tighter around her waist, at a loss for how to comfort her.

Three hours later, as they neared Lush Valley, Marlies straightened in the saddle. Everything looked peaceful from above, but as they flew over the village square, she knew something was amiss. Tharuks were milling around the square, strolling between the stalls in the market, stationed in the shadows and under the eaves of the buildings. Usually the square was humming on market day, but only a few stragglers were out. Not that Marlies blamed them with these beady-eyed monsters breathing their foul stench down everyone's necks.

"I guess you're no longer keen to land in the village square?" Liesar asked.

"You're right about that. I've suddenly lost my appetite for Lush Valley delicacies. Head out along the northern trail toward our old farm."

Liesar swooped over the buildings and flew north over cottages, farms and snow-speckled fields toward Hans and Marlies' old home. A short way out of town, there was a huge plot of freshly-turned earth in the snow-edged cemetery—a mass grave. Marlies' hands clenched the saddle. Only a few short moons ago, citizens of Lush Valley hadn't tolerated dragons, or even been sure they existed. They'd thought tharuks were just rumors from beyond the Grande Alps. For years, Lush Valley had been isolated from the outside world.

Not anymore.

Eighteen years ago, Marlies fled Dragons' Hold after killing Zaarusha's dragonet and settled in Lush Valley with Hans, unwittingly putting the settlement in danger. In hindsight, she should have realized that Zaarusha's dying dragonet had blessed Marlies' twins with special talents. Ezaara's ability to meld with every dragon had definitely come from the tiny purple dragonet. And the compassion the creature had shown her—by blessing Marlies with its last breath—was a trait that Tomaaz had inherited. Even as a littling, he'd constantly brought home wounded creatures and stray waifs that needed feeding. Was it any wonder Zaarusha had come here seeking Ezaara as her new Queen's Rider? Zaarusha's imprinting with Ezaara had drawn tharuks to this secluded valley. So, by settling here, Marlies had endangered them all.

You did what you had to do. Zens is responsible for tharuks, not you." Liesar banked.

Leah pointed over Marlies' shoulder. "Look, down there in that field."

Two boys were jumping up and down, waving.

They circled down and landed in a snow-crusted meadow near a small house that backed onto a copse of trees. Marlies and Leah slid off Liesar, and the boys ran over to greet them. Marlies recognized them immediately—Paolo and Marco. Boisterous and always getting into scrapes, she'd healed them often.

"Marlies? Is that you?" Paolo grinned and pumped her hand.

"You look much older... or sick," Marco said, hugging her leg.

Typical littling honesty. Their faces were gaunt too, and their eyes wary. Things hadn't been easy for them either. "Boys, how you've grown. How's your Ma and Pa?"

"Pa got cut up bad by one of them tharuk's tusks, but he's healing up." Paolo thumped his fist on his chest. "I fought in a battle too, right next to your Hans."

The Egg forbid. At nine summers, Paolo was barely out of his littling years. "I'm sure you were brave." Marlies gestured at Leah. "This is my trainee healer, Leah. She's an important person at Dragons' Hold."

The boys' eyes grew wide and they shook Leah's hand. "Most honored to meet you." Paolo bowed deeply as if Leah were foreign royalty.

It was almost comical. Of course, neither of them knew that Marlies herself was Dragons' Realm's master healer—they'd only known her as Marlies, Hans' wife. "And this is Liesar."

"She's so beautiful. May I touch her?" It was Marco that asked, but at Marlies' nod, they both rushed forward and laid their palms on Liesar's upheld foreleg.

The introductions over, it was time for business. "Where are the blue guards that were protecting Lush Valley? Where's Klaus?" Marlies turned to Leah. "Klaus is the settlement arbitrator."

"There was a big battle two weeks ago," Paolo answered. "There was lots of smoke, and dark dragons attacked us, not pretty like yours." Paolo waved his arms in the air, his fingers flapping like wings. "The blue guards came and drove them away from the village, that way." He pointed eastward.

Marco blurted out, "They said the dragons killed the other dragons, but I don't know. I hope they're still alive." His huge blue eyes brimmed with tears. "I like dragons."

"But not those dark ones." Paolo shuddered. "I hate them."

Marlies pursed her lips, gazing at the eastern sky. So a dark dragon had been here too. More than one. She had to find out if the blue guards were still around, if there were any wounded. "How many dark dragons were there? Where did they go?" she asked, stooping to look Paolo in the eyes.

"Two." He pointed at a high peak to the east. "They flew straight for the Horn."

The Horn was the highest peak in the eastern range of the Grande Alps. At its foot was a densely forested area, far from any homes. A wise choice, given the damage Seppi had sustained from that dark dragon's eyes. "Could you take me there?"

"Me? Ride a dragon?" Paolo's eyes shone. "Of course."

"Can I come too?" Marco bit his lip, waiting.

Marlies shook her head. She didn't know what they'd find. He was far too young, although from the mass grave she'd seen as she flown out of the village, he might've already seen his share of bodies. "Liesar's flown a long way. She's too tired to carry four of us. Maybe she'll give you a ride later."

Behind her, Liesar snorted.

Marco's eyes welled.

"Go inside, and stay safe with your Ma and Pa. Tharuks are about." She gave him a hug. "Thank you for your help."

With Paolo sandwiched between Marlies and Leah, Liesar took to the sky. Below them, the fields were shrugging off their winter blanket, the snow only crusting the shady edges.

"Wow, we're up so high," Paolo squealed. "Look! My house is like a tiny walnut in the fields."

"That's how I felt on my first flight." Leah laughed, but it was nervous, brittle.

Gods, these mere littlings were facing Zens' horrendous monsters.

Are you all right, Liesar? We've flown far—you must be exhausted, Marlies melded.

I'm fine. We have to find them. As tired as she might be, Liesar's wings were still beating strongly as they headed over the forest toward the Horn.

Marlies wanted to ask her dragon not to strain herself, but she couldn't bring herself to do it. The lives of dragons and riders could be at stake. Although what she'd heal them with, Marlies had no idea. First, they'd find them. Then they'd deal with getting more piaua juice.

"They went in that direction." Paolo pointed north.

Liesar veered left.

"The trees look like little sticks. Even the mountains seem smaller," crowed Paolo. "And Liesar's scales are so beautiful in the sun."

True. Liesar's wings sparkling like diamonds had been one of Marlies' first joys when riding her. She exhaled, trying to loosen the tension in her chest, but the tightness remained as the Horn's peak loomed.

"There, see that? I'm going down." Liesar dove toward a vicious slash that scarred the forest below.

"Hold on," Marlies called.

Paolo's grip around her waist tightened and he huddled against her back. The wind flew into Marlies' face, water streaming from her eyes. A swathe of foliage had been crushed, trees tossed aside as if they were splinters. As they drew closer, Marlies spotted a blue dragon.

Leah gasped.

Paolo shifted in the saddle and whimpered.

Liesar landed among patches of ice, broken branches and scattered foliage. Some of the trees were blackened, the tang of char making Marlies' nostrils itch.

"Stay here." She slid off Liesar's saddle. Her boots crunched over smashed branches. The fight between these dragons had turned mighty tree trunks to kindling. Debris hung suspended on the surrounding treetops. Several trails, wider than houses, had been smashed through the forest.

Marlies approached the motionless blue dragon and laid her hand upon his cold hide. *"Are you alive?"*

Nothing.

She was too late. This blue guard was dead. But what of his rider?

She scrambled over trunks and branches, making her way around the dragon. A tree trunk had speared the dragon's side and killed him, spilling his guts over the broken timber. His entrails were dried and cold.

Liesar let a mournful howl into Marlies' mind. Her dragon couldn't grieve aloud, not when the enemy might be near.

Marlies cast about and walked farther into the broken trees, keeping an eye out for the blue guard who had served with this dragon.

As she clambered over a pile of broken foliage, a boot caught her eye beneath a swath of charred leaves. She bent down and swept some leaves aside. A battered body lay beneath the pile of debris she'd been climbing.

Eyes stinging, she flung aside bark, leaves and branches to get to the body, pausing regularly, scanning the forest, keeping an eye out for anything unusual. Finally, she hefted the broken rider in her arms, staggering under his weight, and carried him back to his dragon.

"Well done," Liesar said. *"I can scent the other blue, along there."* She twitched her tail toward one of the channels smashed through the trees.

Marlies bent over, hands resting on her knees, panting. *"In a moment."*

"You're too tired," Liesar replied. *"Let me carry you."*

Marlies straightened. *"No, it's the least I can do for these valiant servants of the realm."*

Liesar crunched through broken branches, nuzzling Marlies' shoulder. *"There's no sense in breaking yourself. You can't save the dead, and we still need you to save the living."*

Backhanding a tear from her cheek, Marlies nodded and climbed into the saddle, the young ones scooting back to give her space. She gripped Liesar's spinal ridge with bloodstained hands. *"Take me to the next blue guard, but beware, the dark dragons may still be lurking."*

Moments later, they found the other blue dragon and a dark dragon entwined among ruined undergrowth. The dark beast's talons were still embedded in the blue dragon's throat, even though in her death thrall she'd blasted the dark dragon's face away, leaving a pale skull with gaping eye sockets.

Paolo whimpered. Leah hugged him, burying his head under her arm and pulling him against her torso so he didn't have to see. "Do you need my help?" she asked briefly, not a tremor in her voice.

"There's nothing we can do here," Marlies answered.

Liesar snarled. *"Oh yes there is. I scent a dark dragon, still alive."*

"Hold on, you two."

Leah flung Paolo against Marlies' back and they gripped her waist. Liesar tensed her haunches and sprang over some trees to land nearby.

A faint scream ricocheted through Marlies' mind. She blocked it out, snapping mind-meld with Liesar. Seppi had warned them of the dark dragons' anguished screams. Ahead, on the charred forest undergrowth, lay a wizened black dragon, a slumped mage dead in the saddle.

Its wings had been burnt off and its side was seared. The swathe of ruined bushes behind it showed it had crawled here to lick its wounds. The dragon raised its head and snarled, a flicker licking from its maw.

Marlies felt it battering at her mind, trying to get in.

"My head. My head hurts," Paolo said, voice ragged.

"Sing a song in your mind," Leah instructed. "Just keep singing. Your song will block the scream."

With a snarl of anger, Liesar pounced on the dragon.

The dragon writhed, yellow beams springing from its eyes, scoring Liesar's shoulder with a deep bloody gouge. With a scream of pain, Liesar snapped through its neck with her jaws, severing its head and tossing its skull far into the forest.

"Liesar, let me dismount." There was something strange about the mage. Marlies had to take a closer look.

Sliding off Liesar, she clambered up the dead dark dragon's scaly hide, shuddering at the feel of its strange skin under her fingers. There was something wrong, off, about this beast.

The mage was slumped over the dragon's shoulders, splattered in black blood from Liesar's killing strike. Marlies pulled her upright. And hurriedly dropped her. From her posture and body shape, she'd assumed the mage was a young girl, but her face was as wrinkled as an ancient woman's. Marlies had never seen someone so old. Never known people that ancient with young supple bodies existed. Once again, something was dreadfully off.

"*Let's get out of here,*" Liesar said. "*I don't like you touching that evil beast. It stinks of death and wrongness.*"

Marlies climbed into the saddle. As soon as they were airborne, she asked, "*Shall we give these blue guards a proper sendoff?*"

"*Of course,*" said Liesar. She shook her mighty silver head and raised it to the sky, howling. Her keening song of loss and love and mourning for these two valiant dragons and riders rang through the deserted forest, bouncing off the mountaintops.

Landing near one of the fallen guards, Liesar opened her jaws, setting the dragon and rider alight, creating a funeral pyre fit for a king.

MONTANARA

Snow fell in soft damp flakes, clumping on the sidewalks and turning to mush under the gray morning sky as Kierion strode down the narrow streets in the seedy quarter of town. He stomped off his boots as he strode up the steps to the Brothers' Arms, then pulled the heavy door open.

"Over here, young whelp," Danion called.

At the back of the taproom was an open door, leading to the captain's office—the Nightshaders' headquarters. The captain, as ugly as the night before but slightly less intimidating, was pouring tea from a pot into porcelain tea cups. Sitting at the captain's table was Danion with Gret tucked under one arm. She gazed at him as if she was a fawning lover.

Kierion nearly spluttered. He didn't know that Gret had *that* in her. Hopefully, she'd tone it down by the time Fenni arrived or he'd set the whole place aflame.

Danion stretched back in his chair, arm slipping down to Gret's back. "So, you considered my offer?"

Kierion shrugged. "I've come to talk it over," he replied, sliding into a seat and stretching his long legs.

The waitress came in. He recognized her from behind the bar the night before: a tough woman, about his mother's age, with a nose ring, and tattoos on her forearms. "Breakfast?"

"I'm fine with tea, thanks." Kierion indicated the captain's cups.

"More tea, Rona," the captain called. She passed out the cups and took the teapot. The captain poured a generous slug from a hip flask into his tea, and took a long sip, his eyes appraising Kierion over his cup.

Kierion sipped his tea too.

Danion arched an eyebrow. "Well?"

Drumming his fingers on the table, Kierion said, "I've considered your offer. As long as I can keep my weapons…" He shot the captain a cheeky grin.

The captain, laughed, displaying half a mouthful of horrendous black teeth again. "You can keep your weapons, matey. And, as long as you obey my creed, then I'll let you keep your fingers too."

Danion smirked. "What do you think, boy?" He gave Gret's shoulder an extra squeeze.

She leaned her head against his upper arm.

The door clunked shut. Without turning, Kierion sensed it was Fenni.

Boots thudded across the floor. Fenni slipped into a chair. Staring straight at the captain, he said, "I'm in." He steepled his fingers on the table, tiny flames dancing from his fingertips.

The captain raised an eyebrow. "Need to siphon off a little power, do we?"

Fenni flashed a wolfish smile. His flames extinguished immediately. He flourished a hand, proffering flowers of green flame to the captain. "Just party tricks, sir."

"I appreciate the sentiment, but there's no *sir* here. Captain is fine with me." He turned to Gret. "My crew tell me you put up a right fight last night, girl." He smirked, eyes flitting between Danion and Gret. "In the alley, I meant. My offer is extended to you too."

Gret winked and nodded. "I'm keen."

"Danion will keep you all occupied showing you the business."

Exactly what business the Nightshaders had, Kierion wasn't sure, but it wasn't selling daffodils. He couldn't help himself, blurting, "Captain, what *is* your business?"

The captain arched a dark eyebrow. "Buying and selling: goods, protection, herbal remedies, and lives. You name it we sell it."

"Remedies?" Kierion blurted. That was odd.

"A lucrative little sideline." The captain grinned. "You'll find that all the apothecaries have gone out of business. The sick now have to come to us."

"For a nice fee, no doubt captain." Extortionists. They'd cornered the trade on life-giving supplies. It hadn't been like that when Kierion had lived here. But now, folk would probably die if they couldn't afford a cure. Not only were the captain's teeth black—his heart was as well.

He knew he was pushing it, but Kierion's curiosity got the better of him. "And if they can't pay?"

"Then we trade in lives." That black toothed grin split the captain's face. "Welcome to the Nightshader crew."

§

When they assembled later that morning on the edge of Great Spanglewood Forest, Kierion was surprised at how many dragon riders he recognized. Danion hadn't been joking when he'd said he'd infiltrated the ranks of the Night-shaders—most of his men had been in the Brothers' Arms last night. Not all at the captain's table, of course. Some at the bar, drinking with tharuks; others playing cards at other tables or popping by for a quick ale.

"How can they stand sitting so close to tharuks, even drinking with them?" Fenni murmured. "It made my skin crawl just to be in the same tavern."

Kierion agreed, but he didn't dare say so out loud.

Danion sat on his dragon before them, pulling on his gloves. "Everyone ready for flight?"

Their dragons stamping in the snow, riders pulled winter scarves around their faces, and tugged up the hoods of their cloaks against the cold. Only their eyes were visible. No wonder the Nightshaders didn't recognize them when they were in the air.

"The Nightshaders eyes and ears have reported tharuks milling around on the streets and in the square," Danion said. "The Nightshader crew are slinking through the city, spreading news that Zens has bred evil dragons and that they're attacking today. They're advising people to stay home."

"How did you fool them into doing that?" a rider asked. "Surely if they got hurt, the Nightshaders would stand to profit?"

"I promised them free ale tonight." Danion grinned. "And that I'd slit their throats if they breathed a word about who instructed them."

Laughter broke out.

Danion delegated pairs of dragons to guard various points around the city perimeter, and more pairs to roam Great Spanglewood Forest. He gestured to Gret on Hagret and Kierion and Fenni on Riona, and three other riders on their dragons. "Come with me. We'll patrol from the Southwestern perimeter of Montanara to Spanglewood." He raised an eyebrow. "I hope you're ready, because that's where they'll probably attack from."

Dragons tensed their haunches and sprang.

Snow flaked off Riona's flapping wings. The temperature had plummeted, so the snow was drier now, tiny flakes feathering against Kierion's skin as they flew into swirling white. They swept toward Montanara without a sign of anything being amiss. They doubled back to Spanglewood, their dragons melding with the closest dragons.

Nothing yet, Riona melded.

"No one else has seen anything either, "Kierion reported to Fenni.

They patrolled back and forth along the border of the forest.

So far, no sign of Zens' dark beasts.

When his gloved fingers were numb and his teeth practically chattering, Kierion pulled a waterskin of tea out of a saddlebag and took a swig. "Not very warm. Want some?"

Fenni held the waterskin before drinking, then passed it back to Kierion. "Try it now."

When Kierion took a swig, the tea's warmth stole through his belly. He wiped his mouth with the back of his hand. "Thanks. Mage fire sure is handy."

"No worries. " Fenni said. "You know what galls me?"

"The way Danion looks at Gret when the Nightshaders are around?" Kierion took another swig.

"It's the way she looks at him. I'm sure she likes him."

Kierion spluttered tea over Riona's back.

"I'd prefer that my tea wasn't secondhand," melded Riona. *"And I'd rather have it in my mouth, than over my neck, thank you."*

"Fair enough!" He laughed, rubbing the tea off her back with a corner of his cloak before it froze. He checked that Hagret was flying out of hearing range. "Come on, Fenni. It's obvious Gret likes you."

"I thought so too. I mean, she even kissed me."

"I heard about your ribald antics from the Nightshaders this morning."

Fenni snorted. "Hardly ribald. Half a kiss and then that sod Danion had a knife at my back."

"I can see how that would interfere with your friendship."

"Friendship? With him? More like coercion."

Kierion passed him back the tea.

Fenni took the skin. "Maybe those tharuks were wrong. Maybe no dragons are coming today."

"They'll be here sooner or later—the question is when." Despite the tea, something cold slithered through Kierion's belly. Seppi was one of Dragons' Hold's most experienced riders, and he'd died confronting a dark dragon. Did Kierion, Fenni and Gret stand a chance?

§

The snow was heavier the next day. Only a few horses and carts were about delivering goods. Most people were at home. Even the market was closed, ostensibly due to bad weather. Tharuks stalked the streets as Danion, Kierion and Gret hurried toward the edge of town to meet their dragons. Kierion huffed through his scarf onto his gloved hands, but it made no difference—his fingers were already freezing. He shoved his hands deep into the pockets of his cloak, but nothing would keep out the bone-chilling cold.

Danion's shoulders were hunched against the snow. "Flaming cold. The captain's even called the crew off the streets."

A horde of tharuks stomped down the street, their stench whirling among the blowing snow. Kierion and his companions narrowed to a single file until the monsters passed. It was the strangest feeling to ignore these brutes instead of fighting them, but they'd be fighting soon enough.

"One thing I've been wondering," Kierion said once they were trudging alongside each other again. "Why is the Nightshader crew's leader called the captain?"

"Didn't you see?" Danion asked.

"See what?"

"Above the door in his office," Fenni replied. "There's an old piece of ship planking, *The Sea Dragon*. I think our captain might have been a Naobian sailor. That right?"

Danion grinned. "Nearly," he said. "The captain's a pirate."

That explained the black teeth, black humor and hip flask. And the blood-thirsty glint in his eye.

"Think we'll see any dark dragons?" Fenni asked. "Yesterday was a waste of time."

"Maybe it was only a rumor," Gret said. "Maybe no dark dragons are coming."

"Seppi's death wasn't a rumor." Talking about it made Kierion's throat tight—a death that could've been prevented. His shrotty fault. He forced himself to speak normally. "Dark dragons are out there."

"They are," Danion said. "The tharuks were right. Last night, some of them were sighted to the south. It's only matter of time."

"It's cold. Are you nearly here?" Riona melded.

"One more street."

Just outside the city, hunched over their dragons, cloaks white with snow, dragon riders were waiting. Kierion strode over to Riona. Her warm breath gusted over him as she butted his stomach. He dusted off her saddle with his gloves, and swung up. Fenni clambered up behind him, while the others climbed into their saddles.

"Same drill as yesterday," Danion called, voice muffled by his scarf and the swirling snow.

They took to the sky, sweeping out toward Great Spanglewood Forest. Not that Kierion could see much other than white. *"How do you know where you're going?"* he asked Riona.

"I have a fabulous sense of direction. I know the landscape as well as the back of my wing."

Landscape? It was all white. *"Remember, Seppi said those dark dragons' eyes burn and slice,"* Kierion cautioned. *"I'm not sure if it's true, but let's not risk it."*

Riona rumbled her assent and shot through the white haze. Fenni's arms tightened around Kierion's waist as the dragon beat her wings to gain height. *"The higher we are, the more chance we have of taking them by surprise,"* Riona explained.

"And the colder we are," Kierion retorted.

"Ask the mage to warm you."

"Hey, Fenni, any chance of some heat?" Within moments, Kierion's back was bathed in a toasty glow. "Not bad. You can come again."

Fenni slugged his shoulder. "Might just do that."

Kierion would much rather have been tucked up by a warm hearth in his cavern at Dragons' Hold. The weather was so foul, it was probably snowing there too. He hoped Adelina was warm, not out in the snow. A memory flashed to mind: her standing beside him on the snowy ledge as he held Seppi's dead body. Kierion's eyes burned. Gods, how was he ever going to fix that?

By doing his duty today, even if it was bitterly cold.

A moment later, a terrifying scream filled Kierion's head. Kierion gritted his teeth and blinked to clear his vision, but his skull seared with pain. Flame it, he couldn't think with that racket in his mind.

Riona's pain shot through him.

Fenni's squeezed his waist in a death grip. "Mind block!"

"Hold on!" Riona yelled above the noise.

Kierion broke mind-meld and focused on remembering his home—the roses growing up the trellis, the knotted front door, and yellow curtains in the kitchen windows—but, no matter how much detail he tried to visualize, the screams broke through anyway. He tried again. No good, he'd have to grit his teeth and bear it.

A glimmer of orange flared in the swirling white below. Riona dove down, talons out. Her descent was too steep for Kierion to nock an arrow. He hung on, Fenni's arms tight around him.

Riona shot a stream of fire at a dark shadow. Her flames crackled through the clouds.

A shadow dragon emerged with a mage on its back. God, the screams—Kierion's skull was splitting.

"Holy mage fire!" Fenni cursed. "It's Velrama."

Velrama—the mage who'd been kidnapped by tharuks. How awful to be coerced by Zens.

Velrama flung out her hands and blasted bolts of green flame at Fenni and Kierion. Riona swerved, and the flame went wide. The shadow dragon roared, charging up at them. Golden beams swept from its eyes past Riona's belly. The dragon swung its head, the rays striking Riona's foreleg.

Riona roared, spouting fire. *"Got my leg. Bleeding."*

"Bleeding? Or burning?" Kierion asked.

"Feels like both," Riona replied.

Kierion snatched his bow and fired an arrow. It struck the dragon in the hind leg. The scream in his head intensified.

Velrama was at Zens' command, maybe imbedded with a crystal. Kierion had to help her. But how? Perhaps if he could capture the dragon…What a crazy idea. He shook his head. It would never work. But the training they'd done, the leap from the tail… Amid a raging snowstorm, with this mad dark dragon and the screaming in his head, who knew what would happen. Was it worth the risk?

The dark dragon and its mage rider blasted flame at Danion as his dragon swept close. Gret and Hagret, charged, roaring fire. The shadow dragon bucked and writhed.

Now, while it was busy fighting the others…

Kierion melded, ignoring the shrieking crescendo in his head. *"Riona. I'm going in."* Riona swung away from the fight so they could sneak up from the rear. "Fenni, I'm going in, from the tail."

"From the tail? You're mad." Fenni leaned to the side so Kierion could turn around and hook a leg past Fenni's body.

"Not entirely," Kierion replied, grabbing Fenni to clamber past him. His knee slipped on Riona's damp scales. His weight dragged him down.

Riona listed to one side, counterbalancing as Fenni gripped Kierion under the armpits to stop him from falling. "I knew we were close, but this…"

Kierion didn't laugh at the gag. Heart pounding like a battle drum, he clung to Fenni.

"Come on, Kierion, you're always up for acrobatics." Fenni's words were light, but his green eyes were grave, his grip strong.

"Sure," Kierion's breath whooshed out of him. He made his way to Riona's next spinal ridge, and the next, as Gret and Danion shot arrows at the dark beast, fire and green mage fire roiling around them.

When he was finally on Riona's tail, she sneaked up from behind while the dragon was busy fighting. Kierion clung on with half-frozen hands, hoping his recklessness would pay off. It was worth it if he could save Velrama's life. Besides, if they could examine the dragon at the hold, they'd glean vital information about Zens' latest monsters.

Ahead, Hagret dove in from the side, belching flame at the dark beast. Its flank bristled with Danion's arrows. Danion's dragon closed in from the other side.

Kierion flicked his head around. With no other dark dragons in sight, it was now or never. *Riona, I'm ready.*

The mighty muscles in her tail quivered and she whipped it up. Kierion let go, sailing through the air. Was he going to make it? Oh gods, the dragon was swerving…

"Ooph!" Kierion smacked into the side of the beast's body, flinging an arm around a spinal ridge. The dragon bucked. Kierion scrabbled with his feet, hoisting himself high on the dragon's back. The beast roared and thrashed. Hagret's flame seared its maw. Gret's eyes shot open wide and Hagret backed off. The dark dragon pursued them. Kierion scrambled his way past two spinal ridges until he was high in the saddle behind Velrama. The mage spun. Kierion ducked as a green fireball whistled past his head.

He whipped a knife out of his belt and held it at Velrama's neck. "Hello, Velrama. I'm Kierion. I've come to help you."

The mage snarled and twisted.

Kierion's blade pricked her skin, blood running over his hand. "Stay still. Tell your dragon, that if it doesn't obey, I'll plunge my blade into its side and jump. Its guts will spill through the air, and you'll both be impaled on the pines below." If there were pines below. He couldn't see a flaming thing.

Velrama stiffened. The dragon stopped thrashing.

"Now," said Kierion, "fly us to Dragons' Hold."

Riona and Fenni closed in, flanking him, staying out of reach. The dark dragon turned and headed northward, through billowing snow.

Kierion glanced back. Jets of flame flared as shadows flitted through the snowstorm.

As they flew farther, the screams in his head receded until there was only soft keening. Odd. The dragon's cry was one of pain. Maybe the screams weren't weapons, after all? Maybe these poor beasts were expressing their agony.

PIAUA

It was nearly dusk when Liesar landed near Paolo's farm. A lone candle winked in the window—a beacon for the boy to come home to. Marlies gave Paolo a tiny pot of her precious healing salve. "Here, this is for your pa's wound. Now, go straight inside and see your mother. Tharuks are roaming. She won't rest until she knows you're safe."

"Thanks, Marlies." Paolo patted Liesar's foreleg. "And thanks for the flight, Liesar." He scampered to the house.

Marlies got out of the saddle and smeared swathes of thick healing salve on the gash in Liesar's shoulder. The pungent aroma of peppermint, arnica and the faintest tinge of piaua filled the evening air.

"Where will we sleep tonight?" Leah asked.

Good question. Marlies was drooping. The piaua juice would have to wait until tomorrow. She pulled herself back into the saddle. "We have a homestead nearby. We'll sleep there."

When they arrived at their farm, Marlies swallowed. She couldn't believe it. Their home was a charred wreck—razed to the ground. She pressed her fingers against her lips, closing her eyes until the urge to cry passed. All those years of sweet memories, gone.

"Where to now?" Liesar asked.

"Ernst and Ana are at Dragons' Hold. Let's sleep at their house."

They landed near Ana's vegetable garden, now a tangle of dead weeds and icy patches. Marlies unpacked some food and a waterskin from her dragon's saddlebags.

"I need to hunt." Liesar winged over the river toward the forest.

Marlies pushed the door open. The house was strewn with debris, smashed furniture and scattered foodstuffs. Sword in hand, she stalked down the hallway. There was blood on the floor in the littling's bedroom, so Marlies took Leah into the master bedroom.

Leah let out a heavy sigh and slumped on the bed. "Master Marlies, I hate tharuks. I'll do anything to fight them. Anything to stop them harming our people."

"We need you to keep learning the healing arts. Some people are warriors, others heal those warriors so they can fight again." She hesitated. "Are you afraid?"

Leah's eyes cleared. Her shoulders straightened and she stared at Marlies. "No, Master Marlies. I'm not afraid. When I remember those beasts slashing my parents, I get so angry I want to scream. I'll do whatever my dragon queen needs."

"We desperately need tree speakers," Marlies said. "How did you discover you had the talent?"

"Trees have spoken to me all my life." Leah lay back on the bed and gazed up at the ceiling. "At first, it was a hum. In time, I understood their whispering. On the day the tharuks came, everything sounded… sort of… wrong, like an untuned gittern, but I ignored it, and played in the forest."

The day Leah had been injured. Ezaara had told Marlies how the girl had turned up at Dragons' Hold, limp-locked, bleeding profusely, with her finger hanging by a flap of skin.

"I'll never ignore the trees again." Leah's throat bobbed once, twice, but she met Marlies' eyes with a steadfast gaze. "When I returned to my village, tharuks had slaughtered most of my friends and family. I ran through the house, calling their names, but a beast turned on me. I fought the tharuk off with a kitchen knife and managed to get away, but not before it'd gashed my hand with its claw." She held up her hand, wiggling the stump of her little finger. "With every breath I take, I vow to avenge the deaths of my parents. If I have to fight those monsters with a splinter or my bare nails, I will."

"Let's pray that you never have to fight barehanded," said Marlies.

"My sword is sharp and ready," Leah replied.

"Let's get some sleep," Marlies said, limbs aching. "We have a long day ahead of us tomorrow."

A knock sounded at the door.

"Quick, under the bed. If anything happens to me, escape through the window and run for Liesar."

Leah scrambled under the bed, and Marlies tugged the covers so they draped over the bedside.

She tiptoed to the door, and cracked it open.

Klaus stood there, scratching his beard and looking awkward. "Marlies, welcome back. I, uh, need your help. The blue dragons who were supposed to defend our settlement have disappeared."

Marlies slipped her knife into its sheath and opened the door. "Come in." She sighed, dragging her fingers through her hair. "I found them in the forest near the Horn, dead."

Klaus huffed out his breath. "Well, I guess that's that, then." He shook his head. "What'll we do if more of those dark dragons come?"

Marlies frowned. "We've only had one dark dragon near Dragons' Hold. How many have you had here?"

"Only the two." Klaus' shaggy eyebrows dropped down over his eyes. "And they were bad enough. Look at the havoc they wreaked in town. You know, I can't help but think what would have happened if Zaarusha had never come here for your daughter." He jabbed a finger at Marlies. "Would tharuks have stayed away from Lush Valley, too?"

Although she'd been wondering that very same thing, something snapped inside Marlies. "Zaarusha came here to imprint with my daughter so Ezaara could lead Dragons' Realm in protecting people like you, Klaus. People who've lived in ignorance, never knowing the threats that the rest of the realm faces." She jabbed her own finger toward him. "Ezaara and Zaarusha did not cause this invasion. It was Commander Zens and his tharuks." She turned and stalked back to the bedroom.

Klaus' chest heaved. "So that's it? That's all the help I get?"

Marlies didn't bother to answer. She shut the bedroom door, leaning against the wood, and sighed, "It's all right. You can come out."

Leah scrambled out from under the bed and sat on it, smiling at Marlies.

Moments later, Klaus knocked at the bedroom door, the reverberations running through Marlies' spine. Marlies waved a hand at Leah to stay seated and opened the door. "If dark dragons come, Klaus, I'll fight them from the air on dragonback, but if I do, I'll need someone to look after Leah."

"Fine," Klaus nodded. "I'll be marshaling the troops and fighting from the square."

After Klaus departed and they'd eaten, she and Leah hopped into the large bed. Within moments, the girl was asleep. Marlies blew out the candle. The soft gurgle of the nearby river drifted through the open window. Melding with Liesar, she asked, *Did you find something to eat? Are you warm and safe for the night?*

I was about to ask you the same. I'm in the trees near the river. You just snuffed out your candle, didn't you, and went to bed?

Marlies smiled. "I did. Good night." She drifted to sleep.

Marlies and Leah were up at dawn. They ate, packed everything into Liesar's saddlebags, and donned their cloaks.

"I'm ready," Liesar stretched her wings, then furled them again.

"We'll walk. It's only a short way," Marlies said. *"Rest up for the return flight,"*

She and Leah picked their way through the trees along the riverbank, over the stepping stones across the river, and into the forest. Memories rushed at Marlies: the twins learning to swim; summers laughing in the sun; teaching Ezaara how to find herbs in this very forest; and her farewelling the piaua tree, collecting the blue berries that had put her in a coma when she was in Death Valley. The very berries that had saved her life—only to give her this wasting sickness.

A tingle ran down Marlies' neck.

"Something's not right," Leah whispered.

Marlies pulled Leah off the track. They stealthily picked their way through the trees on the soft carpet of soggy leaf litter, avoiding patches of snow that would capture their tracks or sticks that could crack. Constantly scanning the woods, Marlies led Leah toward the sacred clearing, eager to see the piaua tree she'd grown to love during her long sojourn in Lush Valley.

When they reached the sacred clearing—or what was left of it—a huge wall of dead foliage met Marlies where there should've been grass. By the dragon gods, no! The giant piaua lay across the clearing, its trunk gouged, hacked, and denuded of branches. Its browned leaves blocked her path.

Marlies bashed her way past the foliage to get to the trunk, Leah following. Not only had the poor tree's trunk been hewn down with axes, the entire length of it had been scarred by tharuk claws, deep violent gouges that had bled precious life-giving sap. She pulled a small metal tube from her healer's pouch and shoved it into a bubble of green sap. The bubble shattered, spraying broken fragments through the air like tiny emeralds.

"We're too late," she whispered. "It's hardened." She sank to her knees, and jammed the tube into another chunk of sap, but it, too, shattered, spraying shards of dried piaua juice over the dead leaves.

Leah scrambled on hands and knees, trying to pick up the pieces.

Marlies shook her head. "It's no good. It has to be fresh. Dried, it has no restorative quality." Clambering to her feet, she raced to the crisp foliage, hunting for green leaves.

Leah joined her search, dry leaves rustling like a rattlesnake. "So, the juice from the leaves works too?"

"Yes, it does. Both the sap and the leaf juice contain the same life-giving substance." She frantically parted the browned leaves, careful not to dislodge the wrinkled dark blue berries hanging from the dried stalks. There was not a living leaf among them.

Marlies took Leah's hands in hers. "Leah, I want you to remember this tree. Look at the pitted, gnarly bark, the shape of the leaves and trunk. We cannot rest until we find another piaua. The fate of Dragons' Realm depends on us."

Leah's straightened. "Yes, Marlies, I understand. The young trees, what do they look like?"

"I'll get Liesar to show you her memory of one." Marlies took one long look at the dried blue berries. Should she? Was this knowledge too dangerous for a young girl?

Leah's quick eyes scanned her face. "What is it? I'm not afraid."

Marlies bit her lip, then plunged in. "These berries create a condition called *witch of blue*. Anyone who eats them slips into an unconscious state, with a slowed heartbeat and very light breathing. The only remedy is piaua juice, a whole vial for a handful of berries. But there's a cost. Once the remedy has been taken, the juice slowly leaches life. Deep exhaustion dogs the person who has taken them, and their life span can be reduced."

"I'd heard you used the berries in Death Valley. Is that why you're so weary?" Leah's shrewd eyes missed nothing. Another reason she'd make a good healer.

Marlies closed her eyes, took a deep breath. "Yes." There, she'd said it.

"If we going to find more piaua, we'd better get moving," Leah said.

A bone-chilling snarl echoed through the clearing. Marlies whipped her sword from her scabbard and spun.

Four tharuks, claws bared, were blocking their path back to Lush Valley. One of them held a bow, nocked with an arrow dripping with green limplock—Zens' poison.

Before Marlies could draw breath, Leah drew and flicked her knife, embedding it in the skull of a tharuk. The other brute loosed its arrow. Marlies pushed Leah to the ground, the arrow whizzing over their heads. She leaped to her feet, sword out, and charged the beasts.

The archer had another arrow ready. An ear-splitting roar rang above the clearing. In a flash of silver, Liesar dove, snatching up two tharuks in her talons and impaling their bodies upon tall pines. Only the archer remained. He shot an arrow that zipped past Marlies' ear as she zigzagged across the clearing toward it.

Liesar got there first. With a swipe of her talons, she tore the tharuk's abdomen open. It dropped the bow, trying to hold its guts in. Liesar blew a gust of flame that burned its head to a charred stump. The tharuk crumbled to the ground, and Liesar stamped its carcass into the earth. *"Come,"* she said. *"There are worse things attacking Lush Valley."*

Roars rang from the village.

STARRUS STRIKES

Tomaaz and Jael entered the council chambers carrying mugs of sopple-berry tea. Although Jael was a master mage and regularly attended council meetings, Tomaaz usually didn't; however, they had to report killing the dark dragon. He nodded at Master Tonio while Jael stopped to talk to Masters Giddi and Starrus.

Master Torston bustled into the room and took his seat between Starrus and Alyssa. Across the table, Masters Derek and Hendrick shared a joke, chuckling quietly.

Lars stood behind the table, his knuckles on the granite tabletop. Tomaaz glanced around. Ezaara and Roberto were missing and way overdue, and Ma and Pa weren't here either. Maazini had told him Pa had left for Lush Valley after seeing a bad vision—and Ezaara's delay didn't bode well.

Tomaaz gripped his mug a little harder. His nose twitched at the scent of healing salve still clinging to his fingers after tending Maazini's injuries. He and Jael took the seats to the left of Master Giddi and Lars began the meeting.

"Another dragon rider has died battling a second shadow dragon—an unfortunate incident." Deep lines furrowed the edges of Lars' mouth. "However, with our healing supplies depleted, no piaua and our healer elsewhere, we must forge on with what we've got." He turned to the leader of the Wizard Council. "Starrus, do you have any mages gifted in healing who could lend us a hand in the infirmary?"

"Jael, but it's not really his strength," said Master Starrus. "He's more valuable in battle."

"Perhaps we could use him anyway," Lars said. "People are dying."

"He's a mage under my jurisdiction," Starrus snapped, "and not yours to command. We need him to fight."

Next to Starrus, Master Giddi shook his head. "If I may interrupt—"

Starrus' head snapped around. "No, you may not. Your superior is speaking."

Tomaaz coughed, fighting not to splutter his tea everywhere. Everyone knew Master Giddi was more powerful than Starrus.

Jael's lips were pressed tight. His hands clenched into fists in his lap.

Lars ignored Starrus' outburst, continuing to address the council. "In our Queen's Rider's absence, as the leader of Dragons' Hold, I issue a decree for the safety of all citizens, dragons, riders…"—he glared at Starrus—"…and mages. No matter how powerful or talented they are, there will be no lone riders or passengers flying outside Dragon's Teeth. This war will not be over in a day. We must think strategically, plan strategically. We can't risk our people. We need them to battle Zens. Whenever possible, two to five dragons should travel together. Have I made myself clear?" His steely gaze roamed around the table.

Master Giddi nodded. Nods and murmurs of assent rippled around the cavern.

Starrus' eyes glinted with cunning.

Jael nudged Tomaaz—he'd noticed it too.

Lars cleared his throat. "Tomaaz and Jael killed a shadow dragon earlier today and faced another five days ago. Maybe the one that killed Seppi. I call on them to report."

Jael and Tomaaz stood, but before they could open their mouths, Starrus blustered, "I've spoken to Jael. As his leader, I'll handle it." He waved them to sit. Tomaaz caught Jael's arm before he could obey, and they remained standing.

The leader of the Wizard Council plowed ahead. "Dark dragons emit a high-pitched scream that subjects hearers to mental anguish," Starrus said as if he'd experienced it himself. "The victims of such attacks, both dragons and men alike, report splitting head pain, throbbing skulls and an inability to think coherently. Our wizards with their flame should be able to combat this."

Jael cleared his throat. "If I may, mage flame is one defense, but not the entire answer," he said quietly but with conviction.

Starrus rounded on Jael. "You mustn't have been concentrating. Did that beast take you by surprise? Or are Naobians unable to think as quickly as we Northerners? Why, I bet if I was out there, dark dragons would be dropping like flies. Why, I'd—"

That trumped-up idiot. "Master Starrus," Tomaaz barked," I suggest that if you were out there you'd risk being sliced in half by the rays that shoot from the beasts' eyes."

"Or burned out of your seat with mage flame from the mages Zens has kidnapped," Jael added.

"Mages?" Lars barked. "What's this?"

Starrus snapped his jaw shut, glaring at Jael.

"We killed a dark dragon, an old, weak one." Jael sighed. "Velrama was riding another dark dragon and tried to kill us."

Master Tonio's fingernails tapped an agitated staccato rhythm on the table. "I told everyone not to trust mages."

"We can't trust anyone," Tomaaz said. "We know Zens uses those crystals to control people. We suspect that's what's wrong with Velrama."

Murmurs broke out among the council members. Lars hushed them with a wave of his hand.

"Where's Velrama now?" he asked.

"Blue guards chased her, but they said she got away," Jael said. "The strange thing is that from the burn marks on its wings, the old dragon we killed was the same one that attacked us five days ago."

"What's so strange about that?" Starrus sneered.

"Silence," Lars roared. "Or I'll cast you from this hold."

"Really? After issuing an edict that no one—mage or rider—must travel alone?" Starrus raised an eyebrow.

"Please continue, Master Jael," Lars said, ignoring Starrus.

"It was like the dragon had aged years in just a few days." Jael shrugged.

Tomaaz spoke up. "Maazini was hurt. The dragon's eyes sliced his leg, just like Seppi's belly."

Lars nodded. "As implausible as it sounds, Marlies suspected that too."

"And there's another thing," Tomaaz said. "I don't think those dragons are deliberately torturing us." Every head in the room turned to him. "I think they're in pain. Zens may have created them, but whatever he's doing to control them is killing them."

A clamor of voices arose, masters shouting at one another.

Jael pounded his fist on the granite table and stood. "Stop! Listen. None of you have dealt with them. You have to believe us."

From the cynical expressions on their faces, no one did—except Master Giddi, who was nodding thoughtfully.

"Let's double our patrols," Lars said. "Be vigilant. Inform everyone they mustn't stray from the hold alone until we know how to defeat these beasts." He smacked his gavel on the table. "Council dismissed."

§

Giddi roamed the hold's warren of tunnels. The stone walls were so familiar, yet it had been so long. Thank the flaming First Dragon Egg that Kierion and Fenni had managed to bring mages and dragon riders together again. Although it had also taken tharuks kidnapping young mages and burning the homes of every mage to the ground.

And what had Marlies' son meant about these dark dragons being in pain? Even dying. Or aging prematurely, by the sounds of what Jael said. Giddi paced on, nodding at people, lost in his thoughts. When he reached the steps to the dungeons, he turned and paced back again. As he passed the mess cavern, he sensed the hum of *sathir* behind him and turned.

Starrus was smiling smugly, his white plaited beard threaded with wizard-leader crystals that he didn't deserve. How many hours that man spent preening in the mirror was beyond Giddi. Didn't Starrus realize they were at war?

"Good afternoon, Giddi." Starrus slicked his greeting with derision; he'd dropped Giddi's honorific.

Two could play at that game. "Good afternoon, *Master* Starrus, *highly esteemed* leader of the Wizard Council. How may I help you?"

A blue vein pulsed at Starrus' temple.

It didn't take much to tip this master mage over the edge. He was as volatile as a hungry dragonet.

"It's good that you asked. I have just the job for you."

Giddi's whole body went still—except for his thundering heart.

"Seppi's dragon, Septimor, needs to stretch his wings. As you can see from that shambles of a council meeting, we need more information about how to kill these dark dragons. The Wizard Council has decided that you would be best suited to investigate their response to mage flame. I hereby assign you and Septimor to hunt down a dark dragon in Great Spanglewood Forest and kill it."

What a load of shrot! The Wizard Council would never sanction anything against Lars' decree. More than one young mage had been burned by following Starrus' personal instructions.

"If you don't go," Starrus sneered, "you will be expelled from Dragons' Hold."

An empty bluff. For a moment Giddi considered refusing, but only for a moment. These dark dragons had been keeping him awake at night. He'd been itching to know what Zens was breeding in Death Valley. This order from his incompetent superior would give him the perfect excuse to figure out how to defeat Zens' creatures.

Giddi remained as still as a dragon about to pounce.

Until the silence crackled with mage power.

He gave Starrus the smile of a dragon playing with dinner. "Excellent. Thank you for doing me a favor." He winked.

Starrus' mouth opened but nothing came out, so Giddi filled the stunned silence. "I'll go immediately. I'm honored that you've chosen me for this difficult task." He flung sparks from his fingers that burst into floral bouquets as they hit the cavern walls—a trick that Starrus had never mastered, although many a fledgling wizard had.

Giddi pushed past a group of riders that had just left the mess cavern, nodding at Jael and Tomaaz, and took the turnoff to Seppi's cavern, melding with the dragon before he got there—a talent he'd mastered in his littling years. *"Septimor, I'm so sorry you've lost your rider. Seppi was a good man, one of the bravest."* He strode through Seppi's cavern, past his empty bed, out to Septimor's den on the ledge. Septimor's mighty blue form was curled under the overhang at the back of the ledge, away from the snow. The air was crisp. Giddi pulled his cloak tighter.

"He was the bravest." The dragon's loss washed over Giddi like winter rain. *"Life is so colorless without him."* He raised his scaly head and large eyes to regard Giddi.

Giddi walked over and stroked Septimor's nose. The dragon leaned into his touch. *"How can I help you, Giddi?"*

"I wish I could help you." Giddi sighed. It felt so wrong to bother a grieving dragon. Why had he agreed to this ridiculous jaunt?

"What is it?" Septimor's voice was so gentle, so peaceful.

"Starrus has asked us to traverse Great Spanglewood Forest to hunt a dark dragon... with your permission of course."

Septimor opened his mind. A band of pain tightened around Giddi's head and that gods-awful scream that everyone talked about became reality. *"Are you ready to deal with that?"* Septimor asked.

"I don't think anybody is," Giddi whispered, mind blocking and shutting it out. Even with his years of experience, the sound battered at his defenses. "Which is why we need to find out what'll work. If we can't defeat them, Dragons' Realm is doomed. Dragons and their riders will be a dying breed. Though I fear Starrus is trying to kill me, we can't let Zens and these beasts win."

The battering at Giddi's head stopped. He let Septimor back into his mind.

"Very well," the blue dragon said. *"And if we die, we'll have noble deaths for the cause of the realm."*

Giddi closed his eyes, took a deep breath, and hoisted Septimor's saddle up from the ledge and onto the dragon's back. Septimor stood, and Giddi cinched the strap under him. He piled Seppi's bow and arrows into the saddlebags and clambered up. With a leap, they were airborne, flying over the snowy vista of Dragons' Hold, the wind streaming in Giddi's face, and his magic thrumming inside him.

He'd missed living here, laughing and fighting with dragon riders. Although he'd enjoyed the time in his solitary cabin in Great Spanglewood Forest, it'd been a mere shadow of the rich, full life he'd had with Mazyka here at Dragons' Hold as the leader of the Wizard Council and the only dragon mage in the realm.

§

A dark blot appeared above the snow-dusted treetops of Spanglewood. And then another. Giddi cursed Starrus for his stupidity—and himself for taking the bait.

"*Let's meet these beasts, head on,*" Septimor snarled.

"*Last time, those screams fractured your skull,*" Giddi said. "*Perhaps we should turn back.*"

"*I'm not doing anything until I've killed one of those beasts.*" Heat surged through Septimor's mind into Giddi's. "*Tomaaz and Maazini said it helped when they broke mind-meld.*"

"*But then we'd be flying blind, unable to communicate.*"

"*Not completely blind.*" Septimor snorted. "*I can still see.*"

Giddi gave a wry smile. "*We'll charge, aim to kill, and dart away.*"

"*Did you think I was going to request a cup of tea and a chat about the weather?*"

Septimor dove down low, whipping over treetops below the dark dragon. With most of the trees blanketed in snow, there'd be little chance of going undetected, but they could try. Giddi hunched in the saddle. They had to avoid those strange slicing eyes at all costs.

Above, the dark dragon spread its black wings, casting a shadow over them. Cries ripped through Giddi's head, even as he tried to block them.

Septimor shot up toward the beast's belly, belching fire. Giddi thrust out a hand, shooting green mage flame at the creature. The dragon wheeled, ducking away, and blasted fire at Septimor. The blue dragon dodged the roiling heat as Giddi sent back a volley of flame—which the shadow dragon nimbly dodged with a spin. Septimor beat his wings, gaining height and swooped at Zens' monster.

Wait, there was a rider on the dragon's back.

As Septimor flew closer, Giddi's jaw slackened. That brown hair. Those blue eyes. *"Sorcha?"* He melded again. *"Sorcha?"*

A man's scream scraped through his head, over the dragon's anguished screeches. Giddi's temples throbbed.

The noise intensified as Septimor melded, *"This is the missing mage?"*

"Yes, it's—"

Another dark dragon rose from the forest. He thrust a wall of fire below them, but the dragon's beams cut through it, slicing his forearm. Gods, that *hurt*. Like a mage burn but more intense. Thank the Egg, it wasn't too deep. Pulling on the *sathir* of the surrounding snow, he built an ice wall around himself and Septimor.

Sorcha laughed. His mage flame and his dragon's yellow eyes melted the ice. The other dragon angled its head and swept past Septimor, yellow beams springing from its eyes and slicing into Septimor's wing.

Septimor bellowed, his wing drooping. Blood sprayed over them. *"They've cut my wing tendon."* They were plummeting toward the treetops.

"Can you land?"

Anguished bellows ripped from the dragon's maw. His wing was bloody, fluttering uselessly at his side. He flapped valiantly with the other wing but was too late. As they approached the forest canopy, Giddi rose in the saddle, flinging his arm out. Roiling green flame churned into a massive molten fireball which split in two glowing orbs. A fireball shot toward each dark dragon.

Giddi gasped. There was a second figure on the other dark dragon. Another rider. Impossible. It was Sorcha again—there were two of him.

The Sorchas lifted their arms, creating a wall of flame. Giddi pushed with *sathir* for all he was worth. A fireball crashed through the fake Sorcha's wall, engulfing the dark dragon and fake mage. The beast dropped, impaled on a spruce. The mage's burning body crashed through branches, spraying sparks, dropping to become a burning dot the forest floor.

The second fireball darted toward the other dragon, catching its tail alight. Giddi pushed the *sathir* and blazing green mage fire engulfed the dragon.

Sorcha's screams rang in his ears. "Oh, gods, oh gods!"

The stink of burnt flesh washed over Giddi. Nauseous, he leaned to the side and retched. His vomit flew behind them in the wind of their downward plunge.

Septimor smacked into the top of a mighty oak. His body smashed through its branches. Tatters of shredded wing flew around them as his head smacked into the trunk. The dragon's blue body came to rest, suspended on the lower boughs.

"Septimor?" Giddi laid his hand on the dragon's hide. With broken wings and the dragon gods knew what else, it'd take some effort to get back to Dragons' Hold, but they could walk if the dragon lived. "Septimor?" He slapped the dragon's bloody shoulder. He pushed with his mind, battering to get into Septimor's head.

Giddi turned.

There was a gaping rent in Septimor's side and a trail of entrails tangled through the blood-splattered branches.

Giddi retched again.

And again until his gut was hollow and aching.

Straightening, he pounded his heart with his fist and closed his burning eyes. "Septimor, may you soar with the spirits of your beloved rider and departed dragons." His voice cracked in a sob.

Even if he was the last mage standing, he'd make Zens pay for this.

He sat for a few long moments, honoring the loyal dragon.

He tore a strip off his cloak and bound his bleeding forearm, using his teeth to tug the knot tight. He checked his little-used weapons were still at his belt and pulled his cloak tight around him. The saddlebags had been torn off Septimor, the bow and arrows smashed beyond repair. Not that he'd need them—his magic thrummed powerfully beneath his skin.

He gingerly climbed off Septimor's back, swinging to a bough, then down to the ground below.

The sight and stench of the gut-strewn branches sickened him. He'd do right by Septimor, give him a proper send off.

Hands shaking, he blasted mage flame at the base of the oak. Emerald fire danced from his fingers, melting away the snow and licking up the trunk. Flames climbed up the branches and engulfed Septimor's body. The sickly-sweet stench of burning dragon flesh filled the air. Despite the stench, Giddi stood there, flinging every last scrap of *sathir* at the tree until the dragon and the oak were wreathed in flame.

At last, he stumbled back and leaned against a strongwood tree, gasping, sweat beading his face. His arm was throbbing. A blazing pillar of green fire and gray smoke rose above the trees, a beacon for every tharuk and dark dragon in Spanglewood. A funeral pyre fit for such a valiant dragon, who'd given long service to Dragons' Realm.

A dragon he'd risked by accepting Starrus' vengeful challenge.

This had to end. Starrus was incompetent. Always had been. Years ago, Giddi had stepped down, ashamed at his own mistakes, and let Starrus lead the council. But he hadn't led them—he'd misled them.

Giddi pulled the fire back, coiling the *sathir*—the life energy—inside himself, and doused the flames. A pall of gray smoke hung over the forest. They could easily find him now.

Panting, boots crunching through snow, Giddi ran. He cast out his mind, searching for a blue dragon on patrol.

No answer.

He kept running, the stench of tharuks drifting on the wind.

VILLAGE SQUARE

A billowing cloud of dark dragons roiled over Lush Valley, their wings blotting out the sun and casting dark shadows upon the snowy landscape. Farmhouses and crops were ablaze. Marlies shifted in Liesar's saddle and fired an arrow, piercing the wing of a low-flying dark beast. It plummeted to a haystack, shooting flame, setting the hay on fire, smoke staining the sky. The beasts swooped over the buildings, picking up villagers and tossing them into the air, blasting fire at people running down the streets.

Marlies spied Klaus yelling and gesturing in the middle of the square. In a blinding flash of white light, her mind was hot, searing. She screamed, clutching at her scalp as shrieks ripped into her head. She grasped at her temples, pressing on them with her thumbs, trying to banish the pain.

Liesar bucked, thrashing her head with her talons. Behind Marlies, Leah hung on.

Gods, there had to be a way past this. She had to mind block, get these creatures out of her head, and get the girl to safety. But the anguished screams of terror in her head made it almost impossible to think straight.

"Liesar, break mind-meld, and drop Leah in the square." Marlies snapped away from her dragon's consciousness. Screeches still bounced around her head, but the pain was lighter.

"Leah, we're taking you down to Klaus." Gods, what if something happened to the girl? Seppi's gut wound flashed to mind. That was less likely if they set her down.

Liesar dove to the square.

"Marlies!" Klaus ran over, snatched the girl from the saddle and ran off with her.

They winged to the air again and a dark dragon bore down on them, the yellow rays from its eyes struck Marlies' boot. She flinched and yanked her foot away. The beams sizzled into Liesar's hide. Blood dripped from the wound. Liesar roared and shot higher.

Marlies nocked another arrow and loosed it at the beast's glowing eye. Its beams shredded the arrow, charred pieces clattering to a rooftop.

Roars and screams filled the air. The stench of burning flesh and fur. On the rooftops, village archers were firing at dark dragons. An arrow struck true, plunging into a shadow dragon's breast. The creature screeched and plummeted through the air, crashing into the square, scattering villagers.

Two dark dragons swept down and snatched the carcass. They shredded it with their jaws in a feeding frenzy, tearing great chunks of flesh and spraying fleeing villagers with black blood.

Oh, Gods.

One of the beasts swung its head and snapped up a man, biting his torso in two, gulping down the neck and head, then slurping up the man's entrails with its long tongue. Marlies fired an arrow into the feeding beast's skull. Then another and another until it slumped over, dead.

The other beast turned, opened its maw, and bit a chunk out of the haunch of the beast Marlies had just killed. Then pounced on a tharuk, shredding it. Fur flew and stinking tharuk blood stained the cobbles of the square.

Liesar melded, the anguished screech of shadow dragons ripping through Marlies' head. She could barely understand her dragon's words, *"Look, Marlies. To the South. Zaarusha and Erob are here."*

§

Zaarusha soared on a thermal beside Erob. The Queen's outspread wings caught flashes of sunlight, sending hues shimmering across her scales. That same beauty had entranced Ezaara when they'd first met in Lush Valley.

"I don't know what I'd be doing without you," Ezaara melded.

"Probably still collecting herbs in Lush Valley," Zaarusha replied. *"And stealing kisses from Lofty!"*

She swatted Zaarusha's hide. *"Don't let Roberto hear you say that. He'll get jealous."* She didn't even like Lofty, never had. Well, as friends, sure, but not like that, not the way she felt for Roberto.

Roberto's deep chuckle echoed through her mind. *"The comparison is insulting."*

At least he'd relaxed a little. Amato had finally fallen asleep, slumped over Erob. They were riding thermals, waiting for Matotoi to catch up to them. Each morning the three dragons flew together, enabling Matotoi to strengthen his wings. After breaking for a midday meal and letting the dragons doze, they continued, Zaarusha and Erob soaring ahead of the old dragon and dancing in the thermals. After three days' travel, they'd made good headway and were nearly at Lush Valley.

"*Good headway? We could've been home within moments if Bruno hadn't stolen that ring,*" Roberto said. "*Look, Matotoi's caught up.*"

§

Matotoi's wings flashed, glimmering jade in the sun. His pale scales had slowly taken on a fresh hue, turning green again as he regained his strength. Roberto was surprised at how fast he'd recovered. No doubt the sunlight, good food and exercise were helping him.

"*That's the bottom end of the Eastern Grande Alps,*" Ezaara shared the image of them, closer up, in her mind.

Roberto looked up to the horizon. There, they were: pristine snow-tipped alps beckoning them in the distance. Although he'd flown over Lush Valley, he'd never been within the horseshoe-shaped formation of alps that protected the valley from the outside world. "*Looks like a storm's brewing.*" Above the Western Grande Alps there was a dark cloud of roiling bad weather.

The mass was moving swiftly over the meadows and forest, rapidly approaching Lush Valley Settlement.

"*Better get our wet weather gear on,*" Ezaara tugged on her jerkin and pulled a weather-proof cloak out of Zaarusha's saddlebag.

§

They were about half an hour's flight away from Lush Valley when something silver flashed in the sky. "*Is that lightning?*" Roberto asked. "*Looks like we're in for a raging storm.*"

There was something odd about those clouds. They seemed to have a life of their own. As they were watching, parts of the mass broke off, drifting downward.

Zaarusha melded with both of them, "*That's no cloud, Roberto and Ezaara…*" A flash of orange shot through the dark clouds—fire. "*It's a swarm of black dragons.*"

"*Are you sure?*" asked Roberto. "*I don't know of any black dragon, only the browns far over the Northern Alps.*"

Another gust of fire spurted from the clouds, blazing against the dark mass.

"*That's not bad weather. It's dragon fire,*" Erob chimed in. "*Tie my tail, if it's not.*"

There was another flash of silver.

Silver? Oh, gods! There was only one thing that could be. "*Roberto, it's Liesar.*" Something had gone horribly wrong. Her mother shouldn't be here. "*If only I had Anakisha's ring, I could be there in an instant.*"

"I still have mine. I'll go." Roberto grimaced, gesturing at Amato hunched over Erob's back. *"I can't go."* He pulled the jade ring off his finger. Zaarusha sidled closer to Erob until the dragons were only a wing's breadth apart. He held the ring up, ready to throw it. *"If we lose this…"*

They couldn't afford to lose it. Ezaara shouted, "No, don't risk it."

Erob swooped up. Roberto leaped from his saddle, landing squarely on Zaarusha's back. He flung his arms around Ezaara, kissed the side of her face, and passed her the ring. Zaarusha ascended slightly as Erob descended, and Roberto leaped back into his own saddle.

Ezaara put the ring on her finger. "Ana."

With a pop, she and Zaarusha were in a golden cloud-lined tunnel, a transparent being floating toward her. *"I've told you to use caution with the rings, Ezaara,"* Anakisha, the former Queen's Rider, mind-melded. *"Look around you."*

Dark cracks in the clouds leaked black mist that swirled and eddied around Zaarusha and Ezaara. The first time she'd used a realm gate there had been nothing but billowy gold clouds.

"The more often you use a realm gate, the higher the likelihood Zens will discover them. Instantaneous travel would be a dire weapon in his hands. Need I remind you of this?"

"But my mother is battling dragons. I must help her."

Anakisha nodded. *"I understand. But I urge you to weigh your choices carefully. It would be a dire tragedy to save the life of one if it sacrificed many lives in the future."*

Ezaara's throat was dry, palms clammy as she and Zaarusha appeared with a crack above the settlement. The sky was teeming with black-scaled dragons, rays shooting from their glowing eyes. Their leathery wings beat like crashing waves. And there was Ma, charging on Liesar, her face fixed in an anguished grimace as she loosed arrow after arrow at the dragons' wings.

A hideous scream ricocheted through Zaarusha's mind. Sharp pain pierced Ezaara's skull. Her head throbbed with a blistering screech that shuddered down her spine. Gods, the pain was awful, spiking down her limbs.

Zaarusha roared, shaking Ezaara's bones.

Despite the crushing pain in her skull and that awful tortured scream, Ezaara nocked an arrow.

§

After transferring Amato to Matotoi's back, it took Roberto half an agonizing hour to reach Lush Valley Settlement, Erob straining every dragon's length of the way. He nocked his bow and loosed an arrow the moment they were in firing range of the shadow dragons, way before Erob's fire could touch the dark beasts that swarmed over the settlement. Zens had outdone himself. Roberto and the Council of the Twelve Dragon Masters had suspected the commander had been breeding dragons when he'd seen large amorphous shapes covered in dark cloth—wings—in Zens' tanks in Death Valley. That'd been less than two weeks ago.

"Let's get closer so I can flame them." Erob roared as they plunged into the fray.

An earsplitting scream rang through Roberto's head, reverberating down his jaw. He clutched his temples, nearly dropping his bow, but snatched the tip at the last moment. The screams seemed to go on and on. He could hardly think, hardly see straight, the pain was so intense.

Erob broke mind-meld.

The scream lessened, an angry echo throbbing in his head. Roberto straightened, letting an arrow fly straight for a dark dragon's head.

The creature turned, yellow beams shooting from its eyes, the arrow disintegrating in a spray of splinters that shredded the wings of a shadow dragon below. The beast plummeted, listing to one side.

Roberto raised his bow and shot again. The dragon turned its golden eye beams toward Roberto, rays slicing through the air. The string on his bow snapped. Gods, what manner of creatures could slice through things by looking at them?

He breathed heavily as he fumbled in the saddlebags for another bowstring. No time.

The shadow creature dove at them. Unable to meld with Erob, Roberto kicked his sides like a common horse. His dragon's neck swung up. Erob blasted flame at the approaching dark dragon. The beast whirled, shrieked and plummeted to the earth, wings blazing, neck wreathed in flames. Two other dark dragons attacked it in midair, shredding its hide with their talons and dragging off bloody haunches to feast upon.

Roberto watched, horrified. The beasts were devouring their own kin. Zens had created living nightmares.

More dark beasts plunged from the sky, flaming fleeing villagers. Thatch roofs caught fire. Houses were smoking charred ruins, a vegetable wagon on the village square was alight. Something pale flashed at the corner of Roberto's eye: Amato on Matotoi. What in flame's name was his father doing?

Roberto snatched his extra bow out of Erob's rear saddlebag and grabbed an arrow from his quiver. A littling ran screaming down a dirt road, chased by a giant dark dragon.

"A littling? Really, those foul things are utter cowards." Erob lunged a taloned foot at the dragon, shredding its wing from above. Its scream shredded Roberto's mind.

Roberto shot the beast through the skull. Ash billowed in the air as it landed on a pile of charred rubble.

Erob wheeled in the air and helped Matotoi burn two more of the vile beasts, searing the flesh from their bones.

Roberto whirled, not daring to meld with Erob. He scanned the skies for Liesar and Zaarusha.

A raging torrent of fire erupted over Roberto's shoulder. Erob wheeled in midair, roaring and belching flame at their attacker's underbelly. The scent of burnt hair filled Roberto's nostrils. They dove, then shot up to attack. Roberto loosed an arrow into the dragon's belly. Blood dripped on him and Erob as they ducked between the dark dragons.

A littling boy screamed, pointing at the sky.

Roberto followed his gaze to see Ezaara upon Zaarusha.

Oh, gods! Ezaara's arrow was sighted on Liesar, who was battling a horde of black dragons—and losing. Liesar plunged earthward. Ezaara waiting, raised herself up in the stirrups and aimed.

Roberto's heart caught in his throat. Cold dread swept over him, trickling through his marrow. Ezaara was aiming at Marlies.

STRANDED

Dusk was creeping over Spanglewood forest, a blazing orange sunset painting the snow-dappled woods—usually Giddi's favorite time of day. But he had no eyes for nature's beauty. One foot in front of the other, he doggedly strode toward Dragon's Teeth looming in the distance above the trees.

"Can anyone hear me?" A few more steps, and then a few more. He'd get there eventually.

"Master Giddi?" A faint voice drifted into his mind. He must be dozing on his feet.

The voice came again. *"Master Giddi."*

Too tired to feel relief or even joy, Giddi kept traipsing. *"Yes, Maazini, it's me."*

"I can't meld with Septimor."

"I'm alone." There'd be time for explanations later. Right now, he had to keep moving or he'd collapse and freeze in the snow. He managed a trickle of magic to warm his hands.

"You're exhausted, aren't you? I can feel it." Maazini's voice was steadily growing stronger. *"Something terrible must've happened for you to feel like this. Can you show me your surroundings so I can find you?"*

Even that was useless—trees were trees were trees—how could Maazini tell one tree from another? Too tired to argue, Giddi obliged.

The dragon kept prattling, chatting to him about anything. The sly beast was ensuring he didn't drop dead in the snow. Grateful for the company, Giddi kept trudging.

§

"Where is he?" Tomaaz asked.

"I have no idea," replied Maazini. *"If I can just keep him talking and thinking, then his voice will grow stronger as we near him."* Maazini swerved to the left. *"This way, it grows fainter."* He swerved back to the right. *"He's in this direction, see?"*

Snow flakes drifted from dark clouds, speckling Maazini's orange hide like goose down.

"I'm not about to start honking, if that's what you think." Maazini quipped. "Now, stop worrying like an old mother hen. We'll find him soon enough."

Tomaaz couldn't laugh. In moments, it would be dark. He gnawed his bottom lip. "I think I know why he left the hold alone."

"I'm afraid I do too," Maazini answered, then resumed his chatter with the dragon mage.

§

When they retrieved Giddi, he insisted that Tomaaz take him straight to Lars, although Tomaaz had no idea why. In Tomaaz's opinion, Giddi would be better off in the infirmary tucked up in bed. Tomaaz had Maazini meld with Singlar. Maazini paused for a moment before they swept into the main cavern, and landed on the rock stage.

On the floor of the cavern, mages and riders were training with swords, arrows, blades and flame. Dragons observed from the stage and ledges high on the cavern walls.

Lars took one look at Giddi slumped over Maazini's neck—and ran over.

Tomaaz shook Giddi gently. The mage roused, pushed himself up off Maazini's spinal ridge and slid to the floor, stumbling like a drunk.

Lars grabbed him and thrust Giddi's arm over his shoulder. "What happened, Giddi?"

Master Starrus was in the middle of instructing a group of junior mages.

Giddi turned, pointing at Starrus. "Him. He happened."

Lars' bushy eyebrows drew down in an ominous frown. "Master Starrus, come here at once," he bellowed.

Starrus whirled to face them, sneering, "I don't answer to dragon riders."

Roars rippled through the cavern.

Lars spoke softly. "The dragons seem to think otherwise, Starrus. I suggest you come here."

Giddi held out a shaking finger, sparks dripping from it and creating molten pools of fire on the floor. "A dragon has died today because of you."

Gasps rippled through the crowd.

"What's the meaning of this? Which dragon?" Lars demanded.

"Master Starrus insisted I take Septimor out to find a dark dragon and unlock the secret to defeating it."

"I did no such thing," Starrus said. "This arrogant master wizard, lusting after power and greed as he always has, insisted that he take Septimor—the poor, grieving dragon—on his own to Spanglewood to search for dark dragons."

Tomaaz slipped off Maazini and strode over to join Giddi. "I was leaving the mess cavern this afternoon, when I overheard Starrus order Master Giddi to go. He threatened him with expulsion from Dragons' Hold if he didn't obey. Knowing it was none of my business, I let the matter rest. But if I'd stepped in, Septimor might still be alive." His hand brushed the hilt of his sword. "Master Starrus is a liar."

"Master Starrus shall be given fair trial for the reckless death of a dragon," Lars said. "We don't dispense justice here. And Master Giddi will also need to face Starrus' accusations."

Master Giddi straightened, pushing Lars aside. "Since I stepped down from the Wizard Council—"

"With good reason," bellowed Starrus.

Giddi continued as if he hadn't spoken. "…you have persecuted me at every move. Your pompous arrogance has cost mages' lives and now the life of a fine dragon. Your energy has been wasted in displays of power and pettiness instead of uniting to fight our true enemy, Commander Zens. I suggest we vote as mages to elect a new Wizard Council."

Starrus smirked. "And I suppose you think you'd be the head of that new Wizard Council?"

Giddi shook his head. "No, I'm no longer worthy of that title."

Wizards murmured. Babble grew as people sheathed swords and stared.

Master Reina held up her hands. "I suggest we settle it now. A vote will be binding, so consider this matter carefully. Any fair trial of Starrus or Giddi will take place afterward. However, I declare the current Wizard Council defunct. And insist that we vote immediately to reinstate another. We are at war. We cannot have bickering among us.

Lars, silent, hovered near Giddi.

Nominations were called for. Tomaaz wasn't surprised that Starrus' name was not among them. Some suggested Master Reina; some, Master Hemlon; and others, Master Giddi. When it came time to vote, Master Giddi was declared the new leader of the Wizard Council.

He shook his head sadly, "I told you, I'm not worthy to lead you."

Starrus' face contorted, red blotches marring his cheeks. "You heard him!" he shrieked. "He said he's not worthy, and I agree." Beard bristling and fingers crackling with power, Starrus flung his hand and a bolt of sizzling mage fire slammed Giddi's chest.

Giddi was thrown backward, smacking into the floor. Without Master Giddi even twitching, a circle of hissing fire sprang up around Starrus, imprisoning him. Giddi scrambled to his feet and faced him. "I may not be worthy, but you are even less so. As leader of the Wizard Council, I now declare you disempowered."

Giddi snapped his fingers.

Blue guards swooped to the stage. The riders manhandled Starrus onto a giant cobalt dragon.

"Take him to the dungeons," Master Giddi said, swaying.

Tomaaz and Jael rushed to Giddi, each giving him a shoulder to lean on.

The reinstated leader of the Wizard Council croaked, "I know why Zens kidnapped Sorcha and Velrama. He's breeding them, the way he makes tharuks and dragons."

"What do you mean? Tomaaz asked. That was crazy. If the two wizards bred, it would take years before their offspring were old enough to wield magic.

"I saw them on dark dragons. Two of Sorcha, both trying to kill me." His voice cracked and he shook his head. "He was a fine student. And now he's dead. I had no choice but to kill him. Twice." His desolate eyes turned to Lars. "And Septimor's dead too. A terrible death, lanced by an oak, with his bowels strung across the tree. I burned him. Neither he nor Seppi deserved to die."

"Gods," whispered Jael, "Zens can now breed an army of Sorchas and Velramas. What hope do we have against countless mages?"

THWARTED

Ezaara stood in the stirrups. *"Kill her. Kill!"* The voices screeched. *"Killing that woman will stop the screaming in your head. She's making the noise, that evil woman on the silver dragon."*

That dark-haired woman had to go.

Ezaara raised her bow. Just a few more moments, and that evil woman's screaming would be gone.

"It's the silver dragon, too," the voice screamed. *"Kill it, and you'll be free."* Shadows danced across her vision. Her arm throbbed unnaturally. *"She did it. That witch injured you,"* whispered the dark voices.

Ezaara eased the bowstring back. That terrible silver beast was bucking and thrashing. Any moment now, it would still, and she could take her shot. She pulled her bowstring taut.

The shining dragon swooped. Soon it would be in range. Ezaara waited, arrow ready.

§

"Erob, quick!" Despite the crushing anguish in his head, Roberto melded with Erob. *"Hurry!"*

Beating his mighty wings, the blue dragon climbed. Erob rose above Zaarusha's tail and banked toward the queen. Roberto let go, flying from the saddle and diving toward Zaarusha. He slammed into Ezaara, toppling her from the saddle. Her arrow flew wide past Liesar, scoring a dark dragon's belly.

Roberto hung on to Ezaara as they tumbled through the air. She fought, clawing at his face. His cheeks were slick and warm. Blood. No, this wasn't like her. Something was terribly wrong. He hung on tight, protectively cradling her body.

"Roberto, are you mad?" Zaarusha's yell reverberated through the screams chorusing in Roberto's head. She dove, the rush of wind from her wings blasting past Roberto and Ezaara. *"Why did you push the Queen's Rider from my saddle?"* She grabbed them with her talons, jolting Roberto's body, but he hung on tight even though Ezaara pummeled his face.

Despite the ear-shredding pain, Roberto melded, *"She was trying to shoot Marlies."*

The queen of the dragons' shock jolted through Roberto. *"Impossible. Ezaara and I flew here to save her mother, not kill her."*

Roberto choked out a sob. *"I know."*

Her face a snarling frenzy, Ezaara grabbed his throat, squeezing until he gurgled.

Zaarusha beat her wings, swooping toward a meadow on the outskirts of the village, containing the charred ruins of a home. She deposited them on the grass.

Ezaara shoved him away, and stood, chest heaving and knife in hand—aimed at him. A broken arrow shaft was stuck in her upper arm.

"What's that?" he asked.

As she glanced down, he tackled her to the ground, and straddled her back. He bent her arm high up her back.

"Drop the knife," he muttered.

She complied, snarling and thrashing her legs

He held her fast. Whatever had caused her treacherous actions, must be on that arrow.

§

Klaus thrust Leah into a corner of the village square to fight alongside young men, littlings and a group of seasoned farmers. As tharuks rampaged through the village, they tried to hold an entrance to the square, barricading it with barrels and trestle tables—anything to stop the beasts from swarming in.

A tharuk charged through the barricade, splintering a table. A boy grabbed a long shard of wood and hefted it.

"Watch out," Paolo called, thrusting his sword into the beast's belly.

It crumpled to the cobbles.

A big tharuk bellowed, "Kill them." A troop of the monsters rushed through the gap.

Waving her sword, Leah deflected a tharuk's claws, but it was so strong she nearly lost her grip. A tall lad thrust forward, jabbing a knife deep into the tharuk's eye. Black blood sprayed over them as it slumped to the ground.

Another replaced it, a beast with a shattered tusk and a gash across its face. The thing's stench wafted over them, making Leah's stomach curdle. What in the dragon's name did these monsters eat? They always stank.

The beast gave an awful guffaw and prowled toward her, beady red eyes glinting. "What we got here? I sick of eating rat. Roast little ones, I say."

The big tharuk slashed the beast with its claws, ripping its throat out in a spray of black blood. "Zens say eat no human. Or you dead." It waved its troop forward. "Now, charge."

Leah batted her sword against a tharuk's claws and ducked as another swiped for her head. Paolo jumped behind her so they were back to back. He swung his sword at an approaching beast, spraying black blood. Leah struck a tharuk on the arm. It howled and she drove her sword into its thigh. It stumbled, dropped to a knee. Paolo whipped around and smote off its head.

She kept fighting as more tharuks flooded the square, kicking in doors, chasing villagers, cutting others down as they fled. A dark dragon swooped overhead, breathing fire over roofs. Thatching burst into flame, blazing above the square. Sweat rolling down her forehead and her hand slick with blood, Leah kept fighting.

A roar reverberated off the buildings, vibrating through Leah's body.

Oh, gods, no. Another dragon, one she'd never seen before—a cream tinged with green like pond scum—blasted flame over the square. A tharuk swiped at her and she ducked, rolling on the ground and standing to face another.

Wait, that pale dragon was flaming the dark ones. It was helping.

Fear dug its claws deep into Leah's belly. Made her blood icy. She still hadn't seen Marlies again. Or Liesar. What if Marlies was dead like those blue dragons in the forest? What if she never came back? A sob built in Leah's throat. She faltered.

A tharuk snatched her, lifting her by her shoulders, its claws stabbing through her jerkin. "Stupid little human," it snarled.

Leah squeezed her eyes shut against its fetid breath. She was never going to get back to Dragons' Hold. Never going to be a healer. It was her turn to die.

The tharuk's grip loosened. Leah fell onto the cobbles on her backside, eyes flying open. The pale dragon had the tharuk clutched in its talons. The dragon tossed the beast across the smoky square. The tharuk smacked into a stone column, splattering it with black blood, and slid to the ground.

Paolo raced over and helped her up. "That was close. If it wasn't for that dragon, you would've been rat meat."

"Thanks," she said, shakily.

The pale dragon swooped again, flame singeing tharuks' fur. Snarling in rage and pain, the beasts fled.

Leah sighed. Thank the Egg they were gone.

A lone tharuk leaped from behind a barrel and roared, launching itself at her.

A skinny dragon rider rushed over, pushing her aside. He raised his sword. The tharuk impaled itself on the man's blade, and they crashed to the ground.

Heart ricocheting in her chest, Leah jumped up. She and Paolo rolled the dead tharuk off the man, and helped him up.

"Y-you s-saved my life," she gasped.

The man panted, pulling his sword from the tharuk's chest with a squelch. He brushed his wispy hair back from his pale face, panting, skinny ribs rising and falling. He nodded. "You're welcome." Then he ran across the square.

"Lucky he was around," said Paolo. "I didn't see that tharuk."

Leah's breath gusted out of her. "Neither did I."

Klaus ran over. "Pails," he wheezed, coughing in the smoke. "We need more pails. The village is burning."

§

Marlies spun in her saddle. *Liesar, what's going on? Where's Erob?* How had the Queen's Rider become unseated? She had good riding technique, was always steadfast in the saddle.

A jet of dark dragon flame shot overhead.

Liesar roared and swooped down to a meadow, Marlies' belly rushing into her throat. *Zaarusha and Erob are distressed. Let's find out what happened.*

When they landed, Roberto was straddling Ezaara's back as she thrashed beneath him. Her arm was bloodied and his face bruised and scratched. By the flaming dragon's claws, what was going on? They were lovers, not enemies.

Marlies slid off the saddle, legs shaky. She strode toward them, unable to manage a run. "Roberto!" Her voice was sharper than she'd intended.

"Didn't Erob tell Liesar?" Roberto panted while struggling with Marlies' daughter. "Ezaara was shot with a crystal implant, one of Zens' yellow ones." Ezaara bucked, and Roberto nearly lost his seating. "Quick, grab a knife. I can't hold her much longer."

"Ezaara, I'm here to help you," Marlies said. "Please hold still."

"Liar!" Ezaara snarled. "You're the witch that put pain in my head."

She was truly far gone. Like Sofia had been. Marlies snatched her blade as Roberto pressed his full bodyweight into Ezaara's back. A lump in her throat, she placed a knee on Ezaara's elbow to hold her upper arm still. She slit Ezaara's sleeve.

Between them, she and Roberto held Ezaara still enough for Marlies to part the edges of the wound with her blade to find the crystal. She reached her fingers into the cut, but the yellow stone wouldn't budge. She tried again. But something was anchoring the crystal to Ezaara's flesh. "It's stuck. I can't get it out."

Ezaara shrieked.

Roberto twisted his head, eyes full of anguish. "I don't care how you do it. Just get that shrotty thing out."

Easing the edge of the crystal to one side with her blade, Marlies thrust her finger into the wound and pulled. Something sharp pierced her fingertip. "Shards! It has barbs on it." She pushed the blade deeper and twisted it up, flicking the crystal out of the wound.

Ezaara screamed.

Worse than the dragons' desperate screams in her head, it brought tears to Marlies' eyes. She was butchering her own daughter. And didn't have piaua to heal her.

"Oh, gods," Roberto sobbed.

Marlies held up the crystal. Shaped like an arrowhead, the yellow stone had two metal prongs at its tip and more metal running through its transparent inside. The prongs had barbed hooks on the ends that wriggled like a dying insect's legs. "By the First Egg, I've never seen anything like it." She showed Roberto. "It's alive, Roberto. Or magicked by powerful mages." Dark terror rose inside her. How could they ever combat Zens' creations? The world he came from was so sophisticated—they'd never be able to defeat him.

§

Ezaara's body went limp under Roberto. His heart was shattered into a million pieces. This desolation and betrayal must've been how she'd felt when he'd been implanted with Zens' yellow crystal and attacked her. She was a better being than him—she'd forgiven him so easily. Taken him back in her arms and told him she'd understood.

"Ezaara, it's all right," he crooned. It wasn't. It wasn't. This was so wrong.

Roars echoed overhead.

She groaned.

Roberto helped her sit up.

Her eyes flew wide and her mouth drooped. "Oh, Roberto. Your face." She touched his cheek and her fingers came away bloody. "I'm so sorry. So sorry."

He put an arm around her, forcing a chuckle. "So now we're even. Except you gouged me with your nails, but hey, I was going to slit your throat." He swallowed—hard—the memory of his blood-stained knife rushing through him again.

Flames crackled in the distance. Smoke drifted over them.

Marlies reached into her healer's pouch and pulled out a bandage and tub of salve. She examined Ezaara's arm. "There's no piaua left, Ezaara. I came here to find some, but the tree's been destroyed." She opened her mouth as if to say more and then snapped it shut.

"We still have some." Roberto took a piaua vial from the pouch at Ezaara's waist.

Marlies held it up to the light. The vial was only a quarter full. "A little," she murmured, her turquoise eyes grave. "Seppi just died of an infection because we're out of piaua at the infirmary. This may be the last we have."

Roberto snatched the vial, tipping a drop on his finger before either of them could protest.

Marlies gasped. "That's not life-threatening. I'll stitch it"

"No, Marlies. She's the Queen's Rider and we're in the middle of battle. We don't have time. We only have four dragons against a swarm."

He rubbed the piaua deep into Ezaara's wound and dribbled another drop in, watching the flesh knit over before his eyes.

Although she'd protested, as any good healer would do, relief washed over Marlies' face. She closed her eyes, taking a deep breath and then opened them again. "Four dragons, you said? Who's the other one?"

§

By the shrotty unfair dragon gods, it couldn't be true. She hadn't, had she?

But it was true. And yes, she had. Over and over in her mind, Ezaara saw herself rising in her stirrups and aiming her arrow at Ma. Hateful thoughts flooded her head. Screams of agony from those dark dragons. Shadows writhed, twisting her mind. An insidious voice whispered, *Kill her. Kill the evil woman.*

She'd drawn her bow and fired.

She clung to Roberto, sobbing. He'd saved her from killing her mother. From hating herself for a lifetime.

She'd seen Roberto turned by methimium. Seen Sofia turned. And she'd understood. Had forgiven them.

But how could she forgive herself for wanting to kill her own flesh and blood?

§

Roofs were ablaze, thatching and wooden shingles burning. Leah cast around. "Quick, this way." She snatched Paolo's hand and ran toward a tavern, its splintered door gaping like an angry jagged maw.

She yanked the door open. Its hinges gave way. "Look out!" She leaped back, thrusting Paolo aside. The door crashed to the ground, missing them by a hand's breadth.

"C'mon!" Her heart beating a crazy staccato against her ribs, Leah tugged Paolo inside.

Dead patrons were slumped over spilled tankards. A bloodied tharuk was on the floor, its skull staved in with a chair leg.

She ignored it all, racing behind the bar to the storeroom, dragging Paolo with her. Paolo sprinted to a keg. "Brilliant idea, Leah."

It took two of them to roll the keg from the back room across the tavern and out the door. They ran back for another keg, and then another. When kegs were jamming the doorway, Leah and Paolo scrambled over them amid bellows, snarls and roars from the square.

Paolo stuck his fingers in his mouth and let out an ear-piercing whistle.

The pale dragon flung a tharuk into the air and leaped toward them.

Steeling her shaking knees, Leah placed a hand on its head. "These kegs are for putting out fires."

"*Good thinking, young one.*" Hooking his talons through the metal bonds around the kegs, the dragon rose above a burning rooftop. He swung the kegs out and smashed them against each other. Honey-colored liquid poured over the flames.

To Leah's horror, the flames belched and soared skyward nearly toasting the pale dragon.

Panting, Klaus arrived. He glanced at the barrels: Heath's Finest Malt Whiskey. "That'll only feed the fire." He thrust aside three of the whiskey kegs. And hefted an ale keg on his shoulder, whistling for the dragon.

Squeezing Paolo's hand in hers, Leah held her breath as the dragon smashed keg after keg of ale over the rooftops, until the fires were reduced to smoldering, steaming char.

SHADOW DRAGON

It was night by the time Kierion and the dark dragon crested the peaks of Dragon's Teeth and flew down into the basin of Dragons' Hold. The snow gleamed in the dark. As usual, a fierce ache built in his chest at the beauty of the hold, making him want to protect his realm against Zens' monsters—monsters like the one he was riding right now.

The air resonated with a bellow—a warning cry that the hold had been breached. A cry that had probably never been uttered in Kierion's lifetime. He'd brought this evil creature to Dragons' Hold. Gods, hopefully they could keep the beast and mage under control so they wouldn't destroy anyone.

§

Jael and Tomaaz got Giddi into a hot bath and then an infirmary bed to rest under Mara's watchful eye. They'd just ambled back to the main cavern when a dragon bellowed.

"The defenses of Dragons' Hold have been breached," Lars roared. "To your dragons!" The council leader leaped upon Singlar. Riders jumped into their saddles and flew out the tunnels in the cavern walls. Tomaaz and Jael jumped on Maazini and broke into the night sky.

Illuminated by a gust of Singlar's flame was a dark dragon swooping toward the main cavern.

Maazini melded, *"It's not screaming."*

It wasn't. And Riona was there too, flying alongside the dragon with Fenni on her back. But where was Kierion?

"Lars says to let the dark dragon go into the main cavern." Maazini bristled.

They followed the shadow dragon into the cavern. It landed, a mage and rider upon its back.

"Nice to see you all," a cheeky voice piped up.

Kierion?

Maazini chuckled. *"So it seems."*

"I've captured you a specimen, so we can figure out how to fight these things," Kierion said. "But stand back, please—it's not tame." His face grim, Kierion held a knife to the mage's throat. "The only thing keeping them subdued is my blade," he said. "I suggest you put them under lock and key in the holding dungeon for dragons."

§

Adelina gasped. He was back. Kierion was here. His eyes swept the cavern and found her immediately. Then slid away. In no time at all, he was hustled out of the cavern, escorting the dark dragon and mage at knife point to the dungeons.

Adelina had no desire to follow. Those were the dungeons where her brother had been held with Erob before he was sent to the Wastelands. She didn't want to relive the memories of her only family member being banished.

She'd see Kierion before he went back to Montanara and apologize. Thank the Egg he was home again—even though the hurt had still been fresh in his eyes.

Adelina went back to her training, Master Jerrick praising her for her aim as her arrows thwacked into target after target.

As soon as she was done, she raced to Kierion's cavern. He wasn't there.

Nor was he in the mess cavern.

Or the infirmary.

"Have you seen Kierion?" she asked Mara.

"He's just gone back to Montanara." She winked. ""Don't worry, there'll be time enough for you to catch up later."

If Kierion ever wanted to catch up with her. Adelina wasn't so sure.

AFTERMATH

Steam rose into the chill air from the entrails of dark dragons ripped open by their peers. Dead tharuks and villagers were scattered over the square like a littling's discarded playthings. Wounded lay among the dead, their feeble moans drifting on the stench.

Wracked with guilt, Ezaara knelt next to Willow, now a newly widowed mother with a broken arm. Last time Ezaara had seen Willow, the young woman had been laughing with her husband, Kieft, at the market. Now, Kieft lay dead, a dragon's length away, with his friend Murray wounded nearby. Those few precious drops of piaua should've been used to save these lives, not for the wound on Ezaara's arm. The Queen's Rider shouldn't take priority over others. It was wrong.

Ma had always taught her there were enough healing supplies for everyone. But not anymore, thanks to Commander Zens.

She fastened the splint on Willow's arm and stood, squeezing the hand of Willow's littling—cradled in his mother's good arm. She had no words. There was nothing to say when your village lay in smoking ruins. When the people you'd grown up with were homeless, wounded, or dead.

Roberto, Ma and Amato were in a tense discussion standing in the corner of the square near the makeshift infirmary—an inn that Klaus had commandeered.

"Ezaara, I think you'd better join us," Roberto mind-melded.

Just seeing her nail gouges on his face made her hesitate. *"I'll be right there."* More guilt wracked her as Ma slumped with exhaustion. Ezaara shook her head to dispel the nagging image of her arrow aimed at Ma, but as she strode over to join them, she couldn't shake it loose.

§

"Amato?" Marlies squinted, hardly able to believe her eyes. He was thin and pale, all bones and angles, a wisp of what he'd been when she'd met him at Giddi's cabin in Great Spanglewood Forest all those years ago. His once-handsome face was sallow, eyes sunken, and hair thin and wild. The years had not been kind to the alluring man she'd once been infatuated with.

But then again, he'd not been kind either. For the thousandth time, Marlies was glad she'd chosen Hans over Amato.

"Marlies." Amato croaked, throat bobbing. "Still as beautiful as ever."

Roberto bristled. Ezaara joined them, placing her hand on Roberto's arm.

Did he have any idea how similar he looked to his father? When she'd first seen Roberto, she'd mistaken him for Amato, forgetting how many years had passed. Then she'd looked again. Roberto didn't have that easy laugh and gregarious nature so common in Naobians. His face was closed, hard, especially now.

She could hardly blame him after what he'd been through at his father's hands.

Overcoming her reflex to recoil from him, Marlies stepped closer to Amato. "I'd heard you'd died in Crystal Lake. How did you survive?"

He shrugged. "Fish and lake weed. I hid in an underwater cave for so long I grew too weak to swim out."

"How long?"

Amato shrugged again, his breath short and shoulders tight. His ribs heaved, pressing through his shirt.

Roberto answered tersely, "Six years."

Marlies gave Amato a sharp glance. "Are you wounded?"

His gaze slid away. "I'm fine."

"By the dragon's talon, you are. Turn around." She didn't wait, but stalked behind Amato, sucking air in through her teeth. The back of his shirt was burnt, angry bubbly skin blistering through the shreds. "We've got to get you to Dragons' Hold. Roberto, Ezaara, do you still have our means of speedy travel?" She wasn't going to mention Anakisha's rings in front of someone who'd been a traitor to the realm.

"Yes, but I'm staying here." Roberto said, eyes flat.

Marlies understood. He didn't care if his father died. Maybe he'd prefer it. She turned to her daughter. "Ezaara, would you take Amato to Dragons' Hold? Once you've given him into Lars' custody, you may return"

"Excuse me, Marlies," Roberto interrupted, "but the Queen's Rider is not taking Amato to Dragons' Hold." Roberto's voice was forged of steel.

"So, you'll take him, then?"

Roberto's only answer was a snort.

"Roberto?" Marlies pressed.

"Take him yourself." Although she knew the venom in his voice was for Amato, Marlies recoiled at the hate in his heart. Roberto flashed a glare at her. "I'm staying here to help clean up."

Ezaara piped up, "Ma, you're not looking so great yourself. And as master healer, you're needed back at the hold. Maybe you should go."

"Back to the hold? When there's so much healing and work to be done here?" And piaua to be found, but she didn't mention that. Not now.

Feeble cries and muttered groans of the wounded drifted around the square on wisps of smoke, weaving between the strands of their conversation.

Ezaara's eyes roamed Roberto's face, and his searched hers. They were melding. Both turned to survey the wounded.

Leah and Paolo joined them. "You were amazing," Paolo said, shaking Amato's hand. "If it hadn't been for you…"

"…I'd be dead," Leah finished. "Thank you for saving my life." She went upon her toes and craned her head to kiss Amato's pale cheek. No mean feat for one as shy as Leah. "Thanks so much for saving me. Marlies, this man's a hero, he saved Paolo and me."

Amato's eyes glistened. "The least I can do is save these littlings, even if I wasn't able to save my own littlings from myself." His eyes didn't leave Roberto's face.

Roberto's gaze snapped to his father. "Get on Erob. I'm taking you to the hold." He strode off.

Ezaara hugged Marlies, eyes still haunted. "Shall we get on with healing?"

Marlies nodded, gazing over the wounded. So many. And no piaua.

REUNION

"What about Matotoi?" Roberto asked Amato. "What's he going to do?"

"He'll help here for a while and then travel to Dragons' Hold." Amato gingerly climbed into Erob's saddle. His back was an ugly mess of burns and blisters.

Roberto climbed up behind him, careful not to touch Amato's back. Seeing Amato couldn't have been easy for Marlies. She hadn't even known he was alive. His father had obviously known her well. Although the way he'd said she was *beautiful* had rankled. As if the memory of his mother was dust.

Well, Amato was dust, as far as he was concerned. Dust he'd grind under his boot.

"How do you know Marlies?" Roberto asked.

"I was the dragon rider who invited her to Dragons' Hold when she first imprinted with Liesar," Amato replied. "We loved each other once."

Roberto raised an eyebrow.

"That surprised you didn't it?" Erob said. *"It was so long ago, it never occurred to me to tell you."* Erob flapped his wings, and they gently rose through the smoke into the sky. From here, Roberto could see that only part of the settlement was damaged. At least Lush Valley's citizens would have somewhere to sleep tonight.

"What happened... with Marlies?" Roberto asked Amato.

"Hans happened. That was the end of it. And then I met your mother."

Roberto shrugged, fighting his curiosity. He didn't want to know. Amato's past was none of his business. "Please close your eyes for a moment and hold on." He kept the jade ring hidden. With a ring, Amato could nip straight back to Zens. Roberto rubbed it, his breath a faint whisper, "Ana."

Lush Valley disappeared. With a pop, they were in the tunnel of golden clouds. In a few short days, it'd changed. Wisps of mist leaked in from dark rifts, swirling around Anakisha's pale figure, making it difficult to see her spirit.

"My grandson, I see you've found your father," Anakisha mind-melded. *"He's been pining for you for years."*

"What about when he beat me bloody? He wasn't pining then."

"No, but he was in Zens' thrall. As you once were, too."

And as Ezaara had been, just today, thanks to Zens' methimium.

Anakisha murmured in his mind, *"Of all people, I'd expect you to understand."*

Roberto clenched his jaw then said aloud, "Please take us to Dragons' Hold, so I can bring my father to justice."

With a crack, Erob was circling down to Lars' cavern. They landed on the ledge and Lars swept out the door.

"I melded with Singlar. I hope you don't mind me letting him know." Erob said.

"No, the sooner I'm rid of him, the better. "

"I've let Linaia know as well," Erob said. *"I thought it only fair that Adelina should see her father."*

Adelina. Roberto swallowed. He'd sheltered his sister from this monster for years, and now he was bringing him to her.

Lars greeted Roberto, face grim.

"He's injured," Roberto said. "The burns on his back need treating."

Lars gave a brisk nod. Within moments, blue guards were swarming onto the ledge. Two of them hoisted Amato between them.

Amato hung his head, his back raw and weeping as he was dragged through Lars' cavern.

Roberto followed. "Careful of his ba—" He stopped himself. What did he care?

The door burst open. Adelina ran in. When she saw Amato, she gaped.

Roberto sprang to her side, putting an arm around her as the blue guards traipsed out, taking their father.

Adelina shoved Roberto away. "I was hoping it wasn't true," she yelled. "How dare you bring that monster back here?" She bolted out the door.

§

Roberto was about to run after Adelina, but Lars put a hand on his arm. "Give her time, Roberto. It's a huge shock and she needs to adjust."

"But I don't *have* time, Lars. Ezaara and Marlies are in Lush Valley helping the wounded. More dark dragons could attack them at any time."

Lars' eyebrows shot up. "Dark dragons have attacked Lush Valley?"

Roberto ran a hand through his hair. "The blue guards are dead and half the village is burned. Dead dragons, tharuks and villagers are strewn over the square."

Lars shook his head. "Then you'd best get back with the ring. Don't worry about Adelina. I'll talk to her when she's had time to cool down. And I'll send more blue guards to Lush Valley immediately."

"Yes, Master Lars." Roberto strode toward the ledge where Erob was waiting.

"And, Roberto..."

"Yes?" He turned at the door.

"Only stay in Lush Valley long enough to get people organized. We need you and Ezaara back at Dragons' Hold immediately."

Roberto nodded, strode outside, and pulled on his gloves. *Erob, take me to Adelina's cavern.*

"Good decision," Erob said, leaping off the ledge.

§

"Why did you bring him back?" Adelina was hunched on her bed, fists balled, shoulders tight. "I've been trying my whole life to forget him."

Roberto clenched his jaw. "Haven't we all?" His world had crumbled the moment he'd seen Amato in that cave. Even though Amato had helped when Bruno and Simeon had attacked, and again in Lush Valley, it was nothing compared to what he'd done to so many.

"I wish you'd just kill him and be done with it." Adelina turned her back and curled in on herself, like a tightly-furled bud. He sat by her, stroking her back, the way he had when they were littlings. Her eyes brimmed with tears. "When we wanted love, he gave us hate. Pain. Sadness. Why should we give him any less?"

"I know." He nodded. "Ezaara said we should be forgiving. That Zaarusha wants—"

"And who is Ezaara to expect that of us? She's lived her whole life cloistered in Lush Valley, safe from the outside world. We had Death Valley in our home. What makes you think I want that again?" Adelina dashed away a tear with the back of her hand. "These are the last tears I'll ever cry for him. I swear it. And guess what? They're not even for him, they're for us. I'm sad that shrotty old man didn't die when he hit Crystal Lake. The world would be better off without him."

Roberto hugged his sister, nodding against her hair, darkness roiling in his belly. "I know, Adelina. I know."

She sobbed. "Why did you bring him back?"

"Zaarusha commanded it." Roberto's breath whooshed out of him. "After what he did to our family, do you believe for one moment that if I had a choice I wouldn't have killed him?"

She sat up. "It must've been hard for you to stay your knife, knowing what he's done. How many lives he's destroyed."

Roberto swallowed. "Harder than you'll ever know. But I've sworn allegiance to my queen." He ran a hand through his hair. "Someone attacked him in Naobia. The hardest thing I've ever done was leap between him and that blade."

Dark eyes wide, Adelina nodded.

Roberto hugged her. "I have to go back to Lush Valley. There's been a terrible battle. The streets are strewn with dead and wounded. I must go to help Ezaara."

Adelina clung to him. "Don't leave me," she whispered.

"I'm sorry, 'Lina. So sorry." He kissed her hair and held her tight. Tears sprang to his eyes and he blinked them back.

There was a thud on the ledge outside her cavern. Erob melded. *"Roberto, we need to leave. Lars wants us back here as soon as possible."*

He stood. "I'll come as soon as I can."

Adelina whispered, "Don't go."

"Roberto." Erob harrumphed impatiently. *"We've been gone too long. Anything could be happening in Lush Valley. We need to get back to Zaarusha."*

He walked to the door, turning back to Adelina's haunted eyes. Tears glimmered on her cheeks. "Good bye, Roberto."

"I'll be back soon." Roberto climbed into the saddle. Eyes burning, he rubbed the ring, and called, "Ana," abandoning his sister.

§

Zens cocked his head, taking his eyes from the tanks of mages he was cloning. There it was again—a ripple in the *sathir*—the life force of Dragons' Realm, the energy that mages could tap into. The energy that he could corrupt with methimium.

He probed with his mind, seeking out the source of the power. There, faintly, on the periphery of his mind, he sensed a ripple. He'd sensed a similar one not half an hour ago. And more of these ripples over the past moons, starting about the time that orange dragon had escaped.

Ripples similar to those he'd sensed when Giddi opened the world gate all those years ago.

Zens rubbed his hands, grinning. Had someone opened a portal? If so, who? And to where? Perhaps this was the chance he'd been waiting for.

Adelina punched her pillow and rolled over. Memories crowded in on her. It was as if the lid had been lifted on a trunk of terrible secrets, letting every dark demon from her past slither out to haunt her. The whip, striking Roberto's cheek. The screams of her mother. The agony Ma had lived through after Amato had injured her. Her dying breaths.

And worse—the choking fear that had engulfed her as a littling, despite her brother's attempts to protect her. That was the worst. The fear. Not knowing when Amato would strike next.

Memories poured from the trunk of secrets, wrapping themselves around Adelina's chest and squeezing. Her breath came in short rasps. The whip. The knife. His boots.

Her forehead broke out in sweat. Her hands shook.

She had to pull herself together. This wasn't real. Her fears were only memories. Amato was contained in the dungeons below.

But what if he escaped?

What if he—

It was no good. Without Roberto, she couldn't control it. The fear hidden in her dark past was driving her into a deep pit of horror—her littling years.

"Adelina, you're distressed," Linaia mind-melded. *"Why does this man's presence trouble you? Lars has him contained."*

That was it. Linaia was her answer. Adelina threw on a warm winter cloak, grabbed some extra clothing, fruit and a waterskin. She rushed out to the ledge and shoved her things into Linaia's saddlebags.

"Linaia, I can't stay here. Not with this man here."

Her dragon nuzzled her hand. *"Is it that bad?"*

"It is. Every dark terrible thing in my life is because of him. He killed my mother." Pulse pounding and her throat choked, she sobbed. *"We have to get out of here."*

Linaia snuffled her face. *"Do you have coin?"*

"Coin?"

"Yes, you need coin if we're to travel to Montanara."

"Montanara?" Gods, she was repeating everything like an idiot, incapable of thought or speech, her whole mind consumed with Amato's face—then and now.

"Yes," said Linaia. *"We're going to Montanara to find Kierion."*

Tonio burst through Lars' door without waiting for an invitation. "This is an outrage. I can't believe it. I won't sanction that venomous traitor staying in our dungeon."

Lars raised an eyebrow. "Where else did you expect him to stay? In a guest cavern?"

"A pile of dragon dung would be a better choice. Or the bottom of the Naobian Sea." Tonio battled to control his rage, holding his clenched fists at his sides.

Lars' blue gaze was steely. "If one hair of Amato's head is harmed before he's put on trial, I will personally hold you responsible for finding out who did it. And if you're under suspicion…"

"Are you questioning my integrity?" Tonio's hand caressed the pommel at his waist.

Lars' eyes flicked down to Tonio's fingers. "No, just your hotheadedness about this situation. You've been exemplary since I appointed you. Apart from the matter of banishing Roberto unjustly because he was Amato's son."

"I seem to recall you supported that decision."

Lars shrugged. "I may have been unduly influenced by your opinion, but I won't be again. Every citizen of Dragons' Realm deserves a fair trial."

Tonio's blood pounded through his temples at the thought of that murderer being at Dragons' Hold. At his being alive.

"I'm giving you one chance, Tonio. As spymaster, you'll head up Amato's interrogation. You will not be allowed alone with him. Two other riders will always be present. If you fail to keep him alive and well, you'll lose your position and standing and be banished to the Wastelands or hung." Lars continued, "I know this is about Rosita—"

"Of course it's about Rosita. He murdered her, and hundreds of others. How you can let this go unchecked? He's a monster who deserves to be shredded by dragons." Tonio snapped his jaw shut, spun, and stalked to the door. "I'll fulfill my duties, so you can bring him to trial and end his life," he snarled, slamming the door.

A Lovely Find

O00 entered the laboratory, stalking up to Zens with a beatific smile on his snout.

"Go on, out with it," Zens mind-melded.

The affection in the tharuk's thoughts warmed Zens, as it always did. 000 was his finest creation, his first prototype, imbued with his own intelligence, but the strong body of a killing machine. He'd ensured all his subsequent tharuks were not as perfect as this one, his first loving creation.

Triple's smile grew wider. He opened his furry hand and passed Zens a curious ring. Made of jade and engraved with whorls, it emanated a strange power.

Without being asked, 000 explained, "It's from Bruno, sir. He passed it to a Naobian troop leader who had it delivered via one of your mage clones riding one of our new dark lovelies." He grinned. "Your mages are proving quite useful, even though they age quickly."

Zens turned the ring over and over in his fingers. "As do our dragons. We have to find some way of making them live longer than a week or so. The accelerated growth gene means we can produce them quickly, but also causes their quick demise." He held the ring up to the light, gazing at the patterns on it. "Did Bruno say what this is for?"

"Yes, sir. He said it used to be Anakisha's. Something about traveling quickly within the realm."

Zens rubbed it and commanded, "Take me to Dragons' Hold."

Nothing happened

Tossing it in the air and catching it, he smiled. "We'll figure this out later. I'm sure it will come in very useful." He scratched 000's forehead, his darling practically purring. "Now, let's get back to these clones." He waved his hand toward the antechamber to his main laboratory. "We need more mages. And dragons. Let's work around the clock to double production and see what we can do to halt the aging process. Soon, Dragons' Realm will be on its knees."

§

Zens turned on the methimium ray, its golden beam springing to life and making a spot on the cavern wall.

000 scratched his tusked snout. "So, this thing takes us through that wall?"

His dear tharuk had misunderstood. "No. I just need a solid spot to aim the ray when I stand in its beam and use Anakisha's talisman."

He held the engraved jade ring in his palm, stroking it with his finger. "I'll open a portal with this ring. The methimium ray will hold that portal open, allowing you to follow me. It can't open a portal on its own, or I'd already be back in our world, wreaking havoc with my new methimium weapons and building more of them.

Zens rubbed the ring again. "We just have to figure out how to activate this ring's power, then we'll pay the Queen's Rider a little visit."

BLACK HEART

Bruno stalked before the hearth, flames casting his shadow up the cavern wall so it towered over Simeon. "In all our years at Dragons' Hold, you didn't even imprint with a dragon despite the many opportunities you had."

"Father, I—"

"Shuddup." His father rounded on him, raising a fist. "And on that raft, you couldn't save your mother. You guzzled the last of the water yourself. It's your fault she died."

Simeon hung his head in shame. It was true—all of it was true. He'd only left her a drop or two.

Bruno jabbed a finger at Simeon's face. "In Naobia, I had that flaming chit paralyzed, and you couldn't even take her. You useless heap of shrot." His father snorted. "I should've shown you how it's done. Should've jammed the Queen's Rider full of my own seed to make baby dragon riders."

The thought of his father with Ezaara made Simeon want to spit. Since he was young, his father had always mocked him, beaten him and bullied him. And now, this lousy bully wanted to take what Simeon most desired.

LAST STOP

After leaving Ezaara in Lush Valley to tend the wounded, Marlies, Leah and Liesar pressed on to Last Stop. Liesar landed on the outskirts of town near a fountain—a bronze dragon with outspread wings, perched upon its rear legs, its maw spraying diamond droplets that sparkled in the last rays of sunset.

They dismounted. Marlies bent to hold Leah's face in her hands. "You're now my daughter and we're seeking a healing remedy for your belly gripe. Here, cover yourself with this." She fished peasant tunics from Liesar's saddlebags, and they donned them and put their cloaks back on over the top. "If we get separated, meet me back here. Try to avoid tharuks, but if one questions you, avoid its gaze. Especially if its a black-eyed mind-bender."

Leah's eyes were grave. "I have my sword. It's tasted tharuks already. I'm sure it would like another bite."

So much bravery in such a young soul. "I'm hoping we won't need to fight," Marlies said. She took Leah's hand, leading her through a back road into town. "Remember, we're here for piaua juice. Nothing else. We mustn't get distracted."

Sure enough, tharuks were milling on the next street and every street after that, as the two women made their way to the town square. The night market was in progress, much subdued from when Marlies had last been here. There was no singing, dancing or revelry. Only tight-faced stall owners, cautiously selling their wares. As they strode through the market at a rapid clip, a tharuk grabbed a stall keeper by the scruff of the neck, bellowing in his face. Hands shaking, the man shoved baskets of produce at the monster.

Leah's hand tightened in hers. Marlies' other hand drifted to her sword, but she stopped herself. Piaua juice. That's all. Although it was hard to ignore the beasts, when they'd just been fighting them half a day ago. Threading their way through the market, the aroma of spiced cheese and ale lingering in the air, they came to The Lost King, the tavern that Anakisha's granddaughter, Kisha, kept. Kisha had once seen a vision of Marlies and kept Anakisha's jade ring safe for her for years. One of a pair of rings that were keys to the realm gates.

Marlies leaned into Leah. "Keep your head down and don't talk to anyone. Don't even look at anyone." She pushed the door open to the clamor of ringing swords, snarls and bellows.

Oh flame it, they'd walked straight into a brawl between tharuks and patrons.

They ducked inside, quickly closing the door behind them so none of the tharuks in the square would notice. There were only five beasts in here—the chances were not so bad. Marlies thrust Leah into a seat at a tiny table in an alcove near the door. "Stay here and don't move."

She drew her sword and leaped into the fray.

§

Leah's heart pounded. She was a sitting duck. Marlies had said she should stay down and remain unnoticed, but here she was, sitting at a table, waiting to be slaughtered.

Marlies dashed over to a tharuk who had a man pinned against a wall and drove a dagger through its back. When she pulled it out, the blade dripped dark blood, and the tharuk crumbled to the floor howling.

Leah scrambled under the table. Not a moment too soon. A chair whizzed overhead and splintered against the wall. Her eyes darted around the tavern. It was complete chaos. Roars split her ears as a tharuk gutted a man. Marlies smote off its head, and its body sprawled across a table, cracking dinner plates. Tankards slid off the table and smashed on the floor, sending glass skittering across the floorboards.

A cry rang out. A tharuk ripped a man's throat out, blood pumping over his body, then ran for the girl behind the bar.

This was awful—watching and sitting here, doing nothing. She had to avoid detection. Or fight.

Leah drew her sword.

§

Three down and two to go. Marlies scanned the tavern. Where had the other tharuk gone? And where was Kisha? Usually behind the bar, Anakisha's granddaughter was nowhere to be seen. Marlies dashed behind the bar and through a door to the kitchen.

A tharuk had its head buried in the meat safe, its rear haunches completely unprotected. It crunched and slurped as it feasted on the flesh inside. Kisha was standing behind it with a cleaver raised in her hands. Marlies held her breath, not daring to make a sound. She hefted her sword and dagger, ready to jump in if needed.

Kisha screwed up her face and slammed the meat cleaver into the beast's neck. The cleaver lodged in its thick fur. Dark blood spurted across the meat locker as the tharuk spun, cleaver still in its neck, and roared at Kisha, slashing with its claws. It bucked and clawed at the cleaver, but the weapon didn't budge. Kisha ran across the kitchen, grabbed a frying pan, and threw it at the beast's head. Yowling, it sprang onto the kitchen counter about to launch itself at the terrified girl.

Marlies' dagger pierced its eye before the tharuk could jump. It crashed to the floor, twitching.

Marlies rushed to Kisha, sweeping her into a hug. "Are you all right?"

Kisha nodded.

A roar ripped through the tavern.

"Flame it, Leah's out there alone." Marlies raced through the door, vaulted the bar and stopped dead.

Leah was panting, her sword black and sticky as she pulled it from the chest of a tharuk that was slumped on the tavern floor. She grinned. "The naughty thing wouldn't play nice."

"Marlies? Is it really you?" Kisha came out from the bar, splattered in tharuk blood.

"Yes, it's me. It's no longer safe here. Come to Dragons' Hold."

Kisha shook her head vehemently. "I promised my grandmother that I would stay here and hold the fort."

"But why? More brutes like these will come, again and again."

Kisha met Marlies' gaze. "I know. But my work is not done here. I was hoping you'd come. I had a terrible vision. I've seen Commander Zens traversing the Dragons' Realm via the realm gate, using it to wage war. I told you, Marlies, only use the ring in times of desperation."

"These have been desperate times, Kisha," Marlies said.

Kisha nodded. "They are indeed."

Piaua—Marlies had told Leah they mustn't get distracted and here she was, forgetting. "I've come seeking piaua juice. Is there any in town?"

Kisha shook her head. "The closest piaua tree has been destroyed, and our tree speaker was murdered by tharuks. We ran out of supplies a moon ago."

Dragon's claws! "Where can I get some?"

"Many apothecaries have closed in the past moon. The Nightshader crew in Montanara are the only suppliers in this part of the realm. Their prices are so exorbitant only the richest people can afford healing."

Marlies' knees faltered. She grabbed the back of a chair.

"Marlies, you're pale." Leah patted the chair. "Sit down."

Marlies gratefully sunk onto the chair.

"I'll fetch you a cup of peppermint tea." Kisha whisked out to the kitchen.

"What do we do now?" Leah asked in low voice.

The Nightshader crew. Marlies had last faced them when she'd been younger, living in Montanara, and had just imprinted with Liesar. The leader back then had been Bruno, a nasty bully who'd terrorized the streets, even stealing from littlings. The same Bruno who'd become a master on the Council of the Twelve Dragon Masters, while she and Hans had been gone.

The same Bruno whose son had attacked Ezaara. And who, with his wife, had murdered two dragon masters.

Leah asked again. "What should we do, Marlies?"

Marlies turned to her. "We'll help Kisha clean up, then pay the Nightshaders a visit."

HOME AGAIN

Marlies neared Montanara in the middle of the night, Leah strapped in front of her, slumped over Liesar's spinal ridge, asleep, smoke and the scent of dead flesh lingering in the air. Oh, Gods, she was so weary. She'd hoped for a reprieve, a day's rest. A chance to see her parents for the first time in more than eighteen years.

She took a deep breath and squared her shoulders. In war, there was no time for reprieve. She'd have to take what she could get. Hopefully, a soft bed for Leah so the girl could sleep for a few hours before all chaos broke out. She squinted through the darkness. *"Liesar, what do you sense? Are there any friendly dragons around?"*

Liesar, concentrated, melding with a distant dragon. *"There's been a battle here today."* They neared the township, tendrils of smoke hanging in the air. Thankfully, there were no flames licking toward the sky. *"They're expecting more fighting."* Liesar winged over the rooftops, the occasional candle glimmering in a window, the street lanterns already dark.

"Thank the Egg, you can see better in the dark than I can," said Marlies. *"Do you think you can find my parents' home?"*

"I remember where they live."

It'd been so long. She'd stopped in a few times after becoming a dragon rider, but when she'd fled Dragons' Hold after killing Zaarusha's dragonet, she'd feared for her life and her family. She'd sent her parents a messenger bird once, telling them she was safe. But she hadn't dared tell them more and left no clue to her whereabouts.

Liesar spiraled down to land in her parents' back yard, her feet crunching in the snow.

A candle was burning in a bedroom window at the back of the house. Marlies slipped out of the saddle and padded through the snow to the back door. She lifted her hand to knock, and dropped it again. She didn't want to startle them…

No, that was an excuse. She was afraid to see them.

"Marlies, so fearless in battle. Surely you can face the ones you love. The ones you've missed for so long."

"I don't know how they feel about me."

"It's how you feel that's important. Do you still love them?'

"Of course."

"How would you feel if Tomaaz or Ezaara went missing for years, hesitated on your doorstep, then left?"

Devastated. Marlies rapped on the door.

Feet thudded their way toward the door. It opened and a candle flared, illuminating their familiar hallway and her father's worn face.

She gasped. Her spare cloak and healer's pouch were still hanging on the hook, right where she'd left them.

"Marlies?" Her father's brows flew up. He dropped the candle in the snow and flung his arms around her, pulling her tight against his chest. His voice cracked, "You're home. You're home again."

Moments later, she was sobbing in his arms. They clung to each other as the candle sputtered and died in the snow. She was home.

"Who's there? Where's the candle?" Ma's voice had aged. Fumbling came from the hallway. Ma appeared, another candle in hand. The years had been hard on Ma, but her radiant smile made her beautiful. She gasped, eyes wide, and thrust the candle at Pa. "You've had your turn. Hold this so I can hug my daughter."

Ma hugged Marlies, then pulled back to look her up and down. "You're as strong and beautiful as ever." Cheeks wet with tears, she hugged Marlies again.

Pa sucked in his breath. "Who's that sleeping on your dragon? Our granddaughter?"

Marlies smiled. "No. Leah's my trainee healer at Dragons' Hold. Ezaara, your granddaughter, is now Queen's Rider. Her twin brother, Tomaaz, is also a rider."

"Ezaara?" Ma said. "We've heard of her bravery, but by the Egg, I had no idea she was my granddaughter."

Marlies smiled. "Let me bring Leah in and I'll tell you everything."

§

Giddi rode at the head of his troop of dragons and riders toward Montanara, power trickling through his veins and coursing through his limbs. It was good to be back in the saddle—literally—as leader of the council on a fine young dragon who'd offered to be his charge. The creature had a delicate balance of courage and intelligence. His keen presence quivered in Giddi's mind as they soared through the dark.

Giddi mind-melded with Master Aidan, *"Any particular battle plan?"*

"It always scares the talons off me when you do that," confessed the battle master—a big admission for one who usually stood on ceremony. *"The plan is to get in, destroy those dragons and get out as fast as we can."*

So, no battle plan at all. Aidan hadn't seen those dark dragons. He didn't understand the power of their minds to shred all conscious thought.

"I suggest I practice mind blocking with mages and riders as we journey," Master Giddi said. *"Those screaming dragons make it impossible for riders to think."*

"Good idea."

Although effective mind blocking took hours of practice, most of the riders had only ever mind-melded with their own dragons, and never with anyone else—until Giddi had recently taught them how to block. Ripples of surprise spread across the troop each time he melded, practicing mind blocks with mages and riders.

He carefully shielded his true thoughts from them—that his own mind blocks hadn't helped him banish those dark dragons, had only reduced the effect of their screams. A little was better than the alternative, which was nothing at all.

§

Within an hour of Kierion's arrival at Dragons' Hold, Lars had dispatched Master Giddi, Master Aidan and Kierion with a troop of riders, dragons, and mages to fight dark dragons in Montanara. Now that the snow had stopped, the world below was silent and white. The rustle of dragon wings and the sighing wind made Kierion restless. He shifted in the saddle. Behind him, Fenni adjusted his grip.

His thoughts flitted to his friends. Hopefully Gret was all right back in Montanara with Danion. But his real concern was Adelina. Her last angry words rang in his head. He'd seen the hope on her face but been too ashamed to meet her gaze, flame it. And now he was fleeing under the guise of duty.

"Kierion, block me." Master Giddi's voice made Kierion flinch.

"You want me to practice mind blocking?"

"Yes. Try now."

He had to fix a picture in his mind, something important to him. Adelina's face popped into his head.

Master Giddi chuckled. *"That'll do as fine as anything. Although I wouldn't choose someone you care about or Zens' minions will torture her to get to you."*

Kierion shook his head and fixed his favorite tree in his mind, one he'd climbed as a littling. The tree burst into mage flame.

Master Giddi chuckled. *"Keep practicing. I'll pop back soon."*

A while later Kierion imagined his cat but was only able to hold the image for a few heartbeats longer.

"What about those archery targets you hate so much?" Riona asked. *"You stare at them so long, you should know them well enough."*

"Cheeky monster." Kierion slapped her hide. *"You know the worst thing?"*

"Aside from your archery? What?" He slapped her hide again, and she chuckled. *"What's troubling you, Kierion?"*

He sighed, letting Adelina's face flit to mind again. *"I didn't even talk to her."*

"Make sure you do next time," Riona said, amid the muted murmur of dragon wingbeats.

The next time Master Giddi jumped into Kierion's thoughts, Kierion took Riona's advice, holding one of Dragons' Holds' archery targets in his head. Pocked with arrow holes, the target had a white ring on the outside, blue middle ring, and a red rim around a black bullseye. Master Giddi jolted and shook the image, but it didn't budge. Kierion could feel the master mage trying to talk with him but blocked the intrusion with his target, imagining every arrow hole and scar on its pitted surface.

A soft whistle came from ahead. In a flare of mage light, Giddi turned on his dragon and tugged his ear.

Kierion let his block drop.

"At least you're listening now. I was trying to say well done."

"Thank you. I don't know how much mind blocking will help against these dragons," Kierion replied.

"Anything is better than nothing," Giddi said. *"Now, where can we rest these riders and dragons?"*

"Pa's farm would work."

"Good, lead the way."

By the time they reached Montanara, there were no signs of dark dragons in the night sky. Or in the surrounding countryside. Perhaps Danion and his riders had defeated them. Riona landed in the field next to Kierion's house, the dragons making gouges in the snow.

He and Master Giddi made their way to the farmhouse. The door opened and his father came out, holding up a lantern. "Kierion, it's you. Who have you brought with you?"

Kierion gestured at the master mage. "Dragon Mage Giddi, meet Pa. Pa, this is Dragon Mage Giddi."

Pa's jaw dropped. He shook Giddi's hand. "My pleasure, Master Giddi. I'll just get a bed ready for you and make a spot in the barn for your dragon." He held the lantern up higher to inspect Giddi's dragon.

A field of dragon scales winked in the light. "H-how many of you are there?"

"Only thirty or forty," Kierion replied.

Pa's brows raised.

"Most have blankets and bedrolls, so they can snooze in the barn," Kierion added. "The riders, I mean, not the dragons."

Pa grinned. "Let's get to work."

An hour later, after Kierion fried a bunch of eggs and bacon, and cut thick slabs of bread for the hungry dragon riders, they were all tucked up safely on bedrolls on the floor, in beds three apiece, or out in the barn in the hay.

Pa jerked his head toward the back door, motioning Kierion to follow.

Kierion stepped over sleeping riders on the living room floor, and went outside. "I know, Pa, I'm sorry. I should have given you notice. I should have—"

Pa waved a hand, cutting him off.

"From what those men and women said tonight, you're a bit of a hero. You captured an evil dragon and mage?"

Kierion shrugged. He wasn't used to praise from Pa. It tasted odd. "We do what we must to protect people and the realm."

"A tail flick? You always did have crazy ideas, Son." There was an awkward pause, then Pa clapped a hand on his shoulder and embraced him. "I'm proud of you."

Kierion's throat choked up. From wild prankster to someone his Pa was proud of. For once, he had no reply.

§

Marlies left Leah at home and visited the Montanarian warrior school to call upon her old friend, now the swordmaster.

Hands scarred from fighting, Louis threw his arms around her and hugged her. "Marlies? What a surprise. The years have been good to you."

She was pretty sure he was lying.

"Come in," he said, ushering her into an office with a ceremonial sword hanging on the back wall. "You may have run into my daughter at Dragons' Hold. Gret's her name."

"A fine rider, Louis. She has your eyes and your aptitude with a sword… although her hair's not as curly."

He gestured to two overstuffed armchairs. "Take a seat."

"Thank you." Marlies sat, and he took the other chair.

"I'm assuming that, in the midst of battle, you haven't come just to catch up. How can I help?"

"We've run out of piaua juice at Dragons' Hold. I'm master healer again, and we desperately need supplies to heal our wounded. Where can I get some in Montanara? Is old Maud still around?"

"Dead, a year now."

It had been too much to hope that the old healer who'd trained her was still alive. But even so…

Louis shook his head grimly. "The Nightshader crew have taken over supply of healing remedies in the city. The flaming criminals have priced everything at a premium."

So, Kisha was right. "And the Montanara guard? I thought they would've run them out of town."

"A new man, calls himself the Captain, set up shop here a couple of years ago. Took over Bruno's crew. A slippery fellow—hard to pin anything on him, although one of his assassins has gone to the gallows recently. He's a tough, old ex-pirate. Quick with a blade, and runs a tight ship—excuse the pun." Louis paused. "You're not going to see *him*, are you?"

Marlies sighed. "As unpleasant as it may be, I have no choice. We must find piaua juice or our riders will die in droves."

§

Marlies tugged her cloak around her against the swirling snow. Although magicked to protect her from damp, it was still cold. She trudged through soot-blackened slush passing dead tharuks, tusked snouts open and glassy red eyes staring at the overcast sky. More tharuks, very much alive, milled around the street, although it was early. She avoided their gazes, head down, striding to Nightshade Alley.

Memories cascaded through her of the time she'd fought Bruno—he'd been hurting littlings, stealing, and beating up Louis—back before Giant John had taught her and Louis to fight. Back before she'd met Liesar, or healed Master Giddi. Back when she'd been young and full of life.

Her bones ached. Curse those flaming berries.

Steeling herself, she strode up the steps to the Brothers' Arms. The building was just as she remembered it, although the paint was now faded and chipped, the gaudy sign weathered. Marlies stamped the snow off her boots and entered the tavern.

Yes, just the same. A few patrons, looking worse for wear, were seated at battle-scarred tables in the dingy interior. The place smelled of ale, and it was barely breakfast time. Her old archenemy Rona was serving behind the bar. With her own eyes changed to turquoise after years of riding Liesar, perhaps Rona wouldn't recognize her. Perhaps. Tugging her hood forward to obscure her face, Marlies swaggered up to the bar with a confidence she didn't feel. "I'm here to see the captain," she said in a tone that brooked no opposition.

Rona—now the proud owner of a nose ring and some badly-drawn dragon tattoos—squinted at her, then gestured to the door at the back of the taproom where Bruno's old headquarters had been. With a curt nod, Marlies strode across the tavern, knocked on the door, and stepped inside.

A dark-haired man sat at the far side of a table. Dragon tattoos on his forearms flexing, the captain dropped his cutlery onto a tray full of fried eggs, bacon and beans. His face broke into a feral grin, stretching the rough stitches on his cheek and exposing half a dozen blackened teeth. His eyes roved over her as if he owned her.

Filthy letch. That rankled.

The aroma of fried eggs and bacon made Marlies' mouth water.

Still grinning, he pulled a knife from his belt, and picked a scrap of bacon from his teeth. "How can I help you, fine lady?" He waggled his eyebrows suggestively.

"I've come to buy some piaua."

Suddenly, he was all business. He reached into his jerkin pocket and took out a slim vial of pale-green liquid.

Marlies' heart soared. At last. The captain passed her the vial. She stalked to the window and held it up to the light. "How much?"

"Oh, for you, pretty lady, only a dragon head."

A whole golden dragon head? Preposterous. Marlies uncorked the vial, and sniffed it. Just as she'd thought. "Smells like mighty expensive lime syrup to me."

The captain's heavy brows furrowed. "Who are you?" he demanded, rising from his chair, knuckles on the table.

"Someone in search of genuine piaua juice."

"Well, you're out of luck—unless you know a tree speaker. If you do, I'd be happy to pay a good price for some. Old Maud's supplies dwindled out last moon."

And sell it for ten times as much as he paid—she knew the Nightshader gang well enough.

"I'm a tree speaker," Marlies said, keeping her demeanor cool. Now, she had the power, something he wanted.

His eyes glinted. "Can you get me more piaua?"

Marlies inspected her fingernails, took a knife from her belt, and cleaned them. She flicked her eyes to him. "If the price is right."

She had no intention of giving this vile criminal piaua. She'd have to journey to the grove near the red guards, in the northwest. She'd found out what she needed to know. Her business was done here. "Thank you for your time, Captain, I'll be going."

There was a clatter on the roof of the tavern. *"Marlies, I'm here,"* melded Liesar. *"Just in case you need me."* Outside the window, a shingle crashed to the cobbles.

"I'm leaving now, Liesar. I won't need you but thanks."

The captain jerked his head around, yelling, "Shrotty dragons, landing on my tavern."

Behind Marlies, the door thudded open, and a deep voice said, "Your tavern?"

Oh Gods, she knew that voice—even though it'd been well over twenty years.

A blade was in the captain's hand before she could blink.

"Marlies, Unocco's in the square. Just warning you in case Bruno's around."

"Too late, I've already found him."

Liesar answered with a snarl in Marlies' mind.

Gods, if he recognized her... She kept her back to Bruno, staring at the captain.

The captain took a step, the table legs grating against the wooden floor. He jerked his chin up, leveling a challenging stare over Marlies' shoulder. "What do you mean?" the captain growled.

"Rona has been holding this crew together for me. She's done well. Tavern could use some paint, though."

The captain sneered, "You mean that lackey behind the bar? She don't hold nothing together. She's lucky I kept her on as barkeep."

Marlies nodded at the captain to take her leave, backing slowly out of the room

The captain's eyes flicked to her. "Wait right there. I can't let a pretty, precious resource like you walk out of my door, now, can I?"

She'd said too much. Made herself too valuable. Marlies swallowed.

"Who's she?" asked Bruno.

The captain shrugged. "Don't know." He grinned, his blackened teeth like ugly gravestones.

Quick as a whip, Marlies surged forward and flipped the tray of food up at Bruno's face. He screamed as hot beans dribbled down his neck.

She drew her knife and bolted. Bruno grabbed her cloak, whirling her around. She spun, kicking him in the chest. He went down. The captain bellowed, leaping across the table, and slammed her up against the wall. She kneed him hard in the groin, and he fell to a knee clutching himself. Marlies kicked him to the floor and ran out the door. She leaped and ran across tables through the tavern.

"*Watch out,*" Liesar called.

A silver-scaled foreleg hit the tavern window. Marlies ducked, covering her face. Glass imploded, flying across the taproom. She ran across the last two tables and leaped through the shattered glass, shards shredding her cloak.

Liesar's forearm was stretched down the building, bleeding, her hind legs gripping the roof. "*Quick, climb on my arm.*"

Marlies grasped Liesar's outstretched limb, but her hands slipped on the dragons' bloody scales.

"*I can't get any lower,*" Liesar said. "*Try again.*"

Marlies grabbed her forearm again. "*Lift me, Liesar. Quick.*"

Bruno jumped out the window and barreled into Marlies' legs. He yanked her by the waist, dragging her hands off Liesar. She crashed to the slushy cobbles, his body on top of her legs. She drove her fingers into his eyes and twisted.

Screaming, Bruno shifted his weight to one side. Marlies rolled toward him, kicking him off her. Then she leaped up and ran.

Liesar shot a jet of flame down the alley. People ran screaming. *"I can't reach him. This alley's too narrow,"* Liesar called. *"I'll meet you in the square."*

Panting, Marlies raced through the familiar alleys and streets of her old hometown, dodging civilians, horses and wagons.

Bruno's thudding boots echoed down the alley. Marlies ducked down a side street past a troop of snarling tharuks. Her chest hurt and her breath was short. Although she'd kept herself fit through all those years in hiding, she hadn't fought like this since she'd taken the piaua berries in Death Valley. *"Liesar, I can't fight Bruno. I don't have it in me."*

His heavy footfalls were was getting closer.

"I'm in the square, ready to leave. Hurry."

"Nearly there."

Bruno's breath rasped behind her.

One more corner and she'd be there.

A roar ricocheted between the buildings. Dark shadows fell over the street. Shadow dragons with piercing eyes. Bruno, lunged, tackling Marlies. She hit the cobbles with Bruno tangled in her legs. Marlies kicked his face. Rolled to her feet. And drew her sword.

He jumped up and freed his sword. He'd trained as a dragon rider. Was bound to be quick. And she was so ill. Already tired.

"After all these years, you thought you could beat me again," he sneered. "I've won, Marlies. My wife destroyed your healing supplies. Tharuks have destroyed the piaua trees. There's no hope for you or Dragons' Realm." He gave an ugly grimace. "Did you know my son has taken your daughter?" he taunted. "In a back alley in Naobia—and he's lusting for more."

Marlies almost gagged. She couldn't believe it. Ezaara would have told her.

Bruno leaped, thrusting his sword.

She parried, blades ringing. Marlies back-stepped. If she could get the last few paces into the square, Liesar could help her.

"Where are you, Marlies? Hurry."

"Nearly there." Marlies let Liesar see Bruno as he drove his sword at her. She deflected it, but her arms were tiring. Letting him think he had the advantage, she took another step back. Then another.

Bruno pressed forward. "Weak, that's what you are, Marlies. I'll best you yet."

He lunged as Marlies broke into the square. Her foot caught a patch of snow, and she stumbled. Bruno slashed at her. Pain burned along her left side. Marlies clutched it with her hand, parrying his next stroke. *"Liesar. Help."* Warmth trickled over her fingers.

"Bleeding like a stuck pig," Bruno crowed. I'd like to see you fight me now."

In a flash of silver, Liesar dove at Bruno.

OLD ENEMIES

Adelina had been silly, so absolutely stupid to flee Dragons' Hold and race after Kierion on a whim. And now, dark dragons were roaring over Montanara, making her break out in a cold sweat. *"I'll only be a moment, Linaia, then I promise we'll go and fight."*

"They need us. There are too many shadow beasts. Be quick." Her dragon was waiting on the outskirts of Montanara. Had been for a while.

"The baker on the corner said he'd seen a green-eyed mage and a blond man going in and out of this tavern. I've got to check." She raced along the alleyway.

"I've told you before, it'll be faster to meld with Riona and Hagret and find out if—"

"No! Sorry, please let me do this my way."

"Hurry."

She strode up the steps to the Brothers' Arms, tugged her cloth hat low and smoothed her peasant's tunic. Tharuks roared farther down the alley. War was raging in the skies above her. Kierion would be among the smoke, dark beasts, and bursts of bright flame, but Adelina didn't want to face him yet. Once she found out where he was staying, she could find him after she was done fighting. She pushed open the tavern door, her boots crunching on shards of glass.

Inside, tables were overturned. Someone was hammering planks over a broken window, remnants of snagged fabric fluttering on the edge of the sill. A man was sweeping glass, while men and women sat at tables, chugging beer as if the chaos of war were as normal as a village market. At the bar, a Naobian with a rugged scar on his cheek was staunching blood on a barkeep's face. Adelina's hand drifted to her hilt. Luckily, she'd missed the brawl. What in the Egg's name had Kierion been doing in a place like this?

"Someone, get a healer," the Naobian called.

"I have a little healing experience," she blurted without thinking.

The man's head whipped around. "Over here, then."

The woman's face was bloody, a piece of glass in her cheek. Adelina removed it and cleansed the wound, the female barkeep glaring and cursing the whole time. The scarred Naobian passed her a strip of cloth.

"I think she'll need stitches," Adelina said.

"Can you stitch her?" the man barked, his obsidian eyes flicking over her.

She shook her head. "No, but I can help you clean up the glass." She couldn't really ask him about Kierion like this. She'd planned to order a lemon water, have a quick chat with a bartender and see what she could glean. So much for that plan…

The man barked at the sweeper. "Brutus, take Rona to the healer, and give the broom to the girl."

Girl? Everyone always thought she was younger than she was, but Adelina buttoned her lip, and took the broom. She wouldn't get anywhere by irritating this man.

"Shrotty, trumped-up dragons." The man paced, grinding glass underfoot as Adelina swept. "Think they can land on my roof, scrape off my shingles, and smash my windows. Useless, cursed creatures. And now these black ones are scaring away business. Not that I can serve drinks without a barkeep. The only good thing that's happened to day is—" He whirled to face Adelina, eyes narrowing. "Know how to pour an ale?"

She stifled a smile. "I'm quick to learn." Now she had a reason to stay and find out more.

"Can you use a knife if things get rough?" His gaze darted to the weapons hanging off her belt.

She whipped a dagger out, twirled it and flung it into one of the new planks on the window, a hand's length above the head of the man hammering.

His eyebrows lifted, appraising her. "Good." He pursed his lips. "A copper an hour. You start now. My name's the Captain. Welcome to the Nightshader crew."

Adelina had guessed right—that weapons were his language. But the ruthless *Nightshaders?* Perhaps she'd be better off with shadow dragons.

Within moments, the captain installed her behind the bar. "You'll fit in with the Nightshaders well, Little One." He laughed and sauntered through a door at the back of the taproom.

Little One. Usually a title like that would rankle, but seeing the men's eyes roving over the other women in the bar, Adelina was glad she was small. That she looked too young. She tucked the pretty gold-and-scarlet dragon scarf—the one Kierion had given her for her name day—under her tunic. No point in advertising pretty wares.

Roars ricocheted through the alley outside.

"More dark dragons. Adelina, are you coming to fight?" Linaia asked.

Adelina padded over to the captain who was seated in a room with egg and beans mashed into the floorboards. "Before I start, I have some urgent business. Can I come back later?"

The captain flicked a piece of meat out of his teeth with his dagger. "Want the job or not?"

She'd spent hours combing Montanara looking for a trace of Kierion, with no results—except here. She couldn't miss him, not after coming so far. Not while Roberto was away. She didn't want to go back and face Amato.

She nodded and went behind the bar to pull ales. *"Riona, I can't come and fight today."*

There was an awkward pause, then Riona answered. *"Then I shall go alone."*

§

Snarls and a scream came from an alley. *"Be there soon, Hagret, I have to help."* Pulling her sword from its scabbard, Gret pounded the cobbles, arriving, just as a man severed a tharuk's head from its body.

Sword bloody, he bent down to a littling with a bloody gash on his cheek. "Go home and stay indoors. There's battle raging." The boy scampered off and the man straightened. His figure looked familiar.

"Donnell?"

"Is that you, Gret?" A familiar voice came from behind her. Gret spun.

Under the eaves of the house, hidden in shadow, was Trixia, her arrow nocked, ready.

Gret took in her flat belly, the absence of a baby, and hugged her. "Trixia, great to see you. Is your baby at home with your mother?"

Sadness, pain, regret and relief flitted across Trixia's face like an eddy of autumn leaves.

"What is it?" Gret asked.

Trixia's mouth opened and shut. And again.

Donnell stepped in. "We lost the baby."

"Oh, I'm so sorry."

Trixia shrugged. "I was, too, but I'm not. If that makes sense."

It did. Gret had always wondered how her best friend could stand to raise Simeon's baby after he'd forced himself upon her. "Stillbirth?" she asked.

Trixia nodded.

Roars raged from the alley around the corner.

Trixia's eyes swept over Gret's riders' garb, her archers' cloak. "Where's your dragon?"

"Waiting for me, so we can fight these dark dragons."

Donnell nodded. "We're fighting with arrows from the rooftops."

Trixia smiled. "And I'm coating them with poison."

Gret gave her a short sharp hug and grinned. "Excellent."

§

Simeon ran across the square. A dragon rider with dark hair was slumped against a building. Clutching her bleeding side, she held her wavering sword out, panting. A silver dragon flew at Bruno.

Simeon wasn't going to let a dragon get the better of him. "Father look up."

Seeing the dragon, Simeon's father ducked and rolled. Unocco roared and leaped for the silver dragon. Above the two fighting dragons, more roars broke out, dark shadows blotting the sky—Zens' lovelies, as Pa called them, had arrived.

Simeon ran over as Pa scrambled up, towering over the rider—a woman he'd never seen before. "Who's that, father?"

"It's the Queen's Rider's mother, you idiot. Maybe I should take her right now to show you how it's done."

Simeon stepped closer to his father, his blade ready.

The woman slid down the building to the slushy cobbles, still clutching her sword.

"She's injured." Pa toed her with his boot. "Maybe I'll just take the Queen's Rider next time I see her instead."

White-hot anger blazed through Simeon. He plunged his blade into his father's back. It punctured Pa's soft flesh. He rammed it in harder, feeling the sickening crunch of bone. As his father sank to his knees, Simeon drove the knife, slamming it with his full bodyweight until it was embedded in his father's back to the hilt.

Pa coughed. Poppy-red blood bubbling from his mouth, he sprawled to the cobbles.

A woman screamed.

"Unocco!" Simeon ran across the square past gaping onlookers. The dragon swooped to land. Placing his hand against the dragon's hide, Simeon gasped, *My father was evil, Unocco. You must know that. I promise I'll treat you better.*

"As much as I love him, it's good Bruno's dead." Unocco's sorrow at losing his rider swept over Simeon. *"Do you promise you won't give me more swayweed tea?"*

"*Of course not,*" Simeon lied and scrambled into the saddle, smirking as the foolish dragon sprang into the sky.

§

Gods, oh gods. Marlies took a breath, blood slick on her fingers as she clenched the searing wound in her side. Thank the Egg it wasn't her gut. Just muscle. But the blood loss had made her weak. She couldn't walk. Couldn't climb on Liesar to get back to Dragons' Hold. Or even get to Leah. She was stuck here, wounded in the square, fair prey for the next troop of tharuks. People were staring, pointing. At her. At Bruno's body. His blood staining the snow. Others rushed past, ignoring her. Liesar nudged her foot with her snout.

"*Liesar, fetch Leah.*"

"*Even better,*" her dragon replied. "*Hans is here.*"

Bronze scales flashed through the air. There was the thud of a dragon landing. Running feet. Hans' face appeared above her. "Marlies, I'm here. Talk to me." He unfastened her healing pouch from her waist and pulled out a tub of salve.

"Stitches, Hans," she murmured.

He nodded and threaded her needle with squirrel-gut twine. "Where's Leah?"

His keen eyes missed nothing. "My parents' place."

"Liesar and Taliesin can collect her," Hans said. "We need to get you back to Dragons' Hold."

"*I'm sorry, Hans,*" Liesar piped up. "*I'm not leaving Marlies. Handel will go.*"

There was a flurry of bronze wings and a breeze rippled Marlies' hair. She shivered. Hans tucked his cloak over the uninjured side of her body.

"*There's no one at Dragons' Hold who can help me, Hans.*" Melding was easier than speech.

"I know, that's why we're fetching Leah." He squeezed her hand. "We have to get you out of here. There's a raging battle above. The sooner we leave the better."

Then Marlies heard it again. She'd been in so much pain, she'd dismissed the snarling coming from nearby alleys, roars above and the roiling cloud of dark dragons, punctuated by flashes of color and bursts of fire.

Handel thudded back to the square. Leah ran over and took the needle from Hans. "You're going to be all right, Marlies. We'll have you fixed in no time."

Hans raised a eyebrow. "*I wonder who she learned that from.*"

Despite the pain throbbing in her side, Marlies smiled.

§

Although Leah had stitched her and bandaged her, pain lanced across Marlies' torso whenever she moved. Hans lifted her, cradling her in his arms. "Let's get you back to Dragons' Hold before the square erupts."

"Piaua" Marlies murmured.

Hans shook his head. "Remember, Marlies, there is no piaua."

He'd misunderstood her. "That's what I meant. We must search for piaua."

"You're not well enough. It'll have to wait."

Leah squeezed her hand. "I can seek piaua, and when I find a tree, I'll speak to it and harvest the juice. You'll just have to tell me how."

"I need to tell you anyhow." Marlies beckoned her closer and whispered instructions in her ear.

Eyes wide, Leah nodded.

At Hans' side, Taliesin straightened. "I'll go with you," he said. "We're young, so no one will think we're carrying anything valuable."

Hans shook his head. "No, we're training you as our successors. We can't lose you."

Leah planted her fists on her hips. "Successors need experience. If I don't learn how to harvest piaua, many lives will be lost. Look at those beasts." She flung a hand skyward at the shadow dragons roaring above Montanara. "We need every rider we can get. If I don't try, none of us will be alive. None of this will matter."

"*She has a flair for the dramatic,*" Hans melded.

"*But she's right, Hans. We need piaua juice if we're to fight an endless army of Zens' beasts. These black dragons are pouring out of Death Valley as fast as Zens can create them. We only have limited riders and dragons.*"

Marlies squeezed Leah's hand. So brave, but so young.

Leah squeezed back. "Master Marlies, I beg you, please. We'll find the piaua and save our people."

Taliesin piped up, "I've just had a vision. If Leah goes alone, she'll die, but with me, there's a much higher chance we'll survive and bring back what we need."

Hans' eyes flicked from Marlies to the two young ones. He nodded. "All right. One of our dragons can—"

"Marlies!" A deep voice rang through the square. A huge figure rushed over to Marlies, his enormous frame dwarfing Hans. "Marlies are you injured?" Giant John shook his head. "A stupid question, I know. Will you be all right?"

She smiled through gritted teeth. "Sure, John, I'm as bright as a vase of daffodils."

His eyes darted to her bloodstained side. "Nothing a bit of piaua won't cure, I hope."

Hans sighed. "We're out. There's none here either."

"Out of piaua?" John's eyebrows shot up. "Even you?"

Marlies nodded. "The tree in Lush Valley has been hewn down and destroyed. Same with the ones in Spanglewood."

"Those cursed tharuks," John said. "If only I were a tree speaker, I'd go to the red guards myself."

That was it! "Giant John, meet Leah, a young tree speaker, and Taliesin." She hesitated.

"What is it?"

Hans spoke for her, knowing Giant John had risked his life for Marlies before and that it was hard for her to ask again. "Giant John, are you willing to take Leah and Taliesin to search for piaua juice?"

Giant John thumped his fist on his chest and nodded. "It'd be my pleasure." He glanced down at Marlies. "Hans, I suggest you get your wife to Dragons' Hold as soon as possible."

He beckoned the young ones. "Grab your things and come with me."

§

Kierion's mighty dragon Riona dove as he fired arrows. Fenni shot flames left, then right, at shadow dragons whirling through the skies. Riona ducked, avoiding yellow rays from a dark dragon's eyes. Then she spun to blast the beast with her flame.

Screams echoed hollowly in Kierion's head, a constant throb and ebb of pain. He'd long since given up mind blocking. Or melding with Riona. It was shoot, duck, race in and dart out. He shot another arrow, catching the edge of a dark wing.

A mage leaned out over the dragon—another fake Sorcha. A volley of mage fire shot from his hands, straight for Kierion. Fenni countered it with a wall of ice.

Danion's dragon plunged after a shadow beast, blazing flame. Maazini was a whip of orange, heading toward the forest.

Riona spun to dive into the fray again.

Far out on the horizon, another swarm of dark dragons was approaching.

§

Something about those shadow dragons nagged at Tomaaz's mind.

"What is it?" Maazini asked as Tomaaz nocked an arrow to his bow and headed back into the fray above Montanara.

"I don't know, they seem familiar."

A dark dragon loomed, opening its maw, and blasting flame that licked at Maazini's talons.

Maazini spun and shot up above the dragon so Tomaaz could loose an arrow at its wings. But the mage on its back blasted green flame at Maazini. Blistering heat rolled over them.

Jael leaned out, sending ribbons of fire into the dragon's hide. It screeched and shot away.

"I need water," Maazini croaked.

"To the river, then. Go, before we're attacked again." Tomaaz hunched low in the saddle as Maazini flew away from the battling dragons, soared over the trees, and crunched down in the snow on the riverbank on the edge of Spangle-wood Forest.

Tomaaz slid out of the saddle to fill his own flaccid waterskin. He'd drunk his fill long before Maazini was finished, so he passed the skin to Jael and paced by the riverbank, snacking on a stick of smoked sausage. He ran a keen eye over his dragon's hide, looking for injuries. Aside from a few small scratches, Maazini appeared to be in good shape. Thank the Egg for that. With no piaua, any wound could be fatal.

Maazini turned his head. "Have you finished admiring my fine shape?"

"Shape, that's it! Those dark dragons have Maazini's shape."

Maazini cocked his head. *"Are you sure?"*

Jael nodded. "You might be right."

"Hold your head like that again. No, tilt it on that angle, as if you're going to ask me a question."

Maazini obliged.

There was no doubt about it, with that head shape and their bulk, the dragons were somehow related to Maazini.

Maazini snorted. *"It's not as if Zens grows dragons from seeds, you know. They can't all look the same. Dragons have differences, like Erob's size or Singlar's large horns. Are you sure you're not mistaken?"*

"Let's take another look at those dragons," Tomaaz said aloud for Jael's benefit, and swung into the saddle.

"Look?" Jael replied. "I won't be looking, I'll be blasting those dragons from the sky."

Tomaaz nocked an arrow. "As will I." They ascended, and he braced himself for their awful mind-splitting screams as they headed back into the roiling heart of the battle.

Yes, every one of Zens dark dragons had the same head shape, approximately the same size and even similar talons. They were all black—exactly the same unnatural hue.

Maazini whipped out with his tail, lashing a dark dragon's wing. *"Well, we know they're unnatural,"* he said. *"But what can we do about it?"*

They climbed high above the cloud of dragons, looked down on several dark dragons. Yes, he was right. They all looked like Maazini. Roberto had said the dark dragons had been grown in tanks inside a cavern deep in the earth. He must grow them from something—not seeds, but something. Perhaps Zens had somehow harvested the flesh and bone to grow dragons from Maazini while he was captive.

If that was true, then these evil dragons were all somehow Maazini's brothers and sisters.

And they were all screaming continually as if they were in constant pain.

Jael broke into Tomaaz's musings, calling, "Over there, look. Something strange is going on." He pointed to a gap that had been smashed in the trees by a fallen blue dragon. A prone rider and mage, flung from the saddle were lying nearby. A cloaked figure was bending over one of the riders.

A looter? Or maybe a friend, grieving. Something furtive about the figure's movements made Tomaaz pause.

"I don't like the look of that," Jael muttered.

"Land over there behind those trees, Maazini. I don't want to be seen."

Maazini had never landed so softly. He and Jael slipped from the saddle and sneaked through the forest.

They peeked around the trunk of a strongwood. Jael stifled a gasp.

The man was cutting locks of hair from the dead mage, chopping off her fingers and taking slices of her dark, Naobian skin. He shoved everything into a pouch hanging from his belt.

"Hey, what are you doing?" Tomaaz yelled, aiming an arrow.

The man spun, hands dripping mage blood. It was Old Bill—the man who'd beaten Lovina and drugged her. Tomaaz loosed his arrow at Bill's heart.

Bill dropped and rolled, then was up, sprinting. Before Tomaaz could fire again, Old Bill put his fingers in his mouth and whistled. A dark dragon swooped down, plucked Bill in its talons, and flew off, Bill's feet bashing snow from the branches of a strongwood.

Jael sent a streak of mage fire after them. It missed Bill and the dragon, hitting the branches, which burst into flame.

"Maazini, chase them."

Maazini roared and took to the air, flapping valiantly. After a few moments, he flew back down. *"They're too far ahead. I'm not leaving you two here, with tharuks prowling."*

Jael incinerated the dead mage's body. He shook his head. "Her name was Sovita. She was so young and sweet, barely seventeen summers. I was hoping when she was older—" He looked up, tears glazing his eyes.

Tomaaz's heart clenched. The girl had been someone special to Jael.

This war could take everyone they loved.

THE CAPTAIN

Ezaara squinted, shading her eyes with her hand. A swarm of dark dragons was visible far from Montanara.

"It's going to be a tough battle," Roberto melded, *"with our dragons weary and already having fought in Lush Valley."*

"I was thinking exactly the same," Ezaara said. *"It's good your father is no longer with us. One less person to worry about."* Ma was ahead somewhere, perhaps stuck in the battle. Was Tomaaz there too, and all the other riders she'd come to care about so deeply?

Why had they tarried so long in Lush Valley? In hindsight, it seemed silly that she, as Queen's Rider, had stayed behind to tend the wounded. But Ma had needed to seek piaua.

Hopefully she'd found some, although Ezaara wasn't holding out much hope. In a couple of short weeks, Dragons' Realm had been overrun with tharuks. And now these dark dragons… It wasn't easy being Queen's Rider. The heavy mantle of responsibility weighed upon her shoulders.

"It isn't easy being Queen's Rider, but you have the ability," Zaarusha said. *"Let's purge these beasts and make our realm safe again."*

Their dragons sped on toward Montanara.

Plumes of smoke hung above the city and nearby trees. Dark dragons were sweeping and diving down toward Spanglewood. Riders were holding them off as well as they could.

Roberto melded as he and Erob peeled off. *"We'll help fight in the forest."*

Zaarusha snarled, *"We stay together."*

"Everyone's fighting without me," Ezaara melded. *"As Queen's Rider, I should have been here for our people."*

"Too late for regrets now," Zaarusha said. *"You were serving your people in Lush Valley. And that was your home."*

True, she'd helped people she'd loved and grown up with.

Zaarusha dove down toward a black dragon chasing a young blue. She stretched out her talons and plucked the rogue mage from the dark's back and flung him into the trees. Then she shredded the dragon's wings with her talons. The beast plummeted, and Zaarusha sent a gust of flame after it.

A fireball shot toward Zaarusha; a mage on another dark dragon zoomed by them. The roiling ball of fire flew over Ezaara's head as she ducked. Screams pounded her mind.

"Block your mind," Zaarusha shrieked, cutting off mind-meld.

Ezaara steeled her mind, envisioning her home in Lush Valley. Surely there was a better way? She could mind-meld with any dragon, perhaps she could reach out and try to subdue these ones.

She risked mind-melding with Erob, Roberto and Zaarusha again. *"What do you think?"* The pain in her head was almost too much, but she had to try. *"Should I meld with these dragons and try to subdue them?"*

"I've been thinking the same," Roberto replied. *"Wondering if we could gain mental control over them."*

"We?"

"You're the only person that can meld with all dragons," Roberto said. *"And the dragons can meld with each other. So why don't I support you, chime in?"*

Zaarusha roared, blasting fire that punched through a wall of flame cast by two dark mages. *"Do it. Anything has to be better than this,"* the Queen rumbled.

Ezaara gritted her teeth. She melded with the blue dragon farthest out, another scream piercing through her thoughts. And then with Riona, no more than a purple flash on the horizon amongst a swarm of dark dragons. And then with a green. Maazini. And another dragon.

And another. And another.

And when she could hear the babble of dragon thoughts from their own dragons and the relayed screams of the dark dragons ripping through their minds, she opened her senses and reached out for Zens' dark beasts.

There was a howl in Ezaara's head. An incessant shrieking, like thousands of swords clashing.

A hurricane of anguish, it shredded not only her ears, but her heart. Her very being.

The screams sunk deep, dragging the tattered shreds of her down.

Until she was drowning in a whirlpool of anguish.

§

Roberto tried to hold steady, tried to hold his mind open for Ezaara. With all the strength he and Erob could muster, he supported her, but the magnitude of the noise in her head drowned out his own thoughts. His own senses. Who he was.

He was losing himself in a deep pit of black.

Like the string on a bow stretched too taut, their mind-meld snapped, sending Roberto's thoughts spinning.

With a scream that pierced the battle-torn sky, Ezaara slumped over Zaarusha's spinal ridge, her eyes rolling back in her head and her hands hanging limp.

"Erob, quick. We must get Ezaara back to Dragons' Hold,"

Erob sidled alongside Zaarusha.

Roberto made the leap onto Zaarusha's saddle. He pulled Ezaara against his chest and cradled her in his arms. He slapped Zaarusha's hide, not daring to mind-meld. Then he rubbed the ring on his finger, calling, "Kisha."

With a pop, they disappeared, leaving the smoking, raging battle behind them.

§

A dark dragon flew at Tomaaz, talons out.

Tomaaz blocked his mind, locking in a picture with all his senses, as Master Giddi had taught.

The mage riding the dark dragon fired a short, yellow-tipped arrow at them. Then another and another.

Maazini swerved, but was too late. An arrow pierced the dragon's neck scales.

It was only a superficial cut and the strange arrow was only the length of Tomaaz's hand. He pulled the arrow shaft. It tugged free—without the arrowhead.

Before his eyes, the arrowhead, made of yellow crystal, burrowed into the flesh under Maazini's scales. As if it were alive. Digging deeper.

Horrors! An arrow that dug itself into flesh?

Tomaaz grasped his knife, trying to prize out the arrowhead.

It was now buried a finger's-length deep in Maazini's flesh.

Maazini bucked and writhed, blasting flame at the dark dragon, driving it back.

Tomaaz's knife was slick with his dragon's blood. He fumbled. The blade slipped, plummeting past his boot toward the trees.

He whipped out his bow and loosed an arrow, hitting the mage's chest. Another struck the mage's throat.

The dark dragon swung its head. Bright-yellow rays flew from its eyes, brushing near Maazini.

Maazini spurted past the dragon, lashing downward, swinging his mighty tail. It smacked the dark dragon's head, cleaving its skull. With a screech and a plume of mage fire large enough to incinerate a house, the dragon and rider plunged into the treetops, impaled and twitching.

Tomaaz risked melding with Maazini, *"Are you all right, boy?"*

Black shadows twisted his dragon's mind. An anguished scream ripped through Maazini.

Tomaaz whipped his head around. Surely, that dragon wasn't still melded with Maazini? He probed deeper, agony ripping through his head. A cry of desolation and pain rippled through him.

As Maazini flailed, losing height, yellow rays sprang from his eyes, slicing the top off a tall spruce.

By the dragon gods!

Maazini wasn't melding with another dragon. The shadows and screams were Maazini's own.

§

Dark dragons were flying in thick and fast, blasting flame and slicing through riders and dragon's wings with their yellow-beamed eyes. Master Giddi flung out his hands. A swathe of emerald fire erupted from his fingertips, engulfing a shadow dragon until it was a molten, flapping fireball. It screeched, plummeting to the earth, its cry reverberating through Giddi's head.

It was no good, they were coming too thick and fast. Although his magic was holding some of them at bay, his mages were flagging, their energy far spent.

Beside him, Kierion wheeled on Riona and Fenni blasted another dragon. Kierion's arrow hit another beast in the head, but the flailing beast nicked the edge of Riona's wing.

Shrieks rent the air—Dragons' Realm's dragons wounded and in pain. It was hard to see who, with everything bursting into flame around him. Giddi swung out his arms, and blasted another diving shadow dragon, knocking its fake mage into the air.

Ahead, a blue dragon roared as it bowled into a dark dragon. Wings wrapped around each other and talons thrashing, they clenched their maws around each other's necks, plummeting to the ground engulfed in fire. The blue rider leaped free, to be swooped up by another blue and flown off to safety.

Giddi swallowed—that noble blue dragon had sacrificed its life to bring the dark beast down. But many more stunts like that, and they wouldn't have any dragons left.

Aidan blew a battle horn. Archers released arrows from dragonback. Some of the archers split off from the formation to fly high, some low, and some charging at the center of the mass of dark dragons. Their formations and tactics could be an advantage. The dark dragons were flying in snapping, warring, disorganized chaos.

Jael and Tomaaz bucked and thrashed on Maazini. Something was wrong, but Giddi had no time to ponder what because a black dragon soared past and shot a volley of flame at his dragon. A blue charged in to blast the dark beast as Giddi's trusty dragon swerved to rejoin the troop.

Screams from dark dragons sliced through his thoughts—and he was an experienced mind blocker. Hopefully the other mages were holding out. Despite the noise in his head, Giddi mind-melded with each mage, one by one, buoying them up. *"You're doing well. Be careful to stay out of the range of their eyes. Slowly but surely, we'll get there."*

When he melded with Fenni, Fenni replied, *"Riona saw shadow dragons heading over the city. Kierion and I are going to track them down. Watch out for the swarm advancing on the horizon."*

Giddi glanced up. A seething mass of shadow dragons was racing toward them. *"Stay safe,"* he answered, ducking in his saddle to avoid a yellow ray. He melded with Aidan, *"We've killed nearly all of this lot, but more are coming. I'll get to the front with a group and face them, head on. You take any that get through."* He cut through the swarm of chaos, a group of riders following him. The mass of dark dragons loomed.

Giddi melded with all the mages at once. *"Incoming shadow dragons. Work our plan."*

Danion peeled off from their formation, sweeping up, a handful following to blast flame at the foul beasts from above. More swooped low, staying together. Still more shot out to each side.

"Hold steady," Giddi told his mages. *"And now, fire."*

A wall of mage flame sprang up in front of them, obliterating their view of the dragons.

The top troop blasted a ceiling of fire at the beasts, and from below the low-flying group sealed them in with a floor of fire. More fire erupted from the sides. These creatures had to retreat or be burned.

"And push," Giddi yelled in their minds. Above the dragons' screams in their heads, shrieks and howls rent the air. Giddi's head wanted to explode.

The heat was blistering.

"Hold fast!" Those stalwart mages held the line.

A gust of orange fire burst through the mage's crackling wall of green flame, taking down a blue guard. The dragon's flaming carcass plummeted into the snow-topped trees with a sizzle and plume of steam.

Sweat ran down Giddi's brow. The heat singed his hair. His throat was parched. And still, he pushed out the *sathir,* trying to burn the invading dragons to a crisp. Gradually the screams in his head died down, and only a faint echo remained.

Nothing was alive in that inferno.

"Stop now."

The walls of crackling, green mage fire flamed out. Chunks of char and cinder fell down onto the forest, spattering the snow with dark flakes.

Giddi's magic was nearly drained. He flicked his gaze to the North and South where only a few dark dragons remained, chased down by the remainder of the blue guards and Danion's troop.

It was over. They'd beaten most of Zens' onslaught.

Giddi slumped on the neck of his dragon, exhausted, and wrapped his arms around a spinal ridge. He melded with Aidan. *"Lead the troops back to Montanara. Send three or four riders to patrol the forest and make sure there are no more shadow dragons or fake mages and pick up any stranded mages or riders."*

"And you?"

"I'll do one more patrol to make sure there are none left. I'll see you back at Kierion's farm later, for a well-deserved ale."

§

The snow on the Montanarian rooftops was gouged with black and red. Cries of the wounded carried on the air to Kierion, Fenni and Riona. They patrolled the outskirts, hunting for dark dragons, then flew over the center of town. Down in the square, bodies littered the streets. Tharuks were fighting Montanara's warriors, roars and the clash of weapons punctuating the cries of the wounded.

"Look. What's that?" Fenni pointed from behind Kierion's shoulder at a dark blob on a distant rooftop, snow blazing orange in the sunset.

"Over there, Riona, swoop closer." Riona let out a weary rumble and angled her wings to dive.

A dark dragon was feasting on the body of a dead civilian. Kierion nocked his bow and aimed.

"Wait." Fenni clenched his shoulder. "Who's that?"

A figure clambered onto the rooftop and crept up behind the dark dragon. It was the captain of the Nightshaders. He drew his cutlass and sneaked up on the dragon, raising it to hack at the beast's throat.

The black dragon spun its head and belched flame at the captain's boots.

The captain nimbly leaped aside and ran across the rooftop. Snarling, the dragon chased him. The captain leaped to the next roof. The dragon pounced and landed a body length behind the captain.

The Nightshader leaped again, feet churning up snow as he slipped on the steep rooftop. He slid down the incline, his legs slipping over the edge, his hands leaving gouges in the snow. The captain caught the gutter, and hung suspended over Nightshade Alley.

The dark dragon let out an unearthly, roof-shaking roar. Clumps of snow drifted down to the alley. It perched on the edge of the adjacent rooftop and opened its mighty maw, lowering its head toward the captain.

Kierion stowed his bow and arrow and whipped out his sword as Riona swooped. Landing on the dragon's back, Riona shredded its wings with her talons. Chunks of wing fluttered down, one landing on the captain's shoulder, like a cloak. The captain's hand slipped, and he hung from the gutter by one arm.

Riona belched fire, fastening her jaws on the beast's throat. Fenni blasted its body with mage fire while Kierion slid along Riona's neck. He leaned out and plunged his sword through the beast's thrashing head. He hung on with his legs locked around Riona's neck and drove the sword through the beast's brain until the quillions smacked its skull. Panting, Kierion hung on.

The beast groaned and slumped to the rooftop.

Kierion straightened. "Captain," he called.

The captain glanced up, shock on his face—the first real emotion Kierion had seen from the leader of the Nightshaders.

Riona turned and held her tail out, laying it on the neighboring roof, forming a bridge between the two buildings. The captain hoisted himself up and clambered along her tail. He scrambled onto the roof and fell to his knees, gasping. "You? A dragon rider?" His eyes narrowed. "Flames and golden dragon heads, now I owe you a life debt."

"Indeed, you do." Kierion hoisted him into the saddle. "What were you doing up here?"

"I hate it when dragons land on my roof."

Riona tossed her head, and took to the sky. The dead dragon's blood dripped down the side of the building, already forming a dark pool in the alleyway.

§

Zens rubbed the ring and felt the *sathir* vibrate. But something was missing. Something essential for opening a portal.

This wasn't what he'd been searching for—this wasn't a talisman to a world gate like Master Giddi had opened with Mazyka all those years ago at Mage Gate. The gate that had let Zens into this realm.

And then closed, trapping him here forever.

He held the ring to the light, sensing its *sathir*.

This was something more subtle. Smaller magic. As 000 had said, perhaps this would take him through Dragons' Realm.

These mortals often used passwords to activate talismans. He gave a bemused smile. These people often went for simplistic words, like names. Perhaps Mazyka's name. He tried it. Nothing happened.

Perhaps the new Queen's Riders name? "Ezaara," he murmured, but still nothing happened.

"Zaarusha." Nothing again.

"Anakisha." *Sathir* hummed faintly in his mind. Then flickered and died.

"Ana… kisha," he said, slowly rolling each syllable off his tongue. On the second half of the name, a shimmering glow enveloped him. He flinched at the brightness and dropped the ring. The glow disappeared.

Zens picked up the jade talisman and turned it over in his hands. Interesting find.

All he had to do now was fetch his methimium ray.

§

Giddi slumped over his dragon's spinal ridge. He was bone tired. Weary, right down to the vibrations in his bones. It was worth it. As reinstated leader of the Wizard Council, *this time* he'd saved Dragons' Realm. The war wasn't over yet, but at least, this battle had been won.

A crack, like a quiet clap of thunder, sounded above him. Wearily, Giddi gazed up.

Bathed in a blaze of golden light, a dark dragon loomed.

It'd appeared out of nowhere. A vaguely-familiar rider was perched in its saddle. An unusually large rider with a bald head and bulging yellow eyes. Commander Zens—grinning triumphantly.

"Master Giddi, I've long awaited the opportunity for us to work together. I appreciate your talents. I would never ban you from the Wizard Council or force you to lock out your beloved wife. Come, work with me. Let's better Dragons' Realm."

Giddi mind-blocked as the next barrage of Zens' insidious thoughts hit his head. He locked Mazyka's beloved face in his mind. It made no bones—Zens knew who she was, and she was now safe in Zens' old world. Zens hammered his head relentlessly, trying to get in. Sweat beaded on Giddi's brow.

Not now, when his reserves were low and he was exhausted. He gritted his teeth, staving off Zens' commands.

Another dark dragon shot through the glowing clouds, a fake mage on its back with a nocked arrow. The dragon wheeled behind Giddi, but the dragon mage didn't dare tear his gaze from Commander Zens. Clutching the dragon's spinal ridge, his forearms corded with tension, Giddi pushed Zens out of his head.

Sharp pain pierced Giddi's shoulder. Then his lower back. And his other shoulder. Something sharp and painful dug inside his body. Three somethings, burrowing into his skin. Searing burning paths through his flesh and muscle. Gods, by the flaming holy dragons gods. He screamed, arching his back. Giddi's mind block shattered. Mazyka's face exploded into thousands of tiny shards which were swept away by dark tendrils.

Shadows whirled through Giddi's mind, mist lurking at the edges of his vision.

"Listen to me, Master Giddi. I now control you." Zens' voice was the most alluring thing Giddi had ever heard.

Commander Zens descended from a gate of billowing golden clouds upon the large dark dragon with fiery yellow eyes. Zens extended a hand.

"Welcome to my army, Master Giddi. Climb upon my dragon." His melodious voice slithered inside Giddi's mind and wrapped itself around his senses like soft dark velvet.

Giddi's arms dropped to his side. His legs moved, clambering upon his dragon's saddle in a crouch.

His body tensed.

No. He fought it, trying to withstand Zens' command.

"Jump, Giddi. Come with me." Zens smiled, beckoning him with a welcoming hand.

Giddi sprang, landing on the back of Zens' saddle.

And wrapped his arms around the monster he'd been fighting for years.

Even as he struggled to withstand Zens' commands, pain radiated from the new channels in his back and shoulders, darkness spreading through him. Bit by bit, he summoned his magic. Tiny lights flitted inside him. But darkness smothered them and they winked out.

He'd wanted to face this monster for years. And now he couldn't even summon a spark. Slumping against the commander's back, Giddi held on, his arms not his own.

Commander Zens rubbed one of Anakisha's travel rings and muttered, "Kisha."

A pop sounded and Spanglewood Forest and Montanara disappeared.

THE BROTHERS' ARMS

The Brothers' Arms got busier than she'd expected that evening. A steady stream of patrons came to drink—or do business with the captain in his back office. Most of them were clientele Adelina would rather not face on a dark street alone.

When the first tharuk stormed into the bar demanding a free ale, Adelina resisted the urge to whip out her dagger. She turned the tap, frothy, amber beer spilling into the tankard, and passed it to the monster with barely a glance. It was a rough tavern, all right, but the only thing she'd managed to glean about Kierion since the morning was that lately he'd frequented the tavern. More tharuks followed and soon they were three-deep at the bar. She raced back and forth, serving beer to the tusked monsters.

At some stage in the evening, there was a terrible clatter on the roof—a dragon, she guessed. The captain muttered and stomped out. Roars shook the tavern walls and thuds rattled the rooftop—maybe two dragons fighting. Patrons paused for a heartbeat, glancing at plaster dust raining from the ceiling, then their raucous laughter broke out again and they kept drinking, playing cards and nukils.

Linaia? No answer. Her dragon must still be out of range. Or hunting after fighting. Hopefully she was all right. Adelina should've been riding her today. She'd pledged to fight to protect Dragons' Realm, not stand here with aching feet in some shrotty bar serving beer to her enemies.

The door swung open, and three soot-covered men and a woman stalked inside, hoods up. She readied a tankard, but they didn't even glance her way, sweeping through the bar to the captain's lair.

"You. More beer." A tharuk blasted fetid breath over her.

Trying not to wrinkle her nose, Adelina poured another ale.

§

Danion had his arm slung around Gret again. He tilted his head and murmured something in her ear. She giggled.

Fenni stifled a snort. She didn't have to make it look so realistic. He battled to control the magic sizzling at his fingertips.

Kierion nudged Fenni. "Watch it, you're leaking."

Fenni curled his hands into fists. They were heading toward the Brothers' Arms. As if they weren't exhausted enough after battling dark dragons and mages, the captain had called a meeting. Fenni wondered idly what it was about.

His eyes slid away from Gret. Did she have to put her arm around Danion's waist? Their body language was too familiar—good enough to fool anyone. Even him, and he knew Gret didn't like Danion. At least that's what she said. The leader of the Montanarian dragon corps had broad shoulders, thick dark hair, a ridiculously handsome face, and an easy laugh. So different from him.

Fenni kicked a lump of snow at the edge of the alley. It flew against the facade of a bakery with a thwack, crumbling. He couldn't assume Gret liked him as much as he liked her. It'd been an age since they'd danced together at Ezaara and Roberto's hand-fasting ceremony. Maybe she *had* fallen for the flashy rider.

Although, when the three of them were together, planning, or with Danion's men, Danion never laid a hand on Gret.

But that didn't stop her eyes from following him around the room.

These thoughts did him no good. They only stoked the jealousy burning in his gut. Fenni trudged up the steps behind Kierion, Danion and Gret, and entered the Brothers' Arms.

§

Kierion strode across the busy tavern, past a window that had been boarded up, toward the captain's back room. The captain was alone, pacing behind the table. In the bright glow from the candles on the candelabra, Kierion noticed a yellow dribble down one of the walls. Not that it was dribbling now. Something runny had dried and hardened there. He edged toward it, curious. Egg. That, and the broken window they'd just seen in the taproom were sure signs of a brawl here earlier today.

Face as dark as a thundercloud, the captain glowered as he sat down at his table.

Thank the Egg, Danion let go of Gret, guiding her to a seat between Danion and Fenni. Kierion didn't want Fenni burning the whole place down.

The captain's obsidian eyes glittered, raking over Kierion. He addressed Danion, "Seems this boy's been hiding things from us."

Danion palmed his knife and twirled it. "Has he, now? We can't have that."

Even though Kierion knew Danion was acting, sweat still broke out on his neck.

"Yes, he's a dragon rider."

Danion's eyes were mean slits. "Want me to deal with him, boss?"

The captain snarled. "It just so happens that this dragon rider saved my life. I owe him a rutting life debt. Make sure he's not harmed in any way."

Danion's face froze. "Yes, Captain. I'll protect him."

"These dark dragons and mages are bad for business," the captain said. "We're losing trade. People are afraid to come out of their homes. We need to defeat or kill them." The captain thumped a fist on the table. "Find me more dragon riders, Kierion."

Danion leaned back, rubbing Gret's shoulders. He gave a winsome smile. "How do you propose he does that, sir?"

"You can help him, by any means you please." The captain flashed an ugly black toothed grin.

Danion gave him a matching grin, but not nearly as ugly.

Gods, if Kierion didn't know better, he'd think Danion was out to murder dragon riders. Kierion's head spun. Luckily, Fenni kept his mouth shut. Kierion whipped his dagger from his belt and spun it on his fingertips. "What if I brought more dragon riders into the Nightshaders? Would that please you, sir?" He flicked the dagger under his fingernails, soot flying onto the captain's scarred table.

The captain narrowed his eyes, voice soft and menacing, "Just what are you planning, Kierion?"

"If I do manage to persuade dragon riders to join us, what can you offer them?"

The captain's chuckle was like a rockslide. "Whatever you want."

§

Adelina was in the middle of pulling a beer for a huge tharuk when the strangers strolled out of the captain's office. Hoods off now, there was a handsome dark-haired man with his arm around a blonde woman, a mage trailing sparks and a man with—

It was Kierion. She braced herself, ready to call out, but his eyes swept past her as if she wasn't even there. He swaggered across the tavern. He'd seen her without a flicker of recognition.

Sure, with her hat pulled down over her face and without riders' garb on, she looked different. But surely a man who loved her would have known who she was. She was about to call out, when she noticed the captain scrutinizing her. By letting on she knew him, would she put him in danger? She grabbed a cloth and began wiping beer and tharuks' spittle off the bar.

Maybe he had recognized her. Maybe she'd hurt him too much. Destroyed his tender feelings for her. Between tharuk grunts and slurps, her own harsh words echoed in her ears, *"Flame you, Kierion. I don't know if we killed Seppi by taking him out into the snow."* She'd practically accused him of murder, when he'd only been trying to help.

Seppi's dead body had brought her mother's death crashing down around her and opened old wounds too deep to heal. Wounds caused by her father—not Kierion. Her accusations had been unfair. She wouldn't blame him if he never spoke to her again.

So, she kept her trap shut. Kept her eyes averted as the dark-haired man kissed Gret and they all left, Fenni trailing sparks out the door.

"Oi, you!" Tharuk claws swiped, just missing her nose. "My beer."

The tankard overflowed, froth spilling over Adelina's hands and beer running over her clean counter. She slammed the glass on the bar and retrieved the cloth. Scowling, she ignored demands for beer while she mopped up the mess. If only it were as easy to clean up the mess she'd made with Kierion.

§

The captain had been watching the new barmaid these past few hours. There was more to that dark-haired girl than met the eye. Onyx eyes glittering below that sloppy hat of hers, she missed nothing. A slip of a girl, she had fine curves hidden under the baggy clothing she wore, but he had no interest in young things like that. And it was better his men didn't notice either.

The girl nodded to a tharuk, face carefully neutral, and pulled the monster an ale. It was a necessity having these beasts in the tavern. Captain wrinkled his nose. They stank. And their business stank too. Although he was the still captain of a pirate ship, he didn't like slaves. Once there'd been a scourge which had wiped out half his crew members. A bright idea of the second mate's, they'd sneaked in through the back entrance to Death Valley and procured a few slaves while Zens wasn't looking. He shook his head. Never again. The condition of those men, women and littlings had horrified him. Dried out husks with barely a wit between them, they'd hardly been able to speak. Within a day on board, most had died. The captain grimaced.

There was something uncanny about this girl, the way she sized up patrons and changed her expression to suit each one. She'd watched those men at the door posturing like bulls over that pretty blonde wench. She had a quick mind and a fast hand with a weapon. Obviously trained. Why was she here? A spy? For whom? Zens? Or the dragon riders?

He snorted again. Not that it would make much difference if the dragon riders were going to be in his crew soon. That bloody Kierion, smooth talking swine, he was. Captain had never even realized the lad was a dragon rider. But the blighter had saved his life. He snorted again. After what they'd done, he'd vowed to hate them forever, now he had one on his crew.

But things had changed. Soon, he might have more riders. The captain turned that fact over and over in his mind, wondering how he could work it to his advantage. And what use he could have for the girl.

§

As they left the Brothers' Arms, a gaggle of Nightshaders was trooping in, led by the hulking Brutus. Ever since that first fight in the alley, Brutus had accepted them—on the surface—although his eyes glinted with malice whenever he looked at Fenni.

On the top step, Danion leaned in and kissed Gret's cheek and then her throat.

Heat seared from Fenni's fingertips in a burst of flame. He quickly clenched them, quelling it.

Brutus glanced at Fenni's hands. His hard eyes flitted to Fenni's face. "Hey Danion, I think wizard boy wants a turn at your girl." Brutus' gaze slid over Gret's curves and down her long legs.

Another Nightshader chortled, "Wouldn't we all?" leering at her.

Danion's head snapped around, his dark eyes blazing at Fenni. "You touch her, boy, and I'll string your entrails from the doorway of this tavern." His glare roved over each of the Nightshaders. "The same goes for any man who lays a finger on her. She's mine. Got it?"

Hurriedly, they looked away from Gret, eyes anywhere except her. "All good. I like my guts on the inside, sir." Brutus said.

A nervous titter ran through the Nightshaders.

Danion took Gret's cheeks in his hands and leaned in, kissing her thoroughly.

Rage simmered inside Fenni, seeing that man's mouth claim her soft lips. He contained it, shoving his anger down somewhere dark and deep, where no one would see it.

Amid catcalls and whistles, Danion released Gret's face and took her hand.

She blushed, smiling, and lowered her eyes, just like a besotted lover.

By the dragon gods, a man could only take so much. Summoning all the courage he could muster and coiling his rage inside him, Fenni followed Danion, Gret and Kierion down the steps. The whole way back to Danion's quarters, Fenni tamped down his anger. But his raging jealousy reared again as Danion held Gret's hand and whispered to her, occasionally stopping to kiss her again. Just like a man in love. Danion must've fallen for Gret too.

Fenni remembered Danion's lewd comments the night Gret had walked into the bar. His anger flared again.

They traipsed along the alley and up the stairs to Danion's room.

The moment they shut the door, Danion dropped his arm from Gret's shoulders and rounded on Fenni, pushing him up against the wall. "Keep your urges to yourself, young man."

He hadn't realized how strong Danion was until those arms pinned his shoulders. "And you keep your mouth to yourself." Fenni snapped. "Kissing her, like that."

"You fool. Your sparks and flaming jealousy incited interest from those Nightshader pigs. Do you want the captain to take her—or one of his stinking thugs? You can be glad I staked a claim to her publicly. It might be the only thing that'll protect her from being ravaged." Danion dropped his hands from Fenni's shoulders, running his fingers through his tousled dark curls. "Although I'm hoping it won't goad Brutus into trying his luck."

Gret paled.

Danion pushed a finger at Fenni's chest. "You think I want this? I have a wife and littlings at home. Flirting with your girl is the last thing I need."

Gret pushed between them, eyes blazing. "Acting like two bulls with locked horns and talking about me as if I'm not even here is the last thing *I* need." She stalked out the door and slammed it behind her, leaving them all gaping.

"Well, you both had that coming," Kierion said, stepping toward the door. "I'll see if I can find her."

§

Gret ran along the alley, head down, boots churning through the snow. She was so mad, she could smite those idiots' heads off. She wasn't a piece of meat for them to fight over like scrapping tharuks. Didn't they know she had feelings?

Feelings that were now so utterly confused. Gods, she'd really liked Fenni. Thought she'd loved him. But then again, she'd never seen the simmering jealously and possessiveness that Danion brought out in him. And now she'd been kissed by Danion. More than once. She'd only been acting, but her body had betrayed her, arching into him, looking into his deep eyes, enjoying the sensation of his lips on hers.

He'd just said he had littlings.

Her blood thundered. Fenni wasn't the only one Danion drove to simmering anger. He was married, with littlings. He didn't need to act his part so perfectly.

Footsteps sounded behind her.

She spurted ahead and turned down an alley. It didn't matter whether it was Fenni or Danion—she didn't want to see either of them now.

The footfalls followed, faster now, splashing though the slush.

Gret dashed around another corner and smacked into a wall of muscle.

Strong hands gripped her arms. Brutus leered down at her. Raucous laughter and clanking tankards drifted from a half open door. The stench of latrines was overpowering. Horrified, Gret realized she was at the back of the Brothers' Arms.

"Just what I was looking for." Brutus grinned. "A bit of entertainment while the boys play a round of nukils."

§

At Gret's scream, Kierion couldn't help it, he melded with Riona without even thinking. *"Riona, help."*

Moments later, he rounded a corner and found himself at the back of the Brothers' Arms. Brutus was holding Gret up against the outside wall of a latrine.

Riona's roar rippled the air. Gret squirmed from Brutus' grip and kicked him hard in the groin. He crumpled to his knees, groaning. Whipping her sword from its scabbard, she held the tip under his throat.

Panting, Kierion ran over. *"Riona, please fetch Danion."*

"You'd be better play this cool, or that man may decide she's an attractive challenge."

"Thanks, good advice." He slowed and swaggered over to Brutus and Gret, waiting until he'd circled them entirely before speaking, "Wait until Danion hears about this." He ignored Brutus' glare. "So, you're keen to display your entrails to the world, are you?"

Moments later, Riona landed on the roof of the Brothers' Arms with Danion on her back. Danion swung down on a rope and dropped to the tavern's yard. Riona swiped at the rope, cutting it. It twisted to the ground like an angry snake. Danion snatched it up and ran over to Brutus, who was still on his knees with Gret's sword at his throat.

Brutus' eyes widened, taking in Danion. "S-sorry, boss," he said, his eyes smoldering with anything but remorse.

Danion ignored him, thrusting one end of the rope at Kierion. "Tie him up, and leave an end trailing."

Kierion knotted the rope around Brutus' belly and tugged it tight.

Danion put his fingers between his teeth and whistled. Flapping wings whooshed overhead—Danion's blue. He threw the long end of the rope into the sky. His dragon snatched it and yanked Brutus above the rooftops, whacking the thug's shins on the eaves of the Brothers' Arms.

Danion chuckled. "I told her not to be gentle and to leave him in Spangle-wood Forest." He turned to Gret. "Are you all right?" Danion took her in his arms and hugged her.

Thankfully Fenni wasn't here to see Danion hugging the woman he loved.

Seeing their embrace hit Kierion in the gut—the pang of missing Adelina's cute perky smile, the way she teased him, her musical laugh at his stupid jokes. Those stunning dark eyes that he lost himself in every time he gazed into their depths. The warmth of her in his arms when he comforted her the way Danion was holding Gret now.

He ground his boot into the stone. He was a fool for ignoring her. Blinded by his own hurt, he hadn't considered her feelings—yet again. Now that the battle in Montanara was over, he'd head back to Dragons' Hold and tell her he cared for her. He swallowed. And hope she cared too.

He'd flaming well tell her anyway. His heart was hers—whether she wanted it or not.

Boots thudded down the alley, and Fenni rounded the corner, panting. "Master Giddi's been taken by Commander Zens!" He froze, staring at Danion and Gret, jaw hanging.

§

Everyone froze. But it wasn't Fenni's news that had shocked them—Danion had Gret in his arms again.

Fenni gaped. He wanted to run, flee, hide. But his feet were rooted to the stone. His legs refused to budge. Gret was *hugging* Danion. This was no show. No one was watching. She'd chosen Danion over him.

His magic guttered and died, leaving him stone cold.

In the flickering light of a lantern on the tavern's back wall, Gret stared at him, tears staining her cheeks.

"Gret, what's wrong?" Fenni blurted. He couldn't help himself. He had to know. If Danion had hurt her—

"She's had a terrible shock," Danion said.

Gret let out a loud sob and raced to Fenni, throwing herself at his chest. His arms closed around her shaking body. She cried into his shoulder. He stroked her hair, murmuring, "It's all right now, Gret. It's all right."

"I-it was awful. Brutus attacked me, wanted to—"

Fenni could well imagine what Brutus had wanted. "You're all right now."

He tilted his head, trailing soft kisses through her hair, murmuring until her sobs quieted.

Her arms slowly crept around his back, and she clung to him, breathing deeply, resting her cheek against his shoulder.

§

Fenni's breath brushed Gret's cheek. The warm hum of his mage power soothed her. He trailed tiny kisses through her hair. Stroked her back. Murmured. And held her safe.

Her swordsmanship and wits had saved her. But then she'd fallen apart. Danion had hugged her, tried to comfort her, but it had felt so wrong. She'd desperately wanted Fenni.

And then he'd been there—shock and devastation on his face. Oh gods, oh gods, she'd never meant to hurt him. Flame Danion's stupid antics. She shouldn't have let him hug her.

"Are you all right?" Fenni murmured.

"I am now," she whispered, gazing at his green eyes.

Gret reached up and traced his lips with her fingers. So soft. He kissed her fingertips one by one. And held her, the hum of his magic surrounding them in a warm glow. Somewhere behind her, a door crashed open and terse voices argued. But Gret ignored them. Ignored the world, held safely in the arms of the man she loved.

§

Kierion and Danion leaned against the back wall of the tavern, arms folded. Kierion gestured with his elbow at Fenni and Gret still embracing in the tavern's yard. "At least you won't have to explain to your wife why you keep kissing another woman."

Danion sighed. "I don't have a wife—or littlings. I was just trying to keep Fenni off my back."

Danion was a slick liar; Kierion had to give him that. "So…" Kierion whispered, "you actually do like Gret?"

Danion shrugged a shoulder. "What's there to not like? Pretty on the eye, a sharding good fighter and a fine dragon rider. She'd do any man proud."

Perhaps he was right, but a different girl flashed to Kierion's mind. One not as leggy, or as blonde. Kierion sighed.

"You like her too?" Danion asked.

"Nah, I like my girls half the height, with raven hair and midnight eyes."

"Sounds tempting."

Kierion glared.

Danion gave a soft chuckle. "I was only teasing."

The back door to the tavern crashed open, hitting the wall. Kierion and Danion palmed their blades.

"Get that rutting dragon off my roof!" the captain roared.

"Kierion stepped into the light. "Ah, sir, Riona's mine. I'll tell her."

"Yours? The one that saved me?" The captain growled, "Riona can perch there whenever she wants. Just tell her not to knock off any shingles, or you'll be replacing them."

Kierion sheathed his blade. "Yes, Captain."

The captain's eyes narrowed at Danion. "If that dragon is Kierion's, why were you swinging down on her rope?" Danion spluttered as the captain continued, "And why were you throwing that blue a rope—the one that took Brutus away?"

Danion coughed. "Ah, I'm her rider, sir."

The captain snorted, waving a hand at the embracing couple. "And I suppose they're riders too?"

Kierion broke in, "Gret is. Fenni rides with me."

"I know that. He blasted a gaping hole in that stinkin' shadow beast." The captain snapped, "Exactly how many riders are there in the Nightshader crew, Danion?"

"A couple." Danion's unruffled nonchalance was back in full swing.

"A couple?" The captain counted the four of them off on his fingers.

"Well a few, then."

"A few what? A few dozen? I suppose you expect me to take them all into my crew, dragons included?"

Kierion grinned. "Not a bad deal in return for a life, Captain. Fast, efficient fighters, who can beat back these dark dragons."

Danion smiled. "I'll introduce you to them all in the morning."

"You drive a hard bargain, Kierion," the captain growled. "I'll see you all here in the morning for breakfast. But…" He held up a finger. "I'm not feeding dragons."

"I'm sorry, captain," Kierion said. "I won't be here for breakfast. The Dragon Mage, Master Giddi, has been taken by Commander Zens. I need to take the news to Dragons' Hold tonight." Although he could let the blue guards relay the message, Lars would appreciate being told in person.

And it was time to see Adelina.

Dragons' Hold

"This may sound a bit harsh, Tomaaz," Tonio told him, "but your dragon has been turned. If we can't extract that burrowing arrowhead, we may have to kill him." Tonio drummed his fingernails upon the council table. "I wish there was another way."

Lars muttered. "It might be the only way."

Several council masters nodded in assent.

Alyssa murmured, "Yes, we can't have rogue dragons."

Hendrik shook his head, "Not a good option, but there may be no way around it."

Even Master Jerrick was nodding.

Lars smacked his gavel. "Any dragons who are turned will be given three days. At the end of those three days, they will be executed. This is war. We can't house enemy dragons at Dragons' Hold."

The council masters' dragons, seated along the back wall, snarled. Zaarusha roared.

Tomaaz's head reeled. Kill Maazini? It'd be like ripping his own heart out. "No!" He leaped to his feet, stalked around the table to Lars and thrust his face close to the council leader's. "No. I won't have it. You'll have to kill me too." He picked up a glass and smashed it against the wall. His boots crunched through shards as he strode out the council chamber's double doors and slammed them.

Tomaaz pounded down the corridor, his boots drumming into the stone, echoes thundering along the corridor like a battle drum. He raced past surprised riders. Mages jumped back against stone walls to let him pass.

Down the spiral stairs that led to the dungeon.

Down, down, to the heart of the mountain.

He melded with Maazini, but a snarl ripped through his head in reply. Not good. Surely, he could save his dragon. He stormed past the blue guards.

Opposite Maazini's cell, Tomaaz slumped against the wall and watched for a sign of the dragon he'd rescued from Death Valley. A sign of his gratitude. Of their bond. They'd imprinted under the most unlikely circumstances. The broken, bedraggled creature had hardly been recognizable as a dragon, with gray washed-out scales, sagging wings, and gray eyes due to the numlocked rat carcasses he'd been fed by dull-witted slaves.

But there was nothing, no glimmering friendliness in Maazini's eyes.

Now his eyes were mean green slits in his head. His maw, a mass of snarling fangs. His talons clawed rock. He gazed at Tomaaz as if he'd shred him if he got within reach.

Tomaaz buried his head on his knees. How was he going to save his dragon?

§

Kierion strode swiftly down the corridors of Dragons' Hold toward Adelina's cavern. He needed to report Master Giddi's kidnapping to the council, but first he had to see her. He'd been such an ass, pressured her when she'd been most vulnerable. Perhaps she hated him. But that didn't change how he felt about her. Even if they'd only just begun their journey, he had so much pleasure in her company—had felt so little joy since they'd argued.

He knocked on Adelina's door, licking his lips and nervously running a hand through his battle-dirty, straggly hair. No answer. Perhaps she was out flying. He hunted around the halls and caverns and eventually found Mara in the mess cavern.

"Oh, Kierion we hear you're a real hero."

Another girl chimed in, "He was already my hero after he rescued Ezaara and Roberto from Death Valley."

Mara replied, "And Adelina. You can't forget Adelina."

Guilt spiked through Kierion. No, he'd never forget Adelina—even if she never chose to speak to him again. How could he forget her cute upturned smile, her laugh and vivacious energy? Not to mention those gorgeous ebony eyes that made his heart melt when she was near. "Uh, have you seen her?"

"Adelina's been gone for ages," Mara said matter-of-factly.

"Where did she go?"

Mara shrugged. "No one seems to know. But I imagine Tonio would. He knows everything."

The other girl giggled. "Ssh, the spymaster might hear you."

Kierion didn't feel like laughing. "Thank you." He spun on his heel and left the mess cavern. He was running out of time. He had to report Giddi's kidnapping to the council and leave again for Montanara. Gods, he had to find her.

He ran to Tonio's quarters. The spymaster was hunched over a map, a group of blue guards gathered around him. He stabbed the map with a finger and then turned, barking, "Kierion, I'm busy. Can't it wait?"

No, it couldn't. "It'll only take a moment, sir. Have you sent Adelina any-where? No one seems to have seen her."

Tonio nodded grimly. "Her father's been brought back here, captive. I suspect she left after she saw him. No one's seen scale nor talon of Linaia or Adelina for two or three days."

Kierion barely managed to stutter, "Th-thank you." He staggered out into the corridor.

She'd seen her father and been hurting. Had probably needed someone to talk to. And he'd shunned her. Flames. If only he'd stayed to talk to her.

Riona mind-melded, *"Kierion, I've hunted and I'm ready to go."*

"I'll be there in a moment. I'm just looking for Adelina."

"Then I suggest we leave Dragons' Hold immediately. She's not here."

"I can't," Kierion replied. *"I haven't reported Giddi's kidnapping to the council yet."*

§

Marlies sighed, smoothing her quilt. It had only been two days since the battle at Montanara, but sitting up was still painful. At least Hans had stopped pacing beside her bed and clucking like a mother hen. Well, he was still clucking—just not as often.

Marlies hadn't heard a thing from Leah since she'd fled with Giant John two days ago. She rolled her eyes. Now who was being a mother hen? The red guards were at least a few days' flight away, longer by wagon. Eventually, Leah would reach them and return with piaua juice. Or not. At least they'd know where they stood.

She shifted, wincing as pain shot up her wounded side.

Without piaua, they'd have to heal riders and dragons the old-fashioned way. Stitches risked infections and required patience—so much patience.

Life was a tide too strong for her to stand against. She was tired and everything ached. Every time the tide surged, she wanted to collapse on the sand and rest in the sun, but the tide just kept surging against her. For the thousandth time, she wondered what would've happened if she hadn't taken piaua berries in Death Valley. She shook her head. There was no point thinking like that. She would've been dead. At least she'd had time to see the twins become dragon riders—the dream she and Hans had long held but never dared to voice in Lush Valley.

Sofia bustled in. "Is there anything I can do for you? With Leah gone and Adelina not around, I thought—"

"Where's Adelina?" Marlies' voice came out sharper than she'd intended.

Sofia shrugged. "No one's sure. She was last seen three days ago. I've asked around, but no one knows where she is."

She tried to recall the name of Adelina's dragon. Ah, yes. "Has Linaia gone too?" Her memory wasn't as sharp as it had been, either.

Sofia nodded. "No talon nor scale seen of her, either." She leaned in, whispering, "I think it's because Adelina's father's here."

Although Marlies didn't like gossip, it sounded plausible. Amato was a beast. "Is Lars aware that Adelina's gone?"

Sofia shrugged. "I'm not sure."

"Then please tell him. And, could you also fetch me a quill, an ink pot and parchment?"

Leah was the only one she'd formally taught about her healing remedies. Of course, Ezaara knew them too, but if anything happened to either of them...

Sofia brought in some parchment, a quill and a pot of blood-red ink.

Marlies shuffled the slips of parchment on her lap and started writing. They had to preserve her knowledge. Too much had been destroyed by Fleur.

TOGETHER

Roberto sat by Ezaara's bed. Two days they'd been home at Dragons' Hold, and she hadn't woken yet. For the umpteenth time, he laid his hands on her temples to test her mind.

Nothing. Her mind was blank. A dark, hollow cavern with not an echo inside.

No light. Not even the tiniest glowworm of a glimmer. There was nothing, nothing of the woman he knew. No spark of life, no vibrancy. No *Ezaara*.

He dropped his hands into his lap. He'd agreed to her crazy plan, encouraged her to mind-meld with the enemy's dragons. He was worthless, had sacrificed the woman he loved for the sake of a war not even won.

The door opened and Hans entered with Marlies leaning heavily on his arm. Her face was pale and her steps slow. "How is she?" Marlies asked, breathing shallowly.

They said she'd fought Bruno, injuring her side. That Simeon had killed him, but gotten away.

"Still sleeping," Roberto replied.

Marlies patted his hand. "She's a fighter, Roberto. Always has been. Always will be. Don't give up."

They sat for a while.

Ezaara's parents rose to leave. Marlies flashed him a tired wan smile. With quiet footsteps, she and Hans made their way to the door and closed it softly behind them.

Roberto sighed and turned back to Ezaara. Her new Naobian tunic and breeches were on the bedside table. He traced his fingers over the exquisite fabric. It rustled, dragons winking in the torchlight.

Ezaara hadn't even worn them.

Roberto stroked her cheek, then slumped in his chair, watching Ezaara's chest rise and fall, counting her breaths long into the night.

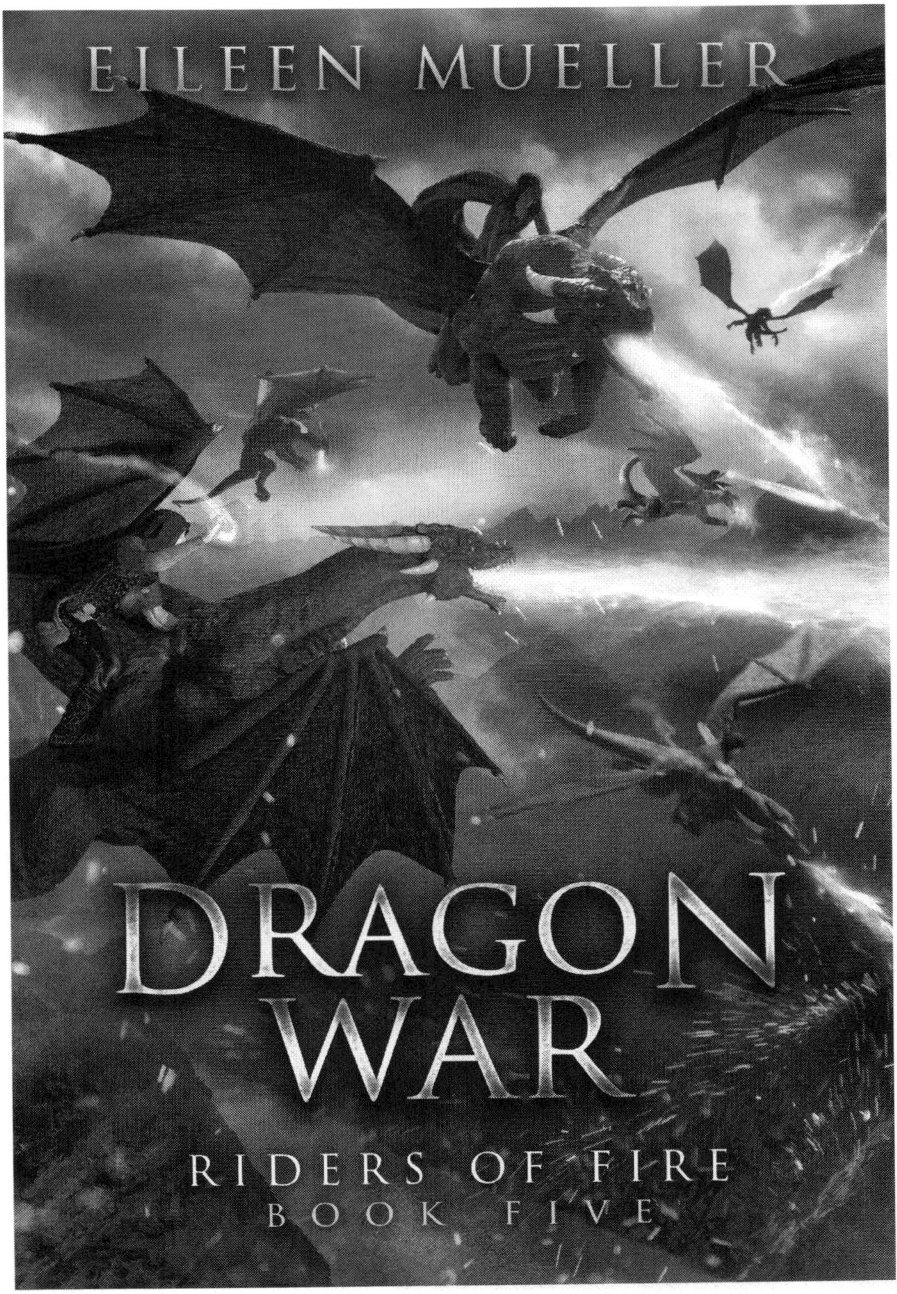
EILEEN MUELLER
DRAGON
WAR
RIDERS OF FIRE
BOOK FIVE

Prologue - Death Valley

Commander Zens pushed the button to activate the stone-clad aluminum sliding door. It hissed open, admitting him to the antechamber to his laboratory, an old methimium mine that he'd re-purposed. His boots struck stone, echoing off rock walls lined with large glass vats. Tharuks tending young mages growing in the fluid-filled vats whirled to attention as he passed. The original two mages they'd kidnapped were still chained to beds, pallid and barely conscious.

"Progress?" Zens snapped.

Tharuk 873 stepped forward, bowing its head and dipping its tusks and furry snout. Its eyes met his. "We've grown twenty full mages from the material Bill harvested and hundreds from the original mages. We have more embryos ready for the accel—um, special stuff."

"Growth accelerant." Zens nodded. Bill had recently harvested DNA from mages he'd killed in battle—fingernails, hair clippings and even hacked-off digits. "Good. Continue. Double the accelerant. We must have more mages fully grown as soon as possible." He waved them back to work, and mind-melded with tharuk 000. *Where are you, my lovely?* His pride and joy usually oversaw the mage cloning process in this antechamber.

In the main laboratory, sir, 000 answered, a wave of warmth accompanying the tharuk's thoughts.

Zens strolled through the hewn rock archway into the lab. He smiled as his gaze swept the rows of huge glass tanks holding his lovelies—*shadow dragons*, the fearful citizens of Dragons' Realm called them, a fitting name for his new beasts that struck terror into their weakling hearts. As his footfalls echoed across the stone, snuffles and grunts ceased. Tharuks turned from their workbenches, placed their test tubes in stands, or climbed down the ladders against the dragons' tanks to face him.

Eileen Mueller

His gaze swept over the lab and he mind-melded with all of them at once, letting a sinister edge lace his thoughts. *"Continue working. All dragons must be fit for flight in a few days. Or else..."* He flashed a malicious smile.

The tharuks turned back to their duties. The largest approached him, its broad shoulders exuding strength and power, the coiled whip at its hip swinging as it prowled between workbenches. 000's eyes gleamed in anticipation. *"Greetings, sir."*

"Come with me, Triple."

Triple Zero, his most-prized tharuk and first creation, followed him through the underground laboratory, past the teams of tharuks working to produce more creatures for the war against Dragons' Realm. Zens' boots crunched on broken glass. He wheeled. "Who made this mess?" he barked, waving a hand at the shards littering the rough stone floor.

A wiry tharuk tentatively raised its hand, its claws automatically springing from its fingers in fear.

"Come." Zens smiled, crooking a finger.

The beast quaked as it approached.

Rightly so. Zens' gaze swept over the tharuk. He sent a powerful wave of mental energy, easily penetrating the creature's weak mind. The tharuk uttered a strangled cry. Its knees buckled and it crashed to the floor amid the shards, gurgling and clutching at its throat. Moments later, it was still. Zens flicked a hand at the creature. "Place its hand in my tank and save its body for the dragons. We have to keep our lovelies well fed."

924, the beast's troop leader, scrambled to grab the body.

"924, have someone clean up this glass." Zens waved his hand. "If more is smashed, you'll be next."

He strode on, 000 beside him. Zens' eyes flicked over the dark dragons, their wings furled in hundreds of fluid-filled tanks. "Everything's going according to plan, 000. We have adequate dragons and mages to bring Dragons' Realm to its knees."

"It's just their aging that's a problem, sir," 000 ventured.

"The growth acceleration gene is problematic, but it's the only way to harvest so many creatures this quickly." If the flaming mages and dragons could live longer than a few days, they'd be able to sustain the pressure on Dragons' Realm and purge the sky of those arrogant dragon riders. "We must combat this premature aging, and keep up constant production."

"The teams are working on it, sir."

"I'm aware," Zens replied dryly. "But it's not enough. To win, we must strike at the heart of Dragons' Hold." He approached the double methimium-powered metal doors, which automatically slid open, admitting them through the short stone corridor to the broad exit tunnel, which thousands of slaves had died digging. A few slaves were a small price to pay for a tunnel wide enough to accommodate the broad wingspans of his shadow dragons in flight. Dragons in the holding area shifted, their furled wings rustling, his cloned mages rigid upon their backs.

"But the mountains around the Dragons' Hold are impenetrable."

Zens turned to his methimium ray, tucked against the tunnel wall. "That's why we have this." He wheeled it out in front of the dragons, turned it to face the wall, and flicked the switch. A beam of golden light sprang from the ray, illuminating nooks and crannies in the rock. Such a lovely warm light. The fools in Dragons' Realm had no idea of the power of methimium. Stumbling upon this corner of the realm where methimium ore was as plentiful as the trees in their forests had been a rich reward for being trapped here with those stinking flying lizards and pompous riders. Riders that reminded him of the bullies who'd taunted him at school, back on Earth before he'd left in 2050 and been trapped here. He calibrated his methimium ray, turning the crude dial he'd made from the inferior materials available in Dragons' Realm. He sighed.

"Do you have the ring Bruno stole for us?" 000 asked.

From any other tharuk, the question would have irritated Zens enough to end its life, but from 000, the query merely demonstrated the foresight and intelligence he'd engineered in his beloved. "Naturally—that's why we're here." Zens drew the engraved jade ring out of his pocket and rubbed it. "Kisha," he said triumphantly.

Over his shoulder, a vortex of swirling gold clouds appeared, riddled with dark cracks that seeped shadowy mist. Just like his test this morning.

A shimmering spirit appeared in the light.

By the cursed dragons, it was Anakisha.

"Zens? How dare you use my ring!" she mind-melded.

"I thought I'd taken care of you," Zens sneered. He'd drive the spirit of the stubborn ex-Queen's Rider to her knees. *"You know I tortured the new Queen's Rider,"* he taunted. *"She didn't stand a chance against me."*

"And yet she lives," Anakisha replied. *"And leads her people in battle against you."*

Those gentle yet defiant words got under his skin. He blasted her mind with enough power to kill ten tharuks.

Anakisha's spirit just smiled. *"When will you learn that there's more power in love than there ever will be in hate or vengeance?"*

Sweat rolled off Zens' forehead as he battled to subdue the woman's spirit and snuff her out like a candle.

The shimmering being remained, hands outstretched, pleading with him.

At his side, 000 shifted, startling Zens. He'd been so focused, he'd forgotten his tharuk's presence. "If you can't kill the human, why not paralyze her with your mind?" 000 whispered.

Brilliant. Zens blasted Anakisha's spirit with his mind.

Her face froze in a scream, eyes wide.

Wiping his brow, Zens turned to 000. "Saddle the strongest dark dragon we have. I'm going hunting."

§

This short scene is repeated from Dragon Strike, Riders of Fire book 4

Giddi slumped over his dragon's spinal ridge. He was bone tired. Weary, right down to the vibrations in his bones. It was worth it. As reinstated leader of the Wizard Council, this time he'd saved Dragons' Realm. The war wasn't over yet, but at least this battle had been won and Zens' shadow dragons vanquished.

A crack, like a quiet clap of thunder, sounded above him. Wearily, Giddi gazed up.

Bathed in a blaze of golden light, a dark dragon loomed.

It'd appeared out of nowhere. A vaguely-familiar rider was perched in its saddle. An unusually large rider with a bald head and bulging yellow eyes. Commander Zens—grinning triumphantly.

"Master Giddi, I've long awaited the opportunity for us to work together. I appreciate your talents. I would never ban you from the Wizard Council or force you to lock out your beloved wife. Come, work with me. Let's better Dragons' Realm."

Giddi mind-blocked as the next barrage of Zens' insidious thoughts hit his head. He locked Mazyka's beloved face in his mind. It made no bones—Zens knew who she was, and she was now safe in Zens' old world. Zens hammered his head relentlessly, trying to get in. Sweat beaded on Giddi's brow.

Not now, when his reserves were low and he was exhausted. He gritted his teeth, staving off Zens' commands.

Another dark dragon shot through the glowing clouds, a fake mage on its back with a nocked arrow. The dragon wheeled behind Giddi, but the dragon mage didn't dare tear his gaze from Commander Zens. Clutching the dragon's spinal ridge, his forearms corded with tension, Giddi pushed Zens out of his head.

Sharp pain pierced Giddi's shoulder. Then his lower back. And his other shoulder. Something sharp and painful dug inside his body. Three somethings, burrowing into his skin. Searing burning paths through his flesh and muscle. Gods, by the flaming holy dragon gods. He screamed, arching his back. Giddi's mind-block shattered. Mazyka's face exploded into thousands of tiny shards that were swept away by dark tendrils.

Shadows whirled through Giddi's mind, mist lurking at the edges of his vision.

"*Listen to me, Master Giddi. I now control you.*" Zens' voice was the most alluring thing Giddi had ever heard.

Commander Zens descended from a gate of billowing golden clouds upon the large dark dragon with fiery yellow eyes. Zens extended a hand.

"*Welcome to my army, Master Giddi. Climb upon my dragon.*" His melodious voice slithered inside Giddi's mind and wrapped itself around his senses like soft dark velvet.

Giddi's arms dropped to his sides. His legs moved, clambering upon his dragon's saddle in a crouch.

His body tensed.

No. He fought it, trying to withstand Zens' command.

"*Jump, Giddi. Come with me.*" Zens smiled, beckoning him with a welcoming hand.

Giddi sprang, landing on the back of Zens' saddle.

And wrapped his arms around the monster he'd been fighting for years.

Even as he struggled to withstand Zens' commands, pain radiated from the new channels in his back and shoulders, darkness spreading through him. Bit by bit, he summoned his magic. Tiny lights flitted inside him. But darkness smothered them and they winked out.

He'd wanted to face this monster for years. And now he couldn't even summon a spark. Slumping against the commander's back, Giddi held on, his arms not his own.

Commander Zens rubbed one of Anakisha's travel rings and muttered, "Kisha."

A pop sounded and Spanglewood Forest and Montanara disappeared.

§

A tunnel of billowing golden clouds engulfed the shadow dragon carrying Commander Zens and Giddi. A transparent wispy figure dressed in white was suspended in midair, her mouth open in shock, and her hand outstretched. With a jolt, Master Giddi recognized the spirit of Anakisha, the former Queen's Rider lost in battle years ago.

The jade ring Zens had used was one of Anakisha's jade rings that controlled the world gates, rings that Ezaara and Roberto had taken on their hand-fasting holiday.

Oh gods, Ezaara and Roberto might be hurt. And worse, Zens could now travel Dragons' Realm at will. Giddi tried to mind-meld. *"Anakisha."* No reply. His heart sank. Somehow she was bound, powerless to guide them through the gate. Giddi tried to buck and thrash.

Zens chuckled. *"Try as you might, you now serve me."*

The commander's insidious tones wound into Giddi's head. His arms stayed wrapped around Zens' thick torso, his body slumped against the commander's massive back. By the dragon's talon, Giddi found himself drawn to Zens' melodious tones. Pain radiated from the crystals channeling into his back and shoulders. Mouth dry and stomach clenched, he tried to summon his magic. Tiny sparks flitted within him, then winked out, one by one, smothered by the darkness of Zens' foul burrowing crystals.

The commander rubbed the ring again and, with a crack, they were above the stark slopes of Death Valley. Devoid of vegetation, the valley was a channel of dusty arid land, a far cry from the lush forested valley Zens had stolen years ago.

The shadow dragon flapped its ragged wings, and they descended behind a desolate mountain. It flew into a gaping hole in the hillside, then winged down an enormous tunnel to a holding chamber.

Bitterness flooded Giddi's mouth as they swooped between rows of dark dragons. Replicas of Sorcha and Velrama sat upon the dark backs—Zens' unnatural creations. The commander had brought abominable dark magic from his world that enabled him to grow creatures, monsters, and people. The two young kidnapped mages had been pliable and eager to learn, but their replicas had hard-edged faces and sneered at Giddi, sparks dripping from their fingers as he and Zens passed. There were hundreds of them. And other mages too, some familiar, mounted on snarling dark dragons, ready to do Zens' bidding. No doubt those fake mages had also been grown in those infernal tanks that Roberto had described.

Giddi tried to thrash against Zens' mental restraints, but it was useless: he couldn't even remove his hands from the commander's waist. Finally, they left the ranks of dragons behind and came to an enormous metal door. The dragon thudded to the rocky floor.

Behind them, a cry rang out. A dragon bellowed. A troop of twenty shadow dragons flapped their wings, the draft sending shivers down Giddi's spine as they flew out the tunnel, fake Velramas and Sorchas astride their backs, headed for Dragons' Realm.

Oh gods, he'd thought they'd defeated the worst of these dark dragons, but what they'd faced was nothing compared to the hundreds of battle-ready dragons lining this tunnel.

Time to dismount, my faithful mage slave.

Master Giddi's arms moved, unwrapping themselves from around Zens' waist. His torso straightened to allow the commander to slide off the shadow dragon's back. His body moved of its own volition—no, Zens' volition—slipping off the saddle and following Zens. His feet felt like clumsy blocks of wood. He traipsed behind the commander, his spirit bucking and fighting every step of the way, but his body was under Zens' control. The door slid open and admitted them to a chamber with row upon row of tanks holding dark dragons. Soft black dragons' wings undulated in clear fluid. Snouts were pressed against the glass, revealing pointed fangs. Talons and tails poked out from the masses of wings. Everywhere Giddi looked were orderly rows of dragon-filled tanks. So many. Too many shadow dragons to ever defeat.

Tharuks looked up from their work, their beady red or black eyes taking in their commander, claws instantly springing from their furry hands. They bowed their heads for Zens, snouts and tusks scraping their breastplates.

"Keep working. No time to lose," Zens barked.

The beasts retracted their claws and went back to their tasks, mixing substances in glass jars, using needles, vials of fluid, and other strange methods to do their work—the work of growing more dragons.

Zens turned and grinned, his bulbous eyes raking Giddi's face. *"See? You never really had a chance. None of you did."* He flung his arms out, addressing his tharuks. "Look who I've captured. The master mage of Dragons' Realm is mine to command."

Tharuk roars filled the chamber, reverberating through Giddi's bones. He tried to summon a fireball, a flame, a spark—nothing.

The largest tharuk paced toward them. Dark saliva dripped from its tusks, one of them broken. A whip was coiled at its hip and 000 was emblazoned upon its inner forearm.

Giddi knew of 000, Zens' only love and first creation. Roberto had recently threatened to harm 000, to bargain with Zens for Adelina and Ezaara's lives, allowing them to escape from Death Valley.

000 stopped before Master Giddi and spat. The stench of rotting carrion hit Giddi and dark spittle splattered his face.

He lifted his hands to wipe it away, but Zens guffawed and waved at him. Giddi's arms slammed against his sides and he was powerless to move. The tharuk's stinking spittle slid down his cheek and into the corner of his mouth.

Panic constricted Giddi's chest. He was a pawn in the evil commander's hands.

"The dragon mage shouldn't have closed the portal all those years ago and trapped me here," Commander Zens said softly. "It's time to teach him a lesson, 000."

000 grinned and uncoiled his whip.

§

Leah glanced back at Marlies—still injured in Montanara's town square—as Giant John led her and Taliesin away. Blood seeped from the wound in Marlies' side, but Hans was already helping her onto a dragon to get back to Dragons' Hold. The square was in complete havoc. Dragons swooped through the air, plucking up tharuks and breathing fire. Ugly tusked tharuks fought villagers, claws out, snarling. The snow was churned with ash and stained red.

"Will Marlies be all right?" Taliesin asked, slipping his small hand into Leah's. Despite their efforts to feed him up, the boy was still waif-thin from being Commander Zens' slave in Death Valley for so long.

Leah squeezed Taliesin's hand. "I'm sure she'll be fine." She wasn't sure at all. She blinked back tears. She had no idea whether Marlies would die from being stabbed, but what else could she say?

She and Marlies had failed to find piaua juice, and the realm needed a supply for this war against Commander Zens. With Marlies now injured, if she and Taliesin didn't find it, hundreds, even thousands, would die. The life-giving juice was essential for healing their injured riders and dragons. And there were no tree-speakers left except her. Although she didn't want to, for the sake of the realm, she had to walk away from her dying friend.

"Come on," said Giant John. "We have to go."

Leah tugged Taliesin and followed Giant John's bulky form out of Montanara's square into a winding lane. She instinctively ducked as dark dragons flapped overhead. Tharuk snarls echoed down alleys either side of them, making the hairs on her arms prickle. The giant ragged wings of a shadow dragon blocked the light as it shot over a building. Giant John pulled Leah and Taliesin into a shallow doorway. The dark beast whooshed a gust of flame between the buildings. A littling cried out as his jerkin caught fire. His mother screamed and batted at the flames.

Giant John leaped to their aid and rolled the boy in a patch of snow to douse his flaming clothes.

Leah's breath caught in her throat.

"Now get home," Giant John said to the mother, handing her back her littling.

The mother cradled her littling to her chest and nodded, then rushed along the alley.

"Let's get out of here," growled Giant John. He snatched Leah up under one arm and Taliesin under the other, and jogged through the alley, past tharuks fighting villagers and dragon riders valiantly swooping over the buildings to battle Commander Zens' beasts. Leah jolted with every one of Giant John's steps, her feet bouncing in the air behind Giant John's large body. Opposite her, Taliesin's head bobbed as Giant John ran. The man was stronger than an ox, no, two oxen. Alley after alley, he raced.

Leah had seen Giant John at Roberto and Ezaara's hand-fasting dance. He'd been sitting in a corner with Master Giddi, gnawing on a goat haunch. His appetite had been amazing, but then again, not so amazing, given his size; the man had downed enough to feed an army of snarling tharuks.

Giant John ducked into a lane and stopped under a sequestered archway, puffing. He lowered Leah and Taliesin to their feet, then crouched down, catching his breath. He looked them both in the eyes. "It's havoc here. If you're to get to the red guards and find the piaua juice we so desperately need, we have to keep you out of sight—otherwise tharuks may take you as slaves." He waved a hand down the lane. "In the stables along here, I have a wagon full of ale and wine barrels. One of the larger barrels is empty and has no bottom. It's on the wagon tray over a trapdoor. I'll hide you in there as we leave town. If there's any trouble, open the trapdoor to escape. You must get to the red guards, the dragons and riders that patrol an area north of Great Spanglewood Forest close to Death Valley. The piaua trees in Spanglewood have been destroyed. Marlies said the red guards are our best chance of finding piaua juice."

"B-but where are they?" Taliesin asked.

"Through Spanglewood," Giant John said. "Travel to the east for a week. When you can see the Terramite range poking above the trees, head north. You'll find them." He cleared his throat and straightened. "Of course, all this talk is just a precaution. Hopefully, I'll be with you the whole way. Now, come. If the stable master asks, I'm your uncle and you two are my niece and nephew. We're rushing home after making the deliveries for my vineyard."

Giant John rushed along the alley with their hands in his and turned into a stable yard. "Good," he whispered. "Tharuks haven't been here yet, but we'd better be quick if we're to get out of town."

A man with a dark mustache stepped out of an outbuilding. "Morning. Got some littlings with you today, have you?"

"Just my nephew and niece returning home from a week in the city with friends." Giant John thrust coin into the man's eager hands. "Thank you for taking care of my horses and getting them ready for the return journey."

Giant John took them behind the stables to the rear of the yard where four horses were harnessed to a large wagon laden with barrels. "It'll be cramped, but this is the best way for you out of here." Giant John lifted them both onto the wagon tray, then leaped up and pried a barrel open. Glancing about, he said, "Quick, while no one's looking. Some citizens of Montanara like to make quick coin by selling information to tharuks." He lifted Taliesin into the barrel. "Stay quiet. I'll let you out again when it's safe." He helped Leah inside.

She crouched on the wagon floor and leaned against the barrel's inside wall. The tang of red wine filled her nostrils. Taliesin's legs were crammed up against hers. She set their rucksack on the floor.

Giant John peered inside. "Not very comfy, is it? Hopefully we'll have you both out soon. Move until you find the bolt to the trapdoor, then try not to sit on it."

Leah shuffled over until she was hard against Taliesin's side and felt around the floor. She found a bolt with a rope attached to it.

"That's my girl. If you tug that rope, the trapdoor will pop open." Giant John reached in and tapped wooden pegs on either side of the barrel above them. "When you open it, hold these so you don't fall straight out. But make sure you don't open it while I'm moving. All good?"

Leah gave the rope a tug. "All good, Giant John."

"If I drum my fingers on the wagon, then you need to flee. Understood?"

Taliesin reached up to touch a peg, then nodded, his blue eyes huge.

"Righty-ho. Off we go," Giant John murmured.

A lid thudded shut above them and everything went black.

Taliesin's hand found Leah's. "Leah," he whispered.

"Yes?"

"I don't like small spaces. It reminds me of when tharuks found me."

"Don't worry, I'm here."

The wagon rocked as Giant John climbed upon the seating. Reins snapped, hooves thudded, and the wagon trundled out of the yard, every reverberation running through the boards into Leah's bones. The jolting got worse as the wagon wheels clattered onto city cobbles. At least she had a little cushioning on her rump. It'd be much worse for Taliesin with his bony backside. She gave his hand a reassuring squeeze.

Taliesin gripped her hand hard as they headed on, surrounded by darkness.

THARUK ATTACK

With their knees jammed up to their chins and their rucksack crammed between them in a wine barrel, Leah and Taliesin headed out of Montanara. Soon, the metal-bound wheels of Giant John's wagon clattered off the cobbled roads and onto a dirt trail. At least the bone-shuddering cobbles were behind them. Leah adjusted her sit bones, but it was impossible to get comfortable. This was going to be a long journey, but every dragon length closer to the red guards was a boon.

Beside her, Taliesin squirmed.

The wagon slowed and stopped.

"Where you going?" a guttural voice snarled.

A tharuk! Leah's heart pounded. Taliesin whimpered. She fumbled in the dark, covering his mouth with her hand and guiding his hands to his ears. His elbow dug into her. Pressed against her side, his bony frame trembled. Leah had seen the old lash scars on his back. The beast's voice must be bringing back his memories of tharuks beating him in Death Valley.

"Good day, kind sirs. I'm delivering wine," Giant John boomed.

Marlies had told Leah tales of Giant John's deliveries across the Flatlands while she was hiding in the secret compartment in the base of his wagon. Back then, Giant John had dulled the tharuks' senses with beer. Hopefully these tharuks would fall for his tricks. If not... Leah gulped.

There was a creak as Giant John clambered onto the wagon tray, then the scrape of a barrel being moved—although how one man could move the enormous barrels on John's wagon amazed her. Giant John thudded to the ground. The wagon jolted and sticks crunched underfoot.

"Here, my fine tharuks, some of Nightshade Alley's finest." The tang of red wine drifted on the air. "Enjoy it." The wagon creaked and shifted as Giant John climbed back on board. He clicked his tongue and snapped the reins, then they were moving again.

Leah let out a breath, not daring to take her hand from Taliesin's mouth yet.

"Wait!" roared a tharuk.

The wagon kept moving, picking up pace. Feet stomped behind them.

Shards, from the sound of the pounding, a whole horde of tharuks must be racing after them.

"Wait. 555 warned us about you, Giant!"

"Whoa," Giant John called.

The wagon careened, everything tilted. With a smash that ricocheted through Leah's spine, they stopped. Giant John drummed his fingers on the wagon tray, the signal for them to flee. Beside her, Taliesin shook harder than ever.

She pulled the rucksack onto her back and leaned in, whispering, "Stay quiet."

He nodded against her shoulder.

As thudding feet converged at the head of the wagon, Leah barely breathed her next words into Taliesin's ear. "Wriggle back against the side of the barrel and hold the pegs. I'm opening the trapdoor." As soon as Taliesin had shuffled out of the way, she held onto the peg above her and felt in the dark until her fingers found the rope. She pulled it, thanking the dragon gods the bolt didn't squeak. The trapdoor flew open. Leah blinked against the bright light.

Taliesin was cowering against the side of the barrel on a scrap of planking, hands on the pegs, the hole in the trapdoor gaping at his feet. Her own heels were on wood, her toes hanging over the edge.

She had to go first or the boy would be paralyzed by fear.

Growls broke out at the other end of the wagon.

"My apologies," Giant John prattled in an overly-loud voice. "One of my horses got away on me. She's been having a lot of problems lately with her front shoe, so it's been hard to control her. I wouldn't want her to go lame, would I? I'll just check on her." His voice grew more distant as he clambered off the wagon. Tharuk footfalls followed him.

Beneath them, dirt and patches of snow beckoned.

A rush of cold air enveloped Leah as she dropped to the ground. Glancing under the wagon, she confirmed what she'd suspected: Giant John had driven the wagon into a tree. The side was up hard against some bushes, so she and Taliesin could escape. John's boots paced in front of the horses, tharuks gathered around him. He chatted away and gave a loud belly laugh—disguising their noise.

That distraction wouldn't last long. She beckoned urgently to Taliesin. He slid to the ground.

With cold fingers, Leah pushed the trapdoor shut and twisted a nail to hold it closed. She and Taliesin crawled under the bushes. Gods, what luck so far! Keeping to the underbrush, they made as much headway as they could. When roars shattered the air, they took to their feet and ran, avoiding the snow and racing along winding dirt paths between the trees so their tracks weren't as visible.

Not that it would help them if there was a tharuk tracker around.

Dragons' Hold

Kierion burst through the council doors, skidding to a stop as his boots hit broken glass. Who in the First Egg's name had smashed a drinking glass in here—and why? All the dragon masters stared at him. Many were missing—most notably, the Queen's Rider. His feet crunching on shards, he approached. "I'm sorry to interrupt, but Master Giddi has disappeared."

Master Lars, the council leader, leaped to his feet, his blond beard bristling as he snapped, "What do you mean, Master Giddi's disappeared?"

Kierion cringed. Shards, he hated being the bearer of bad tidings. "Battle Master Aidan asked me to bring the news."

The council doors thudded open again behind Kierion.

Lars thumped the granite table with his fist. "The Queen's Rider's unconscious, Maazini's been turned, and now the Dragon Mage is gone?"

Shivers skittered down Kierion's spine. What in flame's name had happened to Ezaara? Kierion didn't dare ask with the council masters looking so dire. "We vanquished the dark dragons from Montanara, but then Commander Zens arrived in a flash of golden clouds and took Master Giddi away."

"Realm gates," announced spymaster Tonio, closing the double doors to the council chamber behind him and striding into the room. "When I spoke to Roberto yesterday, he said one of Anakisha's travel rings had been stolen."

Kierion scratched his neck, not eager to share more terrible news. "The strange thing is that Master Aidan reported Master Giddi willingly getting onto Zens' dark dragon."

"Obviously Master Giddi has chosen to side with dark dragons," Master Mage Starrus snapped. "I told you he was no good. I'd like to—"

Master Mage Reina rounded on Master Starrus. "You're only here in Master Giddi's stead," she said. "You no longer have authority on this or any council. You were demoted when Master Giddi was appointed leader of the Wizard Council."

Kierion wished he was a mage himself, so he could blast Starrus with a bolt of mage flame. Couldn't he see that Giddi might have been turned?

Master Lars barked at the new leader of the blue guards, "Dominique, please have one of your guards escort Master Starrus to the main cavern so he may proceed with training the mages. And then have someone clean up these flaming glass shards that Tomaaz made."

Dominique thumped his fist over his heart and escorted Master Starrus out of the council chamber.

"Don't blame Tomaaz," Flight Master Alyssa muttered, flicking a dark brown braid over her shoulder. "You threatened to execute his dragon when it turned."

By the dragon gods, a lot had gone on while Kierion had been gone. He battled to keep the shock from his face.

Lars' steely blue eyes cut through the room.

No one else dared speak.

Kierion pounded his fist on his heart and nodded to Lars, then left the council chambers, the doors thudding shut behind him. Gods, Dragons' Hold was a mess if Ezaara was unconscious, Giddi was gone, and Maazini, Tomaaz's dragon, had been turned to follow their enemy Commander Zens. But he couldn't stay and help. His stomach churned. He had to find Adelina.

Tonio, the spymaster was concerned because she'd been missing for a few days. And Kierion's dragon, Riona, had just told him Adelina had been seen flying to Montanara on Linaia, her dragon. Just the thought of bubbly Adelina with her dark eyes in war-torn Montanara where shadow dragons had burned anyone who moved made Kierion nauseous.

He clenched his fists and ran. *Riona, meet me on the ledge outside my cavern.*

I'm already waiting, Kierion, but you're about to drop. You're no use to anyone hungry and exhausted. I'll be outside the mess cavern once you've slept and eaten.

"But Adelina's been missing for days."

"Then a bit longer won't change things." Riona's tone was final.

Groaning, Kierion slowed down and trudged to his cavern.

§

Ezaara woke in her bed, groggy. Her fingers ran over the white quilt edged with golden dragons, reveling in its billowing softness. From her first day at Dragons' Hold, this quilt had been a safe cocoon for her to retreat to.

A chair creaked beside her bed.

"You're awake." Roberto's voice was husky. He smiled, but the smile didn't chase the dark shadows from under his eyes or the worry lines from his mouth. He exhaled and reached out to hold her hand, rubbing the back of it with his thumb. His dark hair was tangled and messy, and he gave a brittle laugh. "You've been out cold for two days. You really had me worried this time."

"Huh?" was all Ezaara could manage. The last thing she remembered, she'd tried to meld with all of Zens' shadow dragons to stop the battle above Montanara. He slipped pillows under her shoulders and brought a glass of sweet, cool tea to her lips. "Slowly, now."

She sipped, soothing her parched throat. Her head was still fuzzy. Bones, weary. Gods, even her bones were tired. "Roberto?"

He sprang up from his chair and knelt beside the bed, holding her hands. "Yes? What is it?"

"How many were wounded? Dragons and riders? How many dead?" Before Roberto could answer, Ezaara's eyes shut and darkness closed in.

§

Roberto steeled his nerves, banishing the ghosts of his past, and strode down the spiral stairs to the dungeons, pounding out a steady beat on the black stone. He had to confront his father. Get this over with. His mind was numb, body icy with dread, but he refused to allow that to slow him. Instead, he propelled himself forward, barreling past the blue guards with a terse nod, and arrived at the dungeon where Amato was held. Because Amato was how he thought of him now. The cursed murderer from Naobia. Roberto felt no pull of father-and-son relationship.

Jacinda unlocked the cell and let him enter.

He was alone with his dreaded enemy.

Amato, slouched on his mattress, looked up. With surprising agility, he sprang to his feet, posture defensive, hand flying to his hip. Then he realized he had no weapon.

Roberto stood, observing him. Long moments passed. Wary eyes regarded wary eyes.

"Son?" Amato croaked.

Son? After all he'd done. Roberto opened his mouth.

Then snapped his jaw shut. With all his resolve to face Amato, he now had nothing to say. He turned and stalked from the cell.

Ezaara woke slumped on her bed, her mind still ragged at the edges. She'd tried her best but hadn't been able to save her people from Zens' dark dragons. The bodies in Lush Valley haunted her. Dead and broken, scattered over the square, the wounded and injured moaning. She'd barely had time to patch up the worst of them and give instructions before leaving. And these were people she'd grown up with. The people she'd known and loved. Across the realm, others were dying. And she was responsible for them all. *"Oh gods, Zaarusha, when I leaped upon your back that day in Lush Valley, I had no idea…"*

Queen Zaarusha answered from her den next door, her comforting rumble echoing through Ezaara's mind, soothing the ragged edges the shadow dragons had shredded. *"I know. You've come far. You've learned so much."*

"Our people are dying."

"It saddens me too, but they were dying long before you ever met me. Their blood has been spilled for many decades now." Zaarusha's voice took on dark vengeance. "Commander Zens has a lot to answer for."

"And so do I. As Queen's Rider I should be able to head off these beasts, to conquer them. Not watch my people die, their life blood spilling on the snow, in the forests, and in town squares." She'd failed. In the core of her bones, she knew she'd failed.

And the worst moment was her shooting at her mother. She'd failed her people. Her family. Failed Ma. A dark chasm opened inside Ezaara, ready to swallow her.

§

When Roberto returned to Ezaara's cavern, she was stirring. Worn out from sitting up watching her for two days, he kicked off his boots and lay on the bed beside her, his hands clasped under his head, elbows out, staring at the cavern's stone ceiling.

"What is it?" she murmured. "You're mulling something over."

He sighed, turning to her. "I've just been to see Amato. I thought I could talk to him."

Her green eyes regarded him steadily.

Shards, she looked exhausted. He stroked her hair. He didn't know how he felt, how to tell Ezaara. All of his father's actions had been driven by Zens' methimium. As had the actions of others: Sofia when she'd tried to kill Ezaara;

Roberto when he'd tried to kill her too; Ezaara, her mother; and now, Maazini had been turned. All of them had been victims of Zens' methimium crystals. But none of them wore the blood of hundreds on their hands like Amato did. Roberto closed his eyes, but tears still sneaked out the corners.

All of Zens' other victims had been saved early enough, before they'd done too much harm. If they hadn't… The thought made him shudder. The things Amato had done. The things Zens had forced Roberto to do in Death Valley. He also had blood on his hands. Maybe he was similar to his father after all.

"Some scars run too deep for forgiveness," she whispered.

His words. He swallowed, turning to her. "I still don't know how you forgave me. I turned on you. When I close my eyes, I see my knife against your beautiful neck. Your blood welling…" He stroked the satin skin below her ear. "I'm sorry. I think I'll be apologizing for a lifetime."

Her eyes glimmered silver in the torchlight.

"What is it?" he murmured, brushing her stray tear away with his thumb. "You and your ma in Lush Valley?"

She closed her eyes, more tears escaping, and melded with him.

Whispers wound through her mind. That dark-haired woman had to go. Ezaara raised her bow. Just a few more moments, and that evil woman's screaming would be gone.

"It's the silver dragon too," *the voice goaded.* "Kill it, and you'll be free."

Ezaara pulled her bowstring taut. And waited.

Roberto felt the hatred surging through Ezaara, the narrow focus of her darkened vision. He heard the insidious whispers urging her to kill her mother—whispers she had to obey. He felt the implant burning in her arm, burrowing deeper into her skin. Her muscles flexing as she pulled her bow taut and aimed at the woman on the silver dragon.

Now, free at Dragons' Hold, she was drowning in a new sea of darkness. A canker that would eat away at her, consuming her from the inside out.

"Roberto," she whispered. "If I can't even forgive myself, how can I expect you to forgive your father?"

He stroked her hair. "Do you remember what you told me?"

She shook her head.

"That Zens wanted to destroy me." He kissed her furrowed brow. "Knowing that made me fight to make sure he didn't. If you hate yourself, he wins." He kissed the tip of her nose. "And we won't let him win. Do you remember what you told Sofia at her trial?"

She shook her head again.

"We'll never succeed if we let Zens' tools of war drive us apart."

"Did I say that?" Her smile was like the first fingers of dawn peeking over a mountaintop.

"You did. You're very wise. The wisest woman I know." Roberto kissed her.

§

Ezaara threaded her fingers through Roberto's hair, pulling him closer as his mouth explored hers. So much had happened since their hand-fasting holiday. People had fought and died. Zens had battled and been vanquished. It'd only been ten days ago that Amato had surfaced and turned Roberto's life upside down.

But right now, it was them—just the two of them. Lying on her bed—their bed—together in the Queen's Rider's cavern for the first time. She leaned her forehead against his.

"Naobia feels like a million years ago," Roberto murmured, their breath mingling. "Remember dancing on the sand with the surf washing around our ankles?"

"I do. And the lazy mornings in that enormous bed." Her cheeks warmed.

He grinned at her. "The sun-warmed boulder in the middle of Crystal Lake. Gods, you were beautiful."

How could she forget his lean, tanned body cutting through the clear water? Back in Naobia, he'd been right when he'd said they'd make new memories. And right now, they could make more. "Close your eyes."

When his dark lashes were flush against his tanned skin, Ezaara slipped out of bed and stole over to Zaarusha's saddlebags against the cavern wall. She dug past her weapons and cloak, searching for Roberto's gift. It wasn't there. She spun, scanning the cavern. The beautiful Naobian riders' garb Roberto had ordered for her was draped over her chest of drawers. Quickly slipping off her clothes, she changed into it. The colorful dragons winked in the torchlight as she strode back to the bedside.

"When can I open my eyes?" Roberto asked, his deep voice husky.

Ezaara traced her fingers over his lips, then kissed him. "What do you think?"

Roberto opened his eyes, swung out of bed, and stood, placing his hands gently on her shoulders. "You're beautiful, no matter what you wear." He took a long slow breath. "But right now, you're breathtaking."

He kissed her. His river of *sathir* danced around her, entwining with hers, silver flecks glimmering like a thousand glowworms lighting her way through the dark.

$$§$$

Jael followed Tonio into the dungeon with a brace of blue guards. He held the torch up so they could see. A wrinkled old crone in a mage cloak squinted in the torchlight. Behind her, lurking in the shadows, was a decrepit dark dragon. Its skin hung in saggy folds from its bony frame, as if it hadn't eaten in moons.

Tonio spun. "I don't know who this is, Jacinda," he said to the lead guard. "I wanted to see Velrama, the young mage Kierion brought here."

The blue guard stepped forward. "This is the mage Kierion delivered. She's aged decades in three days." Jacinda grimaced. "And so has her dragon."

Tonio approached the dragon.

"Leave my beast alone," the mage snarled. "Let him have his dying days in peace."

Jael had told the council that the dragon they'd seen in the forest had aged, but it was another thing for the spymaster to see the evidence with his own eyes. "Why have you aged so fast? Are you dying?" Jael asked Velrama. If it was really Velrama. It was more likely to be one of the fakes Zens had made.

"I can't die," she snapped. "There are hundreds of me. And I don't have to tell you anything." She flung an age-spotted hand at the blue guards and laughed when they flinched. A lone spark dropped from her finger to the stone.

Jael put the torch in a sconce. When he'd seen Velrama a short while ago at the mage trials, she'd cast more than a lone spark. "What's happened to you?"

She snarled at him, "Nothing."

"At the mage trials you had so much power at your fingertips. You could create walls of flame or ice."

Velrama's wrinkles creased in a deep frown. "What mage trials?" She looked truly perplexed.

Tonio leaned in and whispered, "Test her. Fling flame at her and see what happens."

Gods, he couldn't flame one of his own mages.

"Now," hissed Tonio. "It's the only way to know whether she's faking."

Jael raised his hands then dropped them again. He shook his head.

Tonio's hand drifted toward his blade. "Are you defying a dragon master?"

Jael held his hands up, ice in his voice. "Are you ordering a master mage to attack one of his own?"

The crone cackled with glee. "Go on, fight, fight!"

Jael spun and flung his hands at the wretched soul. Flame burst from his fingertips roiling toward her. She held up her palms and pushed. A green spark flitted from each hand and fell to the stone. She dived to the side. Jael's flames hissed into the wall above her. He pulled the flames back into his palms and clenched his fists, quenching them.

"Happy now?" he snapped at both of them.

The crone crawled onto her mattress, shaking. "I don't know of any mage trials," she whimpered.

Because she wasn't the real Velrama. Zens had replicated her body, but not her memories.

Tonio strode over to inspect the shadow beast. Its scales were patchy, falling out as it stretched then paced stiffly to a water trough. Feeble yellow flashes flickered from its eyes. It was no longer the fierce, young specimen Kierion had brought into the hold just a few days ago.

Jael shot a grim glance at Tonio. "Let's go." They'd seen enough. The council would have to believe him now.

They left the blue guards to lock up behind them and strode along the stone corridors, their boot thuds echoing off the walls. Halfway up the dungeon's spiral staircase, Tonio turned back to Jael. "You know I was just goading you, so we could test her, don't you?"

Jael grunted. Whether he was telling the truth or not, the spymaster was sure slick.

"I'd never pull a knife on a fellow Naobian," Tonio continued.

You could've fooled him. Jael had seen the way Tonio glared at Amato and sometimes at Roberto. He changed the subject. "Do you know what the good news is?"

"What?" the spymaster asked as they reached the top of the stairs.

Jael came up the last step and looked Tonio in the eye. "They can't live long, so to win this war we only have to kill those mages and dark dragons faster than Zens can create them."

"Only?" Tonio raised an eyebrow.

"Yes. Only." Jael strode off, his boots clipping the stone in a rapid staccato.

§

Marlies held up Caldeff's head and helped him sip some feverweed tea. It'd been a day since the older rider had succumbed to a fever after a gash in his thigh had become infected. She wasn't surprised—tharuk claws were filthy. Although she'd used clean herb, she'd had no piaua juice to seal the wound and heal it, so it'd been bound to get infected.

Once he'd finished the feverweed infusion, she peeled back the covers and removed his bandage to inspect the wound. A red line tracked up his thigh. She had no way to fight it. Nothing she could do except make him comfortable and hope his body could fight the infection. At least the tea would help him rest. She cleansed the wound again and changed his bandage. She'd have to watch him tonight.

After washing her hands, she slumped in her chair and propped her elbows on the edge of his bed, her head in her hands. If only she wasn't so tired. It wasn't as if sleep helped. Her bones ached and her muscles were fatigued. And with the constant flood of injured riders and not enough help in the infirmary, it was easy to feel overwhelmed.

The infirmary door clicked shut. A soft tread made its way toward her. "It's late," Hans murmured, rubbing her shoulders. "How's your wound?"

"I'm recovering." At least the gash under her ribs wasn't infected. "We're lucky Bruno's aim is so lousy." A hand's breadth farther and Bruno would've hit her vital organs and killed her.

"Indeed. Come to bed."

"I wouldn't sleep anyway."

"Because you're worried about Taliesin and Leah again?" Hans asked.

Marlies stood, rubbing the small of her back. Gods, her legs ached. At least they were still functioning. She sighed. "Yes, I'm worried about them, Hans. Aren't you?"

Hans tilted his head. "I haven't had a bad vision about their quest. Mind you, I don't see everything. They're probably fine, safely on their way to the red guards with Giant John."

"I'll be glad when they return with the piaua juice. We sorely need it." If they returned.

"And we sorely need you to be rested." He ran a hand through his dark curls, keen green eyes regarding her. "Staying up and watching Caldeff isn't going to help you recover from your stint in Death Valley, Marlies. We need you fighting fit here in the infirmary. You're the only healer we have now—apart from Ezaara, but she's busy running the realm." He hugged her. "Gods, Marlies,

I don't want to lose you. Come to bed. I'll get up and check Caldeff in a few hours."

Marlies shook her head. "I can't, Hans. I just can't."

§

Roberto was gone when Ezaara woke to a soft knock. The door opened and Sofia stuck her head inside. Ezaara started.

No, it was all right. Sofia had changed. She shook her head. Zens' methimium implants were wreaking havoc upon Dragons' Realm. For the Egg's sake, the least she could do was forgive Sofia's attempt on her life. "Come in, Sofia."

Sofia's face fell. "Did you want me to leave?"

Ezaara frowned. "No, I just invited you in."

"You shook your head when you saw me."

"I was thinking about Zens," Ezaara half lied. No point in getting Sofia's feathers ruffled.

Sofia flinched. "He's never far from my mind either. I saw Roberto heading off, so I thought you may want some help."

"Dragons' Realm needs whatever help we can get," Ezaara replied. "I don't know how we're going to beat Zens." She tapped her fingers on the quilt. She was still dizzy, but she got out of bed and pulled on a warm robe. "Could you bring me some ink, parchment, and tubes for messenger birds if you can find some?"

"Messenger birds?" Sofia nodded. "I'll be back in a moment."

When Sofia returned with supplies, Ezaara wrote a message to the Naobian green guards in the South, requesting troops. Another to the people of Lush Valley. More to Last Stop, Montanara, Horseshoe Bend and the villages scattered through Spanglewood Forest. By the time she'd done those, her hands were cramping, but she penned a message to the red guards who patrolled northwest of Spanglewood, near Death Valley, and lastly, to the brown guards over the Northern Alps beyond Dragons' Hold.

Ezaara chewed her lip. There was one more person she could ask for help. She wrote her last message, knowing it was a cry in the wilderness and that the bird would probably die and be scorched in the hot desert sands before it ever reached Ithsar, the young Robandi assassin whose deformed fingers Ezaara had healed. Ithsar had helped her and Roberto escape from the clutches of her mother, Ashewar, the chief prophetess of the Robandi assassins. Perhaps she'd be willing to help her again... if Ashewar hadn't executed Ithsar for treason.

Ezaara sealed the last message in its tube, eyes burning. Was Ithsar still alive? How many fine people was she asking to sacrifice their lives? She clenched her jaw, squeezing back tears. Fewer than Zens would slaughter if they did nothing. "The messages are ready, Sofia."

Sofia swept out with the tubes.

Moments later, Tomaaz entered Ezaara's cavern. His blond hair was ratty, his riders' garb still stained from battle, and his face was gaunt again. After two stints in Death Valley, it didn't take much for him to look haggard. "Thank the gods, you're all right," he said.

She rose from her table.

He rushed over to hug her and held her tight. "They said you were unconscious."

Ezaara clung to him, stifling a sob. "Tomaaz, sometimes it's all too much."

They sat on the edge of her bed.

"It's pretty grim." Her twin shook his head. "A far cry from Lush Valley. I just—" He squeezed his eyes shut, inhaling.

She placed a hand on his shoulder. "What is it?"

His green eyes were bright with tears. "It's Maazini. He has an implant, one of Zens' burrowing ones. And if I don't extract it, they'll kill him at dawn tomorrow."

"What? Kill a royal dragon? Queen Zaarusha's own son? Who decided that?"

"The council, in your absence. Lars decided, but it was a consensus."

"Zaarusha, this is preposterous."

"The council are worried that if they spare Maazini, it will set a precedent for hundreds of our own dragons going rogue and fighting us."

"I was a victim to methimium, Tomaaz." Ezaara met his eyes. "I had an implant too."

"You did?" Tomaaz gripped her hand. "When?"

She didn't want to hold his gaze, but she had to. She had to give him hope. "I was shot in Lush Valley. An arrowhead burrowed into my skin. The evil whispers were so compelling they even goaded me into firing an arrow at Ma."

With a sharp intake of breath he tightened his grip, squeezing her fingers. "What happened? Was Ma hurt?"

Ezaara shrugged. "Roberto pushed me off Zaarusha, so my arrow missed."

"And then…" His eyes were wide with hope, brimming with tears.

"He and Ma held me down and dug out the methimium crystal. Any longer and it might have burrowed too deep."

Tomaaz swallowed, his throat bobbing. He hugged her again, tighter than before. "Gods, I don't want to lose Maazini." This time, tears spilled from his eyes, wetting her hair.

A Stroke of Luck

Leah and Taliesin headed north through Spanglewood Forest, keeping to less-traveled tracks, making for the northern hills that ran through the trees.

As they reached the foot of the hills, Taliesin turned, gazing into the branches of an evergreen pine. "Can you see them?" he whispered, pointing at the foliage.

Tharuks? No, it must be something else. "What?" Leah craned her neck but there was nothing unusual there.

"Spangles." Taliesin smiled. "They're watching over us."

"Where?"

"In the trees among the needles. See those tiny glimmers? Those are spangles."

Try as hard as she could, Leah couldn't see anything but pine. The whispers of the trees were muted, soft.

Taliesin shrugged. "Master Giddi told me only some people can see them. I guess I'm lucky."

"Come on." Leah glanced at the switchbacks leading up the range of hills to a pass. "I don't think tharuks are tracking us or they would've caught us by now, but we'd better keep walking."

It took them over an hour of panting and puffing to get to the top. They didn't dare linger in the pass to admire the broad sweep of southern forest behind them or the swathe of trees with the Northern Alps rising beyond. This high up, they could be spotted. Although the boy was tiring, Leah took his hand and led him down the stony trail.

"Come on, we have to get back into the trees, then we can eat and rest."

Taliesin nodded, following her down the hillside.

Deep in the forest on the other side of the hills, there were high drifts of snow where the sun hadn't peeked for days. Leah's feet were numb, despite her warm boots. Taliesin's nose was bright red from the cold. Leah tucked his cloak closer around him, then pulled his cold hand, leading him on. At least it wasn't snowing now, although from the dark clouds above, it might be soon. They trudged on through the forest, past burnt tharuk bodies, the stink of charred dragon flesh and, occasionally, a dead rider. The trees' whispers here were off, discordant, the way they'd been when tharuks had attacked her village.

Taliesin squeezed Leah's hand tighter as they skirted signs of slaughter.

Maybe she hadn't been courageous when she'd volunteered to seek piaua juice. Maybe she'd just been foolish. If these dragons and riders couldn't survive, she and Taliesin had no chance. She'd thought they might have an advantage by using their small size and stealth to slip about unnoticed, but shadow dragons could burn anyone. And anyone, no matter their size, could succumb to the cold.

Wings flapped overhead. "It might be a shadow dragon," Leah hissed.

They ducked under a tree, peering up through the foliage. Through the canopy, blue wings blocked the sky.

Taliesin let go of her hand and shot out into the snow. He jumped up and down, waving his arms. "Down here. Help us, down here."

The dragon's long sinuous neck snaked down to peer between the trees. It gave a roar and tilted its head to the left.

Taliesin turned to Leah, eyes shining. "She wants us to follow her."

He had the gift of prophecy and said he could see spangles. "Can you meld with dragons too?" Leah asked.

"No," Taliesin replied, "but she jerked her head for us to follow."

"And you know she's female?"

He laughed. "Come on, we're going to be all right."

Leah didn't have the heart to deny him. Gripping his hand, she followed him through the trees, the way the dragon had indicated.

The blue dragon landed, sending a flurry of snow skyward as it folded its wings. The dragon's saddle was empty. Leah approached and placed a hand upon the dragon's hide. *Are you injured?* she asked.

The dragon's slitted green eyes were sorrowful. *No, I'm not injured, but my rider died in battle.*

I'm sad for your loss. Leah hesitated.

What are you doing so far from the nearest settlement? the blue asked.

We're looking for the red guards, Leah said. *We're trying to find more piaua juice.*

Aha, the blue dragon murmured. *So you're Marlies' apprentice healer. Other dragons have spoken of you. We've all agreed we should help you with your quest for the restorative juice."* The dragon turned its gaze to Taliesin. *"And who is this?"*

"*My friend, Taliesin,*" she answered.

To Leah's surprise, the dragon bowed its head, and murmured in her mind, *"Tell the grandson of Anakisha to place his hand upon my forehead so he understands me. I would like to speak with him."*

Leah relayed the message and dropped her hand from the dragon's scales.

Taliesin tentatively laid his palm on the dragon's head. After a moment, he broke into a smile. "Come on, Leah. Amara is going to take us to the red guards." The dragon extended a foreleg so Taliesin could clamber up its side.

Once he was in the saddle, Taliesin reached down and stretched out a hand to Leah. She, too, had to use the dragon's foreleg to climb up. They tugged their cloaks around them, and the mighty dragon took off, leaving nothing but footprints in the snow.

DUNGEONS

Tonio's footfalls rang off the narrow winding walls of the stairway to the dungeons. At the fork, he nodded to the blue guards, two of them falling in behind him as he descended the dank corridor that led to the dragon holding cells. Although Amato had been here three days, his dragon had arrived only a few hours ago and had been put in with his rider. Whoever had decided that Amato should no longer be separated from Matotoi had been mad. Or struck with soft pity for the man who'd become a wretched monster and destroyed so many lives.

Jacinda, the blue guard on duty, rose as he approached. Her keys clanked in the lock and she opened the cell. Tonio stalked inside. Jacinda and another young guard followed him in, staying by the barred door. Tonio placed his torch in a sconce and turned to behold his nemesis.

Amato was mewling in his sleep. His bony body, only partially covered with blankets, was wracked with shivers. Bandages peeped above the back of his shirt. Lars said he'd been burned fighting to protect people in Lush Valley, but that didn't impress Tonio. It was too little and far too late.

Amato's dragon lifted his head, yellow eyes regarding him. Matotoi was only a shadow of his former glory. His scales had faded from glorious emerald to an insipid green nearly leached of color. His bony ribs poked through his sagging skin. Matotoi angled his sinuous neck between Tonio and Amato.

Tonio shrugged. No doubt, Matotoi felt the venom radiating off him. The dragon snorted and Amato awoke, frantically casting around, grasping his blankets and pulling them to his chest.

This skeletal wretch was a far cry from the kind-hearted green guard who'd tried to protect Tonio from his abusive step-brother—before Amato had turned into a power-hungry traitor and given his own son, Roberto, to the enemy.

Amato's eyes widened in fear.

So he'd recognized him. He still had his wits. With a little pressure, Tonio could get some information out of him.

Tonio cracked his knuckles, jerking his head toward Amato. "Stand him up, and let's get started."

The young blue guard pulled Amato to his feet.

"Now, leave us."

"Sorry, sir, but Lars has instructed us to stay," Jacinda answered, her hands hovering near the sword at her hip.

Of course Lars had. Tonio would have to play nice or risk being tried. Lars had threatened as much. He had to be quick off the mark, keep Amato on his toes, so the moment Amato met his eye, Tonio snapped, "You blame your crimes on Zens. How did he control you?"

"Methimium."

"What?" Tonio barked.

"The yellow crystals he implants in people are called methimium. They control *sathir* and harness the life energy, and Zens converts it into hate and rage."

Tonio raised a cynical eyebrow. Amato hadn't lost his gift of the gab, even though Tonio's dragon, Antonika, had told him he'd been in a cave for years. "Tell me more."

Matotoi butted Tonio's hand. Tonio obliged, laying his hand on the dragon's forehead. *"I confirm that Amato was captured by Zens and implanted with a yellow crystal, which forced him to obey Zens."*

"If you don't believe me," Amato croaked, "lift my bandage and look for yourself." He turned and lifted his shirt, exposing his bony lower ribs. "Under my right shoulder blade."

"Shirt off. On the mattress," Tonio barked.

Amato obeyed surprisingly quickly.

Burning with morbid curiosity, Tonio peeled back the bandage. The middle of Amato's back was covered with broken blisters and smeared with healing salve. A mean ridge of scar, thicker than his thumb and half as long as his forearm, scored the skin under Amato's shoulder blade. "On your feet again. Other scars I've seen from these methimium implants haven't been that thick. It could be from anything."

"Most people don't have a dragon performing the surgery with his talon." Amato scrambled to his feet, tucked his shirt in, and wrapped his blanket around him. "When I realized I'd killed my wife, we plunged into the lake to hide in the cave," he said, scratching his matted beard. "I begged Matotoi to rip the vile thing out. It got infected, so we used lake weed to treat it. That scar is my memento." Amato sat on the mattress and slumped, placing his head in his hands. "Once the methimium was gone, I remembered every Naobian I'd given to Zens as slaves for his mines. I was ashamed. Too terrified to go back to Naobia. And when Roberto took me there, all the victims—" He broke into a sob.

As far-fetched as it seemed, it was plausible under the circumstances and aligned with what Erob had told Antonika. "Not a very likely story. How did you survive?"

"Fish and lake weed. We had plenty of water, but by the time I was ready to leave, my lungs were too weak to get out."

"Why should I believe you?" Tonio snapped. "Why should I believe any of this?"

Amato lurched to his knees, clawing at Tonio's feet. "Forgive me, Tonio. Please. I'm sorry about Rosita. I truly am," he cried. "You knew me, the real me, before Zens caught me. I made sure your brother was punished by Master Taren for beating you."

Master Taren, the spymaster who'd recruited Tonio in Naobia and brought him here to train him.

"It wasn't in my nature to hurt anyone," Amato whined. "Zens made me do it. It was Zens. I swear. I'm sorry."

"Not as sorry as I am." Tonio pushed Amato away with the toes of his boot. He would have kicked him if the blue guards weren't present. "Back on your mattress." He let ice slither into his voice. "You murdered hundreds of our loved ones. That's unforgivable, no matter what your excuse."

As Tonio turned to leave the cell, Matotoi butted his back. What did that flaming dragon want this time? Tonio laid his hand on the insipid creature's hide.

"These are Amato's thoughts while under the crystal's influence. I can recall them clearly," the dragon mind-melded, sharing a memory.

Sinister shadows swirled, goading Amato. Nasty whispers dogged his actions. He coldly calculated which Naobians he'd lure away from town in order to supply tharuks with slaves. Rosita's face sprung to Amato's mind, wreathed with shadows. Amato led her to an orchard where tharuks were waiting. The voice in Amato's head laughed as Tonio's wife fought, screaming and kicking. A tharuk slashed her cheek with its claws. Another kicked her in the stomach. The whole time, the voice in Amato's head crooned, "Well done, Amato. Such a pretty one. Tomorrow, bring me more slaves."

"Please, please," gibbered Amato.

Cold dread snaked through Tonio's gut. His palms broke out in sweat. He snapped mind-meld, staring down at the man sobbing on the mattress. It was hard to believe that this rider had once been the leader of the Naobian green guards and one of the best dragon riders in the South. Tonio hadn't touched him or used any implements of torture, yet Amato was a mess.

"Pathetic," Tonio barked. He spun and stomped from the cell, leaving the blue guards to lock up behind him.

§

After Roberto had kissed Ezaara, she'd fallen asleep quickly, leaving him to stare at the stone ceiling. Dark thoughts of his littling years nagged at him—surfacing now that his father was here, in the dungeons. He rose and pulled on his riders' garb, stooped to kiss Ezaara's hair, then made his way through the crowded main corridors and down to the dungeons. He encountered Tonio in the corridor.

"Off to see your father?" the spymaster asked.

Roberto nodded.

"I've just been there, but didn't find out anything," said the spymaster. "Mind if I listen in?"

"I've no problem with that."

Tonio slipped along the corridor behind Roberto and hid in the shadows beyond Amato's cell.

At the clang of the cell door slamming, Roberto's father turned.

"Amato." Roberto sighed, waiting for his father to stop exercising in the far corner. Even though his frame was almost skeletal, Amato exercised every day—and had done so in his cave under Crystal Lake for six years before Roberto had discovered him. "I have a proposition for you," Roberto announced.

Amato's eyes shone eagerly. Matotoi stirred, taking his head out from under his wing to gaze at Roberto, no doubt sensing the interest from his rider.

Roberto could be risking too much by sharing information with Amato. His father could easily use it against them. But then, his father had defended Leah in Lush Valley and Roberto and Ezaara at the cavern when Bruno had attacked. He'd hated his father for years. Been sure he'd never trust him. And here he was, about to throw this mangy dog a bone. A peace offering—a false peace offering. The rage simmering in his heart had never subsided. Still there, it had grown as cold as glacier melt, ice now surging through his veins. "Did you know Zens creates tharuks, not by breeding them, but by growing them?" he asked.

Amato nodded. "Yes, in huge tanks. I'm surprised he let you see that when you were in Death Valley."

"It wasn't on my first visit."

Amato raised his eyebrows, but Roberto held up a hand, preventing any further questions. It was none of Amato's business what'd happened when he'd been held captive by Zens again, recently. "Those dark dragons we fought in Lush Valley were also grown using the same methods," he said.

"I figured as much." Amato waited, expectantly.

Roberto wanted to pace back and forth, but he didn't give himself the luxury of showing his agitation. He forced himself not to move a muscle, motionless, assessing his father. The moon-shaped scar beneath his left eye twitched.

His father's gaze flew to it, showing a brief flicker of anguish.

So the brute felt remorse for whipping him.

Roberto steeled himself against any softness creeping into his heart. Amato hadn't shown softness years ago when he'd repeatedly beaten him and Adelina. "That's not the worst." Roberto glared at Amato. Amato stared back. "Zens is now growing people."

Stark horror crept across Amato's face. "He's an abomination."

"An abomination you served willingly."

"I had no choice. The methimium was too strong. It overpowered my will."

Despite his own misgivings, despite the anger, despite his mistreatment at this man's hands, Roberto nodded. "Numlock, swayweed, methimium… Zens' tools are overwhelming. Including the tortured screams those dark dragons inflict on people's minds."

"What do you want? You didn't come here to tell me a bedtime story, son."

Roberto flinched. *Don't son me.* He'd never be this man's son again. Despite the physical similarities, they were different. Or were they? The methimium-induced shadow voices that had goaded him to kill Ezaara were probably no different than what had driven his father. Roberto had been willing to kill the woman he loved. Just like Amato had killed Roberto's mother. He snapped himself away from that train of thought, vigorously spinning and pacing the cavern, despite his intentions not to.

"All those mages you saw in Lush Valley were grown by Zens, replicated from young mages who were kidnapped." Roberto met Amato's eyes. "And now, Commander Zens has Master Giddi."

Amato tracked Roberto's every movement.

Roberto stopped pacing, forcing himself to stand still. Forcing himself not to show any emotion before this monster. Chin high, he gazed at Amato's dark eyes, so very much like his own. "We must destroy Zens' foul work."

Amato nodded. "I agree. And I know how."

Before he could stop himself, the question shot from Roberto's mouth like an arrow. "How?"

"There's a secret tunnel into Death Valley," Amato said.

Behind him, beyond Amato's line of sight, Roberto heard Tonio's sharp intake of breath in the shadows.

Amato's eyes were bright. "If we can get past the Naobian pirates, I can take you into a hidden tunnel that comes out right in the center of Death Valley."

§

Kierion slept longer than he'd intended. *"A whole day and night,"* Riona commented. *"But at least you're not fatigued anymore."*

Flaming shards. He rushed to the mess cavern and took a bowl of stew to a table in the corner. He dunked a heel of bread into his pepper stew and munched it down. Although the aroma was delicious, he barely tasted it, mechanically chewing as he planned how to find Adelina. Ignoring the babble around him, he mind-melded with Riona. *"Who saw Adelina and Linaia flying south?"*

"A blue guard on patrol. And before you ask when, the answer's a few days ago." Riona snorted.

"How did they know she was going to Montanara?"

"It's the first city to the south, and the largest. It makes sense she'd go there."

"She could be going anywhere. What makes you so sure?" Kierion bit off another chunk of stew-soaked bread.

"Honestly, Kierion. No doubt, she was searching for you. What would you do if your murderous father returned when you'd thought he was dead? Surely, you'd seek solace with your mate."

His cheeks flushed. Of course it was only the warmth of the pepper stew. *"She's not my mate."*

"She will be when we find her."

"Don't be so silly. I don't even know if she likes me." But by the dragon gods, he hoped so.

Riona's only answer was a chuckle.

"Kierion, mind if I join you?"

Kierion glanced up as Tonio seated himself. The spymaster didn't have a plate with him.

Without any preamble, Tonio leaned in. "I still require your services. Return to Montanara. Keep your ear to the ground. We need to find a pirate to guide us through the Naobian Strait south of Death Valley. There's an old pirate tunnel that can lead us to the heart of Zens' territory."

Well, knock him dead with a feather—that was a surprise. "I might already have someone who can help you." Kierion picked up his bowl and slurped the contents down.

"Who is it?" Tonio asked.

"I don't know if he still has a ship, or even if he'll sail." Kierion wiped his mouth on the back of his sleeve and stood. "Captain's an ex-pirate and the leader of the Nightshaders in Montanara. He owes me." Kierion pounded his fist on his heart and nodded to Tonio. "I'll leave right away."

Tonio stood too. "I'll send a team of riders to Montanara the day after tomorrow." He gave a terse nod and passed Kierion a heavy coin pouch. "Gold. One hundred golden dragon heads," he muttered. "If this captain doesn't have a ship, buy one."

§

Tomaaz woke up in the dungeon corridor, still leaning against the rocky wall opposite Maazini's locked cell. Inside, Maazini was slumped on the floor. In the flickering torchlight something yellow glistened on his neck. Shards, the wound from the arrowhead was oozing pus. Tomaaz leaped to his feet, yelling, "Guards, get me a healer, immediately."

A guard rushed along the corridor. "Are you sick?"

"It's my dragon." Tomaaz sucked in a deep shuddering breath. "He needs a healer. Please send a message to my mother—" Tomaaz froze. The guard's lip was curled in disdain.

"Your dragon's to be executed at dawn," the guard sneered. "Why would we waste a healer on him?" The man turned, boots thudding on stone, and strode off.

"Halt," Tomaaz called.

The guard spun around. And raised an eyebrow.

"Please, I beg you to fetch my mother."

"That dragon's been turned. He's evil now, just like those shadow dragons. He'd kill a healer or me or you if we went in there." The guard stalked off.

Gritting his teeth, Tomaaz paced outside Maazini's cage. He couldn't abandon his dragon and time was running out—it would soon be dawn. He whipped his dagger from his belt and pushed the blade into the lock on the barred cell door, turning it. It was no use. Trying to force the lock would only break his dagger.

Flame it, Maazini was worth a thousand daggers. He drove the blade in and twisted. Nothing happened. He angled his blade upward. Pressed again. The lock clicked but didn't open.

Down the corridor, guards muttered. Footsteps headed his way.

Tomaaz slipped the knife up his sleeve and leaned against the bars, crooning to Maazini. His dragon turned its head, snarling and baring his fangs. Maazini's anguished scream shot through Tomaaz's head, making his skull throb. Sweat beaded his brow.

Two guards strolled by. One snorted. "Trying to talk to that wild beast? You'd have more luck hunting for dragon's breath in the snow outside."

"Dragon's breath?" the other asked as they rounded a corner. "What's that?"

This time it was Tomaaz's turn to snort. That idiot didn't even know rare mountain flowers.

"Doesn't matter," the guard replied. "In a couple of hours that demented beast will be dead."

Tomaaz waited until their footfalls had retreated, then, ignoring his pounding skull, he slid his knife out of his sleeve and angled it into the lock.

This time, the lock clicked twice and opened. Tomaaz gingerly pushed the cell door.

Maazini's snarl rumbled through the cavern floor as he approached.

The pain in Tomaaz's head nearly split his skull asunder, but he forced himself to focus. *"Maazini, you're feeling sick. Let me help you."*

Breathing labored, the mighty orange dragon snarled, narrowing his green eyes. He tensed his haunches, about to pounce.

If this was how he was to die, then so be it. He'd rather not live without Maazini. *"Come on, boy. It's me, Tomaaz."* Tomaaz forced the memory of them imprinting in Death Valley past the pain and screams, to the front of his mind. He closed his eyes, concentrating, and was instantly back in Death Valley as the powerful memory played out in his head. He shoved it into Maazini's mind.

A chain rattled. The beast sprang out of its cave, blazing bright orange in the rays of the setting sun. Orange? Yes, and those were the same green eyes that had been peeking through the hole, watching over Ma. But how? A thrum ran through his mind. Warmth spread across his chest. A rush of energy enveloped him.

The folds of what had been saggy gray skin by the creature's side were now orange. They flexed and spread into wings. The beast was a dragon. The thrum turned into words inside his head. "Thank you for feeding me those berries, Tomaaz."

"I, ah—you're a dragon."

"And you're now my rider."

An image of him flying above Death Valley astride the orange dragon shot through Tomaaz's mind. He felt like a mighty eagle soaring above the valley—free and powerful. "Whoa, that would be amazing."

"It will be, when we finally fly together, free of this hell."

With a whoosh, something rushed through him, making him want to dance and yell with joy.

Tomaaz opened his eyes. "We can escape this hell too, Maazini. Just trust me. I can help you again."

Maazini thrashed, clawing at his skull with his talons. He tossed his head, spraying drops of blood. Fangs snapping, he lunged toward Tomaaz.

Gods!

He wouldn't balk, not now. Tomaaz held his ground as hundredweights of dragon surged toward him.

Maazini's fangs loomed. His cavernous maw rushed at Tomaaz.

Then the dragon bucked his head and snatched up his chains in his jaws. Twisting his body, he landed with his injured neck near Tomaaz. Chains still clenched in his fangs, he growled.

"Easy, boy." Tomaaz stretched out his hand to touch Maazini's pale scales. They were hot.

Maazini bucked his head at Tomaaz's touch, rattling the chains in his jaws.

Tomaaz had to be quick. The guards could return at any moment—and Maazini's grip on himself was tenuous. "This might hurt, but stay as still as you can." Using his dagger, Tomaaz scraped pus and gunk from the wound.

Whimpers escaped Maazini's jaws as Tomaaz dashed over to snatch up Maazini's water pail. Tomaaz cut shreds off his shirt, dunked them in water and bathed the site, but still the wound oozed pus. He picked up the pail and tipped the contents over the wound, flooding it. Rivulets of water and globs of pus gushed down the dragon's hide.

"Bring your neck down a bit lower."

Maazini obliged, lowering his neck so Tomaaz could see into the wound. He squinted. That burrowing arrowhead had dug inside his dragon, leaving a deep channel through his flesh. A hand's length into Maazini's body, something yellow glinted. More pus or the arrowhead? There was only one way to find out. *"Maazini, this is really going to hurt."*

Tomaaz eased his dagger into the wound. Gods, the channel made by the arrowhead was narrower than his blade. He'd have to cut Maazini. He hesitated. Then he took a deep breath, climbed onto Maazini's wounded neck, and hooked his legs around the dragon's throat. Ignoring the growl building in Maazini's chest, Tomaaz plunged his dagger into Maazini's neck, and twisted it.

Maazini's fierce yowl ripped through the cavern. Tomaaz hung on, driving the dagger beneath the arrowhead. The stubborn thing burrowed deeper. Gods, his dagger was nearly up to its hilt. Soon it would be too late. Maazini bucked as Tomaaz slammed the dagger into his flesh to the hilt and twisted, dragging the arrowhead upward. With a piercing screech, Maazini went rigid, every muscle in his body quivering.

"Great. Keep holding still, boy," Tomaaz crooned.

Halfway up the side of the channel, the arrowhead caught. Tomaaz pulled his dagger out and pulled the wound apart to get a better look. Amid the blood flooding the wound, the crystal had caught on Maazini's flesh. He inserted his dagger, but the thing was stuck. *"Nearly there, Maazini. Keep holding still."* Maazini's body trembled.

Maazini roared as Tomaaz sliced the sliver of his muscle that the arrowhead was lodged on. He speared the sliver on the tip of his blade and yanked the thing out. *"Well done. We got it."*

The screams in his head died out. Maazini's chains fell from his jaw, clanking to the floor. The dragon slumped, blood flowing from his wound, his mighty body shaking.

Tomaaz clambered off Maazini's neck. Hands covered in his own dragon's blood, he held the crystal arrowhead up to the torchlight. Its nose was pointed, perfect for burrowing into flesh. It had metal legs like fishhooks but more angular and much finer. They wriggled in the air, like feelers. Although the crystal was shaped like an arrowhead, it behaved like a beetle. Tomaaz peered closer. Silver lines, squares, and dots were laid out in a symmetrical pattern inside the crystal. Odd—as if the very stone were man-made. How in flame's name had Zens created this thing?

He shuddered and wrapped it in a shred of his shirt so it couldn't snag on his flesh and burrow into him, then he stuffed it in his pocket.

Maazini whimpered, tail thrashing.

Oh gods. Letting out a sob, Tomaaz cut more shreds from his shirt to staunch Maazini's bleeding. He wadded the rags, shoving them into Maazini's wound. But they soon became sodden with blood. He ripped more strips, until he barely had any shirt left. Shards, he had to get help. Tears pricked Tomaaz's eyes as he beheld his beloved friend, bleeding in a trembling heap. His throat tightened. *"Maazini, I'm sorry."*

"You had to hurt me to help me." Maazini shuddered. *"I'm sorry too. I turned on you, Tomaaz."*

"It's not your fault. Commander Zens did this." Tomaaz rubbed his flank.

"Thank you for not doubting me."

"You would have done the same for me." Breathing labored, Maazini stayed slumped on the floor.

Tomaaz snatched up a blood-soaked cloth, turning it over in his hands. Shards, there was no piaua juice to magically heal Maazini's wound. He'd fetch clean herb from the infirmary to purge the infection and bandages to bind up his dragon's neck. He sneaked out of the cell and eased the door closed so the guards wouldn't suspect anything, then rushed down the corridor.

Amato was at the door of the next cell. His skinny arm protruded between the bars and he pointed at Tomaaz's bloodstained hands. "Did you dig out the methimium?" A shudder ran through the man's bones, making him look like the fish skeletons that littlings shook at winter solstice. "When my dragon Matotoi took my crystal out, my wound was infected. I was sick for days. But he fetched lake weed and put it on my wound. It drew the infection out and healed me." Amato shrugged, his shoulder bones jabbing his ragged shirt. "Up to you if you try it or not. Without it, I would've died."

Tomaaz swallowed. "Thanks."

"I heard what he said," Maazini melded. *"I've asked Ajeurina to help. She and Lovina will meet you on the ledge outside the main cavern."*

"I'm onto it." Tomaaz raced through the tunnels and up the winding stairs into the main network of tunnels that riddled the mountains at Dragons' Hold. He dashed into the main cavern. Thank the dragon gods it was deserted, apart from a lone mage shooting at targets. The mage gawked at Tomaaz's bloodstained hands as he rushed past, but Tomaaz didn't stop to explain. He only had an hour

until dawn, when guards would arrive to execute Maazini. Shards, they could even come early.

He burst onto the ledge, ragged bits of his shirt trailing out from his jerkin. Ajeurina was there, green scales glimmering in the starlight. Lovina reached down and helped pull Tomaaz into the saddle. "What happened? Ajeurina told me Maazini's himself again."

Ajeurina flexed her haunches, spread her wings and they were airborne, a chilly wind nipping at Tomaaz's sweat-soaked neck. "I got the crystal out, but his wound's infected. Apparently, lake weed will help." His breath rushed out of him. "It was touch and go. For a moment I thought he'd kill me."

Lovina tugged his arms tighter around her waist and squeezed his hands. Tomaaz rested his chin on her shoulder and nuzzled her neck as they flew over the stony clearing below the caverns and across the fields toward the lake. The worst was passed, but this wasn't over yet. Unless they got back to Maazini before the executioner, things could go terribly wrong.

Dark fields whipped by beneath them and soon they were over the forest.

Lovina spoke. "Ajeurina says she knows what it's like to be turned, because Fleur used swayweed on her. She's flying her fastest to help Maazini."

"Please thank her." Even though they covered ground with every heartbeat, the moments dragged. Tomaaz gauged the night sky. Soon dawn would come. They had to get back.

They landed on a snowy bank by the lake. Tomaaz kicked a thin layer of ice around the edge of the lake, smashing a hole, and reached his hand into the freezing water. His fingers instantly went numb. He floundered around, trying to grasp the lake weed. "The weed's too deep." Tomaaz yanked off his jerkin and rolled up his sleeves. Beneath the remnants of his tattered shirt, the sweat on his back turned icy, making him shiver. He smashed more ice and waded into the lake until the water was just below his boot tops. Plunging his arm into the lake, he grabbed fistfuls of the lake weed, and tossed them to Lovina. She caught them and stuffed them into Ajeurina's saddlebags.

"I think that's enough," Lovina called. "We can always come back for more later. Look." She pointed at the predawn gray creeping across the peaks of Dragon's Teeth, the ring of mountains protecting Dragons' Hold.

Tomaaz rushed back to the shore. "Hurry. We don't have long."

"I know, but we're not flying until you put this on," Lovina said fiercely, thrusting his jerkin at him and clambering into the saddle. "I'm not having you sick too."

Tomaaz shoved his arms into his jerkin and swung into the saddle, fastening it as Ajeurina tensed her haunches and sprang skyward. "How in the dragon's tail are we going to get the lake weed into the dungeons in time? I shouldn't have left Maazini. Should've stayed with him." Fear tightened Tomaaz's gut.

"Ajeurina knows the back exit that the guards use when they're banishing people to the Wastelands. She says it's how they got Maazini in. The entrance is high on the southern side of Heaven's Peak."

"Isn't it guarded?"

"Not usually. The slope's too steep to be scaled, so no tharuks ever climb it. It's only accessible by dragon." Lovina spun to stare at him.

"Dark dragons," they said together.

"Oh gods, what if they find it?" he whispered. "I bet no one has thought of guarding the tunnel against them."

"Let's hope it's not too late," Lovina replied.

"We'll know soon enough," Tomaaz said. Although the sun hadn't hit the horizon, the sky was already lightening. "Faster, Ajeurina, please."

The forest and fields flashed by. Ajeurina winged over the clearing and up the slope of Heaven's Peak. She crested the mountain. In the glimmering rays of dawn, the dark ravine to the south-east of Dragon's Teeth cut a jagged scar through the fields, but the sky was clear of dark dragons.

Lovina leaned over Ajeurina's neck. "Go, girl, go."

MAAZINI'S PLIGHT

Billowing golden clouds stretched across the horizon, accompanied by the undertone of hundreds of shovels striking stone. Tharuks burst from the clouds, shredding them with their sharp claws. Masses of dark dragons followed, pouring through a dark hole and swarming over Dragons' Realm, breathing swathes of fire over screaming people.

Hans woke, drenched in sweat.

He tossed the sheets aside, careful not to wake Marlies, and paced to the drawers for a clean undershirt. A shiver rippled down his spine, but it wasn't just his sweat in the chill night air. It was the sheer magnitude of that swarm of dragons. Of the hordes of tharuks that had spilled through those clouds—without end. It was a prophecy, but what did it mean? Sometimes his dreams were literal. Billowing golden clouds meant a realm gate. He rubbed a weary hand over his face and then stumbled back to bed. But sleep didn't come. Hans lay awake for hours, trying to fathom what his dream meant.

He'd only been asleep for moments when the dream came again.

More tharuks than before—hordes upon hordes of them. And dragons. Dark dragons—so many—blotting out the sky like a dark cloth. Lone dragon riders fought them, their bursts of flame like tiny stars against the shadows. Then the heavens opened—thousands of shadow dragon maws rained fire on the earth.

Hans woke, panting. Thank the dragon gods and the First Egg—it was only a dream. Hopefully driven by his fears, not one that would become reality.

§

It was an awful job, but someone had to do it. Tonio paced out his agitation in front of his cold hearth as dawn rose over Dragon's Teeth, the ring of mountains that encompassed Dragons' Hold.

"The sun's rising," Antonika, his ruby dragon, reminded him. *"It's time."* His dragon's sadness washed over Tonio.

All too soon, there'd be one dragon less at Dragons' Hold. If these methimium arrowheads were plentiful, they'd soon have more infected dragons that turned against their riders. Zens' new weapons could wipe out their dragons.

Tonio strode down the tunnels toward the dungeon. At the bottom of the steps, he took a torch from a sconce, the flame's warmth welcome after the chilly tunnel. Tonio greeted the troop of blue guards, who fell in behind him. He slid his sword free of its scabbard and strode toward Maazini's cell.

§

Ajeurina wheeled and swooped down the back of Heaven's Peak. Tomaaz's stomach rushed into his throat. The jade dragon backwinged, slipped into a gaping cavern, and flew down a broad tunnel deep into the mountainside. Soon, Ajeurina landed and furled her wings.

"Get down," Lovina said. "This is as far as she can take us." Lovina was already out of the saddle, unbuckling Ajeurina's saddlebags by the time Tomaaz dismounted, limbs stiff from his cold flight.

She lifted the saddlebag holding the lake weed.

"Let me take it." Tomaaz snatched it up in his arms, and they ran around the corner.

"Hey!" A blue guard rose from her post, calling out as they ran past.

Tomaaz's heart pounded. Gods. Dawn was here already. His breath rasped in his chest. And he was cold, so cold. *"Maazini."* All he could gain by mind-melding were snatches of incoherent images: cavern walls, flashes of torchlight and pain. "He's still alive," Tomaaz panted.

They ran through the dungeon tunnels, empty cells lining the walls.

The thud of boots came from the opposite direction.

Behind them, the blue guard stomped after them, calling, "Hey, stop!"

"There!" Tomaaz gasped as Maazini's cell loomed to their left. Lovina shoved the unlocked door open and they rushed inside.

Maazini thrashed, scales pale and breathing labored. His tail lashed the rock. Bloody rags were scattered across the cavern like discarded playthings.

Outside, boots thudded closer. The cell door clanged as someone thrust it open. Tomaaz didn't dare look. Dropping the saddlebag near Maazini, he ducked a flailing leg, thrust open the flap and yanked out armfuls of lake weed.

"Tonio's here," Lovina gasped. She grabbed some lake weed too.

Tomaaz leaped back as Maazini swiped his leg across the floor.

"This dragon is a danger to you and to himself," Tonio barked behind them. "Men, draw your swords. Archers, ready your arrows."

"No!" Lovina screamed. "He's been healed. Tomaaz took out the crystal."

"The girl's right," Amato yelled from the next cell.

While Lovina argued with Tonio, Tomaaz stuffed wet lake weed into his jerkin. Cold seeped through his torso. Maazini's limb swept past them and he ducked it. *Maazini, please hold still.*

His fevered dragon didn't respond. Tomaaz scrambled up Maazini's neck and hooked his legs around the dragon's throat. Holding on with one hand, he stuffed Maazini's wound with slimy lake weed. "Lovina, more."

Lovina spun, thrusting more lake weed up into Tomaaz's hands. Beyond her, blue guards had arrows nocked to their bows.

"We can't afford to have dragons attacking us," Tonio said. "Even if he is of royal descent, I won't have riders killed. Now, step aside. Believe me, if there was another way, I'd take it."

Tomaaz slapped Lovina's lake weed over the wound, patting the damp plant material down to form a covering. He slid to the ground and stumbled over to Tonio. "There is another way," he panted. "Here." Tomaaz reached into his pocket, pulled out a bundle of rags and passed them to Tonio. "That's the methimium arrowhead that burrowed into my dragon."

Tonio's eyes narrowed. He unwrapped the rags, encrusted with dragon scales and Maazini's blood, to reveal the arrowhead.

"Careful," Tomaaz barked. "It'll burrow into you if it touches your skin."

Tonio raised a cynical eyebrow. He tipped the arrowhead onto his other palm. Immediately, the thing's wiry legs wriggled, and one plunged into Tonio's flesh. The arrowhead twisted, aiming its nose at his palm and tried to dig into his skin. Tonio shook it, but the wire clung to the flesh of his palm. "Gods, that sharding thing."

"Hold still," Tomaaz snapped. He drew his blade, grasped Tonio's palm, and flicked the blade under the wriggling crystal. The arrowhead dropped to the cavern floor where it lay, silver legs wriggling in the air like a dying beetle.

Tomaaz faced the archers. "Why didn't you aim at Tonio when the crystal attacked him? My dragon's only fault was being in the wrong place at the wrong time."

"Then why is he still thrashing and trying to kill you with his legs?" Tonio barked, rubbing his bloody palm.

As if to prove Tonio right, Maazini's tail slapped the stone floor.

"His wound's infected. All he needs is to heal."

"That he does," called Amato from the next dungeon cell. "So clear off and give him and his rider a chance to get some sleep."

Tonio stalked to the door. "Shut your shrotty mouth, Amato. No one asked your opinion." He spun to face Tomaaz. "I'll be back."

§

Hours later, Tonio made his way back down to the dungeons, rubbing his palm thoughtfully. That little shrott had stung as it hooked his flesh. Dark shadows had danced across his vision, but it'd be worse to have methimium burrowing through your body, invading your mind and driving you to hate the ones you loved. Not that there was anyone Tonio loved nowadays, apart from his ruby dragon, Antonika. He'd buried those feelings with Rosita.

Outside Maazini's cell, he stopped in his tracks.

With his dragon's tail curled around him and a wing over his legs, Tomaaz was slumped against Maazini's hide, sound asleep. Lovina was nestled against him, her head in his lap. Maazini nuzzled his rider, and looked up at Tonio with mellow green eyes.

This was no untamable rogue dragon, but a dragon bonded with his rider.

Tonio walked into the cell and peeled off a piece of the leaf stuck to Maazini's shoulder. He sniffed it and slipped out of the cell again, leaving the door ajar. He muttered to himself, "Lake weed. How did they learn that?"

"From me." Amato was pressed against metal bars of his cell. "There's plenty more I can teach you. Especially about Zens."

Tonio ignored his arch-enemy, but his mind was whirring. By the tail of the mother of all dragons, he hadn't expected that.

MAZYKA

When 000 was done whipping Master Giddi, tharuks dragged the dragon mage through the large chamber and into a smaller one with beds along a wall. The beasts shoved him onto a bed and shackled him to it. The lashes on his back burning, Giddi pulled *sathir* from the environment around him. Magic hummed and crackled under his skin. He tried to form a flame, but failed. Zens had shackled his magic too. Giddi thrashed on the bed, rattling his chains and yelling.

"Be still. You're disturbing my work." Zens' face came into view. Those bulging yellow eyes swept over him.

Giddi's limbs became heavy and sluggish. He couldn't move. What dragon-gods-forsaken magic was Zen using?

"000," Zens called. "Bring some anesthetic. The dragon mage is going to have a long sleep."

"Yes, Master." The enormous tharuk carried over a needle longer than Giddi's hand. It had some sort of clear tube attached to it, filled with pale-blue liquid.

With horror, as several tharuks held down his limbs, Giddi realized the needle was not for sewing, but to insert the fluid inside him.

"Be still."

With a sharp jab, 000's needle pierced his thigh. Ice flooded Giddi's veins. Darkness crashed in on him.

"Gideon."

Someone was calling. A familiar voice. If only he could open his eyes.

"Gideon. It's me."

Giddi tried to move his head, but couldn't. And then a face swam into view, partially obscured behind translucent golden clouds. The clouds shifted, revealing more. He gasped, sucking in breath.

Mazyka.

His chest squeezed. She was just as beautiful as ever. She'd aged, but what else could you expect in nineteen years? *"Mazyka?"*

Her eyes shone and her lips parted. *"I've yearned for you this whole time."*

"And I, you." As her face neared, Giddi lifted a hand to stroke a wisp of red hair from her cheek, but his hands were chained with heavy shackles, his limbs so tired…

Mazyka's face dissolved and Giddi woke with a rattle of his chains, staring at the rough-hewn walls of Zens' chamber.

MONTANARA

Despite it being the wee hours of the morning, Kierion thumped on Danion's door.

The dashing leader of dragon spy corps in Montanara opened it, bleary-eyed. "What's going on?" Danion scratched his dark hair and squinted in the dim light from the flickering lantern in the ramshackle stairwell.

"I'm looking for a missing friend." Kierion would tear the town apart to find her. The whole flight here, he'd imagined a multitude of worst-case scenarios: Adelina kidnapped by Zens; her body dead on a heap of unnamed victims, mauled beyond recognition by tharuks. He shuddered. "I need help finding her."

Danion glanced along the corridor. "Keep your voice down and come in. You'll wake everyone in the building with that racket."

Kierion ducked inside. "The girl I like has gone missing. She left Dragons' Hold days ago, headed for here, but never turned up. Maybe you've seen her. Short with dark hair. She's about this high." Kierion held his hand up to his chest.

"She's a littling, then?" Danion raised a cynical eyebrow, as if doubting Kierion's intentions.

He spluttered. "No, she's sixteen summers, but petite."

"Where do you think she's gone?"

Kierion slumped into the only chair in Danion's sparse room. Dropping his elbows to his knees, he rubbed his face with his hands. "I have no idea."

Danion sat on the bed opposite him. "It's too late to look anywhere now. Even the Brothers' Arms is closed."

"I know," Kierion groaned.

Danion chuckled grimly. "Here, have one side of the bed." He pulled back the covers and wriggled over to the other side. "Don't snore. Catch a few winks and we'll look for her in the morning."

A Brilliant Idea

Hours later, Ezaara started awake.

Roberto was lying beside her, his ebony eyes scanning her face. "How are you feeling?"

"Glad you're here," she murmured. He grinned and kissed her. Ezaara snuggled against his chest. "All night, I dreamed of shadow dragons hunting our people, burning them with the bright beams from their eyes and scorching their minds with pain. They're too powerful, Roberto. Our people are dying in droves."

Roberto stroked her hair. "There must be some way to defeat them. Something we can do to prevent them from accessing our minds."

Their eyes locked. They spoke at the same time. "The fountain."

His eyes pierced her as he shared a memory of the fountain they'd seen on their hand-fasting holiday, just twelve days ago. Carved from opaline crystal, the entwined sea dragons glittered in the sun, sparkling water spraying from their maws into a wide basin.

She swallowed. When they'd been on opposite sides of the fountain, it'd been impossible to mind-meld with each other or their dragons. *Could it be that simple?* she melded.

"We have to try." Roberto stroked a strand of her hair back from her forehead and dipped his head to brush his lips against hers. *"The opaline crystal blocked our mind-melding abilities. It just might work against shadow dragons."* Roberto sprang out of bed and tugged on his breeches, shirt and jerkin as he talked. "I'm not asking the council. I'll leave immediately and use Anakisha's ring so I can get there and back in a few hours." He sat on the edge of the bed to lace his boots.

Ezaara moved to sit beside him and cupped his chin in her hands. "Roberto, we need enough opaline for every dragon rider and dragon. It's the only way."

He nodded. "Erob and I will make several trips to Crystal Lake. With the ring, it'll only take us—"

Gods, the ring. "The rings are jeopardizing Dragons' Realm. The cracks in the realm gate are growing and seeping that awful black mist. Anakisha warned us that if Zens finds out—"

"I'm sorry, Ezaara." Roberto took her hands, shaking his head. "I really am, but it's too late. Zens has the ring Bruno stole from us." He hesitated.

"What?"

"I didn't want to break this news to you, but while you were unconscious, Zens kidnapped Master Giddi."

Ezaara gasped. "Master Giddi?" By the First Egg, that was dire.

Pursing his lips, Roberto nodded. "Kierion brought the news back after the battle in Montanara. Zens took Giddi through a realm gate. The most powerful mage in Dragons' Realm is in our enemy's hands. An enemy that uses mages to grow new ones. Can you imagine a hundred Giddis firing upon us?" He turned away and tugged his bootlaces, tying them.

Things were way worse than she'd imagined. "How many wounded in Montanara? How many died?"

"The final count isn't in yet." Roberto clamped his lips shut and mind-melded. *"I'll fetch the crystals, Ezaara. Make sure you take time to rest and recover. The war's not over yet. We're going to need you to lead us."* He strode over and picked up Erob's saddlebags.

Her head spun and she lay down again. Gods, she was still so weak. "Roberto, could you please send Adelina to help me while you're gone?"

He turned back to her, face tight. "I can't, Ezaara." His voice was hoarse. A sob broke from him. "My sister's been missing for days." Tension lining his body, he went out to their dragons' den.

The rest of his words were unspoken—he hadn't found Adelina because he'd been sitting with Ezaara while she recovered. And now he was off to save the realm, so he couldn't search for his sister.

§

A few hours later, there was a knock at the door, and Sofia entered Ezaara's cavern. "My Queen's Rider, look." She held up a dark headband. "Alban's making more, but we want you to test this one with Zaarusha. It has an opaline crystal mounted at the front, see?"

Ezaara climbed out of bed, tugged on her boots, riders' garb, and a cloak. She strode through Zaarusha's den onto the ledge. Hopefully, with these headbands and the messages she'd sent, they'd stand a chance against the shadow dragons.

Zaarusha shifted on her haunches in the snow as Ezaara approached, multi-hued scales glinting. Her golden eyes regarded Ezaara. *"I'm worried about you, Ezaara. Although we must ride out in war, your mind was attacked. You need time to recover."*

"That's why I've been stuck in bed." Ezaara held up the headband. *"If these headbands stop us from melding, they might protect us against Zens' dark dragons."*

Zaarusha eyed the crystal. *"Let's try."*

Ezaara tied the headband, adjusting it so the opaline crystal was on the front of her forehead. The Dragon Queen dipped her scaled head to be level with Ezaara's face.

"Zaarusha?" She couldn't feel Zaarusha's mind. Or hear anything. *"Zaarusha, can you hear me?"* Untying the headband, she asked, "Did you try to mind-meld with me at all? Or were you blocking me?"

"I tried, but I couldn't get through. What about you?"

"The same. Are you sure you didn't hear me?"

"Not a thing. Those headbands could block the shadow dragons' screams and help our dragons and their riders focus."

"Exactly." Ezaara smiled at Sofia. "Great work. We believe the headbands will be successful. You can let Master Roberto know."

"He already knows." Sofia flashed her a smile. "He tested his on Erob. The moment he realized it'd work, he headed back to Naobia to get more crystals from the lake." Sofia scuffed the snow with the toe of her boot, staring at her feet.

"What is it, Sofia?"

She gazed up at Ezaara. Her voice came out in a hoarse whisper. "I'm so sorry."

Ezaara sighed. "These yellow crystals do more damage than we can imagine. I don't hold you responsible for those actions."

Sofia tilted her head. "What about Amato? Rumors say he had a crystal implanted too."

Ezaara pursed her lips. He'd committed so many atrocious crimes while under that crystal's influence. "I really don't know." She shrugged. They'd deal with him later. "Would you like to fly with us in battle against Zens?"

"Me, after what I've done?"

Ezaara was about to answer her when Zaarusha melded, *"Ezaara, you're needed in war council immediately. I'll fly you straight there."*

"After days in bed, I need to walk. Tell them I'll be there shortly." She weighed the headband in her hand and said to Sofia, "I'll take this to war council and show them what we've developed."

"Thank you for giving me another chance, Ezaara."

Ezaara nodded and left. She rushed along the corridor, the headband clenched in her hand. It was a symbol of hope, a light shining among the dark dragons that cluttered the skies and drenched their streets in blood.

Riders in the tunnels nodded tersely in acknowledgment, strides crisp and faces taut. Many thumped their hands against their hearts as she passed. The double doors to the council chambers were open. Ezaara strode inside.

Battle Master Aidan rose from his chair and shook her hand vigorously. "My Queen's Rider, good to see you up and about."

Flight Master Alyssa leaped from the chair next to him and hugged her. "I'm so glad you're all right."

"Welcome back, Ezaara," Master Jerrick called.

Ezaara stood at the head of the horseshoe-shaped granite table next to Lars, the head of the Council of the Twelve Dragon Masters. On Lars' other side, spymaster Tonio sat, his black eyes appraising her—no doubt, weighing the effect the dark presence had had upon her. She resisted the urge to cringe. On her other side, her parents' seats were empty. Shards, where was Ma? She hadn't even thought to ask after her or Pa. Surely Tomaaz would've told her if something wasn't right. But then again, maybe he was so distraught by Maazini being turned that everything else had slipped his mind. "I see from your gazes that you're wondering how I am. As some of you know, I have the ability to mind-meld with all dragons. Our own ones—and the dark ones."

Murmurs drifted around the cavern. Wizard Master Reina's eyes widened. Hendrik, master of craft, banged the table with a burly fist, muttering, "Well, I never."

Derek, master of instruction, narrowed his eyes. "That explains a few things."

The smack of Lars' gavel on the tabletop rang through the cavern. "Quiet. Please let the Queen's Rider continue."

Ezaara nodded her thanks to him. "When we were battling over Montanara, Master Roberto and I decided that I would attempt to meld with Zens' dark dragons and command them to retreat." She clenched her jaw, remembering the pain that had ricocheted through her head, nearly splitting her skull; those dark dragons' screams had shredded her mind and left her reeling. "It didn't go well. That was three days ago. Yesterday, for the first time since the battle, I awoke." She shook her head. "Mind-melding is obviously not the right way to battle these dragons."

Master Tonio glanced around the table. "And where is Master Roberto now? As master of mental faculties, was his mind damaged in battle too?"

"I never said my mind was damaged. I simply needed time to recover." Ezaara didn't need aspersions cast on her leadership capabilities now. She was casting enough aspersions on her own. "Master Roberto does not have the ability to mind-meld with all dragons, as I do."

"But Master Giddi does," said Reina. "And now he's with Zens. Imagine the damage he could do."

"Imagine the damage one hundred of him could do if Zens grows more of him, like he has with the other mages. And think of the advantage we'd have if we could control those shadow dragons." Master Aidan narrowed his dark eyes, staring at Ezaara as he scratched his short-cropped blond hair. "Could you try to meld with them again and sway them to our side?"

Zaarusha's snarl echoed off the chamber's rocky walls. *"No. I won't have you hurt like that again."*

Ezaara spun to face the dragons along the back wall. *"It's war, Zaarusha. I can't be precious about myself and neither can you."*

"But you are precious to me. I waited eighteen years for you."

"Our people are precious too."

"No, I forbid it."

"Queen Zaarusha forbids me to meld with them again." Ezaara held up the headband.

Master Hendrik scoffed, "We don't need headbands or fancy adornments to identify us in battle. You'll have us wearing jewelry next."

"These are purely functional," Ezaara replied. "Master Hendrik, please wear one and stand face to face with your dragon and try to mind-meld."

Grumbling, Hendrik put it on, muttering into his dark bushy beard, and stood in front of Drikonia, his dragon. He frowned and muttered some more, then spun. "I can't meld. What is this?"

"Opaline crystal from Naobia."

"Of course," Master Tonio said. "It's been largely forgotten, but opaline prevents mind-melding. I should've thought of that myself."

"Master Roberto is fetching more crystal as we speak," Ezaara announced. "We're planning to make headbands for all of our riders and dragons. What's been happening while I was unconscious?"

Lars shook his head and gestured at Tonio.

"Not good news." Tonio grimaced. "Dark dragons are spreading across the realm. Every day, more villages are attacked."

Ezaara nodded grimly. "I feared as much. We need to kit out our riders and dragons with these new head shields and test them in battle."

Master Hendrik rose and thumped his fist on his chest. "I'll have my craft makers onto it right away."

Lars bashed his gavel on the table again. "Before you go, Hendrik, Tonio has another idea about how to defeat these dark dragons. We all need to discuss it. Tonio, please enlighten us."

The spymaster's chair scraped on rock as he got to his feet. "Amato knows a secret entrance to Death Valley via a pirate tunnel in the Naobian Strait. I've dispatched Kierion back to Montanara to negotiate a crew and ship with an ex-pirate currently running the Nightshader gang. I trust the lad to come through with a crew, but we'll need a small group of riders to accompany them."

Ezaara sagged in her chair. There'd only be one reason Roberto hadn't told her. He must be planning to go to Death Valley with them. A memory flashed to mind: Roberto in chains, being flung into a rocky wall by the power of Commander Zens' mind. Zens' cruel laughter rang in her ears. She smelled Roberto's blood all over again. Saw the gaping wounds on his body. Goosebumps skittered across Ezaara's arms.

§

Sofia sat in the infirmary with Alban, stitching opaline crystals into headbands. It had been Marlies' idea that they could help, after Roberto had returned with the crystals from Naobia. How he'd gotten back within a few hours, Sofia had no idea. But no one was about to tell her. The council had many secrets, and she wasn't one of their most trusted riders—not anymore. She pulled a crystal from a basket and sewed it into a cloth opening in a new headband, careful to stitch around it so the stone wouldn't move. As Alban reached for the thread, his hand bumped hers and he gave her a tentative smile. Not even he'd trusted her after he realized she'd fed him swayweed and corrupted him. She missed his strong arms and their heated kisses.

She attempted a smile back. His gaze slid to his work.

When the crystal basket was empty, Marlies looked up from the young boy she was tending. "Thank you for helping. Your work's appreciated. Master Hendrik is run off his feet making these." She rose, came over, and took a headband to inspect it. "Let's test these and see if they work."

Sofia gulped. "We're about to fight dark dragons?" Since their attempt on Ezaara's life, they hadn't been allowed to even go on patrol with the blue guards who defended Dragons' Hold's perimeter.

Beside her, Alban's large frame tensed. His steely eyes flicked over her face, hope flashing in them.

Marlies shook her head. "I'm sorry, not yet. We'll test our dragons here."

Alban exhaled. "As much as I expected."

They each fastened headbands, ensuring the crystal was in the center of their foreheads, then strode outside to the infirmary ledge.

Banikan, Alban's brown dragon, Aria, Sofia's beautiful purple dragon, and Liesar, the silver-scaled dragon that Marlies rode, were waiting. They stood face to face with their dragons. Sofia reached out and stroked Aria's soft nose.

"All right, now I want each of you dragons to try and mind-meld with us," Marlies said.

There was nothing. Not even the faintest whisper of emotion or thought from Aria.

The door clunked behind them. Roberto strode out to join them. "Any luck?"

"We've only just started." Marlies passed him a spare headband from her pocket. "Here, try this."

Moments later, Erob landed, snow spraying around his feet. He settled, staring at Roberto. Roberto grinned, a sight Sofia had seldom seen on this tough dragon master's face.

"Congratulations," he said. "I think we've nailed it. We've unlocked the secret to withstanding the dark dragons."

"Is it true, Master Roberto?" Sofia blurted. "Can Alban and I ride into battle?"

"More people have been turned by yellow crystals than you'd suspect, Sofia." Pain flashed across Roberto's face, then the harsh angles of his features softened. He laid a hand upon her shoulder. "I now understand what happened to you."

Sofia's jaw dropped. If she didn't know better, she'd think he'd experienced a yellow crystal himself.

§

Zaarusha and Ezaara winged over the edge of Dragon's Teeth, the piercing peaks jutting toward the sky, ready to rip open her dragon's belly if they fell. On either side of them the muted flap of dragon wings broke the still-as-a-graveyard silence.

"Macabre thoughts for such a pleasant evening," Zaarusha melded.

"Ah, yes." Ezaara was in a dark mood, but was it any wonder? Her feelings were still a little fragile, but she wasn't about to admit that to anyone, not even Zaarusha.

Her dragon snorted. *"As if I couldn't detect that myself. Don't worry, Ezaara, we'll win this war. We have to."*

"I thought Handel was the one with the gift of prophecy, not you," she teased, although her heart was anything but light.

"But I have the gift of hope."

Zaarusha had put her in her place—once again. No matter what, as Queen's Rider, she couldn't afford pessimism. She had to inspire their people to fight. Or die trying.

A dark shape rose from Great Spanglewood Forest, spurting fire.

"Let's meet this beast head on and blast it out of the sky—and the mage that rides upon it." Ezaara leaned low over Zaarusha, fastening the crystal on her forehead, making sure it was secure.

Zaarusha roared as a green bolt of mage flame sizzled toward them.

Belching a plume of flame, they flew at the beast, head-on. To her left, Tonio rode Antonika, and to her right, Master Aidan was on Danika. Aidan screamed, clutching his head. Danika clawed at hers as they wheeled off and flew away.

That was strange; Ezaara couldn't hear anything.

Antonika bellowed, her ruby hide flashing as she dived below the dark dragon.

They were trying to escape mental torture. Bizarre—Ezaara and Zaarusha couldn't feel anything.

Talons outstretched, the shadow dragon flapped its ragged dark wings, sweeping straight toward Zaarusha. The Dragon Queen belched a gust of flame and swerved.

Pain ricocheted through Ezaara's head, tearing at her mind. A vice tightened around her skull. In a desperate attempt, she nocked an arrow and fired straight into the dragon's fanged maw.

The beast choked and spluttered, trying to cough the arrow loose. Shrieking in fury, it plummeted to the forest, billowing smoke and flame.

Ezaara's head throbbed. She checked the headband. Still in place. It had worked at first… Oh, shards! *"Zaarusha, I think the crystal has a narrow range, so it protects us from their thoughts when we're face to face, but not from the side."*

"That would explain why the others felt pain. Tonio and Antonika have reported no more dark dragon sightings. Let's head back to the hold."

Hours later, after much experimentation with their dragons, Tonio, Hendrik, Aidan and Ezaara reported back to the council.

Seated at the council table, Hendrik examined a headband, turning it in his large hands. "If Roberto can bring me more stones, I'll make headbands with crystals all over them. I'll place them a hand's breadth apart around the fabric so they encircle each rider and dragon's head."

Ezaara nodded. "That should work."

Roberto scrubbed his neck with his knuckles. "I'll head back right after this meeting."

"Isn't Erob tired?" Ezaara melded.

"With the ring, it's not far to fly." He squeezed her hand under the table. *"We'll be home again soon."*

"I don't like it. The realm gates have been leaking black mist, and Zens used them to capture Giddi. Be careful." She couldn't say much else—this could be their only chance against Zens.

Lars chimed in, "Hendrik, how many extra hands will you need to make enough headbands for our riders and dragons?"

Hendrik chewed his cheek. "Do you have thirty workers?"

Lars gestured to Derek, master of instruction. Derek hesitated, then gave a terse nod. "Consider it done. I've just melded with Reko and asked him to have forty riders report to your work cavern."

Elbows on the tabletop, Lars rested his chin on his steepled hands. "We need battle strategies. The general council is dismissed, but all members of the war council please remain here so we can discuss how to wage battle once we have these new headbands."

Master Hendrik and Master Derek quickly departed, leaving Ezaara, Lars, Aidan, Tonio, Alyssa, Roberto, and Jerrick at the table.

Aidan stood and strolled to the map of Dragons' Realm on the wall, stabbing a finger at Death Valley. "If we can use that pirate tunnel to infiltrate Zens' stronghold, we could wipe out his production of tharuks, mages, and dark dragons." He moved his other hand from Dragons' Hold across the map to Death Valley. "And if our forces can drive his dark dragons and tharuks westward, we could form a pincher between two wings of our dragons and riders and destroy his armies in the middle."

Lars nodded. "I've been thinking much the same thing. We must get a team of riders into Death Valley."

Roberto flinched. "Amato said the only access to the pirate tunnel is via the treacherous Naobian Strait, which is plagued by pirates and sea dragons."

Aidan huffed. "Sea dragons? They're a myth!"

Roberto's eyes turned hard.

Tonio's head snapped around. "Not where we come from, they're not," he growled. "As I mentioned earlier, I've already sent one of my dragon corps' riders to seek a pirate and a ship so we can deploy our riders via the tunnel. I also interrogated Amato further. Apparently this hidden tunnel is along a cliff, only accessible via shark-infested waters at high tide. We can't take our dragons. But if the council thinks this approach will work, I'll take a small party of fighters and see if we can destroy Zens' headquarters."

Aidan pursed his lips, frowning. "I don't want to throw riders away on a whim, but if we can destroy the creatures and mages he's growing, we may have a chance of winning this war."

"We could also rescue Master Giddi," Roberto said. "But I'll have to take Amato with me."

Ezaara stifled a gasp, her hands clenching the base of her chair. *"Roberto, you're not serious. You can't go back to Death Valley. Last time, Zens nearly killed you."*

"And you," Roberto retorted mentally. "If someone's got to do this, it might as well be me," he said aloud to Lars and Tonio. "I don't trust my father with anyone else. I'll watch him like a hawk and make sure he's not double-crossing us."

"So would I," Tonio replied, ice in his voice.

"If you go, I'm coming with you," Ezaara barked.

Roberto's mind flinched at the vehemence in her tone. *"As Queen's Rider, there's no way you're going back. Our realm needs you."*

"And I need you," Ezaara glared at Roberto.

He ignored her, his eyes on Lars.

"We don't need both of you there." Lars' gaze flitted between Tonio and Roberto. "Roberto, I'd like you to get more crystals from Naobia, then return as soon as possible so you can plan how to infiltrate this tunnel to Death Valley."

Tonio opened his mouth to protest.

Lars smacked his gavel on the table. "No, Tonio, we need you here. We can't afford to lose you."

"As if we can afford to lose Roberto!" Ezaara stood, shoving her chair back. It clattered to the rocky floor as she strode from the cavern, her sword slapping against her thigh.

§

"Erob, grab a goat and meet me on the ledge when you're done feeding. I've got to talk to Ezaara." Roberto raced out of the council room after her, pounding the stone.

As he neared their chamber, he saw her. "Ezaara, wait!"

She ran into their cavern and slammed the door.

He shoved it open and stormed into the room.

She wheeled on him, shaking a fist in his face. "Why did you have to volunteer? I'd be happy if we lost Tonio in Death Valley—but not you. You barely escaped last time. Now you're heading off to Zens again."

Roberto stepped back. He'd expected tears, not anger.

Eyes bright, her chest heaved. "I'll have Zaarusha forbid it."

"I think it's a good idea," the queen replied. *"We could save the lives of many riders."*

Ezaara spun toward Zaarusha's den. "I didn't ask you!"

"We have to save Master Giddi, and there's only one way in," Roberto reasoned. "Tharuks will be patrolling the Terramites along Death Valley, so we wouldn't stand a chance of flying over the mountain range." Surely, she had to understand. "If I take a group through that pirate tunnel, we may stand a chance. And I don't trust my father. I have to keep an eye on him."

"All right, when do we leave?" Ezaara thrust her fists onto her hips, jutting her jaw out.

"What?! We?" Roberto scrubbed a hand through his hair. Ezaara was being so sharding stubborn. "You're not going anywhere near Death Valley."

Ezaara stalked toward him until she was nose-to-chin with him. "I'm Queen's Rider, and I'll go where I want."

"No," he barked. "No, you're not going back there. I won't have Zens catching you and replicating you. We can't risk hundreds of Queen's Riders, all able to meld with every dragon at will. Can you imagine the power Zens would have? The torture on our dragons' minds? Can you imagine…" His voice broke. Gods, he was losing control again. "M-my agony if I lost you?"

Ezaara huffed. "I've withstood Zens once. I can do it again."

He very much doubted that indeed, but kept quiet.

"So, you'll go with your father, who has abused and beaten you and been a servant of Zens for years, but I—your most loyal friend, your lover, your wife—can't come?"

"For those very reasons."

"So it's because I'm a woman, is it?"

"No, that has nothing to do with it."

She narrowed her eyes, as if he was on trial. "Anyway, I thought you hated Amato." Ezaara flung an arm out, nearly hitting his face. "What's the sudden change? Have you finally decided to forgive him?"

"No, I'll never forgive him. Never stop hating him."

She folded her arms, raising an eyebrow. "Oh?"

"Yes. As soon as we're done with him, he dies." Roberto tried to take her in his arms.

She pushed him away and turned her back on him. "Roberto, the risk is too high."

"I know," he murmured, coming up behind her and wrapping his arms around her waist. "But if we do nothing, the risk is even higher. I have to go." He kissed the soft skin on the side of her neck.

She disentangled herself from his arms and stalked away. "Go. Get those flaming crystals, and then leave for Death Valley."

§

Hans awoke. Not again. The past three nights he'd had nightmares. Tonight he'd dreamed of spades striking the earth, reverberations running up his arms, the stench of his own sweat, slaves on either side of him as far as he could see, digging. Dust coating his mouth, sweat trickling down his neck and his hands aching and blistered.

He sat up and scratched the back of his neck. The dream was so vivid.

Beside him, Marlies' breathing was peaceful. He was at Dragons' Hold in bed—not underground in one of Zens' mining shafts. He flexed his hands. No blisters. But the dream had been so real.

It could be a prophetic vision. Maybe the other dreams were too. Sometimes it was hard to tell. With creeping horror, Hans realized the dream could become reality. This time, he had to tell Lars, and fast. He swung his feet out of bed, slipped into his boots, and ran for Lars' cavern.

COURTING PIRATES

Kierion woke before Danion, left him a scrawled note, and trudged through the slush to the Brothers' Arms—the best source of gossip in Montanara and the favorite drinking hole of liars, thieves, and tharuks. What if Adelina wasn't in Montanara? He was only operating on a dragon's hunch.

"And what's wrong with my hunches?" Riona melded.

"Where are you?" Kierion asked. *"I thought you were going to sleep at my father's farm?"*

"I decided to keep an eye on the square. Just because there was no sign of tharuks when we arrived, didn't mean none would turn up."

"Any trouble last night, then?"

"No. Surprisingly, all was quiet. None of the blue guards have seen a tharuk for days." Riona snorted. *"We've probably scared them all off."*

"Not likely."

What if Adelina had been captured by tharuks in Spanglewood Forest? He'd search the whole realm to find her. But his first stop was the Brothers' Arms. He huffed on his frozen fingers and thrust his hands deep in his pockets. One of them struck the heavy coin pouch Tonio had given him. Oh shards, he'd almost forgotten that the spymaster had asked him to secure a passage to that pirate tunnel.

Kierion rushed down Nightshade Alley, strode up the steps to the tavern, and pushed open the door.

Bleary-eyed patrons nursed beer tankards, slumped over plates of bacon and eggs, under a fug of stale beer and smoke. Kierion ducked between tables, scanning each guest's face. None of the early morning patrons was short with dark hair. His stomach clenched. Gods, he had to find her. He stepped around a snoring Nightshader's outstretched legs, then knocked before opening the door at the back of the room that led to Captain's lair.

"Ah, Kierion. Back so soon." Captain's scarred face twisted into a grin that showed the gaps in his blackened teeth. "Game of nukils?"

He had to stay bright and breezy, despite how he felt. "Perhaps later, sir. First, I need to discuss a little business."

Captain raised an eyebrow. "Again? Haven't you already wheedled enough out of me?" Captain pushed a beer across the table toward Kierion. "Sit down and drink with me."

Kierion sat and ran a finger around the rim of the tankard, then took a sip of the foul-tasting stuff. "You must miss the sea."

"A pirate feels the same way about his ship as a dragon rider feels about his mount."

Mount! Kierion refrained from snorting. "A dragon's not some horse you ride. We're best friends." It was so much more. He swept his hand in a grandiose gesture. "Imprinting is a strong bond, unlike anything you've experienced."

"As I said, just like a ship," Captain barked. "So, no time for a game, but time for idle chatter?"

The flaming captain was shrewd. It'd be hard to play him a second time.

Because Kierion had saved his life, Captain had taken him into the Nightshaders, but now that Captain knew Kierion, he might as well play this straight. Elbows on the table, Kierion leaned forward. "I have a proposition for you."

The captain folded his arms across his chest. His face didn't even show a twitch. "Go on."

"How would you like to get back into the saddle, so to speak?"

"You mean back on a ship."

Kierion gave a short nod. "Dragons' Realm needs you."

The captain's eyes narrowed.

Pushing his glass aside, Kierion said, "I need to sneak in through the pirate tunnel to Death Valley. But first, I need someone to sail me there."

Clapping the flat of his palms on the table, the captain pushed back his chair and stood. "What for? Slaving? Zens' slaves are useless. Bare husks of people, unable to be trained as warriors. It's a waste of your time and mine, and possibly a waste of our lives. The Scarlet Hand and the Bloody Cutlasses still roam those seas, you know."

"I know," Kierion said quietly, a shiver rippling up his spine at the mention of the bloodthirsty pirates.

The captain's brow furrowed. "If you're not training slaves, then why in the flaming blazes do you want to get into Death Valley?"

"To destroy Zens' headquarters where he creates those foul creatures." Kierion grinned and flicked a hand skyward, sure the captain would remember the dark beast that had drooled over him, about to snap him up as he hung precariously from a rooftop.

"Those shadow dragons?" Captain pulled a red spotted 'kerchief from his pocket and mopped his brow.

"And his tharuks," Kierion added.

The captain's eyes gleamed. "I'm in," he said, slapping his hands on the tabletop again. "With this war, business has all but dried up in Montanara. Do you have a ship?" His eyes narrowed.

"Ah, not yet." Kierion fingered the sack of gold in his pocket.

Captain strode around the table. He slapped Kierion's shoulder. "Just as well I do, then, isn't it? But keep that between you and me. I want every coin you have in that bulging pocket of yours. You can tell your superiors I had to bargain my rump off to secure a fine girl to sail in."

Kierion had never understood why captains referred to their ships as females, but, right now, he didn't care. He pushed back his chair. "There is one proviso."

Captain merely raised an eyebrow.

"I need to bring a select group of dragon riders with me."

"No problem," the captain ground out, sounding anything but pleased.

"And a couple of dragons," Kierion added, watching Captain's eyebrows shoot up.

"Two or three maximum, or they'll sink my ship."

"Deal." Kierion tossed the pouch of gold on the table. "Here you go. That's all I have."

The captain showed him out to the taproom. "Time for a celebratory drink, don't you think?"

Gods, not another beer. Kierion couldn't stand the stuff, but he swaggered out to the bar, nodding at the bedraggled members of the Nightshader crew, and took a seat at the bar with Captain.

"Two beers, my lovie," the captain ordered.

A short barkeep wearing a floppy hat looked up at Kierion. "What will it be, light ale or dark?"

Kierion nearly fell off his barstool. That voice. Those gorgeous dark eyes. Adelina gazed at him, waiting. She was still wearing the dragon earrings he'd given her. Her eyes shot him a warning stare, so he kept his trap shut. Whatever she was doing here, he didn't want to give it away.

The captain cracked his neck. "So when do we leave?"

"I was thinking tomorrow." Kierion pretended to take a long pull, just managing a sip, and put his glass back down on the counter. He wiped the back of his mouth with his hand. Shards, he had to think fast. Maybe he should claim Adelina the way Danion had claimed Gret to keep her out of harm's way. Hmm, that might work. He cocked his head, letting his gaze linger on Adelina, who was chopping a lemon. "How about letting the girl come too? She looks like she's handy with a knife."

A low growl built in the captain's throat. "She's too young for the likes of you," the captain snarled.

Kierion shrugged. "Too young for anyone," he replied, watching a warning fire flicker in Adelina's beautiful, dark eyes. Gods, he was so glad to see her. "But it just so happens she's one of the dragon riders I'd mentioned. She has to come with us."

Captain spluttered his brew over the counter. "Not another bleeding under-cover rider!"

Adelina snatched a cloth and wiped the counter down. She smiled sweetly, pulling off her hat. "Thank the Egg for that, Kierion. I hate wearing this thing. Where are we going?"

"May I introduce Adelina, rider of Linaia," Kierion said, his heart soaring with joy.

The captain tipped back his head and laughed raucously, his belly jiggling against the bar.

§

The next day, Master Roberto strode into the Brothers' Arms, looking like he owned the place. A gaggle of dragon riders wandered in behind him, greeting Kierion and squeezing into seats between patrons slouched over tables and deep in their cups. Kierion couldn't help but admire Roberto's cool assurance as he strode straight for the captain who was seated at the bar nursing an ale. Roberto's dark eyes swept across the captain's face, cataloging every scar and nick.

"So you're our captain," Roberto said. "It's been a while since I've dealt with Naobian pirates."

The captain's eyes flicked over Roberto's tanned Naobian skin, took in his black eyes and hair, so similar to Adelina's. The captain's terse nod was his only reply. He gestured at the riders seated in the taproom, including Kierion, who'd just returned from patrolling Spanglewood Forest with Fenni. "I take it you're the leader of this rabble of dragon riders."

A raised eyebrow was Roberto's only answer.

"Want a drink?" Captain asked.

"Oh gods, Riona," Kierion melded. *"We forgot to tell Erob about Adelina so he could warn Roberto."*

"He's a grown man. I'm sure he'll withstand the shock."

Roberto's gaze swept across the bar, taking in his sister, not twitching an eyelid.

Adelina's dark eyes simmered at her brother.

Was she angry at him? Gods, she'd been angry at Kierion too. What in the Egg's name was going on with her?

Roberto's lip curled. "No, thank you, Captain. I like to keep my head clear when talking business."

Captain spluttered and pushed his own beer back across the bar. He stood and ushered Roberto through the crowded tables past patrons drowning in ale, into his lair. "Feel free to take a seat."

Through the open doorway, Kierion saw Roberto sit, propping an ankle on his knee. "I hear you're happy to provide a crew and ship for my troop of riders."

"Happy's not the word I'd use," Captain growled, slamming the door.

Roberto had ignored Adelina, but his cool gaze had taken in his sister, all right. He hadn't even flipped an eyebrow. That guy was tough. But then again, Kierion supposed he'd have to be tough, what with the abuse he'd withstood at Amato's hands and how he'd twice survived Zens' slave camps.

Death Valley had been bad enough from dragonback. Kierion shuddered. Soon they'd all be back there on foot.

Snared

The forest swept past beneath Leah, snow gleaming in the wan winter sun beyond the blue guard's massive wings. Occasionally, the dragon let them down to stretch their legs or see to their needs, then they were back in the saddle, pressing on. When darkness came, Leah and Taliesin tied themselves into the saddle, the inky canopy bright with stars.

After two days, they reached the edge of the red guards' territory. The blue guard descended to land beside a river. They slid off its back.

The dragon bowed her head and Leah placed her hand upon it.

"You only have a few hours' walk until you meet red guards." The dragon's talons raked the snow. *"I'd like to accompany you, but I've already delayed too long. I must report the slaughter of my fellow dragons and riders to Dragons' Hold and warn them of the dark dragon horde we encountered."*

Leah swallowed. It had been comforting to ride the dragon. Now they were on their own again. *"Thank you for bringing us this far."*

The dragon chuckled. *"You won't be alone for long. Once you find the red guards, they'll give you piaua juice and bring you home again. Take the human food from my saddlebags. I don't need it."*

Leah nodded, lost for words, and crammed as much food as they could carry into her rucksack.

Taliesin waved as the dragon took to the sky over the treetops, its mighty blue wings soon disappearing from sight.

§

"Are you all right?" Leah asked, holding back fern fronds so Taliesin could walk through the narrow trail winding between the woods.

Taliesin was clutching his head and blinking rapidly.

Something was wrong. Perhaps it was because he hadn't had much time to recover from life as a slave in Death Valley. She fished in her pocket for some hard cheese and a crust of bread and handed it to him, hoping he wasn't about to collapse.

Taliesin tilted his head, munching on cheese and bread.

"What is it?" she asked.

"I have a bad feeling. A strong one. I'm not sure what it means, but I know there's something waiting. Something that isn't good."

Leah took a swig from the waterskin, then offered it to him. "So, you haven't seen a vision this time?"

He shook his head.

"Best we proceed stealthily, then." She tugged his hand, leading him forward.

After trudging for an hour, the stench of smoke reached Leah.

Taliesin's eyes widened. "It smells like Lush Valley did after battle."

He was right—the scent of smoke, charred wood, and burnt flesh hung in the air. Leah wrinkled her nose, remembering the stink of the tharuks she'd battled with then; the awful inky blood that had spilled from their fetid bodies. She gave a shiver, wiggling the stump of her little finger—the finger a tharuk had chopped off before she'd been brought to Dragons' Hold for healing.

They slunk through the bushes, staying off the narrow track, raking dead branches in the snow behind them, but even then, their tracks were visible in the snow. And they were leaving a clear scent—tharuk trackers had such a keen sense of smell.

§

1402 snuffled, nostrils twitching, his head swaying to catch the scent carried by the breeze. "Two humans. That way." He waved his furry hand for his troop to fall in behind him. Claws springing from his fingers, he kept his nose in the air, gesturing his troops to tread softly.

They needed a few more slaves to meet their quota before they could return to Death Valley and receive their reward.

Snow muffled the tharuks' footfalls, although some of the grunts behind him were too loud. Halfwits. He'd teach them a lesson later. He motioned them to halt while he crept forward and parted the bushes. Lucky some of these trees kept their leaves in winter.

There the puny humans were. Defenseless and tired. No weapons drawn.

1402 snarled and pointed at their quarry. His troops sprang forward, bashing their way through the bushes.

§

A snarl ripped through the sparse undergrowth. Taliesin jerked his head up. "Tharuks!"

They scrambled to their feet. Leah drew her sword, facing the charging beast, pushing him behind her. "Run, Taliesin. Run."

But Taliesin's blood had frozen. His feet were rooted to the ground. Not tharuks. Not again. He tried to move his limbs, but they were wooden.

He should run. Flee. Anything to avoid becoming a tharuk slave again.

Memories whirled through his head: blood, beatings, awful whippings. He would have died if it hadn't been for Tomaaz. Taliesin gulped as an ugly brute neared and snatched him up, flinging him over its shoulder. He struggled and thrashed in its grip.

"Pesky human." Its claws dug into his thighs, pinning him against its fetid fur as it ran through the sparse snow-laden forest.

§

Leah screamed as a tharuk batted her sword aside and snatched up Taliesin, flinging him over its back. Streaks of blood showed where the beast's claws pierced his breeches. Eyes wide over the tharuk's shoulder, Taliesin didn't scream. Not once. He was so brave.

She'd been a fool—she should've listened when he'd told her he had a bad feeling. The poor boy was destined for the slave camps once again. She'd seen the scars on his back one night as he changed his shirt. Even healed by piaua, there were ugly curling welts where the lash had scored deep.

In front of Leah, a tharuk thrust its ugly snout near her face. Its fetid breath washed over her as it gave a guttural whisper, "Don't fight. Will go better for you."

Better for her? She'd never heard of tharuks being concerned about anyone's welfare. Instead of crushing her in its grip or manhandling her with sharp talons, the tharuk took her hand and led her down a trail among the snarling troop. This tharuk was large, and although the troop leader glared at it, the tharuk led her along in a rapid stumble through the snow, Leah's mind whirling and her feet numb like clumsy stones at the end of her legs.

§

1402 narrowed its beady red eyes staring at 274, who was leading that human with long hair along the trail. No blood was visible. 274 hadn't used its claws, but had taken the small human by the hand and grunted something at it. 274 was fast and good at capturing humans—the reason it was in this troop—but sometimes 1402 wondered whether the grunt was soft in the head.

It snorted. 274 got results from the slaves it commanded, so it'd leave the grunt be—for now.

"Move it," 1402 thundered. The troop increased their pace as they ran back to the meeting point.

§

After half an hour's march through the snow, the tharuk troop brought Leah and Taliesin to the outskirts of a village—or what had been a village. Houses had their thatch ripped off. Doors flapped in the breeze, flurries of snow driven inside hallways. The large tharuk tugged Leah along. Her boots crunched through smashed glass from broken windows. Everywhere, the snow was splattered and smeared with red.

As they neared the center of the village, the crack of whips snapped through the air. Moans rang out.

Taliesin, over the shoulder of the tharuk in front of Leah, had gone stock still. His arms flopped down its back. His eyes were wide, unseeing.

Leah sped up, closing the gap between them. "Taliesin," she whispered.

Not a glimmer of recognition showed on his face. His breath huffed out of him, rapid and shallow, as if he had a terrible injury. It must be the shock of being captured again. The poor boy.

"Taliesin." She grabbed one of his hands and squeezed it. No response. Oh gods, if she were to break free, she'd have to carry him. Throat tight, Leah swallowed.

When the troop reached the village square, cages built on wagons greeted them. People were slumped inside, resting against the bars, eyes vacant. More tharuks converged upon the square, carrying other people. The beasts shoved them into a group. Four tharuks strode among the newly-captured slaves, passing them waterskins and forcing them to drink. The tharuk carrying Taliesin dumped him on the ground nearby and forced his mouth open. Another beast held the waterskin to his mouth. The contents sloshed over his face and neck as he glugged it down, spluttering and choking.

Leah glanced about furtively. No one was watching her. She tugged the loose thread hanging from her sleeve and pulled a dried clear-mind berry off the end, grateful for Marlies' foresight in making them all sew the berries into their rider's garb, weeks before the shadow dragons had appeared. She coughed, holding her hand to her mouth, and furtively swallowed the berry.

A beast forced the man next to her to drink. Trembling, he swallowed the water, eyes wide with fear. His forearm was gashed and bleeding from tharuk claws.

It was Leah's turn next. Her tharuk held up the skin. She drank, swallowing deeply, resisting the temptation to spit out the foul-tasting water. So that's what numlocked water tasted like—muddy, somehow tainted. As the new slaves drank, their moans stopped.

Leah scanned the sky. How had the village been captured so easily when it was supposed to be under the protection of the red guards?

As tharuks herded them into cages, Leah let her jaw drop and her eyelids droop, imitating the villagers around her—no, slaves. They were all slaves now, bound to do the tharuks' bidding.

Her shoulders were heavy. Her body, weak. By letting fatigue and hunger weary her, she'd walked straight into a horde of tharuks. It was her fault. Taliesin had warned her. And now they were captured. Oh gods. They had to get piaua juice. Marlies was relying on her. The whole of Dragons' Realm was. If they didn't get piaua—and soon—there would be no hope of dragons or riders surviving this war. She slumped on the wagon bed next to Taliesin and leaned against the bars of their prison.

Taliesin's worst nightmare had been realized. She never should've brought him along.

Wagon wheels creaked. Teams of horses and oxen pulled the wagons out of the square. Tharuks whipped them mercilessly. More tharuks pushed the wagons from behind. Leah's tharuk pushed the corner of the wagon closest to where she leaned against the bars of the cage. They were like animals being wheeled to a slaughterhouse. Maybe it was better to be slaughtered than to become a slave.

Taliesin was sprawled next to her, eyes glazed and jaw hanging open.

No, she couldn't give up. She had to get him out of here—had to stay alert so they could escape. But the squeaking wagon wheels soon lulled her to sleep.

ARTISTIC FLAIR

Leah jolted awake in the dark and glanced about, letting her jaw hang slack in case a beast was watching. Next to her, Taliesin was snoring softly. Most of the slaves in her cage were dozing. Two wagon cages over, tharuks were waking slaves to give them more numlock and a hunk of bread, but no one was watching her.

She had to be quick. Tharuks could be at her cage any moment. Leah nudged Taliesin awake and shoved some clear-mind berries in his mouth, then also chewed a couple. Then she took a pouch of dragon scale from her jerkin pocket and sprinkled a pinch on his tongue to keep his fingernails and eyes gray like a numlocked slave's. After swallowing a pinch, she tucked the pouch away for safekeeping. Thank the dragon gods none of the tharuks had looked too closely at her eyes or fingernails that day. It was a blessing she'd had her eyes shut. Glad she'd listened to Marlies' lessons on herbal remedies, Leah slumped back against the bars of the cage and waited.

And waited.

Bored, she plucked up some stray sticks and leaves from the wagon floor and wound them together, forming a long snake. She bunched some leaves together to make a head and split one to make a tongue, fingers working nimbly in the darkness. Since she'd been a littling, she'd always made little figurines from twigs and bits and pieces, especially when she was nervous. Eventually, Ma had sold them at the market. But nervousness hardly described the terror that was rising within her. She remembered the tharuk who'd hacked off the end of her finger. Remembered tales of the slave camp in Death Valley. There was nothing she could do. They were trapped here, being led ever closer to Death Valley.

Among the trees, tharuks made a fire, tossing fallen saplings and branches on the heap until it was blazing. In the flickering light, it was easier to work. She completed her snake, turning her handiwork over in her lap to inspect it. A fetid rotting smell wafted over her. Gods, those tharuks stank.

"What that?"

The grunty voice made Leah flinch. Her tharuk was right behind her.

It thrust its snout at the cage, sniffing her. Its eyes fell to the snake in her hands.

Leah dropped the snake into her lap, letting her jaw hang loose, staring straight ahead.

The beast grunted, thrusting a clawed finger through the bars, pointing at the snake. "Give me. Now." The number 274 was tattooed on a bald patch inside its wrist.

She didn't dare speak, but Leah turned her head, desperately trying to look dull-witted. Although this tharuk might be milder than the rest, the threat in its voice was real. And its claws were only a hand's breadth from her face. Mouth dry, Leah picked up the snake and passed it to the tharuk.

The beast hurriedly glanced around, then stroked the snake. "Pretty." It tucked the snake inside its breastplate and thrust a waterskin through the bars. "Drink now." More tharuks converged upon the cage with waterskins and hunks of bread.

Although Leah was hankering for the dried meat and cheese in her rucksack, she didn't dare open it for fear of letting the beasts know she wasn't numlocked. But then again, maybe the snake had given her away already.

As soon as dawn broke, while tharuk snores rumbled through the trees, Leah gave Taliesin more berries and dragon scale. The next day was much the same. As the cage trundled on through the forest, Leah made a rabbit, a calf and even a majestic stag for her tharuk. Each time, he would take her offering and tuck it deep within his breastplate, glancing about to make sure the troop leader and none of the other tharuks noticed.

By sundown, she was out of twigs and leaves. As dusk fell, the tharuks started another blazing fire and roasted rats, crunching down the entrails and slurping as if it was the best meal in Dragons' Realm.

When her tharuk came for her next offering, she shrugged, gesturing at the barren floor of her cage.

The tharuk grunted and rushed off, returning with bits of broken twig.

Leah could've groaned. That wouldn't help her escape. She pretended to craft the sticks, deliberately breaking them and hissing in frustration. She glowered at the sticks, then gestured to the nearby trees. Trees that would provide good cover if she and Taliesin were to escape.

§

With a grunt, Leah's tharuk disappeared and returned with a bundle of keys. Holding the keys so they wouldn't clank, it unlocked the cage and swung the door open. The beast gestured for Leah to come out. But she clung onto Taliesin's hand, refusing to leave without him. The tharuk snorted, waving urgently and glancing at its troop fighting over the remains of rats around the fire. Its message was clear: they didn't have long before they'd be noticed.

Leah shuffled across the cage floor, dragging Taliesin with her. The boy clambered out of the wagon. With a frustrated snort, the tharuk hustled them into the trees. Leah's heart pounded—like a woodpecker was trapped within her chest.

When they were behind the cover of some evergreens, she stooped and picked up sticks, cones, and needles to fashion a dragon. She took her time weaving the complex form, hoping to come up with an idea of how to escape. They were outside now, but still under the watch of this beast. He might be friendlier than the rest, but he'd still slit their throats if they ran.

She wandered farther into the trees and broke a twig off a pine. Soft whispers echoed through the trees. A little farther on, she found a branch with dead buds of tiny cones and used them to create spines along the dragon's back. Then she used a tapered piece of bark to weave a dragon's tail. She couldn't keep this up for long. The beast would soon suspect something.

The tharuk snuffled, eagerly ferreting out sticks for limbs. Taliesin trailed behind her and the beast, still looking numlocked, despite the clear-mind berries. Gods, she hoped he was feigning it.

Leah slowed her fingers, trying to buy time and distance, still weaving, but making her work look cumbersome.

The tharuk prodded her back with an impatient claw. She sped up. No point in getting injured.

Snarls broke out behind them, coming from the cages. A roar shook the trees. Snow thudded from branches. Taliesin flinched—he wasn't numlocked after all, just in shock.

Dark wings blotted out the stars. In a burst of flame overhead, wings gleamed blood-red as a dragon dived toward the tharuk camp. A red guard!

"Wait here. Make dragon toy," 274 said before dashing back toward the cages.

Wait here? That beast had to be flaming joking.

Leah grabbed Taliesin's hand. "Hurry, quick." They ran into the trees.

And kept running.

Snarls, roars, and screams rang out behind them as they thudded their way through the snow. Gods, they'd only a little food left, a few herbal remedies, and no water. No idea where they were. No idea where the piaua was. But providing it survived the encounter with the tharuks, they'd found a red dragon at last—if it could find them.

THE ROARING DRAGON

Roberto stood next to the captain, salt spray hitting his face as the ship's prow cut through the sapphire ocean. It was good to smell the tang of the sea again. And good to be with a fellow Naobian, someone who understood his customs and traditions without even thinking. Someone who didn't know his father—or ignored the fact that he was Amato's son. Someone who'd been through tough times. He tipped his head back and laughed at the captain's ribald joke.

This man had definitely seen the world. But then again, so had he—even Death Valley. He allowed his gaze to wander over the deck, evaluating the members of his troop. It was definitely an eye-opener seeing them on the deck without their dragons or the trappings of Dragons' Hold.

Charcoal in hand, Lovina was sketching. Sitting next to her with his back against the gunnels, Tomaaz bent, his lips brushing Lovina's hair as he pointed to something on her parchment. Roberto snapped his gaze away. Tomaaz's gold hair and green eyes reminded him too much of Tomaaz's twin—Ezaara. He shook his head. How had it come to this? He'd never imagined he could love so deeply, or that love could be edged with so much pain. His heart felt like a trampled rose, its petals bruised and scattered. He scratched his neck. If Ezaara wasn't Queen's Rider, he would've brought her with them in a heartbeat.

No, he was lying to himself. He wouldn't have brought her.

If Zens were to break her, Roberto would be tempted to inflict every terrible torture Zens had ever taught him upon the world. He'd shatter the world. Or shatter himself against it. Now that he'd been in love, he couldn't go back to his half shell of a life before Ezaara. Never. He'd rather die alongside her.

Roberto cocked his head, gazing at the captain's pennant, a roaring dragon, snapping in the wind. "If you hate dragons so much, why is your ship named the *Roaring Dragon?*"

The captain coughed. "Just because you're Naobian, do you think I have to tell you all my secrets?"

Roberto chuckled, his eyes roaming over the deck.

Danion was teaching Gret how to tack. Lines in hand, she followed his instructions, earning a casual pat on the shoulder. Nearby, Fenni paced along the deck, smoke rising from char marks where his sparks fell on the sun-weathered planking. Gret glared at Fenni, then turned back to listen to Danion's instructions. Roberto snorted. The mage was so besotted with Gret and so green with envy over Danion's attention to the girl that he couldn't even see how angry Gret was. According to Kierion, when Danion was undercover, acting as Captain's right-hand thug, Danion had claimed Gret with a kiss to prevent the other thugs from harassing her. Kierion said Fenni hadn't known Danion was a dragon rider, and had disliked him since. Roberto didn't blame him. He wouldn't be happy with someone else kissing Ezaara.

And Kierion—the prankster who could leap from the tip of the dragon's tail and kidnap a mage on the back of a dark beast—had succumbed to seasickness.

The captain nudged Roberto, a hand on the ship's wheel. "So cocky on land, so adrift at sea." He angled his head toward Kierion.

Roberto had to chortle.

Nearby, Adelina stiffened. She stalked over. "Don't laugh at Kierion's misfortune. It could be you next." She spun away in a huff.

Roberto grabbed her arm. "Adelina, please."

She whirled. "Take your hands off me." Her dark eyes flashed.

He dropped her arm. "I just want to sort things out."

"You promised when we were young, you'd never lay a hand on me."

"Zaarusha made me bring Amato home. I had no choice," Roberto hissed, aware of the ears pricking up around them. "You know I would've rather killed him after what he did to us."

Adelina walked back to Kierion, chin in the air.

The captain laughed. Roberto shot him a scathing glance. The laugh died on the captain's lips and he busied himself staring at the horizon.

"At least, the waters aren't stormy," Captain muttered to no one in particular.

§

For the third time that morning, Kierion leaned over the rail and emptied his guts into the choppy sea. Great impression he was making on Adelina, not that he much cared. In the Egg's name, why had he come on this fine adventure? The only thing he'd seen so far, apart from the first day of breathtaking crystalline waters filled with wondrous sea creatures, was the bottom of a pail or the contents of his stomach filling it. He heaved again and again, but his stomach was empty.

Next to him at the rail, Adelina stretched her arms open wide, breathing in the briny air, as if she was hugging the wide expanse of turquoise ocean. She waved a hand at a smudge of orange upon the horizon. "I never thought my brother would survive the Wastelands."

Kierion took a deep breath and grunted. His roiling stomach was wrung out like garments on wash day. Should be safe to speak without hurling. "None of us did. Flaming lucky he and Ezaara got back in time to save Zaarusha."

She turned to him. "And lucky you found the remedy for the poison."

"Ah, that was all skill, not luck." He tried to arch an eyebrow and act cocky, but was sure he'd failed.

"Just like the skill you're exhibiting now?" She slugged his arm, but only lightly, and grinned.

That was more like the Adelina he knew. She'd been stretched as tight as a bowstring. He managed a weak grin back—until the ship pitched. He groaned and slumped on the deck.

Her lips twitched as she gazed at him.

Gods, they were exquisitely shaped and so enticing. When they'd come on board, he'd imagined finding a secluded corner so he could find out how soft those lips really were. But now kissing was the last thing on his mind. He clutched his stomach as another wave of nausea hit him.

"I'll be back in a moment." Adelina disappeared.

She soon returned and passed him a cup of cold peppermint tea. "Here, sip this. The mint should settle your stomach."

Kierion sat up and tentatively took a sip. Adelina held a damp cloth to his forehead, then his neck. "Ah, that feels better." He groaned. "Mara would never call me a hero if she could see me now."

"Is that what she called you?" Adelina laughed, dark eyes dancing.

Gods, she was gorgeous. "I don't care what anyone calls me as long as this ship stops pitching." Kierion moaned as the ship crested a huge wave, sea spray misting their faces, then dropped into a trough.

§

So the girls at Dragons' Hold thought Kierion was a hero. Adelina was glad he was with her on this ship, far away from their compliments, even if he had no sea legs and was as sick as a mooning dragonet. She hoped he had no idea how many young women swooned over him or that he was the topic of many conversations in the girls' sleeping cavern, late at night.

Her laughter died as Roberto's voice cut through her thoughts. At least she'd put her brother in his place. Adelina took Kierion's cup so he could scramble to his feet.

"You all right?" Kierion murmured. Thankfully, his breath now smelled of mint.

She pasted a smile on her face, her weapon against the world. "Sure. It's you that's sick, not me."

Overhead the sails flapped and the mast creaked.

"Why are you mad at your brother?" Kierion's eyes slid to Roberto, who was conversing with the captain as if they were old friends.

It was as if that hardened seaman knew he'd met his match in Roberto—Zens' ex-protégé and the son of Amato the traitor. She huffed. Both the captain and Roberto had nerves of steel and could be just as stubborn as each other. This journey would be hard for Roberto, heading back into Death Valley for the third time.

But that still didn't excuse Roberto from bringing her face to face with the father she'd long thought was dead. And still wished was dead. Gods, the shock had rattled all her terrible memories loose.

Adelina bit her lip. Surely her memories of Amato's abuse paled in comparison to Roberto's—being given to Commander Zens by their father, then enduring months of torture at Zens' hands. Adelina shuddered, but said nothing. She'd also been captured by Zens recently, but only for a few days. Thank the First Egg Kierion had saved her.

Kierion loosely draped an arm around her shoulders and held the railing with a white-knuckled grip as the ship swayed.

She braced her legs, leaning into him. Thank the dragon gods Amato was locked in the brig. Kierion had objected, saying it wasn't fair, but as their leader, Roberto had insisted. If he hadn't, Adelina would've. She didn't want her father roaming the decks. Out of sight, out of mind.

Although just knowing Amato was on board was enough for her thoughts to keep returning to her haunted littling years again and again—the blood on the walls, her mother's screams and Roberto's soft moans in bed late at night after he'd taken beating after beating for Adelina or Ma.

"It's all right, Adelina. I'm here. I won't let Amato hurt you again." Kierion's voice was so soft, she wasn't sure if she'd heard right.

Adelina met his steady eyes—ocean gray flecked with blue. The girls called them pretty. Somehow now, they seemed like a life raft, keeping her afloat. She swallowed and nodded, pushing her anger at Roberto down deep.

Riona thudded to the stern deck with a maw full of wriggling fish. Their stench drifted on the breeze.

Their dragons had been supplying the pirate cook for the two days since they'd set sail from a tiny fishing village south of the Flatlands. Adelina walked over to the dragon and patted her snout. *I suggest you wait until Kierion's below deck, so we don't start him off again.*

Too late. Behind her, Kierion tensed and spun away, leaning over the rail.

So much for the peppermint tea she'd given him.

§

Fenni paced the length of the deck, then turned and paced again. Thank the living flame, Danion was on the other side of the captain's cabin, out of sight. Fishing, he called it. Dangling a string into the sea and hoping something would bite was more like it. The hooks at the end of his line were as barbed as the looks Danion was shooting him. Fenni had found out from Kierion that the idiot wasn't married at all. Danion had just said he was to keep Fenni quiet after he'd kissed Gret, so he could claim he was playing a part. But the truth was that Danion *liked* Gret.

Danion didn't yet know that he knew, but somehow, Fenni would make him pay for kissing Gret. Unless Gret had enjoyed it...

Oh gods, he was doing it again. The sparks trailing from his fingers had left telltale char marks on the deck's weathered planking. He shook his head. Master Giddi had warned him to learn control. And where had all Jael's lessons—throwing underwater fireballs and nearly being killed by strangletons—gotten him? He had to get his emotions under control. Stay cool. They needed to work together as a team. If Zens sensed any division among them, he'd use his mental talents to drive it between them like a wedge, and rip them apart.

§

"I'll be back in a moment." Adelina patted Kierion's shoulder and went below deck.

Gods, he'd been hoping to kiss her, not be patted like a dog. But that was all they could manage with him staring at the inside of his chuck bucket. He groaned as the ship lurched.

Below him, a hatch opened in the side of the ship and cook flung some scraps out far into the ocean. Cook had a good arm on him to turf the food that far. Shark fins cut through the water, and maws rose from the sea, snapping down the morsels before they hit the ocean's surface.

Below the sharks, something large rippled through the water.

Kierion blinked. Gods, was that a… He was seeing things. It couldn't be. He waved at Fenni, who was prowling the deck, looking grumpy. "Flaming claws! Fenni, look!"

A sleek green-scaled maw closed around a shark.

Fenni dashed over. "By the First Egg! A sea dragon! I never dreamed I'd see one."

The sea dragon leaped from the water, the shark flailing in its jaws. Water rushed off its green scales, sparkling like diamonds in the sun. Its wings lifted and flapped, water cascading from them, and then it plunged back into the sea. Cries arose from on deck. Crew and riders rushed over.

"I thought they were a myth," Kierion muttered. "Now I've seen it all."

Roberto laughed. "Not where we come from. Anyone from Naobia knows that sea dragons are real. Look." He pointed out far beyond the sharks. More large shapes rippled through the ocean.

"So there's a whole herd of them. Or whatever it's called." Kierion screwed up his face. "If they're not flying, it is still a wing of dragons? Or are they a school of sea dragons?"

Roberto clapped Kierion on the back. "I'll leave that for you to figure out."

Kierion squinted. "Look again, Roberto." There were dark blobs on the back of some of the sea dragons. "What are they?"

Roberto frowned. "They're too far out to tell from here, but there are legends that sea dragons have riders, people who can breathe underwater using the dragons' magic. I've never met one, but that doesn't mean it's not true."

Long after everyone else had left the rail and gone back to their duties, Kierion stared out at the water, straining his eyes, hoping to catch another glimpse of a sea dragon.

§

Roberto grunted and strode to the center of the deck. The sea dragons were a welcome diversion, but now that they were gone, tension was increasing again between Fenni and Danion, and Adelina was still avoiding his gaze. Gods, he had to do something to let off steam. "It's time for sword practice," Roberto barked. "On your feet." Riders scrambled up and formed a ragged group. Adelina ignored him, studiously attending to Kierion—who was puking again. "Who's first?" Roberto called.

Tomaaz unsheathed his sword.

"I'm in," Lovina said, sliding her sword from her scabbard.

Near the stern, next to Riona, Erob shifted on his haunches and narrowed his eyes, staring at Roberto. *Tut, tut. Taking out your anger on your riders won't help things.*

"They're lazing around on deck. We'll be fighting tharuks in a day or two. They need to stay sharp." Roberto readied his sword.

"If they're half as sharp as your sister's tongue, we'll be fine," Erob replied.

That stung. But not as much as Adelina's anger. She'd been his only family for years. They'd always been tight—until Amato had come between them. And the worst thing was, he wasn't only upset about Adelina. Ezaara was angry with him too, for leaving her behind. Gods, he had to do something or he'd go mad. Better this, than arguing with his sister.

Roberto yanked off his shirt. It was so sharding hot down here in the south.

"Are you sure it's not just you being steamed up?" Erob tucked his head back under his tail and went to sleep.

"You need your beauty sleep, but these riders have had enough rest." Roberto flicked his sword toward Tomaaz and Lovina. "I'll fight you both at once," he called. "And anyone else who's keen."

Danion swaggered over, sword in hand. "Three against one?" He raised an eyebrow. "That hardly seems fair, but if that's what you want, I'll oblige."

That brought throaty laughs from Captain's motley crew of burly pirates. A few gathered to watch.

Gret tied off her lines and came over too, leaning against the railing and folding her arms. "If you're going to duel, I may as well provide some tips."

The first mate, a wiry pirate with three gold rings in his nose, sniggered.

"What? Think I can't fight just because I'm a woman?" Gret glared at him, her hand drifting to her pommel.

The female pirate with a shaved head tattooed with a burning arrow laughed. "Nod knows better than that," she said. "I best him three times out of four."

Nod glowered. "Enough lip from you, Medina."

"I'd watch out if I were you," Fenni growled. "As Montanara's swordmaster's daughter, Gret's been fighting since she was three summers old." He stomped across the deck to stand at Roberto's side. "I'm in. I'll even out Roberto's chances."

So, he wanted to fight Danion. That could get nasty. "All right, but we need a few rules." Roberto didn't want his troop battered and bleeding before they engaged any tharuks. "No mage flame. No sword slashing—only taps with a sword tip." At a groan from the riders, he barked, "Do you want me to cork your tips like littlings? Or make you use wooden training swords?"

"No training swords on board," Nod chuckled, the rings in his nose glinting in the hot sun. "We don't drill, we only fight." He grinned, showing yellow-stained teeth.

"Want to join us?" Roberto asked. "The losers are on galley duty."

"That'll please cook," said Nod. "But I'll watch."

Roberto drew his sword. Beside him, Fenni held up his hands, sparks dripping from his fingers. "No flame," Robert muttered as Fenni's gaze narrowed in on Danion.

Danion gave a cocky grin and twirled his sword.

Lovina lunged, aiming for Roberto's side. He parried. Tomaaz and Danion leaped in, swords flashing. Danion was suddenly buffeted back by a freak gust of wind. Roberto would've laughed if he hadn't been busy blocking Tomaaz and Lovina's blades. The next time Danion lunged, he slipped on a strange ice slick that appeared underfoot.

Fenni did laugh.

Danion snarled, rushing Fenni and scoring a tap to his leg. Then Lovina lunged at Fenni.

Fenni ducked and blew a gust of wind at Lovina, muttering, "Not fair, I'd drive you back with a decent flame."

Roberto's muscles sang as he ducked, parried and blocked. Then he drove Danion hard against the rail—at a cost—Danion scored a tap on Roberto's chest.

The whole time, Gret called out instructions, "Sword higher, Lovina. That's the way. Tomaaz, you're leaving your flank open. See, that's how Danion gets past your guard."

Not once did she mention Fenni. Roberto had the feeling it wasn't only because Fenni wasn't using a sword.

Roberto drove himself hard. Soon his arms were gleaming with sweat, and salt stung his eyes, but he kept on fighting. Driving himself—the way he'd always driven himself when he was unhappy.

§

They'd lost. Fenni sighed. Despite Roberto being an excellent swordsman, having only two of them and him not being able to use his full powers, the others had beaten them. Danion hadn't come back at him again, just focused on Roberto, and Fenni hadn't wanted to blast Tomaaz or Lovina too hard. In the end, the three of them had ganged up on Roberto, and the master had surrendered.

Not wanting to ruin Roberto's day, Fenni offered to do the dishes for them.

When Fenni finished in the galley and came back on deck with a muslin-wrapped package in his hand, he was greeted by the clash of steel upon steel. He came around the corner of the captain's cabin, and his jaw dropped. A bandanna tied around her forehead, Gret had stripped down to her tight undershirt and breeches, her tanned arms and shoulders glistening in the Naobian sun as she leaped and parried—with Danion. Her muscles rippled as she moved. Fenni would've been transfixed, were it not for her opponent.

Older than him and broader through the chest, Danion had stripped down to the waist, his heavily-muscled chest and abdomen gleaming with sweat. He leaped forward, his arms flexing as he parried, then lunged. Danion was stationed in Montanara. How could he be so tan when it was midwinter there? Fenni tugged his cloak around himself, suddenly aware of how wizarding hadn't developed his own muscles. Skin and bone, his mother had said when he was a littling. But he hadn't stayed that way. Sure, his chest was broader now, and his arms too, but nothing like the toned man fighting Gret.

Gret whirled then swung low, making Danion leap, sword swinging wildly in his outstretched hand. She lunged under his guard and struck him on the chest. He grabbed her sword arm and tugged her against him.

She tipped back her head and gave a full-throated laugh. There were both breathing heavily, chests rising and falling. "You'd be dead if we were really fighting." Gret grinned.

Danion laughed. "A gentleman always lets the lady win."

"A fine excuse," Gret crowed. "But I beat you fair and square." Her eyes appraised his torso. "I got you smack in the chest. Admit it, you've met the superior swordswoman." Still grinning, her eyes flicked to Fenni. The merriment in her eyes died.

Danion shot Fenni a look that would have cracked a dragon egg, then turned away, twirling his sword. "Anyone up for another bout?"

Fenni approached Gret. "Uh, I, um, made this for you." He passed her the package and she opened it, revealing a honeyed flatbread.

Her eyebrows flew up. "Thank you, Fenni. That was thoughtful." She bit into it and turned back to watch the others.

Roberto approached Danion. "How about you against me? Everyone else has had a turn." He waved a hand at Kierion, who was still leaning over the gunnels, his lunch kissing the sea. "Except our great dragon-leaping friend here. I'm glad the sea has bested him. I was beginning to think he was good at everything."

Amid laughter, Kierion groaned and then heaved again. Adelina patted his shoulder, biting her lip.

At least Adelina cared about Kierion. Despite Gret kissing him back in Montanara, Fenni had no idea how she felt about him.

§

"Tie off the jib sheet," the captain called.

Gret gritted her teeth and gripped the line, turning her back on Danion and Fenni. Even though the ship was enormous, the space between the creaking timbers was too small for her. Between Danion shooting her flashy smiles and Fenni bristling and dripping green mage sparks whenever he saw Danion, she wanted to flee. It was bad enough that the handsome rogue Danion had kissed her in Montanara and set heat searing through her body before she'd chosen Fenni.

But Fenni's territorial attitude was killing her. She licked a morsel of honey off a finger and gripped the line again.

She'd heard of creatures like groundhogs with enormous spines on their backs that lived in the Wastelands. The males would fight to the death to win their chosen female. It was like having two of them around. Everywhere she turned, they bristled, stabbing each other with eyes like daggers. If only she could jump into the ocean and disappear.

Gret sniffed the salty brine deep into her nostrils and tied off the jib sheet, glad to be busy.

§

Roberto and Danion had just sheathed their swords when a cry came from the crow's nest. "Ship Ahoy."

One of the captain's crew shimmied down the main mast and dashed to the helm. "Red Sails, Captain. Bearing down on us from starboard."

Captain cursed. "That'll be The Bloody Cutlasses. Hopefully the Scarlet Hand isn't on board that ship."

Roberto's spine ran cold. The Bloody Cutlasses were infamous for terrorizing the Naobian Sea. Wherever they struck, they left no survivors. They said their leader, the Scarlet Hand, drank the blood of his enemies.

PLANS

Giddi cracked an eye open, and then the other. He released his breath in a gust. He was finally alone, except for the tanks and the unconscious mages strapped to the beds nearby. He raised his neck off the table and gazed at the tanks—and the people Zens was growing inside them. There were dozens of replicas of Velrama and Sorcha, but others too. Was that Arturo? Yes, but Giddi had seen him struck down dead in the forest, near Montanara.

How could Zens possibly grow his body if he was dead? Unless…

Giddi gagged on the thought. Zens was using material from fresh corpses. He rolled to the side heaving, but his stomach was empty. He hadn't eaten in days.

Zens could be planning to use Giddi's own body the same way to replicate his formidable powers. Gods, no. He was the most powerful mage in Dragons' Realm. There'd be no end to the horror Zens could wreak with a hundred of him at his command.

He glanced around the tanks, but there didn't seem to be anyone in them that remotely resembled him. Thank the Dragon Gods.

Zens must have a darker purpose in mind.

An idea sprang to mind. And took root. Suddenly, Giddi knew what Zens wanted him for. Ice slithered down his spine. Gods, things were much worse than he'd thought.

He flicked a finger, but no spark came forth. That couldn't stop him. Giddi pulled *sathir* from the air around him and stored it deep in his core, where it crackled and hummed.

When Zens came for him, Giddi would be ready.

§

Zens tweaked the dial and stepped back from the methimium ray as its golden beams hit the cavern wall. Behind him, hundreds of restless dragons shifted at the sudden light.

Zens turned to 000. "Assemble my tharuk troops. Gather all of my slaves still healthy enough to dig. Make sure each has adequate tools. We'll move them today so they can start work."

000 stared at the golden swirling portal before them.

"Also bring every dark dragon strong enough to fly," Zens added, "and every mage ready to ride."

His beloved tharuk tore his gaze away from the portal and turned to him. "What's their destination, sir? Have you found a new methimium mine?" A smile tugged the corners of 000's mouth up.

Zens rubbed his hands together, his laughter echoing down the broad exit tunnel from his laboratory. "No, 000, we're going to be mining dragons and riders."

A Suspicious Lull

Roberto had been gone six days already, and still no word. Not that she expected one. Ezaara put down her hairbrush. It was useless fretting. It wasn't like Roberto had taken messenger birds with him. And she hadn't exactly given him a chance to talk to her—she'd been too mad about being left behind, and Tonio had been in such a hurry to dispatch them. Ezaara pulled back her quilt and was just getting into bed—alone—when someone knocked at the door.

Mara came in holding a small tube of parchment.

"What is it?" Ezaara asked.

"A message from Giant John," Mara said. "It just arrived."

"What did he say?"

"The last tharuks they saw at Horseshoe Bend were over a few days ago, and there's been none since. Or any dark dragons. It's suspicious. He believes Zens is planning something. And he said to remind Master Jerrick about the strongwood trees."

"Strongwood trees?"

"They grow throughout Great Spanglewood Forest. In fact, everywhere. They're as common as flies in summer."

"I know that. What about them?"

"You mean you haven't heard?" Mara smiled. "I sometimes forget you're from Lush Valley."

"What are you talking about?" Ezaara asked.

Mara grinned. "There's a rumor that if you exercise under a strongwood tree, you get very strong. And there's a man named Mickel in Horseshoe Bend, probably about your parents' age, who claims that's the source of his strength. His muscles are rumored to be massive and he wins the hog tossing contests every year."

"Hog tossing?" What a strange sport.

"Then again, he's also the local blacksmith. So it could just be years of pounding metal that made him so strong." Mara giggled, passed Ezaara the parchment and left.

So tharuks had withdrawn from attacking villages? And Giant John thought it was the lull before the storm. Late into the night, Ezaara contemplated where Roberto was, what Zens could do with the missing ring, and where and how that storm could strike.

Red Guards

Dawn rose, its gentle rays filtering through the last of the trees. The foliage's soft whispers caressed Leah's ears as she awoke. Leah and Taliesin wandered wearily out of Great Spanglewood Forest onto a vast snowy plain, squinting. Leah wrinkled her nose against a rotting stench. Huge mounds of red earth had been dug up and heaped on the snow.

The earthen mounds were oddly shaped. As they walked toward the nearest, Leah gasped. Oh gods, these were not mounds of earth. Dead red dragons were scattered over the plain. The stench was their rotting flesh.

Leah hunched over, retching until her stomach was empty. She spat into the snow, trying to clear the bitter bile from her stomach. Taliesin shook, whimpering. Feet numb with cold and hearts numb with horror, they wandered through the snow. Here, a dragon's wings were hacked off, bloody stumps leaking lifeblood into the snow. Another dragon's throat had been ripped out. More had their guts slit open, spilling entrails. Some dragons were charred, their scales more black than ruby.

Such terrible, senseless waste.

Salt bit into Leah's cheeks as tears streamed down her face. As far as she could see, the snow was studded with dead dragons.

"What's that?" Taliesin pointed.

No! In the middle of the plain stood a grove of trees, blackened and charred.

Leah's gut twisted as if tharuks were clawing it. Shadow dragons had been here. They were too late. She sank to her knees, her body heavy. Oh gods, not the piaua trees.

"Come on, Leah." Taliesin squeezed her hand with a strength that surprised Leah. "We didn't come this far just to give up," he said fiercely. "A drop of piaua goes a long way. That grove. We might be able to salvage something."

She stood and they strode toward the blackened trees with renewed purpose.

Wings swished above them. Without daring to look up, Leah and Taliesin ran, cowering behind a bloody dragon tail. Only then did Leah glance skyward. A flash of scarlet caught her eye. Her heart soared with joy. Zens' monsters hadn't killed them all.

The red dragon circled down to land near the trees and let out a low, mourning keen.

Taliesin sprinted toward it.

Leah hurried after him.

Taliesin stopped in front of the dragon. His lake-blue eyes were transfixed on the dragon's face. Even amid the carnage of its fellow red guards, the dragon's lips were pulled back, its fangs glinting in a smile. Taliesin was beaming. In the few short weeks she'd known him, he'd never looked so peaceful. The dragon lowered her head, and Taliesin flung his arms around her neck.

§

The moment he saw the dragon, Taliesin knew she was special. Those ruby wings winked in the sun, beckoning him. All her fellow dragons, the red guards, were dead. She was the last of her kind—just like he was the last of his family. And as her keening filled the air, ricocheting among the bodies of her fellow guards, it rattled Taliesin's bones. He had to help her.

He ran until he was face to face with the majestic creature. His chest filled with a mighty power. His bones and senses hummed. Even his fingertips were tingling.

And when she turned her enormous gold eyes upon him, her slitted pupils growing, surprise rushed through him, and then love. Love larger than he'd ever remembered feeling. Every one of her scales was glorious—finer than the most beautiful painting. Rushing filled his head, like the flapping of a thousand dragon wings.

And then she spoke. *"Everything I loved has been destroyed. I have nothing— except my broken heart. Will you accept it?"*

How could he? *"I'm not worthy. I'm only a slave, rescued from Death Valley, broken, without family."* He tilted his head. *"But I do have a new home at Dragons' Hold. Maybe you could come with me."*

"I would like that very much indeed. Taliesin, you are worthy to be my new rider. I shall now be named Esina after you." She lowered herself to her knees.

A rush of bittersweet sorrow and love hit Taliesin. His heart felt like it would snap. This poor dragon had endured so much.

"Just as you have," Esina said.

She understood. More than anyone else could ever understand, she understood. He'd seen his entire family die at the hands of tharuks in Zens' slave camp. She'd fought as hers had died around her. Esina lowered her head. He flung his arms around her warm neck. His beautiful ruby dragon tucked her head over his shoulder and a gust of warm air enveloped him.

§

Not wanting to disturb Taliesin and his dragon, Leah strode over to the grove. Even though a pall of smoke hung over the charred trees, there were no longer active fires. Burnt branches crunched underfoot. The outer trees were mainly strongwoods. Although she was sad so many trees had been destroyed, she breathed a sigh of relief. Thank the egg it wasn't the piaua grove. For a moment there, she'd been worried their journey had been for nothing.

Leah stepped around the remains of a cluster of strongwood trees, blackened but still standing, wearing their ash like dark armor. She walked deeper into the grove. Here, the trees were different.

She gasped. These were piaua. Thick rings of towering strongwoods had been planted around the precious grove to protect them. Here the piaua were broad, their trunks mature, but—like the strongwoods—they'd been burned. Her chest clenched as Leah laid her palm on the smoky trunk of a dead piaua. Its leaves, which would normally be evergreen, were shriveled and gray. The trunk, as wide as a small cottage, was burned and blackened.

The crunch of charred branches alerted her to Taliesin and his dragon behind her. "Esina says that a week ago this was a thriving piaua grove, the source of much of the piaua juice in Dragons' Realm."

"Not anymore." Zens' monsters had destroyed everything. Leah's heart was as heavy as rock. One blow, and it would shatter into a thousand pieces. Her eyes swept the burnt grove and the mounds of dead dragon flesh beyond.

"I've told Esina we're hunting for piaua juice," Taliesin said, catching up to her.

The dragon pushed her way through the dead strongwood trees, knocking them aside with her scaled limbs.

The crashes reverberated through Leah's bones. So many mighty trees. So many mighty dragons. All destroyed. She watched Esina bowl another strong-wood over, clumsy in her grief. The trunk shattered into lumps of charred wood and set off a flurry of ash.

Taliesin had said that they hadn't come all this way for nothing.

They had to try something. Anything. "Let's knock a piaua down to see whether there's anything left at its core—perhaps tiny traces of sap that we could use to treat our injured riders."

"It's worth a try," Taliesin said dubiously. "Esina?"

The dragon rumbled. She pushed against the piaua trunk with her flank. The tree gave a dry groan. Esina pushed again, then wrapped her tail around the tree and shook it. Ash floated down, coating Leah's face, hands, and cloak. Coughing and covering her nose and mouth with her cloak, she breathed through it. Taliesin did the same. His eyes were filled with a light Leah had never seen. At least, if this journey brought nothing else—and Leah was now sure it wouldn't—she'd helped him find peace.

Esina stretched up her forelegs and leaned her weight against the charred trunk. Dead cinders floated onto the snow. Branches thumped down and shattered into lumps of char. Cracks appeared in the blackened trunk. The tree split lengthwise and blackened rubble crashed to the ash-stained snow.

When the ash dust had settled, Leah and Taliesin examined the jagged mast spearing the sky. Leah pressed a hand to the cold heart of the tree. Nothing. No stickiness. No sap. Whatever had existed had been burned clean, destroying one of nature's most precious resources.

Leah sank to her knees, resting her forehead against the trunk of the dead piaua. It was useless. They were at the end of the road. There was no way to help her people now.

Shoulders shaking, she cried, tears running down her face and falling onto her ash-smeared hands.

Taliesin laid an arm around her shoulder and sat with her.

"I'm sorry, Taliesin," she sobbed. "It's just…" She turned to him.

His eyes were bright with hope.

She had to break this to him somehow. Although he'd found a wonderful dragon, they would return home empty-handed. There was no hope for their people. She opened her mouth, unsure of what to say.

"Come on, Leah." Taliesin tugged her to her feet. "Esina has just told me that there are brown dragons who protect a piaua grove far over the Northern Alps. She'll take us there."

Leah's mouth sagged. "What?"

"Esina said there are brown guards who—"

"I heard you!" Leah hugged Taliesin, lifting him off the ground and spinning him around in a flurry of ash. "Thank you, thank you, thank you, Taliesin and Esina. I'd given up hope."

"No need for thanks," Taliesin answered, grinning. "I told you back in Montanara, we'd be successful."

THE BLOODY CUTLASSES

The Bloody Cutlasses' ship was bearing down on them at a rapid rate, red sails billowing. Roberto ordered his dragon riders to prepare.

"Barnacles," Captain cursed. "The wind's favoring them. Nod, fetch barrels of oil." He bellowed. "Medina, ready the rags. Skim and Scupper, into the tops with your bows. Everyone else, haul shields, bows and cutlasses on deck. Line the railing. Let's show those egg-suckers how to fight."

The pirates formed a chain with sleek efficiency and passed metal barrels out of the hold to their mates, who spaced them along the rails. Medina, the pirate with the flaming arrow on her scalp, dipped rags into the barrels, soaking them with oil, and wrapped them around arrow shafts. Other pirates flung open large chests of weapons and passed out daggers, knives, and cutlasses.

Two skinny pirates with tattooed sea dragons entwined around anchors on their forearms, and quivers and bows slung over their backs, swarmed up the mainmast to the fighting tops. They nocked their bows, waiting. More rushed on deck wearing breastplates, holding shields, their weapons gleaming at their hips.

The dragon riders assembled in the stern and pulled on their jerkins, fastened breastplates and strapped greaves to their forearms.

"Everyone got their weapons?" Roberto barked.

They nodded.

"If only we had all of our dragons," Gret said.

Danion scowled. "We've planned for this eventuality. And you know the ship could only hold three dragons at a time. Now, we fight."

Only Riona and Erob were supposed to accompany them. But Tomaaz had refused to come without Maazini. After the recent death threat to Maazini, Roberto didn't blame him, so he'd relented. They needed Tomaaz. He and Lovina had been slaves in Death Valley and knew the layout and tharuk habits. They'd be essential on the ground once they reached their destination.

Roberto nodded. "We can try to summon our dragons, but most of them will be patrolling Spanglewood Forest near the Terramites, far out of range. If you do manage to mind-meld with them, warn them to fly high, out of arrow range. Now, await your orders." He strode through the bustling pirates to the helm. "Captain, what can we do to help?"

"Blast that barnacle bowl out of the water," the captain snapped. "Make sure your dragons don't get in the way of our arrows. When I blow the horn, fall back."

"Will do."

"Mark my words, this will be a bloody battle," Captain muttered.

Not if Roberto could help it.

Captain spun. "What about Amato? We need every fighter we can get."

Roberto huffed. "Leave him in the brig. If the ship's taken, the pirates can do what they like with him."

"So much anger in such a young heart," Erob melded.

"Come on, Erob. You know what he—"

"Pirates are attacking," Erob interrupted. *"Focus."*

"Captain, mind your archers don't hit our dragons," Roberto called.

"Hear that, crew?" Captain bellowed.

"Aye, aye, Captain," the crew roared, arrows nocked and eyes focused on the looming red sails.

Captain bellowed. "I don't want dragons injured or riders lost. Medina, pass those riders some oil-soaked rags so their dragons don't have to get too close. Once we've wiped out the Bloody Cutlasses, they have work to do in Death Valley."

Medina passed each rider a quiver of arrows wrapped in oil-soaked rags.

Roberto strode to the poop deck where Erob, Riona, and Maazini were sitting. Dragon riders were lined up next to them, awaiting orders.

"Adelina, Danion, and Gret, man the rails and use your bows. The crew have shields to protect you from volleys of enemy arrows. Kierion, Tomaaz, and I will ride our dragons out to destroy those blood-red sails. We'll be back before our crew fires any arrows. Lovina, you'll be the captain's runner. Stay out of harm's way. If it comes to the worst, take a rowboat with Danion, Adelina, and Gret and make for land." He made eye contact with each one of them, painfully aware that he couldn't bridge the gap with his sister before battle. Gods, if anything happened to her—or him... "Good luck, everyone. And by the First Egg, our top priority is to stay alive. Take no stupid risks, hear me?"

They nodded, murmuring assent.

Roberto glared at Kierion. "Especially you. You've been sick for days and don't have the strength for heroics. Fenni, ride with him and Riona, and keep both eyes on him."

The mage thumped his heart with his fist. "Yes, sir."

"Thank you, Roberto. I'm terrified of fighting," Lovina's blue eyes were wide. Tomaaz hugged her, then swung into his saddle as she raced to the captain.

Fenni helped Kierion—still green at the gills—into Riona's saddle. Adelina reached up and squeezed Kierion's hand.

"Well deployed," Danion murmured to Roberto before hustling Adelina and Gret to the railing.

Roberto climbed onto Erob's back, tightened his saddle straps and gnawed his lip, watching Kierion fumble with his saddle.

"Riona assures me he's made of strong stuff," Erob said.

"Apart from his stomach. Are you ready to stretch your wings?"

A happy rumble coursed through Erob's body. *"I'd like nothing better."*

Riona tensed her haunches, gently rising into the air, the wind from her wingbeats stirring the ends of the pirates' bandannas.

Gold tooth glinting, Nod winked at Roberto. "Don't get yourself killed."

§

Adelina's throat tightened as Erob and Riona flew out to meet the Bloody Cutlasses. As a littling, tales of the Bloody Cutlasses had made her quake in bed all night long. The Scarlett Hand was worst. Now, the only people she loved were flying into the pirate's maw.

She nocked her bow and held her oil-soaked arrow steady, ready to touch it to the flaming torch mounted on the rail in front of her. She was the last in a long line of archers along the *Roaring Dragon's* gunnels. Behind them, pirates stood with long shields, ready to raise them over their heads against the enemy's answering volleys of arrows.

The ship loomed, red sails tight with wind. It was huge, way bigger than the *Roaring Dragon*.

This was crazy. Adelina had been to Death Valley, faced down tharuks, yet now she was quaking. Gods, if only Linaia was near. She tried to mind-meld but there was no answer.

§

"Ah, Riona, I should have done this earlier. I'm not getting back on that floating pail again." Gods, Kierion had no idea the ocean was so many shades of blue. Below them, dark shapes moved beneath the crystalline ocean surface, mysterious and alluring.

"You feeling all right?" Fenni asked, both arms around his waist, obviously taking his assignment seriously.

"For now, yes. The moment Riona took off, I felt fine." Kierion patted her neck scales. Well, apart from still being weak and dizzy, but they didn't need to know that.

"Let's roast some pirates."

Kierion clung to the saddle as Riona climbed higher. They entered a bank of cloud. Clammy air clawed at Kierion, but it was better than pitching on that wooden bucket in the middle of the sea.

To his left was a bright orange blob between drifting clouds—Maazini and Tomaaz. And to his right, a blue shape—Erob.

The cloud cleared. Below, a stream of churning white trailed the red-sailed ship. He glanced back. The *Roaring Dragon* had turned to meet the Bloody Cutlasses head on.

Shards, Captain was mad. If it were him, he would've turned tail and fled, not angled the ship to ram the pirates. He shrugged. No doubt, Captain had his reasons—as long as he didn't get them killed.

§

"Roberto, let's go," Erob called, furling his wings and diving.

"I don't want you hurt, so we'll use Captain's flaming arrows." Roberto fired one of Medina's arrows.

As it shot past Erob, he spurted a tiny flame. The arrow ignited, leaving a fiery trail through the sky. It fell short of the ship, sizzling into the water.

Cries from the Bloody Cutlasses rang out. They fired at Erob, but he climbed and the arrows fell back, speckling the sea's surface like rain.

Roberto had the advantage because he was firing downward. He took his time to aim, correcting for a light cross wind. The next arrow hit its target: a pirate standing at the stern.

"I'm dying to try just a little flame or two," Erob melded.

"No," Roberto replied. *"I don't want you hurt. Captain's right, we have bigger fish to fry."*

"Please, I haven't flambéed pirates in years. It'll make a nice change from killing tharuks." Roberto would have laughed out loud, but he was too busy concentrating on his next target. He loosed his arrow. Erob flamed it. The arrow tangled in the rigging behind the mainsail. Sparks flitted onto the ropes and a thin stream of smoke trailed from the ship. It wasn't enough.

Maazini dived. Tomaaz's flaming arrow hit the jib sail. Flames licked along the edge.

Fanned by the wind, the fire in the rigging flared until tongues of hungry flame reached the main sail, setting the edge on fire. Smoke billowed into the sky.

On deck, a man in a red cloak waved his hands at the flames. The fire in the rigging and sails died. Shards, they had a mage on board.

Riona swooped from the starboard side. Kierion's arrow struck the neck of a pirate behind the ship's wheel. A bolt of Fenni's mage flame hit him, too. A yell pierced the sky and his body slumped to the deck. Another pirate kicked the dead man aside and grabbed the wheel as Riona shot skyward.

Erob wheeled in midair as a volley of arrows zipped toward them. A spike of pain lanced through Roberto's mind. Erob. *"What was it? Were you hurt?"*

"Just a scratch on my tail, but now I'm angry. Can I kill some pirates?"

A horn blew aboard the *Roaring Dragon*.

"No, Erob, I'm sorry. That was the captain's signal to fall back."

Erob snarled, opening his jaws and sending a lick of flame down toward the ship, but the mage waved his arms and it sputtered out before it hit. Erob snarled, flying back to the *Roaring Dragon*. *"Next time come to a different arrangement with that stupid captain."*

The sky below them was filled with the crackle of flaming arrows as they streaked toward the *Roaring Dragon*.

§

The pirate ship's progress slowed, but they hadn't stopped it. Riona flew back to the *Roaring Dragon*, Kierion's blood charging through his veins. His stomach roiled, but this time, not with nausea. *"Flame it, Riona, I'm starving!"*

"Don't worry, we can grab you a snack."

"What do you mean? It's not as if we can stop by the Brothers' Arms and get a meal. We're in the middle of the ocean."

"Yes, flying right above nature's garden." Riona flew to starboard, out of firing range, and dived, her talons skimming the surface of the sea. When they rose, she turned her neck and raised her foreleg. A fish was spiked upon one of her long talons, flopping about. She breathed a gentle gust of flame over the fish, roasting it, then tossed it in the air.

Kierion caught it. Shards, the thing was hot. He bounced it from hand to hand, trying to cool it.

"Don't burn your tongue," Fenni quipped from behind Kierion.

"*I could dip it back in the ocean if you'd like?*" Riona replied.

"*What? And feed my dinner to the sharks? No thank you!*" Kierion laughed and scoffed down the fish before they flew back to fight.

§

Fenni peered out from behind Kierion as his friend ate his fish. He didn't want to hurry Kierion and Riona, but talk about sharding timing. He sighed. His friend hadn't held down food for days. No doubt the purple dragon knew if Kierion didn't eat, he'd flake out in the middle of this battle. Fenni flung his hand out and quenched a fireball zipping toward the *Roaring Dragon's* main sail. That Bloody Cutlass mage was quick on his feet, shooting fireballs faster than Fenni could control them. The pirate mage had also doused the fires on the Bloody Cutlasses' ship before they could destroy much.

A volley of fiery arrows flew through the air at the *Roaring Dragon*. Fenni stretched out his arms and tried to pull *sathir* from the fires to quench them— and failed. Flames sprang from the rigging at the stern of the ship. Shards, his magic couldn't reach that far. "Kierion, Riona, back to the ship. Go, go, go."

Fenni snatched a rope from the saddlebags and tied it to Riona's saddle.

"What are you doing?" Kierion asked, turning to eye the rope as he scoffed the last of his fish.

"I'm going to land among the tops and slither down into the crow's nest. From there, I can help douse the fires."

Kierion's eyes flew wide. "You're flaming mad."

"If you can jump from dragon's tails, I can do this."

The *Roaring Dragon* was under them now. Riona swooped.

"Maybe." Kierion gauged the distance. "Quick! If you're going to do it, jump now."

Hanging on to the rope, Fenni leaped. "Ooff!" The rope went taut and he flew toward the masts.

§

The horn blew. It was time to fall back. "*Let's go,*" Tomaaz melded. "*We're in our own men's firing range.*"

"*Tomaaz, what's that thing?*" Maazini asked. He showed Tomaaz an image of a long object on the Bloody Cutlasses' ship, like a spear but as thick as a big man's upper arm. It had a sharp barbed nose and was mounted on a stand. A rope was coiled on the deck beside it.

"Not sure. Perhaps we should take a closer look." Tomaaz hunched over the saddle as Maazini dived toward the ship. Hopefully, the pirates were too busy scrambling to notice them.

Four Bloody Cutlasses were gathered around the long shaft. As they got closer, one of them looked skyward and yelled, pointing at Maazini. The other aimed the nose of that spear up and released it. The giant thick-shafted spear flew into the air, its rope uncoiling as it gained momentum, firing straight for Maazini's belly.

"Maazini, flee!"

His dragon broke his dive and shot skyward, frantically beating his wings.

Maazini zipped to the side and the thick spear shot past them, the wind of its passage ruffling Tomaaz's long hair. "Shards, that was close!"

"It's not over yet." Maazini swerved again as the projectile hit the end of its tether above and started falling seaward—toward them.

"Heave-ho!" A cry rang out below them. The pirates were pulling the rope, leaning sideways to alter the spear's path.

"Fly to your left, fast!"

Without questioning him, Maazini obeyed. The rope swayed and the enormous spear, as thick as a man's thigh, arced toward Maazini.

"Faster, boy, faster."

Tomaaz angled his body over Maazini's back. Maazini flapped and arched sideways as the heavy projectile fell toward them. "Hang on." Maazini rolled, twisting his body over. Tomaaz's arms ached as he hung on, upside-down. There was a flash of horizon, sea, more sea, and then sky again. Tomaaz's head spun.

"Hold on again." Maazini dived, blasting flame at the thing, but it fell harmlessly into the sea, creating an enormous splash that sprayed the pirates' bowsprit.

"Heave-ho," came the cry of Bloody Cutlasses.

"No!" Tomaaz cried. The Bloody Cutlasses were hauling on that thing's rope, yanking it back on board the ship, so they could fire again. "There are more of those things along the gunnels and in the stern."

"Curse that battle horn," Maazini said. "Despite that scare, I was just beginning to enjoy myself."

After being stuck in the dungeons at Dragons' Hold for so long, Tomaaz had to agree. "Nothing ventured, nothing gained. At least we slowed them down," Tomaaz replied as they shot higher and winged back toward the Roaring Dragon.

A Rare Find

Giddi was dreaming of Mazyka again. But this time, he was actually awake. Her face swam in and out of his mind, her lips moving as she called his name. Dreams like these had taunted him years ago, when he'd first locked the world gate. Occasionally now, they still did. Perhaps the substance Zens had plunged into his veins had started these infernal dreams again. There was no other explanation. He longed to wrap his aching, empty arms around Mazyka and embrace her after all these years.

She'd opened the world gate and let Zens into their world.

So what? Giddi no longer cared. Gods, he missed her with a vengeance. And even though he'd had to lock her out for the sake of Dragons' Realm, he wished he'd gone with her. And wished he could open that world gate again.

§

Zens stalked into the antechamber, glancing over the young mages growing in the tanks. They'd soon be ready to fly on his latest batch of the black-winged beasts he'd created from the scales and flesh of that orange royal dragon. No doubt, the foolish creature didn't realize he'd been used for cloning. He padded over to Giddi, the dragon mage. There were rumors this man could mind-meld with any man or dragon. Jealousy surged through Zens' veins.

By controlling the mage, that power would be his. He stared down his malformed nose at Giddi, probing his helpless mind with his own.

The methimium beetles had bored through the mage's muscle. They'd keep boring until they connected with his central nervous system, allowing Zens to take control of the mage's mind permanently. He snapped his fingers at 000. "Bring the slave in for the mage's test."

000 was soon back with a hunched elderly man covered in methimium dust. "This miner hurt his hand yesterday. He's useless now."

Indeed. The miner's wrist was bent at an odd angle, probably broken. Zens snorted at the pathetic human. Then smiled. "Excellent choice, 000."

000 stalked to the drawer where it kept a set of torture implements—just in case someone needed persuasion.

"Not now, my pet. Today, I want you to watch and learn."

On the benchtop, the master mage was lying peacefully, staring at the ceiling.

Zens released his shackles. "Master Giddi, it's time to rise."

And rise he did. The methimium beetle saw to that. The smirk grew on Zens' face as the most powerful mage in all of Dragons' Realm rolled off the bed and stood next to the table.

"Good morning, my beloved Commander Zens," Giddi said. "How may I help you?"

A thrill ran through Zens. He flexed his fingers. Oh, it felt good to be in control. He waved a languid hand at the numlocked slave. It was a shame the wretch was too drugged to know what was going on. "Please kill him."

Without a blink of an eye, Master Giddi stretched forth his hand. A bolt of mage fire slammed into the old man's chest. He screamed and writhed on the stone floor as his body was engulfed in fire.

Zens took a deep, slow breath through his nostrils, inhaling the satisfying stench of burning human flesh.

As cool as an ice-laden pond, Master Giddi raised an eyebrow. "What would you have me do next, sir?"

"Bring another slave," Zens barked at 000.

000 carried a young, shirtless boy—eyes shining bright with fever—into the lab and dumped him on the floor. The weakling gasped, his skin sucking up under his bony ribcage every time he breathed.

Zens slipped into Giddi's mind. *"Kill him now."*

This time, when the mage stretched forth his hand, frost coated the boy's feet. It moved up his legs and encased his torso and arms. Through the thin layer of frost, the boy's torso took on a bluish-gray tinge. The boy whimpered, but it was too late. The frost crept up his neck, over his face, until his hair was stiff with it.

The frost thickened into ice. The boy stopped breathing. His eyes rolled back in his head. He fell to the stone floor, ice shattering around his dead body.

"He's dead. What would you like me to do next?"

This mage was powerful. Stronger than Zens had realized. He'd turn this power to his advantage… "Excellent. 000 will teach you everything we know about creating clones. You will work for me. Understood?"

"That will be interesting. I thank you for this opportunity, Commander." The mage's voice seemed genuinely friendly.

Warmth stole across Zens' chest, making him gasp. He'd only ever had that feeling with 000. He clamped it down, stowing his memory of 000's creation deep at the back of his mind so the mage couldn't access it.

"Let's get started," the master mage said. "We'll need more of these mages if we're to conquer Dragons' Realm."

Zens rubbed his hands together, grinning. The dragon mage—the man who'd trapped him here in this world—was now his.

§

It had been an interesting few days, learning how to 'clone' mages. The process had involved all sorts of contraptions that Giddi didn't fully understand, but his part had been simple: taking what Zens called 'tissue samples' and putting them through various procedures before finally placing them in tanks of solution. Then Zens added an 'accelerant'. Within hours, tiny bodies formed, growing over days into full-sized versions of Sorcha and Velrama.

Today, Giddi had hauled those same mages out of the tanks. Tharuks helped the mages out of the clear membranes around their bodies and taught them how to flex their limbs, bend, and even walk. They were fast learners. Within an hour, all of them had mounted dark dragons under Zens' beaming gaze. Now they were waiting in a tunnel beyond Zens' main workroom.

In the main, larger chamber, tharuks worked around the clock. Luckily his own activities in the antechamber were restricted to a few hours a day, due to the lack of glass tanks for growing mages.

Giddi was exhausted. The food in Death Valley consisted of stale bread and thin gruel that did little to quench his hunger—a far cry from his favorite: wizard porridge. He couldn't wait for the tharuks to raid Dragons' Realm again and bring back decent spoils. As he passed Zens' workbench, something flashed in the yellow glare of the methimium-powered lights. Something familiar.

Giddi moved closer. His heart battered against his ribcage. He reached for the teardrop-shaped crystal necklace and held it up. Suspended on a fine chain, it swung, glimmering in the light.

He'd had a similar necklace, but lost his years ago. Memories flooded him.

Anakisha had made these necklaces to help rare couples who could mind-meld to maintain contact over long distances. Back then, only a few couples had been able to mind-meld: he and Mazyka; Anakisha and Yanir; Hans and Marlies; and now, Roberto and Ezaara. How had this precious treasure fallen into Zens' hands?

He doubted his new master knew how to use it. Perhaps he'd show Commander Zens when he returned from teaching the cloned mages how to fly their new dragons. Giddi slipped the necklace over his head and then tucked the crystal under his clothing. It vibrated against his chest—the same comforting, reassuring vibration that had helped him mind-meld with Mazyka when she'd first gone through the world gate, years ago.

Dark shadows whispered in his mind, *"There's no point thinking about the past. Zens is the future."*

Yes, they were right. He'd use the power of Anakisha's necklace to aid his new master.

SEASICK

Dragons thudded to the deck behind her, but Adelina had no time to look. The gap between their ship and the Bloody Cutlasses' was narrowing fast. The Bloody Cutlasses' mainsail was blackened and scorched, but the damage was only superficial, curse it. The rest of the sail caught the wind and strained at the rigging. Sea spray showered the bowsprit as the ship plowed through the brine alongside them.

Something thudded against the foremast behind Adelina. She spun as a grappling hook whipped through the air. She twisted out the way and it caught on the railing. Ropes flew and more hooks caught on the railings. One hit a ship hand in the head. He sprawled on the deck, unconscious. No time for that now. Pirates were scrambling along the ropes, curved blades in their teeth.

Adelina swung her sword over the edge of the railing. Her blade thunked off the sea-soaked rope. She slashed again and again, but her blade kept sliding off. The rope went taut as a leering pirate seethed across it, making his way toward her.

There was only one thing for it. She hooked her legs around a sturdy piece of timber and leaned out over the edge of the ship, sawing at the rope with her dagger. A thread gave. Then another.

Blade glinting in his teeth, the pirate growled, scrambling faster along the rope. Adelina sawed, arms aching and legs trembling as the sea pitched below her. She clamped down on her roiling stomach but nausea washed through her. Oh gods, this was how Kierion must've felt. Flaming arrows zipped in both directions. The rope sagged as the pirate neared, now only a few body lengths away.

Frantically, Adelina thrust her dagger back and forth. Just a few more cuts.

A piece of rope gave. The pirate's eyes widened. He lunged up. The ship pitched. Adelina's stomach heaved and she vomited.

Spew hit the pirate's face. Yelling, he let go to bat at his eyes—and plunged into the sea.

Heart pounding, Adelina hung onto the railing. Then she snatched her sword and smote the rope, cutting it free. It fell into the sea, and she shimmied back onto the deck.

Beside her, Captain's crew were firing arrows and cutting ropes, but several Bloody Cutlasses had made it on board. Roberto was fighting a pirate with a scraggly brown mane. Erob bit another and tossed him into the ocean. Flaming arrows rained down, thudding into shields. Adelina grabbed a pail and doused a small fire on the deck.

Strong arms snatched her, lifting her off the ground.

"A fine little bit of girly here," a voice growled, the stench of foul breath wafting over her. "I like 'em extra young, I do."

She slashed down with her dagger, scoring the pirate's thigh. In a spray of blood, he dropped, screaming. Adelina spun and drove her dagger into his groin. A sword slashed past her, plunging into the pirate's heart.

Roberto flashed her a grimace, then spun to parry the blade of another pirate.

Fires sprang up on the deck around them, as the crew fought the Bloody Cutlasses. Riona dived, purple scales whipping through the air. Holding the bottom half of a weapon chest, Riona dunked it in the sea and returned to tip water over the flaming topsail, helping Fenni, up in the tops, to douse the fire. Again, she filled the chest and poured water over the fires on deck.

Fenni lobbed fireballs at pirates and waved his hands to quench new fires in the rigging and springing up on deck. Suddenly, he flung up his hand. The railing grew slick with ice. Vertical icicles grew from the railing, spiking into the air and growing as high as Adelina's head. Then higher. They coalesced. A thick ice wall sprang between the *Roaring Dragon* and the pirate ship, making everything appear murky and distant. Fireballs and the flaming arrows thudded into it and died.

"Man the oars," the Captain bellowed.

As the crew rushed below deck to row, the captain, the dragons, and Roberto turfed the dead pirates overboard. "Thank the Egg the Scarlet Hand wasn't on board that ship," Captain muttered as they carried a corpse to the other non-icey railing.

Fenni stayed put, keeping the ice shield intact, forehead dripping sweat and body trembling.

Lovina rushed up to Adelina, holding a bloody sword. "I killed a pirate," she crowed, eyes gleaming with triumph. "After all those years of being beaten and hurt, I finally fought back."

Adelina hugged her.

Above in the tops, Fenni slumped over the edge of the crow's nest. The ice wall shattered and crashed into the sea.

Adelina and Lovina watched as the *Roaring Dragon* pulled away from the Bloody Cutlasses, leaving the pirates' masts on fire and their scorched, tattered sails fluttering in the wind.

SNOWBOUND

On the third day flying north-east upon Esina, Leah, and Taliesin hit a heavy snowstorm. After clinging to the dragon's back with their cloaks bunched around them and limbs shivering, they found a cave high in the Northern Alps and sheltered overnight.

"How far to the brown guards?" asked Leah, prodding their fire with a stick.

Taliesin turned the haunch of mountain goat that Esina had killed for them on its spit.

It certainly was handy traveling with a dragon who could catch your dinner and then light a fire to cook it. Leah edged closer to the crackling flame, holding out her hands to warm them.

"Only half a day from here, when the storm stops," Taliesin replied.

When the storm stopped.

It could be days before they could fly farther. And when they did, would they find another grove of desecrated piaua and more death and desolation? Or would their luck finally change? Leah kept that slim hope stoked inside her as the goat's fat dripped, hissing, into the fire.

PORCELAIN TREASURE

Yesterday had been a long day, but after repairing the rigging and sails, the *Roaring Dragon* had made good speed. They'd be on land soon. Roberto's gut tightened. He'd been dreading this since they'd embarked upon the ship—today he'd comb through tunnels with his father, hunting tharuks and revisiting the very place where his father had sold him to the enemy.

Nearby, Adelina was sharpening her sword on a whetstone. Her eyes met his, mouth grim. She gave a terse nod.

Only she knew how he felt. Although she still hadn't spoken to him, at least her nod was something.

A heavy hand fell upon his shoulder. Roberto turned. The captain gave a command. "Step into my cabin, Master Roberto."

"Yes, Captain." They'd developed a mutual accord, not complete trust, but a good working relationship. Roberto followed him.

"We'll be disembarking soon," the captain said. "I suggest your dragons fly inland now."

"Erob, take the others and meet us near Death Valley, but be careful. Don't get hurt."

Erob snorted. *"Make sure you take your own advice. All of us would like our riders intact, thank you."* His dragon shared a glimpse of the sea beneath him, orange and purple wings flashing to either side of him as the dragons departed.

Captain shut the door behind them and gestured Roberto to a red velvet-covered chair at a highly-polished table with fancy curved legs. The tabletop was inlaid with beautiful wood of various shades and grains, in the shape of sea dragons. Strange—Roberto hadn't picked Captain as someone who liked pretty things.

Captain paced to an ornately-carved wooden cabinet. Behind the cabinet's glass were porcelain cups, ranging from dainty to tankard-sized, each decorated with various dragon motifs—all different. "Did I ever tell you about the time Old Blood-eye knocked on my door?"

Captain knew full well he hadn't. Roberto shook his head.

Captain poured him a cup of tea out of a porcelain teapot painted with blue and green dragons flying over a vast ocean rippling with multi-hued fish. He passed Roberto a teacup that was also painted with green dragons wheeling in midair over an ocean—Naobian green guards, by the look of them. Captain's own cup was covered in fire-breathing dragons, fighting. Roberto had to refrain from gaping. It was ludicrous to see a collection this beautiful here, in the middle of the sea surrounded by rough tattooed pirates with nose rings, scars and belly piercings. He accepted the cup and leaned back in his chair. "Thank you, this'll probably be my last tea in a while." Inhaling, he asked, "Peppermint or spearmint?"

"Keen nose. Try it and see." Captain barked one of his laughs and took a delicate sip, holding his cup as if it would shatter. "Anyway, back to my tale. Captain Blood-eye had been my foe for years. He'd even set one of my ships on fire, back in the days when I had a fleet. One day, he stole onto my ship and knocked at my cabin door. It was all I could do not to run a sword through him." He took a sip of tea, his keen eyes peering at Roberto over the top of the flames on his cup. "He stopped me by saying he knew the whereabouts of something precious to me. Something I'd want above all else, if I knew what it was."

Captain ran a finger around the top of his teacup, eyes distant. "He begged for an audience. But I told him I'd rather feed him to the sharks than listen to his words. I had him whipped and locked in the brig. Even locked up and bleeding, he yammered at my crew, telling them he had to talk to me."

"Sounds persistent." Roberto chuckled, but his laughter died on his lips at the serious expression in Captain's eyes. He took another sip of tea.

Captain swirled his cup, lost in thought. At long last, he spoke. "The Scarlet Hand and his Bloody Cutlasses had taken my wife and littlings."

Roberto raised an eyebrow, unaware that the captain even had littlings—or a wife.

"I'd kept their identities and location secret. Well, so I thought, but one of my ex-mates had betrayed me, selling their names and whereabouts to the Scarlet Hand for a sack of golden dragon heads, so he could buy his own ship. After days of pleading, Blood-eye convinced Nod, my first mate, that I'd regret it if I didn't hear him out." The captain fell silent, sipping his tea. When his tea was finished, he set it down, examining the flaming dragons.

Captain looked up. "By the time I listened to Blood-eye, it was too late, although I didn't know it. Despite me treating him so badly, Blood-eye helped me scour the seas, looking for them, but my wife and littlings were dead. You see, the Scarlet Hand and the Bloody Cutlasses had taken Blood-eye's family, years before—which is why he raged upon the Naobian Sea, inflicting pain and mayhem on everyone, vowing that if he ever came up against the Scarlet Hand he'd reward him with a slow torturous death."

Captain traced a finger along a sea dragon's tail on the pretty tabletop. "Captain Blood-eye was a good man who'd been dealt a bitter hand. In the end, after years of fighting the Cutlasses and losing a duel against the Scarlet Hand, Blood-eye died in my arms."

Roberto placed his cup in its saucer, trying to hide his impatience. They must be nearing the pirate tunnel. He didn't have time for reminiscing.

Captain poured them both another spearmint tea. Taking a sip, he continued his story. "You see, Master Roberto, Blood-eye did something important for me. After his death, I lost my lust for pirating. So did most of my crew. I became a trader and let my crew run my trading ship, while I traversed Dragons' Realm until I came to Montanara. I ousted the weak leader of the Nightshaders but kept his gang, even the ones I wasn't so keen on, including Brutus." Captain chuckled. "I'm quite glad he got carried off by your lad's dragon."

What? "Which lad?"

"Brutus was trying to have a go at that girl with long blonde braids. The one Danion has Fenni spitting sparks about."

Gret. "And what did they do?" He obviously hadn't heard Kierion's whole report. Then again, Kierion was notorious for secrets.

"Danion's blue dragon carried Brutus off into Spanglewood forest and dropped him among tharuks—where he belonged." The captain chortled. "Eventually, some of my pirating crew joined the Nightshaders. We had quite a tidy, if shady, business going."

"That still doesn't tell me why you hate dragons so much."

"I asked the green guards for help when my family went missing, but the dragons and riders never came. I vowed never to trust a dragon or rider again..." Captain glanced out the cabin window at cliffs looming across a short stretch of ocean. "We don't have much time." He reached across the table and grasped Roberto's arm. "Amato's been talking to my crew. Says he was implanted with a crystal by Zens and couldn't help what he did."

Oh, that was Captain's point—Amato. Although Blood-eye and Captain were enemies and had wronged each other in the past, they'd pulled together to fight a common enemy.

Captain arched his brows. "Your future is up to you, Roberto."

It flaming well was. Who did Captain think he was, meddling in his affairs? Roberto drained his cup—embellished with Naobian green guards flying through the sky. His throat constricted. The rider in the foreground looked exactly like his father.

Captain met his eyes and nodded. "Even though I hate dragons, I've kept this flaming crockery because it belonged to my beloved wife. She had each one especially commissioned. I knew Amato years ago. He was a good man before Zens turned him. When I took up pirating, she wanted me to remember that."

The captain's words were like a knife twisting deep in Roberto's gut. The last thing he or Adelina needed was to remember the man behind the monster.

"Thank you for the tea." Roberto's thanks stuck in his throat as he turned and left the cabin.

LAND BOUND

Yesterday Riona had flown around the ship dousing fires long enough for Kierion's fish to digest. As soon as she'd landed back on board, seasickness had hit him again and it hadn't stopped. Thank the First Egg it was time to disembark. Kierion couldn't have been happier—except they weren't disembarking onto nice flat dry land, were they? No, huge cliffs rose straight out of the sea, barren and pockmarked with thousands of holes.

It'd be impossible to find the pirate tunnel into Death Valley without Amato to guide them.

Confronted by jagged rocks, the captain maneuvered the boat as close as he dared and then weighed anchor. "This is far as I can take you all. I won't enter Death Valley again."

"Fetch Amato, please," Roberto commanded in a voice that could've frozen the ocean.

Nod dragged Amato from the brig.

Looking like an emaciated skeleton and squinting against the light, the frail man rested his hands on the railing, scanning the cliffs. His wispy hair stirred in the sea breeze. No one spoke as he scanned the cliffs.

Waves slapped against the hull.

Finally, Amato pointed. "There, there it is, I'd know it anywhere. See, it's shaped like a dragon's maw."

Nod grunted.

"It's been a few years since I've used this entrance. Eight years ago, actually, last time I was here."

Leaning on the railing at Kierion's side, Adelina flinched. He brushed her hand with his. Roberto remained cool, not even acknowledging that his father had spoken, his gaze riveted on the cliff.

"There should be a few meager supplies inside, above the high tide line—unless a freak tide has washed them away," Amato said.

Kierion tried not to look, but the churning gray waves under the gunnels of the boat were too much. The deck swayed. Gods, now he had to get into another boat, a pitifully light craft that Captain's men were now lowering over the side.

Instead of watching the sea, he focused on a tattoo rippling across the large bicep of one of the pirates lowering the rowboat—of dragons with their necks entwined, forming a heart. Scattered at their feet were a horde of dragonets, among fractured shards of eggs. Blood dripped from the shards, trickling onto a banner: *In blood we are born. In blood we die. Together.*

Kierion shuddered.

He risked a look over the railing. Dark fins peeked above the ocean, were swallowed by waves, then cut through the choppy sea. That didn't help his nausea. Kierion swallowed and looked away, willing his stomach to behave. He didn't fancy leaning over the low side of that rowboat with sharks so near.

"Heave-ho." The rowboat splashed down into the churning brine, Medina sitting inside it. She used the oars to keep the boat close to the ship. A wave crested the side, leaving a pool of water in the bottom. Nod tied a rope to the railing and cast it down to Medina, who by some miracle grabbed it. "One at a time," she called.

Kierion rolled his eyes. As if she thought they'd scale the rope in threes.

"The quicker we're out of here, the better," Roberto said. "Into the boat. Danion first, then Tomaaz, Fenni, and Gret. After them, Amato, Lovina, and Adelina. I'll take the rear with Kierion."

Captain passed Danion a bulging rucksack. "You'll need these to get into the tunnel. Amato knows how to use them."

Danion shouldered the rucksack, grabbed the rope and launched himself off the edge.

Captain and Roberto clasped each other's arms and nodded, Naobian style, to farewell each other. Then Tomaaz was over the edge.

Oh gods. Kierion groaned. It would soon be his turn.

Captain strode to the railing next to Kierion. "Chew this. It'll settle your stomach." Captain shoved a piece of dried ginger root into Kierion's hand. Staring out at the ocean, he muttered, "I didn't have much, so I saved it for this leg of your trip because the waters are notoriously choppy here."

No kidding. "Thanks." Kierion stuffed the root into his mouth and chewed rapidly. It nearly burnt his tongue off, but he'd eat a Naobian hot pepper, seeds and all, if it stopped his stomach churning.

Captain slugged him on the shoulder. "Thanks for saving my life, Kierion, and introducing me to dragons again."

Kierion swallowed the ginger, throat burning. "You're welcome, Captain." He was aware of Fenni, Gret, Amato, and Lovina going down the rope to that tiny boat bobbing in the churning sea, but he kept his eyes on Captain. "I was glad to serve my people in Montanara, and to serve you."

Adelina squeezed his hand, then went down the rope.

Kierion turned back to Captain and pounded his fist over his heart. "Thank you for bringing us here."

Captain winked. "Just don't mention to the dragon masters that I already owned the ship you bought for me." He chortled.

"What?" Roberto asked from behind them.

Kierion grinned. "Um, nothing."

Roberto smiled back. "I guess it's one of those secrets that I really don't want to know."

Kierion shrugged.

"Next," Medina yelled from below.

Captain gestured to the rope. "Your turn, Kierion. Don't ever keep a lady waiting."

Kierion grasped the rope, launched himself over the edge and walked down the side of the ship. Carefully studying his hands on the rope, he avoided looking below.

"Two more steps, then leap," Adelina called.

He didn't trust himself to answer. Clenching his jaw shut against rising nausea, Kierion swung out to the rowboat and found his footing. Sighing, he sank down onto a bench.

Moments later, Roberto's weight hit the boat. The rowboat dipped then lurched on a wave.

Ginger burned its way up Kierion's throat. He grasped the side of the rowboat and leaned over, depositing Captain's chewed-up gift into the choppy gray waves. His nostrils burned too, the cloying stench of ginger smothering the salty brine. Oh, by the flaming dragon gods, no. He clung on as the world wobbled on the swell. Squeezing his eyes shut, Kierion waited for his nausea to pass.

When he opened his eyes, a dark fin was cutting through the water. He slumped back on the bench, holding his middle. No one spoke. There was just the hiss of the waves against the boat, the creak of Medina's oars in the oarlocks, and the slap of the tide against the pockmarked cliff.

§

Roberto had to admire Kierion. Not everyone could descend from a ship to a rowboat while suffering from crippling seasickness, and keep their head. Or their midday meal. Kierion had nearly mastered it, until that wave hit the side.

Tucked in the rowboat between himself and Danion, Amato pointed at the tunnel high up the cliff face. "See, it looks even more like a dragon maw from down here."

Roberto grudgingly nodded.

An enormous wave crested, smashing on the cliff face and sending spray high inside the dragon's maw. The next wave did the same.

This way led only to certain death. "So how do we get in?"

His father replied, "There are two ways: either you ride a wave and chance it throwing you up there—"

Medina interrupted. "Hopefully the wave won't throw a shark at you." She laughed. "You wouldn't be the first to be eaten here."

Amato glared at her and continued, "Or you hop out of the rowboat and cling onto the rock while the tide hits you, and then clamber up."

Anger surged inside Roberto. "You never mentioned this. Is that what your game is? To bring us here to die?" Was his father still carrying a methimium crystal, buried deep somewhere inside him? "You're still working for Zens, admit it."

Amato held out shaking hands. "Pass the rucksack, Danion." He opened it and fished out three short lengths of rope. "This is how we'll do it. There are rings mounted in the cliff, leading up to the cave." He pointed them out, then threaded the first piece of rope through his belt, and looped the other two onto it. "We get out of the boat, one at a time. You tie one of these ropes onto the first ring. When the wave hits you, you hang on."

"And pray that a shark doesn't spot you." Medina cackled.

Amato shook his head. "Before the next wave comes, you tie yourself onto the next ring with the other rope. Then wait out that wave, and untie yourself from the one below. Then you do the next—"

"And the next." Roberto eyed the steep cliff streaming with backwash from the wave. At intervals, rusty metal rings were mounted into the stone. "If the rings hold, you'll gradually make your way up the cliff, always anchored by at least one rope. Amato, distribute the ropes. Do we have enough for everyone?"

Amato nodded. "And spare. Captain made sure of that."

"All right, everyone. Did you hear Amato's instructions? It'll be slow progress, but doable." It'd take iron nerves and steady hands. Hopefully, Kierion was up to this. Flaming Amato—if he'd mentioned this, they could've had a dragon ferry them up the cliffside. Hmm. Maybe not, it was pretty steep and would require a huge leap from dragonback. Anyway, he hadn't given Amato a single chance to speak with him since they'd boarded the *Roaring Dragon,* despite his requests. Oh gods, just like the captain and Bloodeye. Roberto cleared his throat. "If any of you don't think you're up to it, speak now and you can go back to Naobia with the captain. No one will think less of you."

No one spoke.

Kierion had paled. His hands were shaking.

Danion growled, "And then we freeze, climbing through a tunnel in sea-sodden clothing to find Zens? Is that your brilliant plan?" He glared at Amato.

"We must tie our knots firm and fast, or the tide will take us," Amato said, ignoring Danion. "Let's practice until everyone knows how."

They tied their ropes around their waists or belts and threaded the others through.

"No, Gret, the top piece has to go through the bottom one. There, that's right," Amato said. They all practiced the knots several times. Kierion's hands were shaking and he looked greener than a Naobian dragon. Roberto vowed he'd be the last off the boat with Kierion right in front of him to make sure the lad didn't fall.

Medina rowed closer to the cliff. The boat rose on the swell to a tiny rock platform with only room for one person. The rowboat bobbed up and down, the rock awash with brine.

Danion was first out and reached high, fastening his rope to the second ring. Even though Fenni glowered at him, he reached down to steady Gret on the rock. They both moved higher, using footholds and handholds cut into the rock. The boat rose on a swell and the tide washed up Gret's calves.

Roberto glanced behind then.

Sharks were prowling farther out. If someone slipped…

"Next," Roberto called as the tide receded. Fenni was out in a flash, fastening himself to the first ring and reaching for the second when the tide hit him. He clung as the backwash tried to pull him back into the sea.

"And next," Roberto called.

Amato tried to help Adelina clamber out of the rowboat but she waved him off and sprang, slipping on the rock. In a flash, she was on her feet, tying herself to the ring. Roberto watched, heart in mouth as the water rose to his sister's thighs. Gods. If she got washed away he'd be powerless to help her. And they hadn't even sorted things out yet.

Another Blood-eye of sorts. He vowed he'd talk to her as soon as he could.

Above, Danion led the way, calling instructions to the others about footholds and handholds.

Tomaaz helped Lovina out, then followed. Next, it was Amato's turn. He scrambled onto the platform and threaded his rope around the ring as if he'd done it a hundred times. Perhaps he had.

Roberto cringed. No one knew how many foul deeds his father had done in Zens' name.

"There's only you two left." Medina waved a hand at the sharks. "Better be quick. Your sister let blood into the water."

Roberto's gaze shot up to Adelina, halfway up the cliff. She'd gashed her knee when she'd fallen. Blood ran down her leg and stained the stone where she was climbing. Below the tide mark, the rock was clean.

"They say a shark can smell a drop of blood from a hundred dragon lengths away," Medina said. "This time, I'm not joking. They'll be in a frenzy soon and may even jump into my boat. Get out. Now."

Curse the dragon gods, there wasn't enough space on the platform for both of them. Roberto gripped Kierion's biceps. "You can do this, Kierion. Once we get in to that tunnel, you won't have to look at the sea again. But be prepared. Your legs won't be steady. You'll feel as if the rock is pitching."

Kierion groaned.

Roberto shook him. "Come on, Kierion. You're the man who can jump onto a dragon's tail. Imagine the seawater is a cold bath and hang on. Imagine the rope is a test of skill. We'll get you to the top. I'll be behind you every step of the way."

Kierion's panic-stricken eyes met his.

Glancing up, Roberto saw Danion leading the others into the cavern.

"Move it. The sharks are closing in," Medina called.

Roberto grabbed Kierion's chin between his hands. "Don't look. Get on the rock now."

Kierion leaped onto the platform as a massive fin cut through the water. He grabbed his rope and threaded it through the first ring. And hung on as a high wave drenched him to the waist.

Roberto glanced behind them. The shark was getting closer to the rowboat.

Another wave drenched Kierion. He clung on, but didn't move.

"Up. Next step, Kierion," Roberto called. "Make it lively."

Kierion climbed up a few footholds. Roberto leaped onto the platform and tied his first rope.

"The dragon gods be with you," Medina called, pushing off with an oar.

Freezing water clawed at Roberto's legs, dragging his feet across the rock, but he clung to his anchoring rope. Now the rowboat was gone, there was nothing but water between him and that massive fin. The shark sped toward him.

Gods, he couldn't rush Kierion, or he'd likely slip. Roberto waited as another wave crested. It smashed against his thighs, splashing his backside and lower back.

Oh gods, Kierion had gashed his elbow on the rock above. His blood dripped into the sea.

Roberto tried to tie his second rope to the ring above, but it was tangled in his belt. He yanked it from his belt and reached up, but the rope slipped through his fingers and plunged to the sea. A fanged maw rose from the water. A shark snapped its jaws around the rope.

Medina cried out a warning.

Roberto grabbed a handhold, hoisting himself up the rock. The next wave smashed around his knees, but he ignored it, untying his first rope.

A wave slapped at his calves. There was an almighty yank on his waist. His face slammed into the rock. Blood ran into his eyes. And dripped down onto the last rope around his waist. Oh gods. He screamed as another freak wave splashed higher. There was another yank on his waist.

He risked a glance down.

The giant shark had his rope firmly in its jaws. It yanked again, thrashing its tail.

Other sharks, excited by its thrashing, shot toward it. Gods, oh gods.

As the wave receded, Roberto freed his knife from its sodden sheath and severed the rope from his belt.

He scrambled up the slippery cliff face, leaving a frenzy of sharks fighting over the rope in the churning waters.

§

Barely breathing, Adelina lay at the mouth of the tunnel, head over the edge, staring down at her brother and Kierion. There they were—the two men she loved most in the world, battling for their lives on the cliff. Below them, sharks churned the water into a frothy white mass of snapping jaws and thrashing tails.

Shards, Roberto wasn't even tied on. She'd struggled and slipped, gashing her knee. Only the flimsy ropes had saved her. Her fists clenched the rim of the ledge.

Just a few more handholds now, and Kierion would be in the cave. His face was pale and limbs trembling. He'd barely eaten these last few days. It was a wonder he could climb at all.

Roberto, blood trickling down his face, was much farther down. His voice drifted up to them. "That's it, Kierion. You can do it. You're nearly there."

She swallowed. He'd gone last so he could help Kierion. Roberto was always looking out for others. Always trying to help wherever he could. He'd even let himself be banished and sent to the Wastelands so he could save Ezaara.

She groaned. She'd been such a fool. So stubborn and so blind. Shocked at Amato being alive, she'd lashed out at her brother, who must've been just as stunned as her.

"Careful there, Adelina." Danion spoke softly, crouching beside her. "Don't move now, but be aware that you're gripping the edge of that ledge mighty hard. When you let go, you might send stones down on them. I don't want either of them to be startled."

"Oh." She glanced at her fists, then at him.

He angled his body to hold his hands in the air under hers. "Let go now."

Some pebbles came loose from the rock. Danion caught them and straightened, casting them into the tunnel behind them. "How about you shuffle back so I can help Kierion into the cave? He looks pretty tired."

Adelina wriggled back a pace or two, glad someone stronger and bigger than her could help. She was so tiny, if Kierion fell, he'd take her with him.

Kierion's panting was audible before his head appeared.

Danion called, "Look out, Roberto." He grasped hold of Kierion's arms and yanked him into the cavern. Adelina looked over the edge to see a scatter of loose shale bounce down the cliff. Roberto ducked his head and waited until it passed, then kept climbing.

She spun to Kierion and threw her arms around him. He shuddered, legs trembling and gave her a wan smile. "Those poor sharks missed out on their main course."

She squeezed him. "I'm glad they did."

"I only teased them with second-hand ginger and a bit of blood. They'll probably ask for their coin back."

"Come on, sit down while we wait for Roberto." She pulled a soggy length of smoked meat from her pocket. "I've been saving this for when you were back on land and could stomach it."

"Thanks." Kierion sat down and leaned against the wall. He ripped off a piece of meat with his teeth and groaned. "Oh, this is good. Maybe that's what the sharks were after."

"You're nearly there," Danion called down to Roberto. "Just a few more handholds."

Her brother's grunt was his only reply.

Adelina hung back until Danion heaved her brother into the cavern.

Roberto staggered a step or two.

Adelina flung her arms around his waist and hugged him, murmuring, "I'm so sorry."

His arms tightened around her and he tucked his chin on her head, the way he had when she was a littling. "It's all right, 'Lina. I understand."

§

The moment Roberto released Adelina, Amato was there. The rest of the riders tensed. Fenni instinctively held his hands up, ready to fling mage flame.

"Son, I'm sorry, perhaps I should've explained about the cave," Amato started.

Roberto waved a hand. "It's all right. We're all safe and alive."

"I tried to tell you about it."

"I said, *it's all right.*" Roberto snapped. He took a deep breath. "We've made it. Let's have a short rest before you lead us to Zens." He deliberately made it sound simple, but this was Death Valley—they'd be walking into a nightmare. "Danion, got anything to eat in that bag of yours?"

Danion shot Roberto a shrewd glance. "As a matter of fact, I have." He fished around in the rucksack.

As Roberto intended, everyone's attention turned to Danion. Roberto slumped against the wall next to Kierion, glad to be off his shaking legs. Gods, that climb had really taken it out of him. Not the climb itself, but the scare with the sharks. He leaned in to Kierion, murmuring, "Thank the sharding First Egg those sharks are far behind us."

"Well, below us, actually," Kierion quipped, accepting some hardtack, plump figs, and dried apricots from Danion. "Mind you, we could throw them some of this to break their jaws on." He waved his hardtack in the air, then bit into it. "On second thoughts, that would be a waste. It's not too bad when it's soggy."

Roberto chuckled and chewed his own hardtack.

After that one short climb, they were all exhausted—except Amato and Danion.

Lovina sat next to Tomaaz, her head leaning on his shoulder as they ate. Gret stared out the cavern mouth. Fenni was leaning against the cavern wall a few paces behind her, face wistful. Danion was still rummaging in his rucksack.

Roberto's gaze flitted to Amato hovering near the back of the tunnel.

Adelina grabbed her food off Danion, then sat against the wall on Kierion's other side. She leaned over Kierion and whispered, "So, Roberto, who's going to break the ice with Amato—you or me?"

She didn't call him *Pa* either.

Roberto chewed on his hardtack without answering, ashamed of the surge of relief that ran through him as Danion strode to Amato and offered him food, then started discussing strategy, their soft murmurs humming through the cavern.

DEATH VALLEY

They'd been walking for hours when Amato froze, holding up a hand. "Tharuks." His voice was barely a whisper in the stale dry air of the tunnel.

Roberto inhaled. Yes, there was a faint stench of fetid rot. The scrape of everyone's swords sliding from their scabbards thundered in his ears.

Fenni adjusted the mage light bobbing above them, dimming it until it emitted a faint green glow. They crept forward, putting their weight on the outer edges of their boot soles so they made as little sound as possible.

Soon, light was visible around a corner. Fenni extinguished his mage light.

Danion moved to the front, Roberto at his heels. They peeked around the corner, hanging back in the dark.

A group of tharuks were sprawled on the tunnel floor, leaning against the walls. Some guards these were—although if Amato was right, there hadn't been an attack for years, so it was no wonder they weren't on high alert.

Danion nudged him. Motioning the others forward, they rushed the tharuks.

The beasts roared and leaped to their feet, claws out. Danion's sword swung, hacking through the first tharuk's neck. The beast's ugly tusked head bounced along the floor, hitting Roberto's boot. He leaped over it, landing on blood-slicked stone. Catching his footing, he charged into the midst of the tharuks.

Roberto slashed the belly of a small tharuk. It slumped to the floor, its entrails sliding to the stone. Gret drove her sword into a tharuk's chest. Its claws raked her side, its last breath rattling. Blood welled through the slice in her jerkin.

"You all right?" Roberto called.

With a quick nod, she spun to an attacking beast.

Adelina plunged her dagger into the back of a tharuk's thigh, while Kierion drove his sword into its throat. Amato swung his blade at a tharuk's head. Roberto ducked claws, then drove his sword up into a tharuk's side. It was chaos. Danion swinging. Fenni blasting the beasts with glowing green mage flame.

Suddenly, the tunnel was quiet, except for their panting and the gurgle of the last dying tharuk.

"I'll take care of these." Fenni snapped into action, throwing the tharuks into a pile. "All of you get along the tunnel behind me."

Roberto marshaled the others deeper into the tunnel.

Fenni turned back the way they'd come. He flung out his hands. Flame blasted from his fingers, engulfing the tharuks and creating a wall of fire that sealed the tunnel behind them.

Roberto wrinkled his nose. By the dragon gods, those beasts stank even worse when they burned.

"Anyone hurt?" Roberto asked.

"I don't think so," Danion said. "We were lucky."

Gret met his eyes. "Just a scratch."

"Fenni, light, please," Roberto barked. Light flared at Fenni's hands. He held them near Gret's side while Roberto inspected her wound. "Adelina, come and help."

"Danion, pass your rucksack, I need some supplies." Adelina fished out some bandages and clean herb. She cleansed and bandaged Gret's wound, making short work of it. "If only we had piaua, but this will have to do. You all right to continue on?"

Chin up, Gret gave a short nod.

"We'll help you," said Danion.

"I will." Fenni was at her side in an instant, glaring at Danion.

Gret glared at them both. "I said I'll manage."

The wall of flame died down. Stinking smoke billowed from the bodies.

As much as he hated to address his father directly, Roberto had to. "Amato, how close are we? Will tharuks have heard us fighting? Will they smell the smoke?"

Amato shrugged his bony shoulders. "Depends where the next guards are stationed. I guess we'll find out."

The greenish light cast the stark bones of his father's face into shadow. With his wispy hair and his skin stretched tight over his skull, he looked like a monster.

Roberto turned away, trying not to shudder.

§

They'd crept along Zens' secret tunnel for hours. Up ahead, beyond Danion, Amato, and Roberto, it was getting lighter. Tomaaz wrinkled his nose at the familiar stench of ripe sewerage creeping down the tunnel and working its way into his nostrils. He was tempted to pinch his nose, but with his bow nocked, his hands were busy. He snorted, trying to clear the stink.

At his side, Lovina wrinkled her nose too. Occasionally, their arms brushed as their group sneaked along the tunnel, weapons at the ready, toward the entrance. They hadn't encountered any more tharuks. Something must be up. It was unlike Zens to leave any area unguarded.

Sure enough, as he'd suspected, they came out of the tunnel into the latrine area. The memory of that littling drowning in the sewage canal still roiled in his stomach. His inability to save her—or any of the other slaves in Death Valley—ate away at him. No, he couldn't think like that. He'd saved Lovina from Old Bill, preventing her from having a life of abuse and maltreatment. And he'd managed to get Maazini, Ma, and Taliesin out. He'd always thought he'd come back and save more slaves. There were thousands, all dosed with numlock-laced water to keep them subservient.

Roberto held a hand up just inside the tunnel entrance and halted. He gestured Tomaaz and Lovina forward because they knew Death Valley. Danion and Amato fell back.

Together Tomaaz, Lovina, and Roberto scanned the area—the ramshackle latrines, the long open sewage channels leading into the stinking pond. There was retching in the tunnel behind them. Tomaaz glanced back. Kierion again. Poor guy.

A lone slave stumbled out of a latrine, heading back toward the main valley.

Bowstring still taut, Tomaaz nudged Roberto with an elbow. "Where are all the tharuks and the rest of the slaves?"

Lovina answered, "Something's happened. Death Valley has never been this quiet."

Roberto shrugged. "We'd better keep moving. A tharuk troop could round the corner at any moment." He waved the others forward, and Tomaaz, Lovina, and Roberto led the party past the latrines toward the main valley. "Be careful," he cautioned. "It could be a trap."

§

In all his time in Death Valley—a year when he was only twelve summers old as Zens' protégé, and then his recent stint when he'd been captive—Roberto had never seen Death Valley like this. The hills were still barren, devoid of plant life, and stinking mist still wreathed the mouths of the mines, but it was quiet. No whips cracking. No tharuk snarls or guttural beastly commands. No endless tromping from teams of slaves—because there were no teams, only a few listless slaves lounging, jaws slack and gray eyes dull, against the cliffs and buildings. One limped aimlessly along the valley, staring at his feet.

It was as if Zens had disappeared altogether. Roberto motioned the party forward and they huddled in a group behind a sleeping hut.

"Where is everyone?" Kierion whispered.

"It's time to find out," Roberto answered. "You three," he gestured to Fenni, Danion, and Gret. "Zens has a place where he grows the dragons. It's usually manned by tharuks, so be careful. I'll show Fenni where it is."

He placed his hands upon Fenni's brow and mind-melded with him, showing him the gaping maw that led into the hillside, the wide passage with a narrow winding side tunnel that went deep into the bowels of the hillside. *"Keep following this route until you get to this door."* Roberto showed Fenni the large stone door, how it would slide open with a hiss if he pressed one side.

"This is where Zens grows his dragons." Roberto shared his memories of the chamber with tanks lining the walls—filled with black dragons, their ragged dark wings undulating in fluid. *"We must destroy this chamber."*

"Will do." Fenni raised his eyebrows. "I know Master Giddi can mind-meld with anyone at will, but I had no idea you could too."

"Only when I'm touching their foreheads."

"I guess that's why you're the master of mental faculties," Fenni said.

Roberto's talent often surprised people. Not many knew that he'd learned everything at the hands of Zens—the man they were now hunting. He'd paid a dear price for those talents. Every time he used them, it left a bitter taste in his mouth.

"I'll check Zens' lair," Roberto said. "Amato, Adelina, and Kierion, come with me."

He turned to Tomaaz and Lovina. "Could you—"

Lovina reached for Tomaaz's hand. "We'll stay here and help these slaves," she said. "Somebody has to. I believe Zens is gone, Roberto. He's only left the weak and injured. Look at them."

Although most people taken as slaves weren't in their prime, the few here now were definitely in bad shape. "Be careful," Roberto said. "It could be a trap. These mountains are riddled with tunnels. Zens may have withdrawn deeper into the hillside and be hiding in wait."

"I know," Tomaaz answered. "Zens used a secret tunnel to ambush me as I was escaping." He nodded at Roberto. "You be careful. My sister would never forgive me if anything happened to you."

§

Fenni led the way through the gaping hole in the mountainside. Gret stepped up to his side and walked with him. Danion hung behind, perhaps intentionally. Fenni's mage light lit the rocky walls as the track sloped down, narrowing as they went. The acrid stench of the mines hit Fenni's nostrils, making his eyes water.

Gret glanced up at Fenni and gave him a grim smile.

He wrinkled his nose—and not just at the smell. "I've been a regular donkey, haven't I?"

Gret shrugged.

She wasn't making this any easier, but he guessed he deserved it. "Well, you can't blame me. It looked like you enjoyed his attention." Oh shards! His big mouth.

Gret gave him a glance. "Maybe I did. It certainly beats talking to you when you're so snarky." She hung back. "I'll just wait for Danion to catch up."

Fenni strode deeper into the bowels of the mountainside.

§

Lovina and Tomaaz herded the slaves into a sleeping hut where it was easier to tend them. Here, they'd be hidden if Zens and his tharuks attacked. There were around a hundred slaves, all injured or unwell—as she'd suspected. Lovina tugged the thread hidden in the hem of her jerkin. Dried orange clear-mind berries appeared, threaded like beads on a necklace. "Thank the First Egg we have so many clear-mind berries." She kept pulling until she had a handful of berries, then bent, giving a berry to a slave with a gash on his arm, and then another to a young littling who was so thin his ribs poked against his saggy shirt. She dispensed the berries, tugging the thread whenever she needed more, until every slave had eaten one.

"Let me look at your leg," Tomaaz addressed a slave with a festering gash. He opened the healer's pouch at his waist to find a needle and twine.

"I'll try to find them something to eat," Lovina said to him. The rations in their rucksack were pitifully low. She beheld these people's faces: their jaws, slack; eyes vacant and unseeing. Is this how she'd looked all those years as Bill's slave? She must have. A shadow of her true self. Something sharp twisted in her belly. These people were only a tiny fraction of the number that had been in Death Valley. Where were the others? Her chest grew tight. If Zens had killed them all...

Tomaaz gazed up at her, his green eyes steady. He squeezed her hand. "One step at a time, Lovina. We'll get there."

"I'll search for some bread." She walked along the deserted valley into the cooking hut, where she'd often prepared food as a slave. Her memories were dim and hazy. This small hut had loomed much larger in her mind when she was numlocked and regularly beaten by tharuks. The hearths were cold. Large tubs held stale bread, ripped into chunks. Lovina picked up pieces, sniffing them.

No numlock. That was a start. This tough stale bread and thin gruel filled with weevils and bugs was all she'd eaten for the years that she lived here. If it hadn't been for 274, the tharuk overseer who'd enjoyed her art, and prevented her from beatings so she could draw animals, she wouldn't have survived. It was strange that she owed her life to a tharuk. She picked up a pail and filled it at the pump outside, amazed at how light it felt now that she was stronger. Then she grabbed the handle on a large bread tub and took the bread and water back to the sleeping hut.

Tomaaz had his head bent over a woman's lacerated back, hands busy treating her infected lash marks. Lovina shivered. It had not been so long ago that he'd healed hers. The slaves sat there staring at him, most still too dazed to speak.

Lovina dispensed water and bread to the waiting slaves—no, not slaves, people. Her people of Dragons' Realm.

"Tomaaz, we have to find the rest and save them too."

Tomaaz met her gaze. "I know," he said, his mouth grim.

§

Before Roberto confronted Zens he wanted to make sure they had a means of escape. *"Erob, are you around?"*

"So you've made it to Death Valley. Welcome."

"We're just north of the latrines, past a sleeping hut," Roberto replied. *"Where are you?"*

"Just keep walking."

Around the next corner, dark-blue, purple, sky-blue, red, green, and orange wings glinted in the sunlight as Erob, Riona, Linaia, Hagret, Matotoi, Ajeurina,

Maazini and Danion's blue swooped over the Terramites, stretching their wings in the sun. In a blaze of flame, they incinerated the tharuk guards and their lookout. *"Now they're taken care of, we can land,"* Erob said.

His midnight-blue dragon thudded to the floor of the arid valley, sending up a puff of dust. He wrinkled his snout. *"I'd forgotten about the stench."*

Roberto ran to Erob and flung his arms around his dragon's neck. *"I'm so glad to see you."*

Beside him, he was aware of Kierion hugging Riona and Adelina embracing Linaia. Amato shifted his weight from foot to foot, then tentatively patted Matotoi's snout.

Erob nuzzled his shoulder. *"You injured your face. Is everyone else all right?"*

"A few scrapes, but everyone's in one piece."

"What's the plan now?" Erob's yellow eyes regarded him.

"The others have gone to destroy the shadow dragons."

"And you?"

"I'm hunting down Zens."

§

She'd done it again. Gret knew Fenni had been about to apologize. It was just his way, his roundabout talking until he warmed up. Why had she snapped at him? Things were so much easier with Danion. Although she enjoyed Danion's attention, it didn't matter. He wasn't important to her. He was just playing a part, and she sensed it.

Danion grinned at her. "Lover boy still being difficult?"

She elbowed him. "It's not as if you're helping."

"On the contrary," he replied. "I saved your skin back in Montanara at the Brothers' Arms."

Their feet chewed up the rocky tunnel floor, which was coated in fine yellow dust.

She sighed. "I know that, but he doesn't."

Danion, sword at the ready, tilted his head. "Then isn't it about time you told him?"

Maybe. Gret didn't answer. Instead, she followed the dim light glowing at Fenni's fingertips deeper down the spiraling tunnel into the mountainside.

§

Roberto was keenly aware of his father's shaking hands as they approached Zens' lair. It was obvious, his sword was trembling like a leaf in a storm.

"This tunnel's as dark as a dragon's innards," Kierion whispered.

"Could you head back outside and get Riona to light us a torch?" Roberto asked.

"Back soon," Kierion replied, leaving Roberto, his sister, and his father alone for the first time since they'd found Amato alive.

Adelina was fuming. "Why are you shaking?" she barked at Pa.

Oh gods, he'd sworn to never call Amato his father again, and here she was…

Amato's gaze slid away from them.

Adelina tapped her foot. "Well?" she demanded. "I bet it's some trick to make us feel sorry for you."

"It's nothing," their father croaked.

Moments later, Kierion returned, his blazing torch casting flickering shadows over their faces.

They approached Zens' lair. The door was ajar. Perhaps Zens was down with the dark dragons. Roberto led the way, slipping through the door and checking the quarters. Kierion followed, holding up his torch so they could inspect every corner.

There, against the rear wall, was Zens' trophy tank.

Amato gasped. "So full. When I last saw this tank, there were only a few hands and ears."

"Zens has been busy." So many tharuk and slaves' hands, human ears and fingers floated in the yellow water that there were more body pieces than fluid. Stomach turning, Roberto looked away.

"A fair share of them are probably from people you helped tharuks kidnap for Zens," Adelina snapped.

Kierion flinched, but Roberto didn't blame his sister. She'd been barely six summers old when their father had turned. She'd hardly remember him from when they were younger—the lovely times in the sun, fishing and hunting goats.

Apart from the tank, the room was deserted.

Despite his awful memories, Roberto's eyes were drawn to the cell next door.

He opened the heavy wooden door, blocking the others from entering with his body, and peered into the room.

000's implements of torture were still hanging on the wall. Roberto shuddered, remembering how Zens had picked up Ezaara with his mind and smashed her against the stone. Right there were his own dark bloodstains on the rocky wall. He'd nearly died at that monster's hands.

Roberto left the room and slammed the door. "Come on, let's go. We've no time to lose. There's a chance Zens is down with those dark dragons. Kierion, Gret, and Danion may need our help." They ran out of the tunnel, Roberto leading the way.

ZENS STRIKES

Ezaara adjusted her weight in her chair behind the granite horseshoe-shaped table. It was already dark outside. She was spending altogether too much time in the council chamber lately.

Zaarusha's voice rumbled in her mind. *"I agree. Flying would be more preferable to sitting here. However, although brute force may help to win a skirmish, strategy will be the key to winning this war."*

The door opened and Dominique, the new leader of the blue guards, entered.

"I agree. Zens has strategy, but so far all we've done is react to his attacks."

"We have to win. I won't see Dragons' Realm destroyed."

"Neither will I. I love it as much as you do, Zaarusha." Ezaara shifted her attention to Dominique, who was striding past the other council masters toward her.

Dominique thumped his fist over his heart and bowed his head to Zaarusha, then he nodded to the other dragons sitting along the back wall and finally bowed to Ezaara. "I have my patrol report, my honored Queen's Rider."

"Thank you, Dominique. Anything new?" Ezaara asked.

"We found two dark dragons south of Dragon's Teeth, milling around the chasm." The blue guard grinned. "Our troop slaughtered them and the fake mages riding them."

"Any casualties?"

"Rocco has a flesh wound, but he's being tended to by the healers as we speak."

Lars piped up. "Make sure Rocco gets his wound cleansed regularly. We can't afford infection and deaths from neglect." He shook his head. "If only we had piaua juice."

Exactly what Ezaara had been thinking.

"Excuse me, if I may," Hans said. "Marlies and I sent Leah and Taliesin to retrieve piaua juice from the red guards." Pa's brow crinkled. "They have a large grove so we should get more supplies soon."

Derek huffed. "The future of the realm in littlings' hands. What have we come to?"

Pa's green eyes met Derek's. "They're hardly littlings, and they're traveling with Giant John. If he could get Marlies to Death Valley across Flatlands crawling with tharuks, then surely he can get two young future riders to the red guards."

The spymaster pursed his lips. "Young ones might have more chance of slipping by unnoticed."

Hans nodded. "Exactly what Marlies and I had thought."

"How is she?" Tonio asked, brow furrowing.

"Not quite healed, but not too far off." The worry lines in Pa's face deepened.

So, Pa didn't want them to know Ma was still exhausted. She hadn't been the same since she'd taken piaua berries to put herself into a coma in Death Valley so she could fool Zens that she was dead. Back home in Lush Valley, she'd had so much energy. Ezaara took a deep breath and turned back to Dominique. "Anything else in Spanglewood Forest? How are things at Mage Gate?" They'd first encountered Zens' shadow dragons at the massive clearing in Spanglewood where Mazyka and Giddi had once created a world gate. The blue guards had been patrolling there since the dark dragons had been spotted.

"My Queen's Rider, there are a few isolated tharuks in the forest, but apart from them, we haven't seen much. It's as if Zens has given up."

Ezaara shook her head. "He hasn't given up, believe me. I've met that man, and he'll never give up. He'll be planning something."

"Makes sense." Dominique nodded. "Maybe he's gathering more troops in Death Valley."

Battle Master Aidan strode over to the large map of Dragons' Realm mounted on the wall and stabbed a blunt finger at Death Valley. "Master Roberto and his riders should be here soon, striking at the heart of Death Valley. Hopefully, they'll force Zens out from his stronghold and across the Flatlands. We agreed to fly from Dragons' Hold and form a pincher, trapping Zens' army between two troops of dragons and riders. With mage fire on our side, we might stand a chance."

Tonio snapped, "We've been over this already. Zens now has mage power too, and Roberto has pitifully few riders with him. Anyway, we'd be too far from our supplies at Dragons' Hold. I say we drive the tharuks back across the plains to Death Valley."

Ezaara's fists clenched around her seat. Drive Zens' whole army back toward Roberto—no. He'd never hold them off with his small band.

Master Hendrik broke in. "Weapons, supplies—how can we fight without those? We must stay near Dragons' Hold."

"We need an advantage," Ezaara said. "I want ideas. Something. Anything."

Master Jerrick spoke up. "In Horseshoe Bend where I grew up, there was a man named Mickel who claimed that exercising under strongwood trees increased your strength. He swore on it—and he was the strongest man in the village. We should get our riders to try that."

Tonio laughed. "That's an old dragon tale."

Hendrik chuckled too. "Stupid gossip, that's all."

Jerrick drew his eyebrows down in a frown, mouth grim.

Lars smacked his gavel on the table. "We need a comprehensive strategy. Hans, as Master of Prophecy, what do you think? Have you had any visions that might help us know Zens' plans?"

Hans opened his mouth, but before he could speak, the door to the council chambers clunked open again. A bedraggled blue guard staggered in—a man Ezaara had seen around, although she didn't know his name. Dominique sprang to his feet and guided him to a chair in front of the council table.

The blue guard thumped his hand over his heart. "My Queen's Rider, I've come from the red guards. Flown two days without a stop." Deep worry lines cut into his face. His eyes were bright with unshed tears. "All the red guards are dead. Slaughtered by Zens' forces." His gaze flitted from master to master and came to rest upon Ezaara.

His words were met with stunned silence. The distant boom of Master Hendrik's blacksmiths hammering weapons in the depths of caverns echoed through the chamber. Then everyone started talking at once.

"I'll lead a troop of dragons myself," Alyssa, master of flight, said. "My cousin was a red guard. I have the right of vengeance."

Master Tonio shook his head. "Dragon Corps should investigate what's happening before we rush headlong into—"

"I think we have to—"

"Silence." Lars smacked his gavel on the table, the crack echoing like thunder.

"Please, someone bring him some water." Ezaara gestured to the man. "Then let him finish."

The guard gratefully accepted a cup from Dominique, gulped the water down, and handed it back for a refill. "Red dragons and their riders' bodies are scattered across the plains, their blood staining the land. The piaua grove has been desecrated. What chance do any of us have?" He placed his cup on the floor and dropped his elbows to his knees, burying his face in his hands.

The scratch of talons on the stone floor echoed through the chamber as the masters sat in shocked silence. Far below them, the blacksmiths still pounded. Faint vibrations ran under Ezaara's chair legs.

Ezaara met Pa's eyes.

"That's what Marlies found in Lush Valley too." Pa addressed no one in particular, his face haggard. He massaged his temples.

"Handel says that Hans is now thinking he sent Leah and Taliesin to their deaths," Zaarusha melded. *"Your father has already melded with your mother and told her. She's beside herself with guilt and grief."* Zaarusha also relayed what the guard's blue dragon had seen.

Nausea churned in Ezaara's stomach at the blue guard's memories of the bloody carnage of murdered dragons and riders. The chances of Leah and Taliesin being alive were slim. Ezaara rose and walked around the council table. She crouched before the sobbing guard, her hand on his shoulder. "Do you know how long ago the attack on the red guards occurred?" she asked gently.

"Days ago," he sobbed.

"Were any dark dragons still in the vicinity?"

He shook his head. "They're gone. The whole way here, I didn't see a single one."

"Thank you for coming straight here to report." Ezaara rose. "Dominique, please ensure he gets a decent meal and some rest."

Dominique nodded, thumping his hand on his heart, and guided the guard out of the council chamber.

Ezaara addressed the council. "We'll adjourn until morning. Keep me updated if anything changes." As everyone filed out of the chamber, she hung back. Pa was still seated, his eyes closed, rubbing his forehead.

She sat beside him. "How is Ma?"

"Much better. Her ribs are recovering. She's not in the prime of health, but what can you expect at our age?" Pa gave a chuckle, but it rang hollow.

"You're not the only one worried about her, Pa," she said softly. Her eyes stung at the thought of losing Ma.

"Don't worry, Ezaara. You have the weight of the realm on your shoulders." His voice was tender. "You don't need to worry about her."

Her heart cracked a little. She'd taken her parents for granted all these years. She squeezed Pa's hand.

He squeezed hers back. "It'll work out," he said. "If only that flaming booming in my head would go away."

"Booming?" Ezaara asked. "Oh, you mean the blacksmiths hammering out new weapons?"

"In all my years at Dragons' Hold, I've never been able to hear the blacksmiths from the council room." Pa cocked his head.

The booming was louder now, coming deep from the stone. The rock under Ezaara's feet shuddered.

"You can hear that, too?" Pa's eyes flew wide. "Oh gods. It's like the prophecy I told Lars about: Zens digging a tunnel with hundreds of slaves." His mouth sagged, his eyes wide with horror. "Shards, I should've realized. The signs have been right in front of my nose: I've had the dreams; Zens' armies have been absent; and then Dominique saw shadow dragons around the southern chasm. They must be tunneling through the chasm to attack Dragons' Hold! Ezaara, raise the alarm!"

§

Ezaara threw on her winter cloak, her father at her side as they ran across the council chambers.

"That flaming booming. I should've known," Pa panted. He yanked the door open. "If Zens is really digging in the chasm, the tunnel should come out near the main cavern." Horror crept across his face. "Hundreds of riders are training there tonight. Quick, we've no time to lose."

They leaped upon their dragons. Zaarusha swooped off the ledge into the dark sky, angling down the mountainside to the main cavern. Handel was only a wingbeat behind.

Ezaara burst into the cavern on Zaarusha's back, her bow nocked.

Training was in full swing. Riders were dueling, firing arrows at targets and swooping on dragons with mages seated behind them. Bolts of mage fire flew into painted targets high on the wall. Master wizards called instructions. At the back of the cavern, littlings played while their parents trained. Hundreds were here.

The rear walls of the cavern shuddered, a boom jarring Ezaara's bones.

"*That's not a good sign,*" Zaarusha rumbled.

A littling cried, blocking his ears. People pointed at the rear wall. Others paused for a moment, then continued with their training.

Ezaara melded with their dragons. "*We may be under attack at any moment. As a precaution, please gather your riders and leave the main cavern in an orderly manner.*"

A flurry of questions pelted Ezaara's mind, making her head reel. "*Zaarusha, please help.*"

"*Don't worry, I'll explain.*"

Another boom made the walls shudder.

People gathered up littlings and fled through the tunnels. Riders snatched up weapons, leaping on dragons.

Another boom rang out. Now a constant barrage of thuds was coming from the wall. A crack appeared.

Blue dragons swooped into the cavern to collect people. Other dragons were trying to leave. The tunnels were chaotic.

"*Use the west tunnels to enter, the east ones to exit,*" Queen Zaarusha ordered.

In a shower of shale and granite, a hole was punched through the rear wall. A spray of rocks flew into the cavern, knocking down riders, hitting dragons and burying a handful of littlings at the back of the cavern.

Handel dived. Pa dismounted, plucking up four screaming littlings and throwing them onto Handel. The bronze dragon shot out of a tunnel to take them to safety.

Dark dragons swarmed out of the jagged hole in the rear wall, flame bursting from their maws. Fake wizards rode them, blasting green mage fire. Hundreds of tharuks rushed through the gap.

Ezaara melded with all of their dragons. "*Attack! In the main cavern!*"

"*How dare they,*" Zaarusha snarled, charging to meet their foes. Even as screams rang in their heads, she blasted flame at the nearest shadow beasts.

Pa drew his sword. Riders on either side of him formed a ragged wall. They rushed to meet the tharuks.

Ezaara fired an arrow and then another, and another, but still more dragons poured through the gap.

Blue guards swooped into the cavern, their arrows finding tharuks and shadow dragons.

Tharuk archers fired arrows. Dripping with green grunge, the arrows zipped toward dragons.

"Oh no, Zaarusha, limplock," Ezaara cried. "They'll paralyze our dragons."

Zens' mages fired arrows tipped with methimium beetles. Dragons screamed, writhing in midair as the arrows met their marks. Two blue dragons collided. A ruby dragon snarled, attacking a blue. Amid snarls and thrashing tails, dragon fought dragon. With necks intertwined, they bit and clawed at each other. The ruby dragon ripped a chunk from the blue. It roared, its deafening bellows ringing in Ezaara's ears. Shards, it was like Maazini all over again. Like herself attacking Ma.

Their people were running, screaming. Dying all around her.

Zaarusha roared and shot flame at a shadow dragon. Engulfed in fire, it writhed and fell to the ground, killing a fleeing family.

"Gods, no! We have to get our people out of here," Ezaara melded with the dragons. "Retreat. Everyone, assemble outside."

Dominique charged a shadow dragon, firing an arrow straight through its eye. A fake mage shot a plume of green flame at him as the beast plunged to the cavern floor, squashing people. Every time someone felled a dark dragon, their people died beneath the flailing body.

"Stop! We need to get everyone out of here," Zaarusha's message swept through Ezaara's mind like a thunderstorm.

While their people fled, Ezaara and Zaarusha hung back, flaming dark beasts, dodging tharuk arrows and blasting fire and arrows at the tharuks below.

"Get Zaarusha out of here," Handel melded with Ezaara. "Now!"

"Zaarusha," Ezaara sobbed. "We have to go. Our people need their queen. We can't risk losing you."

Zaarusha roared as a tide of tharuks and shadow dragons surged through the main cavern, burning, slashing and murdering their people.

§

"Flee, Marlies. Tharuks and dark dragons are overrunning Dragons' Hold." Liesar's command ripped through Marlies' mind.

Marlies had heard bellows, felt the infirmary floor ripple beneath her feet as roars reverberated through the mountainside. The wall beside her shuddered.

"I'll be there soon. Don't take too long." Her dragon knew she'd grab healing supplies before she left. "Where are we fleeing to?"

A roar thundered out on the infirmary ledge. Something thunked against the doors.

Marlies grabbed Liesar's empty saddlebags and swept her remedies off the tabletop. They clattered into the saddlebag. She snatched up her large travel rucksack and stuffed it with the three loaves of bread on her table, meant for patients' breakfasts, a half-full sack of apples and some full waterskins. They'd need everything they could carry.

She shoved blankets and candles into the saddlebags. Oh gods, how she wished she had piaua. Bandages were next. Marlies ran to the alcove and shoved more remedies into a sack and put them in the saddlebags too.

Now she could hardly lift the saddlebags. She dragged them along the floor and tucked them by the doors to the infirmary ledge.

Throwing on her winter cloak, she mind-melded with Liesar. "Where are we going? How many dragons are coming to transport my patients?"

Liesar's snarl ripped through Marlies' head. She saw her dragon's talons ripping the neck of a tharuk, then swiping another's belly, its entrails spilling to the stone.

Tharuks were inside Dragons' Hold? Dragon's talons! Things were worse than she'd thought.

A moment later, Liesar melded again, "I'm sorry, Marlies. There are no spare dragons to bring your patients. Make sure you have adequate weapons and leave the rest. This is war."

She glanced at Caldeff, and another elderly rider with a heavy chest cold, the woman who'd broken her shin, and Kion, the littling boy who'd come to get his arm stitched. She roused them all.

They sat up, bleary-eyed.

"Quick! Into my alcove. Tharuks have overrun the hold. Pull the curtain and stay quiet. They may not find you there. You." She gestured to Kion. "Pull on your cloak, boots and warm clothes and come with me." If she had to choose, she'd save the young.

Her patients raced into the alcove and yanked the curtain shut. One of them started coughing. Marlies' chest clenched. They had no chance. Leaving them broke her heart, but there was nothing she could do. With Leah most likely dead with the red guards, she was the only healer Dragons' Hold had left, aside from Ezaara. If they were to have a chance in this war, she had to get out of here.

There was a thud against the door to their quarters by the infirmary.

Someone was outside.

"Quick!" she hissed at Kion. "Grab that bed."

Together, they pushed it in front of the door to form a barricade. It wasn't much, but it'd win them a few moments.

They dashed toward the infirmary ledge. Marlies thrust the doors open. Kion helped her drag the saddlebags outside.

The bed grated on the stone behind them.

The boy shut the outer doors—it was a flaming shame there was no lock on them.

Marlies spun as Liesar landed on the ledge, spraying slush. She hoisted the saddlebags and managed to get them over Liesar's back.

"*Quick,*" Liesar melded.

"*No kidding,*" Marlies snapped.

Roars broke out in the infirmary. Please, oh gods, please… It was too much to hope that the tharuks wouldn't find her patients.

Screams rang out. Kion clutched her sleeve, wide-eyed.

Liesar raised herself on her legs.

"Quick," she hissed to Kion. "Get under Liesar's belly and pull this strap through."

The boy ducked under and passed her the strap. Marlies fastened it, then threw him up into the saddle and leaped up behind him.

Tharuks thrust the doors open. Behind them, one of the beasts ripped back the curtain, exposing her quaking patients. The tharuk slashed its claws across Caldeff's body. The old dragon rider sank to the stone in a pool of blood.

She covered Kion's eyes, glancing back to carnage and bloodshed, as Liesar leaped off the ledge—into a swarm of dark dragons.

§

The main cavern was chaotic. Hans leaped onto Handel, nocked an arrow, leaned over his side and shot a tharuk, then another. A dark dragon swooped down, talons out. Hans fired an arrow through its throat. It bucked and writhed, its mage rider flinging wizard flame. Handel swerved, nearly veering into a blue guard, then backwinged and twisted.

"*We have to get higher,*" Hans melded. The screams of the dark beasts ripped through their minds. Gods, he could hardly think straight.

Handel ascended, belching flame through a swathe of dark dragons. He snapped at a black ragged wing, shredding it. The shadow beast plummeted, shrieking, onto a troop of tharuks, splattering black blood on the stone.

Its screams skittered through Hans' skull. He loosed arrow after arrow at tharuks and dark dragons. Streaks of color shot through the cloud of dark beasts, cries of anguish from men and women, as they were struck, burned or sliced with those awful rays from shadow dragons' eyes.

Blue guards had tattered wings, rents in their bellies. Carcasses from good dragons littered the floor. Hundreds of tharuks swept in, shooting numlocked arrows.

Handel swerved to avoid the numlock. *"We don't want you trying any of that again."*

"No, thanks," Hans said. *"Once was enough."* Recently, he'd nearly died from Zens' paralyzing poison in Death Valley.

"Look out!" Hans ducked, lying against Handel's spinal ridge as a mage shot a volley of green flame over his head, scorching the ceiling. He reached for an arrow and shot it straight into the mage's neck.

The mage slipped from the saddle, blood streaming down his neck. His body toppled into the chaos below.

"Handel, I'm out of arrows." Handel flamed his way through the cavern, staying near the roof, sending a billowing trail of flame over the dark dragons thrashing below.

They shot out of the main cavern among shadow beasts fighting blue guards. Bursts of orange and green flame lit up pockets of the sky, flaring like shooting stars. A dragon with burning wings plummeted to the ground.

"To the infirmary, Handel. We must find Marlies. Quick."

Handel flew up the snowy mountainside and landed on the infirmary ledge. Hans slid to the ground and ran through the open infirmary doors.

Blood splattered the infirmary beds, floors and walls. A man lay dead on the floor, his throat slashed by vicious claws. A woman had been flung sideways across a bed, her head staved in. A mutilated body was in the alcove. Nausea churned in his belly as he checked each patient. Dead—tharuks had killed them all.

Only the young lad was missing. With luck, he'd escaped.

He scanned the bodies, relieved when he didn't find Marlies. And guilty for feeling relief when so many had died.

Hans raced next door into their sleeping cavern and snatched up quivers of arrows, more daggers and an extra sword and bow. He grabbed the thick winter quilt off the bed and ran back out to the ledge, stuffing everything in Handel's saddlebags.

Not a moment too soon. Behind him, the infirmary doors smashed open. Tharuks snarled.

Hans leaped into the saddle. The battle was still raging in the sky.

"We've been ordered to flee." Handel tensed his haunches and sprang, beating his bronze wings.

"Where to? Spanglewood? Montanara?"

"Look behind you," Handel howled.

Hans glanced back.

Swarms of seething black dragons blotted out the sky. They'd be upon them in moments.

§

Singlar wheeled in midair, so Lars could scan the main cavern littered with their dead. The overpowering reek of burned flesh and the coppery tang of blood stuck in his throat. Down there, caught between his smoldering dead dragon and a horde of tharuks, was a rider battling for his life. His sword gleamed black with tharuk blood.

"Save him," Lars commanded.

Singlar dived down to the fighting beasts, his purple scales flashing in the light from dark dragon flames. He snatched the rider in his talons and blasted the tharuks with fire.

Their dying snarls ripped through Lars' mind. He smiled grimly. They'd got what they deserved.

"Zaarusha is commanding us to flee," Singlar said. *"Never in my hundreds of years, did I ever think we'd abandon Dragons' Hold."* His purple wings were bathed in the shadow dragons' blood as he sped across the cavern.

Dark dragons were landing on the floor of the cavern, feasting on the dead—dragons, dark dragons, tharuks and riders alike. Lars' stomach roiled.

Most of the exit passages were swarming with dark dragons, but high up near the ceiling was a seldom-used tunnel. Singlar blasted flame at a shadow dragon's head and swept his mighty wings upward. He grunted as the yellow rays from a dark dragon's eyes gashed his foreleg. Lars swept into the tunnel upon Singlar's back, Singlar still carrying the brave rider in his talons.

§

With a bone-shuddering roar, Zaarusha burst out of the main cavern into the night, dark dragons on her tail. Hordes of shadow dragons swarmed over the top of Dragon's Teeth, snarling. Their flames lit up the sky. Fake mages shot bolts of mage fire from their backs. Overhead, a canopy of ragged black wings blotted out the stars. Roars and shrieks tore through the dark.

Despite the screams ripping through her skull, Ezaara melded with Zaarusha, *"The opaline headbands—we can't fight without them. Quick, back to my cavern."*

Zaarusha whirled, blasting flame at the shadow dragon tailing her. Ezaara ducked as yellow beams from its eyes lanced through the dark and sliced off the tip of her braid.

"Lower, Zaarusha."

Zaarusha swooped. They raced to the mountainside, climbing until they reached Zaarusha's den and the ledge outside Ezaara's cavern.

Slipping out of the saddle, Ezaara dashed inside, slamming the door to the ledge behind her. Across her cavern, snarls and stomping feet came from the tunnel outside her main door. Tharuks were overrunning the hold. She ran over and slid a bar across her door. Then, she shoved a chest of drawers against the door too. Ezaara strapped extra weapons to her waist, slung quivers over her shoulder and had just grabbed the sack of opaline headbands when something large thudded to the ledge outside.

Roars shook her cavern, the outside doors rattling on their hinges. There was a flurry of thumps and snarling.

"Zaarusha?" Ezaara caught rage, snatches of talons and the flash of beige scales.

"It's that traitor, Unocco," Zaarusha roared.

Unocco—fighting Zaarusha. Gods, no! Ezaara snatched up the sack of opaline headbands and raced outside, flinging the door open.

A dark figure pounced on her, slamming her back against the rocky face. Her sack and quivers thumped to the snow.

"Now I can finish off what I started in Naobia." Simeon pressed his body against hers, his chest mashing her breasts, his hands grasping at her breeches.

She kneed him in the groin. And jabbed her elbow up under his chin.

He reeled back, staggering in the snow, and snatched a dagger from his belt.

Dark dragons fought their dragons in the sky behind them. Zaarusha and Unocco fought too, snarling and thrashing at one another with their talons. *"Unocco's been turned with swayweed. I don't want to flame one of my own kin."* She roared. *"Kill Simeon."*

Simeon snarled, his face twisting in an enraged grimace, and rushed at Ezaara, dagger flashing.

Ezaara drew her sword and lunged. Her blade met Simeon's belly as he flew at her, piercing his flesh. His momentum drove the blade deep inside him.

Simeon's eyes flew wide and he clutched his gut. He staggered to the edge of the ledge, his bloody fingers around the blade.

Ezaara stood, stunned. Simeon's blood ran off her blade, dripping into the slush. He stared at her, pulled her sword from his belly and threw it into the snow.

She picked it up. By the dragon gods, should she kill him? That was three times he'd tried to rape her. And he'd already raped Trixia, Gret's friend. Dragons' Realm would be better off without him.

No, that was someone else's job—a job Roberto would relish.

Simeon sank to his knees, clutching his belly. "Unocco," he screamed.

So he couldn't mind meld. He hadn't imprinted with Bruno's dragon. He was merely riding it. Ezaara turned her back on Simeon. Hands shaking, she slung the quivers over her shoulder and picked up the sack of opaline headbands.

Snarls ripped through the air. There was a thud on the ledge behind her.

She spun.

A dark dragon was perched near Simeon, its eyes slitted in greed as its nostrils flared, sniffing his blood. It licked at the entrails poking from his wound. Simeon screamed. The beast snatched him up by the ankle. His head whacked the granite ledge as it took to the sky.

With a violent snarl, another dark dragon closed in. Snatching Simeon's arm in its jaws, it yanked. Simeon's screams sliced through Ezaara, chilling her to the bone. Dropping the sack and her sword, she clapped her hands over her ears, unable to look away as the snarling dragons slashed Simeon's body with their talons.

His screams stopped. Simeon's blood rained over the ledge. Chunks of his body fell down to the valley. A horde of dark dragons dived, squabbling and flaming each other in a race to devour what was left of him. Ezaara tiptoed to the edge of the ledge. Thank the flaming dragon gods, it was too dark to see. She fell to her knees. Gods, oh gods. Her stomach convulsed. She vomited.

Oh gods. She retched again.

Ezaara? Still writhing in the sky with Unocco, Zaarusha unfastened her jaws from around his neck. With an anguished roar, Unocco flapped off, dodging dark dragon flames. Zaarusha thudded down beside Ezaara, her mighty chest heaving and head covered in soot.

"Are you hurt?" Ezaara asked, battling to keep the screams of the dark dragons at bay so she could think. Her breath shuddered out of her. She shook her head, trying to dislodge her memories of Simeon grasping at her breeches, trying to violate her.

"A few blisters and scratches. I know you're shaken, but we must leave. Shadow dragons are still exiting the main cavern and more are flying over Dragon's Teeth."

Ezaara fastened a headband around her forehead, and thrust her weapons and the sack of opaline headbands into Zaarusha's saddlebags. She stopped to retrieve her sword and retched again at the sight of Simeon's blood—the memory of his shredded flesh raining over Dragons' Hold.

Wearily, she wiped her mouth on the back of her sleeve and cleaned her sword in the snow. Then she clambered into the saddle and slumped over Zaarusha's spinal ridge, hugging it tight. She wouldn't wish that horrific end on anyone.

Zaarusha took to the sky, leaving Dragons' Hold and the remains of Simeon behind.

Zens' Lair

In the very first chamber Fenni entered, he let his mage light die, squinting against the yellow light bathing the roughly-hewn cavern. Velrama and Sorcha were tied to beds, breathing as if they were asleep, but with open unseeing eyes that stared at the ceiling. Strange clear tubes ran out of their arms and necks. Fenni grimaced. Both mages were only wearing undergarments, their skin tinged blue with cold. Slivers of their flesh had been sliced away. Tiny puncture wounds ran up and down their arms, torsos and legs. He shuddered.

Along the stone walls at the back of the room on either side of an archway were tanks. As tall as Fenni, the tanks contained forms that resembled Velrama and Sorcha, smaller, but somehow fully-grown.

"What manner of evil is this?" Danion waved his sword at the tanks and imprisoned mages. "This must be where Zens made those evil mages."

"There may be tharuks about. Let's take a look around before we do anything else." Fenni jerked his head toward the tunnel to the larger chamber that Roberto had shown him during their mind-meld.

"Good idea." Danion nodded.

Danion and Gret prowled toward the archway, swords drawn. Fenni held his hands at the ready.

Before they could peek into the next chamber, a noise sounded behind them.

Fenni whirled. The door slid open.

Roberto, Amato, and Kierion rushed inside, panting.

Fenni held a finger to his lips. Roberto nodded and took the lead, taking them into a massive cavern. Benches ran in rows along the length of the cavern and, beside them, tharuks grew in tanks the height of fully-grown men. Still more enormous tanks lined the walls, the size of houses.

Floating in the tanks were what looked like bundles of black rags. Apart from that, not a single tharuk was in the room.

"Zens' dark dragons," breathed Danion. "I've never seen anything like it."

Neither had Fenni. "Or this strange yellow light." He waved a hand at the huge overhead methimium crystals emitting a yellow glow that bathed the chamber.

A roar reverberated through the cavern.

"There is someone here after all," Roberto whispered. "That sounded like a shadow dragon. Hopefully it's alone. Danion, take Kierion, Adelina, and Fenni, and see if you can find out what's out there." Roberto motioned toward double metal doors at the rear of the cavern, so shrouded in shadow that Fenni hadn't seen them. "Those doors are huge. That must be how Zens gets his shadow dragons out when they're ready."

No doubt. Fenni nodded, his mouth dry. It was one thing to face a shadow dragon on dragonback with Kierion as Riona flamed her way through the skies. It was another thing entirely to face one on foot.

§

Kierion, Adelina, Fenni, and Danion dashed across the cavern. It could take them forever to open those metal doors. Kierion couldn't see any sign of a handle or a lever, and they were large enough to need more than one man to push them apart.

He nearly jumped out of his skin when the double metal doors hissed open as they approached. They plunged into a short tunnel large enough for a dragon to walk through. Yellow light glowed from around a bend. Danion and Kierion edged along the wall and craned their heads around the corner to get a better look, while Adelina and Fenni hung back.

An enormous tharuk with a broken tusk was standing before a strange metal contraption that streamed yellow light against the cavern wall.

Rows of shadow dragons mounted with fake mages were waiting, the dragons' ragged wings furled against their sides and their feet shifting, talons scraping rock. Their mental cries drifted through his head. The mages leaned forward, hunched in their saddles as if they were about to launch themselves into the air.

Kierion frowned. It made no sense. They were facing the lit-up wall. There was nowhere to go.

The huge broken-tusked tharuk was bathed in the yellow light. It held up a gleaming jade ring, too small to fit on its large furry fingers, and rubbed it, calling in a guttural voice, "Kisha."

Billowing golden clouds appeared before the wall, swirling in midair, lit up by those unearthly yellow rays.

"Go, now," Broken Tusk bellowed, saliva dripping off its tusks and its dark eyes glinting. The tharuk stepped aside.

Kierion cut off a gasp as a shadow dragon and mage leaped at the clouds and disappeared.

"It's a realm gate," Danion breathed in his ear.

Kierion nodded. He'd thought so. Somehow Zens had created one with that metal contraption.

Another shadow dragon and mage jumped and vanished. And another pair, and another, until there were only a handful of tharuks left, milling around, pushing and shoving. A wiry tharuk leaped, tusky snout first, into the rays and disappeared into the billowing clouds.

Danion tugged Kierion back and they crept to the others.

"There are only a handful of tharuks left. Let's attack," Kierion whispered, quietly drawing his sword.

Danion nodded. "There's a strange metal box producing yellow rays. I think it sucks people through a realm gate. Stay away from its light." He and Adelina pulled their swords from their scabbards.

Fenni held his hands at the ready.

Adelina nudged Kierion. They spurted around the corner, feet hammering on stone, swords out. Broken Tusk roared and dived into the billowing clouds, something clattering to the rocky floor behind it.

Tharuks spun to meet them, slashing with their claws. Adelina deflected one, then plunged her sword into its side. Kierion finished it off with a blow to the head. Dark blood splattered him as Danion took another beast down. Fenni shot plumes of mage fire from his hands, blowing holes in two tharuks' chests.

Kierion spun and ducked the last tharuk's claws. Adelina jumped on its back, knocking it to the stone. The beast snarled and bucked, trying to throw her off its back. She clung on.

"Head back, Adelina!" Kierion charged in, raised his sword and hacked through the tharuk's neck, bone crunching and his sword thunking wetly through its flesh. Blood spurted up, raining on the stone.

Adelina stood, panting.

"My apologies if I got your riders' garb dirty." Kierion bowed and sheathed his sword. "That one was rather messy and you were in the splatter zone."

She wrinkled her nose. "Sure was."

He kicked the beast onto its back, staunching the bloody fountain, turning it into an ever-growing pool. "You all right?"

She nodded and retrieved her sword from where she'd dropped it. "You?"

He grinned and took her hand. "I am now."

She grinned back and leaned against him.

"Come on, you two, we'd better show Roberto what we've found." Danion gestured at the metal box, which had strange dials and levers and an aperture through which the rays still shone.

"That's not all we've found." Kierion tugged Adelina over to where the big tharuk had stood. "Fenni, a little light over here, please."

In the gleam of the mage light, Kierion found what the tharuk had dropped—the jade ring. Kierion passed it to Danion. "At least now we know where the dark dragons have gone," he said.

"Do we?" asked Adelina.

Kierion shrugged. "Not really, we can only guess, but now we know how to get there."

"Good work," Danion said. "Now we can take the battle to Zens. Let's get back to Roberto."

Kierion gestured up the broad tunnel they were standing in. "Adelina and I will take a look at the rest of the tunnel and see if there's a way to get our dragons in. There's no point in chasing Zens without them."

"Be careful," warned Danion. "We don't know what's up there."

§

As Danion and Fenni went back into the shadow dragon chamber to report to Roberto, Adelina wrinkled her nose and toed a tharuk with her boot. "These beasts always stink."

"Let's get some fresh air," Kierion replied. "Wherever this tunnel leads, it's got to be better than this."

"Fresh? We're in Death Valley, remember?" She elbowed him.

He laughed, his hand warm in hers as they strode along the tunnel, leaving the humming box with its yellow rays and the dead tharuks behind. "That box is handy. We can finally explore a tunnel without Fenni to guide us." Kierion leaned in. "I'm so glad we're here together. It was absolutely awful when I didn't know where you were. I thought I'd lost you."

She sighed. She'd been so silly, running off to Montanara—angry with Kierion. With Roberto, Amato, with the world, actually.

"Are you all right now?" he asked. "I know this trip hasn't been easy for you with your fath— um, him along."

Her flash of anger was instant: the moment he'd been about to say *father*, Adelina had wanted to rage at Kierion all over again and scream that Amato was no longer her father. That he didn't deserve that title after all the horrific things he'd done to their family. She expelled her breath in a whoosh. "It's a little better. It was such a shock knowing he was alive. We all thought he'd died in Crystal Lake. Do you know what's funny?"

She stopped walking and tilted her head to look up at him. The light wasn't as bright here, but she could still see his pretty eyes, now gazing down at her in concern. "He survived by living in the very cave that Roberto and I used to hide in when he was on a rampage. We didn't know, because after we thought he'd died in the lake, both of us refused to go there again. If Roberto hadn't shown Ezaara his littling haunts on their hand-fasting holiday, then—"

Kierion pressed their clasped hands against his chest, her hand right over his heart with his warm palm on top. His heart thrummed beneath her fingers. "I don't think that's funny at all, Adelina. No one should have to live in fear of a family member."

"He's not my family." She shook her head fiercely. "Not anymore. Roberto's my only family now."

"I don't think that's right," he said.

She was about to protest when Kierion took his hand off hers and cradled the back of her head, slipping his other arm around her. His head descended and his lips brushed hers.

"I'd very much like to be part of your family, Adelina. I swear I'll protect you with my life."

Kierion's warm soft lips found hers again. His heart pounded beneath her hand like a wing of rampaging dragons. Adelina's own heartbeat raced, trying to keep up with his as she reached up, wrapping her fingers into his blond hair and pulling him even closer.

The coil of tension that had been wound tight inside her since she'd first seen Amato at Dragons' Hold—and gotten ever tighter since—unwound with each brush of Kierion's lips, each caress of his fingers over her cheeks, with the trail of kisses he left down her neck.

He groaned softly, kissing her earlobe.

The coil sprang loose inside Adelina. She grabbed Kierion's cheeks and kissed him, soaring like a dragon on the wind. She felt free—really free—for the first time in her life. She'd always buried her feelings, hidden her fear and pain behind a cheerful wall of bubbliness. No one suspected there was a terrified little girl hiding inside her. But Kierion saw that little girl. And loved her for who she had been, who she was, and who she one day could be.

Kierion pulled back from her lips. Foreheads touching and arms wrapped around one other, they gazed at each other. He smiled, their breath mingling. "I guess that means yes, you'll count me as part of your family?"

She nodded.

His face lit up like a thousand methimium rays. He flung his arms open wide and tipped his head back. "Yahoo!" Kierion's cry echoed off the tunnel walls and bounced back and forth as he picked Adelina up, spun her around, then kissed her, still holding her aloft.

She laughed. And laughed again as he carried her along the tunnel, kissing her again and again.

Suddenly, the flap of wings filled the tunnel, coming toward them.

In a flash, Kierion set her on her feet and was running up the tunnel, sword drawn.

Adelina ran, yanking her sword from its scabbard. Of all the stupid things! They'd forgotten they were in enemy territory. Shadow dragons were coming. Their wingbeats echoed off the tunnel walls around a corner. By the sounds of things, there were a few of them.

A flash of purple scales rounded the corner, and sky-blue scales followed.

"Riona!" Kierion called. "Linaia! How did you find us here?"

Linaia mind-melded with Adelina, *"Kierion's mating call was heard by all of us."*

From the red tinge that covered Kierion's face right to the tips of his ears, Adelina guessed Linaia had shared the same message with Riona. *"Mating call indeed!"* she huffed. *"We were merely—"*

"Doing what humans do as a prelude to mating, or hand-fasting or whatever you riders call it. But I know a mating call when I hear one, and his echoed through this tunnel and off the mountainsides."

Laughing, Kierion sheathed his sword and wrapped an arm around Adelina's shoulders. "It's nearly official. We're family now." He beamed.

Adelina couldn't help laughing.

She laughed even harder when Kierion said, "We'd better get back to our big brother before he tells us off."

§

Most of the slaves hadn't yet recovered from the effects of numlock. It was still too early. Lovina's attempts to help them bake bread and teach them to help themselves were failing. Tharuks had stored ample barrels of stale flour and supplies for feeding the thousands of slaves they'd captured from villages across Dragons' Realm. It was just that these people couldn't think for themselves anymore. After months of being drugged with numlock and underfed, their reserves were sapped and minds drained.

She shook her head as a man dropped yet another round of flatbread dough on the floor.

"Come on, pick it up," Lovina encouraged.

He stared at her, then bent to retrieve the bread, now covered in dust. Forgetting to wipe it off—as she'd just shown him when he'd dropped the last—he placed it on the flat iron over the glowing hearth to bake.

Lovina wiped sweat from her brow. After her leap from the rowboat, her trek along the tunnel and now helping these people all day, she was exhausted.

Tomaaz placed a gentle arm around her shoulder. "Lovina, we can't leave them here like this. They're as helpless as littlings."

Lovina leaned into his comforting embrace. She'd been thinking the same thing. "But we can't stay here with them."

"Then there's only one option." Tomaaz's kind green eyes regarded her. He smiled. "I knew you'd agree. Let's take them with us."

She shuddered. "Wherever Zens has gone, his tharuks and dark dragons are with him. We could be leading these people into a death trap."

Tomaaz nodded. "Until they've recovered, they don't have much chance if we leave them here alone. I'll go through first, and you can be the rearguard. If anyone's not in good enough condition to travel tomorrow, we'll leave them with fresh bread and water, and come back in a few days."

Lovina shrugged, her gaze skimming the people in the food hut shuffling about their work.

"Let's leave a few of the more able-bodied to tend them and tell them we'll be back in a week," said Tomaaz. "If we bake all this bread"—he indicated the mass of dough they'd kneaded—"they should have enough to last that long."

His brow furrowed. They both knew he could be lying—they had no idea what the next week would bring, whether they'd even be alive.

COURAGE

Gret bent over Sorcha, examining the clear tubes leading out of his neck and arms. They went right into his veins. This must be some strange magic from Zens' world. She touched his skin. It was cold, still bluish. Not a good sign. She leaned in. Pale-blue fluid was flowing through the tube into the mage. Perhaps this was how Zens controlled their magic or even gave them magic. She tugged the tube to Sorcha's arm gently. It pulled at the skin inside Sorcha's elbow. Gret let go. Who knew what would happen if she took it out.

Bellows came from outside the huge metal doors at the back of Zens' shadow dragon cavern. A sword rang on stone. The others were fighting. Gret dashed back into the main cavern.

Roberto and his father were bent over a workbench, investigating Zens' paraphernalia, arguing.

Gret slid her sword from its scabbard. "Roberto, should I help them?"

Roberto cocked his head.

Gods, Fenni was out there fighting and she hadn't even told him how she felt.

Thuds rang outside. The roars died. The murmur of voices reached them. "I think they're all right now." Roberto said. He pointed to something on the bench and mumbled to Amato.

Gret paced, waiting.

The doors hissed open. Danion and Fenni strode inside, splattered with dark tharuk blood. Danion held up a ring of green stone. "Zens has opened a realm gate and this might be the key."

"This ring is Ezaara's. It was stolen from us on our hand-fasting holiday." Roberto took it from Danion. "We suspected it had ended up here. Thank the Egg you've found it."

"You might not be that pleased when you hear that every last shadow dragon has fled Death Valley," Fenni said. "We killed the remaining few tharuks."

Roberto grimaced.

Gret hadn't expected the master of mental faculties and imprinting to show his emotions.

"Shards, I would've liked to question those tharuks who knew where Zens went." Roberto shrugged. "We've no time to lose. If Zens has traveled by realm gate with his army, he could attack anywhere. Gret and Fenni, could you free those mages and destroy the ones Zens is growing, while Danion and Amato and I take care of things in here?"

Fenni's keen green eyes flicked to Gret, then he nodded. "Sure. Back soon."

Gret accompanied Fenni into the chamber where the mages were kept.

"These are attached. I didn't try to take them out, because I didn't want to hurt her or Sorcha," Gret said, waving at the tubes leading into Velrama's arm and neck. "Maybe you could help."

"I'm not sure if I can." Fenni scrubbed his hair with a hand. "We may kill them. But it's better than leaving them here." He examined Velrama's arm.

Gret noticed that Fenni kept his eyes averted from the thin fabric barely covering Sorcha, only looking at her arms or face. It was sweet, really. Endearing. Her cheeks burned. She remembered enjoying Danion's face, allowing her eyes to roam over his tanned torso on the deck of the ship, even though she'd already known she loved Fenni.

Fenni didn't really deserve her. He was too sweet. Mind you, she'd been sweet and innocent too. Until Danion had kissed her, she'd only ever kissed Fenni. And only once.

Fenni pointed at Velrama's elbow. "This tube is attached to a slim piece of metal, like a needle, that enters her vein. See it?"

"Yes, I can. Do you want me to hold the tube steady while you try to pull that needle thing out?"

He nodded. "That idea's as good as any. Let's try."

Gret tried to swallow but couldn't. "Fenni, what if we kill her?"

He turned, his green eyes steady. "Zens will kill them both anyway. You can guarantee that. At least we're giving them a chance of survival." He tilted his head. "Does that help?"

Gret nodded, unable to trust her voice. A tear slid from her eye, down her cheek.

"Hey, Gret." Fenni cupped her chin in his hands. "What is it?"

Another tear slipped from her traitorous eyes. "Um, nothing. It's not important."

His hands slipped from her chin to her shoulders. He straightened and pulled her against him. "Whatever you feel, it's never nothing. Your feelings are always important to me."

And that was it, in a nutshell: her feelings were important to him. He cared about what she felt for Danion, or for him. And she'd hurt him. She'd been so cruel. And so confused. For a moment, Gret let herself cry in Fenni's comforting arms. He held her tight until she stopped crying. Then he gazed at her tenderly, wiping the tears from her eyes with his fingertips.

"It's just that…"

"I know," he said gently. "It's one thing to kill monsters in battle with a sword or mage flame. It's another thing to accidentally kill two young mages."

That was exactly how she'd felt. "Thank you for understanding." But that wasn't all. She'd felt bad for hurting him.

Fenni squeezed her hand. "We have to give them a chance."

They turned back to Velrama. Gret held the tube steady while Fenni pressed against Velrama's skin and eased out the needle. Blood seeped out of Velrama's tiny wound.

Gret yanked open a drawer on a cabinet against the wall. "Look, here are their wizard cloaks and clothing." She opened another drawer and found bandages. She wrapped one around Velrama's arm, while Fenni extracted the needle from Velrama's neck. Although tiny, her neck wound bled profusely. Gret bandaged it up too.

"Should I extract Sorcha's needles now?" she asked. It didn't look too hard.

"Sure," Fenni waited with the bandages and patched up the mage's wounds when Gret was done.

"All you needed was some encouragement," Fenni said. "Um, Gret…" He scratched his head again, looking awkward, but hopeful. "I, uh—"

Behind them Velrama and Sorcha groaned. Velrama sat up. "Where am I? What's going on?" she moaned.

Gret rushed over to her. Fenni rushed to Sorcha.

They helped Velrama and Sorcha get dressed and led them into the main chamber. Roberto gestured to where they should sit and asked Amato and Danion to watch the mages.

"Now, come with me." Fenni took Gret's hand, his fingers warm. "We're about to have some fun." They strode back into the antechamber. "Let's destroy this place so Zens can never use it again." Fenni bowed graciously and waved a hand at the tanks. "After you."

Gret whacked her sword against the glass. It gave a ringing clank, but the tank didn't smash. She picked up a chair and heaved it at the tank. The legs splintered. "This glass must be thicker than it looks."

Fenni held up his hands. "Stand back, and enjoy the show." Fire danced at his fingertips. He wound it into a flaming fireball and hurled it at a tank. The tank shattered, fluid spilling over the floor and rushing around Gret's boots.

He spun his hands in an arc. The next tank, and the next, shattered. Fake Velramas, Sorchas, and other mages tumbled onto the floor amid fluid and dangerous glass shards as long as Gret's thigh. Those mages looked so much like real people. For a moment, Gret wanted to rush over and help them. But these were Zens' monsters, just as much as tharuks were, so she stood, sword at the ready in case one of them blasted Fenni.

Fenni turned to her, mouth gaping and eyes panic-stricken.

"What is it?"

"I've met some of these other mages at Mage Gate, during the mage trials. I thought they'd died in battle."

Gret nodded. "Tomaaz told me he saw a man harvesting body parts off mage corpses and taking them to Zens."

"Body parts?"

"Well, he said hair, fingernails, stuff like that."

Fenni grimaced. "So he made people from the dead."

Gret nodded grimly.

Fenni shot flame at the corpses. Despite the fluid sloshing around them, he burned every one of them to ashes.

§

"Erob, please get Maazini and Ajeurina to bring Tomaaz and Lovina down here. Show them the way."

"Right away," the royal blue rumbled in Roberto's mind.

Roberto faced the other riders and Fenni. "Erob is summoning Tomaaz and Lovina. They should be here soon. We'll discuss our plans once they arrive." He paced, his boots striking the stone floor of Zens' large chamber, the echoes ringing off the glass tanks, which no longer held dark dragons. There were hundreds of empty tanks. And other tanks containing dragons that were still growing. And the tanks filled with half-formed tharuks. Zens could've filled and refilled these tanks countless times. All those dark dragons were out there hunting their people. If only they knew where.

In a flash, Roberto remembered the time he'd mind-melded with Zens when he was imprisoned in Death Valley. Dragon's claws, no wonder that man was so evil. His parents had tortured him and changed his body using strange methods from their world—the very methods Zens was using here to grow the mages and monsters. With needles and tubes and strange lights. He shook his head, trying to rid himself of those awful memories, but they persisted: Zens' father beating him; locking him in a cupboard until he wet himself as a tiny littling; the way his parents had altered Zens' skull shape and face with their odd magic; how they'd changed his body, everything about him; then the taunting from Zens' friends until Zens had killed to silence them; finally, the surge of elation flowing through Zens as that first body hit the floor.

Roberto shook his head again. There was no point in feeling pity for this man—he'd maimed and killed too many. There was no space for forgiveness. Zens deserved to die.

Kierion interrupted Roberto's thoughts. "If I was Zens, I'd use that realm gate to get to Dragons' Hold."

No! Roberto spun to face Kierion.

Kierion nodded.

Roberto froze. That was exactly what Zens would do—strike at their heart when no one suspected it. His blood chilled. Ezaara and Zaarusha were at Dragons' Hold—with their main body of dragons and riders.

Tomaaz and Lovina came through the double metal doors, eyes wide as they took in Zens' enormous mage-and-dragon-growing scheme.

Roberto passed Tomaaz a jade ring, the twin to the one he wore on his own finger. "This belongs to your parents. If you use it correctly, it will take you anywhere in Dragons' Realm."

"I'm aware," said Tomaaz. "My parents and I used these to escape Death Valley when I rescued Maazini. Is this Ma's or Pa's one?"

"Your mother gave it to Ezaara. Zens has found a way to hold the realm gate open long enough for his entire army to travel through it. He's left the sick and poorly slaves. He must've taken those who could fight. I'll use my ring so we can get through. You can use Ezaara's to join us when you're done here."

"Good plan, I agree." Tomaaz stuck the ring on his finger.

"Remember, Tomaaz, we can always come back to Death Valley to help these people. There's a war raging out there. Our first duty is to the realm."

Tomaaz nodded tersely. "We'll join you as soon as we've organized the slaves to sustain themselves for a few days."

Roberto grabbed his arm. "Tomaaz, don't stay too long. We're about to destroy Zens' life's work. If he finds you, he'll kill you. I'd hate to lose you two and your dragons." Roberto hesitated. "You can come with us now instead, if you want."

"No!" Lovina snapped. "We're not abandoning Zens' slaves. We were slaves too, remember."

"We'll be quick." Tomaaz said and took Lovina's hand. They rushed out of the metal doors, back to their waiting dragons.

Roberto sighed and looked around the chamber. Earlier, when he'd heard Fenni smashing tanks in the next cavern, he'd been itching to do the same here. Now it was time. "There's a lot of work to do here."

"Or undo," Kierion piped up.

He was holding Adelina's hand. When had that become a thing?

"All right, everyone, let's make sure Zens can never create another monster again." Roberto gestured at the tanks. "Destroy them all."

Amato was the first to move. With a grimace and a yell that made everyone flinch, he flung equipment at the tanks. Adelina and Kierion joined Amato, throwing heavy tools. Cracks appeared in the glass, weeping fluid. They expanded. Rivulets cascaded onto the stone. Tanks burst in a gush of fluid.

Roberto and Danion picked up a workbench and heaved it. A tank smashed, spraying glass and fluid. Water flooded the floor, up to their calves, and rushed down wide drains covered in metal gratings that ran the length of the room.

"Take cover!" Fenni yelled. Everyone ducked behind benches.

Fenni sent arcs of fire crashing along a row of tanks, smashing the glass into thousands of pieces. The shadow dragon embryos slumped on the floor, squawking, flapping their half-grown wings and scrabbling with their soft talons.

Their mewling rippled through Roberto's mind.

Fenni set them alight, grinning at Roberto. "Luckily, mage fire burns through water!"

Gret strode among the flapping shadow dragons, plunging her sword into their tiny heads, even as their wings burned with green mage flames. "Roberto, look."

He rushed over. A bloody methimium crystal was lodged in each shadow dragon's skull. "So that's how he made them so evil." He stabbed his sword to end the tharuk runts scrambling in the debris.

Adelina and Danion joined Gret, massacring Zens' monsters with blood-darkened blades.

The stink of burning flesh filled the room. Smoke billowed among broken glass. Velrama and Sorcha started coughing.

When all the tanks were smashed and dragons and tharuk runts slaughtered, Fenni nodded at Roberto. "Let's get out of here."

"Danion," Roberto called. "You and Fenni take the mages. I'll look after everyone else."

Fenni picked up Velrama and rushed, Gret at his side, into the tunnel. Danion staggered after them, holding Sorcha. Adelina, Amato and Kierion were next. Roberto took one last glance back at the flooded floor, the sodden charred remains of the slaughtered shadow dragons, and the glass and debris littering the cavern.

He and Amato had tried to figure out Zens' equipment, to see if there was anything here that could benefit their realm. He was sure there was, but Zens' techniques had been beyond them. It was better to destroy this equipment than have Zens wield it against them again.

With a twinge of regret, he walked through the open metal doors, the water lapping at his boots as he strode into the broad tunnel.

§

The methimium ray still lit the walls of the broad exit tunnel. Roberto strode past Danion, who was on his blue dragon with Sorcha slumped over his dragon's neck. Next to him, Gret had Velrama draped over Hagret's neck. Adelina rubbed Linaia's snout and climbed into her saddle.

"You all set?" Roberto asked Fenni, who was in his customary spot behind Kierion on Riona.

Fenni nodded. "The sooner we leave, the better."

Amato was leaning on the rear wall, waiting for him. Matotoi sat on his haunches nearby. That was everyone.

"Except me, Maazini, and Ajeurina," Erob rumbled, *"and Tomaaz and Lovina."*

Roberto faced them. "Kierion, how does this all work?" He waved at the thing producing that yellow light.

"Stand in the light and rub your ring while saying the special word," Kierion said. "Then get out the way so our dragons can jump at the gold clouds without trampling you down. That's all there is to it."

So simple, yet so terrifying.

Kierion piped up again, "Not that we'd mind trampling you. You're a tough taskmaster."

Riding Riona behind him, Fenni laughed.

Roberto flashed them a grin as nervous laughter skittered among the riders. Trust Kierion to crack a joke when they needed it.

"It's always terrible, sending troops into battle," Erob ventured.

"Blindly. I have no idea where they're going. Whether this is a trap." Roberto twisted the ring on his finger.

"Then it's best we get it over with and find out."

There was nothing for it. This was it. Roberto addressed them all. "Before you go, good luck. We don't know what'll greet you. Kierion, please go first but be careful. Fenni, be prepared."

Kierion and Fenni nodded somberly.

He could be sending them all to their doom.

"Or you could all die here, waiting," Erob said.

Roberto stood in front of the yellow rays and rubbed his ring. "Ana."

He jumped out of the way as Riona thundered toward him, and turned to see Kierion and Fenni disappearing into the swirling gold clouds of a realm gate.

Adelina was next. Danion and Gret followed.

Only he and Amato were left. Matotoi sank to his haunches near Amato, gazing at Roberto.

"Father."

Amato started. "M-me? Y-yes." He blinked, his eyes glittering.

"Before we go, I have a question. Why were you trembling when we were in Zens' den?"

Amato's chin slumped to his chest and he held his face in his hands. For a long moment, the only sound was the hum of the metal box making the methimium ray.

Amato looked out. "I was remembering the day that I gave you to Zens." His face crumpled. "The shadows were goading me, forcing me to hand over my own son, but somewhere deep inside I didn't want to." Matotoi shifted nearer to Erob. Amato reached out, grasping at Roberto's sleeve. "Son, you have to believe me. All these years, I've dreamed of seeing you and Adelina again, never knowing if…" His voice trailed off as he broke into sobs.

This was the man who'd murdered his mother—just as Roberto had attempted to murder Ezaara. Roberto swallowed. Hard. Zens had forced them both to do terrible things.

Taking Amato's hand, he led him to Matotoi and helped him up into the saddle. He clambered up onto Erob and they dived into that billowing yellow cloud. With a pop, Death Valley disappeared.

DRIVEN TO MAGE GATE

Dark dragons hounded them. Swarms of them filled the sky, driving dragons and riders from Dragon's Teeth over the northern part of Great Spanglewood Forest. Antonika flew until the sky was lightening to the gray of pre-dawn. Tonio was hunched low in the saddle. The beating of tired dragon wings surrounded him on either side, above and below.

Ahead, Ezaara rode like the wind on Queen Zaarusha.

"The queen is asking us to stick together."

"We don't have much choice," Tonio replied, trying to mind-block the awful shadow dragon screeches ripping through his head. *"There are so many of them. If we separate we'd be picked off."*

A blue dragon and hunched rider broke off, wheeling to the north.

"Antonika, tell them—No!"

A shadow dragon dived and the blue's wings burst into flame. It plummeted, lighting up the foliage in the forest.

Every wingbeat, they'd been chased by Zens' shadow dragons who'd shot mage fire, dragon flame and those awful slicing beams from their eyes. The chill cut through Tonio's cloak. It'd been a long night, with no sleep, after a difficult council meeting and running patrol yesterday morning since dawn. Many of the riders were weary. Their only chance was to out-fly their enemy.

There was shadow on the horizon. Tonio squinted.

More dark dragons rose from the forest ahead, their flames igniting foliage as they rose through the trees. The dark beasts charged toward the front ranks. The shadow dragons behind them roared. Those on either side drove them closer together.

Shards! They'd fled into a trap. Their dragons and riders were hemmed in. The snarling shadow beasts circled, driving them toward...

... Mage Gate.

Tonio should've realized that Zens would want to reopen that dragon gods-cursed gate to his world. After Giddi's wife Mazyka had gone through, the council had ordered Master Giddi to shut the world gate, locking out his wife and most of Dragons' Realm's mages. Zens must want to bring more tharuk reinforcements through the world gate.

Or some other means of annihilating Dragons' Realm completely. He doubted the commander wanted a trip home.

CHASM

When Roberto entered the realm gate, Anakisha's figure was frozen in midair, her mouth open, anger lining her body and face. Instead of the golden clouds bathing him in their light, the tunnel was fractured with dark rifts and swirling black mists. Anakisha's fear had been realized. Zens had corrupted the realm gate.

With a crack, the realm gate disappeared and Roberto was in darkness on Erob's back. Muffled voices called to each other and talons scratched rock. A tiny flicker of green glowed in the distance.

"I assume you'd like some light on the matter?"

"Thank you, Erob."

Flame flared from Erob's maw, illuminating a deep gully lined with rocky walls stretching high above them. The sky was a distant black ribbon of stars. Erob's talons crunched on rubble.

Fenni's voice carried back to them. "It's a tunnel. It goes on a long way." His green mage light bobbed above Riona's back.

Adelina and Danion turned to Roberto. "Shall we follow him?"

If the dragons kept their wings tightly furled, there would be room enough for them to walk.

Climbing over scree, they traipsed down the tunnel. "Oh, shards!" Fenni cried.

Erob raced down the tunnel with his long legs, coming upon dead slaves with picks and shovels still in hand.

The ribbon of sky above them disappeared as they headed farther underground and deeper into the bowels of the earth. The tunnel soon became wide enough for two dragons, then three, but they walked single file avoiding the piles of scree up the sides of the tunnel walls—recently excavated by the looks of things.

"Erob, shine a flame on that scree," Roberto asked. A sweet cloying stench hung in the air–a stench that was only too familiar.

A hand stuck out of the gravel pile. Oh gods, that's where all the slaves were. Buried here after dying digging Zens' tunnel. As they went deeper, Roberto saw legs, even a head sticking out of the piles. His stomach churned at the waste of so many lives.

Erob trudged along the passage. Eventually, they reached a ragged hole at the end of the tunnel, which opened out into a wide cavern.

"No!" Fenni, still in front, let out an anguished scream that echoed through the gully, chilling Roberto's bones.

Their dragons sprang through the hole into the main cavern at Dragons' Hold. Except it wasn't the main cavern as they'd left it. They'd come through a gaping hole in the rear wall onto a pile of rocks and carnage several dragons high.

Bodies littered the ground: shadow dragons, tharuks, mages, slaves, dragons of every color—and riders. They were steaming. The air was filled with smoke and the stench of death.

This had happened not even an hour ago. "By the dragon gods," Roberto whispered. "We're too late."

§

In the distance, spurts of flame gusted above the dark forest over Mage Gate. *"Nearly there,"* Maazini said.

Flying through the night beside them, Lovina was huddled in her cloak on Ajeurina.

They'd arrived at Dragons' Hold a few hours ago, too late to save their people. In the end, he and Lovina had brought Death Valley's former slaves with them through the realm gate. With a little decent food and the clear-mind berries, many of them had showed good signs of recovery.

The carnage they'd seen back at the hold was worse than anything Tomaaz had ever witnessed—and that was after living in Death Valley. They'd found injured blue guards—dragons and riders—among the debris and the dead. Lovina had discovered Mara hiding in a cupboard in the girls' sleeping cavern. A few of Hendrik's workers had hidden at the back of the storerooms and others had taken refuge in a dungeon deep beneath the areas the tharuks had ransacked.

Although everyone was still reeling in shock and grieving, Tomaaz had organized the survivors to camp in the council chambers until they returned. Situated at the highest point in the mountain's cavern and tunnel complex, he hoped the chambers would provide a refuge. He'd then organized them to clean up the hold. A task of momentous proportions—tharuks had rampaged through the place, smashing furniture and destroying possessions. It would take a massive effort to clean up.

They'd left the slaves under Mara's command, guilt prickling their consciences because the injured riders had to deal with a hundred people. Hopefully, they'd help rebuilding Dragons' Hold—their new home.

The bursts of flame were closer now. A few hundred wingbeats farther. Pressure began to build in Tomaaz's head. He called out to Lovina, "Have you got your headband?" He'd found two opaline headbands on Ezaara's bloodstained ledge, amid signs of a scuffle. Gods, he hoped his twin sister was all right.

"I'll let you know as soon as I can mind-meld with one of our dragons," Maazini said, the screams in his head rattling Tomaaz's senses.

Lovina pulled the headband from her pocket and fastened it around her head as Tomaaz fastened his own. The pressure eased. He shook his head, unsure whether these dark dragons' screams were a battle tactic to distress dragons and riders, or whether dark dragons were constantly in pain. The effect was the same—unable to meld with Maazini any longer, Tomaaz was literally flying in the dark.

BATTLE

Zaarusha's sides were heaving when she and Ezaara landed at Mage Gate. Ezaara dismounted and rubbed Zaarusha's snout. *"Thank you for being so swift."*

"Rally our people and make a battle plan," Zaarusha replied. *"Shadow dragons will be on us in no time."*

Ezaara melded with all the dragons overhead, requesting them to land.

Dragons dived to the clearing, their feet churning up old snowdrifts and turning patches of emerging grass to mud. Some dragons arrived carrying three or four people. Littlings were sandwiched between parents or thrown up on top of dragon's necks clinging to their spinal ridges. They jostled to make space in the forest-ringed clearing.

"Zaarusha, please summon Dominique," Ezaara asked as the dragon masters gathered around her.

A burst of color broke away from the approaching cloud of dark dragons. The cloud scattered, becoming individual dragons that swooped to the clearing. A dark-blue dragon led them.

"Erob, Roberto. Is that you?" After all this time—and she'd been so angry at him when he'd left. Her heart pounded against her ribs.

The masters' dragons shuffled back to make space for them to land.

"It is indeed. We flew like the wind to catch you and dodged the swarm of shadow dragons. But I have bad news: still more dark dragons are coming."

"Thank the First Egg you're safe." Tears pricked Ezaara's eyes. "How did it go?"

"We've destroyed Zens' facilities. He can no longer create his monsters." Roberto dismounted and embraced her.

Dominique strode between the assembled dragons, toward them. "How can I help, my honored Queen's Rider?" The leader of the blue guards thumped his hand on his chest.

"We must find refuge for our littlings. What would you suggest?"

Dominique paused, tilting his head, then nodded. "Iniquo, my dragon, tells me Horseshoe Bend is safe. Our guards finished patrolling there a few hours ago."

"Good. Dispatch the littlings and those too weak to fight."

"Yes, Queen's Rider." Dominique departed.

Marlies spoke. "Your father and I have scouted the area and found a place suitable for a temporary infirmary for anyone injured at Dragons' Hold."

Or in the upcoming battle, but Ezaara didn't mention that. They all knew what they were facing. "How many wounded do we have already?"

"More than I'd like," Ma answered, shaking her head grimly.

Ezaara gestured to Battle Master Aidan. "Please organize foot archers to protect the new infirmary. Where is this clearing, Marlies?"

Ma gestured eastward. "A hundred dragon lengths away in a copse of trees between a small clearing and the river—an ideal spot for dragons to land and bring in wounded."

Ezaara scanned the skies. Shadow dragons were rapidly approaching.

Lars barked, "Master Aidan, we also need adequate dragons to transport our wounded there."

The battle master nodded. "Our blue guards will take them there immediately. Master Jerrick, please select foot archers."

The master of archery nodded and departed.

How were they going to feed an army? Ezaara nodded at Derek. "Get everyone to divide what food we have among us to ensure that no one goes hungry."

Derek nodded. "I'll relay the message."

With logistics organized, now Ezaara had to rally their riders. *"Oh gods, Roberto what am I going to tell them? We've been driven from our homes. Dragons' Hold has been destroyed. People are homeless, and we're facing our worst enemy in years."*

Roberto's thoughts were calm. *"You can do this, Ezaara. You're Queen's Rider. You saved Zaarusha from poison. You saved me from the Robandi silent assassins. Our people will rally behind you. I know you can save us from Zens."*

Then he knew more than she did. Ezaara wasn't sure at all.

"Ezaara, don't give up hope. Zens destroys from a sense of hatred. We fight out of love. Our riders will meet the shadow dragons in battle and defeat them."

The dark blot across the sky was rapidly approaching.

Ezaara climbed upon Zaarusha's back. The queen stood tall and proud. Ezaara stood upon her saddle and held her hands up for silence. Quiet fell over the clearing. Distant dragon wings rumbled, like an approaching storm in the sky. Faint echoes of mental shrieks rippled through her mind. She didn't have long.

"My dear people, we've been driven from our homes. Tonight, many of you will be hurting or grieving. But if we don't fight back, we'll lose everything. Zens is formidable, but he's just a man, susceptible to an arrow or a well-aimed spear. He's not fireproof. And neither are his beasts. We face many more than we ever imagined. But we are many, and know how to fight too." Ezaara took a deep breath.

"I have a secret to share: these dragons age prematurely. Roberto and this team made their way into Death Valley and have destroyed Zens' means of creating more tharuks, shadow dragons or fake mages. The mages and shadow dragons that now exist won't live longer than a week or a few days. If we can kill them all, we can end this onslaught against Dragons' Realm forever."

For a moment there was stunned silence in the clearing.

"Why don't we outrun them?" someone called.

"We have to fight," Ezaara answered. "They've surrounded us, and if we run, they'll slaughter our people."

Kierion thrust his fist in the air and yelled, "Let's go! Let's fight!"

There was a rousing cheer. Riders pounded their chests with their fists. "Let's take to the skies for Ezaara."

Ezaara's eyes pricked with tears. Shards, she could be sending them to their slaughter.

"Zens has given us no choice, Ezaara," Zaarusha melded.

She was right. Ezaara held her arms high again. "We are not defenseless." She reached into her pocket and drew out one of the opaline headbands. "As you landed, blue guards handed you these headbands. Opaline crystals are inserted inside them to protect you from the shadow dragons' screams. You won't be able to mind-meld with your dragons, but the enemy will no longer be able to mentally torture you. Good luck in battle. Some of our riders and dragons may fall, but we will fight on and purge Dragons' Realm of Zens and his abominations."

A cry came up from the back of the crowd as arrows flew from the bushes. Tusky faces appeared. Tharuks smashed through trees, running toward them.

Blue guards turned and flamed the tharuks.

Ezaara punched her fist in the sky. "Now, we fight! To the skies!"

BROWN GUARDS

After only one night sheltering against the storm in the cave, the snow cleared. Wan sunlight glancing off her wings, Esina descended from the Northern Alps over a snow-shrouded forest, then glided over a plain toward a cluster of hills.

Hugging Taliesin's waist, Leah said, "I never knew what was beyond the Northern Alps. The map hanging on the wall of the hold's training cavern doesn't show anything."

Taliesin nodded. "Hans once told me that the territory has never been mapped in order to protect the brown dragons."

"What do the brown guards do up here?"

"I'm not sure," said Taliesin. He pursed his lips. "The feelings I have are mixed—sadness and hope. Last night in the cave I dreamed of sick, dying dragons, but also of piaua flourishing. It was very confusing."

That *was* confusing. Leah was glad she was a tree speaker. Although she had no idea how to use that gift—apart from a few hurried instructions from Marlies. She held on to Taliesin's waist a little tighter.

They flew over some small snow-covered hillocks, approaching a chain of larger hills. A bellow rose, shattering the stillness. Esina replied, her roar rumbling across the plains and echoing off the hillside. Mighty brown wings flapped, taking off from the highest outcrop and soaring out to greet them.

The brown dragon roared again, a mournful sound that floated over the tiny knolls. Its rider's eyes flicked over them and he nodded. The dragon turned, escorting them to a plateau on the hillside. Esina followed the brown into a large cavern at the back of the plateau. As Leah's eyes adjusted from the blinding white landscape outside to the dim flickering torches in the cavern, she saw around twenty brown dragons. The brown they were following was distinctly larger than the others.

The cavern rippled with murmurs, snorts and snuffles. Huge feet thudded as the dragons came forward to sniff Esina. About a hundred riders approached, faces gaunt and posture listless.

"Something's gone wrong here," whispered Taliesin. "Very wrong."

Leah could feel it too—as if these people's very bones were sad.

The brown's short stocky rider slid from his saddle and strode over, a long dark plait hanging over his shoulder. The murmurs and snuffles died as he whipped out his sword and held the point at Taliesin's belly. "It's been a long time since we asked the red dragons to come to our aid. Why did you not turn up sooner?"

Taliesin spoke, his voice surprisingly clear and confident. "I'm a new rider. It's been barely five days since I imprinted. My dragon Esina has asked me to convey her condolences for your dead." He placed his fist on his heart. "However, she is the only remaining red guard. All the riders and red dragons have been slaughtered by Commander Zens."

Gasps echoed through the cavern. Dragons shifted, talons scraping stone, sending shudders down Leah's spine.

The stocky rider's eyes narrowed. "How is this possible?"

Once again, Taliesin's voice was clear, even commanding. "We don't know. We came upon the massacre a few days ago. Esina told me they were ambushed by Zens' dark dragons: beasts who shoot fire from their maws; aim strange yellow light from their eyes that slices through skin and scales; and use mind screams that torture our riders and dragons."

Leah spoke up. "I'm a healer at Dragons' Hold." How her heart swelled to say those words—although she was only in training. "We've come seeking aid to fight them, and piaua juice to heal our wounded. Our trees have been destroyed by Commander Zens and his tharuks. Every grove is gone." Her eyes teared up and her voice choked.

Exclamations of outrage came from the riders. The stocky rider, obviously their leader, held up his hands for silence.

"Our injured riders are dying in droves," Leah said. "Shadow dragons are attacking villages across Dragons' Realm. Lush Valley is laid to waste. I witnessed the screams of the dying around me, the earth peppered with the bodies of people, tharuks and dragons."

The leader sheathed his sword and motioned them to dismount.

When they slid from the saddle, he shook their hands. "I'm Darynn, leader of the brown guards and rider of Rynnlak. Dragons' Realm must be in dire trouble to send two so young on such an important quest. Welcome to our hearth." He waved a hand at his people. "Prepare some food and ready bedrolls for our guests."

He turned back to Leah and Taliesin. "Come with me." Their boots echoed hollowly on the tunnel leading to the mouth of the cavern. "Recently, a scourge came upon the land and our dragons were weakened. Many died. The sickness that took them could not be battled with piaua. I'll show you."

He stopped at the edge of the ledge where they'd landed. Below, hillocks dotted the plain all the way to a grove of trees in the north.

Darynn turned to them, sorrow etching harsh lines around his mouth and on his brow. "These humps you see are not hills. They're dragons, lying dead beneath the snow."

Leah's hand flew to her mouth. Taliesin gaped.

Shoulders slumped, Darynn shook his head. "Our dragons were too sick to give our dead a decent funeral pyre. For now, they rest. When the thaw comes, we'll dispatch them to the land of departed dragons with respect." Eyes bright with tears, he bowed his head, silent.

§

Leah was itching to get going. Sitting around in the cavern for a night during the snowstorm and, now, for another night while these people deliberated how to help them wasn't aiding the injured riders at Dragons' Hold. To ease her agitation, she sat by the fire, weaving animals out of sticks, wondering whether the tharuk who'd unwittingly helped her had perished when Esina had attacked.

She bent twigs to form the body of a hare. If only she was as fleet-footed, she'd run straight home with piaua juice tucked in her healer's pouch. She passed Taliesin the hare.

He studied it. "I wonder what happened to that dragon you made?"

"I think I lost it when I fled." Leah picked up more sticks, fashioning them into a piaua tree.

Darynn came over to the fire and sat beside them. "Our own supplies are low, and our tree speaker also died in the scourge. We've no spare piaua juice to give you."

Leah turned to him. "I'm a tree speaker. That's why I was sent on this quest."

Darynn raised his eyebrows. "So you know how to harvest the juice? Good, perhaps you can help us replenish our supply. Tomorrow I'll take you and Taliesin to the piaua grove to the north."

"Thank you." Leah touched his arm. "My people will be indebted to you."

Darynn gave her a grim smile. "Good, we need all the help we can get." He rose and left her and Taliesin in front of the fire, the murmur of soft voices around them.

Leah closed her eyes, the flames casting bright patterns behind her eyelids. Marlies had only whispered a few hurried instructions before she and Taliesin had headed off. She'd hoped to find another tree speaker here who could teach her, but it was all up to her now.

Taliesin squeezed her hand. "Do you know what you're doing?"

Leah opened her eyes, gazed into his, and whispered, "I have no idea."

§

Darynn led Leah through the snow to the trees. "This is our sacred grove."

Two denuded oaks stood on either side of a trail leading deep into a growth of strongwoods, pine, yew, holly, and eucalyptus. She hesitated. After seeing the barren grove of the red guards and the desecrated sacred clearing in Lush Valley, it was almost too much to hope that any living piaua remained. Leah turned and waved to Taliesin, waiting on Esina, bundled up against the light flakes that danced across the plain. He lifted a gloved hand and waved back.

Darynn placed a hand on her back and gave her a gentle push. "Go on," he said, kindness lighting his eyes. "You've journeyed far. Don't be afraid."

Leah squeezed her hands into fists, resisting the urge to pluck twigs to make a woodland creature. Whispers from the trees drifted around her in the snowflakes. She strode between the leafy foliage, the whispers caressing her ears. Her fingertips hummed with the peculiar sensation she always experienced in a healthy, vibrant forest.

She forced herself to relax, exhaling. Avoiding a deep snow drift, she rounded a bend in the narrow trail and came face to face with an impenetrable wall of trunk and foliage. A mighty living, breathing, piaua was before her, its foliage kissing the sky. Large enough to shelter several dragons, its leaves were dusted with snow, green peeking through where the wind had rustled its branches. Her heart soared. There was hope for her people.

If she could harvest the juice—and that was a big 'if'.

Whispers built, crashing upon her mind like waves on a shore. *"Tree speaker, you come in peace."*

Leah nodded, in awe of the mighty tree. "Yes, I come in peace, seeking your juice to save my people."

"I do not give my juice lightly."

Leah's knees plunged into the snow, her chin touching her chest. "I seek not for myself, but for my people—the dragon riders who are wounded, the citizens of Dragons' Realm who are dying."

"I sense the piaua trees in the south are all dead. Why?" The sadness in the tree's voice made Leah's arm hair prickle.

"An awful being has invaded the realm. His monsters wreaked this havoc."

The piaua's leaves rustled. Hissing filled Leah's ears. "We must fight this enemy and protect our people and our realm. I will strengthen your injured riders with my juice so they can do so. Step inside my most sacred grove."

Leah was already in the sacred grove. What did the tree mean?

"Behold your future," the tree whispered. One side of the piaua rustled. The leaves and branches bowed, creating a gap.

As Leah walked through, the tree sealed the way behind her.

She gasped. She was inside a ring of giant piaua trees. Not as large as the one she'd spoken to, but still enormous. Within the ring were piaua saplings as tall as her waist, her shoulders and her head—a piaua nursery. Tears streamed down Leah's face. Never in her wildest dreams had she imagined such abundance. She could harvest what they needed and come back for more.

On the far side of the clearing, a brown dragon was curled in the snow, his head raised. He opened his maw and breathed warm air over the young trees.

His rider, a handsome boy not much older than her, looked up from brushing snow off the saplings' leaves. He shook his light brown hair back from his eyes. "Welcome. Um, I'm Eryk." The dragon rider stared at her with wide eyes. "This is Beryk." He gestured at his dragon.

"I'm Leah."

A breeze built in the clearing and the leaves of the mighty tree shook. "A tree speaker must never be greedy. Take only as much as you need."

Leah pulled Marlies' small metal spigot out of her pocket and cast about, wondering which tree to take juice from.

As soon as she had the thought, the mighty tree's leaves rustled again.

Leah strode to the tree. Apart from Marlies' brief whispered instructions, she was still in the dark. Oh shards, if only Marlies were here. Swallowing, she placed her hand on the pitted gnarly bark. "Please, mighty piaua tree, I come requesting thy juice to heal the wounded and dying. I promise to use it sparingly."

She waited. Marlies had told her of a hum she'd feel beneath her fingers. Leah would never have described the sensation that ran through her hand as a hum. Elation coursed through her arm, her body vibrating with a peculiar energy as if she was being filled with light. She tapped the spigot against the trunk. The tough bark parted like soft butter. She held out a vial under the spigot. When it was full, she stood the vial in the snow as she filled the next, and the next.

When all her vials were full, she corked them and stowed them in her healer's pouch and rucksack. "That might be enough now." She placed her hand on the spigot to remove it, but the tree's rustling voice filled her head again.

"You'll need more for war. What else can you fill?"

Leah rummaged through her rucksack and found a flaccid waterskin. Marlies would be thrilled. She could hardly believe it, her hands shaking as she held the waterskin under the spigot.

When the skin was half full, a shudder went through the tree's trunk. *"I must replenish my resources before I provide you with more. Please use the juice of my brothers and sisters."*

Leah went to the next tree, and the next, taking a little juice from each until the skin was full.

"I heard you talking to them." Eryk bit his lip, his eyes upon her. "You can hear the trees speak?"

Leah nodded.

"My people need piaua too. Do you think you could ask for them?" He gestured at some waterskins hanging from the back of his saddle.

"I'll try."

Eryk passed her the waterskins.

Leah took them. "I'm sorry for the scourge that hit your people."

He ducked his head, a lock of his hair falling over his eyes. "I'm just glad it's over. Well, I hope it is."

When Leah had filled his skins, Eryk knelt on one knee and thumped his hand over his heart. "Thank you for the gift of life. I'll take this to Darynn for our people. It's an honor to be in your presence, tree speaker."

In her presence? She was no one. An orphan. A humble trainee healer. It was the piaua who gave life, not her.

A PEACEFUL WORLD

Tharuks had stealthily been surrounding the riders while Ezaara spoke, rousing her people. Master Giddi shook his head. The foolish dragon riders would all be killed.

"*Good riddance,*" the shadows whispered. "*Such unruly disorganized rabble deserve to die. They lack Zens' impeccable sense of order and strategy.*"

Giddi agreed. Commander Zens certainly had impeccable strategy. His plan to take Dragon's Hold had been flawless. The vermin had been driven from their burrows, and now, all that remained, was to finish the job.

Tharuks burst from the bushes, firing arrows dripping with limplock and tipped with methimium at dragons and riders. Rustling, flapping wings thundered in Giddi's ears as hundreds of riders scrambled to their dragons and took to the sky above Mage Gate. Roars ripped through the sky as Zens' shadow dragons met them.

A surge of elation ran through Giddi. For once, it was good to be on the winning side.

A troop of tharuks marched Giddi through the trees into the clearing. Hundreds of brightly colored flapping wings whirled above Mage Gate. Giddi tilted back his head. Zaarusha was there, too, leading them all.

The teardrop-shaped crystal was warm against Giddi's chest. His magic thrummed under his skin as he pulled *sathir* from the trees, waiting until Zens gave him the signal to release it.

"*Your time will come,*" whispered the shadows. "*Zens will help you create a world where chaotic human relationships, anger, and pain are replaced with order and peace. There will be no dragons fighting, no petty politics, or councils.*" Master Starrus' face flashed to mind—and Septimor's entrails strewn across the tree as he'd died. That had been stupidity—caused by a power-hungry wizard. And Giddi's lover had been banished due to such power games by dragon masters. All of them deserved to die.

"*Open the world gate when Zens commands you,*" the shadows hissed. "*And welcome a better world.*"

A vision opened in Giddi's mind: Dragons' Realm was a barren wasteland with not a living thing. Forests had turned to marshy swamplands. Caverns were long abandoned. The air was free of creatures. And everywhere Giddi walked, he sensed quiet solitude amid trees devoid of leaves.

"Even plants need no longer struggle. Zens will take care of them all. There is beauty and simplicity in following Zens." Transfixed by the vision, Giddi let tharuks lead him into the middle of the clearing as the shadows kept whispering. He was looking forward to a peaceful world. *"Will you obey the commander?"*

"Yes, I will."

§

They'd flown hard and caught up with the riders from Dragons' Hold at Mage Gate. Ezaara had dispensed opaline headbands to them all and ordered them into the air to fight the shadow beasts. Dark dragons swarmed around them as Fenni, at the front of the saddle, ducked their flame and shot mage fire. Kierion wriggled down Riona's back. It was tricky maneuvering with Riona bucking to duck flames and those slicing eye beams, but he hung on, edging along bit by bit until he was halfway down Riona's tail.

She flicked her tail. Kierion sailed through the air and angled his body to land behind a mage on a dark dragon. Kierion aimed his dagger between the mage's spine and shoulder blade and drove it into his back and through his heart.

The mage slumped, blood streaming down his back. Kierion kicked him out of the saddle, hoping the dark dragon would feast upon the carcass as it tumbled earthward. Sure enough, the dragon dived. Kierion leaped off and Riona caught him. If only there was some way to get from her talons up to her back again. With the opaline headband on, he couldn't meld with her.

She dived over a dark dragon below, giving a twitch of her talons. Who needed to mind-meld? Her signal was clear enough. Kierion squeezed her foreleg, readying his arms and legs. Riona dropped him smack on top of a mage. He plunged his dagger into the mage's throat. Eyes rolling back, she slumped over her dragon's spinal ridge.

Tucking his knife in his belt, Kierion pulled his sword from its scabbard and smote the dragon's neck. Its howl shuddered through Kierion's bones. He launched himself off its saddle into the air.

Riona plucked him up again. Thank the First Dragon Egg that she had good reflexes. Riona ascended through a swathe of dragons as Fenni cleared a path with blazing green mage fire. Riona threw Kierion onto another dragon's back, and he swung his sword, cleaving the fake mage's head from its body. In a spray of blood, the head bounced on the dragon's spinal ridge and again on its foreleg, then ricocheted off another dragon into the forest.

Beasts swarming around it, the dragon he was riding snarled, turning its neck and breathing fire at Kierion. Without thinking, he leaped, scanning the sky for Riona.

But she wasn't there.

Above, she was fighting tooth and talon for her life as Fenni shot flame at a dark dragon with its jaws clamped around Riona's neck. Gods, no. His dragon was going to die.

And so was he.

Kierion plummeted ever closer to the spear-like tips of the trees.

He squeezed his eyes shut. They said it was easier to die if you didn't look.

Not that he was a coward or anything.

Still he fell.

Something thwacked against Kierion's backside and bounced him in the air. His eyes flew open. Danion's blue dragon had tail-slapped him. She dived under his body and caught him neatly between her spinal ridges. Kierion clung onto Danion, trembling. They were barely above the sharp pines piercing the forest canopy. Moments later, and he'd be dead.

Danion laughed as his dragon ascended.

Kierion couldn't even lay his hand on his dragon's hide to mind-meld, thanks to the opaline headbands. "Tell your dragon thank you." He panted.

"Her name is Onion," Danion replied with a chuckle. "She wanted me to name her when we imprinted. I was young and cocky with a terrible sense of humor."

If the way Danion had been goading Fenni was anything to judge by, his humor hadn't improved. "Thank Onion for me, please."

Onion beat her mighty blue wings, ascending above the forest and the swarm of dark dragons. She dived upon the dragon attacking Riona, shredding its wings with her talons. Riona released her jaws from its neck. The beast scrabbled with its talons, gouging her side, and then fell, roaring through the air to be impaled upon the very pines that had almost claimed him.

HOMEWARD BOUND

Leah and Taliesin wrapped themselves in their warm cloaks and climbed upon Esina.

Darynn came to the cave mouth to see them off. "My riders are preparing as we speak. Half will stay behind to guard our sacred piaua grove, the other half will leave tomorrow for Dragons' Hold." He reached up and shook Leah and Taliesin's hands. "Our numbers are no longer great, but we'll do what we can to aid Dragons' Realm."

"Thank you," Leah said.

"We appreciate your help." Taliesin waved.

Saddlebags bulging, Esina leaped off the ledge and flew toward the Northern Alps. When they crested the alps and swooped toward Dragons' Hold, Leah breathed a sigh of relief. They were heading home.

Dark clouds rolled in from the west, but at least there was no storm to hamper their progress yet. "We did it, Taliesin. I can hardly believe it."

In front of her in the saddle, Taliesin turned, his lake-blue eyes grave.

That somber look didn't bode well. "What is it?" she asked.

He shrugged. "I'm uneasy."

"Perhaps it's that approaching storm." Leah gestured at the dark cloud racing toward them.

"Could be." He squinted. "There's something odd about those clouds, though."

Strange, there wasn't a strong wind, but the cloud was breaking up and moving quickly.

Taliesin's fingers tightened on Esina's spinal ridge. "Dragon's claws! It's not a cloud."

Then what was it? One of the smaller clouds speared toward a mountaintop, gusting orange flame.

Dark dragons.

"Quick, Esina, faster. Perhaps we can out-fly them." At Taliesin's urging, the red dragon flapped her wings valiantly, spurting ahead.

Within half an hour, shadow dragons surrounded them and blasted flame at Esina, the beams from their eyes cutting dangerously near.

Leah's stomach lurched. No. Only a day's flight from Dragons' Hold…

A male mage upon a dark dragon lobbed a green fireball at Esina. She snarled, twisting her neck aside, and the fireball sizzled past, barely missing her snout. He tossed another fireball back and forth between his hands, his dark dragon swooping so close overhead that Leah had to duck. The wind from its wingbeats shook them in the saddle.

The mage yelled, "Land at once or I'll blast your dragon out of the sky and toast it for our mounts to eat."

The resounding roars from the dark dragons rocked Leah's bones.

Taliesin turned to her, panic on his face, his shoulders tight. "I'm telling Esina to go down. I won't risk her life."

Leah nodded. Not that it mattered either way. They were all going to die. She couldn't trick these ferocious beasts with little emblems made from sticks and leaves. Nor could she talk her way out of this, or slip away without anyone noticing.

And no one was going to rescue them.

Their piaua would be taken. This whole journey had been a waste.

Esina spiraled down toward a mountaintop. Leah's breath caught in her throat as she saw the gleaming peaks of Dragon's Teeth in the distance. So close, yet impossible to reach.

In years to come, would anyone find their bodies, frozen up here on this mountain, and wonder what had happened to two young riders and their dragon? Her throat constricted, making it hard to breathe. She'd never see Marlies again. Never heal another wounded rider. And never get to bring this precious piaua juice home. Many lives would be lost because she'd failed.

Taliesin reached back and squeezed her hand. "Never give up hope," he said. "When the tharuks whipped me, I thought my life was ending, but look at me now: I have a dragon."

From tharuk slave to dragon rider. His had been an amazing journey. And so had hers. From an injured villager to trainee healer to a tree speaker who had found the remedy that could save her people. But was her life worth anything if it was now destroyed?

Never give up hope, Taliesin had said.

The dark dragons swarmed around them, herding them away from the mountain that Esina had been aiming for, pushing the red dragon down into a narrow valley between two peaks. Below, troops of tharuks were waiting. Shadow dragons swarmed above Esina and shot flames either sides of her wings, forcing her to land.

§

Tharuks rushed forward and surrounded Esina. Mages mounted on dark dragons landed—identical to the mage who'd spoken—all wearing a sneer, venom lacing their eyes. What were these bizarre creatures? Was this man one of the mages who'd been captured by Zens? Tharuks swarmed around Esina. She let out a small gust of flame, driving them back, but tharuk archers raised their bows, dripping green with limplock.

Esina ducked her head, trembling.

"What were you doing so far north?" the mage asked.

Leah straightened her spine, holding her chin up. "We sought allies for the war, but found no one willing to help us."

The mage snapped his fingers. "Search them. See what you can find."

Tharuks swarmed up Esina's sides. A tharuk with a scarred snout grappled with the healer's pouch on Leah's belt. She released it.

The beast ripped her pouch open with its claws and threw the contents into the snow. All her remedies, her weeks of training, the precious substances that could save lives. Tharuks stomped on them with their boots, smashing the vials of precious piaua. Staining the snow pale green, they ground the herbs with their strong boots, snorting and laughing.

"She won't need those healing supplies anymore," the mage said.

A chill ran down Leah's spine. He was going to kill them.

The mage slid off his dragon and stalked through the snow, kicking at the shattered vials and strewn leaves with his boots. "So little after traveling so far."

Taliesin's eyes slid over the bulging saddlebags to the waterskin fastened behind them.

The mage jerked his head at the waterskin. "Bring that to me."

The same scarred grunt tossed the waterskin to the mage.

He opened it and sniffed the contents. Then, laughing, he poured the precious piaua juice over the snow.

§

"*Why are you trembling?*" Esina asked.

"*Whips. Blood. Pain. Every time I see or smell tharuks, I remember. Then the shaking starts and I can't move for fear.*"

"*Use my strength, little one.*" Esina's love washed over Taliesin, calming his shaking hands.

He rested them on her spinal ridge. "*Thank you.*"

"*You're stronger than these monsters. You have freedom and strength of spirit, but they are slaves to a terrible master.*"

That had never occurred to Taliesin. These monsters obeyed Zens' every whim: murdering, slaughtering, and doing his bidding. But he was free to choose for himself. "*I guess that does make me stronger.*" Taliesin breathed deeply, willing his legs to be steady in the stirrups.

Suddenly, a vision appeared in his mind. He was riding Esina in battle, firing arrows as Esina slew dark dragons with fire. Was it a vision? Or merely a dream of something that would never be? He frowned. It felt like a vision.

"*Even in the face of all adversity, anything is possible. You told Leah to have hope, now take some hope yourself, and nurture it.*"

As Taliesin's dragon's strength coursed through him, his hands grew steady on her spinal ridge, and he sat high upon her back, looking down upon the mass of snarling tharuks.

§

"You're pathetic," the mage said, his eyes sweeping scathingly over Leah, Taliesin, and Esina. He scoffed, "The last poor desperate red dragon with two riders barely older than littlings." He laughed. "Let's see how far you get with a one-winged dragon." A fireball flew from his fingers straight for Esina.

The red dragon ducked, but the edge of her wing caught, dancing with flame. Her shrieks bounced off the mountainsides. The scent of charred wing itched Leah's nostrils. Esina bashed her wing against the snow to quench the flames, but the damage was done—her wing was tattered.

Her eyes narrowed, and she growled. Tharuks jumped back from her thrashing tail.

Leah's hand drifted toward the dagger at her belt.

"Archers, aim," the arrogant mage called. His head swung to Leah, snarling, "Hand off your knife or I'll put a hole in her other wing and then another straight through her head."

Leah held her hands in the air.

"You useless lot won't get far on foot." The mage clapped his hands.

All the shadow dragons took to the sky en masse. They snatched up the tharuks in their talons and flew off toward Dragons' Hold.

Taliesin flung his arms around his whimpering dragon's neck. "Esina!"

Leah strode to the green-stained snow. "Esina, come over. We'll see if this works."

The red dragon dragged herself over and sank to her haunches near Leah.

"Taliesin, help me. Smear the green snow over her burnt wing. Hopefully the cold will help numb the pain and the residue of the juice may help heal her."

"I'm glad they didn't ransack our saddlebags." Taliesin dismounted. "What about the piaua vials you hid under your clothes?"

Leah nodded. "It would take every last drop to heal her, and we'd have nothing left for our people. But a whole waterskin full of piaua was poured onto this snow."

Esina gingerly lowered her injured wing to the stained snow. They shoveled armfuls over the burned tip. The dragon shuddered, whimpers escaping her jaws.

"Careful, we don't want her to get snow burn too." Leah strode over to retrieve the discarded waterskin. She sniffed it. The skin still smelled of piaua. "Esina, shake the snow off your wing."

As Taliesin and the dragon shook the snow free, Leah slit the skin along the seams with her dagger. The inside gleamed with green juice. She rubbed it over the tattered raw edges of Esina's wing, not knowing whether it would be enough to heal her.

STRANGLETONS

Dawn peeked over the edge of the forest above Mage Gate, and still the battle raged. Maazini twisted to duck flame and a methimium-tipped arrow. Tomaaz fired an arrow into a flurry of dark dragons. He nocked and fired again. A roar broke out and a beast plummeted toward the forest. Maazini wheeled back, avoiding the gust of flame that shot up from the black dragon's fanged maw. The mage upon its back thrust green flames at Maazini's tail. He swerved, blasting fire at a shadow dragon's belly above him.

Glad for his opaline headband, Tomaaz reached into his quiver. He only had a handful of arrows left.

Breaking out of the horde, a shadow dragon flew at Maazini and Tomaaz. By the flaming dragon's tail, the mage on its back was the spitting image of Jael's sweetheart, Sovita.

No, Sovita was dead on the forest floor. This was a fake mage, made from the fingers, skin and hair that old Bill had stolen from her. Gods, there was no end to Zens' depravity—he was bringing the dead back to life.

Tomaaz recoiled, clutching his bow tighter, and fired a shot at the mage's head, making sure he didn't miss.

§

A dark dragon streaked through the sky, green mage flame rippling along its broken wings. Its bellows rang in Fenni's head. Gods, his headband had slipped. Riona banked. Fenni clutched Kierion's waist. With his other arm, he sent a volley of flame at another dark dragon. As Riona straightened, he tightened his headband.

A blue guard flew alongside them, and a whistle rang out. Fenni started. Jael was riding behind the blue guard. His teeth flashing in his tanned face, Jael grinned and pointed earthward.

Fenni leaned out, craning his neck to see what Jael was gesturing at.

Dark shapes were marching through the forest, approaching Mage Gate. Tharuks—hundreds of them. There was another whistle. Fenni snapped his head up. Jael was pointing behind them at a ribbon of murky green winding through the forest. A river. With a jolt, Fenni recognized it. He'd trained here with Jael and nearly been killed by a strangleton.

Yet another whistle. This time Jael, still grinning, motioned frantically with his hands.

Fenni gave an answering nod and tapped Kierion on the shoulder.

"Kierion, can Riona drop me down by that river?" He pointed.

Kierion leaned out and glanced down. "No, that's crazy. Hundreds of tharuks will be upon you within moments. What can one mage do against so many?"

"Believe me, I know what I'm doing." A thrill ran through Fenni's veins as he gauged how far the tharuks were from the river. "Just give me a moment. The timing has to be right."

The blue guard shot away, veering around the tharuks to land behind them. Fenni waited until Jael had dismounted. Soon, a raging wall of mage fire sprang up behind the monsters, driving them through the dense forest along a narrow trail leading straight to the river. "Tell Riona I'm ready," Fenni called.

Kierion released an arrow, hitting a shadow dragon's temple, then leaned forward to yell the message to Riona.

Riona descended into the forest.

Hopefully, Fenni could time this right… They sank through the tree line, spiraling down to a clearing on the far side of the river from the terrified snarling tharuks, who were now racing with a wall of green flame at their backs.

"What's the best thing Riona and I could do?"

"Remain hidden until the tharuks are nearly upon me, and then flame them from the air."

"But how are you going to stop them single-handedly?" Kierion asked.

Fenni leaned in and told him his plan.

§

Tharuk 1967 had been traversing the forest for days, sending its troop through the trees in small groups so no one could detect them. Last night, they'd reassembled. Now they were marching to Mage Gate. Commander Zens would be happy with such obedience. Perhaps the kind commander would give him a reward—if 1967 was lucky, perhaps even some dream time.

"Fire coming," a tracker snarled, twitching its nostrils in the air. Snarls broke out behind it, then roars of fear.

1967 turned to see a wall of crackling green flame. Behind him, tharuks pushed and shoved. Some fell. The green fire rushed for them. 1967 spurted forward. "Run," it bellowed, goading its troops on.

The stench of burning fur and cooked meat filled the air. 1967 coughed on the smoke from the bodies of its burning grunts. The flame raced on. Tharuks screamed, pushing and shoving to get past one another. Whips cracked amid the horde, the overseers' attempts to move the troop faster.

1967 had seen fire like this before. It had sprouted from the fingers of cloaked beings on dragonback, scorching the mountainsides in Death Valley and massacring many tharuks. Zens had not been happy—he'd ordered all the mages in Spanglewood Forest to be killed. And many more throughout Dragons' Realm.

That's what those cloaked beings were called: mages. There must be one behind this firewall.

1967 gestured 835 over. As they ran, 1967 said, "Take five grunts. Go around flames to behind fire. Mage sprouts flames from fingers. Chop off its hands. Bring me its head."

835 grunted and, taking five other tharuks, sprinted off into the trees.

1967 glanced back. It panted, hot air surging into its lungs. The fire crackled and licked, now a towering inferno. Over the screams of its dying grunts, 1967 heard a welcome sound: a river was thundering nearby. 1967 bared its fangs in a grin. That mage had no idea that they could find refuge in the river.

"Come," 1967 bellowed, urging its troop onward. "To the water."

§

Marlies knelt next to yet another rider lying on a blanket on the forest floor and threaded her needle with squirrel gut twine. At least the light was better now that morning had come, even if the conditions weren't. Injured men and women were crammed two or three to a blanket, tucked under the trees. She'd tried to spread cloaks beneath them too, to keep out the damp, but many injured would end up dying from chills.

Piaua. She swallowed. There was little hope that Leah and Taliesin had survived, but she nurtured her hope—feeding the spark and refusing to let it die out. The future was too grim without it.

It was no coincidence that Commander Zens had captured Master Giddi, then driven them all to Mage Gate—where Giddi had sealed the world gate. By why? Was Zens bringing new monsters through the gate to conquer Dragons' Realm? Or did he have some other sinister plan in mind?

Marlies focused on the rider's gashed arm. "We'll have you sewn up in no time," she said cheerfully.

Archers ringed them, keeping tharuks at bay. Hopefully they'd hold them back for a while. But Marlies didn't fool herself. They couldn't go on like this for long.

Above the moans of the wounded, a bellow rang out. A short distance away, something smashed through the canopy and crashed to the forest floor. The stench of burning scales and dragon flesh wafted through the trees. Marlies' heart clenched. Shards, not another dying dragon. It gutted her not being able to get to those who'd been injured in midair and were now dying in the forest.

Marlies tied off the stitches. "Make sure you get adequate rest before using your arm again."

The rider blustered, already getting to his feet. He swayed.

Marlies placed her hand on his shoulder. "You're no use to us or yourself, dead. Rest for a few hours before going back into battle."

He nodded and sank onto his knees.

Marlies quickly moved to her next patient. Dark blood rained down, splattering the leaves above. She glanced up. A dark dragon ensconced in mage flame screeched through the air and crashed into the forest.

She cleansed a wound on the rider's shoulder and stitched and bandaged it as fast as she could.

Adelina swooped down on Linaia and landed in the clearing behind Marlies. She slid off her dragon and came over. "With Leah gone, I thought you could use a little help." Adelina's usually cheerful demeanor was gone. Her face was haggard and her eyes were shadowed with weariness.

Marlies gestured to the young boy she'd rescued from the infirmary. "Kion is new to this. I've asked him to establish which riders have the worst wounds. Perhaps you could give him a hand for a while, but first, grab an apple from that sack." She gestured toward their meager supplies. There would never be enough to feed everyone. They were all running on empty stomachs and no sleep.

While crunching on her apple, Adelina scanned the patients and showed the boy how to sponge a wound and dress it.

There was the thud of dragons landing. Archers dragged two more injured riders over.

Marlies waved them to the nearest cloak spread on the ground, scanning the horrendous burns on one man's leg and the gash across the other's back.

She gave the burnt rider a bright smile—one she didn't feel. "Please, have one of our wonderful beds."

The rider, a young man with dark tousled hair and stormy blue eyes, gave a grim bark, "What's the going rate? Two golden dragon heads?" His eyes rolled back in his head and he collapsed in the archer's arms.

"Quick. Lie him down." She snatched up a waterskin and sloshed water over the man's leg, then handed the skin to the archer. "Is there any way you could refill this and the other one over there? We're out–and we'll have more burned riders here soon."

"There's a fire raging by the river. I'll sneak upstream." The man nodded grimly and, taking the skins, departed.

She examined the rider with the gash on his back—another clean slice from a shadow dragon's eyes.

Hands bathed in blood, heart and bones wearier than a dragon who'd just lost her mate, Marlies staggered from patient to patient, trying to lift their spirits and heal their broken bodies. By the cursed dragon gods, her patients were laid out like dead fish to dry. Only there was no drying here, just the constant drip of blood and the moaning of the wounded.

§

Fenni made it to the river before the tharuks. The heat wave from the oncoming fire rushed at him from across the water, making his skin prickle with heat. He used his mage flame to clear a section of the river from strangletons—the plants that choked waterways, devouring any who entered the river—searing through the plants to kill them. After selecting a long hollow reed, he positioned himself underwater among some harmless plants and waited, breathing deeply and slowly through the reed.

It wasn't long before thundering feet neared the riverbank.

Even underwater, the tharuks' snarls reached him. The reflected light from Jael's green mage fire glimmered on the surface of the water. When shadowy figures appeared at the edge of the forest, Fenni sucked in *sathir* from the river plants and surrounding trees. Concentrating his magic, he pushed flames through his fingertips.

He teased the flames into fireballs and waited until the shadows loomed. If only he could see better. Power singing through his veins, he shot his fireballs through the water, aiming for the middle of the dark horde chased by flickering green mage flame.

Screams rang out. Figures faltered, engulfed in flames. His fireballs tore holes in the tharuks. One splashed into the water, thrashing.

Fenni scrabbled away, bubbles escaping his lips. Thank the Egg, he'd hung onto the reed. He jammed it between his lips again. The tharuk floated face-down past him, its long tusks nearly grazing his reed. There was a gaping burned hole in its middle, leaving black bloody trails in the water.

Fenni sucked air through the reed, trying to ease the tightness in his chest. Roars rang out above him. He lobbed more fireballs into the mass of tharuks. These beasts were destroying his home, killing loved ones. They deserved to die.

Thank the First Egg Master Giddi had insisted Jael teach him to master underwater fireballs. As he shot more flaming balls of molten fire from the river into the swarm of Zens' monsters, two questions chewed at his mind.

How long could he keep this up?

And where in the Egg's name did Zens have Master Giddi?

§

The fire crackled behind 1967. The tharuk ran on. The narrow trail widened as the troop came to the riverbank. Tharuks thundered toward the river, snapping saplings and trampling bushes in their eagerness to get to the water.

When they were a few body lengths from the water, a ball of molten green flame shot out of the river. 1967 ducked. There was a scream behind him. 1967 spun. The fireball ripped a gaping hole in 795's chest and went straight through the grunt, hitting another tharuk in the thigh and ripping off its leg in a spray of blood.

1967 crouched by the riverside, sheltering behind a dead underling. Grunts leaped over him straight for the water—only to be blasted by flame and flop dead into the river.

Behind them, the green blaze grew ever closer, tongues licking out and eating into his troop. The stench of burned flesh and fur cloyed in 1967's nostrils, ramming itself up his snout, making it hard to breathe. Muffled screams and groans of dying tharuks rang amid the crackling fire.

1967 had to get across the river. It could swim well enough—if only there weren't molten balls of flame in its way. It narrowed its eyes, scanning the riverbank. The fireballs were only coming from one section of the river.

1967 waved its arm, gesturing to its grunts. "Follow me."

The troop leader stomped over the bushes in its haste to get to the deep water and, taking a deep breath, dived into the river. 1967 would've laughed if it wasn't underwater. Those mages thought they'd had the troop trapped with fire behind them and fireballs shooting from the river. 1967 poked its head above the water to grab a breath. Halfway across the river now, not long to go.

Something thick wrapped around 1967's thigh and yanked, nearly pulling its hip from the socket. Another tendril wrapped itself around 1967's chest. The troop leader tried to slash the plant with its claws. To 1967's horror, the spongy plant tightened its grasp, squeezing 1967's lungs. Breath escaped 1967's snout, bubbles trailing to the surface as more tendrils wrapped around 1967's arms.

The tharuk troop leader opened its snout in a silent waterlogged scream as the strangleton reeled the tharuk down to the bottom of the river to ingest its next meal.

$

The hours dragged by as Marlies tried to heal wounded rider after wounded rider. Her arms and legs grew heavy, and her heart too. Without piaua, their plight was hopeless. Her breezy smile faded as the battle wore on, turning into grim determination. Riders who had died had their bodies laid to one side in the forest. Before nightfall, more would succumb to their wounds, their spirits leaving the battlefield to fly with departed dragons.

Adelina had long since taken to the sky to fight shadow dragons. Now only the boy, herself, and a couple of patched-up riders were helping with the flood of wounded. Marlies felt a woman's forehead. "More feverweed tea," she barked at Kion, who looked so exhausted he'd soon drop. It'd only been yesterday that he'd been a patient himself. They didn't even know if his family had made it out of the hold alive. She softened her voice. "You're doing well. Keep it up."

Marlies crouched next to an unconscious man and took his pulse. Still weak and thready. She tugged his cloak tighter around him. They'd run out of blankets hours ago. Thankfully some riders had had the foresight to stuff a few in their saddlebags before fleeing.

"Incoming, bleeding badly." An archer staggered between the trees, carrying an unconscious young woman. Her arm was ripped at the elbow, blood and bone gleaming wetly.

In the infirmary with bone knit, slippery elm powder and piaua, Marlies could've saved her, but here on this dirty grim battlefield, the woman didn't stand much chance. But she had to try. "Bring her here." Marlies gestured to a patch of ground closest to her supplies, eying the wound as the man lowered the woman to the ground.

"It's my daughter," he gasped, tears pooling in his eyes.

"Good, then you can spare your belt."

While the man removed his belt, Marlies grabbed swathes of bandages. On second thoughts, she put some back for other patients. "Can you spare a few strips from your shirt?"

He passed her the belt and drew his knife.

Tearing fabric ricocheted in Marlies' ears. "Keep an eye on her breathing." She fastened his belt around the girl's upper arm, thrust a stick through a loop and twisted it. The tourniquet should cut off the blood supply and stop the girl from bleeding out.

"She'll lose her arm, won't she?" the archer asked, hands shaking as he passed Marlies strips of his shirt.

She nodded. "Better than losing her life," she said softly. "See if you can staunch the blood with those strips." Infection was a risk, but the girl wouldn't have the arm for long and they'd need the clean bandage when they severed her arm and cauterized it.

An hour later, Marlies tied off the bandage and rose, stretching her aching back. She blew air out of her nose, trying to clear the smell of the cauterized flesh. At least the girl now had a chance.

"Stay here and watch her," she said to the father who was openly weeping now, his daughter's good hand in his bloody fingers.

A small cloaked figure broke through the trees, a slim boy following her. "Marlies," she called.

Marlies rubbed her eyes. For a moment she'd thought it was Leah. Impossible. Leah was probably dead with the red dragons. Shards, she was tired.

"Marlies."

Gods, the girl even sounded like Leah.

"One moment, please," Marlies called, turning away to wipe her hands clean on a damp rag. She had to get a grip on herself. She picked up a waterskin and sloshed water onto her hands, asking over her shoulder, "What is it?"

"Marlies, I've brought piaua juice."

She spun, staring at the girl. Smoke-smudged, with a smile on her face, *it was Leah*. Taliesin, too.

Marlies rushed over to hug her protégé, squeezing her tight. "When I heard the red guards had died, I thought you had too. By the dragon's tail, it's good to see you." Her heart surged. Now, here was some good news.

Leah gave a grim laugh. "We nearly did die, more than once, but now we're here and have piaua with us. Only a little, though."

Taliesin grinned at Marlies. "I told you we'd do it."

Something had changed about the boy. He stood straighter, was more confident. Marlies grabbed him by the shoulders and embraced him. "So you did. Thank the mighty dragon gods."

§

Tonio stumbled into the clearing, a wounded young blue guard in his arms. "Please, Marlies, help this boy."

Blood dripped from a gash in the lad's throat. Her eyes met Tonio's dark ones, grave. She swallowed. "I'll do my best."

"You always do." Tonio laid the boy on a blanket beside her.

Marlies quickly cleansed the wound and stitched it together clumsily, her fingers weary. She was tired, so tired. Would these battles never end? She steeled her shoulders. Not until Zens was purged from the realm and his evil monsters were dead.

Ignoring rustling in the nearby bushes, Marlies tied off the last stitch in the lad's throat and dribbled a few drops of piaua over the wound.

"Look out, Marlies!" Tonio yelled.

She spun. An arrow was heading for her.

Tonio lunged, slamming her to the ground. Marlies stared in horror as the arrow pierced Tonio's breast. He slumped to the earth, the arrow protruding from his chest, its shaft slick with limplock.

"We're under attack!" an archer yelled, shooting the beast that had just hit Tonio. More archers raced into the brush, checking for further tharuks.

"Marlies, I'm dying." Tonio clutched his breast. "You helped me understand him. Thank you. Tell Roberto I apologize for banishing him to the Wastelands."

Marlies sank to the ground, cradling Tonio's head in her lap, stroking his hair. "It was nothing, Tonio."

"He's a better man than Amato. Anakisha's and Lucia's blood run strong in his veins." Tonio's eyelids fluttered.

"Yes, my friend." She stroked his hair. He smiled as his eyes drifted shut.

After all the years of bitterness, Tonio finally understood. But it was too late. Nothing could restore his beloved Rosita or his former friendship with Amato. He'd wasted much of his life in anger and resentment. Marlies' tears fell on Tonio's eyelids. She squeezed his hand, her chest cracking in two. "Please,

Tonio, please hold on." She opened a vial of piaua and dribbled juice into his wound, but the red stain spread across his chest until it drenched his jerkin. His head slumped.

For a long moment. Marlies sat, the battle raging above her and the wounded moaning. Roars rang in the distance. Fireballs shot above the trees.

A roar of grief rang through the forest as Antonika, Tonio's ruby dragon, shot overhead. She circled the trees, calling for him, her plaintive cry tugging at Marlies' heartstrings. Her wail was answered by blue guards as she shot into battle to avenge her rider.

Marlies recalled Tonio telling her how he'd stolen Antonika's egg from a Naobian street gang when he was young.

Tonio's time was up. He'd saved her. She had to make it count. And although she'd worked for years among the wounded and injured, it hadn't always been like that. In her early days at Dragons' Hold, she'd fought tharuks along with the rest of them. She'd had her fair share of kills.

Her next kill would be to avenge Tonio—her friend and former dragon corps master.

Marlies kissed Tonio's forehead and laid him on the earth, folding his arms over his chest, his feet facing Naobia, his origin.

She rose and stepped around patients, pacing to Leah and Taliesin, who were doing an admirable job of tending the wounded. Taking off her healer's pouch, she fastened it around Leah's waist.

"Go and fight, Marlies." Leah kissed her cheek. "I'll see you soon." Her smile did not touch her eyes. "Thank you for everything you've taught me."

Taliesin hugged her.

Marlies ripped off her opaline headband. She had always fought while mind-melded with Hans and their dragons. Today would be no different. As the anguished screams of the dark dragons tore through her mind, she met them with a ferocity she hadn't felt in years. As if the screams were her own. Screams for her friend who'd died. The screams of a nation overrun with monsters. Screams for a sweet dragonet she'd accidentally killed years ago. For every rider or dragon she'd laid to rest.

Marlies opened her mind to her dragon. *Liesar, I'm ready to fight.*

In a flash of silver, her dragon dived between the trees and landed, her talons tearing up earth and spraying slush. Marlies swung into the saddle, grabbed her bow, nocked an arrow, and they ascended into the broiling swarm of dark dragons.

A flash of silver shot past Handel into the sky. Hans' heart soared. Years ago, he and Marlies had fought together—it was only fitting that they do so again today. He ripped off his headband so he could speak with Handel, but his dragon was already on Liesar's tail, riding the way they had all those years ago in Anakisha's final battle.

Marlies loosed an arrow into a shadow dragon's ragged wing, shredding it. Hans fired at the mage upon its back. Liesar flamed the beast while Handel blasted any dragon that tried to come near.

Liesar wheeled and shot through the dark cloud of dragons like a silver arrow.

Far off in the distance, Hans saw a flash of orange—Maazini carrying Tomaaz. A streak of rainbow cut through the black dragons, Ezaara's blonde hair flying in the breeze as she loosed an arrow.

When they'd fled Dragons' Hold all those years ago, Hans had never dared hope to one day fight in battle with the twins at their side. Here he was, protecting the realm with his entire family. With a jolt, he realized the prophecy he'd seen of himself in battle with Ezaara as he'd left Death Valley months ago, limplocked and dying, had come true.

He prayed to the dragon gods that they'd all live to see another day.

§

Dragons roared and screeched, talons out, as they flew toward Erob, aiming for his wings. Roberto aimed an arrow, but the beast swerved and a volley of flame gusted from its maw, narrowly missing Erob's tail.

Erob flapped his wings, shooting higher. The yellow beams from another shadow dragon's eyes swept toward his foreleg.

A bellow of pain ricocheted through Erob's body. Another shadow dragon dived at Erob. Roberto gulped. He was surrounded. Gods, this was it. If only he didn't have the opaline headband on, he could mind-meld with Ezaara and tell her how much he loved her one last time.

A volley of flame shot from overhead, catching on the shadow dragon's wings. Flames licked along its wing struts. Soon the beast was engulfed in fire. Another volley of flame shot from the air, engulfing another shadow dragon above him. The beast plummeted to the ground in a trail of smoke. A third volley shot at yet another shadow dragon. In a flash of color, Zaarusha was upon its back, shredding its wings with her talons and beating its body with her tail. The beast dropped.

Erob and Zaarusha shot skyward, free of shadow dragons—but not for long.

"Are you all right?" Ezaara called.

"Yes, but I think Erob's hurt," Roberto bellowed back. "Can you take a look?"

Zaarusha dived below Erob. Ezaara craned her neck up, scanning his underbelly. They shot back up beside Roberto. "He has a gash on one of the toes on his right foreleg. I don't think it's too bad," she yelled.

"Look out," Roberto cried. "Behind you." He nocked his bow and fired as Zaarusha wheeled and shot off to fight more shadow dragons.

Chaos Reigns

A shrill whistle cut through the water. About time. Fenni's lungs were strained. His last few fireballs had sputtered and fizzed out before they'd even made it as far as the riverbank.

He burst from the water, hands at the ready.

A floating tharuk corpse bumped him. He shoved it away. The river was choked with dead and dying tharuks. Fenni had to swim through them, pushing their bodies out of the way to get to the shore.

They'd done it.

Jael leaned down, panting hard, and gave him a hand out of the water. Fenni's feet churned on the muddy bank, which bore deep gouges from hundreds of tharuks. They stood there, puffing for a moment.

Fenni shook his head, gazing at the hordes of tharuks burnt and charred behind them in the forest. At the bodies being swept downriver and clogging the riverbanks. "At least the strangletons have enough to feed on."

Master Jael clapped him on the back. "They certainly do. Well done."

"I would never have been able to do it without you making me freeze my backside off during the mage trials." He shook his head again. "We did it. We really did it." Something loosened in his chest and he bent over, holding his hands on his knees to get his breath.

Jael embraced him, using his magic to dry Fenni's garments.

"Thanks, that's much better," Fenni muttered.

Jael tilted his head back, frowning. "By flaming *sathir*, what in the Egg is that?"

Fenni didn't want to know. He was spent. Wearily, he turned and gasped. No. A beam of yellow light shone above the forest, cutting into the dark mass of dragons above. "Oh, no."

Jael shook his shoulder. "What is it?" he asked urgently.

"A methimium ray. Those yellow crystals Zens has can keep the realm gates open," he groaned.

Jael frowned. "Do you think he's gone to Death Valley to fetch more dark dragons?"

"No, he couldn't have." Fenni took a deep breath. "I destroyed them all."

"You?" spluttered Jael, eyebrows shooting up.

Fenni nodded. "Yes, me."

"So Ezaara's right. If we can kill these ones, the battle might be over." Jael bit his lip. "They age quickly and die, so they don't live long. All we need to do is wipe them out."

"Either way, we'd better help."

They raced along the trail toward Mage Gate.

When they got there, they hung back in the trees. Master Giddi was standing in the clearing where they'd held the mage trials.

"At last, he's here." Fenni tensed his muscles, about to run and greet Master Giddi.

But Jael restrained him. "Something's wrong. Look."

Commander Zens was standing behind Giddi, speaking to him, his luminous yellow eyes fixed on the dragon mage's face.

"That man is plain creepy." Fenni shuddered.

"We can't risk hurting Master Giddi."

A figure ran into the clearing from the other side, long white beard flowing and cloak billowing out behind him. Master Starrus! He thrust up his hands, about to unleash his magic.

Starrus yelled, "Kill Master Giddi. He's under Zens' influence." He raised his hands, shooting a volley of flame at Master Giddi.

Master Giddi didn't react. He simply stood there, gazing up at the yellow beam streaming from a small metal contraption in the middle of the clearing.

Instinctively, Fenni flung up his hands to counter Master Starrus' flame. An arc of fire leaped from his hands toward Starrus.

Before Starrus' flame hit the mage, Zens spun, staring at Starrus. Master Starrus dropped to the ground twitching, then went still.

"He's dead," Jael whispered.

Fenni's flame hissed over Starrus' dead body into the trees. Master Giddi, oblivious, stared along the shaft of the yellow beam piercing the sky.

For a moment, the forest seemed to pause and everything went silent. Even the distant roars of the dark dragons were muted.

Fenni swallowed. If it hadn't been for Zens, he would've killed Master Starrus.

Zens turned, slowly scanning the forest.

"Quick, flee." Jael dragged Fenni deeper into the trees.

They ran, then stopped to catch their breath.

"The question is," Jael said, "whether Master Giddi is working for us, or Zens?"

"Zens, from the look of it," Fenni said. "I just couldn't bring myself to let him die."

Jael laid a hand on his shoulder. "Don't fret. I was close to blasting Starrus too, but you got there first. There's no wizard blood on your hands. Master Starrus' death was clearly Zens' doing."

Only by a hair's breadth. He'd aimed to kill. Fenni shuddered. He still felt like a murderer.

Snarls broke out in the forest behind them.

§

An enormous dark dragon flapped in front of Maazini, blocking Tomaaz's view. Its rider was older—which was unusual—and not a mage—which was even stranger. The man loosed an arrow, its head gleaming yellow in the sun.

It was one of those methimium arrowheads, the burrowing, cursed things. Maazini shuddered. *"I never want another one of those."*

"Neither do I." The hate Tomaaz had felt from his dragon had been so real. Maazini would've killed him if he'd gotten too close.

The arrow hit Antonika, Tonio's dragon, on the flank and burrowed into her flesh. The man shot another, which entered her shoulder. Antonika was riderless, but Tomaaz had no time to wonder where Tonio was as Antonika snarled and chased a blue guard.

Maazini tailed the dark dragon. Tomaaz whipped out an arrow as the man loosed an arrow that hit a yellow dragon in the neck. The man laughed as the beast started bucking and trying to dismount her rider. The dark dragon spun toward Maazini.

Tomaaz's dragon dived and the enemy's arrow went wide. The man nocked another arrow and laughed again—a familiar laugh that sent a chill down Tomaaz's spine. He'd heard that voice before. A memory sprang to mind: Old Bill jumping on Lovina's arm in Lush Valley to break it.

By the First Egg, no! Old Bill was on dragonback, turning dragons against their riders and kin. Tomaaz leaned low, urging Maazini to go faster. His orange dragon sped forward, tailing Bill's obsidian dragon. Tomaaz fired, but his arrow bounced off the dark dragon's spinal ridge, missing Bill and falling harmlessly to the forest below. He bit his lip. He had less than a handful of arrows left. Every shot had to count.

With a roar, Danion's blue dragon, Onion, burst between them, spitting flame at Bill's shadow dragon.

As quick as a whip, Bill fired a methimium-tipped arrow into Onion's hide. And then another.

Tomaaz loosed an arrow that lodged in Bill's back and knocked him forward as Bill's third arrow plunged into Onion's hide.

Old Bill turned. "You!" His face warped with anger. "You stole my slave."

Tomaaz shot another arrow straight through Bill's throat. Zens' spy, the man who had beaten and tortured Lovina, fell from his dragon, crashing into another and another before hitting the trees below.

A green dragon swooped—Ajeurina. "Thank you," Lovina hollered.

A dark dragon lunged for Ajeurina. "Look out!" Tomaaz yelled.

Ajeurina turned and spurted flame at the beast.

Danion's blue was entwined, talon to belly, with another blue guard, their jaws around each other's throats. As they bucked and twisted, Danion fell from his saddle.

"Maazini, save Danion!" Tomaaz shrieked.

They dived, but too late.

A shadow dragon blasted Danion's body with fire. Danion lit up like a funeral pyre, plunging to the forest.

His dragon twisted and clawed the other blue guard, leaving bloody gouges.

His chest cracking, and tears blurring his vision, Tomaaz shot an arrow into Onion's head, and then another and another, until his quiver was empty and the dragon fell limply into the trees.

§

Zens' excitement was barely contained, images spilling through his head with wild abandon as he neared his goal. Remaining in Zens' mind as a silent witness, Giddi sifted through those images, his gut roiling at Zens' intentions. The commander did not want to go through the world gate to create more tharuks. No, he could do that here. He had more devastating plans than that.

Beings made of metal with sweeping methimium gazes stalked Zens mind. They bore weapons, not bows, spears or swords, but long metal tubes with flashing lights and fire spouting from their ends. Hot yellow fire that destroyed everything in its path. These metal men moved with surprising fluidity, sweeping their weapons across masses of people, who fell to the ground, screaming, in flames. Dragons fell from the sky, felled by tharuks mounted on dark dragons.

Using the same metal weapons, Zens' monsters shot yellow streams of flame farther than any dragon could breathe fire, destroying every dragon in their path. Ash coated the trees in Great Spanglewood Forest. The snow melted from Dragon's Teeth, leaving Dragons' Hold a barren wasteland. Rivers were clogged with strangletons, their tendrils waving above the water and snaring any wildlife that came near. Lakes turned into stinking swamps.

And then Giddi saw Zens sitting supreme upon a large dark dragon, weapons belted at his hips, leading thousands of tharuks back through the world gate to conquer his own world.

He saw himself at Zens' side, flying through the world gate on a shadow dragon. A strange world greeted him, with tall structures that twinkled like hundreds of stars. As far as his eyes could see, these structures spread across the surface of Zens' world, their tiny lights glittering like diamonds. They dived lower and Giddi saw streets teeming with people in strange garb. Zens signaled him. The commander shot his weapons, making those people writhe in pain while Giddi burned them alive with his mage fire.

The shadows called him, *"See, we can rule both worlds. And more. Imagine all the worlds we can conquer."*

The magic inside Giddi built, thrumming through him. It swirled around each of the methimium arrowheads, making them vibrate within his flesh.

Zens smiled at him. "See what we have in store for both of our worlds? We can rebuild these worlds, purge them of weaklings, and make new beings, strong, capable, and ready to obey. Together, we have the power to create worlds of order."

Giddi smiled back, showing his teeth. "I do see, my honored Commander." He bowed his head, thumping his fist over his heart. Under his fingers the teardrop vibrated.

"Good. Wait here for your instructions."

The commander needed him. Zens couldn't open a world gate without a mage as powerful as him. But what Commander Zens didn't know was that Giddi had never opened a world gate on his own. No, for that, he needed Mazyka. He had closed a world gate on his own, but it was only their power combined that had opened it before. Could he do it alone? Or would Zens kill him for failing?

He remained, with his fist over his heart, awaiting Commander Zens' instructions.

§

Taliesin ferried supplies, cleansed wounds, and bandaged injured limbs. They saved piaua juice for the worst injuries, but even then he knew they'd soon run out. More wounded riders were flooding the clearing—and injured dragons were landing too. He glanced up at the trees, seeing the glimmer of spangles on their branches—tiny sparks, flickers of hope in the forest.

Master Giddi had once told him that, although many had forgotten, Great Spanglewood Forest had been named after the spangles and their power. But how could they help in this raging battle?

Snarls shattered Taliesin's thoughts.

Above him, a red dragon and green dragon fought with a blue, making Taliesin's flesh crawl. Those yellow-tipped arrows had turned both dragon and rider, pitting allies against one another.

A vision opened in his mind: all the dragons in Dragons' Realm fighting each other. Dead corpses lay heaped upon the land. The hillsides were desolate. Great Spanglewood Forest was reduced to stumps and smoking ash. If Zens had his way, the entire realm would look like Death Valley, barren and stinking. All these beautiful forests would be gone, and the riders and dragons with them.

Taliesin couldn't let that happen. He had to stop Zens' monsters. But how?

He stretched his mind, letting the glimmer of the spangles wash through it. He shared his vision with the tiny pinpoints of light that danced among the trees.

"We will help you," they whispered.

But what could they do other than give him hope? A hope that would be crushed just as Zens' forces were crushing Dragons' Realm.

§

Adelina was sneaking through the forest, with Amato at her side, retrieving arrows for their riders' empty quivers. Quite how her father had managed to be the one to help her, she didn't know. But here he was, dogging her footsteps and making ingratiating comments. Not that it helped. He'd beaten her too often for her to forgive him now—with or without methimium having caused everything.

She pointed to some tharuk corpses bristling with arrows near the foot of a strongwood. "Why don't you retrieve those?"

Without waiting for an answer, Adelina stalked through the underbrush to retrieve an arrow from a pine. Stepping over a dead tharuk, she stretched up, yanked an arrow from the pine's trunk, and deposited it in her quiver. Then she bent and plucked an arrow from a snowdrift at the base of the tree. That'd been a wasted shot.

The tharuk had two arrows embedded in its corpse: one in its arm and another through its eye. Wrinkling her nose against the beast's stench, she plucked the arrow from its arm, then placed her foot against the monster's snout and her fingers around the second arrow shaft.

Nearby, a twig cracked. Adelina spun.

She snatched one of the bloody arrows, fumbling to nock it, but she was too slow. A numlock-covered arrow sped at her. Adelina ducked, and it thudded into the tree.

Four tharuks smashed their way through the underbrush, surrounding her and the pine.

Adelina's arrow grazed the first's ear. Her next arrow narrowly missed the second beast. She flung a knife at it, but it thudded off the monster's breastplate and landed in the dirt. The tharuk guffawed, grinding the knife into the dirt with its boot as it ran at her, claws out. Another arrow zipped past her.

Shards! Adelina scuttled around the pine, but another beast was there. It slashed its claws, ripping her cloak. She snatched her sword from its scabbard and swung, but the beast parried it with a kick.

Tharuks sprang around the pine. Suddenly, she was outnumbered, backed up against the tree with four salivating beasts staring at her with beady red eyes, sharp claws at the ready.

"No, not my daughter!" Amato charged the monsters. Swinging his sword, he smote a beast on the neck, and it fell to the earth, blood spurting out over the patchy snow. A wiry tharuk raked its claws along Amato's thin body. Blood welled from three gashes in Amato's side, but he spun, hacking at the tharuk's shoulder with his blade.

A tharuk ran at Adelina. She drove her sword into its belly. It grabbed the blade and stumbled backward, ripping the pommel from her grasp. The tharuk slumped to the ground, rasping.

Shoulder bleeding, the wiry tharuk pulled the sword out of the fallen tharuk's gut and ran at Amato.

Another beast charged Adelina, waving its snout and tusks. She instinctively snatched at her hip to grab her knife, but her belt was empty. Shards! She dived as the tharuk neared, rolled away, then scrambled to her feet.

The beast smashed into the tree, then roared, spinning to face her. Dark blood trickled from its snout over its wicked tusks. "I gut you." It roared again and lowered its head.

Adelina snatched her bow, whipped an arrow from her quiver, and loosed the arrow. It hit the tharuk's snout with a meaty squelch. She released another. The beast fell to the snowy forest floor, her arrow protruding from its eye.

Her father was tiring, still fending off the wiry tharuk. Adelina trained her arrow on the beast, but they were lunging and moving too fast. She had to find a better angle. She raced between the trees, coming up behind the tharuk.

The beast lunged and struck Amato on the chest with her sword as Adelina let her arrow fly. It hit the back of the tharuk's neck. The beast swung to face her. She fired another arrow. It pierced the side of the tharuk's throat. The beast slumped to its haunches in a spray of black blood.

Amato grunted and clutched his bloody chest. He staggered a step or two and crumpled to his knees.

A snort came from behind her. Adelina whirled.

Through the bushes, yet another pair of red eyes observed them. Adelina loosed her arrow, aiming right for the center of those eyes. There was a crash and the tharuk hit the ground.

Spinning, Adelina checked the area. All clear.

She ran over to Amato and sank to her knees, cradling his head on her lap. Her father had saved her life—the man who'd beaten her bloody when she was a littling and given her brother to Zens.

Blood bubbled from the corner of Amato's mouth. His lungs were punctured. There was nothing she could do, except comfort him.

But how could she comfort the man who'd ruined her littling years?

Maybe, with the truth. Adelina sniffed and cleared her throat. "You know, Father…" Even that was strange, calling him *father*. "I don't remember much of the man you were before Zens harmed you." Her veneer of cheerfulness and optimism cracked. The years of sorrow she'd stowed behind it trickled out.

Amato reached up to touch the tears on her cheek. She steeled herself not to flinch.

His fingers were gentle. "I know," he said, his eyes lined with silver tears. "I've regretted every moment."

One of her tears dropped onto his cheek. Glistening in the sun, it carved a clean path through the dirt and soot on his face.

She nodded. "But I can see the good in you now."

"Thank you," Amato murmured, bubbles foaming from the corner of his mouth. He coughed, blood splattering his shirt, then his eyes and body stilled.

Adelina sat for a moment.

Then she rose, leaving her father in the forest, determined to make Zens pay.

A Losing Battle

Roberto had been sweeping over the forest when he'd seen Adelina—and his father saving her. He called out to Adelina, but she didn't hear him and ran into the forest with her full quivers and bow. No doubt off to fight tharuks. The battle was still raging around them, but that was his father down there dead on the forest floor. Sympathy and old hurt and anger warred in his chest.

Without him even asking, Erob landed. Roberto peeled off his opaline headband, wincing at the dark dragons' screams.

"We should honor him," Erob said. *"For being the honorable green guard that he once was. And for saving your sister's life."*

Roberto slid off Erob's back and ran to Amato. Blood stained his chest. His dark eyes were unseeing, staring at the sky.

Had Amato still loved Lucia, Roberto's mother? Had his heart still yearned for her, even as he'd died? Remorse had haunted his father for years, without Roberto even knowing he was alive.

Roberto felt bad enough about what happened between him and Ezaara when he'd been controlled by methimium. How awful Amato's burden must've been—the blood of hundreds upon his hands, and destroying the very people he loved. Living alone for years in that underwater cavern, never seeing the people he loved. Knowing he'd ruined their lives.

Roberto bowed his head for a moment, closing his eyes. But for a few twists of fate, his life might have been the same.

Erob snuffled his back. *"At last, you understand."*

Roberto gazed into his dragon's golden eyes, fire lighting the sky as dark dragons wheeled above the forest. *"I do."*

He lifted Amato's body—so light. His father had been so frail, but still remarkably strong. Roberto climbed into Erob's saddle, Pa cradled against his chest.

Erob took to the sky, winging away from the dark dragons, rising higher and higher.

Roberto melded, *"I'm ready."* He slid Amato off Erob's back.

His father's limp body fell through the sky. Erob dived after Amato. Opening his maw, he set Amato's body alight, flaming him until he was only ashes on the breeze.

"Father, may your spirit fly with departed dragons." Roberto took a shuddering breath and released it. *Let's get back down to battle.*

Zaarusha was a speck of color amongst a horde of dark dragons below. Dragons were fighting each other, riders valiantly trying to stop them. Guilt shimmied through Roberto's belly, twisting in his gut. He'd allowed himself the luxury of grief, while his people were battling for their lives.

"You needed that time. Don't regret it." Erob roared and dived back down into the fray.

Roberto saw Ezaara fire an arrow at a mage. The mage countered with a volley of bright-green flame. Zaarusha swerved, ducking it.

But Zaarusha and Ezaara hadn't seen another mage behind them with his hands outstretched. Fire bloomed at the mage's fingertips.

Roberto screamed, "Ezaara, behind you!"

She turned.

Erob furled his wings, shooting like a spear through the sky. Roberto's stomach flew into his throat. Oh gods, he was going to be too late.

§

Something was moving down in the forest, cresting the hill south of Mage Gate. Hans slapped Handel's flank. "Down there." His dragon banked to the right, speeding over the trees to take a closer look. As Handel swooped over the trees, Hans kept his bow nocked, ready for anything.

A large figure bent back saplings, leading an army of men, women and youth. Bows ready, they crept through the underbrush.

Hans squeezed his knees into Handel's sides as Handel descended to take a closer look.

It was Giant John leading a team of warriors—probably from nearby settlements.

"Let's say hello," Hans called to Handel.

Handel landed on the rear side of the hill. Hans strode down through the trees. "Giant John," he called.

Giant John, brow beaded in sweat despite the cold, wrapped Hans in a bear hug. He waved a hand at the hundreds of foot warriors cascading through the forest behind him. "We received a messenger bird from Ezaara. These men, women, and littlings from Horseshoe Bend have come to help fight Zens. Master Mage Reina and Master Archer Jerrick are from Horseshoe Bend, so the settlers are fiercely loyal."

So many. Hans shook his head in wonder. Now it was his turn to hug Giant John. "Thank the Egg. We'll need every one of them," he said.

§

Leah gazed above the river, hardly able to believe her eyes. The sky was filled with gleaming brown scales. She hurried out from under the trees. With a flurry of wings, brown guards landed in the clearing near the healing post. Leah rushed over to Darynn as he dismounted.

Hoisting two large waterskins out of Rynnlak's saddlebag, Darynn pressed them into Leah's hands. "I know you left with enough piaua to last for months," he said, "but here, take these, just in case."

A lump rose in her throat and she tried to swallow. "Th-thank you. We barely have any left. Tharuks destroyed our supplies en route." She squeezed her eyes shut, trying to stop her tears. Tears for those who had already fallen, for the men, women, and dragons who had bled out at her hands.

Darynn hugged her, not heeding the piaua skins between them. "Leah, whatever you've done has been enough," he said. "As grim as it looks, if we all play our part, maybe we can win this battle." He pulled away, holding her out at arm's length. "You're a strong young woman, Leah. No matter what happens, I want you to remember that. I thank you for giving the brown guards this opportunity to fight." Then he was gone.

Darynn leaped onto his dragon and took to the sky with a battle cry.

The other brown dragons, many still thin and bony, shot behind him like arrows into battle.

But even as they rose into the sky, Zens' mages shot two with methimium-tipped arrows. They snarled, turning upon one another. A dark dragon swooped and grabbed a brown dragon's neck in its jaws. The snap was audible. The dragon crashed through the trees. The ground shook as it landed, killing a group of injured riders who were making their way toward the healing post. Rynnlak blasted fire at the shadow dragon and they rose higher in the sky, fighting.

A hollow opened in Leah's chest. She clutched the piaua skins tightly. Oh gods, so many people to save. So much bloodshed. Would it ever end?

§

Although they'd marched for days, Giant John fought with ferocity and vigor. Beheading tharuks and tossing their bodies aside, he waded through the horde, smashing, crunching, and slowly pushing back the dark tide of fetid stinking beasts.

Still more tharuks came at him, like a giant wave, cresting around him and his warriors. Cries rang out. Dark blood sprayed. Red blood, too, as men, women, and littlings fell, trampled by beasts. Others had their guts slashed by claws. More were felled with poisoned arrows. Still, John and his band of warriors fought. Mickel and Benno were at his side, the men's strength lending him courage as they fought together, smashing through the tharuk troops.

But still more came. And more.

Mickel slashed a tharuk's head from its body. Benno plunged his sword into a tharuk's chest and kicked the beast to the ground. Yanking his sword out of the furry body, he turned. "Our warriors are being crushed like eggshells, John. But we won't give up. Even if we're the last ones standing at your side."

Grim determination fueled Giant John as he drove farther, making inroads into the tharuk troop, snarls and cries echoing around him. The roars of dragons punctuated tharuk battle cries, and the tang of spilled blood was heavy in the air.

§

"*Giant John is here,*" Hans melded, his distant thoughts barely audible in Marlies' mind above the screaming of the dark dragons. But she would not put her headband back on. No, these beasts would not sunder the lifelong connection that she and Hans had shared with their dragons and each other.

She nocked her arrow and shot a fake mage in the throat. Liesar spun to avoid the slicing rays from its dragon's eyes. Liesar shot through the sky, a flash of silver lightning, spearing a dark dragon's belly with her flame.

The tiredness Marlies had been feeling for weeks dissipated as her blood sang in the thrall of battle. She reached for an arrow from her quiver. Only two left.

As a healer, she hated bloodshed, but this is what she'd been born to. Healing her friends, and killing their enemies. Fighting to protect Dragons' Realm.

From the corner of her eye, she caught a multi-hued flash amid a cloud of black, and turned.

Her daughter was surrounded by dark dragons. "*Liesar, to Ezaara's aid!*"

Liesar angled down, blasting two more dark dragons on the way.

One of Marlies' two remaining arrows took out a mage that had been aiming for Ezaara. The other, she embedded in the belly of a dark dragon. The beast fell, momentarily blocking her view of her daughter. Then the blood in Marlies' veins turned to ice.

A mage flung a plume of mage fire directly at Ezaara's back.

One moment, Marlies was screaming from Liesar's saddle. The next, she'd leaped and was flying through the air into the path of that mage's fire. *"Hans, I love you. Tell Tomaaz and Ezaara I love them too."*

§

A streak of silver shot through the sky. Ezaara turned, grasping for an arrow, but she was too late. Mage fire was roiling through the air toward her. A woman's body flew through the air, dark hair streaming.

Mage fire slammed into Ma's stomach. Catching, it roared over her body until she was a pillar of bright fire, whistling through the air.

"Ma! Ma!" Ezaara screamed. "Zaarusha! No, not Ma."

Zaarusha roared, diving after Marlies. Liesar dived too, the dragons nearly colliding in their quest to snatch Marlies' burning body.

It was too late. The towering pillar of green mage fire flared in the sky and then snuffed out, ashes swirling in the wind from the dragons' wingbeats.

Her mother was gone. The mother who'd given her life, who'd spent her own life in hiding in Lush Valley to protect them. The mother who'd forsaken her identity for the sake of her twins. The mother who'd loved her with fierceness. And healed others with unbounded compassion.

Ezaara's throat squeezed shut. She gasped for breath. Hooking her bow over Zaarusha's spinal ridge, she held her hands to her chest to ease the squeezing pain. She was going to break, fly into a thousand pieces if she didn't do something.

Letting out a mighty scream of rage, she cried, "This is for my mother." She snatched up her bow.

§

As Marlies' ashes rippled on the wind from her wingbeats, scattering over snarling dragons, Liesar threw back her head and howled. Her mourning cry shattered through the roars of the shadow dragons. But she didn't care, her rider was gone.

Far below, skimming the treetops, her mate Handel twined up through the fighting dragons to join her.

Together they would rip apart these beasts as vengeance for the rider she had missed for eighteen years—and only had back for these few short moons.

Liesar howled again, allowing herself a moment longer for her grief.

And then, flaming dragons left and right, Liesar and Handel speared through the fighting masses to hunt down the beast and mage that had killed Marlies.

§

Beside Giant John, Benno swung his sword, his mighty arms flexing as he hewed a tharuk's legs out from under it. Giant John was drenched in blood, but he didn't stop. Whether the blood was from the dragons above, the tharuks before him, or his own men beside him, it didn't matter. The only thing that mattered was killing the next tharuk. And the next.

These beasts had roamed Dragons' Realm too long. It was time to end them.

Far off to his left, Mickel's cry rang out, "Incoming."

Giant John spun.

He and Mickel had been separated, a few warriors between them scrambling to hold the line. But the line had just disintegrated as a fresh troop of tharuks—vigorous, swift and strong—came crashing through the undergrowth toward them.

This flaming carnage would never end. There was little hope. Dark beasts blotted the sky, outnumbering their own dragons. And here, down in Spangle-wood Forest near Mage Gate, tharuks outnumbered the men.

Gritting his teeth, Giant John ran to meet the new beasts and plunged his sword into the troop leader's side, aiming up under its breastplate. All that mattered was killing the next tharuk.

And then the next.

And the next.

§

Giddi remained with his hand clenched in a fist over his heart, unmoving, awaiting Zens' instructions. Beneath his hand, the teardrop crystal under his clothing radiated warmth into his fingers and palm. He closed his eyes, taking a deep breath, and focused.

Mazyka's face swam into his mind, shimmering as if it were at the bottom of a deep pool. Her voice reached him, as if from far underwater. *"Giddi, I am with you. I always was."* Her face was just as beautiful as it had always been—with those luscious lips, large dark eyes and that flaming red hair. She smiled. He noted the shadows beneath her cheekbones and tiny creases at the corners of her eyes. She had aged too, gracefully.

"Has the other world been kind to you?"

"I've missed you terribly, my love." Her words were double-edged, laced with pain.

He'd banished her, not knowing how to save the realm, not knowing that his efforts had been too little, too late. And now, he was too late again. Zens would force him to open the world gate, then let his metal men sweep through the gate with their blasting weapons to obliterate Dragons' Realm.

Giddi's eyes stung, but no tears came. If he couldn't protect this world, perhaps it was just as well that it would be destroyed.

"No," Mazyka cried.

The dark shadows swirled and eddied, covering Mazyka's face and drowning out her voice. *"Yes,"* the shadows said. *"You must help Zens destroy this pathetic world."*

§

Giant John, Benno, and Mickel were side by side again, fighting to stem the endless tide of tharuks. It was no good. More kept coming.

At the edge of the forest, Giant John spied a boy with dark hair and deep-blue eyes. He wanted to yell at the boy to flee, but that would only draw the tharuks' attention to the lad. The boy raised his hands, lips moving. Tiny sparkles of light shot from the trees, swirling around the boy's legs and over his torso.

"Spangles," Giant John called to Benno, in wonder. "I've heard of them, but never actually seen them." Hope surged in his heart.

Suddenly, the earth around the boy seemed to move, teeming with life. Beetles crawled out of the ground and swarmed the tharuks' legs. The beasts batted at them. The trees seemed to ripple as squirrels scampered down from their trees and raced toward the boy. He thrust his hand outward, glimmering light streaming toward the tharuks—and the squirrels followed, attacking the monsters, climbing up their bodies and biting their arms and legs.

Everywhere the boy's light touched, nature awoke. Foxes crawled from holes, racing toward the tharuks. One opened its jaws, fastening upon a beast's leg. Another leaped, aiming for a tharuk's throat.

Tharuks faltered, swiping their claws at the creatures.

A pack of wolves howled and raced for the tharuks. More beetles poured out of the ground, swarming Zens' monsters. Dark furry forms as large as dinner plates scurried from their homes under loose bark in trees. Gargantula spiders swarmed the tharuks and bit into the monster's limbs, injecting venom with their fangs.

A tharuk lashed out with its claws, ripping a fox's belly open. The woodland creature dropped dead at its feet. "Kill them!" the tharuk bellowed.

Zens' monsters leaped into action, slashing squirrels and foxes with their tusks and claws. They crushed the gargantulas underfoot, splattering their insides on the snow.

Mickel and Giant John pressed forward with a handful of men, hacking, hewing and doing their best to kill the tharuks. Even more tharuks poured through the forest, stomping on beetles, firing arrows at wolves.

The boy still stood there, light swirling around him, calling nature to fight. More spangles glittered amongst the trees. Their branches swayed, knocking tharuks down. But the stinking beasts soon scrambled back up, charging toward Giant John and his band of warriors.

HOPE DASHED

Grief still a ragged hole in her chest, Ezaara had replenished her arrows and was back in the sky, shooting dark dragons. There were so many—too many to kill them all. Roberto and Erob hadn't left her side, flying alongside Zaarusha, staying melded every step of the way. She shot an arrow into the breast of a mage and nocked another. Her arrow hit a dark dragon's eye. The dark dragon's screams ricocheted through her head, but were drowned out by her own roar of grief and pain.

She nocked her bow again and fired, downing dark dragons as fast as she could—aiming arrows between their eyes, into their hearts, through their maws. Anything to assuage her grief at losing her mother, her people, and probably Dragons' Realm.

Zaarusha blasted flame at shadow dragons and shredded their wings to tatters with her talons. Shrieking beasts plunged to the forest below. Erob did the same. Roberto's arrows zipped on the wind, burying themselves deep in the flesh of their foes.

"Oh no, not more dark dragons," Roberto melded.

Ezaara had seldom heard such despair in Roberto's thoughts—but then again, he'd only just found and lost his father. She glanced up and gasped. Dark specks converged on the horizon—yet more shadow dragons were flying for them. Not as many as they were fighting now, but still a sizable wing. *"So that's what you meant."*

"I just want this to be over."

As they fought on, the new wing of dragons flew nearer.

"Roberto, we're wrong." The roar in Ezaara's head died. Her world went still for a moment. *"They're not dark dragons."*

The dragons were all varieties of green and blue: aqua, turquoise, jade, cobalt, lapis, emerald, and moss. Their wings were tinged with flecks of silver, glimmering in the sunlight like rays of hope sparkling upon a vast sea. Riding each dragon was a woman with dark skin, clothed in orange.

"Zaarusha, Roberto, Erob," Ezaara melded, *"it's Ithsar and the silent assassins."*

Ithsar's dragon was jade, sparkling with silver like the ocean.

The deep timbre of Roberto's thoughts was tinged with happiness as he replied, *"Yes, and they're riding sea dragons."*

"And look." Behind them were green guards, riding their valiant emerald dragons. *"The green guards from Naobia are here too."*

§

Straight ahead, Ithsar saw the landscape as she'd seen it in her vision: a winter forest sprawled before her, patches of snow in dark shadows and grass peeking through in the sunlit clearing. And there was the metal chest she'd seen with the strange yellow beam of light jutting from it. Above it all, spread like a giant awning above an oasis, was a legion of foul beasts spitting fire and shooting yellow beams from their eyes.

The Naobian green dragons had joined them in the south, flying beside her own Saritha whose jade scales glinted with silver like a brooding sea. Joy thrummed inside Ithsar's breast, a surging, bucking beast, almost as wild as Saritha.

Moons before, Roberto and Ezaara had helped her become the new Prophetess—not that they knew that yet. Ezaara—she with the golden hair—had healed her, making her fingers whole, and helped Ithsar discover the power of her *sathir*. And Roberto had restored her faith that kind men like her father still existed.

And now she could help them. "Avanta!" Ithsar called, the battle cry of the Sathiri—the Robandi silent assassins.

Their mighty sea dragons charged into the mass of dark dragons.

§

"Erob, there behind Ithsar's dragon's left flank." Roberto loosed an arrow, but it only glanced off the spinal ridge of the dark dragon angling for them.

With a mighty beat of his wings, Erob lurched forward, gusting flame at the beast.

But another replaced it, and then another.

Dragons and riders had rallied when Ithsar's silent assassins joined them, but now they were exhausted after fleeing then fighting half the night and all day. Now, as day waned, Ithsar's dragons were flagging too.

Brown and green dragons darted in and out among Zens' cloud of black dragons, spurting fire at shadow dragons, then nimbly speeding away.

Tree trunks seethed with creatures that leaped onto tharuks from above. Someone had rallied the animals to attack the tharuks. Birds flew into dark dragons' faces, clawing at their eyes. Golden eagles swooped from their craggy nests out over the forest, clawing at dark dragons' wings. Many had been shot down by mages or ingested in a single bite by a fiery maw, but others bravely fought on.

Giant John and his warriors bashed their way through hordes of tharuks, leaving casualties and dead in their wake. But now they, too, were exhausted.

They were doing all they could, but still the dark dragons outnumbered them. His whole life, Roberto had trained for battle, but it wasn't enough. There were too many foes.

And what was that strange beam of golden light stabbing through the sky from the clearing? *"Erob, let's take a closer look."*

Erob swooped lower. Master Giddi was standing in the beam from the methimium ray. Bathed in its golden light, his hand was clasped in a fist over his heart, his head bowed. Beside him stood Zens, grinning.

Oh gods, the dragon mage was about to unleash his power at Zens' command.

Giddi Strikes

For long hours, Giddi stood in the clearing, watching the battle range around him, seeing mages' brave and foolhardy actions. Through it all, his people were dying. Trapped in Zens' mental thrall, he couldn't do a thing.

"Yes, you can do something," the shadows whispered. *"Put those foolish mages, dragons and riders out of their misery. Zens has a better plan and you will help him achieve it."*

The teardrop crystal thrummed underneath his hand. His magic coiled and bucked inside him, prickling under his skin.

Every moment, Mazyka whispered from the other side of the world gate.

But the dark shadows wrapped around his mind. *"You will obey the commander and use your power to help him."*

Giddi's gaze swept over the tharuks fighting his people and slaughtering his mages. *"Yes, of course I'll obey my commander."*

§

Without any warning, the dragon fighting Ezaara turned, speeding away from her. A swarm of shadow dragons followed.

Zaarusha, about to give chase, melded, *"They're all leaving. I wonder what Zens is up to."*

"Don't follow them," Ezaara answered. *"We'll wait and see."*

More dark dragons and those turned by methimium flew away, leaving the dragons of Dragons' Realm milling in the air in confusion.

"I don't understand why they're fleeing in different directions," Erob said.

"At least it'll give us respite." Roberto plucked two apples from Erob's saddlebags and threw one to Ezaara. He called out to the riders around them, "Replenish your strength. Eat while you can."

The riders in the sky around them quickly grabbed bread, dried beef or apples from their saddlebags and slumped over their dragons' necks to eat.

"You're lucky dragons don't eat that often." Erob sighed. *"Not that an apple would make a difference. A herd of oxen would be more like it."*

Roberto patted his scaly neck, too tired to laugh.

About forty dragon lengths away, the shadow dragons stopped fleeing and formed a loose ring, flying around the dragons and riders. The dark beasts chased each other, nose to tail.

"What are they up to?" Roberto asked.

Some shot overhead.

"Oh gods, I bet they're going to try to herd us somewhere." Roberto tossed his apple aside.

Sure enough, the ring of dragons swooped inward, growing tighter.

The dragons above them belched flame.

"Everyone, fight back!" Ezaara mind melded with all of their still-loyal dragons.

Blue guards shot out toward the perimeter of the ring, blazing flame. Browns flapped upward, blasting fire at the shadow dragons above. Gradually, the shadow dragons pushed from the north, forcing them toward the yellow methimium beam streaming into the sky above the clearing.

"Don't get near those rays," Ezaara warned everyone. *"Break through their circle. Destroy those beasts."*

Zaarusha rushed at the shadow dragons, Erob alongside her.

A distant cry came to Ezaara's mind. *"Ezaara. Help me."* Her gaze locked with Roberto's. Still melded with her, he'd heard it too.

"That was Master Giddi," Roberto said.

Ezaara nodded. Erob and Zaarusha swooped toward the clearing at Mage Gate, but a volley of methimium-tipped arrows shot toward them. Tharuks were battling with warriors in the surrounding bushes, preventing anyone from getting close.

"Fall back," Zaarusha trumpeted to Erob.

Zaarusha and Erob swooped over the trees to land on a small hill with a view of the main clearing. As Ezaara slid to the ground, Roberto dismounted, sword in hand, and ran toward her.

"Ezaara, you have to go," Zaarusha melded. *"You're the only one who can meld with Giddi to stop Zens. Take your mage cloak. It may come in handy. We'll be in the air above you keeping watch. But be careful—I don't want to lose you."* She nuzzled Ezaara's shoulder. Ezaara pulled her invisibility cloak from her saddlebag and put it on, leaving the cloak hanging open and the hood undone, so she could still be seen by her friends.

Erob and Zaarusha took to the sky as Roberto and Ezaara descended the hill, sneaking through the trees, making their way to the clearing. The stench of tharuks clung to Ezaara's nostrils.

Fenni and Jael broke through the trees. Master Jael greeted them, clasping their hands.

"We must get to Master Giddi," Ezaara said. "He needs our help."

"We've scouted the area," Jael replied. "There were too many tharuks for us to get past, but with four of us we might have a chance."

Roberto gave a grim nod. "It's risky, but we don't have much choice." He took her hand firmly.

"Master Giddi's trapped by Zens," Fenni replied. "They say he's working against us."

"We'll find that out when we get to him," Ezaara answered. "If you can help me battle through the tharuks, I'll sneak up wearing my mage cloak, so Zens can't see me helping Giddi." Below the copse on the hillside, screams and roars rang out as tharuks and people fought.

Master Jael cocked his head. "Even though you'd be invisible, you could still get hurt. We're coming with you."

Ezaara nodded. "Once we're in the clearing, I'll need to go deep inside myself to give Master Giddi mental aid to fight the methimium. I'll be vulnerable."

Master Jael thumped his hand on his chest. "It'll be our pleasure to protect you."

"My honored Queen's Rider." Fenni bowed. "Let the fight begin."

"Begin?" Jael raised an eyebrow. "Where have you been?"

Ezaara had to smile.

Roberto addressed Jael and Fenni. "Do you mind giving us a few moments alone?"

Jael glanced at Fenni and shrugged. "Sure. We'll wait just down there." He pointed down the slope, then he and Fenni disappeared into the trees.

Roberto placed his hands on Ezaara's shoulders, his ebony eyes burning through her. "There's a risk in all of this. Zens might sense us via Giddi and control us. With our powers and Giddi's combined, there's no doubt he'd be able to command all of our dragons and destroy Dragons' Realm."

Ezaara studied Roberto's beautiful soot-smudged face and trailed a finger along his cheekbone. "I know." She took a deep breath and smoothed back a lock of his hair. "But if Giddi really is in Zens' thrall, and we don't help him, then Zens already has the power to destroy us all."

Roberto pulled her against his chest, cradling her head in his hand and wrapping his other arm around her waist. "I don't want you hurt. And I don't want to lose you," he murmured against her hair. "Don't go up against Zens alone."

Ezaara leaned into him, wishing they had hours instead of moments. She gazed at him. "I've withstood Zens before. I'm stronger now."

Above, dragons were waging battle as dusk began to creep across the sky.

Roberto nodded. "I agree, you are stronger, but not as strong as Zens. Although it's risky and I could lose you, having you meld with Giddi is our best hope—but I'm staying melded with you the whole way. You don't get to do this on your own."

Ezaara's breath caught in her throat. "But you won't be focused on fighting if you're mind-melding with me. You could get killed."

"So could you," he murmured. His hands slid to her cheeks. Suddenly, his lips were upon hers, his dark-blue-and-silver-flecked *sathir* wrapping around hers, intertwining with her many hues and creating a warm comforting blanket that sheltered them from the snarls of the tharuks below, the groans of dying men and the roaring dragons blazing fire in the sky.

It all faded. Right now, there was only them, arms around each other, desperately kissing each other for what could be their last time.

"Ezaara, you're the best part of me. You've given me the strength to face my past and become a better man."

"And I would've been nothing without you."

"No, you're everything, even without me." He squeezed her to him. "But we'll face this together," he whispered, "and then build our future."

A future neither of them might see. Or only one of them. "I'll never forget you," she said fiercely. "Ever. No matter what—"

"Ssh." He put a finger to her lips. Then kissed them. Softly, one last time. "Together."

They closed their eyes and stood, nose to nose, breath mingling.

"Stay melded with me, Ezaara. Whatever happens, don't let go."

"I won't. I promise."

A flash of green lit up behind Ezaara's eyelids. She and Roberto pulled apart, spinning. Down the hill, green mage flame lit up the trees. Roars cut off. The stench of burning fur and flesh wafted up the hillside.

Roberto grasped Ezaara's hand and they ran, half sliding through slushy patches, gouging trails down the hillside until they reached Fenni and Jael among the strongwoods.

A tharuk lay at Fenni's feet, a smoking hole in its chest. Another was slumped against a tree with its neck bent at an odd angle and mage fire licking up its side. More tharuks were strewn on the ground, still smoking. The stench of mage fire, burning flesh and charred fur hung between the trees.

Jael bent for a moment, resting his hands on his knees to catch his breath.

"You all right?" Roberto asked.

Straightening, Jael flicked out his hands. The fires quenched. He turned. "About time you two showed up."

"I suggest we get going," Fenni said. "Our mage fire is bound to attract the tharuks."

Zaarusha melded, *"I saw the mage fire. Are you all right?"*

"Yes, but perhaps we should all stay melded, so you and Erob can see what's going on," Ezaara suggested. *"Despite the screams of those infernal beasts."*

Snarls echoed through the bushes. They slipped quietly through the trees in the opposite direction, angling down the hillside toward the clearing.

Tharuks darted out of the undergrowth, swarming up the hill at them. Mage flame sprang from Jael's fingers, blowing off the head of the nearest tharuk, a spray of dark blood staining the snow.

Fenni flung out his arms and whirled, sweeping fire at the approaching beasts. Five went down in a blaze of flame. Above, Zaarusha roared. Roberto ducked as a tharuk swiped at him with its claws. Ezaara ran full tilt, ramming her sword into the belly of another.

"Follow me," yelled Jael.

He took off to the left, thundering through the trees, Ezaara, Roberto, and Fenni close on his heels. An arrow zipped through the air. Ezaara ducked. It narrowly missed her, thudding into the trunk of a tree. Roberto grabbed her hand and tugged her forward.

They ran and slid down the hill, joining warriors who were fighting ten deep against the troops of tharuks guarding the clearing.

"There's Giant John," Ezaara cried, pointing to a huge figure battling three tharuks. Two men with broadswords were fighting at his side, a wedge of warriors driving their way through the beasts. Further along the line, warriors were falling, the clash of swords against claws echoing among snarling tharuks and the cries of dying men and women.

Roberto melded. *"Giant John will be our best chance of getting through."*

"To Giant John," Ezaara yelled.

Jael and Fenni surged forward. Fenni lobbed an arc of fire over Giant John's head and hit two of the beasts John was fighting. Giant John swiped his sword through the neck of the other. The men beside him dispatched the remaining tharuks with a blow to one's head and a slash to the other's belly.

Bellowing, more tharuks flooded in to replace them. Ezaara parried a tharuk's claws with her sword and then jabbed it under the armpit. The beast roared and lunged. She ducked and Jael finished it off with a fireball to the chest. The scents of smoke, blood and cooked meat clawed their way up Ezaara's nostrils. She stomped over the body of a dead tharuk to face another.

She thrust her sword, but the tharuk spun, slashing at Roberto. He parried the blow, but only just.

"That was close," he melded.

"Too close. Oh, shards!"

A methimium arrow shot through the air. Ezaara ducked, but the arrow embedded itself in Giant John's upper arm.

"Take it out. Now!" Ezaara yelled and leaped over a body to Giant John. Jamming her bloodstained sword into its sheath, she snatched a dagger from her belt.

Giant John's eyes widened in surprise as she grabbed his arm and dug her knife in under the methimium arrowhead. "That'll burrow into your flesh and turn you faster than a dragon can backwing."

She flicked out the arrowhead, made of yellow crystal with wriggling metal feelers, and ground it into the mud with her boot heel. Ezaara tore a strip from the archers' cloak she was still wearing under her invisibility cloak and bound Giant John's wound.

"Thank you." Giant John gestured with his sword at the two well-muscled warriors fighting with him. "My honored Queen's Rider, meet Benno and Mickel, two of our most valiant warriors from Horseshoe Bend."

"So you got my messenger raven." Ezaara tied off the makeshift bandage. "Please thank them for coming to our aid."

Giant John raised an eyebrow. "Why? This is not just your battle. We're fighting for our homes too."

A tharuk lunged at Giant John and he spun, smiting off its arm.

Another beast plunged its claws at a young man who fell to the ground, a gaping rent in his belly. Giant John bellowed and sprang to dispatch the tharuk.

"Follow us," Jael called. He and Fenni pushed past Giant John and Ezaara and stood side-by-side with their arms out. A wall of fire sprang up in front of them, pushing the tharuks back.

Limplocked arrows flew at them. Zens had seen the mage fire and decided to counter them.

"That mage flame's not exactly subtle," Roberto said, slipping his hand into Ezaara's.

Green fire licked through the tharuks in front of them, killing them in a haze of stinking smoke.

"Now," Roberto yelled above the din of the battle. "Get your cloak on, Ezaara. I'm taking you through."

As Ezaara tugged her cloak around her and pulled the hood over her face, Giant John gave a belly laugh. "The disappearing Queen's Rider. Quite a party trick. Do you want a hand?" He jerked his head toward the clearing. "Giddi is an old friend of mine. I guess that's where you're going. I'd gladly give my life to rescue him."

"You may well do," Roberto said, sandwiching Ezaara between his side and Giant John's.

Fenni and Jael parted the wall of fire, creating a narrow tunnel through the middle and blasting their flames out sideways to engulf tharuks. On either side of the passage, Zaarusha and Erob blasted fire, killing more of the beasts and opening up a channel in the monsters' defensive wall.

Giant John and Roberto charged through the mage fire tunnel with Ezaara pressed between them. A tharuk leaped through the flames, swiping at Roberto's belly, but Roberto's sword drove it back into the tongues of mage fire. The beast screamed and writhed, burning on the ground.

"Troops, charge!" Giant John bellowed and rushed forward, sweeping his sword ahead of him, aiming for the tharuks waiting at the end of the tunnel.

Warriors surged behind them.

"Quick, Roberto, come!" Ezaara raced behind Giant John.

Roberto shot past her. And with the thundering feet of a hundred warriors behind her, Ezaara burst into the clearing to hundreds of bloodthirsty tharuks.

§

"Open the portal. Now." Zens' voice cracked like a whip through Giddi's mind.

Giddi flinched.

"Do it now, my friend," Zens' sinuous voice wound through his head, cloying and sweet, lulling Giddi into a sense of wellbeing.

"Yes, Commander." But Giddi had worked for days, gradually managing to wrest back control of a tiny corner of his consciousness without Zens noticing, keeping it barricaded from Zens.

"I'm here, helping you," Mazyka melded. "I won't let Zens claim that part back." Her face shimmered before him.

Giddi's body was still under Zens' control. His arms flung out, green flame licking its way up the shaft of golden light that pierced the sky.

Dark shadows danced at the corners of Giddi's vision and drifted across the clearing. Fire blazed a channel through the ranks of the tharuks fighting on the clearing's perimeter, then warriors flooded through the blazing gap. Tharuks surged to fight the warriors, riders, and mages—his people. But with his will still locked to Zens' command, Giddi was powerless to help them.

SILENT WITNESS

Oh gods, he'd lost Ezaara. Roberto floundered around, afraid to wave his sword in case he struck her. *"Ezaara, where are you? How can I protect you if I don't know where you are?"*

"I'm right behind you. Just keep going."

"Good. I was hoping you'd—" Roberto broke off as a small wiry tharuk dived at him, grabbing his legs and sinking its talons deep into his thigh. He crashed to the ground. Ezaara's sword appeared in midair and hacked off the beast's head. With a spray of dark blood and a gurgle, the tharuk slumped on top of Roberto. He kicked its body off and scrambled to his feet. *"Thank you. Quick, put your sword away before someone sees it."*

It vanished.

"That's better. Now, hold my hand," he said.

"I can't," she said. *"We're both right-handed. If I hold your hand, only one of us can wield a sword."*

"Stay behind me, then. I'll make my way to Giddi." Thigh throbbing, Roberto ran.

In the center of the clearing, Giddi was standing, arms outstretched to the heavens, plumes of green mage fire licking from his fingertips up the yellow ray of light.

"What's he doing?" Ezaara asked.

Roberto dodged out of the way as a tharuk aimed its claws at him. *"It's a methimium ray. It holds the realm gates open. That's how we got so many people and dragons back to Dragons' Hold from Death Valley."*

"By the mighty dragon gods! Zens must be opening the world gate."

"I'm afraid you're right," Roberto answered.

A group of tharuks charged at him. Shards, he was wounded and outnumbered. But Ezaara had to get to Giddi. *"Ezaara, run. I'll join you when I can."*

Roberto swung his sword at the biggest beast, but its claws glanced off the shoulder of his sword arm, gashing it. Gods, that hurt. If only he could see where Ezaara was. He was terrified of hitting her by accident.

"I told you to focus on fighting. I'll take care of myself."

It was uncanny hearing her, but not being able to see her. He whirled his sword, slashing through fur, doing what he could for the realm—for the people he loved. Around him, mages and warriors fought, blood—black and red—staining the clearing. A huge tharuk rushed at him, four others flanking it. Two rushed his right side. He swung his sword, but they grabbed it. Not caring about the slices he left in their hands, they yanked his sword, wrenching his shoulders. He let go and they stumbled backward. Roberto drew his dagger.

The enormous tharuk slashed at him with its claws. He jumped back, but a tharuk had sneaked up behind him. It jabbed his back. The large tharuk lunged and grabbed his neck. It raised its arms, lifting him off the ground. Roberto kicked and slashed at the tharuk's face with his dagger, but his reach was too short.

This was it. He didn't dare send Ezaara one last message of love or he might distract her. If Giddi melded with all the dragons or opened the world gate and let an army in, Dragons' Realm could come crashing down around them. Shielding his thoughts from Ezaara, Roberto prepared himself for his end as the tharuk's hands tightened around his throat.

The tharuk laughed, its stinking breath wafting over Roberto's face. It mind-melded with him, *"So we meet again, Roberto."*

In horror, Roberto saw 000 emblazoned inside its wrist. This was Zens' prized creation, the tharuk Roberto had threatened to kill in Death Valley to blackmail Zens into setting Ezaara and Adelina free.

"My, how you've grown," Roberto melded back.

"How small you are," 000 growled, its tusks dripping with dark saliva. *"I'll enjoy pulling you apart. Stripping the flesh from your hide and crunching your puny bones beneath my boots."*

"Very poetic," Roberto stalled. Shards, how was he going to get out of this?

000 looked perplexed. *"Poetic?"* it repeated.

Roberto scoffed, *"No matter how you pretend, you'll never be enough for Zens. After all, you're only his minion. You're just like the rest of his slaves, obeying his every command, never thinking for yourself. How long until he tires of you and kills you too?"*

With an enraged roar, 000's hands tightened around Roberto's throat, constricting his windpipe. Roberto gurgled, clutching at his throat and the monster's hands. Oh, why had he let his mouth run away on him? It was going to get him killed.

Spots danced before Roberto's eyes.

Then heat swept over him as the side of 000's face was set aflame with green mage fire.

The beast dropped Roberto, clutching at its face. Roberto sprawled on the ground.

Jael and Fenni ran toward them, shooting fireballs to clear a path between Roberto and Master Giddi.

Roberto snatched up his sword and swung. *"Ezaara, where are you?"* He ran. *"Ezaara?"* he called again. There was no answer, and of course, she was nowhere to be seen.

§

Luckily, no one had noticed the dark drops of blood dripping from Ezaara's sword hidden under her cloak, or the footprints she'd left in the churned up mud as she raced across the clearing toward Giddi and Commander Zens. Before she reached them, she slowed to quiet her breathing. Ezaara stepped over a dead tharuk and made her way around a troop fighting with warriors and mages.

There was only one place to take shelter so tharuks wouldn't stumble into her. She ducked down behind the metal box that was streaming yellow light into the sky. She peeked around the edge.

Commander Zens stood near Master Giddi, no doubt controlling the entire battle with his mind and his methimium implants. Around them, a wall of tharuks stood, fur bristling and claws out. Giddi's arms were thrust skyward as green flames from his fingertips climbed up the beam of light. He was trying to open the world gate. She was sure of it.

As long as Zens didn't detect her, she'd be safe. But the moment he suspected something…

She swallowed, her mouth drying at the thought. Roberto had taught her how to be a silent witness, to slip into someone's mind and listen to their thoughts without leaving a trace. But the dragon mage, the most powerful wizard in Dragons' Realm, knew more about mental faculties than most—except Master Roberto and Commander Zens themselves.

Gently easing her mind open, Ezaara felt Roberto's comforting presence. *"I'm behind the methimium ray and I'm going in,"* she said.

"Good. I'm here if you need me." His thoughts faded until he was a silent witness in her mind.

Gently probing, Ezaara slipped inside Giddi's head.

§

When Ezaara slipped into Giddi's mind, Zens' dark shadows were roiling across Giddi's vision as his words slunk through his consciousness. *"Come on, Giddi, you can do it,"* Zens urged. *"Open the portal."*

Zens must mean the world gate.

Ezaara closed her eyes to concentrate. Slumped against the metal box and entirely covered by her mage cloak, she deliberately kept her thoughts tightly under control to escape the commander's notice.

She let herself wander the corridors of Giddi's mind. Something bathed in gold flickered in a corner. Ezaara crept closer. A woman's face. Accompanying it was a love so fierce and bittersweet it made Ezaara's chest ache. Even though she'd never seen her, Ezaara knew it was Mazyka.

"Now, Giddi," Zens commanded. Zens' dark energy stretched Giddi's arms higher.

She felt *sathir* swarm from the center of Giddi's being and flow along his arms and out his fingers into the methimium beam. She opened her eyes. Above the forest, a volley of green mage flame licked up the beam of golden light.

It was happening. Whatever Zens' reason, Giddi was opening the world gate. But was Zens in control or Giddi? Perhaps some small remnant of him remained, calling out for help.

Zens' excitement ran through Master Giddi's thoughts. Metal-clad figures were shooting metallic tubes of flame, laying waste to Dragons' Realm. Lakes were dried mud patches; the skies were empty of dragons. Strangletons choked the rivers, turning them to stinking marshes full of dead fish. The hills were barren. This was the future Zens envisaged.

Ezaara slipped out of Giddi's head so her shock wouldn't break through his thoughts. *"Roberto, this is a million times worse than what we thought."*

"I know," said Roberto. *"We have to help Giddi stop Zens. I know he's inside there somewhere or he couldn't have called us for help."*

"I'm going back in." Ezaara slipped back inside Giddi's mind.

§

Giddi tuned in to the *sathir* around him, surprised when a tendril of silver, like a thread, spiraled from his core, down his limbs, and out his outstretched fingers. The thread wound around the golden beam stretching skyward beyond the flickering green mage flame.

"Giddi, I feel you reaching for me," Mazyka whispered into that tiny protected corner of his mind.

Another voice whispered too. *"We're here for you, Giddi."* Ezaara, with Roberto. Their combined *sathir*, his dark-blue flecked with silver, and hers, multi-colored, flooded through him.

He would've danced for joy. Except he couldn't—his limbs were still controlled by Zens. He hoped like egg shards that Zens couldn't detect Ezaara. If he did, they'd be dead in an instant.

Giddi coiled the flickering *sathir*, tamping it down until the buzz of magic was like a hive of wild bees under his skin, dying to be set free. He let a tendril escape from his fingers. It shot along the silver thread, pushing it higher along the beam piercing the sky.

"I feel you, Giddi. A little more and I can reach you," Mazyka encouraged.

Ezaara pushed more *sathir* at him. Giddi took it, swelling the power until it ran out of his fingers. The silver thread wound higher.

"That's the way," Zens' voice slithered through his head.

Giddi locked down his thoughts, hiding them from the commander.

A tiny crack in the sky appeared, and a thin gold filament slipped through it, winding around the beam and stretching down toward the silver thread.

After nineteen years, they were finally opening the world gate—and Mazyka was still alive on the other side. Seeing his wife again was more than Giddi had dared hope for.

Before Giddi could rejoice, dark mist wafted from Commander Zens' hands, racing up his silver thread of *sathir*. By the dragon gods!

Mazyka's gold thread raced downward.

With a push of Ezaara's *sathir*, his silver thread shot up, stretching to meet it...

But the dark shadows were climbing faster, now two-thirds of the way up his silver tendril.

"Mazyka, faster. Ezaara, more."

The silver had to reach the gold before Zens' shadows overtook them.

§

Roberto grunted, gritting his teeth, shoving hard, letting his *sathir* flow into Ezaara so she could feed it to Giddi. A tharuk swung at him and he ducked, his *sathir* waning. He didn't have time to fight—the mental battle was more important. He rammed his sword up under the beast's chin and kicked it aside.

Another tharuk leaped, landing on his back, and Roberto hit the ground with a thud, landing on a dead warrior's thighs.

Worried his pain would break through the silent witness and alert Zens, he slipped out of Ezaara's mind. The tharuk's claws dug into his back. Roberto twisted, ripping his jerkin, and cried out as the creature's claws gouged his back.

With a roar, Erob dived, plucked the tharuk off him and tossed it into the forest.

Not a moment too soon. The silver thread was shriveling, shrinking back on itself, and dark shadows were gradually consuming it.

Gently, Roberto slipped into Ezaara's mind, once again connected through her vibrant colorful *sathir* to Giddi. He gradually built the flow of his *sathir*, letting Ezaara use it to aid Giddi. The silver thread wound upward along the yellow beam, barely the length of a dragon's thigh above Zens' clawing shadows.

§

Ezaara's head was going to crack open with the pressure building inside it. Roberto had pushed his *sathir* at her for Giddi, but she couldn't release it all at once or Zens might detect them and order his tharuks to kill her and Roberto. Without them, Giddi wouldn't stand a chance against Zens—and Dragons' Realm would become a wasteland.

Inside Giddi's head, Zens' voice was relentlessly bellowing, *"Open the gods-forsaken portal."*

Ezaara released more *sathir,* trying to keep Giddi's silver tendril above the dark shadows.

Suddenly, Zens skittered into Ezaara's mind. *"So, Ezaara, you're here too? Two can play at that game."*

"Or three," Mazyka roared, revealing her presence.

With every particle of *sathir* she had, Ezaara gave a mighty shove, flooding Giddi's mind.

The cords in his neck standing out, the dragon mage fell to his knees and screamed.

§

Giddi fell to his knees, screaming, "Mazyka!"

Dark shadows enveloped his mind and shrouded the silver thread, rushing up to meet the gold. He kept Mazyka's face in his mind and shoved *sathir* at his silver tendril with every last scrap of his strength. The silver thread shot above the clawing shadows. The world exploded in a flash of light.

A rift appeared in the sky and a golden dragon flew through, a woman with flaming red hair upon her back, screaming at the world. His heart sang. She was home. Mazyka was home again.

Smaller golden dragons poured through after her, ridden by mages with blue light springing from their fingers.

"Mazyka," Giddi cried hoarsely, spent.

Zens thrust his hands higher. With a surge, the shadows raced up their entwined threads and a dark crack opened in the sky. Metal beings glimmered behind it. A shining metal weapon poked through, blasting flame. A golden dragon dropped from the sky, dead.

Giddi grimaced, battling with Zens to squeeze the dark world gate shut. Ezaara flooded him with *sathir*, Mazyka too, and Roberto. He poured it all into their bond. Their threads grew thicker, twining around one another to form a golden rope threaded with silver.

Zens shoved at him, thrashing and screaming in his mind. Dark shadows whirled across Giddi's vision. Voices called at him to sever the rope.

Head swaying from side to side, Giddi struggled to his feet. He held out his hands and roared.

Mazyka was strong, steady in his mind. *"I'm with you, Giddi, we can do this. Resist the methimium."*

Zens laughed as a metal figure flew through the dark rift, shooting its weapon, felling green, gold, and blue dragons.

The legs of more metal beings poked through the rift. Another dropped down. Its metal body gleaming, it fired at a blue dragon, destroying its wing in a burst of flame. The dragon plummeted, roaring in agony.

The metal being chased it, propelled by some unseen magic, blasting more fire.

"Reverse the flow," Ezaara called. *"Reverse it! Close the world gate."*

Giddi pulled the *sathir* until it flowed from the gold-and-silver rope into him. Sweat broke out on his forehead, his cheeks. Even his arms were sweating. He ripped off his cloak, his shirt, standing with his torso naked against the world.

Dark tendrils of mist leaked from the methimium arrow wounds in his back, winding around his neck and face.

"Time for you to die, wizardling," Zens laughed. *"You've served your purpose."*

The shadows writhed into his nostrils, around his eyes, hissing at him.

Still, he pulled the *sathir* back inside himself. The crystal teardrop thrummed against Giddi's skin, growing hotter, burning like a brand on his chest. White light burst from the crystal and swept around the clearing, banishing the shadows. Zens was thrown onto his back. Tharuks and warriors fell to their knees, shielding their eyes.

The light from Giddi's chest blazed through the sky, hitting the dark rift. The crack closed, the metal beings shut out forever.

Mazyka's golden dragon swooped upon the remaining metal beings. She blasted them with plumes of blue mage fire. They exploded, metal shards spraying across the forest.

CHASE

When the blast of light hit the clearing, everyone had shielded their eyes or fallen to their knees. Despite the burning sensation on his chest, Roberto's only concern was Ezaara. The box holding the methimium ray had collapsed in a heap of molten metal. She'd been hiding behind it.

"Ezaara?" Roberto scrambled over to the wreckage, feeling around the ground by the remains of the box to find her. If she was unconscious, passed out... Blast those flaming mage cloaks—invisibility, at a time like this!

Around him, tharuks and warriors were rising to their feet and starting to fight again. Gods, any one of them could trample Ezaara.

"Ezaara!" He felt around the ground. Nothing. But he kept searching. He stumbled over something he couldn't see. Bending, he pulled back something that felt like fabric. A leg appeared, then her boot. He shook her calf. "Ezaara!"

She stirred and sat up, her hood falling from her face and mage cloak spilling open to reveal her rider's jerkin.

"Thank the Egg you're all right." Roberto pulled her into a hug. "Did you black out?"

She took off the mage cloak, bundling it up. "I'm not sure; maybe. My chest is burning."

"Mine too."

Ezaara pulled open her jerkin. Above her right breast was a new white scar in the shape of a teardrop.

Roberto pulled his jerkin back too. He had the same burn etched into his chest. "What caused these?"

"It's the same shape and size as your grandmother Anakisha's heirloom, the crystal necklace you gave me that helped me mind-meld with you over long distances."

"But you're not wearing it." Roberto frowned. "It was stolen on our hand-fasting holiday."

Ezaara shrugged. "Bruno gave Zens the ring. I bet he gave him the necklace too. Maybe that's what Giddi used to open the world gate."

"Makes sense. There was a light blazing from his chest."

"That could've been the crystal. Maybe it's the key to the world gate."

Roberto helped her to her feet.

Zaarusha and Erob swooped, breathing flame at the tharuks. Fenni and Jael were still lobbing fireballs into tharuk troops. A shriek of jubilation rang above the clearing as Riona dived. Kierion punched the air with his fist and hollered again. Above him, golden dragons swooped and flamed dark dragons. A woman with flowing red hair rode the largest gold, her fingertips thrusting blue mage fire at Zens' creatures. Giddi was standing , arms outstretched, his face painted with joy, staring at her while dark vapors hissed out of the wounds in his back.

"At last, the tide is turning," Roberto melded. *"Thanks to you and Giddi."*

"And you." Casting about, Ezaara frowned. *"Where's Zens?"*

An enormous shadow dragon swooped down to the clearing. Commander Zens scrambled into the saddle. The dragon shot off toward the forest.

No. Not after all he'd done. *"Zens mustn't get away,"* Roberto snapped. *"Erob, let's hunt down that murderer and finish him off."*

"My pleasure." Erob thudded to the ground, Zaarusha on his tail.

Roberto and Ezaara sprang into their saddles, and their dragons leaped into the sky, speeding after Zens.

§

With their mighty wingspans, their royal dragons caught up to Zens' shadow dragon quickly. Erob lashed out with his talons, tearing a strip of wing tissue from the dark dragon. The dragon pulled away, ascending. Zaarusha stretched her neck and belched a cloud of flame, her rumble resonating against Ezaara's thighs. Smoke billowed from the shadow dragon's burning tattered wing. It roared and bellowed, its screeches ricocheting through Ezaara's head.

Zens' dragon listed, and it sank toward the forest. Its belly raked by foliage and high branches, it crashed through the trees and landed in a river. Leaning over, the dragon doused its burning wing in the water. Zens snatched a whip from his belt. He lashed the dragon, but it moaned and sank deeper into the river. He drove the whip into its flesh, scoring deep gashes in the dragon's haunch, but the dragon refused to move.

"Our headbands," Ezaara mind-melded. Gods, they couldn't forget those. *"Otherwise Zens could kill us with his mind."*

"Good idea. Ezaara, whatever happens, I must avenge my family."

"And everyone else in Dragons' Realm," she replied.

"I want to kill him myself," Roberto replied grimly. He fastened his headband.

As Zaarusha descended, Ezaara donned her headband too. It was strange having silence in her head after the screams, roars and constant stream of thoughts from Master Giddi, Zens, and Roberto. Almost peaceful.

Zaarusha landed on the riverbank.

The dragon turned, yellow beams slicing toward Ezaara, but Zaarusha ducked and moved out of range. Zens slipped out of his saddle into chest-deep water and waded to the far bank. Erob landed there, trapping Zens and driving him back against a cliff with a jet of flame.

Roberto dismounted and strode to meet Zens.

Zens laughed, a cold sound that made ice skitter along Ezaara's scalp. Grunts, snorts and the fetid stench of tharuk wafted from the burnt foliage beyond the river. Furry, tusked monsters rushed from the trees, claws out and beady red eyes gleaming as they eyed Roberto.

"Look out, Roberto," Ezaara yelled. He hadn't heard her, hadn't seen them. And they couldn't meld.

She jumped off Zaarusha and raced over an icy log that spanned the river upstream from Roberto. When she was halfway across, a thick tendril whipped out from the water and wrapped itself around her ankle. It tugged. Gods, a strangleton. It'd haul her underwater, suffocate her and devour her. She slashed at the slimy brown tendril, but it tightened its grip and yanked her foot. Ezaara slipped and fell on the log. She thrust out a hand, landing on one knee. She hacked again. Green gunge oozing from the strangleton's half-cut tendril, the plant pulled her foot off the edge of the log and out over the river.

Tharuks were snarling, racing for Roberto.

Ezaara gave the strangleton one last whack, just missing her ankle. The tendril released, thrashing into the water.

Breath shuddering and legs shaky, she scrambled across the log and leaped onto the riverbank to face a tharuk troop leader.

Already battle-weary and exhausted, she swung her sword at its throat, spilling its dark blood on the ground. More tharuks replaced it. She swung again. With a thud that made the ground shudder, Erob landed near her and sprang into the tharuk troop, ripping their bodies apart with his teeth and talons. Fur and black blood showered the riverbank.

Still more beasts charged from the forest. Erob blasted them with a wall of hot orange fire.

Among the roars, snarls, and crackling flame, Zens was laughing.

He'd summoned these beasts. Even though Master Giddi had opened a world gate and a new band of dragons and mages were here to help them, Zens still had his army under his mental command.

A gust of heat rose at Ezaara's back. She spun.

Zens' dark dragon advanced across the river, hissing flame, boulders rumbling beneath its feet. Erob now at her back destroying tharuks, Ezaara held her sword high and faced the beast.

Beams sprang from its eyes, hitting her sword arm. Her jerkin sleeve flew open, revealing a deep gash. Ezaara's sword clattered to the stony riverbank. The beast advanced, a feral smile splitting its maw. It lunged for her.

A roar rent the air. The dragon jerked back on its haunches.

Heart pounding and breath short, Ezaara stared as Zaarusha dragged the dragon back across the river, her jaws clamped around the beast's tail. The beast's feral grin turned into an agonized grimace as it stretched its neck skyward and bellowed. Zaarusha pounced on its back and shredded the beast's hide with her talons, blasting its head with flame.

Transfixed in horror, Ezaara stared as the shadow dragon's skin melted from its skull, chunks of its flesh falling into the river. Hundreds of slimy strangleton tendrils snatched the pieces of dragon flesh and hauled them under the water to devour them.

UNEXPECTED

Giddi's throat choked up as Mazyka swooped through the sky, red hair streaming, those dark eyes thunderous. Her glorious golden dragon landed in the clearing and she slipped out of the saddle. Her grace hadn't left her, even after all these years. His throat tightened further, stealing his breath as she strode toward him with her long legs, hair rippling in the breeze from dragon wingbeats.

His magic surged inside him.

Mazyka held up one of those metal tubular weapons and aimed straight at his groin.

He was so shocked, he could only stare as a tiny projectile flew from the barrel and pierced his thigh. Giddi flinched, staring at the fletched metal object protruding from his leg.

He looked back up to Mazyka and thundered, "What have you done?" He'd thought she still loved him. His knees buckled and his vision went black.

§

Mazyka grinned as Serana's dragon landed behind her. She gestured Serana forward.

Serana joined her, staring down at Giddi. "So that's my father?"

"It certainly is. And he hasn't changed one bit." She bent and pulled the tranquilizer dart out of Giddi's thigh.

Surrounded by riders and warriors battling tharuks, she shrugged. "We may as well operate here." She jerked her head at Giddi. "Let's flip him on his front." Serana helped Mazyka turn Giddi over.

Sure enough, there were puncture wounds with soft scabs in his naked back. "These look like methimium beetles, all right. Those shadows oozing from his back were a sure giveaway." Mazyka took a surgical kit from the inside pocket of her coat and pulled latex gloves from the side pocket on her tailored combat pants. Not that gloves would make much difference here with so much dirt.

"Really, Mother?" Serana said. "It's hardly a sterile operating environment."

"Good habits die hard." Biting her lip, Mazyka made quick, clean incisions around the wounds. "Hold the edges, please."

Serana pulled the first wound apart so Mazyka could hunt down the burrowing microchip in Zens' methimium arrowheads. Yellow crystal glinted way beneath Giddi's skin. It was in deep, obviously days old. "Tweezers."

Serana passed them.

Mazyka removed the methimium beetle. Tiny scraps of Giddi's muscle clung to the barbed claws that propelled it through human tissue until it latched onto the nervous system to transmit Zens' commands. "Although these are common where we've just come from, everybody here will think they're magic." She dropped the microchip into a tiny plastic receptacle on Serana's palm, then removed the other two, closed the container and dropped it into her pocket. "These are still programmed to Zens' transmitter, so we'd better keep them safe."

Serana gazed around them. "So many dragons," she said, scanning the sky.

"And from what I can tell, the dark ones have been created by Zens. Probably by cloning one of the royals, from the look of them."

"Dragons have royalty here?"

Mazyka nodded. "I told you things are different in this world, but I think you'll like it."

A red dragon thudded to the earth nearby. A thin blue-eyed boy with a shock of dark hair was riding her. "What are you doing to the master mage?" he called out.

About time someone noticed. "I've drugged him so I can take out his methimium crystals. What I used is stronger than woozy weed, but only lasts a short while." She asked a question of her own. "Do you have any piaua juice?"

The lad grinned and slid out of his saddle, carrying a waterskin over to Mazyka.

That was no good. "I don't need water," she snapped. "I asked for piaua."

Serana rolled her eyes. "As if that legendary juice even exists. I've always doubted it."

The boy said nothing. He knelt beside Giddi, placed the waterskin on the ground and dipped his finger into it. He dropped pale green juice into the wounds on Giddi's back. His serious deep-blue eyes stared at Mazyka as the wounds' edges knitted together. "Now I've seen to Master Giddi, I must go and heal others." With that, he strode back to his ruby dragon.

Tiny glimmers of light danced along the dragon's spinal ridges. Spangles? Mazyka couldn't be sure. It had been so long since she'd seen them.

Giddi groaned.

"The tranquilizer's wearing off. Get ready," Mazyka murmured.

A grim smile on her face, Serana said, "I've been ready for years. It's him you have to worry about."

Giddi pushed himself to sit upright and scrubbed at his face with his hands. "Why did you shoot me?" He groaned. "Oh, my back's burning." Those infamously bushy eyebrows pulled low over his deep-set eyes, and he glared at Mazyka.

Still kneeling in the mud, Mazyka laughed. "You haven't changed one bit."

He shot her another glare. "And you're just as much of a mystery as always." Giddi tugged her onto his lap, wrapped his arms around her, and kissed her.

§

By the fire-spitting dragon gods, she was back. And she felt better in his arms than ever. Giddi pulled back to look into Mazyka's eyes.

"Your kiss tastes exactly the same," she said, cheekily tweaking him in the ribs.

"Do you think we're still young spring chickens?" he said. "Carrying on like this?" And then he kissed her again.

Nearby, a woman laughed. He heard dragons landing, tharuks snarling, the battle raging around them, but he didn't care. Giddi kept his eyes shut and enjoyed kissing his wife.

"Ahem." Someone cleared their throat. "Master Giddi, if you don't mind..."

Oh shards, that was Lars. He stopped kissing Mazyka. They scrambled to their feet. She smoothed her clothes. Giddi pulled on his shirt, jerkin and cloak, then stood there, holding her hand, not caring what the world thought. If they sent her back through the world gate, this time, he'd go with her.

Aidan stalked over to Lars. The battle master gave Mazyka a curt nod.

Lars folded his arms, his legs astride and planted firmly on the ground. "What's the meaning of this?" he glowered at Mazyka. "You were banished years ago. If you hadn't brought Zens into our realm, none of this would've happened." He swept an arm around the clearing, indicating ash-coated bodies and smoldering dragons.

Giddi opened his mouth to speak, but of course, Mazyka, ever quick, answered first. "I can't change the past, Master Lars, but I can help clean up." She took a deep breath. "But before I do, I'd like my husband to meet his daughter, Serana."

Giddi spluttered, staring at the girl before him. He should have realized they were related the first time he saw her: She was a blend of him and her—his hawk nose and Mazyka's eyes and high cheekbones. Her hair took after Mazyka, too, as red as a blazing sunset. And with her slightly heavy brows and tall gangly frame, there was no mistaking that she was his daughter.

She hugged him.

Happiness welled inside Giddi's chest, which threatened to explode.

"It's about time we met." Serana kissed him on the cheek. "Mom has told me so much about you."

Aidan, the battle master, smiled, but it was tinged with sadness. "Too many have lost their families today. I'm pleased you found yours, Master Giddi."

Lars' face softened. He unfolded his arms and took a step toward Mazyka, holding out his hand. "So, Mazyka, how do you and Master Giddi propose we clean up?"

Mazyka shook his hand and swept her other arm at the sky. Dark dragons and dragons implanted with methimium were still fighting sea dragons, green and brown dragons, and the dragons of Dragons' Realm.

Mazyka nodded at Serana.

Giddi still couldn't get over the fact that he'd had a daughter all this time. Mazyka must've been pregnant when he'd closed the world gate. He shook his head. That made his actions even more despicable.

Serana put her fingers to her mouth and gave a piercing whistle.

Immediately, two small gold dragons arrowed toward the clearing, mages astride their backs. Mazyka gestured them over. The dragons strolled forward.

Such majestic small creatures. *"How did you breed them?"* Giddi asked Mazyka. She'd stolen a dragon egg—a secret that Giddi had never revealed. But, just like humans, it took two dragons to breed a clutch.

"Cloning," she replied. *"I'll tell you all about it later."*

Remembering Zens' huge tanks, Giddi replied, *"I think I already know."*

"We're not here for a reunion," snapped Lars. "This is war. Now that you've offered us help, what's your plan?"

Mazyka grinned, calling to the mages on the golden dragons, "Bring a dead dark dragon down to this clearing. I want its body as meat for the others to feast on."

The mages nodded and their dragons took to the sky.

"Lars, I need thirty riders with steady hands and good aim. Archers might be best."

Lars nodded gruffly and hollered for some of the warriors fighting nearby to come over. He sent his dragon Singlar to battle tharuks in their stead.

Mazyka turned to their daughter. "Serana, pass them out the tranq guns and give them a run down on how to use them."

"So you're teaching our archers how to use those?" Giddi winced, rubbing his thigh.

Mazyka laughed.

Gods, it was good to have her back.

But although his wife was tempestuous, strong-willed, and just as good a mage as he was, Giddi couldn't just let her take command. He was still Master Wizard and Leader of the Wizard Council. After years of not fulfilling the role, it was time to step into those shoes—with Mazyka at his side, if she was willing.

Master Giddi stretched out his mind, melding with all of the dark dragons still fighting in the skies. *"Kill dark dragons."* He imitated the tone and feel of Zens' thoughts. *"Kill each other,"* he snarled. *"Kill."*

"Very clever," said Mazyka. "I'm wondering why I didn't think of it myself."

Their gaze met. Giddi laughed. He felt light and carefree in a way he hadn't for decades.

Aidan's eyes flitted between them. "What? What is it?"

Mazyka gestured skyward. "Now that he's been freed from the methimium's sway, Giddi has set the dark dragons against themselves." She dusted off her hands as her eyes flicked to Lars. "We should have this mess cleaned up soon."

Above them, dark dragons turned away from battling those of Dragons' Realm. They roared and snapped, their yellow-rayed eyes raking each other's hides. Blood dripped from deep wounds. They flew at each other, wrapping their jaws around throats, gouging and shredding with talons, and engulfing one another in fire.

Two golden dragons winged down, carrying a dead dark dragon between them. The dragons let go and the beast plummeted to the earth, blood splattering the mangled melted metal of the methimium ray.

Mazyka gestured at the carcass.

"I suppose you want me to call our dragons currently controlled by methimium down here to feast so you can knock them out with those projectiles?" Giddi asked, raising an eyebrow.

"*Same eyebrows. Same angle. Same stern look. You haven't changed.*" She grinned. "Tranquilizer darts, they're called. Why don't you call them now?"

Giddi stretched out his mind, calling only the methimium-controlled dragons of Dragons' Realm. It was easy to tell them apart by the shadows wrapped around their minds.

They angled their wings and sped down to the clearing, the breeze from their wingbeats stirring the hair of the assembled council members and mages.

§

By the First Egg, Master Giddi had done it. As much as Lars had been annoyed to find Mazyka back, he had to give it to the mages—they had turned the tide of the war. Methimium-controlled red, green, blue, and brown dragons fought over the carcass of the shadow dragons in the clearing. They snarled and snapped at each other as they tore chunks of flesh from its body.

The archers were ranged around the carcass, their metal tubular weapons glinting as they took aim.

Tonio's ruby dragon growled at a blue who tried to muscle in on her spot, baring her fangs.

"I guess Tonio didn't make it," Aidan said sadly.

"When I got my arm treated, the healers told me he died defending Marlies." Lars flexed his forearm, glad they'd had to piaua to heal it. "But I haven't seen Marlies."

"Danika told me she went down in a blaze of flame."

"That'll be hard for Hans, Tomaaz, and Ezaara." He swallowed. They'd only just found her again, to lose her so quickly. It was a sharding shame.

The archers squeezed levers—Mazyka called them triggers—on their tubular weapons. Short fletched projectiles hit the dragons' haunches. Some flinched. Some went right on eating.

"*Rather disgusting, don't you think?*" Singlar melded. "*Such cannibalistic behavior.*"

"*Privately, I agree. But Mazyka says she can use the distraction to extract these methimium beetles. These dragons will be flying with us again soon, so we'd better not make our opinions known publicly,*" Lars replied.

"*You're ever the consummate politician, Lars.*" Singlar snorted. "*I still think eating dragon flesh is revolting. Any dragon caught doing it—no matter the excuse—should be banished.*"

"A lot of things have happened in this war due to Zens' methimium. I think we should be glad that we've been spared and turn a blind eye, my friend."

Singlar's rumbling approval was comforting.

A blue dragon's head slumped onto the dead carcass. Then that of a green. Soon a red was slumbering, and a brown. Antonika staggered on her feet, then curled up and tucked her head under her tail.

Mages on gold dragons landed in the clearing and dismounted. Each mage retrieved a small kit from Mazyka and crawled over a dragon, inspecting it for arrow wounds. They removed the burrowing crystals with metal implements and called for piaua to heal the wounds.

Lars sighed, tension ebbing out of his shoulders. "I'm glad we didn't have to kill more of our own." That had been the worst: watching their dragons turn on each other in a mad killing frenzy, seeing their blood on each other's fangs and talons. Too many good dragons and riders had died today. Too many good friends, like Tonio and Marlies.

"It's a relief," said Aidan. "I was worrying about having to kill more of our dragons when we'd already lost so many."

Lars nodded somberly. "It's going to take a while to recover." He glanced around the clearing. "Did you see what happened to Zens?"

Aidan's startled glance said enough.

"Singlar," Lars melded. *"We have to hunt down Zens. Now."*

Singlar, busy trampling a tharuk, answered, *"No, we don't. Master Roberto and the Queen's Rider are already on it."*

§

Kierion couldn't believe it. All of a sudden, golden dragons were amid the battle, mages shooting blue fire from their fingertips at the fake mages upon the dark dragons' backs. Every time the blue fire hit one of Zens' mages, the fake mage disintegrated in a spray of ash.

Behind him, Fenni muttered, "By the holy mother of all dragon gods, what in flames name is that power?"

Ash floated in the air, coating their hair as they flew through it. "I have no idea," Kierion said. "And who was that woman riding the giant golden dragon?"

"I think I can answer that," said Fenni. "Mazyka, Master Giddi's long-lost wife who opened the world gate years ago and let Zens in. She's returned to help us."

Riona roared, a tremor running through her body beneath them. And the golden dragons answered, opening their maws and shooting flame at dark dragons, setting the sky ablaze with color.

§

Once the dragons were knocked out, it didn't take Mazyka, Serana, and their mages, who had all trained as medics on Earth, long to remove all the implants from the dragons' hides and patch them up with piaua. By then, ash from the incinerated dark dragons and cloned mages was drifting through the air, coating the clearing and the unconscious dragons' scales.

Mazyka straightened, rubbing her aching back. It had been a while since she'd had to work so arduously, and this was nothing like the surgical operating theaters back on Earth. But it was good to be home again. To see Giddi's kind eyes. Hear his gruff humorous comments as he barked at young mages. It took her back to years ago, when she'd first met him.

A young blond mage with green eyes approached her. "Um." He scratched his neck.

"I'm Mazyka." She held her hand out. "How can I help?"

The man shook it. "I'm Fenni. I've always wanted to meet you."

She frowned, perplexed. "Oh, ah, the pleasure is mine, I'm sure."

Fenni glanced over to check Giddi was busy, then leaned in, whispering, "Anyone who has Giddi's undying loyalty is a friend of mine. He never spoke of you, but we could all tell he still cared about you." He blushed, cheeks cherry-red, and strode off. On his way back to the purple dragon and rider waiting for him, he spun and blasted a tharuk with a fireball.

Mazyka smiled. She'd guessed it, but it was still nice to hear that Giddi, with his fierce heart, had never stopped loving her.

ZENS

"So, Master Roberto." Zens spat the word *master*, as if it were dirty.

Roberto snorted. He'd more than earned the title, deserved it, despite everything Zens had done to break and corrupt him.

Zens' powerful frame rocked with cold laughter—the insidious laughter Roberto hated. In Death Valley, he'd seen Zens laugh at people he'd tortured and slaughtered. At families he'd broken. At dragons who'd died at his whim. And Zens had laughed at Roberto when he'd been Zens' captive, grooming him as his protégé, forcing him to murder dragon riders or watch Zens kill littlings.

Roberto's anger roiled inside him.

A tharuk burst from the trees, the fur on its snout and face blackened. 000 snarled, prowling toward him. The largest of the tharuks, its body rippled with menace. It slashed its claws in the air. "Fight, coward!"

Roberto ran for 000, sword out.

He parried 000's claws with his blade and ducked its swipes. Dancing around the enraged tharuk, Roberto darted in, striking its sides, back, and shoulders. Eventually the beast tired and stumbled.

Roberto struck home, driving his blade through the tharuk's eye.

000 slumped to the earth. Its head rolled to the side. Dark blood foamed around the blade and leaked onto the ground, leaving a black stain.

"No!" With a bellow of rage and grief, Zens raced at 000, his bulging biceps—larger than most men's thighs—flexing. Zens scooped up 000. "You killed my lovely. My pride and joy." Tears escaped Zens' eyes as his face contorted in grief and anger.

Towering over Roberto, Zens snarled and tossed 000 aside.

Zens was much bigger, his reach longer, but Roberto had an advantage—Zens, in his arrogance, had assumed he could defeat any foe with his mental talents, so he'd failed to bring a sword.

The commander flung out a hand and cocked his head, frowning.

In moments, he'd realize he could no longer penetrate Roberto's mind. It was now or never. Grateful for his opaline headband, Roberto lunged, aiming straight for Zens' chest. The commander whirled, springing up and kicking

Roberto's sword from his hand. It skittered across the stones. Roberto dashed, stones crunching underfoot, and snatched it. He spun, facing Zens.

Again, that cruel laughter rang around the riverbank, bouncing off the cliff face. "You'll die today to pay for what you've done."

Zens leaped through the air with a jump Roberto would have thought impossible, his foot aiming for Roberto's chest. Roberto rolled and scrambled to his feet to slash at Zens' back. He missed. The commander spun into a crouch and then flew at Roberto, his hands grasping for his neck.

Roberto sidestepped. The commander fell heavily onto the ground. Zens rolled and grabbed Roberto's ankle, pulling him off balance.

Roberto's shoulder hit the stones. He sprawled on the ground. Zens scrambled on top of him, pinning his chest with his torso and wrapping his legs around his, immobilizing him.

Roberto thrashed his arms and swung his sword, but the angle was wrong for a killing blow.

Zens ripped off his headband, and his large hands closed around his neck. "You pompous dragon rider, I'll throttle you like a weak and lowly slave." The commander's breath blasted him. His hands tightened around Roberto's windpipe.

Roberto gurgled. Shards. He struggled for breath. Spots of light sprang before his eyes.

"Die, you cursed worm. Die." Zens' thoughts rippled through Roberto's head.

He melded with his dragon, *"Erob!"*

"Your mind is no longer barricaded," Zens sneered in his head.

Gods, last time he'd been captured, Commander Zens had thrown him around the cavern with the force of his thoughts. He was as good as dead.

"No, you're not." The tip of Erob's blue wing flashed beyond the trees. *"Last time, I wasn't there to aid you."*

A wave of Erob's power rippled through Roberto. His veins thrummed with fire. His body roiling with dragon energy, he rolled, toppling Zens off him, and surged to his feet.

"Never forget that you're a Rider of Fire," Erob called.

Power thrummed through Roberto—and anger.

On his knees, Zens flung a hand at Roberto. *"Choke and die, scum."*

An invisible band tightened around Roberto's neck.

Zens laughed, thrusting his fingers out and clenching them.

The band tightened. Zens' jeers ricocheted through Roberto's head like a landslide.

"*No, Zens. You've destroyed enough already.*" Dragon power surged through Roberto. His veins, his muscles, his very bones burned until they were molten with heat.

The hold on his throat broke. Roberto drew in deep breaths.

"You burned me," Zens cried, shaking his hand. He flung his hand out again, but nothing happened. With a cry of frustration, he tried to scramble to his feet, but Roberto thrust out his foot and kicked Zens to the ground. In a heartbeat, his sword was poised at Zens' throat.

The commander lay on the stone, his massive chest heaving. "Go on, kill me."

Roberto hesitated.

"You don't have it in you, do you?" Zens sneered. "You were always a coward, too weak to torture or maim."

Roberto took a deep breath, clenching the pommel with both hands, ready to drive his blade through this monster's blasted throat.

But images flashed to mind—scenes Roberto had seen in Zens' nightmares when they'd accidentally mind-melded in Death Valley. Zens as a littling, strapped to a metal workbench, strange implements from his world around him. Zens' father locking him in a cupboard, refusing to let him out, and then beating him when he'd wet himself in terror. His mother and father had malformed his body and mind, turning him into this monster and making him an ugly subject of ridicule. Roberto had seen the bullies teasing Zens for being so strange—and felt the pleasure rushing through Zens as he'd stopped the taunting—by leaving a boy who'd tormented him dead on the floor.

Despite everything he'd done, this evil monster was the result of his parents' actions.

Roberto understood that sense of helplessness, that desire to punish the world for being wronged. He'd experienced helplessness during his father's beatings. And a burning vengeance that could've destroyed him.

Zens smiled, his enormous yellow eyes glinting. "See, I knew you couldn't do it. You're not strong enough."

Roberto should kill Zens. He had to. This monster had destroyed so many lives.

But over and over again, Roberto saw Zens' cruel father locking him in the cupboard, and the littling Zens whimpering when he'd needed to pee—his father's refusal to let him out and, buttocks burning with urine burns, Zens cleaning up the mess while his father bellowed.

Echoing Roberto's own father's bellows of rage.

If it wasn't for Erob and Ezaara, he could've been the same. Trapped in a hell of hate and torture.

Zens' silky voice caressed Roberto's ears. *"Come, Roberto, together you and I could—"*

A sword flashed past Roberto.

Zens' gut was rent, blood staining his shirt. A moment later, Ezaara drove her sword two-handed through Zens' throat. Blood sprayed over Zens' face and ran down the blade embedded in his neck.

Ezaara panted, staring at Roberto. "Are you all right?" she huffed. "I had to do it. After what he's done to you, to our people..." Her voice trailed off. Eyes wide, chest rising and falling, she struggled to regain her breath.

Roberto's gaze fell to Zens' bleeding body. Yes, he and Zens had been shaped by their parents' evil actions, but he'd chosen differently.

Ezaara pushed her boot against Zens' shoulder and yanked her sword out of his neck. Stepping back, she spun, revealing a bloody gash on her sword arm.

"Oh gods, your arm."

"That's why I used both hands to kill him."

Roberto slashed a strip off his shirt and bound her bicep. "There's a rumor we now have piaua. We'll get your wound seen to." He picked up his opaline headband, then barked, *"Erob, burn him."*

As he led Ezaara away, his dragon landed behind them, turning Zens' body into a flaming heap.

Ezaara took off her headband. *"My right hand's free now,"* Ezaara melded, hefting her sword in her left and holding her hand out to him.

Roberto grasped Ezaara's hand. *"Look at the mess."*

The riverbank was littered with tharuk body parts and char. The river seethed with strangleton tendrils as they feasted on the dark dragon's carcass and tharuk corpses. On the other side of the riverbank, Zaarusha flamed a tharuk troop. Now that the commander was dead, tharuks on this side of the river were fleeing through the bushes.

Roberto pulled Ezaara into his arms. Never wanting to let her go again.

Above them, the sky roiled with fire. Flashes of gold and streaks of blue stabbed through the flames to incinerate dark dragons. Thick clumps of ash floated down, coating the river, the dark dragon's remains, the tharuk corpses scattered over the riverbank. Ash flakes fell into their hair. Onto their faces.

Heart pounding, Roberto clung to Ezaara, her heartbeat thrumming against his chest as she held him tight.

RETURN TO DRAGONS' HOLD

As dragons battled the remaining few shadow dragons and fake mages, the sky blazing with blue, green, and yellow flames, Giddi felt the *sathir* in the environment around him lighten, as if a great shadow had lifted. Instantly, he knew Zens was dead.

Mazyka's eyes met his and the words fell from her lips, "Zens is gone."

It was the end of an era marked by bloodshed, slavery, and wanton killing. And the beginning of a new era, which he'd face hand-in-hand with Mazyka. "By the dragon gods, I've missed you," he said.

Mazyka's eyes shone. "I felt like I was only half alive without you."

He kissed her, cupping her face in his hands. Her hair swirled in the breeze from hundreds of wings above. Behind her, the dragons who'd had their crystals removed still slumbered, slumped over the shadow beast's carcass. Giddi slid his fingers down Mazyka's neck to touch the teardrop-shaped crystal resting against the exquisite porcelain skin under her collar bone. "These saved us."

"They did. You know that with these we can go back to Zens' world any time"

He arched an eyebrow.

She laughed. "That's one thing I never forgot about you—your eyebrows." She traced one with her fingertip.

Giddi kissed the tip of her nose. "You created enough havoc going through last time. I don't think we'll be doing that again anytime soon."

"Zens came from an amazing world with technology and science."

Giddi frowned. "With what?"

"Well…" She tilted her head. "Science is like magic. It takes a long time to learn. First, I was overwhelmed, but, little by little, I started to understand. Eventually I trained and became a doctor and scientist myself. Technology is the magic of making things."

Giddi frowned again. "If you understand all that magic, does that make you a master wizard in Zens' world?" Mazyka's laugh reminded Giddi of a tinkling stream. *Sathir* coursed through him. He reached for her hand, feeling years younger—ready to face the world and finally be the leader of the Wizard Council and the master mage that Dragons' Realm so desperately needed. She bit the edge of her lip. Even after all these years, the familiarity of her old habit knifed through him.

"No, I'm not a master wizard," Mazyka said. "A doctor is like an advanced healer. A scientist understands life around us. I could take you there and show you, although, now that I'm back, I'd like to stay."

"Perhaps we should visit Zens' caverns where he grows tharuks. You might be able to make sense of his, um, what did you call it?"

"Science? Technology?"

"Yes, that stuff." Giddi glanced around.

Lars and Aidan were issuing orders. Blue dragons were landing in the churned-up mud of the clearing. Their riders were loading passengers onto dragons to leave for the hold. More dragons fanned out over the forest to scout for remaining tharuks or shadow dragons. Ezaara and Roberto landed and a cheer rippled through the clearing.

"Let's slip away quickly and make sure Zens doesn't have reinforcements growing in his caverns."

Mazyka nodded. "Makes sense. Serana has gone to help the healers. I doubt anyone else will notice."

She held her crystal and Giddi held his. *Sathir* hummed between them, growing in intensity as threads of gold ran from her fingers and silver from his. When the threads reached each other and intertwined, they were enveloped in billowing gold clouds. Giddi pictured Zens' work caverns in his mind. They shot through the glowing clouds and landed on their feet in ankle-deep water in the cavern where he'd been held captive.

The benches and beds were buckled. Zens' equipment was smashed. The stench of stale mage flame and burned flesh hung in the cavern. Char decorated the rocky walls.

Mazyka wrinkled her nose. "I saw this place through the world gate when we mind-melded. Is this where Zens implanted you with methimium?"

"No, he did that with arrows in battle. This is where he made fake mages."

"Ah, cloning," Mazyka muttered.

"I didn't see Anakisha in the realm gate," Giddi said. "Since she died, her spirit has usually guided our passage. I wonder what happened to her?" He scratched his beard, looking around at the mess. "Come with me." He led Mazyka into Zens' laboratory.

Floating ash swirled around their ankles as they splashed through the water. Bodies of half-burnt tharuks and shadow dragons blocked the gutters and drains. The huge tanks at the rear of the cavern were now nothing but jagged shards jutting above the waterline.

"What's this?" Mazyka asked, pointing to a door tucked behind a rocky outcrop.

"I've never noticed that before. We should probably take a look."

Mazyka opened the door. Giddi conjured a mage light. The green blob of flame lit up a small area and a few stairs leading up to a larger cavern.

They sloshed through the water and ascended the stairs. Mazyka mind-melded, "I'm glad not to have wet boots anymore."

"Are your boots not waterproof?" Giddi asked, glancing down at the durable silver fabric. "Perhaps you need to rub the leather with pig fat."

"Gortex is waterproof without the need for, um, pig fat. I was just glad not to be standing in tharuk soup."

Giddi's laugh came out as a bark.

The mage light bobbed ahead of them, illuminating two glass boxes the size of coffins. Giddi approached, holding his hands at the ready. Mazyka strode confidently over and pushed a knob on the wall. Everything was suddenly bathed in a yellow methimium-powered glow.

Giddi doused his puny mage light and gasped. Two bodies were prone in the glass boxes. "Oh, my holy dragon gods. Yanir." He fell to his knees, arms on the glass lid to the box holding Yanir, Anakisha's husband, immersed in clear liquid.

"And Anakisha." Mazyka's voice echoed in the rocky chamber. Something hissed.

Giddi rose and came over to Mazyka. Anakisha' body was not immersed in fluid, but had long tubes running into her mouth and arms from small metal boxes with blinking green lights. One of the metal boxes hissed and the other buzzed quietly, like a hummingbird's wings. Anakisha's skin was covered in wrinkles. "What in the Egg's name are those?" Giddi waved his hand at the boxes.

"A life support system." Mazyka gestured at tubes running into Anakisha's mouth and arms. "These supply Anakisha with everything she needs to stay alive. See how her chest is rising and falling? That's because this tube provides air. The other tube provides food straight into her blood."

Food in her blood made no sense, but Mazyka had said Zens' magic wasn't easily understood. "And Yanir? He doesn't have any tubes. Is he alive too?"

Mazyka turned to Yanir's tank. "No, he's dead, but preserved in saline, a salty solution."

Oh gods. "Zens pickled our King's Rider like an onion." The very thought had Giddi's fingers twitching and dying to fling mage flame at a wall.

In a billow of gold cloud, a transparent shimmering figure appeared.

"Anakisha!" Giddi and Mazyka spoke at the same time.

Anakisha's spirit held out her hands. *"I implore you, release me. Turn off Zens' magic and let me be free."*

"And Yanir?" Mazyka asked. *"What should we do with his body?"*

"Release him too. We belong with our kin. Please take us back to the Lost King Inn at Last Stop to be laid to rest."

Giddi addressed Anakisha's spirit. *"To Kisha, your granddaughter. Wouldn't you rather we brought her here for a last chance to talk to you? What about Zaarusha? She'll want to talk to you too."*

Anakisha shook her head. *"No, this is unnatural. Let us go, so we can fly with departed dragons."*

For a moment, Giddi hesitated. So many people and dragons would give a talon to have one last chance to speak with their beloved ex-Queen's Rider.

Mazyka shot Giddi a shrewd look. *"So be it,"* she said. *"Farewell, Anakisha. I'm sorry I let you down."* Bright tears glimmered on Mazyka's cheeks.

"And I am too," Giddi bowed his head, throat tight.

"You're both forgiven. Tell Lars I said that, and give my love to Taliesin, Kisha, Roberto, and all of my grandchildren. Give my love to Ezaara too." Anakisha's spirit hovered over her body for a moment, then sank into the flesh and disappeared.

The hiss and hum of Zens' metal boxes was the only sound in the cavern. In her lidless glass box, Anakisha's chest rose and fell in an even rhythm. Strange that he hadn't noticed that before, only now, when it was about to stop.

Mazyka laid her hand on a slim rectangle on the metal box. *"Ready?"* she melded.

He'd never be ready. He'd thought he'd lost their beloved Queen's Rider so many years ago, only to lose her again now. Giddi nodded.

Mazyka pressed the rectangular thing on the box. There was a click. A tiny red light flashed three times, then the hissing stopped. Anakisha's chest was still. With another click, Mazyka turned off the other box.

Giddi's breath rasped from his chest. Mazyka opened her arms and he stepped into her embrace willingly, burying his face in her hair. She held him, crooning, as his chest shuddered with grief.

A cluster of brown guards were gathered at the northern end of Mage Gate's clearing, their dragons' hides flecked with dark ash. When Esina thudded to the ground, two short riders broke off from the group, striding toward them. Leah recognized Darynn and Eryk instantly. She and Taliesin dismounted and ran to meet them.

"Is it time for you to go?" Leah asked Darynn.

Darynn nodded and grasped her hand. "We're humbled that you chose to visit us in your hour of need, but we must get back to our people. Will you visit us soon to replenish our piaua supplies?"

"I will," Leah said. "Thank you so much for helping to save Dragons' Realm." She flung her arms around Darynn, then he stepped aside to hug Taliesin.

Eryk glanced at his boots and then looked at her shyly, his mouth twitching up into a smile.

"Thank you." She hugged him too.

He whispered something. Tilting her head, she strained to catch what he'd said. "Sorry, I didn't hear that."

Eyes wide, Eryk whispered, "I've never seen anything as beautiful as when you were harvesting piaua juice. Your face was radiant, lit by an inner light." He ducked his head shyly again. "And you have really pretty eyes. I just wanted to tell you."

Leah gaped, eyebrows high, not knowing quite how to answer. "Well, um..."

"Darynn told me it was the first time you'd spoken with a piaua tree."

Now it was Leah's turn to duck her head. "Well, it was. But I hope it's not my last. Hopefully, I'll visit again."

He leaned in to hug her again, then stepped back and held her hands gently. A smile lit his face, making it shine like the morning sun. "I'd like that very much indeed."

"So would I," Leah answered, a surge of joy blossoming inside her chest until her skin felt too small to hold it.

Eryk and Darynn climbed upon their dragons and waved. The brown guards leaped into the air and flew off over Great Spanglewood Forest toward the Northern Alps.

Taliesin nudged Leah. "I just had a vision, a prophecy about your future."

"What is it?" Leah asked. "Something to do with the brown guards?" She hoped so.

"Maybe." Taliesin grinned. "But you have to find out some things on your own. I wouldn't want to ruin all of life's surprises."

"By the First Egg, you're infuriating." Leah laughed, linking arms with him and giving one last wave to the brown guards winging northward.

§

Gret was running through the clearing, ducking between dragons, making a beeline toward Fenni, braids flying. Above Mage Gate, dragons wheeled in the air, carrying passengers back to Dragons' Hold. Fenni helped an injured rider into Riona's saddle behind Kierion.

"Be back soon," Fenni said to Kierion, then strode out to meet Gret.

She was panting, eyes worried. "Have you seen Danion? I can't find him anywhere."

Fenni took Gret's hand, and led her away to the trees where no one could hear them. He rubbed the backs of her hands with his thumbs, searching her brown eyes. "I'm sorry, Gret, Danion fell in battle. Kierion told me his dragon, Onion, died as well." Although Danion had some annoying habits, Fenni knew he was a good man. His death was a sore loss to Dragons' Realm.

She gasped. Her hand flew to her mouth. "Danion died?"

Fenni nodded. "I'm afraid so. He and Onion saved Kierion before they were killed."

He wiped a tear from her cheek, but more streamed from her eyes. "I'm sorry to bear bad news." He fumbled in his pocket for a kerchief and dabbed at her cheeks and eyes, but she kept on crying. Perhaps she did love Danion more than him after all. "I'm so sorry. Danion was a good man. I feel terrible, Gret. Maybe it would have been better if it had been me."

Gret stopped crying, staring at him with wide eyes. "Oh gods, no! That would be much worse," she said, her lip trembling. "I'm glad it wasn't you because that would leave a hole wider than a dragon inside me. Danion was my friend, Fenni, that's all. He was an amazing man, but you're my future."

She nestled her head on his shoulder. Fenni pulled her close and swore he'd never let her go.

§

It was dark when Ezaara's bedraggled group of dragon riders and mages neared Dragon's Teeth. There were still tharuks roaming around Mage Gate, but most of the dark dragons had been killed. Ezaara ran a hand through her tangled hair and shifted in the saddle.

Nearby on Erob, not letting her out of his sight, was Roberto. *"I know how you feel,"* he melded. *"My sit bones are aching."*

"And my bow arm."

"How's the gash on your other arm?"

Ezaara shrugged. *"The piaua's healed it up fine."*

Gold wings glinted in the moonlight on either side of them. They were coming home with more than a hundred mages who'd left through the world gate with Mazyka years ago. And their littlings, who'd grown up on Earth.

Ezaara felt a little overwhelmed at the sheer number of gold dragons among the colored dragons from Dragons' Hold, the brown guards, green guards, and sea dragons. The golds varied in hue—orange-gold, brown-gold, beige with a golden tinge, and burnished gleaming gold, like Mazyka's grand dragon, who was large, but still smaller than the Dragons' Hold royals—Zaarusha, Erob, Maazini, and Ajeurina.

"It looks like a gleaming chest of treasure, something Captain would covet."

"I have to meet this captain of yours someday." She smiled.

"Of mine? I'd say he's his own man. Did you know he knew my father before he turned?" Roberto's gusty sigh echoed through Ezaara's mind.

They all had scars that needed healing. Her own stomach felt hollow at the loss of Ma. And Pa had just regained his new life as a dragon rider, only to lose his wife. A tear tracked down Ezaara's cheek. She wiped it away with a grimy hand. But another slid down to replace it, and then another.

What she needed was a long bath, but, as Queen's Rider, there wasn't much hope of that tonight. They still needed to hunt down any remaining tharuks at Dragons' Hold and clean up the slaughter. Gods, it had only been yesterday that the wall of the main cavern had been staved in and Zens' troops had flooded into Dragons' Hold on their killing spree.

The first time the hold had ever been breached—and it had happened while she was Queen's Rider.

"And while I was Dragon Queen," rumbled Zaarusha. *"You've done admirably. No one has ever been able to vanquish Zens, yet you killed him. You've stopped the senseless slaughter of our people. I'm proud of you. Don't you ever forget it."*

Ezaara tilted her head. *"One thing I've always wondered is how you knew where to find me."*

"I'd heard there was a skilled healer in Lush Valley. Handel had prophesied my rider would be one of Marlies' progeny, so I went searching." Zaarusha chuckled. "He said you were meant for Roberto, which is why he insisted that the council appoint him to train you."

Ezaara smiled. "That wily old dragon."

"He certainly is," Zaarusha replied. "Ezaara, don't forget what I said: I'm proud of you."

Zaarusha's love washed over her, filling her with sweet—no, bittersweet—satisfaction, despite her tears. Many friends had fallen today—and over these past few months. From now, a new era could start at Dragons' Hold. Hopefully an era of peace and prosperity, now that Zens' shadow no longer darkened the land.

The fierce peaks of Dragon's Teeth glinted in the moonlight. They swept over the mountains, across the basin. Dark blobs littered the stony clearing beneath the southern wall of Dragon's Teeth where their caverns were located. No doubt, carcasses of dragons, riders, tharuks, and mages.

As Zaarusha and Erob landed on the ledge of the council chamber, dread coiled in Ezaara's belly at the massacre and wreckage that would be awaiting them.

§

Linaia's wingbeats slowed as they neared Dragon's Teeth. "You're tired too, aren't you?" Adelina asked.

"Yes, those flaming shadow dragons were quite nimble. It was hard work ducking their beams and fire, but I suppose we won't get much rest tonight."

Adelina was dog-tired, exhausted, and wanted nothing more than to snuggle into her bed and sleep. "I doubt that there'll even be a bed left at Dragons' Hold if tharuks have rampaged through the place."

"If worst comes to worst, I'll shelter you under my wing."

"Nearly there!" Kierion called. He and Riona were flying only a few wing-spans away. He'd been attentive throughout their journey, waving, calling out to keep her spirits buoyed. After finding her father, hating him, then losing him again, her heart was broken into so many pieces she could never imagine being whole again. At least she had her trusted friends with her as they surged over the peaks of Dragon's Teeth and headed down to the basin.

Linaia melded with her, "Riona has asked us to follow her. Kierion wants to show you something."

"All right then."

As Linaia spiraled down, Adelina soon realized they were heading to the clearing where, only a few days ago, she'd breakfasted with Kierion in the snow on her name day. Gods, she'd thought her littling years had been rough, but she'd seen more death and carnage in the last few days than in her whole life.

Linaia thudded to the snow. It was still icy cold here. The only sign that they'd been here was the bench, shrouded in snow. Adelina held onto the saddle and slid down Linaia's side, dropping to the ground.

Kierion snatched her up in an enthusiastic hug.

"Shards, how can you have so much energy after that battle?"

"No matter how tired I am, I always feel great when I'm with you." He grinned, leading her to the bench. He retrieved a blanket from Riona's saddlebag, kicked the snow off the bench and laid the blanket on top.

"Did Riona forget to put the bench back?" She sat down and he joined her.

Kierion shrugged. "I decided to leave it here in case we wanted another romantic picnic." He sighed, dragging his fingers through his grimy soot-streaked hair. His face was blackened with dragon char.

She probably looked the same.

Kierion took a deep breath and let it out slowly. He pulled an apple out of his pocket, cut it into wedges with his knife and offered her a piece.

She hadn't realized how hungry she was; her stomach rumbled. Adelina bit into the juicy apple.

"A copper for your thoughts," Kierion said.

"I'm not looking forward to going back. To finding what's been left behind."

"Neither am I. This war has taught me a lot."

His perspective was always interesting, different. "Apart from bloodshed, desolation and robbing people of hope, what has it taught you?" Adelina felt hollowed out at the memory of Amato's dead body and the hundreds that had fallen.

Kierion's pretty gray eyes blazed. He took her hand, lifted it to his lips, and kissed it softly, never taking his gaze from hers. "It's taught me that I never want to lose you. How fragile life can be. And how I should never waste time again, telling you every day how much I love you."

His words stole Adelina's breath. She gasped. "You what? I mean, I know I love you, but I never thought... I didn't know..."

Kierion gave her a lopsided smile. "Adelina, I'm serious. And for once, I'm not pranking. I'd like to be hand-fasted to you. Um, I mean... ah, if you'll have me."

Emotion rushed through her chest, tightening her throat. Tears pricked her eyes. She flung her arms around him, pulling him close, crying—smelling the ash in his hair, the dried salt on his forehead, the tang of mage flame from riding with Fenni, and the musky scent of dragon.

"Yes, Kierion. I would love to be hand-fasted to you. I can think of nothing more perfect than being hand-fasted to the man I love."

§

She loved him! She loved him! She *loved* him! Kierion squeezed Adelina tight, vowing that he'd follow her to the ends of the realm and back if he ever had to. Never again would he let a misunderstanding come between them. Never again would he let his stubborn pride rob him of the woman he loved. "I promise you, Adelina, never again."

"What? You'll never hug me again?" Dark eyes dancing, she gave him that cheeky grin he loved so much.

"I'll never ever let you sneak out of my life again." He laughed, picking her up and spinning her around and around in the snow. "Gods, you're beautiful. I want to spend every living moment with you."

§

The door to the council chambers thudded open and people rushed out—people Ezaara had never seen before. From their tattered clothing, gaunt faces and hollow eyes, they must be slaves from Death Valley. Someone must've saved them.

Roberto slid from his dragon and helped her down off Zaarusha. Squeezing her hand, he murmured, "This'll be Tomaaz's doing. I left him and Lovina in Death Valley to care for the slaves. They must've brought them here through the realm gate."

A blue guard with her arm in a sling and a gash across her cheek pushed her way through the crowd and fell to one knee in front of Ezaara, pounding her heart with her fist. "My honored Queen's Rider, Zaarusha alerted our dragons that you have vanquished Zens. I, Jacinda, vow to serve you with love and humility, thankful for the lives you have saved." She swallowed and rose to her feet. "My husband and family were murdered at Zens' hands. Now they can have peace, flying with departed dragons, knowing he is gone."

Roberto melded. *"She and her dragon were injured, so I told them to come back to the hold and prepare for our return."*

"You knew we'd return?"

"I hoped so," said Roberto, *"but for a while there, it wasn't looking too promising."* His ebony eyes were warm in the glow of the torchlight.

The guard continued, unaware of their mind-melded conversation. "We've cleared the chambers and caverns of tharuk corpses, although a few live tharuks remain in the dungeons. Half of the infirmary is ready for patients. The wounded dragons who returned to the hold have burned many bodies in the clearing, but there are still more. There are many more slaves from Zens' mining crews who're currently clearing the main cavern as we speak, piling bodies in the clearing and dragging rubble outside." She tilted her head. "Ezaara, for years, Dragons' Hold has been impenetrable, inaccessible to the people of the realm. If we can clean up the tunnel Zens made and guard it well at the chasm end, we could share this beautiful basin with all the citizens of the realm." She blushed. "I know it's probably too early to be thinking of these things, but I have a lot more ideas if you'd like to hear them."

Ezaara was gob-smacked. Here they were, battle-weary and exhausted, yet Jacinda already had plans. As she opened her mouth, struggling to think of what to say, Roberto tipped back his head and laughed.

He clapped the blue guard on the shoulder. "Your plans sound very interesting, Jacinda. But let's hear them tomorrow after we've cleaned off our battle grime and had some sleep."

§

Roberto put a protective arm around Ezaara and helped her back up into Zaarusha's saddle. He climbed up behind her, and Zaarusha flew toward the Queen's Rider's cavern. Roberto cradled Ezaara in his arms, nestling his chin on her shoulder. "I suggest we take a long hot bath while our dragons hunt."

Ezaara leaned back, enjoying his comforting warmth at her back. "That sounds so nice," she said wearily.

"Do you know what sounds even nicer?" he asked.

"What?" The breeze ruffled her hair.

"Spending our lives together, without living in Zens' shadow. A bright new future that I never dreamed would be possible." He kissed her neck. "I'm glad you had the courage to jump on Zaarusha in Lush Valley."

"I'm glad you did too." Zaarusha belched a gust of flame, heading toward their ledge, her triumphant roar rumbling through the night.

Her mother was dead and their realm in tatters, but they had each other. And a new future ahead of them. *"I'm glad too."* Ezaara smiled, turning in the saddle to meet Roberto's lips.

Roberto kissed Ezaara. Kissed away the memory of the battlefield. The loss and the pain. And welcomed her home.

Zaarusha landed on the ledge, waiting patiently until they were finished. *"About time,"* she said as they dismounted. *"I'm hungry and need to hunt."*

Ezaara and Roberto laughed, walking hand in hand into their chambers.

A New Dawn

Dawn peeked over the tips of Dragon's teeth as Maazini touched down outside the infirmary. Tomaaz helped Jael out of the saddle.

"Go and find Lovina," Jael muttered. "I'll be fine from here."

"You sure?" Tomaaz gestured at Jael's stomach wound. "That looks painful."

It was. Jael gritted his teeth and held his hand over his belly as he staggered to the infirmary doors.

Tomaaz swung down and came over to open the heavy door for him.

"Thanks," Jael grunted, sweat beading his forehead.

Tomaaz was haggard, his face lined with grief. "I'll check in on you later. I just want to make sure Lovina's all right."

"Rightly so." Jael had never known what it was like to have a mother burned to cinders in midair, but from where he stood, it looked pretty grim. He supported himself with a hand as he stepped over the threshold. The rear part of the infirmary was in chaos with people righting overturned beds, scrubbing walls and bustling about, putting tharuk damage to rights. The area closest to him had already been tidied up and the beds made up with fresh linen. Some were occupied with wounded; many were waiting for the influx of patients from Mage Gate.

A tall redhead who'd come through the world gate was checking patients and issuing soft-spoken commands to the people tending them. If he wasn't mistaken, many of the mages tending the ill and wounded were riders of those magnificent gold dragons. He guessed that made them dragon mages of sorts.

A girl came over. "Please sit down." She ushered him to a bed and examined his wound.

Jael winced. "It's not that bad."

She felt his forehead. "You have a fever. Your wound could be infected. You'll need Serana to see you. She'll be here soon. In the meantime, I'll bring you some feverweed tea."

She bustled over to the redhead, who glanced up and nodded, then continued her work.

Soon the redhead was at Jael's bedside, wavy locks tucked over her shoulder. Her jade eyes swept over him, taking in his bent knees, his bloody hand clutching at his wound, the layers of ragged clothing that had been sliced through by that horrible shadow dragon's eye beam. It had only been a glancing blow as the dragon had fallen to its death, enough to hurt like wildfire, but not enough to spill his guts like Seppi's. But it had happened last night, and now he wasn't feeling so great.

She grabbed a pillow and tucked it under his knees. "I know it's painful, but try to relax your muscles so I can see what's going on." She felt his forehead and waved away the girl who'd brought feverweed tea. Her hands were gentle, almost tender, as she peeled back his clothing, exposed his wound. Her eyebrows drew down, fine lines wrinkling her forehead as she examined him. "It's not too deep, but you may already have an infection." Her eyes grazed his torso. "Not surprising given the amount of blood and ash on you. You were fighting in the thick of battle, weren't you?"

"You could say that, but I think we all were." Jael cocked his head. "You're Mazyka's daughter, aren't you?"

She laughed, her eyes lighting up like the ocean splashing in the sun. "I am. Serana's my name."

Gritting his teeth, he stretched his hand out to shake hers. "Jael."

"You're Naobian."

He nodded, unable to speak as a dizzy spell hit him. Shards, it was so cold in here. The sweat pebbling his brow made him shiver.

She put something on the bedside table that looked like a leather-bound book, but when she opened it, it was full of sharp metal implements. "This is my medical equipment." She picked up a long needle with a clear tube on the end.

"What's that?" he asked, eying it.

"You'll feel a prick, but it shouldn't hurt much. It's an antibiotic which will take your fever down and fight what's gotten into your body. It's like sending small warriors into your blood to fight the infection."

Jael squinted at the sharp needle. It couldn't hurt worse than his wound. "All right. Send your littling warriors in and get this over with." He squinted again. There was a hazy glow around Serana, probably caused by the torchlight.

She moved, but the glow remained. No, not the torchlight then. With a jolt, Jael realized he was seeing her *sathir*. Magic thrummed beneath his skin. Did Serana realize how beautiful she was? Dragon's teeth! He'd never felt like this before.

Serana prepared the syringe. Oh gods, explaining antibiotics and modern medical procedures to a man who'd never heard of an immune system was tricky. The fact that he was handsome, dark-haired, dark-skinned, and dark-eyed with a gaze that spoke of honesty and honor had nothing to do with it. She fastened her tourniquet around his bicep.

"I assume you're not amputating my arm."

"No, this will make your veins stand out."

"So you can send the littling warriors in. I'm relieved you're not sticking that thing straight into my wound."

"So am I. Are you all right?"

"A bit dizzy. It's nothing."

"That'll fade as the antibiotics work." When she injected him, he didn't flinch, moan, or look away.

His lips twitched into a smile. "Let the battle against my fever begin." His eyes flitted to one of the male medics who was administering an antibiotic injection to another fevered warrior. "I'm glad you're my healer, not him. You have gentle hands."

Her eyes met his. Warmth rushed to her cheeks. Not enough that she'd be noticeably blushing, but enough for her to feel it. She pushed the plunger down.

"That's an unusual sensation. It's so cold. What causes that?"

By gods, he was gorgeous—those dark eyes, tanned skin, and thick luscious hair. Her eyes drifted to his lips. She hurriedly glanced down at the syringe. She had to focus.

"So, I'm just wondering how a troop of warriors can fit inside that needle." He raised an eyebrow, eyeing it. He obviously had a keen, inquiring mind and a sense of humor. "From what I hear, there are amazing things in Zens' world. Things that we can't comprehend." He gestured at the needle. "I guess this is one of them."

"There are many things that would seem like strong magic to people here. They're all perfectly logical if you learn about them, bit by bit."

"Try me."

"Right now, you need to heal. Maybe another time."

His ebony eyes met hers. "That would be nice."

Hang on—what had she just committed to? Serana laid the syringe aside and swabbed his stomach wound. His lean muscled torso was quite a sight, but she kept her eyes focused on his gash. Interesting. He didn't wince, shudder, or grit his teeth, even though she could tell from the slight flare of his nostrils that he was in pain.

Brave, then. Perhaps even courageous in battle. "How did you get this gash?"

He shook his head. "Rather silly of me, really. I wounded a shadow dragon. As it was dying, it plummeted past me. I got distracted for a moment and the beams from its eyes did this." He gestured at his stomach. "It's not as bad as what happened to Seppi." He flashed a genuine smile. The effect was dazzling. "I'm lucky, I guess."

Oh man, she was in deep trouble.

§

There was a thud on the ledge outside Zaarusha's den. *"You have visitors,"* Zaarusha mind-melded.

Ezaara's quilt was so soft, her muscles so tired, she didn't want to get up.

Roberto's eyelids fluttered open. He rolled over and kissed her. "Morning."

"Someone's here." Ezaara tugged on her shirt and breeches.

Roberto sat up in bed. Ezaara sighed, her gaze lingering on his tanned muscular chest. "I'd love to relax here all day with you, but there's work to be done."

"Come on, sleepyhead. Don't let these young ones wait all day," Zaarusha harrumphed impatiently.

"Young ones? I'll be out right away."

"I'll come with you." Roberto swung out of bed and slipped on his breeches, shirt and boots. He flung a cloak over Ezaara's shoulders and put his arm around her waist, kissing her hair as they walked out to the ledge.

A beautiful ruby dragon was waiting with Taliesin and Leah in her saddle.

Ezaara rushed to them and squeezed their hands. "Thank you for bringing piaua, for giving us hope." Her throat choked up and she couldn't speak.

Leah nodded, wiping her eyes. No doubt thinking of Ma too.

Taliesin gave a lopsided grin. "Meet Esina." He waved at the ruby's head.

The dragon snaked down her neck, bowing to Ezaara, Roberto, and Zaarusha. *"My honored Queen, Queen's Rider and Master of Mental Faculties, I am Esina, the last surviving red guard."*

Images flitted through Ezaara and Zaarusha's minds: shadow dragons swooping through the air with outstretched talons and fiery maws; huge armies of tharuks streaming from forests and rampaging across the plains; methimium-tipped arrows turning the red dragons against one another; yellow eye beams slicing through red dragons' bellies; blood raining on the ground; and Esina fighting valiantly, but losing her rider—a young woman with blonde hair streaming in the wind—as a shadow dragon plucked her from the saddle and tore her body apart with its talons. They heard bellows of rage as Esina fought harder against great armies of tharuk archers felling dragons with limplocked arrows. She battled tharuks hewing down piaua trees and rampaging through the piaua grove with axes. Finally, Esina fled, chased by a horde of shadow dragons.

"I took refuge in the Northern Alps to heal. When I returned, everybody I knew and loved was gone. Dragon carcasses lay in stinking mounds upon the plain." A shudder rippled through the ruby dragon. *"I am the last survivor of the red guards. I beg forgiveness for outlasting my brethren. Perhaps I, too, should've fallen in battle."*

Ezaara flung her arms around the dragon's neck and nestled her head against her warm scales. *"No. Please, don't feel guilt for surviving. Without you, Taliesin and Leah would never have found piaua juice in the North. You have saved countless lives. As we speak, healers on the battlefields at Mage Gate are treating people, readying them to be brought home by the blue guards. If it weren't for you, your noble rider Taliesin, and his generous-spirited friend Leah, many more would be dead. Thank the dragon gods, you all survived."*

Esina snuffled Ezaara. The dragon's warm breath tickled her cheek. Ezaara scratched her eye ridge. "Be at peace."

Roberto spoke up. "We're indebted to you, Esina."

Ezaara nodded. *"We are."*

"Thank you, your words mean much to me."

Leah gestured Ezaara over. "Our Queen's Rider, we have something special to show you." Although smoke and blood were smudged on Leah's face, her eyes were bright with excitement. "We would've come sooner, but we were tending the wounded at Mage Gate and helping the blue guards get them onto dragonback."

"Go on, Leah," Taliesin urged.

Leah loosened the straps on a rear saddlebag and lifted the flap. Esina settled low on her haunches so Ezaara could reach inside.

Ezaara thrust her hand into the saddlebag. Her fingers brushed against something pliable, then closed around a slender supple stick.

"Take it out." Leah and Taliesin were grinning.

Ezaara pulled out a small piaua seedling with its roots wrapped in damp cloth. She gasped. "A piaua seedling. Where did you get?"

"From the brown guards." Taliesin leaned past Leah and pulled out two more seedlings, holding them up. Their slender green leaves weren't even as long as Ezaara's little finger. "We have thirty of them. We can go back to get more when we need them. We had much more piaua juice, but tharuks caught us and destroyed it on the way. We were lucky they didn't search the saddlebags," he babbled.

Ezaara had never heard that many words come out of Taliesin's mouth before. When he was a newly-rescued slave boy, it'd taken ages before he'd even spoken.

"Esina said she's happy to take us any time," he said.

Leah grinned. "The brown guards would be grateful to have us back. They've lost their tree speaker, so we'll have to visit them regularly so I can harvest piaua juice for them and us, until our trees mature. They have an enormous grove full of saplings, which are kept warm by dragon's breath so the trees grow, even in the dire northern winter."

"That's wonderful news." Ezaara cradled the seedling against her chest. "You've both done a fabulous job. Thank you."

Leah smiled. "Although we had a difficult journey, I remembered how you healed my little finger and stopped me from dying from limplock. That kept me going. I wanted to share the same hope with others."

Roberto leaned in and kissed Ezaara's cheek. *"You've given so many of us hope, Ezaara. Never forget it."*

Zaarusha rumbled in agreement.

§

Ezaara and Roberto had just sat down to breakfast in their cavern when another thud sounded on the ledge.

"Another visitor," Zaarusha announced. *"I think you'll want to come out and meet this one in person."*

When Ezaara and Roberto strolled out to the ledge, Ithsar was perched upon a massive jade dragon whose scales shimmered with silver. Her orange robes billowed in the breeze, reminding Ezaara of the Robandi desert sands.

"Ithsar!" Ezaara ran to greet her friend. Ithsar nimbly leaped off her sea dragon and embraced Ezaara. "Thank you, Ithsar. You changed the tide of battle. Your dragons and the Naobian greens helped save us."

"Before I ever met you, I had a vision of us riding into battle together," Ithsar said fiercely. "And then again, when my mother captured you."

Ezaara clasped Ithsar tighter. "I was afraid your mother had killed you, that I'd caused your death. Gods, I'm glad you're alive."

Ithsar's dark eyes flashed. "Ashewar lives no longer. I am now chief prophetess of the Robandi assassins." She waved her fingers in the air. "And my fingers work again. Thank you. None of that would've happened without you, Ezaara, she of the golden hair."

"How in the Egg's name did you become prophetess? And how did you meet your beautiful dragon?"

"That's a long story," said Ithsar. "Saritha is hungry and needs time to recover from battle."

"As do you." Ezaara took Ithsar's hand. "I suggest Zaarusha takes Saritha hunting and to our lake so she can swim, while you and Roberto and I catch up over breakfast."

Roberto laughed and embraced Ithsar. "We'd love to hear your tale."

"That would suit us well. Although she hankers for the sea, Saritha likes your northern lakes." Ithsar's white teeth flashed in her tanned face. She adjusted her orange headdress. "And I am famished."

After the War

One Year Later

Riona's purple wings glinted with gold shimmers in the bright Naobian sun, a contrast to the aqua ocean glistening below them. Kierion tightened his arms around Adelina's waist. Although Adelina could've chosen to fly on Linaia, they enjoyed snuggling together whenever they flew. He murmured in her ear, "It's nice to have you here, tucked safely in my arms."

She grinned against his cheek and swatted his hand. "As if I was all yours," she replied, twisting around to gaze at him cheekily.

He lowered his head, and she kissed his cheek. Suddenly, he couldn't help himself. His lips were in her hair, on the back of her smooth neck, and his arms tightened around her tiny waist, pulling her against his chest. "You're all mine, and I'm greedy. I'm never going to share you with anyone else."

She laughed, elbowing him in the ribs, and leaned over Riona's spinal ridge, pointing down at the sea. "Look, there's a whale." A fountain of foaming water shot above the sea as a dark shape surfaced. Her voice was full of joy. "The last time I remember seeing one was with my father when I was a littling and he took me for a ride on Matotoi."

Matotoi, Amato's trusty dragon, had died in the battle at Mage Gate. It was wonderful to hear Adelina's voice tinged with joy as she spoke of her father. Occasionally, shadows passed across her face when was she sitting quietly in the evenings and Kierion knew she'd been thinking of her troubled littling years. Yet today she was remembering the joy her father had given her.

"I like it here," said Kierion. "I'm glad we stayed."

"I never thought you'd want to settle in Naobia."

He kissed her again. "It's your influence," he said. They'd come down to a seaside cottage for their hand-fasting holiday, but neither of them had wanted to leave. After a fleeting visit back to Dragons' Hold to pack up their belongings, they'd returned to stay and help the green guards fight smugglers and pirates.

"Are you sure it wasn't the captain and your great seafaring expedition that convinced you?" Adelina asked, adjusting the pretty gold scarf with scarlet dragons he'd given her on her name day, so long ago.

Kierion groaned. "Sure, I loved the view inside Captain's chuck bucket. That must be it."

"Great," she said. "There might be more where that came from." She waved a hand at some red-sailed ships cresting the horizon.

"Not the Bloody Cutlasses again!" Kierion groaned.

"I'm afraid so, but they're a way off so I suggest we enjoy the peace while we can." Adelina kissed him some more.

§

Two Years Later

"Are you nervous?" Gret asked as she and Fenni crossed the floor to open the front doors.

Oh, flame it! Those stupid sparks were dripping from his fingers again. Fenni grinned. "How could you tell?" he quipped.

Gret just laughed, her blonde hair swinging over her shoulder.

He tilted his head. "When you wear your hair down, I get to see all the beautiful shades of caramel and honey among the blonde. I like it."

She glared at him.

He laughed. "I love your braids too," he added hurriedly.

She raised an eyebrow. "Did you know my hair was actually chestnut when I started training at Dragons' Hold?"

"You're joking."

"No, I started washing it with wood ash and vinegar to bring out the blond, back before I met you."

It was Fenni's turn to raise his eyebrows. "I'll love it, no matter what color it is. Any more surprises?"

"Maybe." She pursed her lips, raising an eyebrow. "You didn't answer me. I asked if you were nervous."

"Of course I am. It isn't every day you get to open a Dragon Mage Academy."

She chuckled. "With an expert swordswoman at your side."

"That's the best part," he murmured. "Our mage riders have to be able to fight too." He leaned in and kissed her, feeling her smile beneath his lips.

"This place has scrubbed up quite well," Gret said.

Captain had given them the Brothers' Arms. Running his eyes over the room, Fenni admired their handiwork. They'd widened the doorway, mounting it with double brass doors, and sanded back the battle-worn scratched tables, polishing them with oil until they gleamed. Parchment and inkwells sat on the tables, not that they anticipated the mages would be taking many notes. And the rooms upstairs and out the back had been converted into dormitories or smaller classrooms.

Now their academy was due to open.

"Come on," said Gret. "Let's show the people. The streets of Montanara are humming with excitement."

Fenni grinned.

They took each other's hands, strode to the double brass doors, and flung them open. Fenni and Gret stood at the top of the stairs, gazing down to the crowded cobbled street on the corner of Nightshade Alley.

"Welcome to the Dragon Mage Academy of Dragons' Realm," Fenni boomed. He thrust out his hands and sent bouquets of green-flamed flowers cascading over the crowd.

People roared and shoved, pushing to clamber up the stairs.

Gret turned to him and kissed his cheek. "I told you there was nothing to be nervous about."

Fenni grinned again and ushered their eager new students inside.

§

Four Years Later

As the sun rose over Death Valley, Tomaaz kissed Lovina on the cheek and rolled out of bed. He padded to the window overlooking the glorious view. The once-barren hillsides had been replanted, the young saplings now showing the lush green growth of spring.

He and Lovina had rehabilitated as many slaves as possible, buried the latrine pits and stinking cesspools that Zens had left behind, and tilled the land for the last four years. Dragons from all over the realm had participated, raking and turning the earth over with their talons and providing dragon dung to feed the dry and arid soil. There was a long way to go. Much of the land farther south near the old pirate tunnels was still arid, but they'd get to that one day. For now, this little corner of Dragons' Realm, which had once been their hell, had become their heaven.

Lovina stirred and slipped out of bed, padding to join him. Tomaaz put an arm around her. The sun warmed their shoulders through the window.

She murmured, "After my family died, during all those years in Death Valley, all I ever wanted was a home and someone who'd treat me kindly." She turned, her cornflower-blue eyes bright and full of hope. "And you've given me both."

Tomaaz's gaze flitted to Lovina's easel standing near the window. Although she was often too busy to draw, the portraits of hundreds of slaves now thriving here in the valley were nailed to the walls. He brushed her hair with his lips, murmuring, "Wherever you are is my home."

There was a knock at the door. Tharuk 274 entered, holding a tray of fresh bread and cheese. "I milked goats," it said, giving them a tusky smile. 274's gaze slid to the portrait Lovina had drawn of it after they'd found it wandering in Great Spanglewood Forest after the Battle of Mage Gate.

274 had been clutching a dragon figurine made of stick and leaves, and had never lost its love of art. In fact, it still had one of Lovina's charcoal sketches on bark from when she'd been a slave in Death Valley. Tomaaz had hardly been able to contain his surprise when the tharuk had shown them its stash of precious things hidden in Zens' old warren of mine tunnels. Since they'd spared its life, 274 had proven loyal and loved to serve them.

He often wondered how many more tharuks could've been rehabilitated if they hadn't been thoroughly wiped out.

"Feed black scales next?" 274 asked, bringing Tomaaz back to the present. The tharuk took a tiny dragon made of twigs and leaves from its breeches pocket and stroked it—a dragon that Leah had apparently made when she and Taliesin had escaped. "I like black scales."

When they'd cleaned up Zens' caverns, they'd discovered some dragon embryos that hadn't been destroyed. Although the dragonets had mind-screeched when they were taken out of their tanks, Tomaaz had insisted that Mazyka operate on them. Once she'd removed the methimium implants from their brains, the creatures had also proven friendly and not aged like those that'd had methimium.

"Yes, we'll hunt with our black scales this morning." Tomaaz or Lovina always accompanied the black dragons when they hunted to prevent the citizens who lived in Spanglewood Forest near the foot of the Terramites from worrying about whether stray shadow dragons had survived. 274 often rode behind them.

"Very good." The tharuk smiled again and left, closing the door.

Lovina leaned her head on Tomaaz's shoulder. "Sometimes I wonder if 274 will imprint with one of our black dragons one day. It's certainly devoted to them."

Tomaaz inhaled the floral scent of her soap and kissed her again. "After what we've seen, I'd say anything is possible."

§

Six Years Later

Ezaara put down the rest of her roast fish and leaned against a rock. "I'm full. I can't eat another bite." She gazed at the lake shore where their daughter was skipping in and out of the shallow water. Nearby, Erob and Zaarusha were curled up in the sun.

"I wonder if she'll be the next Queen's Rider?" Roberto asked, dropping to the grass beside Ezaara and stretching out his long legs.

"Are you planning my demise already?"

"Never." Roberto leaned over and kissed Ezaara's lips, his dark eyes eating through hers. "Why would I have saved you from the Robandi Desert assassins if it was just to plot your demise now?"

She whacked him on the shoulder. "As if you saved me." She snorted, a habit she'd learned from him over these past six years. "That's not how I remember it, at all."

He laughed. "Where would I be without you?"

"Sometimes, I do wonder whether Tyra will be the next Queen's Rider. After all, she's shown remarkable ability so far, and she's still so young," Ezaara mind-melded.

"I wonder too," said Roberto. *"It's strange how she has a pale birthmark over her chest, like the burns we got at the Battle of Mage Gate."*

"That might explain her ability to mind-meld with animals." Ezaara pursed her lips, remembering the first time Tyra had surprised them by mind-melding with an injured goat and telling them where it was hurt. *"I didn't even realize I was pregnant back at Mage Gate."*

Tyra squealed, running toward them. "Ma, Papa, look what I found."

Ezaara scrambled to her feet and strode over. A tiny dragonet lay in Tyra's hands, its tail curled around her wrist. Its scales were a splotchy turquoise-jade, and shimmered silver in the sun. "Where did you find it?"

"Over there in the rocks."

Zaarusha and Erob lifted their heads out from under their wings. Erob stood and walked over to the lake. He stretched his long neck down behind the rocks. *"There are egg shards here. I think this little one has just freshly hatched."*

The dragonet crooned, rubbing its head against Tyra's chest. A shard of eggshell fell off its chest and its tongue flicked out, licking her cheek. She giggled. "She says she's hungry. And that her name is Zatyrob."

Roberto leaped to his feet and speared Ezaara's discarded fish on his knife. He crouched beside Tyra. "Honey, you're imprinting."

"Imprinting?" Tyra squealed with glee. "You mean with Zatyrob?"

Roberto chuckled. "I think you'd better feed her." He held out the fish on his blade.

The dragonet's nostrils quivered as it gazed up at Tyra, ignoring the meat.

"Oh Roberto." Tears pricked at Ezaara's eyes. *"Honey, she's gorgeous. Zatyrob's asking Tyra's permission to eat."*

Tyra took the fish. "I have to feed it to her. You can't, Papa. She's my dragonet."

Once again, Ezaara's eyes pricked. Her own mother had missed Ezaara imprinting and had never had a chance to meet her granddaughter. "Roberto, she's only five summers old. What are we going to do?" she whispered.

Roberto laughed and kissed Ezaara again. "I'm sure we'll figure it out, just like we've figured out everything else so far."

Zatyrob snaffled the fish and licked Tyra's fingers. "It tickles." Tyra laughed. "She wants to swim now."

Swim?

Ezaara and Roberto followed Tyra to the water's edge. Erob and Zaarusha joined them.

Zatyrob scrambled out of Tyra's hands and leaped into the crystalline waters. She dived, then shot above the water into the sky, her wings dripping sparkling droplets, only to twist and plunge back underwater again. The next time Zatyrob surfaced, she had a small fish in her tiny jaws. She swam to the lake edge and clambered out with clumsy feet—much too large for her body. Then she pounced on the flapping fish, killing it with a swipe of her talons.

Erob rumbled his approval at Zatyrob's first kill, while Zaarusha snuffled the dragonet like a proud mother. Tyra danced on the shore, clapping her hands together. "I've got a dragon, Mama. My very own dragon!"

Ezaara couldn't help laughing. "Yes, you have, sweetie. Zatyrob is a sea dragon."

Roberto raised an eyebrow at her. *"And where did she come from?"*

"When Ithsar and her Robandi guards visited a few weeks ago, one of their sea dragons was clutchy. She must've left an egg behind," Ezaara replied.

"*How in the Egg's name are we going to take care of a sea dragon, here at Dragons' Hold?*"

Ezaara laughed again. "*Don't worry, we'll figure it out.*"

They stood arms around each other, watching their daughter and the dragonet frolic in the warm water, the fierce snow-tipped peaks of Dragon's Teeth rising behind them against a pristine blue sky. Ezaara leaned her head against Roberto's. Yes, they'd figure it out somehow.

§

Hans opened the door and strolled out of his cottage onto the porch carrying his soppleberry tea—Marlies' favorite drink. Tears stinging his eyes, he took a sip. Liesar and Handel were curled up in the sun-warmed grass, sleeping.

"*Well, you thought we were sleeping,*" Handel rumbled in his mind, making Hans chuckle.

Life had been like this for some time, the sweetness tinged with sadness; his happiness tinged with tears. He missed Marlies. Would do as long as he lived. He glanced out at the group of young piaua trees growing on the edge of his land—Marlies' Grove, Taliesin and Leah had named it. Every day the three of them tended the trees and Leah harvested the piaua juice needed for the healers at Dragons' Hold and others across Dragons' Realm. Now that Mazyka was the new master healer at Dragons' Hold and had many trainees, Leah was only occasionally needed in the infirmary.

After Marlies' death, it had been too painful for him to remain at Dragons' Hold. So he'd opted to live here, near where she'd died. Raising Taliesin and Leah had kept him from being too lonely—not that they needed much raising anymore, now that they were of age. And here, on the edge of Great Spanglewood Forest near Mage Gate, he was close enough to the hold to still be useful, and close enough for Taliesin to train.

And sometimes, just sometimes, if he listened closely...

Hans took another sip of tea and closed his eyes, listening to the whisper of the trees from Great Spanglewood Forest telling him how much they missed Marlies.

When he opened his eyes, Liesar's turquoise eyes regarded him, sorrow in their depths. And he knew, with certainty, that she would not imprint again. Just as he could never love another with the same fierce love he'd felt for the woman who had first saved him from tharuks, so long ago when he was a foolish, headstrong, young rider on Handel.

Handel chuckled. *"I remember that battle well. Marlies really saved your backside."*

Despite the tears rolling down his face, Hans had to laugh. *"She saved the rest of me too,"* he said. *"It was a very close call."*

EILEEN MUELLER

SEA DRAGON

RIDERS OF FIRE
BOOK SIX

PROLOGUE

These short scenes are repeated from Ezaara, Riders of Fire book 1

Ithsar was used to hiding in the tunnels. Used to avoiding the unwanted gaze of her fellow assassins. Used to crawling into tiny spaces to escape their taunting. But she wasn't used to the new strength in her fingers, the strange energy that had surged along her half-dead nerves as Ezaara, she of the golden hair and green eyes, had healed her. Ithsar had never experienced such kindness from anyone. And although the *dracha ryter* from a far-off land had given her a vial of healing juice, Ithsar honored Ezaara, so she hadn't dared use any on herself.

So, Ithsar ran for her life and for Ezaara's. Having hands that didn't work well had helped her hone the rest of her body. Whenever she was off-duty, she practiced the *sathir* dance for hours on end, her limbs nearly brushing the walls of her tiny cavern. Her legs were strong, feet agile, and her endurance was akin to the legendary *Sathiri*, who had established the ancient dance. Not that any of her fellow assassins realized. She'd hidden her prowess, deliberately acting clumsier than she was. Deliberately fooling everyone—especially her mother, Ashewar.

On through the dark, Ithsar ran, through winding tunnels to a hidey-hole they'd never suspect. When pursuers passed her, she doubled back until she reached an alcove near where the Naobian lay healing. Healed. She'd healed him with that little vial of juice. He of the dark eyes shining like ripe olives under the sun. No wonder Ezaara loved this man—Roberto, she'd called him—it was evident in her *sathir* when she'd asked after him. And he had cried, calling Ezaara's name in his fever with such love, babbling about her color. The color, Ithsar had understood. Ezaara's presence radiated all the colors in her mother's prism-seer. Another talent Ashewar was unaware of—Ithsar could see without a prism. And she'd seen a vision of these two *dracha ryter*.

The Naobian had also ranted about banishment, murder and poison. It appeared he'd saved Ezaara, the healer. For that, Ithsar owed him.

Chief Prophetess Ashewar planned to breed him with her women and then kill him.

But no, Ashewar would not kill this man, loved by her healer. Ithsar would see to that. He would go free to love Ezaara. Perhaps one day, she, Ithsar, would have a man like this, who called her name with a voice that ached with tenderness.

Her breathing now quiet, Ithsar stepped out of the alcove. The Naobian had only one person guarding him at night—but tonight it was Izoldia. Ithsar's birth defects meant she was smaller than other girls her age. Izoldia, the largest, had led the bullying, and was always the last to finish beating her—the most savage, the cruelest. Bruises, black eyes, and, later, cuts and burns had been Izoldia's mark—until one day, Ithsar had wrestled the brand off her and burned Izoldia, keeping her brutality at bay.

Ashewar, noticing Ithsar's hurts, had said nothing. Disciplined no one. If Ithsar had been the daughter of another assassin, Ashewar would've been ruthless in punishing Izoldia. But she wasn't. She was Ithsar, Ashewar's only daughter—the chief prophetess' malformed disappointment.

Perhaps Ithsar owed Izoldia, for driving her to artistry in *sathir*, for making her stronger than she otherwise would have been, but Izoldia had also twisted what the Naobian had said, conjuring up stories so Ezaara—she of golden beauty, the girls called her in hushed whispers over their evening meal—would die.

Not while Ithsar breathed.

Opening the healing room door, Ithsar kept the anger from her face, instead, offering congeniality and supplication.

"What do you want?" Izoldia snapped.

"Did you hear the disturbance?" Ithsar asked, eyes downcast.

"You think I'd miss that lot, thundering around like a herd of Robandi camels?"

"I came to fetch you because you're stronger. You'd be better at fighting an intruder than me."

Izoldia sneered at Ithsar, her chest swelling with pride, but then her eyes narrowed in suspicion.

Although she hated groveling, Ithsar had to be quick. She held out her twisted fingers, hiding the healed ones in her palms. "My hands... I'm useless, afraid..." She let her lip wobble.

"You miserable wretch, Ithsar. I should make you go and face the danger." Izoldia's bark was harsh, loud. She'd never been good at silence—gloating didn't sound right in a whisper. Izoldia got up, hand on her saber. "Watch that man."

The moment Izoldia shut the door, the Naobian's eyes flicked open.

"I am Ithsar," she murmured. "Ezaara's friend. I'll take you to her so you can escape."

"My hands and legs are fastened." His whisper was papyrus-thin. He was obviously used to stealth—good, that would serve them well tonight.

The ropes on his hands and feet were quick work for her saber. Ithsar thrust the cut ropes into her pocket and pulled some clothing and a headdress from a drawer. He threw them on. On close inspection, he wouldn't pass for a woman, but it was better than the *dracha ryter* clothes he wore underneath. She passed him his sword and dagger. They slipped out the door, sliding through the shadows along the walls and nipping into side tunnels or alcoves whenever someone neared.

Finally, they made it back to Ezaara, hiding under the bridge.

When she'd crawled out and they'd retreated to a nearby side tunnel, Ezaara whispered, "Ithsar, quick, give me your unhealed fingers."

In the darkness, something dripped onto Ithsar's fingers, then Ezaara rubbed the oil into her skin. The slow healing burn built until her bones were on fire and moved and straightened. An ache pierced her chest and her eyes stung.

She was whole.

Ithsar clutched Ezaara's hand for a moment longer, placing it on her wet cheek. "My life is yours."

The Naobian's hand rested atop theirs, enclosing them both. "Thank you, Ithsar," he whispered. "Thank you for risking your life to save ours."

They stood in the darkness, her and these two strangers, their breath flowing and ebbing together in the inky black. And then the vision descended upon Ithsar again—these strangers on mighty *dracha*, with her beside them on another. *Sathir* built around them, tangible, like a warm caress full of color and life, a force connecting the three of them. She belonged to these people. This was her destiny.

From Ezaara's soft gasp and the grunt the Naobian gave, they'd sensed it too.

Footsteps slid over rock nearby. They froze, waiting until they retreated, then Ithsar led them into a tunnel far away from the main thoroughfares. Winding under the heart of the lake, deeper and deeper into the earth, she took them toward a hidden exit on the far side of the oasis.

Ithsar and the strangers stooped to avoid sharp rocks protruding from the ceiling and slithered over piles of rubble nearly as high as the tunnel itself. Ithsar led them on, the tiny lantern at her waist a star in the inky blackness.

When they were near the tunnel's end, there was a ripple in the fabric of the sathir, a rip in the cloak that surrounded them. Ithsar turned to the *dracha* ryter, holding up her lantern.

They were no longer holding hands. The Naobian's face was stoic.

Ezaara's… Ezaara's look haunted Ithsar. Hollow-eyed, bereft of hope.

Something terrible had passed between them. "What is it? What ails you?" Ithsar asked. "With such disunity, Ashewar will feel the disharmony and find us immediately. If you are to be reunited with your *dracha*, you must put this pain aside."

They nodded and stared at each other for long moments—counted by the pounding of Ithsar's heart. Expressions flickered across their faces—no doubt they were mind-melding—and the ripple of *sathir* died.

She nodded. "That's better."

Ithsar turned and shone her lamp on a series of handholds and footholds in the rock, leading up a chimney into darkness. She went first, Roberto next, and Ezaara took the rear. Her hands bit into the dusty rock handholds. The footholds were gritty with stone particles, her feet sending pebbles and sand cascading onto the couple below.

They climbed in silence, making their way up to the surface of the oasis.

When Ithsar's new strong fingers brushed the tangled roots of a date palm over a handhold, she whispered, "We're here." She put out the lantern hanging on her belt and reached above her to part the rustling foliage of the desert brush.

The cool kiss of night air rushed in to meet her. Ithsar climbed out to a sky scattered with stars, and date palms whispering in the breeze like hundreds of silent assassins. Moonlight cast a shaft of brightness across the lake. Beyond, a strange new hillock was silhouetted among a fringe of trees—the enormous blue *dracha* that had brought these strangers here. The sky was dark, but it wasn't long until dawn. She had to get them out of here.

The Naobian scrambled up and reached down to grasp Ezaara's hand. As he pulled her up into the open, she stumbled on the edge of the chimney. He grabbed her and she landed with her cheek against his chest.

The Naobian leaned in to kiss Ezaara.

"No," Ithsar whispered, but it was too late. The Naobian's lips touched Ezaara's hair, lighting up the *sathir* connection between them like a million stars. Any assassin tuned into *sathir* would know where they were. So much for stealth.

On the other side of the lake, a sand-shifting roar split the air. A belch of *dracha* flame lit up the palm grove, and the mighty blue-scaled beast took to the sky.

He was coming. Both *dracha ryter* would be saved.

"Traitor." Izoldia stepped from behind a date palm, saber out.

By the *dracha* gods, Izoldia had seen through her ruse. She had to think fast.

Ithsar snatched her own saber and pointed it at the Naobian. "Now, you're coming with us!" she cried.

The Naobian spun, flinging Ezaara aside. He was fast. When had he unsheathed his sword?

"You," he spat at Ithsar, lunging at her. "You've outlived your usefulness."

He was absolving her of blame. Ithsar parried with her saber, letting it fly out of her hand as he struck, as if her fingers couldn't hold it. Izoldia wouldn't know any different.

The Naobian held his sword to Ithsar's throat. "Drop your weapon," he said to Izoldia. "Or the girl dies."

Izoldia threw her head back and laughed. "She's worthless. Kill her. It'll save me the trouble."

The slow burning anger that Ithsar had harbored all these years blossomed like a bruise, staining the *sathir* purple-black. The stain spread across Ithsar's vision, blotting out the stars, blotting out the date trees, blotting out Izoldia.

Ithsar had never deserved such scorn. Despite her deformed fingers, she had tried her best. Izoldia had seen to it that everyone despised her, including her own mother.

A breeze stirred at her feet, whirling the sand into a flurry. It rose, faster and higher around her, whipping her clothes in the wind. It shook the date palms, rustling their fronds and swaying their trunks. Thrusting out her anger, Ithsar's whirlwind made the date palm over Izoldia tremble.

A huge bunch of dates fell, hitting Izoldia's head, knocking her to the ground.

Instantly, the purple stain was gone.

The Naobian released Ithsar and spun, checking for more assassins. Ithsar could sense them across the lake, running toward them.

Ezaara rushed over to Izoldia. "She's unconscious." She hesitated for a moment.

"I'm sorry," whispered Ithsar. "I've never done that before."

"A good job you did," the Naobian said, putting a comforting hand on her shoulder.

Ezaara opened her pouch and took out a tiny sack of powder. "Ithsar, quick," she hissed, "fetch a little water."

Ithsar snatched the empty waterskin at her belt and collected water from the lake.

Ezaara threw a pinch of powder into the skin, and they held up Izoldia's head, letting the water trickle down her throat. Izoldia swallowed reflexively.

"This is woozy weed," Ezaara said. "It will make her sleep and leave her confused about what happened over the last few hours. She probably won't remember any of this."

Ithsar had been prepared to die to free these strangers. She let relief wash through her, not trying to control it. If anyone had seen the dark bruise in *sathir*, they'd believe the *dracha ryter* had caused it. She fished the ropes she'd cut off the Naobian's limbs from her pockets and thrust them deep into Izoldia's tunic. "Hopefully, they'll think she's the traitor who led you here."

Cries carried on the crisp pre-dawn air as the assassins raced between the palms, getting closer every moment.

The *dracha* bellowed and landed with a flurry of wings.

"Fast," said the Naobian, "go back to your quarters through the tunnel." He snatched the dates that had hit Izoldia and flung them into a saddlebag, then helped Ezaara on Erob's back.

Ithsar flung herself down the chimney, and he pulled foliage back over the entrance. Only when she reached the bottom and turned on her lamp did she realize she'd forgotten to farewell the *dracha ryter* and tell them about her vision.

TREACHEROUS SECRETS

The roar of the mighty blue-scaled *dracha* shook the ground above Ithsar's head, sending sand into her hair. She clambered down the rough-hewn hand and footholds and scurried along the tunnel, more sand dusting her head and shoulders. Blinking grit out of her eyes, she hurried on. Yells from outside drifted through the foliage and down the dark passage. Another roar came, more distant now. Ithsar was glad—hopefully it meant the *dracha* was escaping, whisking Ezaara and her Naobian lover, Roberto, away from the oasis.

She scrambled over a pile of scree and shale from a fall in, her stomach coiled as tight as a rust viper in the hot desert sand—hoping like the blazing sun that the Naobian had pulled the foliage over the tunnel entrance well enough to fool her fellow assassins. Most people had long forgotten the secret tunnel. She prayed the *dracha* gods would be kind and help it stay that way.

If she got caught aiding the *dracha ryter*—the northern dragon riders her mother had captured—to escape, her life would be in danger.

Although fear prickled along her scalp, Ithsar tried her best to remain calm so no one would detect a ripple in her *sathir*—the life energy binding every living thing—as she made her way along the secret passage under the lake. The lantern at her waist flickered, casting looming shadows on the walls, shadows with long fingers that leaped out grasping as she ran.

When she reached the entrance to the tunnel, Ithsar was panting. She paused to catch her breath and cocked her head. The tunnels riddling the silent assassins' underground lair were quiet. Her only chance was to sneak back to bed and pretend she'd missed everything—but Izoldia was a major thorn in that plan. Izoldia had been on duty watching the Naobian who'd still been tied to his bed in the healing quarters when Ithsar had relieved her. Ezaara had said that after having woozy weed Izoldia may not remember everything, but which of her memories would be hazy? Those in the healing room, or only the recent fight by the lake?

For long moments, Ithsar waited in the shadows. If she went to the healing quarters and pretended she'd been asleep, she'd probably encounter people who'd wonder why she hadn't rushed to help capture the strangers when the alarm had been raised. But if she went to her sleeping alcove and pretended she'd missed everything and then Izoldia later remembered her sitting with the Naobian, she could be accused of treason and executed. Had anyone checked her alcove to see whether she'd still been sleeping? By the *dracha* gods, she should have thought everything through before she released the prisoners, but she'd been so desperate to set them free she hadn't spared a thought for her own life.

It didn't matter. Ezaara, she of golden beauty, the new Queen's Rider who'd healed Ithsar's damaged fingers, was now her friend. Roberto, Ezaara's beloved Naobian man with olive-black eyes that gleamed with love as he beheld the Queen's Rider, was her friend too. Since Ithsar's father had died when she was a littling, she'd yearned for human friendship. With only her lizard Thika to keep her company, she'd been lonely. But now, she had two new friends. A smile traced her lips and she flexed her newly-healed fingers in wonder. Now, she could hold her head high and fight with the other assassins. She need no longer be afraid of not being worthy. No longer be afraid of being the deformed one, the only assassin unable to fight.

Light footsteps and the faint rustle of clothing sounded along the northern tunnel. That ruled out going back to the healing cavern, then.

Ithsar's newly-healed fingers doused the light on her lantern. She plunged into the darkness, fleeing along the southern tunnel, trailing her fingertips along the wall to sense her way to her sleeping alcove. Fingertips that could feel, sense, and move again with newfound freedom.

§

Ithsar woke to something burrowing into her armpit. Thika popped his orange scaly head onto her chest and looked up at her with his yellow eyes. His tongue flicked out and tickled Ithsar's chin. She smiled and rubbed his eye ridges. The lizard's eyes hooded and his body thrummed with pleasure as he leaned into Ithsar's touch. Without the old pain shooting up her fingers, things like stroking Thika were more pleasurable—Ezaara had not only healed her, she'd given her the power to enjoy such simple things.

Ithsar sat up and cradled him in her lap. Running her fingers over the dark bands on Thika's orange back, she whispered, "I'm so glad Ezaara healed you too." Someone had recently poisoned Thika. Ezaara had managed to detect which poison it was by sensing the *sathir* of various poisons and remedies to see how they affected the lizard.

Ithsar swallowed. Everyone knew her father had given her Thika before her mother, Ashewar, the chief prophetess, had executed him when Ithsar was only four. Ithsar blinked, seeing her father's pleading dark eyes as he'd begged her to take care of herself and be strong, before they'd killed him.

The best way to hurt her was to strike at Thika. After enduring Izoldia's taunting and physical torment for years, she knew Izoldia was most likely the poisoner.

Distant footsteps scraped the dry dirt in the tunnel outside her tiny alcove. Ithsar's keen ears caught the whisper of fabric. She popped Thika on the bed and pulled on her orange robe. She tapped her belly. Thika clambered over her legs, along the voluminous fabric, and crawled inside the front of her robe. He flattened his body, settling himself above her waistband as she pulled the stays shut.

The curtains across the narrow opening of her alcove slid open, their iron rings rasping against the brass bar. Thut, one of Ashewar's most trusted guards, thrust her head inside. Thut's eyes slid over Ithsar and, curling her lip, she crooked her finger, motioning Ithsar to follow.

Ithsar nodded demurely and kept her eyes downcast as she rose and left her tiny alcove.

More guards were waiting, one on either side of her nook, flat against the wall. Without a word, they each grasped one of her arms and dragged Ithsar along the corridor toward the chief prophetess' grand hall.

§

"Where were you last night?" Ashewar hissed, her dark fiery eyes burning through Ithsar like the desert sun. The chief prophetess was seated on her grotesque, ornately-carved throne depicting hundreds of female assassins murdering men.

Ashewar's personal guards—a semicircle of stony-faced female assassins standing behind her throne—didn't even look at Ithsar.

Ashewar thrust her chin forward, the diamond studs in her beaked nose glinting and the beads in her hundreds of tiny braids clacking. "I said, *where were you?*" Her whisper echoed off the walls. Torches guttered, as if Ashewar's voice controlled the brightness of their flame.

No one's gaze shriveled Ithsar's heart the way her mother's did.

Ithsar flexed her fingers, keeping them hidden in her long sleeves. Her mother didn't yet know that they were healed, and now was not the right time to reveal that surprise. "Asleep," she murmured, meeting her mother's gaze for a fleeting heartbeat before she lowered her eyes and stared at her dusty feet. Grains of sand clung to her toenails. She marked the passing time with her thundering heartbeats, surprised the rhythm wasn't reverberating off the walls of the grand cavern.

"Asleep? The alarm sounded, yet you slept?"

The alarm—hundreds of feet slapping against the floors as the silent assassins had sought Ezaara and then Roberto in the maze of tunnels between the caverns. The assassin's vows of silence meant they were attuned to hear the faintest noises in the tunnels. Attuned to feel the subtle shifts in *sathir*. Their muted footfalls should have been enough to wake the deepest sleeper.

The guards would be sensing her *sathir* now. Ithsar had to maintain a sense of calm and keep herself as cool as the lake waters above them—or someone would sense a ripple in the colored fabric that joined them together. "Yes, most revered Chief Prophetess." She breathed slowly through her nose and kept her head lowered so her mother wouldn't see the pulse racing at her throat. Her waistband was damp with sweat where Thika pressed his body against her skin.

Ashewar despised Ithsar and Thika. She always had, but Izoldia's snipes and jeers had fueled her mother's hatred into something wild and pulsing that bashed at Ithsar's skull.

The door thunked open. A heavy tread on the stone marked Izoldia's arrival. Two female assassins, both much shorter than Izoldia, guided the burly guard into the cavern. She was sporting a black eye and an egg on her forehead the size of a small sand dune. Izoldia sank to her knees and bowed low enough to scrape her ugly nose on the floor.

One push, and Izoldia would fall flat on her face.

"My honored Chief Prophetess," Izoldia's harsh whisper cut through the cavern. She'd never been good at keeping their vows of silence, but it didn't matter because she could fight. Ashewar overlooked Izoldia's shortcomings because of her size, sycophantic attitude and sadistic streak.

Hands still hidden in her sleeves, Ithsar subtly dug her fingernails into her palms—the only movement she dared make to calm herself. A new movement—her fingers had refused to bend properly until Ezaara had healed them. Thika's tail shifted slightly, his scales slithering across her hip.

Ashewar's voice hissed again. "What were you doing last night, Izoldia?" She snapped her fingers.

A guard stepped forward and dropped to one knee in front of Ashewar, holding out two pieces of hacked-off rope.

Rope that Ithsar had cut to free the Naobian with the olive-black eyes, then stuffed into Izoldia's pockets. Would Izoldia remember what she'd done? Or had the woozy weed numbed her memory, as Ezaara had promised? Ithsar let her gaze slide around the room, examining each guard's face for a reaction, for a sign that they'd seen her shake the very palm trees with the power of *sathir*.

Roshni, a slight guard with piercing blue eyes and ebony skin, from the deep South, was watching her every move. Despite her knees wanting to melt like camel butter in the midday sun, Ithsar met Roshni's gaze squarely, pretending she had nothing to fear.

"What are these?" Ashewar addressed Izoldia, flicking a finger at the ropes as if they were bugs on her robes.

Izoldia's eyebrows rose, and she shrugged. "I don't know. Um, ropes?"

"What were the prisoner's bonds doing in your pocket?" the chief prophetess' dark eyes flashed with venom.

Izoldia stayed on her knees, arms prostrated on the floor before their leader. Her voice shook like palm fronds in a sandstorm—something Ithsar never thought she'd hear. "I—I do not remember." Her face rippled with fear.

Ashewar's dark eyes narrowed, glittering like burning coals. "If you do not remember, why are you afraid?"

Cunning stole over Izoldia's features. "An assassin likes to keep her wits about her, my revered and highly intelligent Chief Prophetess. I don't know what happened and woke with a bump on my head and found out that the scrawny *dracha* and its two *ryter* had escaped while under my watch. It was enough to cause fear in anyone." Izoldia remained prostrated on the floor, her arms practically touching Ashewar's feet. Ashewar flicked a beaded slipper toward Izoldia's hand.

Those slippers, traditional *yokka*, didn't fool Ithsar. Underneath the hundreds of tiny orange beads glinting in the torchlight, there were blades hidden in the soles that would spring out if Ashewar pressed her big toe down. Izoldia's wrist was within a finger's breadth of those blades.

"The prisoner was under your care, my loyal guard," Ashewar crooned, caressing the inside of Izoldia's wrist—along a pulsing vein—with the toe of her *yokka*. No doubt, considering setting the blade free. "How did the Naobian escape if you were watching him?"

Izoldia leaped to her feet. Her head hanging, she whispered, "I do not know. I don't remember anything."

Ashewar's head spun to glare at Ithsar. "And you? Why weren't you fighting last night?"

"I slept deeply."

Ashewar's eyes narrowed, flitting between them both. The chief prophetess' smile turned into a feral grin. "Izoldia, the prisoner escaped on your watch. Although you are my most fearless and courageous personal guard, I have no choice. You will be whipped twelve times and tied to a palm tree in the hot desert sun until mid-afternoon." Leaning against the hideous carvings on her throne, Ashewar waved a languid hand. "If she cries out, rub salt into her wounds."

Ashewar's whisper died, the slap of bare feet the only sound as the guards grasped the stunned Izoldia and marched her from the room.

After the years of torture, burns, and bullying at Izoldia's hands, Ithsar knew she should feel jubilation at Izoldia's punishment. But, twelve lashes in the hot sun? It was her fault that Izoldia's flesh would turn into a bloody pulp. Ithsar tried not to cringe. She wouldn't wish that upon anyone.

Ashewar gestured at Bala, one of the more vicious guards and a close crony to Izoldia. "Once Izoldia has been whipped, arrange for a tonic to heal her head and restore her memory. We must get to the bottom of this."

Her gaze snapped to Ithsar, her black eyes glittering more brightly than the diamond studs in her beaked nose. "Someone who sleeps through the alarm needs to gain strength. You are on drill, doing the *Sathiri* dance in the training cavern until nightfall. No food nor water." She waved to her guards.

"Bala, once you've ordered the healing tonic, you will oversee her dance." Ithsar's mother flashed a terrifying smile that reeked of bloodlust. "If the deformed wretch collapses, leave her. Anyone who helps her is under the threat of death."

DANCE OF THE SATHIRI

I thsar kept her fingers tucked inside her palms and hands inside her too-long sleeves as she executed the movements of the ancient dance of the *Sathiri*. She pointed her toes, kicked and spun, then lifted her knee and swung her arm, pretending to wield a saber. Even though her chest felt as if it would crack in two for causing Izoldia's whipping, the smooth rhythm of the dance soon soothed her. The women around her moved as one, flowing like the tide on a shore, the hissing and slap of their feet against the sandstone floor and the soft huffs of their breaths echoing around the chamber. The other women's sabers glinted in the flickering lamplight, but, due to her mangled fingers, Ithsar had never been allowed to wield a saber. Maybe tomorrow, after she'd danced all day to prove herself, when she showed her mother her healed fingers, she would at last earn a real blade instead of the dagger she'd once stolen from the weapons cache when no one had been around.

Thika stayed pressed against her belly, adjusting his weight to compensate for her movements, the harmony between her and the lizard filling her with quiet peace. Her father had found the tiny hatchling abandoned in the tangerine desert sands and gifted Thika to her. Ithsar had fed Thika, catching flies and bugs for him and oiling his dry scales during the molting season. Sometimes the lizard disappeared for hours to hunt around the oasis, but his favorite place to sleep was nestled around her belly. She carried him under her clothing to help him avoid detection. Izoldia had made more than one attempt on Thika's life. It wasn't enough that Ithsar was scorned and hated by all the women— no, Izoldia wouldn't even allow her the small privilege of loving the lizard her father had given her.

Ithsar's breath caught in her throat as her father's face flashed to mind: his handsome face; the kind smile lines around his mouth; and the way he used to hold Ithsar on his lap and tell stories of his life beyond the oasis out in the wild desert. Stories of taming camels, fighting rust vipers with a knife, or the story of him nearly dying. Dehydrated, he'd been taken in by the female assassins to breed an heir to the chief prophetess. Often, he'd stroked Ithsar's hair, saying,

"You are Ashewar's heir. Never forget it. You are the most precious thing in my life." His love had warmed Ithsar's heart, sinking down deep into her bones.

One day, when she'd been a littling of four summers, he'd found her crying.

"What's wrong, my beautiful princess?" He stroked the tears from her cheeks and scooped her into his strong arms, the scent of camel enveloping her.

"The older girls say I'm weak because my fingers don't work. That mother will kill me when I come of age," she whispered, terrified someone would hear her speaking aloud and punish her. Although no one punished Izoldia when she spoke.

"Was it Izoldia, Bala and Thut?"

Her lip wobbled as she nodded. More tears came. "They did this." Ithsar held out her arm, swollen and mottled with rapidly-forming bruises. "They hurt me. They'll snap my arm if I tell anyone, but I can tell you, can't I?"

Her father had nodded, eyes burning with rage, and gone off to find the girls who'd hurt her.

That night, she'd heard voices in Ashewar's sleeping chamber. Raised voices—unheard of in the lair of the silent assassins—her parents arguing.

Her heart had rejoiced that her father was championing her. She'd rolled over and gone back to sleep.

The same heart had broken in the morning when she learned her mother had ordered his execution.

Tears had glimmered in her father's eyes, then, as he stole a few last moments with her. "Remember," he whispered, his voice a flutter against her ear, "I will always love you. Be strong, practice the *Sathiri* dance every day. Even if no one sees you, I will be watching over you. One day, you will rise above your mother's petty hatred, for you are my precious daughter, strong beyond words." He kissed her hair and caressed her fingers with his bound hands.

The guards yanked his rope, pulling him away from her. They dragged him down the tunnels.

And then her mother had collected her and made her watch.

Ithsar faltered, her foot slipping on the cavern's sandstone floor.

Bala's eyes flicked to her as the women around her continued moving in rhythm. Lip curling, Bala snapped her fingers, the sharp sound whipping through the natural echo chamber of the training cavern.

All movement stopped, women freezing mid-pose, arms extended and knees bent. Waiting.

Bala stalked, feet barely making a whisper on the dusty cavern floor. Ithsar angled her head, holding her cheek up, ready.

Humiliation washed over her. She could never be a true Robandi assassin, despite her healed fingers. She was too weak. Too full of what her mother called fool's sentiment. If just the thought of her father made her falter, how could she kill? She didn't have it in her. She was a failure.

The ominous faint scrape of Bala's feet on sandstone reverberated off the cavern walls, reminding Ithsar of the night she'd unlocked the cell in the corner and let Ezaara loose. Ezaara had dropped her saber, the clattering echo raising the alarm for the assassins, but at least Ithsar had helped the Queen's Rider and her lover get free.

Bala stopped in front of her, leering.

Ithsar drew in a breath and braced herself. *You are my precious daughter...*

Bala drew a knife from her belt and slapped the flat of the blade against Ithsar's cheek.

Despite her stinging cheek, Ithsar kept her gaze steady, her spine straight and her chin up... *strong beyond words.*

A figure moved from the shadows, beads on tiny braids clicking softly as Ashewar made her way through the ranks of silent assassins, still frozen in place. She clapped her fingers and the assassins stood down.

"Not you," Ashewar hissed, glaring at Ithsar. She motioned with a flat hand.

Ithsar quickly raised her arms again and lifted her knee, and froze in *Sathiri* stance.

The other assassins retreated to line the walls, leaving Ithsar standing alone in the middle of the voluminous cavern. One by one, they filed into the barred cell where Ezaara had been captive and helped themselves to a dipper of cool water from the natural spring.

Ithsar licked her lips, throat dry. She hadn't even eaten or had the barest sip of water before the guards had manhandled her to Ashewar, but now was not the time to ask.

Ashewar nodded, eyes glittering with malice, not with the love Ithsar longed for. She motioned Ithsar to continue.

With a heavy heart, hands still hidden in her sleeves, Ithsar spun on her left toe, her right leg flung out, and then landed and raised her arm in a defensive block, flawlessly executing the next *Sathiri* movement.

Ashewar's eyes blazed.

Ashewar had never seen her complete the full dance. Because of Ithsar's bent, scarred fingers, she'd been assigned menial tasks, rarely joining the assassins' training. But since her father's death, Ithsar had practiced every night in her tiny sleeping alcove, her fingertips and toes nearly brushing the walls. So Ithsar continued, sweeping her arm wide in a blow that would dismember any attacker—if she had a saber. But now was not the time to ask Ashewar for a saber. Not until she'd proved she could perform the killing dance. Ithsar spun and leaped again, kicking an imaginary attacker's chest. She landed, following through with a left arm flick as if she were throwing a knife. Keeping her hands still buried in her long sleeves, she twirled and executed a series of slashes. On and on she danced, until she'd executed all thirty movements of the *Sathiri* killing dance.

Ithsar stood before Ashewar, head high and chest heaving, controlling her breathing so she didn't huff. Surely her mother was proud of the way she'd executed the dance. Surely now she could have a drink.

Ashewar's eyes fell to the ends of Ithsar's sleeves. Her lip curled and she motioned for Ithsar to start the sequence over.

She would try harder, and earn her mother's love if it killed her. Ithsar slipped into the starting stance again, and spun, kicked, and slashed. She sprang higher, moved faster, leaped farther until, at last, she stood before her mother, the dance complete. Surely now...

Ashewar's nose wrinkled. She gazed down at Ithsar and motioned her to begin again.

When her mother found out that her hands were healed, Ithsar would join the ranks of the assassins, but now, she had to prove she was worthy. Her hollow belly rumbled, but Ithsar unleashed her full power, spinning, turning, and flying through the air. *Sathir* swirled around her in reddish waves, tendrils flying from her as she attacked imaginary assailants. Waves of pale blue *sathir* flowed from Roshni, her ebony braid glinting in the torchlight as she watched Ithsar's every movement with those piercing blue eyes, stony-faced. More *sathir* flowed from three others, until the blue, red, orange, and greens of their intertwined *sathir* danced in time to the rhythm of Ithsar's movements. Too tired to figure out what the merging *sathir* meant, Ithsar kept dancing.

Her legs shook as Ashewar motioned her to start yet again.

Ithsar made a cupping gesture, the sign she and her silent sisters used when they needed to drink.

The chief prophetess' face hardened and she waved her to continue dancing. The four assassins whose *sathir* was now intertwined with hers shifted against the wall, but said nothing.

Shoulders aching and legs trembling, Ithsar began the dance again, arching her back with more agility, putting in extra effort to impress her mother. *Sathir* swirled as she danced and finished, landing with her head high and a smile on her face. That was it. Any moment now, her mother would smile back, then she'd show Ashewar her healed fingers.

The corners of Ashewar's mouth drew down and she thrust her hand out, motioning her to start over, then held up her hands, her fingers splayed. Once. Twice. Thrice.

Thirty more times?

Ithsar's smile froze, but she didn't dare show her displeasure, so she kept her forced smile in place as she started the next thirty rounds of the *Sathiri* dance. Her head spun from lack of food. Her throat was dry and scratchy, like she'd swallowed sand. Perhaps she'd breathed in the grains that had flown around her as she'd danced. No matter, she could do this—she could prove herself to her mother.

Ashewar gestured to the other assassins to go to the mess cavern for food, as if she knew Ithsar's belly ached from hunger. She gave Bala a grim nod, motioning her to keep watch on Ithsar, and, robes rustling, stalked from the cavern—not toward the mess cavern or her throne room, but out toward the entrance—to witness Izoldia's whipping.

Under Bala's glower, Ithsar finished a cycle and began the dance again, limbs leaden and her movements hollow. Her gnawing belly matched the emptiness of her heart. Her whole life she'd endured scorn, abuse and dismissal because of her deformed fingers. Couldn't her mother see that all she wanted was her love?

No, not love—the chief prophetess wasn't sentimental. Approval—the barest nod or hand motion to show her mother was satisfied.

As Ithsar finished the next cycle, the *sathir* around her washed scarlet. Blinding red pain flashed through her mind. She faltered and gasped. Izoldia—it had to be. The *sathir* was the color of blood. Blood that would be running down Izoldia's back—and all because she'd planted the prisoner's bindings in the burly guard's pocket. Ithsar stumbled as the *sathir* ran off her in rivulets, pooling like water at her feet.

Bala sneered. "Tired?" she hissed, not daring to use a louder voice and have it echo around the cavern and bring assassins running.

Ithsar kept dancing, completing that cycle and the next, and the next, her mind searing with Izoldia's pain and red *sathir* spraying from her hands. Bala's teeth flashed in greeting as a new shift of assassins filed into the cavern. They joined Ithsar in allotted positions, twirling and slashing in time with her. Not one of them gave her a second glance. None of them could see the blood-red *sathir*. None of them could sense Izoldia's pain.

But, from a young age, Ithsar had possessed the gift of seeing without the aid of her mother's prism-seer. Especially when events directly affected her. She'd seen a vision of her future: flying into battle on a mighty green *dracha* with Ezaara flying on the multi-hued queen of Dragons' Realm and Roberto on his blue *dracha* Erob. Ezaara had given her a new chance to be whole, so Ithsar had set them free.

And let Izoldia take the blame.

Limbs nearly giving out and movements growing clumsy, Ithsar drove herself harder. But dance as she might, she couldn't shake the visions of blood-red *sathir* coating her hands and pooling at her feet.

Yes, she was responsible for her tormentor's pain.

LASHED

Four assassins manhandled Izoldia along the tunnels underneath the oasis. Her head spun. The huge bump she'd somehow gotten last night ached, making her head throb in time with the guards' footfalls. She couldn't remember anything past her midday meal yesterday. Her face was covered in bruises and her body as battle-weary as if she'd been on a killing spree. Vague dreams of a storm—palm fronds slashing among purple clouds—flitted at the edges of her mind. But that couldn't be right. She'd even asked Thut, and indeed, there'd been no storm yesterday.

Besides, Ithsar's face featured in those dreams, full of rage and strength. Izoldia snorted. That runt Ithsar was anything but strong. No, it must be just another nightmare about that pathetic heir of the chief prophetess, the useless sniveling thing. Izoldia should have poisoned her too, not just that slimy lizard that Ithsar insisted on carrying around like a crutch. When Izoldia was finished with her lashes, she'd kill the lizard and Ithsar too.

Then no one could stand between her and the chief prophetess.

And, when the chief prophetess was dead, there'd be nothing between Izoldia and the beautiful throne Ashewar sat upon—made from the bones of murdered men and carved with the Robandi Assassins' killing rituals. Deep at night, when no one was around, Izoldia sneaked into the throne room and ran her fingers over the carved patterns, reveling in the exotic depictions of women murdering men. By studying the carvings, she'd learned new methods of torture, and had been hoping to test those methods on the Naobian prisoner as she forced him to breed with her sisters. But now, he was gone.

A sun-blasted shame—she'd hoped they'd spawn fine daughters from him. Daughters they could raise to be strong assassins in true Robandi tradition. Ashewar had assigned Izoldia to kill the Naobian when his time was up. Izoldia had planned a slow and torturous death, peeling his skin under the desert sun while she carved holes in his pretty face.

And then there were the other deaths she would've enjoyed—the newborn babes, his rejected spawn—all males or deformed females. Slicing littlings open while they screamed and watching the vultures pluck their bones clean had been her delightful pleasure when they'd last kidnapped men for their seed. There was no place for men or cripples among the assassins. No place for soft emotions. No place for that runty heir, Ithsar.

Yes, it was a sun-blasted shame, but the guards had found the ropes in Izoldia's own pockets. She couldn't remember releasing him, couldn't remember anything. Had he unbound his own ropes, fought with her and hit her head, escaping? Her cheeks burned with shame. Whatever had happened, it was obviously her fault. She'd failed the prophetess, failed her people.

Their chances of replenishing their ranks were gone. Unless she hunted down more men.

Yes, she'd find more men for her sisters to spawn from, so she could earn her way back into Ashewar's good graces.

As they clambered up the tunnel toward the daylight, Izoldia stumbled, her head throbbing. A guard hefted her arm to help her up—Thut, who wouldn't dare disobey Ashewar, but was a loyal crony. Izoldia kept her head high. She would not falter. She'd take her lashes without a scream. The prisoner had escaped on her watch, so she deserved them.

They stepped through the entrance into the shade of the date palms. Sentinels parted, letting them pass. Izoldia's feet shuffled through the cool sand as Thut and the other three guards led her under the palms out to the edge of the oasis. Vast orange sands shimmered with the sun's haze. Heat beat down upon Izoldia's face. The sand was already burning the soles of her feet. She squinted against the brightness, then bowed her head against a palm trunk. Thut and the others tied ropes around her wrists, and bound her to the tree. Izoldia let them. She deserved this. The chief prophetess' prime breeding stock had been lost on her watch.

Thut uncoiled a whip from her waist, and moved in, murmuring so quietly it couldn't be deemed as treason, "I have no wish to lash you. I am only obeying Ashewar."

Izoldia gave the faintest nod. It made no difference. She'd accept her scars as trophies, a symbol of her submission to the prophetess. But one day, she would no longer submit. Then she would pay back every assassin who had ever caused a wisp of harm to her.

The whip cracked, slicing through Izoldia's robes into her flesh. She clenched her jaw against its stinging bite as rivulets of warm blood trickled down her back.

Another crack. Pain lanced across her shoulders. Gritting her teeth, she kept her head bowed so the whip wouldn't mark her face. When the third lash came, she clamped her teeth down, biting the edge of her tongue. Her mouth flew open in a grimace. She arched her back against the pain, but refused to cry out.

The next strike of the whip cut deep into her flesh, driving Izoldia's body into the date palm. Her forehead smacked against the knobbly trunk. She gasped and shuddered as her back burned.

Sand hissed as Ashewar's orange-slippered feet came into view. She stepped from the shade into the blazing sun, her rings glinting. The prophetess' cool voice rang out, "Not only the tip, Thut. Let her have the full brunt of the lash."

The next stinging lash made Izoldia's knees falter and her body sag. The impact nearly wrenched her shoulders from their sockets, the ropes on her bound arms the only thing holding her in place. The lash bit into her back again and again, agonizing blows that shredded her back, blood splattering the tree trunk and streaming down her legs.

On the twelfth lash, her jaw unlocked and a cry ripped from her throat, shattering the silence between the whip cracks.

"You," Ashewar's voice hissed. "Rub salt into her wounds. It's not becoming for my strongest warrior to cry out in pain." Ashewar turned and strode back under the date palms to their underground lair, her rustling robes nearly kissing Izoldia's face as she passed.

Drida—their oldest assassin, a silver-haired woman who could strike a man dead with one well-aimed kick—paced to Izoldia and untied a pouch of salt from her belt. Not a lick of sympathy showed in the harsh lines of her ancient wrinkled face as her eyes flicked over Izoldia. She rubbed salt into Izoldia's wounds. Roughly. The scrape and grind of the grit made Izoldia scream. Tears of pain ran down her face in rivulets, wetting her orange robes.

And then the assassins left her out under the heat of the beating sun.

A Test of Endurance

Bala was relentless, insisting that Ithsar keep dancing long after thirty cycles were done. After forty. And fifty. Until Ithsar lost count. Until time was measured by the slap of her feet, the whirl of her body and the blood pumping in her ears. Every time she slowed, Ithsar received another smack with the flat of Bala's saber—on her arms, cheeks, or legs. But Ithsar accepted it. It was less pain than what she'd caused Izoldia.

The others filed off for their evening meal. Bala left, and Thut replaced her to watch Ithsar. Still, Ithsar danced, her limbs slow and sluggish. Thut picked at her nails with her blade, leaning against the wall, occasionally gesturing that Ithsar should speed up. At last, the assassins joined her for the late evening dance.

Ithsar swiped a hand at her dry, pounding temples—she'd stopped sweating long ago. There was little fluid left in her. Giant dark spots swam before her eyes, obscuring the assassins to her left. Not *sathir*. Exhaustion.

Her breath rasped, dry and hot in her throat. She leaped and stumbled, then flung her arm weakly. She jumped and thrust out her foot to land. Ithsar's knee buckled and she slammed into the sandstone. Her body flew across the floor, gashing her cheek. A warm gush of blood pooled under her face. Although she tried to push up with her hands, her elbows collapsed and she lay amid the dancers, slumped on the cool stone. At least, here, she could rest.

Thut barked at her, threatened her, but she couldn't respond. So Thut motioned at the other women to keep dancing and ignore her.

Ithsar's head spun as the slap and scrape of feet thrummed through the sandstone against her aching, bloody cheek. Then darkness claimed her.

§

Ithsar woke, cold and shivering, to something scraping her cheek.

No, not scraping, but licking. "Thika?"

The lizard squirmed under her face, trying to rouse her. Ithsar's breath shuddered out of her. Everything ached, her head spun, and the blood on her cheek had congealed. She tried to swallow but her mouth and throat were as dry as the desert sand. Thika wriggled again. How had he squeezed under her face?

The scuff of feet carried along a passage. More than one pair of feet. Were Bala and Thut coming to gloat over her? Gods, what had happened to Izoldia?

Heart pounding, Ithsar froze on the stone, the last nearly-dead torch sputtering. It must be the deep of night. Thika wormed his way under her neck, hiding.

A shadow fell over her body as someone bent over her. Ithsar braced herself for a kick or jab.

"Thank the *dracha* gods you're still with us," Roshni breathed so softly, Ithsar wondered if she'd imagined it. Roshni knelt beside her and lifted her aching head, gazing at her with those piercing blue eyes. "Look," she rasped faintly, her voice croaky from disuse, "your lizard tried to protect you. He slunk under your cheek to stop you from swallowing your blood."

A low moan threatened to escape Ithsar, but she held it in. No need to set the chamber echoing—that would only bring people running.

Roshni held a waterskin to her lips. The cavern dipped and swayed as Ithsar sipped. The cool, refreshing nectar of life slid down her throat.

In the shadows at the edge of the cavern, someone moved. An assassin materialized from the gloom, her silver hair glinting in the torchlight—Drida, holding a blanket.

Drida motioned that they must leave, and Roshni nodded and scooped Ithsar into her arms. Drida tucked the blanket around Ithsar and picked up Thika, depositing him on Ithsar's belly. Then she pulled a bandage from her robes and pressed it to Ithsar's cheek. Her eyes flitted around the cavern and she made the hand gesture for leaving swiftly.

When they were deep in the passage, halfway to Ithsar's sleeping alcove, Drida murmured, her voice as soft as a moth's wing, "I was on duty in the healing cavern tending Izoldia, but all I could think of was you, lying there, broken and wounded."

Ithsar's only reply was a violent shiver.

"You're cold." Drida took her hand. Her brows shot up. Eyes wide, she stared at Ithsar's hand.

Roshni stopped walking, staring too. "Your fingers…"

Although it made her head pound, Ithsar managed a weak nod and wriggled her healthy fingers.

Roshni said nothing more, slipping through the tunnels, Drida nipping ahead to make sure the way was clear. When they reached her sleeping alcove, Drida lifted the curtain without drawing it, so the rings wouldn't scrape along the brass rail. Roshni ducked inside, carrying her, and Drida followed, letting the heavy curtain fall.

Roshni deposited Ithsar gently on her bed, but instead of the two women leaving, Drida took a tiny lantern from her belt and lit it, and the two assassins sat beside Ithsar on her mattress, Drida at her head and Roshni by her belly. Thika crawled straight back into her robes to rest against Ithsar's stomach. Warm, familiar, comforting—despite the raging aches rippling through her muscles.

Roshni held Ithsar's fingers, examining them, wonder in her eyes.

Ithsar didn't dare tell Roshni how she'd been healed. Two of Ashewar's most trusted guards, these women could've been sent by the chief prophetess to wheedle out her secrets.

Drida drew a needle and twine from her robe and stitched Ithsar's cheek, her smile warm and her fingers nimble.

Roshni pulled some flatbread and dates from one of the many pockets in her robe and passed them to Ithsar. "Eat and gain strength, for I'm sure the dawn shall bring new trials." Her blue eyes were concerned—such a strange color for a southerner, vividly bright against her dark skin.

Ithsar took a piece of flatbread and chewed it, nearly gagging.

"Here, more water," whispered Drida, eyes darting to Ithsar's curtain. The water helped ease the passage of the flatbread down her dry throat. As Ithsar chewed the sweet, succulent dates, Drida continued, "You know, you should leave. Ashewar hates you and will find another way to hurt you."

"And if she doesn't, Izoldia will," Roshni whispered.

Drida leaned in so close, Ithsar could barely hear, her breath tickling Ithsar's ear. "We can prepare a camel for you on the far side of the oasis and wake you in two hours so you can leave."

Their *sathir* didn't show the dark shadows of betrayal, just a calm yellow tinge around Roshni and an orange glow around Drida, but where would Ithsar go? What would she do? She'd only ever lived in the lair beneath the oasis. For a heartbeat, Ithsar hesitated. Leaving didn't feel right, despite her maltreatment at her mother and Izoldia's hands. "I can't," murmured Ithsar. "This is my home."

"But what good is a home where you must hide who you truly are?" Drida whispered urgently. "You danced an entire day without food or water. You have great strength and talent, yet you've masked it. And now, Ashewar knows. She will not make life easy for you." Drida tilted her head, her voice a faint breath. "Are you sure you don't want to run away?"

Ithsar nodded.

The women stood and slipped out her curtain.

They'd seemed to be genuine. Their *sathir* had even appeared so, but Ithsar couldn't help a dark foreboding that Drida and Roshni were working against her. That they were scheming for Ashewar, trying to catch her out so they could hurt her.

So far, everyone but her father and Thika had.

Ithsar sipped the water they'd left and chewed the remaining flatbread and dates, cradling Thika against her belly as a lone tear slipped down her cheek.

AGONY

With a start, Izoldia awoke, lying on her stomach in the same bed that stinking Naobian had lain in when he'd been healing from his slit gut. The bed he'd been in the night he'd escaped. The night she'd been watching him. Had that only been yesterday?

By those slimy reptilian *dracha* gods, what had happened?

Irritation flashed through Izoldia at the constant dribble of water—the underground stream flowing through the edge of the healing cavern. Despite it being the deep of night, that cursed water made it hard to drift off again. She shifted, her head still foggy—and now throbbing from the long hours under the desert sun. Her back burned. By the cursed sun gods, she could barely move.

With such terrible gut wounds, how had that Naobian managed to run and evade everyone hunting him through the cavern tunnels? Ashewar had reported that he'd flown off on his giant blue *dracha* with that woman of the golden hair, but managing to climb on a *dracha* with such shocking wounds was about as likely as rain in the Robandi desert.

She tried to push up on her hands, but her back screamed in agony, so she slumped down again.

Robes rustled and a cool hand was laid upon her brow. Those same hands held a reed straw to her lips.

Curse it, so much pain that she couldn't even sit up. Glowering, Izoldia tugged water through the straw, then laid her head down again. The healer's footfalls padded away.

Izoldia's eyelids fluttered. They'd put healing tonic in her water to make her doze so her body could recover. She fought the tonic, battling to stay awake as a memory niggled at the edge of her mind.

In a flash, Izoldia remembered Ithsar requesting to take over her post guarding the Naobian, suggesting that Izoldia should fight. With a lurch in her gut, Izoldia knew that despicable worm had betrayed them. That sniveling good-for-nothing hangdog with the broken fingers, that softhearted piece of camel dung, had fooled them. She must have planted the ropes in Izoldia's pockets after helping that foreign scum escape. Izoldia hadn't betrayed Ashewar at all. Ithsar had.

Ithsar had cheated Izoldia of her fun with that man. Cheated her of forcing him to breed and create daughters. Cheated her of the chance to slay any male offspring he would've sired.

And it was Ithsar's fault Izoldia had been lashed. Ithsar's fault that Izoldia's back was a mess of fleshy, bloody tatters and searing pain. Due to Ithsar's cunning, Izoldia had fallen out of Ashewar's favor.

Izoldia's burning back was nothing compared to the hatred that burned through her gut as she contemplated her revenge. Then the tonic claimed Izoldia and, try as she might, she could no longer battle her drooping eyelids, so she drifted into a restless sleep.

STEALTH

Izoldia screamed in pain, begging Ithsar not to whip her. But Ithsar gave a grim smile and flicked the whip again, scoring deep into Izoldia's bloody, tattered back.

"Enough! Please!" Izoldia begged.

Ithsar struck her again and again.

"Please, Ithsar, be true," her father pleaded. "You are my precious daughter, strong beyond words."

"Thank you, Father." Ithsar smiled, whipping her enemy's back until she collapsed dead on the sand. Still, Ithsar lashed her, again and again.

Until Izoldia's body disintegrated into tiny blood-red sand grains, carried away by the wind.

Ithsar's chest heaved as she stared down at herself. Her robes were splattered in Izoldia's blood, her whip slick in her hand, and her arms stained red to the elbows.

She turned to her father, but his eyes were dead, soulless black holes that sucked her toward him, step by step. His body grew, towering over her, wreathed in black shadows. A whip appeared in his hands. "Now it's my turn, princess," he crooned, his words as soft as gossamer as he raised the whip to beat her.

Ithsar jolted up in bed, sweat beading her brow, gasping.

Thika crawled out of her robes and clambered up her torso to perch on her shoulder. He nuzzled her neck.

"It's all right, Thika. It's only a dream." She stroked the lizard's soft scales, trying to steady her breath, but it still shuddered out of her. "Gods, Thika, it's my fault. I have to do something." She plucked Thika from her shoulder and put him back on her bed.

Ithsar reached under her bed. Dislodging a stone that leaned against the far wall, she pulled out a slim vial of pale-green juice. She tucked it in her pocket and slipped out of her sleeping alcove, striding quickly on bare feet, ever watchful. She had to be fast.

Footsteps sounded around a corner. Ithsar nipped into a crevice, pressing her body flat against the wall as two assassins passed, returning from night patrol. Then she slipped out and continued winding her way through the tunnels to the healing cavern. She hid in the curtained alcove of supplies just outside the door and waited.

When the night healer slipped out for a latrine break, Ithsar stole into the room, Ezaara's vial of precious green juice clutched in her hand.

Izoldia was asleep, face down on a bed. Two other patients were fast asleep. The sight of Izoldia's swollen back wrapped in bloodied bandages made Ithsar's stomach churn. By the *dracha* gods, she'd been so callous, letting Izoldia take the lash for her own crimes.

But she'd had to rescue Ezaara and Roberto from the clutches of these evil women. Women who were her only family—even though they maltreated her. As she neared the bandaged carnage that was Izoldia's back, Ithsar's belly heaved. She battled, clenching her stomach muscles. After not eating yesterday, she couldn't afford to lose the meager flatbread and dates she'd had only a few hours ago.

Swollen, angry flesh tugged at the sides of the bandages. The lash marks must be deep, then. Whoever had welded the lash would've been one of Izoldia's friends. Ashewar constantly played the assassins against one another, ruling with iron claws of fear that dug deep into the gut of every assassin, teaching them they could never trust, never give in to any emotion—except the terror of being punished by the chief prophetess or their peers. Izoldia may have been different if Ashewar had let her. All of them could have been different if Ashewar had drilled them with love instead of hate.

Ashewar could punish her, but Ithsar wouldn't have Izoldia's lash marks on her conscience. She quickly loosened the bandages, biting her lip at the deep tracks cut into Izoldia's flesh. Too many to count. So many to heal.

One at a time, then.

She let a drop of the piaua juice fall onto Izoldia's skin and rubbed it along a wound. The muscles and flesh knitted over beneath her fingers, weaving the fibers together until there was nothing but a rough red scar. Ezaara had used a second drop of juice on her fingers to rid Ithsar of scar tissue, but Izoldia had so many wounds and she had so little juice, that was a luxury she couldn't afford. Ithsar selected another gash and dribbled another drop, rubbed it in as Izoldia moaned in her sleep. Yes, the healing juice had burned through her flesh as Ezaara had straightened her finger bones and healed her twisted flesh, but the Robandi healers drugged their patients into a deep sleep, so hopefully Izoldia wouldn't wake. Ithsar worked quickly, aware the night healer could return any moment.

When the worst of Izoldia's cuts were healed and only a few small nicks remained, Ithsar shoved the empty vial into her pocket. Izoldia groaned and tossed.

Heart pounding, Ithsar raced to the door. Perhaps she should find Drida, and be rid of this awful place, after all. It was the only home she'd ever had, but there must be a better life out there.

As she eased the door shut, footsteps approached. She ducked back into the supply alcove, huddled under the shelves, and tugged a linen bedspread down to cover her.

The footsteps stopped right outside her hiding place. Someone drew the curtain, the scrape of the brass rings impossibly loud. Through the bedspread, a light shone. Ithsar tensed, ready to run. A shadowy figure leaned in. There was a rattle on the shelves above. A scrape as the curtain was pulled half shut. Then the door to the healing cavern opened and shut.

Ithsar inhaled. Thank the—

A loud gasp came from behind the healing cavern door, then a muttered curse.

Ithsar clambered out, thrust the bedspread back on the shelf, then raced down the tunnel, every nerve in her body taut. Gods, her *sathir* was brilliant yellow—screaming fear.

Near her alcove, she slowed, letting her eyelids droop as if she'd just returned from a sleepy walk to the latrine. She mentally rolled her eyes—as if she'd need the latrine after not drinking all day yesterday. A sound came from her sleeping alcove. Ithsar ducked back around a corner, just in time to see Bala exit her alcove and slide the curtain shut.

Gods, Thika!

Bala disappeared down the hall toward the larger, more spacious sleeping caverns reserved for Ashewar's personal guards.

Pulse hammering at her throat, Ithsar slipped into her quarters.

Thika was still asleep on her bed, his tail curled around his body. Ithsar crawled back under her blanket, wondering why Bala had been here.

BLESSED BY THE GODS

Izoldia awoke. Her wounds were burning, way worse than when she'd dozed off into a fitful sleep. The pain draught must've worn off. She flexed her back, muscles searing, but different than before. She grabbed fistfuls of sheet. The fabric tore beneath her hands with a satisfying rip.

Something crashed to the stone floor and glass skittered across the healing cavern.

"Izoldia, by the mighty *dracha* gods!"

"What?" Izoldia growled, sitting up. She turned.

A hand flew to the healer's mouth. "Your back. It's healed."

Izoldia snorted. That idiot. "Of course it's healing." It wasn't as if anyone was standing there, making the wounds worse. She stopped, mid-thought. The burning had faded to a warm glow. She flexed her back. The glow slowly faded.

"No, I said it's *healed*."

Surprise rippled through Izoldia. She swung her legs over the edge of the bed and stood, flexing her arms and bending her torso. "The pain is gone."

The healer nodded and whispered, "The wounds have disappeared. The *dracha* gods have blessed you."

Izoldia felt a slow grin spreading across her face. She pointed at the shattered glass. "Then you'd better clean this up, hadn't you? You fool, the chief prophetess won't be pleased you've smashed her glassware." Izoldia backhanded the woman so hard that the healer's head flew back, the audible crack of her blow ricocheting through the healing cavern.

TREASON

The heavy tromp of guards woke Ithsar. It didn't bode well, but she wasn't expecting much after yesterday. Thika slithered out from under the blanket, and scampered up the wall to the low rocky ceiling of her alcove. Thika's throat puffed in a brief, brave show of defiance as he angled his head toward the doorway, then the lizard pressed himself flat into a crevice—one of his favorite hidey-holes—his orange and brown striped hide blending with the sandstone.

Ithsar closed her eyes again, pretending to sleep.

Guards stopped outside her curtain and flung it open. One of them strode in and shook her shoulder roughly.

Still clothed in her robes, Ithsar rolled to face them and sat up. A moment later, Thut's saber was at her throat. The guard hauled Ithsar outside. Others grabbed her upper arms and dragged her, like a criminal, along the corridor to the throne room. Ithsar didn't bother asking what they wanted her for. There was no point.

Thut thrust the heavy doors open and pushed Ithsar inside.

Gods, her muscles still ached. She was still shaky. If Drida and Roshni hadn't fed her, her legs would've collapsed. As it was, Ithsar stumbled into the cavern, but regained her footing and straightened her spine.

With fiery eyes burning like the Robandi sun, Ashewar, sitting on her grotesque throne, raked her gaze over Ithsar. Behind her throne, her guards were arrayed like vultures on a dead branch, Drida and Roshni among them, faces harsh and shadowed in the flickering torchlight.

Ithsar met her mother's fiery stare without flinching, without apology.

Ashewar set her elbows on the arms of her throne and steepled her fingers. "On the night the strangers escaped, I saw a purple bruise of *sathir* staining the sky around them, and the palms swaying violently in the breeze. One of those palms dropped a cluster of dates right onto Izoldia's head. I wonder what caused that? Magic from the strangers? Or something, someone, closer to home?"

Oh gods, oh gods, her mother knew.

Or suspected.

"But no, there is no one here with that sort of skill," Ashewar continued, her eyes never leaving Ithsar's face. "I must consider this an act of war from the North. Soon, we must strike back at these *dracha ryter* and their worm-scaled beasts. But first, I've to deal with you, an heiress who sleeps through a vicious attack upon my guards by our enemies. Once you are dealt with, we'll ride to war and slay those *dracha ryter* in their sleep."

Ithsar had really messed things up. Instead of saving Ezaara and Roberto, she'd consigned them to a war against the blood-thirstiest assassins.

The doors thunked open, making the guards twitch. Izoldia was in the doorway, her huge frame rigid with tension. Bala rapidly gestured to her. Izoldia's posture softened and a grin broke out on her face.

Then Izoldia stalked across the tiles to stand in front of Ashewar's throne. "My revered Chief Prophetess, Seer of all, and the ultimate Wise One, I have reason to believe your heiress is plotting against you. She wishes to murder you."

"No!" The cry broke from Ithsar before she could check herself.

Ashewar waved Ithsar to silence. "Does she, now?"

Bala piped up, "Last night, I heard the weakling mutter something about killing you, right before she collapsed."

"No, I didn't," Ithsar cried. "You weren't even there. It was Thut on duty when I fainted."

"Fainted, did you? Not a good trait in an heir." Ashewar's eyes flashed, as hard as diamond. "Bala, take witnesses and search her quarters."

Bala bowed, thumping her hand on her chest, and then exited the throne room, taking two other guards with her as witnesses.

Ithsar breathed a quiet sigh of relief. There was nothing in her alcove that could incriminate her. Nothing except Thika. She swallowed. She hadn't thought of bringing her friend with her.

"My most revered and wise Chief Prophetess, please let me explain—"

Izoldia's words died as Ashewar waved her to silence.

Good. Izoldia's fawning attitude rubbed Ithsar's scales the wrong way.

Ashewar rose from her throne with the grace of a feline predator. Her feet slipped across the tiled floor. Noiselessly, she glided between Ithsar and Izoldia, her quick eyes measuring every breath, every twitch of a muscle, every heartbeat. She stalked, circling them both.

Ithsar's heart thundered. As her mother's icy gaze slid over her, she lowered her eyes, staring at her dirty toes on the clean tiles.

"Izoldia, you appear to be in remarkably good health after just being lashed."

Izoldia preened, meeting Ashewar's gaze. "My rapid healing is a sign of the gods' approval, my revered Chief Prophetess." Izoldia inclined her head and gave a deep bow. "I took each lash with pleasure, knowing you had bestowed them upon me. However, the gods have seen fit to heal me while I slept."

As quick as a rust viper, Ashewar sprang, slitting Izoldia's robe with her knife.

The collective sharp intake of breath from the gathered guards ricocheted like a scream in Ithsar's ears. Her heart raced like a herd of camels, their hooves thundering inside her chest.

Ashewar's eyes narrowed. "Bring a torch," the chief prophetess hissed.

A guard sprang into action, fetching a flaming brand.

"Bend." Ashewar snapped, kicking Izoldia in the back of the legs.

The guard fell to her knees on the tiles, bowing her back. A crisscrossed mash of thin, red scars gleamed on her healed flesh.

Ithsar let her eyebrows shoot up in surprise, staring like the rest of the assassins.

Ashewar spun, her sword a flash in the torchlight as it sliced toward Ithsar.

Ithsar dropped into a defensive crouch, ready to roll, raising her arms to block the blow, her sleeves sliding down her arms.

Ashewar's sword stopped a hand's breadth short of Ithsar. Her mother's control was impeccable. What had she been trying to prove? Ashewar's cackle bounced off the walls, reverberating around the throne room, making the hairs on Ithsar's neck rise. Then her mother's glittering gaze landed on Ithsar's healed fingers outstretched before her face.

Her mother's glare made something inside Ithsar curl up and die like a stray plant out of the shade.

Ashewar sheathed her sword, her eyes never leaving those fingers.

Surely now, her mother would rejoice that she was healed. Ithsar sprang to her feet, smiling. "Mother, I—"

Her smile froze as her mother sneered, "So, you've been healed, too? I wonder how that happened?"

Although her mother's words sounded harmless, the venom of hundreds of rust vipers laced her words, sending icy trickles of fear through Ithsar's bones.

§

Ashewar stalked back to her beautiful bone throne. That scheming snipe of a girl had been healed. In a flash of insight, Ashewar knew the vile blonde Queen's Rider had been responsible. Her limbs shook with savage rage. Her prisoner had not only escaped, but she'd healed her daughter. The girl that, one day, would be the end of her. Ashewar tried to control her trembling hands. She'd heard rumors of the miraculous piaua juice in the northern lands—in Dragons' Realm—but she'd never believed they were true. Now before her eyes was evidence that, not one, but two people, had been healed. Perhaps the man she'd captured for breeding stock had been too. How else could he have negotiated the caverns without his guts spilling out of his belly wound?

She wanted no trial for her daughter. Slaughtering her on the spot would be more fitting for such a despicable runt.

Izoldia rubbed her hands together. "If I may, my revered Chief Prophetess."

Ashewar narrowed her eyes at the fawning sycophant who'd dogged her daughter for years, but had not been able to quell Ithsar's stubborn streak— or break her spirit. The daughter whose long slim fingers now moved with dexterity as she tucked them into her sleeves.

"But, Mother," the girl cried, eyes bright with tears—another weakness not to be tolerated. "Mother, my hands are healed, so I can now train as an assassin. Please let me be a true weapon in your hands."

Ithsar dropped to the tiles, her forehead kissing the floor and her out-stretched, now nimble, fingers within a hand's breadth of Ashewar's deadly *yokka*. An act of trust. A fool's trust. She should snap the girl's neck and end this now. "Stand, you weakling."

As the girl scrambled to her feet, Izoldia crooned, "Chief Prophetess, Ithsar wants to be trained as an assassin so she can end your life. It was Ithsar who set the prisoners free and planted the ropes in my robes. I fear Ithsar has plans to kill you."

The door to the throne room burst open and Bala marched inside, holding up an earthenware pot. She strode between Ithsar and Izoldia and laid it at Ashewar's feet, then bent and touched her temple to the ground near Ashewar's *yokka*. *Yokka* that could slit her throat if a single word from her guard displeased her. Ashewar gave her coldest smile and waved Bala to speak.

Bala swayed back on her haunches. "We found this pot under the runt's bed." At a nod from Ashewar, Bala uncorked it and held it up, waving the fumes toward Ashewar.

The reeking poison stung Ashewar's nostrils. "Dragon's bane," she spat.

Bala bowed. "We believe that the deformed runt was seeking to end your life, dear Chief Prophetess."

Ashewar coiled in her strength, refraining from smiting the rutting snipe dead on the spot. This useless hunk of flesh that had been born of her body with blood, sweat, and pain had been a bitter disappointment since her first cry. Although she hadn't been male, perhaps it would have been just as good if she'd had her guards feed that runtling to the desert vultures.

She needed strong women to fill the ranks of the Robandi Silent Assassins. Women who would not betray her. Unlike this snipe—the spawn of that attractive man who'd produced nothing but male spawn and this useless deformed waste of flesh. She would end this once and for all.

§

No. This was not the beginning of a new life with strong, healed fingers. A life fighting among her cold-hearted sisters, the Robandi assassins. Pain lanced through Ithsar's muscles. If she hadn't already been lying on the floor, then she would have fallen at the ice-cold rage she'd seen in her mother's eyes. For years she'd been working to please her mother, to gain her love. And now? Now, there was nothing.

Nearby, Izoldia smirked.

Izoldia had poisoned her mother against her. Rage built inside Ithsar. She quelled it. She only had one chance. And that was to submit to her right for a trial before her execution. "But, Mother, that poison's not mine. In fact, someone used it to poison Thika."

Ashewar sneered at her. "You named that despicable lizard from that useless man?"

Her father was not useless. Her father had taught her to love, to believe in herself. *Precious, strong beyond words.* Above all else, he had given her Thika, a special friend to carry with her. Ithsar habitually placed her hand against her belly. Her robes were empty.

"We searched her quarters but never found the spiteful lizard," Bala snapped.

Ithsar hid her smile. No doubt, Thika had evaded them. She sprang to her feet. "I request the right of a fair trial."

"I'm sure you do." Ashewar turned to Izoldia. "My most trusted guard, it's the runt's fault I had you whipped. What do you suggest?"

Izoldia bowed so low her hair scraped the floor. "It would be my humble pleasure to assist you in dispatching this traitor. I have long wanted her bleached bones to lie strewn under the hot desert sun."

"I'm aware," Ashewar said dryly. She turned, her cold eyes slicing through Ithsar. "This has been trial enough," Ashewar announced. "Tomorrow at dawn, this outcast will be thrown off the edge of the Robandi cliffs into the Naobian Sea." Ithsar's mother stroked an elegant finger along the carved arm of her bone throne. "Although I pity the sea monsters who will devour her. She won't make much of a meal."

FAITHFUL FRIEND

Guards dragged Ithsar, kicking and fighting, down the narrow passages in the deepest dungeons. When they reached a tiny cell at the tunnel's end, they unlocked the door and threw her inside. Ithsar landed on the hard stone floor and immediately leaped to her feet, rushing to the doorway. Thut lashed out, kicking Ithsar beneath her rib cage.

Winded, Ithsar stumbled, hitting the stone, then rolled to her feet. She lunged, but the bars clanged shut in her face.

Thut stalked down the passage, laughing with the other guards—they made no attempt to keep their vows of silence now that they were so far from Ashewar.

Ithsar yelled, "No!" But after years of disuse, her voice only echoed in the tunnel like a rasping ghost.

She refused to give up, pacing the length of her cell, running her hands along the crumbling walls, straining her eyes in the flickering shadows of the distant torches. Here, near the back of the cell, the sandstone wall was damp. She scrabbled with her fingers, gouging tracks in the dirt, but Ithsar knew they were under the heart of the lake. Even if she could dig up high enough, the sandstone would cave in, the cell instantly flooding, burying her in a pile of waterlogged silt.

She ran her hands along the back wall and turned toward the cell door again, barking her shin on something hard. Her newly healed hands ran over a natural stone shelf with the remnants of a tattered blanket lying on it.

Ithsar slumped onto the bed and wadded the scrappy blanket into a ball, hugging it against her chest. Without Thika snuggling against her belly, she felt empty. And even though she'd seen a vision of herself flying into battle with the two *dracha ryter* she'd released, it must've been nothing but a dream. Her belly gnawing with hunger, and her muscles still aching from her *Sathiri* dance yesterday, she choked back her sobs and drifted into a nightmare-plagued sleep.

§

The bars clanged open and Ashewar swept into the cell. The blaze of the torches in her guards' hands made Ithsar squint as she scrambled to her feet, still clutching the tattered blanket. Ashewar waved a languid hand and her personal guards filed out of the cell, leaving them alone.

Ithsar considered dashing past her mother to snatch the torch the guards had left in a sconce outside her cell and burning her way out, but there were too many guards waiting along the tunnel. There was no point in fighting here where the odds were against her. Better to wait until she had a chance. For the first time in years, she did not hide her hands inside her sleeves. She would not back down. If she had the chance again, she'd still free Ezaara and Roberto.

Dark shadows played across Ashewar's face. "So, I finally get to kill you. Believe me, the pleasure will be all mine."

Ithsar's chest tightened, making it hard to breathe. Her fingers were healed, so why did her mother still hate her so much? "I would gladly train with my sisters."

"The likes of you? Train with the Silent Assassins?" Ashewar wrinkled her nose. "You're a useless chattel, only worthy to fetch and carry, or bow and scrape. My clan have undergone extensive training. They have discipline."

As if dancing the *Sathiri* dance yesterday from morn until deep into the night had not taken discipline. As if *bowing and scraping* and hiding her strength from these monsters she'd lived with all these years had not taken discipline.

"Izoldia has told me everything. You freed those dirty *dracha ryter,* going against your own flesh and blood." Ashewar pointed to the dusty sandstone floor. "At my feet."

Ithsar complied, prostrating herself for the chief prophetess. There was no point in fighting. Not here. Not now.

"You loved your father, didn't you?" Ashewar gave the feral, wild smile of a panther about to pounce. "Did you know you were his downfall? One day as I sat with my hands cradled around my prism-seer, seeking glimpses of my future, I saw you killing me." Ashewar stalked around Ithsar, a shark circling its prey. "How could a despicable tiny slip beat me, the best fighting weapon the Robandi has ever had? I scoffed at the idea, assuming the vision must be wrong. But I kept seeing it: you, killing me in a hundred different ways." Ashewar paused by Ithsar's head and then lashed out with her foot, kicking Ithsar's chin.

Ithsar's head snapped back. Her jaw clamped so hard, her tongue was already swelling, the tang of blood in her mouth. *Precious, strong beyond words.* She held onto her father's words.

"It was your fault your father died," Ashewar hissed. "I killed him because of you. For impregnating me with such a vial loathsome specimen of the human race. A daughter who could not even hold a weapon properly. A daughter who would turn against her mother. A daughter more treacherous than a rust viper. I, Ashewar, rule the Robandi with an iron heart. I sit upon a throne made of the bones of my enemies. There is no place for weakness in my clan."

Strong beyond words. Sometimes there was strength in waiting, in biding your time.

"I shall laugh tomorrow morning as your body is ripped to shreds by the vicious fangs of those monsters in the deeps. I'll cackle with glee, breaking my vow of silence as they tear you limb from limb and feast upon your flesh and bones."

Ithsar didn't point out that Ashewar was already breaking her vow of silence, right now.

Ashewar towered over her. "Because I'd foreseen your treachery, I decided to systematically destroy you. I fostered hatred among the other girls. Izoldia was a perfect tool in my hands, torturing you for years. You'd come to me, begging for justice, unaware that I was behind her cruel actions." A deep-throated laugh burst from Ashewar's throat. "To your feet, you weak fool." Her mother's hands twitched as if she wanted to throttle Ithsar.

Ithsar rocked back to her knees and then stood. She'd looked to her mother for support.

Looked to her mother for love.

Looked to her for solace from Izoldia's torment. Her mouth grew dry, her tongue thick and clumsy. She tried to answer, but all that came out was a croak.

"Killing your father gave me double the pleasure, knowing it would destroy you."

Ashewar's words stole Ithsar's breath. Pain lanced through her chest. Her knees faltered. Her father had died because of her. There was no blow Ashewar could've dealt that cut as deeply as that truth.

As quick as an asp, Ashewar's foot struck Ithsar's gut with so much force Ithsar flew across the room, crashing into the wall and striking her head on stone.

The walls of the cavern spun as dark memories swirled through her: *Ashewar taking her on a special trip to the desert; seeing her father sinking to his knees, grasping his gut as blood sprayed over the tangerine sand; palm leaves rustling overhead in a hot, arid breeze; her father staring at her until his eyes glazed over and he toppled into the sand, unseeing.*

One day, you will rise above your mother's petty hatred, for you are my precious daughter, strong beyond words.

Her screaming, screaming.

Ashewar gloating, her face radiant with joy as assassins tied Ithsar's father's dead body to a camel and dragged it over the dunes, leaving him far out in the desert so his bones would be picked clean by vultures. Ithsar, on camelback, being squeezed against Drida's chest firmly, despite squirming and kicking and fighting, as they followed the trail of blood and the camel hauling her father's bloody body away.

Pain throbbing through her skull, Ithsar tried to clamber to her knees, but Ashewar was already there, pinning her underfoot, her pretty *yokka* on Ithsar's throat.

"You deserve to die." Ashewar pressed her big toe down.

The lethal blade from Ashewar's apricot-beaded *yokka* pricked against the artery in Ithsar's throat. One move, and she'd be dead.

"But not now," Ashewar gloated. "I will have no greater pleasure than watching the fanged monsters of the deep rip your body to shreds. You, Ithsar, will not be my downfall. I will be yours."

The blade slid back into Ashewar's *yokka*. The chief prophetess spun, robes swishing, and stalked from the dungeon.

As the cell door clanked shut and Thut turned the key in the lock, leering at her, Ithsar clambered to her feet and cradled the blanket to her belly, blinking back bitter tears.

The guards' footsteps retreated, leaving her alone.

Her mother had never loved her, always hated her. Worse, she'd done everything in her power to destroy her. Sorrow and rage surged through Ithsar. A dry breeze rustled her robes, and she sensed purple bruised *sathir* forming at her fingertips.

Rise above your mother's petty hatred, my precious daughter.

Ithsar quelled her rage and waited.

§

Ithsar woke to a faint rasp across the stone in her cell. Her eyes flew open to something slithering along the floor. Orange scales flashed in the torchlight. A rust viper! She clambered onto the stone bed, standing with her back hard against the wall.

The viper skittered over to her bed.

Skittered? She gasped. "Thika."

Her little lizard leaped onto the ledge and Ithsar gathered him in her arms. He nuzzled against her cheek, his tongue flicking out to tickle her nose. She gave a quiet chuckle. "At least you're here, Thika. I may not have a knife or a weapon, but I have you."

To Ithsar's dismay, Thika cocked his head and scurried off, leaving her alone in the dark.

§

Ithsar's sleep was plagued with dreams of drowning, snapping sharks hurtling toward her body, and scaled maws and talons ripping at her flesh. She woke in a cold sweat. Tugging the scrap of blanket around her, she sat up and tucked her knees against her chest, trying to get warm. Another day without eating or drinking. No wonder her body was so cold and her limbs sluggish and leaden.

Ashewar's words came crashing down on her again, a heavy smothering blanket weighing on her, making it hard to move. She was responsible for her father's death. If she hadn't loved him, held him so tightly in her heart, then perhaps her father with his warm brown eyes and soft laughter would still be alive. She squeezed her stinging eyes tight. Her world had crumbled when he'd died, leaving no one to protect her from the taunts and jeers of Izoldia, Bala, and Thut.

It was worse now, knowing that her mother, driven by hatred and fear, had caused every burn, punch, kick, or knife wound those bullies had inflicted upon her.

Still clutching her knees to her chest, Ithsar rocked on the hard stone bed. She sat there, unable to shake the guilt threatening to choke her.

Something ominous scraped along the corridor. She cocked her head.

There it was again. The only other sound was the guard's soft snoring further down the passageway. The scraping—metal along the stone—was approaching her cell. A blade, then.

Had Ashewar changed her mind and come to finish her off?

A quick kill might be better than the vicious fangs waiting in the Naobian Sea. Ithsar shuddered.

Balancing on the balls of her feet, she tiptoed across the cell and peered out the bars. Something glimmered. There was a flash of silver in the torchlight, light catching on a blade. But low, at floor level.

The blade drew closer, and in the flickering light from the nearest sconce she saw a pale glimmer of orange. It was Thika—tugging Ithsar's knife along the floor, dragging the ornately-carved handle by a decorative tassel.

"Thika!" Ithsar fell to her knees, took the knife from Thika, tucked it inside her breeches, and tightened her belt securely. There, it would be hidden by her voluminous robes. She embraced her lizard, patting his warm, scaly hide.

The snoring in the passage stopped. Stealthy feet made their way along the corridor.

Ithsar slunk onto her bed, and Thika slithered inside the front of her robe. Nestling the lizard against her belly, she drew her knees up and closed her eyes, breathing evenly.

The bright flame of a torch danced, casting yellow and orange shadows behind Ithsar's eyelids. There was a grunt, and the footsteps receded. She cradled Thika, glad of the solid knife hilt against her hip, grateful for her only true friend among these cutthroat, male-hating assassins.

Desert Trek

The unmistakable clip of Ashewar's boots echoed on the stone walls. Faint and weary with hunger, Ithsar stood with her chin high. She tugged her robes so they hung loosely around her waist to disguise her dagger and Thika's presence. She would release Thika in the desert. At least one of them would live to see another day. Because, if she didn't let him go, Ashewar would kill him.

Ashewar and her guards arrived at her cell. Ithsar winced, blinking against the light of many torches. The diamonds glinted in her mother's hooked nose—a nose that wrinkled at the sight of Ithsar.

Keys clanking, Izoldia unlocked the door. Bala's rough hands gripped Ithsar's biceps, sending sparks of pain through her arms. Izoldia bound her wrists far too tightly, the ropes biting into Ithsar's flesh. She tensed her muscles, hoping that when she relaxed the bonds would loosen.

"None of those tricks," Izoldia hissed.

Ithsar ignored her, staring, unseeing, at the walls. *Precious, strong beyond words.*

Izoldia drove her thumb into a pressure point on Ithsar's elbow, spiking pain down Ithsar's arm and releasing the tension in her palms, while Bala bound her wrists more tightly than before.

Resistance was futile. There were too many of them. Her head held high, Ithsar mustered her dignity as the guards led her down the passage. Bala followed closely, her breath huffing against Ithsar's neck. Through the winding corridors Ithsar traipsed, up past the caverns and out into the hot desert. It was still early morning, so the sands didn't burn her feet, but she had no illusions. By the time they reached the Naobian Sea, those same orange sands would be blistering hot. No one offered her boots or sandals.

No one cared whether she died with blistered feet.

Thut mounted a camel. Izoldia hefted Ithsar as if she weighed no more than a scrap of parchment, and threw her over the bony haunches of Thut's camel. Thika squirmed beneath her belly, moving so he wasn't so squashed, as Bala and Roshni tied her to the saddle and bound her feet, so she couldn't slip off and run. Roshni tried to meet her gaze, but Ithsar looked away.

Ashewar's fine camel knelt. Izoldia stooped to let Ashewar step upon her back to seat herself in her elegant leather saddle, ornately painted with desert flowers and encrusted with jewels. Around them, guards mounted their camels.

Ithsar's head spun with fatigue. Dread pooled in her stomach. With each rise and fall of the camel's haunches, Ithsar bounced against Thut's beast's bony rump as they plodded off into the blazing orange.

§

Joy surged in Ashewar's breast. Never before had she had a righteous reason to execute her daughter. At long last she would be free of the visions that had plagued her, showing her daughter's dominion over the Robandi assassins. Although Ashewar had tight control over her assassins, in the visions she'd seen of Ithsar, her women had been devoted to Ithsar, joy and admiration in their faces as they followed her. Instead of fear.

Rage ripped through Ashewar every time she remembered that vision. That girl must die.

She glanced back at the small figure draped over the back of Thut's camel, tied to its saddle, head lolling and limbs flopping in time to the camel's gait as its large feet plodded through the sand. The sun blazed down, warming Ashewar's heart. Tonight she could rest easy, no longer plagued by the nightmares of her daughter usurping her and stealing what she'd worked so long to create—her tribe of loyal well-honed assassins who hated men, cold-blooded killers not afraid to destroy weakness.

Izoldia sidled over on her camel and inclined her head.

Ashewar waved a hand, giving the fawning guard a chance to speak.

"My revered Chief Prophetess, there is dissension among the ranks. Some believe the girl should not be executed."

Ashewar glanced back at the group of orange-robed women traveling behind them. Her best guards were on the perimeter on camelback, bows nocked toward the young figure slumped over Thut's camel's haunches. She lifted an eyebrow.

"Would you like me to name them, most revered Chief Prophetess?" Izoldia asked.

Ashewar inhaled a thin stream of warm air through her nostrils, and gave a half nod.

"Roshni, she of the blue eyes. Bala believes she helped the runt when she collapsed."

No surprise there. Ashewar raised her other eyebrow.

"Drida, she of the silver hair and many wrinkles, helped her as well."

How dare that runt influence one of her best assassins. Ashewar's rage bucked inside her like a wild beast straining to be set free. She pursed her lips, letting Izoldia squirm under the hot sun for a hundred camel paces before she replied. "Tonight we'll purge our ranks of these weaklings. At midnight, slaughter them both in their beds."

Eyes glinting, Izoldia licked her lips. "Yes, most revered Chief Prophetess, it shall be done."

Only when Izoldia had pulled her scarf over her face and fallen back to ride with the clan, did Ashewar allow herself to smile.

§

Ithsar's throat was parched and gritty by the time Ashewar halted at the foot of the enormous slope jutting up against the sapphire sky. They'd reached the drop off, where the steep sandstone cliffs that edged the Robandi desert fell into the Naobian Sea. Although Ithsar couldn't see it, the hiss of the ocean rose over the sand.

Thut dismounted and yanked Ithsar to the ground. She collapsed in a heap, then used her bound hands to push herself up. Gods, the sand was hot. She wriggled her tied feet, burrowing beneath the surface to find a cooler patch, hoping there were no lurking scorpions—although it made no difference, because today she was due to die.

Her efforts weren't much use—her feet still ached from the heat.

Ashewar snapped her fingers.

Bala sprang forward, thrusting a spear at Ithsar's back.

Izoldia's blade flashed, slashing the rope around Ithsar's ankles. The burly guard picked up the pieces and waved them in Ithsar's face. "Cut ropes, just like the ones you hid in my pockets. Now you'll pay for your treachery." Her spittle landed on Ithsar's cheek.

If she could get to her knife…

"You're too afraid to release my hands, aren't you?" Ithsar said. "Afraid I'll beat you."

Izoldia's eyes flashed. Her blade flew at Ithsar's wrists. A moment later, Ithsar's hands were free, the ropes falling to the sand, her wrists throbbing as the blood rushed back into them.

Through her robes, Bala's spear pricked Ithsar's back.

Her hands and feet still prickling with pins and needles, Ithsar stumbled up the sandy dune, trailing Ashewar and her personal guard to the top of the cliff. The rest of the assassins followed them—Ashewar was taking no chances.

Every time Ithsar placed a foot on the burning sand, rivulets of orange grains ran down past her. For every three steps she took, she slipped back two. Ithsar wished she were as small and insignificant as a grain tumbling down the dune. Too small to bother with. Not worth killing.

Bala's spear prodded her back again. She rushed on, feet searing, assassins arrayed behind her and to either side—lethal weapons in Ashewar's hands.

She could never fight them all. Never hope to beat them.

SACRIFICE

"Face your destiny." Ashewar's boot-clad feet were planted in the sand above Ithsar on a large flat space at the pinnacle of the dune. Ithsar's gaze traveled up her mother's legs and powerful lithe body to her stony face. "There is no hope for you," Ashewar said. "What use was your love for your spineless father, for that pathetic lizard, if it all led to this?"

Bala's spear jabbed Ithsar's back, and she scrambled up the last few body-lengths to the flat area at the top of the cliff, Bala and Izoldia on either side of her. Behind them, the assassins formed an impenetrable wall several women deep. The front of the cliff fell away in a sheer drop to the raging sea. The thundering of foam-speckled waves crashing against the orange sandstone was drowned out by the pulse pounding in Ithsar's ears.

Her breath stuttered. Her heart fluttered against her ribs like the Naobian starling she'd once seen trapped in a cage at the oasis, beating its wings against the bars—under the illusion it could get free. Dead within hours, that tiny bird had never soared under blue skies again.

Ashewar's chuckle shuddered through Ithsar's bones. Her mother prowled along the cliff, and kicked a loose clump of sandstone. It skittered off the edge and dropped in a spray of orange sand into the sea. "Give the monsters their due," Ashewar smirked, snapping her fingers.

Misha, a slim assassin who'd been adopted into the clan when Ithsar was a littling, took a Naobian flute made of opaline crystal from her robes. She held it to her lips, the sun glittering off the eagles carved along the instrument. Misha's deep brown eyes latched onto Ithsar's. A few high crisp notes trilled from the flute, then broke into a haunting melody that wrapped itself around Ithsar's heart and carried it out soaring above the open sea, sweeping her off to far distant lands. The sea breeze danced through Ithsar's hair. Pink *sathir* wended from the flute, wrapping itself around her in a soft cocoon, then billowing out over the ocean.

If only the melody were a giant-winged eagle that could whisk her far away to Naobia.

Ithsar's knees trembled. *Precious daughter, strong beyond words.* She forced strength into her muscles, holding them rigid. She'd go to her death proudly, honoring her father.

Roshni, of the piercing blue eyes, took a pale-brown satchel from her shoulder and dropped it in the sand, kneeling next to it. Every detail etched itself into Ithsar's mind: the worn, tan leather; the gleaming brass buckles; the pale half-moons on the tips of Roshni's fingernails as she opened the buckles with deft fingers; and the way Roshni averted her gaze.

A cool breeze danced off the sea, clashing with the arid desert air. Izoldia's fingers tightened on the hilt of her saber. Bala's dark eyes scanned Ithsar, missing nothing.

Roshni flipped the lid of the satchel open, revealing dark red stains and a slab of raw meat. The scent of blood filled Ithsar's nostrils—from sacrificial goat flesh, an offering to rouse the monsters of the deep.

As if their appetites needed rousing.

Still kneeling at Ashewar's feet, Roshni held the chunk of meat in her blood-stained hands, her head bowed and eyes down.

So much for Ithsar's camel ride off the oasis. Roshni and Drida's support had crumbled in the face of Ashewar's wrath. Had the offer been genuine, or just a means of trapping her?

A vision washed through Ithsar.

Hundreds of dragon riders wheeled in the air above a forest pockmarked with snow, their colored wings flashing like jewels in the wan winter sun as they fought shadowy, foul dragons with ragged wings and yellow beams slicing from their eyes. Riding the multi-hued queen, Ezaara, with Roberto on Erob at her side, led her dragons and people into battle. Bolts of fire shot through the sky at Ezaara and her dragon riders, the shadow dragons blotting out the horizon with their dark leathery wings. Below, a strange metal chest sat in a clearing with a brilliant beam of golden light streaming from it into the sky.

Ithsar resisted seeing the rest of the familiar vision—the part where she joined Ezaara in battle. This vision was not to be. Ashewar had triumphed.

With a flash of her hard ebony eyes, Ashewar said, "Awaken the beasts from the depths and stir them into a feeding frenzy."

§

Roshni stood, her blazing sapphire eyes connecting with Ithsar's. With a jolt, Ithsar realized Roshni's eyes were blazing with anger—she'd only averted her gaze to hide her fury from Ashewar. Roshni threw the meat high in the air and whipped her saber from her belt. With two slashes, the meat fell onto the sand in four pieces. Blood dripped from Roshni's ceremonial saber, but she did not clean it and sheathe it, as was custom. Instead, Roshni speared the hunks of meat upon the tip, bowed her knee, her eyes downcast once more, and offered them to Ashewar.

The chief prophetess was so filled with glee that she didn't appear to notice the lapse in custom.

Ashewar plucked a piece of meat from the tip of the saber and threw it off the edge of the cliff. The harsh sunlight caught ruby drops of blood as the flesh arced through the air, then plummeted to the sea. Ithsar couldn't tear her gaze from that tiny piece of goat. It hit the water. Dark fins sped through the sea, and the water foamed as sharks fought over the morsel.

"More," Ashewar spat. "Work them into bloodlust, ready for this traitor."

Izoldia plucked the next piece from Roshni's saber and tossed it off the edge of the cliff, sliding a sly grin at Ithsar. "You're next," she muttered, malice glinting in her eyes.

The sea became a churning mass of thrashing tails and fins as the sharks ripped the flesh from one another's jaws, devouring it.

Farther out, a dark shape rippled under the ocean's turquoise surface. Longer than three camels, it cut through the water toward the frenzy of the fins and snapping jaws. Another dark shadow followed in its wake; and farther out, many more. Those giant, fanged monsters would rip her body to shreds, as Ashewar had promised.

Bala hurled the third piece of meat. It flew from her bloody hands. An enormous shark rose from the ocean, its gray and white maw snapping down the meat.

Ashewar flashed her teeth at Roshni. "You may throw the last piece."

Her saber still dripping blood, Roshni took the meat from the tip. She tossed the flesh high into the air, off the cliff. As Ashewar's eyes tracked the chunk of goat, Roshni whirled, her saber flashing toward Ashewar's heart.

The chief prophetess deflected it. With a kick to the chest, she knocked Roshni off balance, then slammed into her with her shoulder. Roshni teetered on the edge of the cliff, saber flashing as it was flung from her hand, arcing, blade-over-hilt-blade-over-hilt in a spray of ruby droplets. Roshni's body followed, her scream shredding Ithsar's heart, her sapphire eyes stark with fear.

Dark hair swirling around her face, her body hit the sea, and her scream was silenced in a spray of white.

Sharks dived in. Within heartbeats, Roshni's body was a churning froth of red.

A scrap of her orange robe floated upon the ocean's surface as sharks prowled, waiting for their next meal. Waiting for Ithsar.

§

Ithsar tried to swallow, but couldn't. She gasped, but couldn't draw air. Her chest felt as if it had been kicked, the life driven from her lungs. She clasped her hands to her breast.

"See what happens to those who disobey me?" Ashewar crowed.

Roshni's only failing had been to show kindness. Despite the broken feeling in her chest, anger flickered inside Ithsar and spread like wildfire to her belly. How dare her mother end lives on a whim. Ashewar hated Ithsar, had always planned to kill her, disobedient or not. Ithsar refused to stand in the shadow of her mother. If she was going to die, she'd go down fighting.

Ithsar spun, facing her mother. Behind Ashewar, the assassins were an impenetrable wall. Drida's eyes were misty, her mouth gaping. The Naobian flute dangled from Misha's fingers, her jaw slack. Nila, a lively assassin with black curls, stood beside Misha, eyes glinting with hatred. The rest of the assassins were stoic, immovable.

"You killed Roshni." Wildfire burned bright in Ithsar's belly, spreading through her core.

Ashewar held a hand out, examining the nails at the end of her long slender fingers. "Oh? So I did." She snapped her hand shut.

Ithsar spun, executing the tenth move of the *Sathiri* dance, kicking out at Ashewar.

Ashewar ducked, and rolled away.

Izoldia and Bala lunged. Grabbing Ithsar's arms and torso, they kicked her knees out from under her, slamming her into the sand, and dragged her to the edge of the cliff. They thrust her upper body out over the edge. The wildfire guttered and died, leaving Ithsar's belly hollow. There was nothing between her and the raging sea—nothing except Izoldia and Bala's grip. She gasped, head spinning at the vertical plunge into that wild ocean writhing with sharks and the huge, dark shadows of terrifying sea monsters.

"No, no, my beloved guards," Ashewar drawled. "She's mine."

Bala and Izoldia dragged Ithsar back to her feet and spun her to face Ashewar.

With a feral grin on her haughty face, Ashewar whipped her saber from its sheath.

§

As Bala and Izoldia backed off, Ithsar balanced on the balls of her feet, ready. Like a deadly rust viper, Ashewar struck, saber flashing. Ithsar whirled, but the saber caught her robes. A scrap of orange fabric fluttered free, and was caught by the wind and tossed out over the sea.

Ithsar's limbs trembled, not from fear this time, but from rage. The trembling grew until her whole body shook. Her fury pooled in her gut and burned along her veins. She thrust her hand into her robes and yanked out the hidden dagger from her breeches. Ashewar's eyes widened. She slashed again. Ithsar blocked, the reverberation clanging through her blade and running down her forearms into her elbows. Ashewar spun and kicked Ithsar's ribs, then followed through with a lunging swing of her gleaming saber.

The blade whispered past Ithsar's head as she rolled to the side and leaped to her feet, sand crumbling beneath her and cascading down the cliff. She rushed forward as Ashewar struck again, her saber slicing a rent in Ithsar's flowing breeches. Her mother's face was mottled with fury, her cunning eyes slitted as she swiped her wicked blade at Ithsar's legs. Ithsar leaped over the blade and kicked her mother's jaw. Ashewar grunted as her head snapped back, but recovered her footing and slashed at Ithsar again, going straight for her belly.

No! Not Thika! Ithsar shrieked the ancient *Sathiri* battle cry, "Avanta!"

Her robes ripped and Thika leaped out, landing on Ashewar's face. His claws scrabbled bloody gouges in Ashewar's cheeks. Ithsar leaped, slashing at Ashewar's ribs.

But Ashewar grabbed Thika by the tail and held the squirming lizard up, the tip of her saber at his belly. "Move a hand's breadth and I'll spill this despicable creature's guts."

Ithsar froze.

"See, love is a weakness," Ashewar sneered. "Something to be used against you. A weakness I do not tolerate."

Ithsar's heart pounded like a herd of stampeding camels. Ashewar was determined to destroy everything that meant anything to her. Everything precious. Just as she'd killed her father. Rage blazed through Ithsar. A purple bruise of *sathir* built at her fingertips. A dark bruise blossomed on the ground beneath her feet, and the earth shook, tremors running up her legs and through her body. She knew she was causing the quake, but she didn't care. White-hot fury surged through Ithsar's veins. A flurry of sand swirled around her feet, whipping into a dust storm around Ashewar, Thika, and Ithsar.

Ashewar dropped Thika. He scrambled up Ithsar's leg, clinging to her robes.

She slashed her dagger at her mother. Ashewar deflected her knife and barreled into Ithsar. The *sathir* bruise blackened and the sand shifted. The edge of the ledge crumbled, and, in a thrashing pile of limbs, Ashewar, and then Ithsar, fell from the cliff, plunging toward the sea.

INTO THE DEPTHS

Wind tugged at Ithsar's tattered robe as she plummeted through the air, Thika's tail wrapped tightly around her wrist. By the *dracha* gods, what had she done? Ithsar's rage had cleaved the edge off the cliff. She, Ashewar, and Thika would die—and it was all her fault. Ashewar flailed, her saber flying from her grasp and the beads on her braids clacking. The roar of the waves grew louder, water pounding against the sandstone cliff and drenching them in spray. The sea was swarming with sharks and dark ominous shadows.

Ashewar's body hit the water first.

Ithsar smacked into the ocean, plunging beneath the surface, the impact of the water driving the air from her lungs. She flailed and kicked up, holding her hand over Thika's nose so he wouldn't ingest any water. She burst through the surface, gasping, holding Thika aloft. An enormous, wicked fin arrowed toward her.

Treading water, Ithsar spun, but there were more sharks behind her, closing in fast. Beyond them, the giant, green-scaled tail of a sea monster whipped above the water, sending a spray over the sharks. Thika climbed upon her head. Spluttering, Ithsar swam in the only direction she could—toward the sheer cliff. She couldn't scale it, but Thika was nimble, good at climbing. If she could toss him onto the cliff face, maybe one of them would survive.

She glanced back. That shark was getting close. In a few heartbeats, it would be here.

Ashewar burst out of the water behind her, Thika's scratches on her cheeks still bleeding.

Ithsar screamed, "Look out!"

But it was too late. The shark lunged and opened its cavernous jaws. White fangs gleaming, it crunched down on Ashewar's body. Her blood leaked from the shark's maw. It shook her broken body like a dog worrying a big, bloody bone. Fins sliced the water and sharks dived at Ashewar, tearing off her limbs and severing her head. The sleek creatures ripped her apart in a feeding frenzy, snapping her bones and thrashing their tails.

Ithsar turned away, unable to unsee the carnage and clothing scraps—the only remains of her mother. Giant shadows of sea monsters roamed the depths below Ithsar. Gods, she had to flee. She shoved Thika's tail off her face, his claws digging into her scalp as she frantically kicked toward the cliffs. Her arms were tired. Her sodden robes dragged her down. For every few body lengths she swam, the strong ocean currents sucked her back a length or two toward the enormous sea monsters.

Something nudged her stomach. Ithsar glanced down, wanting to scream.

A shark butted her again, then dived and angled back up toward her. This time, it nudged her thigh. It was playing with her, toying, before it closed in for its meal. Her breath rasped as she kicked and thrashed. There was no way to get Thika to the cliff now, the current was too strong. The shark, too close. Should she lie limp on the water's surface, pretending to be a piece of driftwood, and hope the shark would leave her alone?

No, it was hopeless.

Heart hammering and gasping so hard she could hardly breathe, Ithsar plucked Thika from her head and held him aloft while she trod water. A wave crested, swamping them, but she kept her legs moving and held her precious friend as high as she could. Waiting.

Far above her, assassins in orange robes peered over the lip of the cliff. Their cries drifted on the wind, drowned out by the thundering waves smacking the sandstone. One of them gestured, pointing. Ithsar turned as a wave broke over her. She gulped in mouthfuls of salt water, throat burning, and stretched her arm up again to keep Thika aloft. His tail was curled so tightly around her forearm that her hand was going numb.

The shark's blunt nose rose out of the water, the pale underside of its jaw gleaming. It turned, its curved fin speeding away, but then circled around and raced toward her. Ithsar strained, churning her legs and stretching to keep Thika high, but it was no use. This was it.

Sobs broke from her chest. "I'm sorry, Thika. Sorry, Papa. I just wasn't strong enough." Her visions had been for nothing—she would never see Ezaara again.

The enormous fin neared.

A huge shadow rippled underwater.

The shark surged up from the sea, opened its maw and leaped, its jaws angled to crunch through her forearm and snap up Thika.

A giant green-scaled head speared out of the churning ocean and opened a gaping maw, revealing the dark cavern of its throat. Water streamed from pointed fangs as long as Ithsar's forearm. Its fiery gold eyes locked onto hers as it dived through the air, spraying brine. Those enormous jaws engulfed the shark, crunching its body in half. The monster flicked its head, and the shark's remains went flying and splashed into the sea.

Then the sea monster opened its jaws again. Grasping Ithsar in its fangs, it dragged her under the water.

Izoldia's Decree

Ashewar's saber flashed and her arms flailed. A purple bruise stained the sky and sand grains whipped through the air. Izoldia squinted and pulled her headscarf over her mouth. There was no need to intervene. This would soon be over. Besides, if Ashewar died at the hand of that runt, Izoldia would easily finish the girl off afterward. And if that scrawny thing died?

As head guard, Izoldia would be heiress to the chief prophetess—and then only Ashewar would stand in her way.

The dune shook. Izoldia gaped as a chunk of the cliff broke off. In a flurry of sand and scrabbling limbs, the chief prophetess and her daughter tumbled off the cliff.

Izoldia rushed to the edge and peered over. Her sister assassins surged forward to join her, head scarves whipping in that strange wind. Suddenly, the wind died and the purple stain vanished.

Ashewar hit the water first and disappeared. Ithsar's turn came a moment later. The sea turned into a choppy frenzy of snapping jaws. When Ashewar burst to the surface, the sharks made short work of her, turning the sea frothy red.

That deformed fool was down there, struggling in the sea, but the enormous fanged monsters were heading toward her, their tails lashing the water.

Nila and Misha called out, trying to warn her. Izoldia glared at them, but they were too busy yelling and pointing to notice. She dragged her gaze back to the ocean below. A giant green head and shoulders rose from the surging surf. Its jaws wrapped around Ithsar's pathetic, weedy body and dragged her under the surface. Izoldia's heart thrummed. She waited, licking her lips, but the monster didn't resurface.

The day couldn't have turned out better.

Snatching her saber from her hip, Izoldia thrust it high into the air. "Ashewar is dead. The chief prophetess is no more. And her traitorous heir has been swallowed by the mighty beasts that patrol the depths of the Naobian Sea." She spun, grinning, still holding her saber high.

The women fell into line, staring at her, stone-faced.

"I, as Ashewar's most loyal guard, will take her place. I now anoint myself Chief Prophetess." Izoldia smirked.

Not a brow rippled.

Drida, that wrinkled old crone with ugly gray hair, stepped forward, eyes blazing. "A chief prophetess is not self-declared," she croaked. "The *dracha* gods anoint the new chief prophetess, one with gifts. Stand down, Izoldia, or we will—"

Izoldia flicked her wrist, throwing the blade hidden up her sleeve. Her dagger hit the woman's throat before she finished speaking. A spray of red drenched the nearby assassins and the woman collapsed in a puff of orange sand.

"Any more objections?" Izoldia surveyed them all.

Among the women arrayed before her on the hot desert sand, not a single muscle twitched. They each met her gaze with hard eyes.

She gestured to Bala and Thut. "As the chief prophetess' elite guard, these two women will help me enforce new rules among the Robandi assassins. For too long, the chief prophetess has only let us glean lousy pickings from the desert, but there's fine hunting to be had among these dunes. We shall now take the lion's share, and spill the blood of the male vermin that dare inhabit the Robandi Desert sands. Their spoils shall be ours."

Izoldia twitched her saber at the dead woman whose blood was seeping into the hot desert sand, her glassy eyes staring skyward. "You two." She gestured at Misha, a young, skinny assassin, and Nila, who was a wild, wicked fighter. "Toss this carrion to the sharks and join us. We'll ride out now, and make men quake and scream with terror."

§

The sun beat down mercilessly. Sweat prickled Misha's forehead and slithered between her shoulder blades, snaking its way down her back. She traipsed over to Drida and Nila. The other assassins were following Izoldia down to the camels, their nimble feet making short work of the steep dune.

Wiping a black curl from her face, Nila leaned over Drida's body and pulled Izoldia's dagger from her neck.

Misha winced, trying to hide her horror at the wet sucking sound. At Drida's beautiful, silver hair now splattered in gore. And the gaping wound in her neck.

After examining and cleaning the blade, Nila gave a sly grin and pocketed it deep within her robes. She shrugged and wrinkled her nose at Izoldia's hulking back as she led the assassins away.

So, Nila wasn't a fan of Izoldia either. That was handy to know. They might as well get this unpleasant job over and done with. Misha bent her knees and slid her hands under Drida's shoulders. There was nothing for it. Even though Drida had held the admiration and respect of all of her sister assassins, she was better off with the sharks than the vultures circling overhead. Anything but vultures. Misha shuddered at memories of her father and brothers' bodies strewn across the sands. They said vultures picked out the eyes first—that eyes were a delicacy for those foul birds. At least those sharks would finish Drida's remains quickly.

Nila picked up Drida's legs and Misha hefted her shoulders, the wound leaking more blood as Drida's head flopped back. They crab-walked over the flat area to the lip of the cliff. Drida was dead. Roshni was dead. Sharks had just devoured Ashewar, and a sea monster had gobbled up Ithsar. Misha shook her head. Ashewar had been bad enough as a leader, but Izoldia would be worse— way worse.

When Misha was a littling, her father and brothers had died at the hands of these Robandi assassins, but one of their killers had taken mercy on her and adopted her into the clan. Without a choice or a say in the matter, she'd been raised to fight among these violent women. It had been her only chance of sur- vival. She'd never dared disobey.

And the harsh lines that carved Izoldia's face and the hate that glittered in her dark eyes, had Misha obeying now, too.

They tossed Drida's body to the sharks. Misha spun away before it touched the raging ocean, keeping her face impassive.

Nila bounded to her side, sand streaming from every footfall as they half- slipped down the dunes to their camels. But as they mounted, Nila slid her a sidelong glance, raised an eyebrow, and gave her a jaunty grin.

With a jolt, Misha realized Nila's ebony eyes were bright with unshed tears.

SEA MONSTER

The sea monster's fangs pressed through Ithsar's tattered sodden robes, against her torso. She and Thika were dragged down, down, her heart hammering and lungs threatening to explode. She hadn't even caught a proper breath. They'd only last heartbeats before they drowned. Not that it would matter. This ravenous beast was about to eat them. She clamped her hand over Thika's nose, squeezing his nostrils and mouth shut, but the lizard lashed his tail against her arm and squirmed.

Gods, Ithsar's lungs *burned*. Dark spots danced before her eyes. Her chest ached as they dived deeper.

Thika fought and thrashed. He bucked out of her grip, hooked his tail back around her shoulder, and opened his mouth. No, despite all she'd done, her best friend would die. Ithsar gasped, drawing in breath—

Air filled her lungs—not water.

Another breath. More air.

Ithsar drew in great gulps, easing the pressure on her chest. She was breathing—still alive. A shimmering silver bubble filled with glorious air surrounded her and Thika. Thika nestled against her face. Thank the *dracha* gods, he was all right. Thank the sea gods, too, that they both were. For now.

The sea monster opened its fangs and released her. Ithsar floated, suspended in the water before the monster's golden gaze. Its eyes glowed like a lantern in an oasis welcoming home a weary traveler. Silver *sathir* danced around the creature. A strange surge of warmth bubbled in Ithsar's chest and belly.

A current tugged Ithsar away from the beast. Its forelegs snaked out and it cradled her in its talons. *"You are precious, noble and strong, fated for great things,"* a warm voice hummed in Ithsar's mind. *"I am Saritha, renamed after you, Ithsar."*

This monster was talking to her? She'd heard of the naming convention in Dragons' Realm, where dragon or riders took upon a syllable of each other's names upon imprinting, but surely these sea monsters—

"Sea monster? I'm not a monster. I'm a dragon, a sea dragon."

"You're not going to eat me? But I've seen Ashewar feed other traitorous assassins to your kind."

"True, we have killed some orange-robed women in the past, but only because their sathir had turned rotten, hatred eating like a dark canker through them. But your sathir is pure. You proved it by trying to save our cousin."

Wonder wove through Ithsar. Like the oasis lake's soothing kiss on the hottest day. Reminding her of how she'd felt as a littling, sitting on her father's lap listening to his stories, wrapped in his warmth. Awe filled her and, for the first time, Ithsar *really looked* at this wondrous creature, at her head and body coated in green scales that gleamed silver in shafts of sunlight cutting through the sapphire ocean. Saritha's *sathir* danced around Ithsar and Thika. Now she recognized the source of the beautiful silver bubble: it was Saritha's shimmering *sathir*. *"You didn't want to eat me. You were* saving me *from those sharks."*

And from a life with cutthroat assassins.

"Just as you saved little Thika, my distant cousin from the desert sands."

The skin along Thika's sides twitched and a groove appeared. Tiny buds sprouted from his body and unfurled into wings. Thika lunged, swimming around in glee, fluttering his new wings like fins. Her lizard looked like a tiny orange sea dragon.

"Land lizards are the ancient ancestors of our kind," Saritha said. *"Some of them have the gift of transformation."*

Despite being underwater, that strange warmth burst from inside Ithsar's chest and radiated through her body, from the roots of her hair to her toenails. She wanted to sing, dance, shout at the top of her voice. And as Saritha's gossamer *sathir* wrapped around her, and Thika swam in happy circles, Ithsar felt as if she could propel herself into the skies, into a life full of wild possibilities.

Her life with the Robandi assassins had been a cage she'd been trapped in for too long. But she wouldn't die like that Naobian starling. She was never going back. She'd swim to the ends of the sea with Saritha. *"You've given me hope and freed me from my shackles. I can now be anyone I want."*

"Ithsar, you need only be yourself. You will always be enough for me." Saritha lowered her muzzle into the silver bubble and huffed warm breath against Ithsar's cheek. *"Always."*

Ithsar's throat caught. A tear slid down her cheek. *"I'm enough?"* Something was unfolding inside her, something small and sweet that had been lying dormant since Ashewar had killed her father and that camel had dragged his dead body into the desert. *"Thank you."*

Someone understood her—Saritha understood. *Sathir* swirled around her in a silvery dance, wrapping her in a warm cocoon and cradling her.

"Yes, I do understand."

She reached out a tentative hand and scratched the sea dragon's nose. This was no monster, just a beautiful giant creature who was now her friend.

"Yes, Ithsar, you are now my rider."

Rider? "So, I should ride you, like I'd ride a camel?"

Saritha snorted, shooting a stream of water from her nostrils. *"Not quite like a camel. Climb on my back."*

§

Saritha swam through waving fronds of green weed, Ithsar on her back with Thika perched upon her shoulder. The fronds brushed against Ithsar's legs, tickling, and she laughed as a tiny yellow-and-turquoise-striped fish darted away into the towering green forest around them. They broke out of the weed and swam along a coral reef. Growths of purple-and-orange-striped mushrooms clung to rocks. Enormous clusters of flat yellow plates formed towers that rose above them. Pink coral formations waved tiny tentacles with white stars on the ends, and red puffy balls drifted along the pale sand of the ocean floor, like tumbleweeds. Orange and tan starfish darted among small trees of pink, yellow, and vibrant turquoise, and turtles swam past Saritha, their mottled shells blending with their surroundings. And the fish—Ithsar had never seen such a variety—banded, spotted, spiky, and sleek, with more colors than the rainbow.

"At home, everything is so... orange."

Saritha's foot disturbed a red tree with undulating fronds, and yellow-and-silver-striped fish burst from its foliage, shooting away. A diamond-shaped ray floated past, its mantle flowing in the current and tail streaming out behind it.

"Avoid those barbed tails—they're poisonous," Saritha rumbled.

As Saritha approached, a school of purple-banded yellow fish with enormous bellies and bulging eyes fled into a clump of yellow and blue coral.

Ithsar gaped. And gaped. This was a whole world she'd never suspected existed. She glanced up to the pale-gray underbelly of an enormous sea creature, nearly as large as Saritha. Mournful keening filled her ears.

"What's that?"

The dragon chuckled in her mind, a comforting rumble. "A whale. They're peaceful, our friends. Although sometimes their songs do get tedious."

The whale's song floated through Ithsar, filling cavities inside her that she hadn't known were empty. Sadness, happiness, pain, and joy flitted inside her.

Tears trailed down her cheeks as she remembered her father's laugh, his warm dark eyes, losing him, loving Thika, Roshni's bright blue eyes wide with fear as she'd tumbled from the cliff.

"*Who pushed your friend into the ocean?*" Saritha asked.

"*My mother, Ashewar, who hated me for the crime of being myself.*" Ithsar saw Ashewar's screaming face as sharks snapped up her body. Her throat tightened and she thrust her hands to her aching chest, trying to staunch the pain. A splintering sob broke from her. "*She destroyed everything I loved, and wanted to destroy me.*"

"*I'm sad that your mother is dead, but she deserved to die,*" Saritha said. "*However, crying will only use your air supply faster. Believe me, we don't want you to run out of air down here.*"

Her dragon's sweet voice soothed Ithsar. Ashewar was gone. She and Thika had a new life.

Dolphins swam overhead, chittering. Thika darted off, following them. Saritha trumpeted, and the lizard whirled, his tiny wings fluttering, and zipped back to Ithsar's shoulder.

They dived under a coral archway festooned with conical pink spires. Anemones the size of her torso wafted tentacles in the water. One snaked out its tendrils and plucked up a silver fish, forcing it inside its cavernous mouth. The tentacles shrunk, pulling in on themselves and closing over the fish until the anemone was a small dark ball, no larger than Ithsar's head.

"*I wouldn't want to get caught by one of those.*"

"*Indeed.*"

On the other side of the archway was a forest of waving yellow weeds that towered above them. Saritha dived and the plants parted to let them through.

Another sea dragon appeared out of the undulating plants. Then another, and another. Through the yellow fronds, Ithsar spied hundreds of sea dragons in a variety of greens and blues as vast as the ocean's moods, all radiating silver *sathir*.

As Saritha burst out of the forest, the scaly long-bodied dragons formed a ring around them. Sharp talons sprang from their feet, and their tails lashed the water. Their snarls rippled through the water, making Ithsar's head pound.

QUEEN AQUARIA

The sea dragons' snarls rippled through the water. Then turned into roars that crashed through Ithsar's head. The water quaked. Fish darted into hidey-holes. Thika's claws tightened on her shoulder.

Fear rattled Ithsar's bones, making her tremble. *"Why are they so angry?"*

"They say that women with orange robes are murderers, destroying the life energy of living beings. They see your robes and fear you have come to harm us. I've told them you're my new rider, but they're distrustful because it's been so long since any of us had riders."

Thundering roars crashed into Ithsar, ricocheting through the water around her and lashing her like a storm.

"They're insisting I take you to my queen."

"Your queen?"

"Yes, my queen. You didn't think we were a lawless bunch, did you?" Saritha chuckled, her rumbling belly tickling Ithsar's legs, but the bared fangs and slitted eyes of the dragons around them weren't so convincing.

"Am I in danger?"

"Is anyone ever out of danger? You leaped into the jaws of the ocean and found me. Now, prepare to meet Queen Aquaria."

Saritha's reassurance did little to calm Ithsar's racing heart. They dived between two coral spires, the other sea dragons trailing them. They speared down until the water was darker, the fish drab, and the coral brown, then leveled out and swam toward a mountainous rock bigger than the assassins' oasis. Saritha entered a gaping tunnel in the rock, and the sea dragons followed them into pitch black. Thika's tail twined tightly around Ithsar's neck and he nestled into her face as they angled down into the black. Cool currents streamed past Ithsar's legs. Pressure built in her ears, and her lizard squirmed—no doubt, feeling it too.

Glimmers of distant light appeared, growing larger.

Strange fish with vicious jagged teeth and light-bearing stalks protruding from their heads surrounded the sea dragons, illuminating the darkness, and led them through the base of the rock until the tunnel angled upward toward the light.

Saritha kicked strongly and shot up. *"I'll open my mind so you can hear."*

Ithsar was about to ask exactly what she'd hear when they burst out of the tunnel onto a broad shelf of pale sand.

Shafts of sunlight spilled through the water like the pillars in the assassins' throne room, striking a majestic dragon seated on a coral-festooned rock, lighting her green scales with a silver shimmer. The dragon angled her head. *"Be seated, my daughter. Be seated, my loyal subjects."*

"Daughter? Does that make you a princess?"

The barest murmur of assent rippled through Ithsar's mind followed by a whisper, *"Keep your thoughts still. Everyone can hear you."*

A titter from one of the smallest dragons ran through Ithsar's head, but the queen silenced the dragon with a glare. The water undulated as the sea dragons arrayed themselves on the sand in front of their queen.

The queen's voice thundered through Saritha and Ithsar's minds. *"My daughter, what have you done? Why have you brought this creature with you?"*

Ithsar's hand shot up to cover Thika with her hand. Until the queen's gaze leveled at her. No, the queen did not mean Thika. She meant Ithsar.

"Why did you bring this vile beast to our innermost sanctuary?" Venom laced the queen's thoughts. *"These orange-robed murderers are the vermin of the desert sands. For years they've left a trail of carnage in their wake."*

"Their ruler is dead," Saritha replied. *"And this is her daughter."*

The queen's eyes glinted with feral menace. *"Ah, so you brought her as a sacrifice to appease the gods. Well done."*

"No, we've imprinted. She's my rider." Saritha straightened.

Queen Aquaria's head snaked down from her perch. Eyes narrowed, she glared at them. Ithsar's legs trembled, but she held her head high, meeting the queen's blazing gaze. Queen Aquaria's derisive snort wound through Ithsar's mind. *"Rider?"* The queen leaped from her coral throne, the scratch of her talons amplified by the water, skittering through Ithsar's bones. She landed, her mighty talons raking the sand and stirring up a cloud of dust that obscured Ithsar's vision.

Ithsar's traitorous pulse raced at her throat, and despite the shimmering bubble around her, her chest grew tight.

The eddying sand settled and the waters cleared to reveal the queen's giant maw outside Ithsar's bubble of *sathir*. A long tongue darted from her jaws. *"Let me taste you."*

Saritha had tricked her to gain her trust and bring her as a sacrifice to the queen. Swallowing hard, Ithsar knew her time was up. *"Take care of Thika,"* she begged Saritha. Her only regret was not helping Ezaara in battle against those dark dragons, but she would not quake. She would not fear. She had already faced death twice today. And she had lived to see wonders that even her father and Ashewar had not seen. It was enough.

She was enough.

"Of course you're enough," Saritha harrumphed. *"I told you so already. Now stretch your hand out of the bubble so my queen can taste you."*

Ithsar gulped. Her fingers tingled as they brushed through the silver bubble and plunged into cool water, but the bubble stayed intact. She sucked in a deep breath, relieved she wouldn't drown.

The queen licked her palm and gazed at her quizzically. *"I do not sense death upon your fingers, yet you wear orange robes. Please explain."* Queen Aquaria nuzzled her hand.

Oh gods, the queen had wanted to scent her, not eat her. She felt like such a fool. As the queen touched her hand, her life flashed before her: the years of taunting and jeering; Izoldia burning and cutting her; her mother's hatred; her father's brutal death; Ashewar throwing Roshni to the sharks; and finally, Ithsar fighting Ashewar and them both tumbling into the sea.

Her memories swept on, revealing the vision she'd seen.

Above pristine snow-tipped mountains and carpets of lush forest, dark-winged beasts blasted dragons from the sky, beams from their eyes slicing into the dragons' flesh. The foul creatures' screams ricocheted through Ithsar's mind. Amid plumes of flame, Ezaara dived on a dragon with scales that flickered with all the colors from a prism-seer, firing arrows. But there were too many beasts. Ezaara and her troops were nearly overwhelmed. Then Ithsar arrived, riding a beautiful green dragon whose scales flashed silver—Saritha.

Ithsar inhaled a sharp breath. The prophecy was already coming to pass.

They swooped into battle, trails of sea dragons bearing Robandi riders behind them, followed by Naobian green guards. Their arrows found their marks. The sea dragons killed foul beasts, shredding their wings and breathing fire. Ezaara and her warriors rallied, but the battle was not over.

"So you see visions, too?" The queen inclined her head, not breaking contact with Ithsar's hand. A vision swept through Ithsar, and she knew it was the queen's. Sea dragons, wings dripping with water, rose from the sea with orange-robed women on their backs.

"I fought this vision for years, knowing these women were killers, but after meeting you, I relent." Queen Aquaria's eyes were steady, softer. *"You are heralding in a new age where sea dragons will take to the skies with riders again, to protect the freedom of my far distant cousin, Zaarusha, Queen of Dragons' Realm. If we fail, the entire realm will become a barren wasteland."*

Another vision roiled through Ithsar's mind—the same land she'd seen in her vision.

Instead of gleaming snow gracing the mountain peaks, they were brown and barren. At their feet, desolate sludge and swamp stretched as far as Ithsar could see. The oceans were clogged with dead fish and carcasses of dragons, and the waterways were green and stagnant, choked with waving tendrils of flesh-eating plants.

Ithsar pulled her hand back into the *sathir* bubble with a pop, clutching her stomach.

"The visions are upon me now, young Ithsar. I realize that for us to help prevent this awful fate, you must find us new riders among those orange-robed killers, fierce women with pure hearts."

Impossible. How could she ever convince those bloodthirsty women to fight for good? She'd be slaughtered, cut down by Izoldia, Bala, and Thut within a moment of setting foot in the desert. *"I'm only one person. One small, insignificant person."*

Saritha leveled her gaze at Ithsar, then looked at the queen. *"My Queen, I'll accompany her and ensure the job is done."*

The queen nodded sagely. *"To prove their goodwill, these new riders must make a leap of trust: every new rider must throw herself from the cliff into the sea, just as you did."*

Ithsar opened her mouth to protest.

The queen gave a flick of her tail, scattering a school of brown fish. *"Do not fail me or you'll be failing the whole of Dragons' Realm."*

Ithsar snapped her jaw shut and nodded.

"Good," said the queen, stirring. *"My beloved dragons, our fate and the fate of our lands are in the hands of a chosen few. Ithsar is one. Zaarusha's rider, the golden-haired girl, is another. There is yet another."*

She gestured Ithsar to lay her hand upon her snout.

Ithsar saw an older man with dark hair, a goatee and extraordinarily-bushy eyebrows standing in a forest. His gaze was piercing, his stature, tall, and he wore a forest-green cloak. Green flame danced at his fingertips. A mage, then. *"Who is he?"*

"The dragon mage, Master Giddi. Years ago, he saved my life. Aid him in any way you can and send him my greetings. His role in this war is essential, but without your support he will fail, and Dragons' Realm will be lost. I cannot sense more than that. Let this suffice for now." Queen Aquaria turned and swam back onto her coral throne. *"Bring forth the blade."*

A small green dragon swam from the assembled crowd toward the queen, something shiny flashing in his talons—Roshni's ceremonial saber.

Ithsar's fingers tingled as they passed through the bubble and grasped the hilt. She would use this saber to honor Roshni.

Queen Aquaria's golden eyes glowed. *"Swear you will never use this for cruelty or revenge, only to protect the downtrodden and the weak."*

"I swear." Ithsar pounded her heart with her hand, her head reeling.

"Good. Revenge will never bring you happiness," the queen said.

Ithsar didn't want to go back. She wanted to flee the assassins, never visit the oasis again, but now she had no choice.

A weight settled upon her, like a thick blanket warding off the bitter cold of the desert night—but heavier, much heavier. The weight sank down through her flesh and settled in her bones. She had to face Izoldia and the other assassins. If Dragons' Realm were to survive, she had no choice.

BLOODY TRAIL

Wings dripping and seaweed dangling from her foreleg, Saritha burst from the Naobian Sea with Ithsar upon her back. The bubble around Ithsar popped and fresh air rushed into her lungs. She hadn't even noticed that the air she'd been breathing had grown stuffy and thin, until she was above the surface. The orange sandstone cliffs rose above them—so impossible to scale when she'd been drowning and holding Thika. The blood in the sea had dissipated. The only thing left of Ashewar and Roshni was a shred of orange fabric floating on the sea. As Ithsar watched, a wave crested and swallowed the cloth, dragging it under. Ithsar shut her eyes, drawing in a deep breath. When she opened them, the orange sandstone was rushing past them as Saritha ascended.

Thika curled his tail around her neck and spread his little wings, drying them in the breeze.

"Who would have known you could sprout wings?" She scratched his nose. His wings fluttered and slid back into the tiny slits in his scales. "Now you look like a normal lizard again, but I always knew you were special." He nuzzled her cheek.

Saritha crested the cliff and landed, puffs of tangerine sand stirring at her feet. She held her snout up, nostrils flaring, scenting the breeze. *I smell fresh blood.*

A dark satin marred the sand amid scuffed footprints, and splatters of blood led from the stain to the cliff's edge. More blood than just the sacrificial goat had been spilled here today. *Someone's been killed. It looks like they were thrown into the sea.*

There was no doubt in Ithsar's mind that Izoldia had murdered someone. But who? "Stay here." Ithsar popped Thika on Saritha's back, slipped off the sea dragon and dropped to the scorching sand. She hopped from foot to foot. If only she had *yokka* to protect her feet.

Come here, my littling. Saritha thrummed.

I'm hardly a littling. If I'm to rally my people for more riders, perhaps you should find another term of endearment.

"*But you're such a small slip of a thing to fill such large* yokka," her dragon replied.

"*You know the name of our footwear?*"

Saritha dipped her head in a nod. "*Littling will do until your feet have grown.*"

"*I never knew sea monsters could be so cheeky.*"

Saritha disentangled the seaweed from her foreleg, and held it in her jaws. "*Wrap this around those tiny feet, my littling. And, by the way, I told you: I'm not a monster. Sea dragon is the correct term.*"

"*If you're going to be so cheeky about my size, perhaps monster will do,*" Ithsar said as she sat and wrapped the weed around her scorched feet.

A low throaty rumble echoed from Saritha's throat and skittered through the dragon's belly.

"*You're laughing!*" Ithsar tilted her head. "*I never knew dragons could laugh.*"

"*Yes, my littling, monsters laugh too.*"

Littling? Hah. Ithsar slugged Saritha's foreleg and sprang to her feet. Although her dragon had tried to distract her from the bloodstain, it was time to face what had happened while she'd been gone. The seaweed wouldn't last long—the hot desert sand would soon dry out its moisture and it'd become brittle. She stalked along the bloody trail and followed it to the stain.

So much blood. It had gushed freely and stained the sand dark crimson. Someone had definitely died here—especially with that awful trail to the cliff's edge. Ithsar knelt and examined the bloody sand. The blood was dry, but that didn't mean much—the hot desert sand would dry out warm blood in a heartbeat. Silver glinted among the red-caked sand. Ithsar picked up strands of silver hair coated in blood.

Her other hand flew to her mouth and her belly tightened. "No. Not Drida." Had Drida paid with her life for helping her? Ithsar swayed and sank to her haunches, dizzy. No…

Saritha pounced, landing beside her. "*You need nourishment. We must find these murderous vipers, but you'll collapse without food in your belly.*"

"*You're right. I've barely eaten in two days.*" Gods, oh gods, was Izoldia going to destroy anyone who got close to her, anyone who tried to help her? If she tried to recruit more riders, would Saritha be in danger too?

The dragon flew off and returned with a flapping silver fish in her maw. She tossed the fish into the air, speared it on a talon, then breathed fire over it. The aroma of roasting fish made Ithsar's mouth water. "*I'll just cool it, so it won't* burn your fingers or mouth." Saritha leaped into the air and flew a circle around Ithsar before landing and proffering the fish.

Ithsar bit into the succulent flesh, juice running down her chin. "*Oh, this is good.*"

"*One of my favorites. I scoffed a couple too.*" Saritha extended a foreleg.

Ithsar clambered up, reaching up to grasp her spinal ridge. "*It's much easier to climb onto your back in the water.*"

"*Everything is easier in water,*" Saritha replied, cocking her head and gazing at the desert. "*Especially hunting and swimming. I don't see any tasty fish flapping their fins around here. Or any water to swim in.*"

"*Don't worry, at the oasis we have a lovely big lake.*"

"*Any fish?*"

"*Small ones.*" Such a huge beast wouldn't survive on oranges, dates, and couscous. "*But we have goats. They're quite tasty and have none of those nasty scales that get caught in your teeth.*"

"*Nasty scales?*" Saritha bristled, her own scales standing on end. "*I think scales are beautiful.*"

"*Yes, of course, so do I,*" Ithsar replied hurriedly as Thika nestled inside her tattered robes against her belly. "*Especially the way the sun makes your emerald scales glisten with silver.*" Then she realized what her dragon was doing. "*You distracted me again.*"

"*I don't like seeing you sad about your friend dying.*" Saritha sprang into the air. "*I spotted camel tracks when I was cooling your fish. Let's hunt down those murderers.*"

The breeze of Saritha's wingbeats fanned Ithsar's face, a change from the stifling heat of the desert air. Now *all* she had to do was hunt down her archenemy, and convince a band of highly-trained bloodthirsty assassins to join her in defending Dragons' Realm. Dread pooled in Ithsar's stomach as they swept over the dunes, following the camel tracks across the shimmering tangerine sands.

COLDBLOODED ATTACK

To Izoldia's left, camel tracks led up over a dune. A thin trail of smoke rose up into the blazing sky. Good. Someone was making camp. With her hand upheld, she motioned her band of assassins to stop. She shaded her hand over her eyes against the mid-morning sun as the women silently dismounted and hobbled their camels. Izoldia motioned Thut to watch the others and make sure no one slipped off. Although she had them under control for now, it would only take a few to rebel for that control to slip. Tonight, she would make sure any dissent was extinguished.

Izoldia and Bala sneaked up the dune, slithering the last camel length on their bellies, and peeked over the top. Bala's eyes glinted and her teeth flashed in a fierce grin. Izoldia licked her lips as she gazed down at their prey. In a hollow between the dunes, six men were seated around a bed of smoldering coals, heating a steaming pot. A large, dark-bearded man with a yellow headdress took the pot and tipped a thick brew of tea into the waiting mugs of the others. Behind them was a caravan of twenty camels, still hobbled, their backs heavily laden with goods. The rolled tents tied to their beasts' backs suggested that these men had stopped for the night and were ready to head out again after a lazy morning.

What luck. Six men and such a fine caravan laden with goods. A great way to start her reign.

Izoldia and Bala slithered backward on their stomachs until they were hidden from view, then Izoldia motioned to the assassins with a series of quick hand signals.

A third of the assassins headed around the dune and sneaked up the left flank of the hill, a third took the right, and the rest made their way up to join Izoldia and Bala. When they were all a camel length from the top, Izoldia gave a quick flick of her hand, which each woman repeated, sending the message rippling along the ranks. As one, they slid their sabers from their scabbards and rose. They crested the dune and charged downhill, the only sound the rustle of the robes and their feet on the shifting sands.

The man with the yellow headdress and dark bushy beard cried out, dropping his mug, the dark contents splattering his white robes. His companions leaped to their feet. Four of the men drew sabers and faced them, while two raced to their camels, desperately yanking at the hobbles. The assassins swarmed past the hot coals and were upon the men in moments.

Izoldia gave a feral snarl and slashed her saber across the big man's face, laughing as blood sprayed over the sands, coating her hands.

§

The man's yellow headdress was drenched in red. Misha was aghast at the blood, her stomach roiling. Although she'd been raised to fight with these assassins, she'd usually found excuses to stay back at the oasis by tending someone in the healing cavern, volunteering for kitchen duty, making meals, or feigning illness. It had escaped Ashewar's attention, but she knew Izoldia had noticed.

Izoldia's saber plunged into the man's gut and he fell to his knees. Their new chief assassin's grin made Misha even more nauseous.

At her back, Nila whirled to fend off a man, her blade scraping against his saber. Misha slashed her saber halfheartedly at another, disarming him in a heartbeat.

"No, p-please, I have ch-children," he gibbered.

No, not more children left orphaned at these women's hands. Misha pretended to stumble—and let him run. Thut lunged past her, saber slashing another man's calf, and raced after him. The short man's paces were no match for Thut's long legs. She caught up to him easily, and plunged a dagger into his back.

His body hit the sand, a red stain spreading across his white robe. Misha's knees wobbled.

Nila squeezed her hand, then dropped it, glancing around. "Stay standing," she whispered, lips barely moving. "I think Thut's onto you."

Thut kicked the dead man over. His unseeing eyes stared up at the lapis sky. Thut growled, "You two, come here."

For the hundredth time, Misha wished she were a bird and could fly away from the oasis, these awful assassins, and this terrible life. She mustered up as much bravado as she could and swaggered across the sand, Nila at her side. As they neared the man, she gave a disdainful sneer at his prone figure and nudged his body with her boot. At least his wound was against the sand now, the blood no longer glaring at her.

"You two were too slow," Thut growled, eyes glinting as she twirled her dagger, scattering droplets of the man's blood. "You have a weak stomach, don't you, you coward?" She glared at Misha. "Don't think I haven't noticed you skiving off and missing the action. Let's see how you enjoy this." She plunged her dagger downward and ripped open the man's belly. His pale, steaming entrails spilled over the hot sand.

Misha fell to her knees, retching. Nila reached down to comfort her. But another dagger flashed in Thut's hand, aimed at Nila. "Leave the weakling. We don't need her. Izoldia asked me to kill her in her sleep tonight anyway. This'll save me the job."

Saber out, Nila lunged at Thut. Thut parried, the sun glinting on her flashing blade.

The earth shook. A spray of sand flew over them, pelting them like gnats. Flame surged overhead.

A giant beast had landed, jolting the sand and making it shift between Misha's knees. The green-scaled monster bared fangs the length of her forearm, flame dripping from its jaws. It snarled, sending shivers down Misha's spine.

Ashewar, Roshni, and Ithsar had not been enough to satisfy the hunger of this mighty sea monster. It had come for them. With trembling hands, Misha stood and drew her saber. Nila and Thut flanked her, their fight forgotten as they faced the wild beast with billows of sand clouding around its taloned feet.

§

Ithsar frowned. Something was wrong, dreadfully wrong. There was an agonizing shudder of *sathir* in the desert below them. Screams rent her ears. Someone had just died a violent death. The mighty sea dragon beat her wings upon the hot desert wind, speeding over the dunes. Ithsar strained her eyes. It was difficult to see the Robandi Silent Assassins' orange robes against the sand below; however, their hobbled camels, a large caravan, and the bloody bodies of men who'd been slaughtered were all too clear. The clash of sabers rose on the air.

A short distance from the main fight and the men's smoldering campfire, Thut was attacking Nila and Misha.

Ithsar gasped. *"Saritha, over there. Save those women."*

Saritha swooped between the dunes and landed, showering sand over the assassins. She roared, shooting a jet of flame over Thut's head. Thut dropped her dagger, gaping. Misha leaped up and snatched her saber, tossing it to Nila.

Nila shoved it under Thut's ribs. "Hands up. Misha, grab some rope and bind her."

Misha dashed to the caravan of poor camels, who were bleating at the chaos, and sliced a length from a lead rope, then raced back to bind Thut's hands.

Ithsar whirled. *"Look, Saritha."*

Izoldia was chasing a man, tufts of sand spraying up behind her. He had no chance. She was faster, fitter. She drew a dagger and raised her arm to throw. Saritha swooped and knocked her to the sand with her foreleg. Cursing, Izoldia rolled to her feet and threw her dagger at Saritha's belly. Saritha twisted aside, and blasted fire at the dagger until the wooden hilt burned and the blackened blade dropped to the sand. The sea dragon roared, swooped, and snatched Izoldia in her jaws.

Croaky screams issued from assassins who hadn't spoken in months. They stared skyward, faces rippling with shock and horror. One of the men bellowed in fear, raising his arms in supplication, then fell to his knees.

"I am rather awe-inspiring, you know," Saritha quipped, landing and sending a spray of sand over the smoking fire pit. Izoldia's kicking legs and thrashing arms hung out of either side of her jaw. The burly assassin was still cursing. Saritha gave her a rough shake.

Four men were dead and another's calf was bleeding and his shoulder stabbed. Only one man was unharmed. Ithsar shook her head. How was she supposed to convince these bloodthirsty women that they should trust sea monsters and defend the dragon riders in the North? It would be impossible.

"Shall I finish this miserable wretch now?" Saritha mind-melded, shaking Izoldia again.

Although Ithsar wanted nothing more than to see Izoldia dead, Queen Aquaria's words rang in her mind: *revenge will never bring you happiness.* She sighed. *"Saritha, we shouldn't act in anger or for revenge."*

"Put me down, you great, galumphing, ugly beast," Izoldia yelled, waving her arms at the assassins. "Attack! Kill this beast and free me from its jaws."

Eyes on Saritha, none of the women moved.

"She's asking me to put her down." Saritha's eye ridge twitched. She opened her jaws and dumped Izoldia unceremoniously on the sand.

Izoldia sprang to her feet and smiled, bowing graciously—the last thing Ithsar expected. "Oh mighty fine beast of the sea, there seems to have been a grave misunderstanding. Please take two of these fine camels as an offering to appease you." Izoldia gestured at the caravan.

Those camels weren't even hers to give. Ithsar should've known Izoldia would try flattery, given her fawning, pernicious attitude toward Ashewar.

Saritha tilted her head and asked Ithsar, *"Why would I want those camels? I've already had my fill of fish, and those beasts are stringy and not nearly as tender."*

Ithsar spoke up. "Izoldia, those camels are not yours."

Izoldia's head shot up so fast, Ithsar thought she'd break her neck. The orange-robed assassins shifted, eyes flying wide.

Saritha snorted. *"I believe your friends were so impressed by me that they didn't even see you upon my back."*

"You!" For a heartbeat, Izoldia's lips contorted, then they smoothed into a smile. "Oh, Ithsar, I'm so glad you survived your terrible fall into the sea," she said sweetly. "How awful of your mother to push you."

Now it was Ithsar's turn to snort. She ignored Izoldia, addressing the assembled women. "I've tamed this ferocious monster from the deep. She's my friend and a foe to my enemies. No doubt Izoldia has tried to lay claim to my lineage." Misha and Nila gave surreptitious nods. "However, I am the true heir of Ashewar, our deceased chief prophetess."

Bala, at the front of the assembled assassins, shifted on her feet, looking everywhere except at Ithsar. Thut, hands still bound, glowered.

"You're a liar, a traitor," Izoldia screeched, hand drifting to her empty scabbard. "You fought your mother. She hated you."

Thika pounced from Saritha's back, his wings unfurling, and flew at Izoldia, scratching her arms with his claws. Izoldia's eyes nearly bugged out of her head. Then she whirled and batted Thika away. Saritha snarled.

All the assassins except Bala and Thut leaped into action, drawing their blades and surrounding Izoldia.

The lizard flew back to Ithsar, panting and heart thrumming. Ithsar stroked Thika, crooning.

Misha and Nila tied Izoldia's hands together. The assassins led her and Thut over the dunes and tied them onto the back of their camels. The camels harrumphed and shifted their hooves in the sand.

The remaining man turned to them, trembling. "Anything you want, anything, I'll give it to you." He gestured at the heavily-laden caravan and brightly-colored burdens stacked high on the camels' backs.

"The sea dragon thanks you for your kindness," Ithsar said. "We apologize for the tragedy that has befallen your companions. You may depart in peace. Please, feel free to take your dead with you."

The man hefted his injured companion onto a camel and unhobbled the beasts. His hands shook as he waved farewell. "No, no. Thank you, thank you for sparing my life." He mounted the lead camel and the caravan plodded over the dunes, leaving his dead companions behind.

Ithsar sighed. "*I didn't want their bodies to be picked apart by vultures.*"

"*That, I can fix,*" Saritha replied. She piled up the bodies, and then incinerated them, dark smoke scorching the sky.

A NEW STAND

Saritha flew above the desert, dancing in the hot breeze. Ithsar's hair ripped loose from her headscarf as they rode the thermals, lazily spiraling up on the warm air, then swooping down, making her belly somersault. Growing up in the subterranean caverns and narrow tunnels of the assassin's lair, she'd never imagined such freedom. Even among the dunes, there'd always been hills closing her in. Flying in this vast azure sky with her hair whipping in the wind and the world spread far below made her heart soar.

The assassins rode their camels, trailing between the dunes toward the oasis, as tiny as dates. In the distance, the oasis beckoned, the turquoise waters shining among the palm groves.

Saritha mind-melded, *"You did well back at that skirmish. We quickly stopped those bloodthirsty women."*

"They only listened to me because you were there." Ithsar sighed. *"Once I'm back in the lair beneath the oasis and you're above ground, how will I retain control? Bala, Thut, or Izoldia could kill me at any time with a flick of their wrists and a well-aimed dagger."*

"You have a noble spirit. Count upon your friends to rally around you and protect you."

Friends? Up until now, she hadn't had any. What part of persecuted and despised had Saritha not understood?

They spiraled down to the edge of the palms and waited for the assassins to arrive.

Soon the camels traipsed over the dune and descended into the oasis. Ithsar signaled for the women to tether the camels in the shade of the date trees near the water's edge. The women moved with efficient well-trained movements, their muscles packed with power.

"I'm not fit to lead them. Look how they move, how strong they are."

"You move similarly," Saritha said. *"You have the same strength and power in your frame."*

"I do?"

Saritha's only reply was a chuckle.

Ithsar remained on her dragon's back between her spinal ridges, with Thika on her shoulder. She stroked the lizard absentmindedly as he nestled into her neck.

Once the camels were settled, the assassins quickly fell into a disciplined formation in front of Ithsar.

Ithsar's voice rang out, "As Ashewar's heir, I claim my place leading the Robandi Silent Assassins. We will break from tradition, so be prepared for change, and change with us—or be left like a tumbleweed to be blown in the hot desert sands without purpose or meaning to your existence."

Women shifted uneasily.

"The first change I'll introduce is that we need not maintain the vow of silence. Ashewar demanded silence unless it was necessary to speak. I expect to hear your voices, raised in speech, song or laughter. I suggest you now speak to the women on either side of you."

At first there was stunned silence, then murmurs flitted between the women. A nervous laugh broke out. Thut and Izoldia, hands still bound, glowered at her from the back ranks, Bala beside them.

"You must show them they have no chance, or they'll be forever scheming against you," Saritha rumbled in her mind.

"I know." Ithsar gestured to Misha, Nila, and two other guards, who fastened Izoldia and Thut to the trunks of two nearby palms.

Ithsar stood on Saritha's back and raised her arms for quiet. "My mother used her power to maim and harm others. We've been trained, honed as weapons, to spill men's blood. Ashewar pledged to hate men and honor women, yet you're all aware of the suffering I've endured at Izoldia's hands, suffering sanctioned by my mother."

Saritha roared, shaking a neighboring date palm. Dates fell from the tree, scattering around the dragon's feet.

Ithsar flung her arms out toward the desert. "There's a whole world out there beyond this oasis. As your new chief prophetess, I've seen visions of our future. Visions that show us using our power to love, protect, and defend those who cannot defend themselves."

"Love is weak," Izoldia snarled. Her *sathir* muddied, turning murky brown.

Some women nodded, murmuring their assent.

"What is weaker?" Ithsar called. "To hate the people who despise you, or to love them despite what they've done?"

"Just like you loved your mother?" a slim assassin jeered. "Look where that got you."

Ithsar spun. "Just like I loved my mother. Despite her hatred, which destroyed her. Without love, there is no future. We will eventually destroy each other. I have seen this in a vision."

"How can you have visions?" someone called. "Your mother has the prism-seer under lock and key. No one can see a vision without a prism."

A larger assassin, dark hair streaked with silver, interjected, "It's uncommon, but not impossible. Some naturally have the gift of visions and don't need a prism."

Ithsar nodded. "I've had visions since I was a littling on my father's knee." Some of the women scowled—no doubt, at her referring to a male. "I've seen terrible, dark dragons plaguing Dragons' Realm, the land of the prisoner I released—Ezaara, she of the golden hair."

Startled gasps rippled through the gathered assassins.

Ithsar paused, straightening her spine. "Yes, I released Ezaara and Roberto. I did not touch Izoldia. Although she threatened me, the strangers protected me. But my *sathir* shook the ground and a palm tree swayed, dropping a bunch of dates that struck Izoldia upon the head, knocking her out."

"I saw those dates and wondered how they'd fallen," a woman said, awestruck.

"That explains the purple bruise in the sky," murmured another.

"And the fierce wind that whipped our hair as we ran around the lake." The women stared at her.

"How is it that we missed your power?" one asked.

Another fell to her knees. "I'm sorry we mistreated you."

Bala glowered, her hand drifting toward her saber. "You think you can fly back here, spin these lies, and everyone will believe you? You're the useless spawn of a dead chief prophetess."

"And you framed me by putting poison in my sleeping alcove, convincing Ashewar I was a traitor."

Bala's eyes blazed. "You have no proof."

"Oh, but I do. Saritha will show you."

Ithsar motioned Bala forward, and Bala swaggered over to stand near Saritha. Despite her bravado, her eyes nervously flitted to the dragon and her hands shook.

The dragon bowed her head, and Ithsar slid down her side. "I need three witnesses," Ithsar called.

The women hung back, eyes darting to Saritha.

"Come, be fearless. We are the Robandi."

Three women stepped forward.

"Place your hands upon Saritha's brow, and she will show you my memory of that morning," Ithsar instructed.

The women tentatively placed their hands on Saritha's brow to mind-meld with her. Ithsar also put her hand on Saritha's head, remembering yesterday morning. Saritha showed them Bala slipping into Ithsar's sleeping alcove to plant the poison.

One gasped, turning to Bala with venom in her eyes. "All these years we believed your lies about Ithsar," she hissed.

Bala lunged. In a flash, they had their sabers at each other's throats.

Ithsar motioned to the others to break them up. Misha and Nila dragged Bala over to the palm next to Izoldia's and tied her up. Ithsar's bones felt hollow. How could she command this band of bloodthirsty women?

"Show them," Saritha ordered.

"Form a line before Saritha. It's time you were introduced to her properly. You all need to witness why I have been called as your new chief prophetess."

Despite three women having just laid their hands on Saritha's brow, for a few heartbeats, no one moved.

"This challenge may be difficult, but for those who succeed, there are great rewards," Ithsar said. Good, that had made their eyes glint in anticipation, even Izoldia's. "If I, the least amongst you, can survive being thrown into the sea, overcoming my fear, and imprinting with a sea dragon, then surely you can greet that same dragon." She waved her healed fingers.

The woman with silver-streaked hair thrust her shoulders back and paced to Saritha, meeting her gaze. Alarm flashed across the faces of the others, but not wanting to be outdone, every woman joined the queue—except the three tied to the palm trunks.

"Clever," Saritha said to Ithsar. *"These fierce women like a challenge."*

§

Saritha regarded her new rider, Ithsar—so much smaller than these other orange-robed women, but more generous and courageous. As Ithsar challenged these women to find out why she was Chief Prophetess, Saritha was determined to show them exactly why. To show them everything—much more than Ithsar intended. And to measure the mettle of every assassin in this dusty dry oasis.

The women came, laying their hands upon her scaly brow, one by one. She sensed not only the weapon-worn calluses on their palms, but also the timbre of their minds and the nature of their hearts. She of the silver-streaked hair and finely-wrinkled skin bore no malice. But not every woman was the same. Some carried dark secrets in their hearts. And even without them touching her, Saritha could see that those bound to the trees burned with violent red *sathir* and a hatred of Ithsar that made her talons itch.

When she saw dark dragons blasting Saritha's majestic cousins of Dragons' Realm with flame, the assassin with silver-streaked hair whispered, "How dare they!" And as strange yellow beams shot from the shadow dragons' eyes and sliced through the flesh of riders and dragons, her blood roiled in anger and her other hand drifted to her knife. The woman muttered when green flame shot from the hands of mages on dark dragons—mages that all looked the same.

And when Saritha shared the vision of the carcasses of dragons and riders strewn across the land, and the beautiful rivers and green pastures becoming a buzzing fly-infested swamp, and the towering snow-laden mountains becoming dry dusty gray slopes, the woman turned to face her people. "We must fight to protect Dragons' Realm before it's turned into a wasteland."

As she turned to walk away, Saritha touched her shoulder with her snout and mind-melded again. *"Wait, sister, there is more."*

The woman laid her hand upon Saritha's brow once more.

Towering sandstone rose above Saritha, waves crashing against its base. Spray misted her snout as she thrust her head above the surface to watch the tiny orange-clothed figures dancing along the top of the cliff. She and her sisters had heard the sharks in a rowdy feeding frenzy, demolishing the lone body of a woman who had fallen from the cliff.

Saritha didn't usually like to interfere with the affairs of sharks and men, but something *had whispered that she should go forth and see what this fuss was about. Queen Aquaria had also heard that* same something *whispering. So Saritha had decided to heed the call.*

She yawned, the green scales on her jaw glimmering with salty water in the sunlight. At the top of the cliff, two figures fought, clothed in orange. They fell—more fodder for the sharks.

She sank below the ocean, prowling the depths with her sisters, diving among the coral formations, keeping an eye on the surface. A woman with rotten sathir *as black as night plunged into the water, thrashing, hundreds of tiny braids swirling around her face as she fought her way back up to gasp air. Saritha sensed the hatred burning in this woman's heart, sensed the blood of many lives upon her hands, and turned away, diving deeper.*

Then something surged inside her. She spun, her tail lashing a baby squid.

A slip of a girl was sinking into the water, holding a lizard, pinching its nose. How dare that girl torture this lizard—a distant land cousin to Saritha. Her scales bristled. She swam closer. Above, sharks thrashed and the scent of blood wafted on the current as they devoured the evil-hearted woman. Saritha meandered along the seabed, swimming among the coral towers and waving seaweed. Her siblings dived and frolicked, scattering schools of fish.

What was that?

That tiny slip of a girl was swimming toward the cliff.

A shark butted her, dived, and butted her again, playing with its food. Saritha was about to swim away when she noticed what the girl was doing. Under the water, her legs and one arm thrashed, trying to keep her afloat. Had the littling only one arm?

Curious, Saritha swam closer. The shark was speeding at the girl, who held her other arm high out of the water, holding the lizard aloft, trying to keep it from drowning. She hadn't been torturing the lizard at all, but protecting it. And then Saritha felt the girl's sathir as a rush of pure love enveloped the lizard, and the girl cried aloud, "I'm sorry, Thika."

A shimmering radius enveloped the girl and the sweetest music coursed through the sea dragon's breast.

The shark reared out of the water and opened its jaws, leaping for the girl and lizard.

Saritha surged to the surface and slapped the water with her tail, sending a spray over the shark. Opening her maw, she crunched the shark in half and tossed its broken body over her head to its companions, who devoured it.

And then she plucked up this precious loving girl and her lizard in her jaws, careful not to hurt them, and sank beneath the ocean as her blood sang with joy. She had found a rider and her name was Ithsar.

The assassin with the silver-streaked hair met Saritha's gaze, her dark eyes shiny with tears, and nodded. Her voice was barely a whisper of breath as she said, "I pledge to follow Ithsar, the noble new chief prophetess, and will do whatever she requires."

§

Each assassin had obviously mind-melded with the beast. Izoldia knew her turn was coming. As the knowledge settled in her bones, she was determined to use it to her advantage. This beast did not know that she was stronger than Ithsar, more worthy of owning a sea dragon than Ithsar had ever been. And she'd only have one chance to convince it. So, despite her bonds, Izoldia sat tall and proud against the palm's trunk, and waited for the foul beast to approach. It paced toward her, its strong limbs rippling with muscle under its gleaming scales.

Oh, to harness such a beast and use its power—she could conquer many more enemies than with her saber and a camel. Many more than with the entire band of assassins behind her. Why, this beast could fell men, villages, and armies with a swipe of its talons or the flickering flame from its jaws.

Izoldia held her smile. Now was not the time to reveal her plans. First, she would earn this beast's trust and reveal Ithsar for what she truly was—a deformed weakling.

The monster curled its lip back, exposing gleaming white fangs, some nearly as long as her forearm. That runt stalked alongside the dragon, so close to those fangs. If only Izoldia could convince the beast to turn its head and snap Ithsar's head off, then she could ride upon its back in her rightful place.

That runty girl reached up, placing her hand inside the beast's maw to pluck out a piece of seaweed.

By the holy *dracha* gods. Izoldia gulped, fear skittering through her bones. Her hands shook.

The sea dragon snapped its jaw shut, its yellow eyes forming mean slits as it lowered its head toward Izoldia, nostrils flaring.

Ithsar, unbearably close to that glorious, powerful beast, said, "It's your turn, Izoldia. Lay your hand upon Saritha's brow."

Saritha? Izoldia nearly snorted, but refrained. Terror was a better name for this creature. Or Fang. When she killed Ithsar and imprinted with this monster, she would rename it. But for now, she would bide her time and plan. Until that opportunity arose.

A skinny assassin cut her bonds so she could touch the beast. Izoldia forced a charming smile, stretched her hand forth and placed it on the monster's snout.

And as the monster showed her a vision of the future—of a queen and her dragons waiting in the Naobian deeps for new riders, and then waging warfare in the sky—Izoldia formulated a plan. A plan that would see her triumph over that scrawny runt.

·

A New Challenge

Once all the women had been shown visions of their future, including Izoldia, Thut, and Bala, Ithsar stood before them as they waited in formation in the shade, protected from the hot desert sun. "If we are to imprint with sea dragons and help our sisters in the North, we must learn new skills. Who is prepared for this glory?"

Everyone thumped their fists on their hearts, although Ithsar caught Thut giving Bala and Izoldia a sly glance.

"*Very clever, my friend,*" Saritha mind-melded. "*You have convinced everyone to follow us.*"

"*There are still those who will betray me,*" Ithsar replied.

Saritha rumbled, "*And I have my eye on them.*"

"It has been a trying morning. Later, we'll learn new skills for battle on dragonback. But now, we shall eat. Please fetch food from the mess cavern and bring it up here into the shade of the palms."

Murmurs broke out. "But we always eat inside in the heat of the day."

"We usually do, but today is different. We're keeping many of our traditions, but will also usher in a few new ones. And today, we are celebrating." She motioned to six women, who scurried below ground, and then she asked four others to pick dates and oranges.

The assassins settled in the shade of the date palms while some fetched fresh water from the lake. Soon, women carried large cauldrons of warm goat stew and couscous and rounds of flatbread out under the palms.

Ithsar gaped. So much food. What was going on?

Misha sidled over. "There was a feast prepared for, ah… for your demise."

Ithsar's gut hollowed. Speechless, she stared at Misha.

Misha smiled. "I would've choked on every mouthful," she whispered, and sauntered off to help serve the food.

§

After the feast, Izoldia, Bala, and Thut were taken to the dungeons. Thut protested every step of the way, saying all she'd ever done was obey the commands given by Izoldia, and insisting that the sign of a good assassin was obeying those in command. Bala muttered under her breath.

From late that afternoon until the sun slipped in a blazing red ball toward the distant dunes, Saritha and Ithsar trained the women in dragonback archery. One at a time, Saritha took the assassins into the sky. All experienced at archery on camelback, they had to adjust their angles and perspective as they shot at the targets they'd set around the perimeter of the oasis. Most of them missed the first time, and many the second, but slowly, they learned to compensate for the breeze of the dragon's wingbeats and adjust the trajectory of their arrows.

"Leave the other three in the dungeons. I refuse to carry Bala, Izoldia, or Thut, until they have a change of heart," Saritha growled. *"Their malice for you is like a dark canker rotting them from the inside out."*

"I know." Ithsar sighed. *"You're doing a fine job, but it's frustratingly slow with only one dragon."*

"If we put up more targets, I could carry two women and they could fire arrows at targets on either side of me, so we could train them doubly fast."

"But not as fast as if they had their own sea dragons. We must get them battle-ready or they'll be slaughtered."

"It's too early to ask them to imprint. They need more time to trust us. We can't build a new reign in a day."

"You're a wise dragon." Ithsar scratched Saritha's eye ridges, and the sea dragon leaned into her touch.

"You know, I wouldn't mind that swim we spoke of," Saritha said, eying the lake as the assassins trooped down into the entrance tunnel. *"My scales are dry and itchy. I'm not used to being out of the water so long."*

They waited until the last of the assassins had departed, and flew to the far end of the lake where they wouldn't be disturbed. As the setting sun turned the lake fiery orange, Saritha dipped beneath the surface, her bubble of *sathir* encompassing Ithsar.

Ithsar breathed deeply, letting her aching muscles relax as Saritha swam through liquid gold.

§

Ithsar sat on the grotesque throne carved from the bones of her mother's enemies, the tortured faces of dying men glaring up at her from the armrests. She gingerly placed her hands in her lap, unwilling to have her body touch more of the seat than was necessary. She wouldn't have used it, but Izoldia, Bala, and Thut had requested the right to speak and, bound by tradition, Ithsar was required to hear them. This was the only seat that would bring her remotely near Izoldia's eye level.

All the assassins were present, arrayed at the far end of the chamber near the back wall.

The doors opened and her guards Nila and Misha, flanked by four others, marched the prisoners into the throne chamber. Bala and Thut's eyes glittered.

Izoldia did nothing to mute her footsteps upon the cool tiles, her boots ringing throughout the cavern like jeers echoing off the walls. She also made no effort to disguise her labored breathing. The guards led Izoldia and her cronies toward the throne. When they were half a camel length away, Ithsar flicked her finger, motioning them to stop. Standing in front of the throne, Izoldia dwarfed Ithsar—the way she'd dwarfed and demeaned Ithsar's entire life. Her broad shoulders were wider than the throne, her bulky body towering over Ithsar. Her eyes lowered, she stared at her feet.

Bala and Thut stood motionless behind her.

Ithsar motioned to the guards to fall back—but not too far, in case Izoldia decided to attack. Her heart thrumming in a frenzied tattoo against her ribs, Ithsar said coolly, "You may speak."

Izoldia kept her gaze downcast. "I beg your forgiveness, my Chief Prophetess."

Should Ithsar trust her? The years of taunting, insults, and pain coiled into a hard ball inside Ithsar's stomach. As Chief Prophetess, she had been preaching benevolence to her people. The gathered guards' gazes settled upon her. Unless she led by example and showed that benevolence now, none of them would respect her and do what she required in order for them to imprint with the sea dragons and help Ezaara—she of golden hair and vivid green eyes—from the North.

Ithsar drew a long, slow breath of cool subterranean air in through her nostrils. "You require my forgiveness. What will you give in return?"

Guards shuffled, eyes shifting. Bala and Thut glanced at each other, something passing between them. What was Izoldia planning?

Izoldia fell to her knees and bowed before Ithsar, her tied hands outstretched and her forehead kissing the tiles. "I pledge my undying loyalty."

Better than Ithsar had hoped for, but it had to be a trick. Izoldia was up to something. Although she wanted nothing more than to throw her dagger into this scheming sycophant's back, Ithsar forced her fingers to be still. She'd pledged to show everyone love and kindness, including this woman. Perhaps Izoldia had had a change of heart.

Fraught with risk, there was only one way to test her. Very well. "Please stand."

Izoldia rose, her face expressionless. Without her sneer, curled lip, or a glint of malice in her eyes, she looked completely different. Her face was quite pleasant. It was a shame hatred and twisted emotions had driven her to bullying.

"So you will pledge your undying obedience to me, your new revered chief prophetess?"

Without hesitation, Izoldia thumped a hand on her breast and nodded. "Yes, Chief Prophetess. I promise to obey you."

Ithsar's eyes roamed the chamber. At the back of the room, Bala was smirking. Not a good sign. "Very well," Ithsar replied. "Unbind her hands. You may live among us, but at the first sign of discontent, you will be cast out into the desert."

Izoldia closed her eyes and nodded. "I understand. As you wish, my revered Chief Prophetess."

"Bala and Thut?" Ithsar asked.

"We also pledge to obey you," Bala said.

"Yes, we do," Thut added.

It was all too easy. Misha and Nila's expressions were grim as they cut the ropes around the prisoners' hands.

Izoldia remained contrite as guards on either side led her out of the cavern. At the door, they all turned to salute Ithsar, the thud of their hands against their chests echoing in the chamber. Izoldia's eyes flashed. Bala and Thut smirked, falling in behind her.

Something cold slithered through Ithsar's belly. She swallowed. She was not Ashewar; would never be Ashewar. Perhaps her compassion would be her downfall. But she did not want to rule like her mother. She had meant what she'd said, and wanted a new reign—a reign of fairness and justice.

Everyone filed out, leaving Ithsar sitting upon her throne in an empty chamber, her belly hollow, wondering if Izoldia would murder her in her sleep.

RAVEN CALLS

Ithsar sighed and held her hand outside the bubble of *sathir*, trailing her fingers through the deep blue lake, making a silvery trail of water as Saritha swam. The sun was rising, dawn giving the water a pale pink tinge. It was beautiful, but still wasn't as glorious as the Naobian Sea. Here, there were no coral, just endless sand and weeds and a few species of fish: tiny silver ones; some with yellow stripes and brown tails that blended against the sand; and other larger predators with jagged teeth that snapped up the small fish whenever they got too close. Still, it meant Saritha could swim—even if it was only before dawn or after dusk when their training didn't demand the sea dragon fly in shifts with the assassins.

Training had been progressing well over the last moon and a half, so well that the only time Ithsar had on her own with Saritha was during these early morning or late night swims. She cherished this time when they could relax, laugh, and be themselves. Most of the assassins had long since mastered dragon-back archery and were now learning flight maneuvers and the best techniques for throwing knives from dragonback. Their usual training continued—the *Sathiri* battle dance, saber fights, and hand-to-hand combat, keeping Ithsar busy from dawn until dusk.

Despite one attempted poisoning that had never been proven, Izoldia, Bala, and Thut had been model students, acting with humility and learning the ropes as fast as anyone else. Occasionally, Ithsar caught a malicious glint in Izoldia's eyes or thought she'd glimpsed a curl of her lip, but it had always been so fleeting, she'd never been sure if she'd imagined it.

"Have you had enough? I wouldn't mind hunting fish," Saritha asked.

"Set me ashore and I'll rest while you fish." Ithsar yawned. She'd been tossing and turning half the night, wondering whether the assassins would be called upon to fight the dark dragons she'd seen in her visions. And how in the name of the flaming sun she'd convince the women to throw themselves into the Naobian Sea to meet their dragons. Yes, she'd omitted that tiny detail when she'd spoken to them about imprinting. She hadn't dared let Saritha know.

The sea dragon held out her foreleg, creating a bridge between her shoulder and the shore of the oasis. Ithsar slid down her limb, but Saritha yanked it away at the last moment, and she tumbled into knee-deep water.

Laughing, Ithsar scrambled to her feet and splashed Saritha. *"You really are a sea monster."*

"Ah, yes, I was a wild beast until you tamed me."

Ithsar slugged her dragon's dripping, scaly arm, and Saritha pretended to slash with her talons, splashing Ithsar back.

The pink tinge of dawn peeked over the tangerine sands. Drips running down her face, and saturated below the knee, Ithsar said, *"I'm going to dry off while you hunt."*

"Did you know there are mages in the North that can dry you with the touch of their hands?" Saritha winked at her and dived back under the surface of the lake.

Queen Aquaria had mentioned the dragon mage. Did he possess such wondrous powers?

For a moment, the silver sheen on Saritha's scales glistened pink in the dawn's rays, making Ithsar's chest swell, and then the dragon submerged, her tail sending one last splash across the water. Fighting was all well and good, but these were the moments she lived for.

A trail of bubbles rose to the surface, the only sign that a terrible sea monster now inhabited the lake. Ithsar gave a chuckle and laid down on the sand. It was still cool, but wouldn't be for long. Within moments, she dozed off, waiting for the sun to rise and dry her clothes.

§

Ithsar woke to a dark speck on the horizon. Her robes were nearly dry, but she lay there, watching the speck grow as it drew closer to the oasis. It was a bird, a raven, drooping with exhaustion. It fluttered its wings and dived, collapsing in the sand at Ithsar's feet with a wing outstretched and its sides heaving.

Ithsar scooped the raven up and took it to the lake. The bird trembled in her hands, its soft feathers tickling her palms. She knelt and held it near the water. The raven bent its head, eagerly scooping up water with its beak. She stroked the soft feathers between its wings at the base of its neck. "Easy now," she crooned. "Your belly will burst if you're not careful."

The raven squirmed, and something scraped against her arm. She examined the bird and found a small tube attached to its right leg—a messenger bird, then. Here in the desert? Not unheard of, but extremely unusual. This bird must've come from Dragons' Realm beyond the Naobian Sea. She cradled the tired raven in her hands, strolled back to sit under the shade of a date palm, and popped the bird in her lap. Using her dagger, she gently cut the twine that bound the tube. She uncorked the end and tapped the tube on her palm. A small scroll of parchment fell out.

Ithsar unrolled it.

My dearest friend Ithsar,

I trust that this message finds you well. I write in the hope that you are able to come to our aid.

A scourge has risen upon the lands of Dragons' Realm. Commander Zens has created foul shadow dragons—dark beasts who are destroying towns and villages, enslaving our people, and killing our dragons, riders, and mages. As well as dragon flame, beams of golden light from their eyes slice the flesh of dragon and rider. Using his dark methods, Zens has also grown strange mages who ride these beasts, searing our dragons, riders, and mages with wizard flame.

I am calling upon all my friends in the far reaches of the realm and beyond to come to our aid. Without help, I fear the destruction of the entire realm. Our people are dying by the thousands. These beasts are clogging the skies. If there is any way you can entreat your mother and the Robandi assassins to come to our aid, I would deeply appreciate it. And if this brief letter falls into the hands of someone other than Ithsar, I plead that you will come to the aid of Dragons' Realm and help save our people from extinction.

Ezaara, Queen's Rider

Of Zaarusha, the honored Dragon Queen of Dragons' Realm.

Ithsar's hands shook as she rolled the scrap of paper and tucked it into the folds of her robe, sliding it against her skin. *"Oh, Saritha, Ezaara has requested our help."*

This was it—the visions she'd seen were coming true. Ezaara needed them. There was no time to waste. She set the bird onto the grass under a palm.

Oh gods, how was she—the deformed, useless daughter of a cutthroat assassin—going to do this?

Saritha rose from the lake, dripping, and landed nearby, shaking droplets over the sand. *"This is the moment we've been training for. We must go to their aid. My cousins in the North need us. Go, and gather your sisters."*

Ithsar swallowed. *"But, I'm just a lowly—"*

Saritha cut her off. *"Ithsar, shake off the shackles of your birth and rise to the occasion. Dragons' Realm needs you."*

Swallowing, Ithsar nodded and rushed toward the tunnel to the subterranean caverns.

§

As Ithsar ran through the tunnels, Saritha melded with her. *"Prepare the women for imprinting. If you tell them what's required of them, they'll rise to the occasion. It's an honor to ride a sea dragon, and now that they've grown used to being with me, they're bound to imprint when they leap from the cliff."*

Saritha didn't understand. These fearless women did not like the sea or the monsters that lurked in its depths. Asking them to submit themselves willingly would be the ultimate test of Ithsar's grip on them. Asking them too soon would ruin everything. She'd wait until they had no choice. Ithsar reached the cavern and waited at the front, pounding feet rushing along the tunnels and echoing through the training chamber.

As her assassins assembled in front of her, she was too aware that she only reached the shoulders of the tallest. The women stood, hands out, poised on the balls of their feet—battle-ready. Ithsar waved a hand toward the floor. As one, the women sat.

She let her eyes travel over them, meeting everyone's gazes. Izoldia, Bala, and Thut were near the back of the cavern. Their eyes slid away—not a promising sign.

Ithsar dived right in. "A messenger bird arrived today. The vision that Saritha showed you is coming to pass. Even as we train here in the desert, isolated by the broad Naobian Sea, hundreds of people are dying in Dragons' Realm, slaughtered by evil dragons, their carcasses left to rot across the land. Ezaara—she of the golden hair, and the Queen's Rider of Dragons' Realm—has asked for our aid. I have pledged to help her. And you have pledged to obey me. So prepare your camels, pack clothes, weapons, food, and waterskins for an extended trip. We'll ride out in an hour, so you may imprint with the waiting sea dragons."

Their fists pounding their chests, the silent assassins bowed their heads. No questions asked.

Ithsar swallowed. Would they be so compliant when they got to the drop-off and realized they were required to throw themselves into the sea to prove their trust? Sharks prowled those waters. Suspicion of sea monsters was as much part of their Robandi culture as camel butter on couscous.

Perhaps she'd be flying to Dragons' Realm on her own, an army of one to fight against Commander Zens' evil shadow dragons.

A Test of Trust

Camels snorted, saddlebags creaking as the assassins tightened them around the girth of their beasts. Hooves shifted in sand, like hissing rust vipers. Ithsar strode through the camels, nodding at her women as she made her way to the front, Thika nestled on her forearm.

"*I assume you've told these women what is required of them? They look resolute and willing to fight,*" Saritha rumbled.

Ithsar avoided answering, helping Thika onto Saritha's back. "*I assume you're ready for the long trek across the desert?*"

Saritha snorted. "*It's a mere wingbeat or two. We could be there in no time.*" As Ithsar climbed into the saddle, Saritha flicked her tail toward the camels. "*Those creatures will take half a day.*"

"*I'm afraid we will too. I dare not take my eyes off those three at the back.*" Ithsar glanced at Izoldia, Thut, and Bala.

"*A little jet of flame will sort them out, no problem.*"

"*I know, but you might spook their camels,*" Ithsar replied.

Saritha's talons kneaded the sand, and she turned, angling her head to gaze at Ithsar. "*Well, we couldn't have that, could we?*" A mischievous twinkle gleamed in her golden eyes.

"*I'm trying to lead my people by example. I can't have you upsetting them.*"

"*Upsetting them? Who said anything about upsetting them? I was merely contemplating setting their camels' tails on fire.*" Her fangs gleamed in a dragonly smile, and she tossed her head, facing the camels again. "*Are we ready?*" Saritha's body quivered with impatience.

Ithsar scratched her neck. "*I don't blame you. You've been cooped up here for so long.*"

"*With nothing but stringy goats, the odd fish, and desert vultures to eat.*" Saritha eyed one of the camels.

"*No, you don't. They're our transport! You can't eat them.*"

"*Well, I could… but they do have a rather unpleasant scent.*" The dragon wrinkled her snout.

"*Lucky for them.*" Ithsar stifled a smile as she turned to her assassins. She drew her saber from its sheath and raised it in the air, calling, "We'll ride out across the desert toward the Naobian Sea." Her eyes flicked to Izoldia, Bala, and Thut. "Saritha and I will ensure that nobody gets lost."

Bala leaned across her camel to say something to Izoldia, who grinned. Thut sniggered.

"*Those three are trouble, all right. It's not too late to leave them behind,*" Saritha rumbled.

For a heartbeat, Ithsar considered it. It would be safer for all of them if Izoldia, Bala, and Thut didn't come. "*What harm can those three do against a mighty dragon like you?*"

Saritha preened her scales. Gasps echoed through the ranks of the assassins as her majestic green wings unfurled, glinting in the morning sun. She sprang into the air, spraying sand over the nearest camel's haunches, and then spiraled upward until the camels were a mere speck below them in the sand.

Exhilaration sang through Ithsar's blood as the wind swept her headscarf back, the ends trailing in the sky behind her. The full force of the hot summer sun beat down upon her, but instead of sapping her strength, she felt energized, alive, as if the world was full of wonder and possibility. Saritha's pleasure shot through her, the sea dragon's delight setting her veins on fire.

Saritha swooped, and Ithsar's belly flew straight into her throat. As far as she could see, tangerine sand was spread before her, enormous dunes rolling into hillocks. The Naobian Sea winked deep sapphire-blue in the distance.

Ithsar drew in a deep breath, the tension of these long weeks training the women unfurling and rushing out of her in a whoosh.

They dived and shot out across the desert, camels trailing them, and then Saritha circled and swooped in behind the camels, driving them forward. "*Go on, just a little flame? Please?*"

"*What a tease you are.*" Joy blossomed inside Ithsar. Too big to contain, it felt as if her skin would burst. She whooped and laughed.

Some of the assassins gazed up, surprised. Some smiled. Others waved.

She'd soon see whether they'd still be smiling when they found out they had to throw themselves off the cliff to the monsters of the deep.

§

The lapis sea was sparkling in the blazing sun when they arrived at the Naobian coast. Saritha landed upon the dune where Ithsar had fought Ashewar, only a moon and a half ago. The rugged sandstone cliff cut away beneath them where the cliff had crumbled when she'd fought her mother. The giant waves that had battered Ithsar were only tiny crests of white from way up here. The sea rushed in, roaring as it pounded the cliff, then hissed as it was sucked back out again.

Dark brown flecks—Drida's blood—were half covered in windblown sand. This was a place of death.

And of the birth of her new life.

Ithsar shook a trickle of unease from between her shoulder blades. Hopefully, no more blood would be shed today.

Saritha rumbled, *"I've signaled Queen Aquaria. She and the sea dragons will be arriving shortly. I'm glad these women know what to expect."*

Ithsar slid from the saddle, not meeting Saritha's gaze.

The sea dragon nudged her shoulder. *"You have told them, haven't you? They need to be ready to jump, so they can imprint."*

The camels sat at the base of the dune. The women were traipsing up, their orange robes making the sand ripple with movement. They reached the top of the hill and stood in formation, pounding their fists upon their chests.

Misha approached. "The women are hungry, and more than a little nervous. Is it all right if we eat first? It may help settle their nerves."

Ithsar nodded. "Yes, you'll need your strength."

Nila spoke up. "Are the sea dragons meeting us up here?"

Ithsar's belly coiled tight and a trickle of unease rippled through her. "You'll see," she replied softly.

But Saritha heard. She nudged Ithsar again, this time a bit harder. *"So you haven't told them? Ithsar, I warned you—"*

"I know what I'm doing." Ithsar broke mind-meld and joined the women. She hadn't been prepared when she'd imprinted with Saritha.

She bit into her fresh flatbread, but it tasted like sand. She tried a poppyseed cake, but its usual sweetness eluded her. Even her dried fruit was tasteless pap. So, she melded with her dragon again. *"Saritha, these are my people. I know them well. Please trust me."*

A low rumble issued from Saritha's maw, but she nodded, yellow eyes glinting. *"Very well. But I hope it won't cost us the safety of Dragons' Realm. Since the messenger bird arrived, I've felt something dark slithering under my scales. But at the same time, I sense sunshine filtering down through murky waters."* Her golden eyes met Ithsar's. *"Hopefully, we shall be all right."*

Saritha unfurled her wings and leaped to perch upon the edge of the cliff. She opened her maw and roared.

Below, the water churned with shark fins. Green and blue scaly heads rose out of the sea. In the depths, more long shadowy shapes sped toward the base of the cliff.

Ithsar raised her arms and faced her fellow assassins. "Have you pledged to follow me?"

"Yes," the women cried.

"Do you trust me?"

"Yes."

Although Izoldia's eyes narrowed, and Bala nudged Thut.

Bala asked in a booming voice, "Should we stand back to leave space for the dragons to land?"

"Soon we'll be riding dragons into battle." Ithsar flung her arms out. "The sea dragons are waiting."

The women cast about, looking behind them and into the sky.

She gestured to the cliff. "In order to imprint with a sea dragon, you must show great trust. They require us to leap from the drop-off and meet them in the sea. There are more than enough dragons for all of you, but this is the test you must pass to become a rider." Ithsar waited. No one moved. "You may choose to go back to the oasis, and we will not think less of you."

Wind hissed across the sand. Waves pounded on the cliffs below.

"Misha, you've shown courage. Would you like the honor of going first?"

Misha's eyes shot wide. Her face paled and she opened her mouth, then snapped it shut.

"Your most loyal follower, gaping like a stranded fish," Saritha melded. *"I thought you knew your women."*

Ithsar turned to Nila, who gave a barely perceptible shake of her head.

Panic dug its claws deep into Ithsar's belly. If nobody imprinted, Dragons' Realm would be lost. Her eyes flitted across the women, but no one met her gaze.

A voice rang out. "I'll go first." Izoldia swaggered toward Ithsar, barely restraining herself from an arrogant sneer. "I, Ashewar's greatest warrior, do not hesitate to leap into the deep. I shall conquer a wild beast."

Shaking her head, Ithsar replied, "These dragons don't require conquering, Izoldia. They require an equal, a friend."

As quick as an asp, Izoldia's arm flashed out. She whipped Roshni's ceremonial saber from Ithsar's sheath and kicked out at Ithsar.

Ithsar palmed her dagger and spun, countering with her own kick, but Izoldia leapt off the cliff, her bellow slicing through the air. "I *will* conquer a sea dragon."

Saber flashing, she plummeted toward the sea.

Izoldia's Plot

The wind ripped Izoldia's head scarf from her head and flung it into a wild breeze. Triumph and rage thrummed through Izoldia's veins. This was it. This was her final chance at leadership. If she could obtain a dragon—the largest dragon, the queen she had glimpsed in Saritha's mind—then she had a chance of leading these people. Her last chance of being a mighty ruler.

She would subdue the beast and bend its will to hers, and then destroy the deformed runt on top of the cliff, laughing as the sea monster blasted Ithsar with flame and melted her bones.

Izoldia hurtled through the air and hit the sea, feet first, the shock jarring through her leg bones into her hips. She barely had time to snatch a gust of breath before she plummeted down deep.

When her descent slowed, she kicked up, aiming for the surface. Still holding Roshni's saber tight, she burst from the ocean.

A giant green-scaled beast, the hugest of them all, plowed through the water toward her.

All she had to do was mind-meld, and this beast would be hers. Izoldia grinned, tucking Roshni's saber in the back of her waistband, and swam closer. The beast's majestic head rose from the ocean, its jaws dripping seawater and its golden eyes glinting. Fin-like projections from the side of its face glittered like emeralds in the sun. Its maw, longer than Izoldia's torso, opened, its snarl making Izoldia's bones skitter.

Nearby, a shark cut through the water. The beast lashed out with its tail. The shark arced through the air and landed in the water a hundred camel lengths away. The power of this beast was thrilling. With such a mighty creature fighting for her, the world would be hers.

Izoldia swam nearer.

The monster slitted its eyes and lowered its head, gazing at her. A deep growling voice burst into her mind, *"You would dare imprint with me?"*

It stole Izoldia's breath. A wave lapped, crashing over her head. She spluttered and kicked upward, projecting her thoughts outward. *"Oh yes, wondrous creature of the depths, I have come to imprint with you and be your new rider."*

A dark, roiling cloud drifted through Izoldia's mind. *"You, who killed so many and taunted my daughter's rider?"*

Fierce rage surged through Izoldia's breast. Not that deformed little runt again. Ithsar had always stood between Izoldia and everything she'd ever desired. She quelled her rage, dampening it and shoving it down deep where the sea monster couldn't detect it. *"I have seen the evil of my former ways, dear gracious, wondrous sea monster. I am here to offer myself to willingly serve you and Ithsar."*

She rotated her feet and thrashed her arms, treading water, to stay above the crashing waves.

"You held her saber as you plunged into the ocean—the saber of the one who sacrificed her life to save her. Your heart is full of canker. The rotten fire of hatred burns within you."

"No, no, honored Sea Queen, you sense only the trace of my old life. I have changed."

The monster tilted its head, regarding her. Izoldia's pulse pounded against her temples. At last it spoke. *"I do believe in giving the darkest, foulest creature a second chance. Come here and I will test you."*

Izoldia swam closer. Dangerously close.

The beast lowered its head, jaws underwater, only the eyes and top of her head above the surface. *"Swim alongside me."*

Izoldia splashed, gasping, until she was alongside the queen's giant head.

"Now place your hands upon my brow so I can see your true essence."

This stupid monster was obsessed with its dung-filled rituals—the beast had no idea what she was up to. *"I am too weary, not used to swimming. Please let me climb upon your back, for I fear I will drown."* She spluttered, letting herself be dragged under for a moment, then kicked up again, gasping in great chestfuls of air. *"Help me."*

The monster's eyes narrowed. *"Very well. Climb upon my neck."* It lowered its head, its eyes gazing at her from underwater. And then that giant head swooped under Izoldia's body.

Izoldia grasped a spinal ridge on the top of its neck, but as she laid her hands upon the beast's hide and it raised its head from the sea, a violent wave of black fury ripped through her mind.

"You have the darkest heart. You will never be my rider. The blood of too many men stains your hands, and your mind is full of foul intent."

If Izoldia could never have this beast, no one would. She wouldn't face the humiliation of another assassin imprinting with the queen of the sea dragons. It was bad enough that Ithsar had taken her rightful place as heir after she'd worked so hard to curry favor with Ashewar. Izoldia whipped Roshni's saber from the back of her waistband, and raised it high above the beast's head. Then she drove the curved blade into the monster's head above its eye. The queen of the sea dragons let out an agonizing shriek. Izoldia jumped upon the saber, driving it through the beast's skull with her full body weight.

Blood sprayed from the dragon, bathing Izoldia, but she didn't care. Hanging on as the queen's neck drooped, she drove that saber with all her strength until the monster's body went limp and slumped under the water, taking her with it.

§

Izoldia disappeared over the ledge in a flash of orange robes and a silver glint of Roshni's saber. Ithsar rushed to the edge and stared down at the churning waves. Queen Aquaria was racing to meet Izoldia, her jade body undulating through the sea.

A shudder skittered through Ithsar's bones. Nothing good could come of this—Izoldia was always scheming. A cry broke from Ithsar's lips, "Saritha."

In a flash of green and silver, Saritha was beside her. Ithsar scrambled onto her back. Saritha's mighty haunches tensed, and they dived down the sandstone cliff, the wind rushing through Ithsar's hair, the churning surf beckoning.

The queen of the sea dragons surfaced, raising her head. Izoldia burst from the ocean and clambered upon the dragon. *"No, what is Queen Aquaria thinking?"*

"She wants to test Izoldia," barked Saritha. *"I've warned her not—"*

In a flash of silver, Izoldia drove Roshni's saber deep into Queen Aquaria's head, and then leaped upon it, driving the blade through her skull.

The dragon and Izoldia submerged, disappearing from view. A bloody trail of red frothed in the sea.

An agonized roar burst from Saritha's throat, and she and Ithsar plunged into the ocean, a bubble of silver enveloping Ithsar.

It was chaos underwater. Sharks swarmed around Queen Aquaria. Saritha tore into them with her claws, rending their bodies and flinging them aside. More sharks dived in, biting at the queen's carcass, whipping the sea into a bloody frenzy with their thrashing tails.

Izoldia's limp body floated past. Saritha smacked it with her tail, sending Izoldia into the mass of frenzied sharks. In horror, Ithsar watched as they devoured the burly guard, crunching through her bones and ripping her apart. Feasting upon her remains.

More dragons dived through the water, swimming toward their queen, slashing at sharks with their talons, and driving them away with their tails. Blood swirled around Ithsar, clouding the water, and the sea reverberated with anguished cries of hundreds of dragons.

§

The sea dragons formed a ring around Queen Aquaria, protecting her from the ocean's finned vultures. Anguish ripped through Ithsar's mind as Saritha opened her maw. A mourning keen reverberated through the water, shattering through Ithsar's body. The dragons joined in. Keening came from all around her, bouncing off her—an eerie lament, muted by the water, rippling through her body and echoing in her mind.

They hung, suspended in the water around the queen's limp carcass. Ithsar lost all sense of time—there was only the eerie cry reverberating through her again and again.

The dragons dived, weaving under the queen and lifting her body. Driving upwards with their mighty forearms and lashing with their tails, the loyal dragons pushed their queen's body up toward the daylight.

Ithsar clung on, the keening still filling her ears as the dragons broke the surface. The dragons grasped hold of Queen Aquaria and flew, wings dripping, up into the clear sapphire sky, carrying their queen—a huge ring of creatures honoring their valiant leader. Their mournful cries tugged at her heartstrings, threatening to split her chest in two. This was her fault. If she'd kept Izoldia in the dungeons and not given her a chance, none of this would have happened.

Ithsar shielded her thoughts from Saritha. Her poor friend was grieving her mother and her queen. She didn't need Ithsar's guilt added to her burden.

Ithsar tasted the tang of Saritha's sadness. Izoldia was no more, but, by murdering the sea dragon queen, Izoldia had destroyed their future.

The dragons rushed upward, startling the assassins gathered on the clifftop as their wings beat higher into the sky. When the cliff and the assassins were no more than specks below, the dragons dropped Queen Aquaria. She plunged through the air. Saritha and the other sea dragons dived, belching flame at the queen's body.

Her carcass caught, blazing as it plummeted toward the sea. Burning, burning, until it grew into a towering inferno, a plume of gray smoke staining the sky. The dragons dived, flaming her until the queen of the sea dragons was nothing but ash, swept away on the surface of the sea.

SEA DRAGONS

The moment Izoldia jumped and Saritha and Ithsar dived after her, Misha whipped out her saber and stood back-to-back with Nila facing off Bala and Thut.

"Any trouble, and you'll feel our blades," Misha called in a strong voice—a strength she didn't feel. She willed her arm not to shake.

Nila leaped forward. "We'll wait for Ithsar. Anyone who chooses not to follow Ithsar may leave now." Behind Bala and Thut, women's hands drifted to their hilts.

Bala lunged toward Nila and Misha's legs, trying to knock them off the edge of the cliff.

Misha leaped high, spinning over Bala's body, and landed. Nila dived over Bala as she barreled toward her, then rolled to her feet.

Bala stopped, fists grasping crumbling sandstone, her head hanging over the edge of the cliff, eyes on the sea. A filthy curse rang from her lips. "Shrott and camel's dung! Izoldia's dead."

Thut cried out and flung herself forward, gazing down at the churning, bloody sea. Fins cut through the water. The sea roiled with sharks and the long undulating bodies of sea dragons. The beasts dived, pink froth staining the ocean's surface.

Misha kept her grip on her saber firm. She poked the tip into Bala's back. "Would you like to return to the oasis, or imprint with a sea dragon and follow Ithsar, or join Izoldia?"

Bala scrambled to her feet, glancing over the cliff, her face pale and hands trembling. "I'm not jumping into the mouth of some horrible monster."

Nila, pointing her saber at Thut, snapped at Bala, "Those beasts are not horrible. Izoldia was. She killed a sea dragon and caused the shark's feeding frenzy. She deserved to die."

"I'm not jumping." Bala grimaced, baring her teeth, eyes wild like a trapped beast.

Misha repressed a shudder. If it came to a fight, Bala was larger, more vicious, and desperate. "Then go back to the oasis."

Bala jerked her head toward the camels. "Come on, Thut."

But Thut stared at her feet, mumbling, "I don't care if I have to jump. I liked flying on Saritha. I'm staying."

Bala snarled at her former ally as the assassins parted, hands on hilts, letting Bala through their ranks. She stomped down the dune, sand spurting around her feet, then clambered upon a camel and made her way off into the desert in a cloud of dust.

Misha released a sigh. She and Nila sheathed their sabers.

Roars and moans filled the sky as dragons burst from the sea, carrying the body of an enormous dragon up, past Misha and the others, up, until they were as small as finches. Jets of flame plumed. The dragon's body dropped, blazing and smoking, through the sky. The dragons dived, too, burning the body until there was nothing but ash, and then dived into the sea.

"Ready to jump?" Nila asked, quirking an eyebrow.

Misha's heart pounded. She swallowed, gazing down. Waves pelted against the cliff and sharks prowled the ocean. "Ah, sure."

§

Saritha howled, arching her neck, her grief roaring through Ithsar. Tears streamed from Ithsar's eyes, dashing across her cheeks, swept away by the rushing air as they plummeted toward the sea. Oh gods, oh gods, by the flaming burning *dracha* gods, Queen Aquaria was dead. And it was her fault for not imprisoning Izoldia. The pounding waves neared, thundering against the sandstone cliff.

They plunged into the ocean. Suddenly, the thoughts of the sea dragons clamored inside Ithsar's head. *"We mourn Queen Aquaria's death."*

"Princess Saritha, you are now our queen."

"We claim you as Queen."

"Hail Saritha, the new queen."

They dived down through the archway, past the undulating fronds that brushed against Ithsar's thighs and arms, and through the inky-dark tunnel in the rock, lit only by the fish with vicious jaws and lights hanging from their heads. On they swam, through the darkness, the pinpoints of light illuminating the fishes' jagged fangs. They shot out into the sunlit spot where Ithsar had first met Queen Aquaria, weeks before.

Saritha howled, the sound reverberating through the water in waves that washed over Ithsar's body. Beneath her, the new queen's body thrummed as she howled again and again.

Saritha alighted upon the coral throne that had belonged to her mother, her talons scraping. *"It is true. I am now your new queen, a responsibility I was not anticipating this soon. I will endeavor to serve you with an open heart and a steadfast spirit to the end of my days."*

A rush of sweetness washed over Ithsar as the sea dragons bowed their heads to the sandy ocean floor.

"You need never bow to me," Saritha said. *"You are my equals and my friends. Long, we've swum these seas together, vanquishing foes, facing pirates, and restoring justice in the briny deep. My mother enjoyed the traditions of old; however, I shall usher in a new reign with this rider upon my back. Together we'll make decisions to protect the fate of Dragons' Realm. You saw Queen Aquaria's vision. Let us all find new riders, so we can help our dragon cousins in the far north."*

"These strangers have brought calamity upon us," a fierce voice growled. An older dragon at the back of the crowd charged through the water and back-winged to hover in front of Saritha. *"These strangers killed Queen Aquaria, one of my dearest friends."* She flicked her tail at Ithsar. *"Dismount, and leave us in peace. We want no part of your visions, nothing to do with you terrible orange-robed women."* She bared her fangs in a snarl.

Saritha hissed. *"You have lost your friend, but I have lost my mother. I choose not to judge everyone by the actions of one. There is greater evil afoot in Dragons' Realm, and we must aid our cousins and their riders. Will you fight with us against Commander Zens and his shadow dragons?"*

The elderly mare bowed her scaly evergreen head. *"As you wish, Queen Saritha; however, I do not like it."*

"Then you do not have to come with us."

"You're not commanding me? What sort of queen are you?" The dragon's eyes slitted.

"A queen who will let everybody have their say. I trust you. You are my family. Those who wish to stay behind may do so, but let me warn you, Queen Aquaria saw these visions. My rider Ithsar has seen them too, and shared them with me. If we do not vanquish Commander Zens, whose armies and shadow dragons are terrorizing the lands, there will be nothing left but a wasteland."

"Wasteland," a young voice called. *"That's what the northerners call the Robandi Desert."*

Saritha's gaze turned to a young turquoise dragon near the front of the crowd, his talons raking the sand.

"It'll be much worse." Ithsar opened her mind and shared her vision with all of the assembled sea dragons.

The entire landscape was barren of vegetation, the mountains bare, the forests charred blackened stumps. The swamplands issued foul stenches. What were once beautiful crystalline lakes had turned to sludge. Strangletons choked the rivers. And there were no people. No dragons. And the bodies of hundreds of sea dragons, dead fish, and carcasses of sharks littered the ocean.

Mighty roars rippled through the water from dragons, young and old. "Save the realm."

"We must stop this!"

"Fight to defeat these shadow dragons and tharuks."

"Then I suggest we rise and meet your new riders," Saritha said. "These orange-robed women know how to fight. With them upon our backs, we can be a fierce force in preventing this destruction. Ezaara, rider of Queen Zaarusha, needs us. Will you come to her aid?"

The dragons roared, ripples radiating through the current and surging through Ithsar's body. Saritha leaped from the rock throne and swept her wings and legs, powering them up toward the sunlight.

§

Roars funneled up from the ocean. Misha and Nila peered over the cliff as a teeming, seething horde of dragons broke from the sea, rushing up at them. The sea monsters were all shades of blue and green—lapis, sapphire, emerald, jade, turquoise, and moss. Their bellows filled the sky, their wings spraying droplets, glimmering in the sun.

A massive turquoise dragon rose above the cliff, its golden eyes fastened on hers. Misha gasped, clutching her chest. She'd never seen anything as beautiful. The sea dragon landed, thrashing the sand with its tail, eyes still fixed to hers. The rushing of a thousand seas filled her ears and she gasped again, her breath stolen as exhilaration swept through her. Warmth surged through her veins, flooding her limbs with energy. Before she realized what she was doing, she was on her knees in front of the glorious sea dragon.

It lowered its head, not breaking their gaze. A gravelly voice crooned in her mind, "You were born to be my rider, Misha. I shall now be known as Ramisha in your honor."

Misha's fingers twitched. She was dying to touch those wondrous scales— deep turquoise, shimmering with silver in the sun. "May I?"

"*You may indeed.*" A rumble filled Misha's mind, like a cat's purr, but louder. Warmer.

She ran her fingers along the scales on the sea dragon's snout. So warm, soft, and supple. She'd thought they'd be hard, like armor. Happiness blossomed inside her.

Ramisha nudged her shoulder. "*Climb on my back. I know you're dying to fly.*"

"*I've always wanted to fly, to be a bird, be free.*"

"*Believe me, this is better than being a bird. There's a whole underwater world awaiting you. Hop on.*" Ramisha crooked a foreleg and held it out for Misha.

She climbed onto the dragon's leg, clambered up his shoulder, and sat between two spinal ridges. Misha ran her hand over Ramisha's sleek scales, then grasped the spinal ridge in front of her. Energy rushed through Misha as her dragon unfurled his wings, spraying cool droplets onto her warm skin.

Ramisha tensed his haunches and sprang. They shot up, out over the sea, and swept down over the lapis waters, Ramisha's shadow chasing a school of silver fish. Through the clear waters far below them, dark shapes of enormous sea creatures roamed the depths, and pretty-colored coral sped by.

A happy sigh broke from her. Misha rested her cheek against the dragon's spinal ridge, hugging it tight. "*You know, I lost my family when I was young. But now I have you, I have a home again.*"

Ramisha rumbled and chuckled in her mind. "*I know, so do I. We belong together.*" He turned and huffed warm breath over her, then flitted over the ocean's surface, flying back, the air above wheeling with dragons and the excited cries of their new riders above the pearly waves breaking at the foot of the sandstone cliffs.

§

Thut stared at the turquoise dragon that landed in front of her, sending up puffs of sand with its mighty taloned feet. She licked her lips. Although she wanted to approach, her legs were wooden, stuck like tent pegs in the sand.

The creature stalked toward her, its scales shimmering silver and blue, like a raging ocean. The dragon flared its nostrils, scenting her.

Thut's heart hammered against her ribs. Camel's dung! Could the *dracha* hear her fear? Smell it? She licked her lips again, then stretched out a shaking hand.

The dragon's wild gold eyes narrowed. It slid its snout under her outstretched fingers. *"Do not fear, Thut. You shall be my rider."*

Wild energy coursed through Thut's veins, like a lightning storm, making her skin crackle and her hair prickle. She wanted to burst out of her skin, but she held steady, regarding the fine sea dragon. *"You're my sea dragon?"* Only the lure of riding one of these fine creatures had swayed her to follow Ithsar here today. In fact, Bala had nearly convinced her to flee the oasis instead.

"So you don't like your leader?" the dragon snarled, a rumble building in its throat.

She'd displeased the beast already, but it had read her thoughts, so there was no point in lying. *"Not really. She's new and she's... um..."*

Before Thut could explain exactly why she hated Ithsar, the dragon replied, *"That's good, because I don't like my new leader either."* The beast tossed her head. *"I shall be known as Lethutle in your honor. Together, we shall have dangerous adventures, and be rid of this new lily-livered queen and her scrawny rider."*

Thut found herself drawn to the dark menace in the dragon's words. "When?" she spluttered breathlessly, forgetting to mind-meld.

"As soon as you climb upon my back."

Thut clambered onto Lethutle's back. The dragon tensed her haunches and sprang into the sky among the cavorting sea dragons and riders. The assassins laughed and called out to each other as their dragons dived playfully.

But no one called to Thut.

Savage pride surged in her breast. She hadn't found a playful frolicking beast. Hers was strong and courageous. Willing to break rules. She'd imprinted with the best sea dragon of all.

§

Ithsar and Saritha swept over the assembled assassins. Sea dragons landed and women imprinted, clambering upon their backs and flying out over the ocean or up over the desert. Dragons wheeled in the sky, their scales glinting jade, emerald, turquoise, and lapis, as women imprinted with cries of joy that echoed out across the desert. Something tight unfurled inside Ithsar, and joy blossomed in her heart, expanding until she felt as if she'd explode.

"I don't understand," Ithsar said. *"Queen Aquaria said the women would have to jump to prove themselves."*

"Ah, but I am queen now, and I know that they have trained hard, proving themselves already." Her dragon turned a reproachful eye on her. "Besides, someone forgot to mention that fact until we got here, and that seemed a little unfair."

"Thank you." Ithsar swallowed, staring out over the desert. Far in the distance, a camel was heading back across the tangerine sand.

Saritha mind-melded, "That's Bala."

"I'd be surprised if she's at the oasis when we return."

"It doesn't matter," Saritha said. "We have more important things to deal with. We must save Dragons' Realm." Saritha landed near the camels, who danced back on the sand, gazing at her, their thick double rows of lashes blinking against the gust of sand from her feet.

Ithsar clambered down and unclasped the camels' saddlebags, dropping them to the sand. When their backs were bare, she slapped the camels' haunches and sent them traipsing off after Bala toward the oasis.

Saritha spied the departing camels. "Not even a little flame?"

"Not even a little flame. You'll terrify them."

"I'm surprised those beasts can feel terror. Or find their way home. Don't those silly creatures get lost in those vast sands?"

"They've made this trip many times—they know the way. Besides, do you get lost in the sea?"

"Good point, although I do have superior intelligence." Saritha chuckled. "It won't matter if I give them a hurry up, then." Before Ithsar could protest, she opened her maw and roared.

Ithsar couldn't help but laugh as the camels took off at a rapid pace, their hooves kicking up a sandstorm as they raced across the desert after Bala. She attached extension straps to the saddlebags. Crafted by the assassins over the past moon, they would allow the bags to fit around the sea dragons' large bellies. "In time, we'll make proper saddlebags to fit you all, but for now these will have to do."

Saritha snorted. "I suppose we can deign to wear the garb of camels, although the bags are rather small."

Ithsar playfully slapped her dragon's scaly thigh. "There's nothing wrong with small things." She drew herself up to her full height, which made Saritha chuckle. "Now, please call your friends over so we can fit them." As she clambered under Saritha's belly to cinch the strap, she asked, "Are you sure you can keep our supplies dry?"

"I told you, we'll be fine: our sathir *bubbles can expand to encompass the supplies, you'll see."*

Sea dragons landed, their new riders' faces flushed with exhilaration and joy. The assassins busied themselves, fastening their improvised saddlebags upon the dragons' backs.

Eyes bright with anticipation, Misha asked, "Are we flying to Naobia? Wow, I've never been there, but I've heard the markets are stunning."

"We'll fly some of the way," Ithsar answered, tugging her robes shut.

"If we're not flying the whole way, how will we get there?"

"We'll be swimming." Murmurs rippled through the crowd of assassins. Ithsar climbed onto her dragon. "Follow me and Saritha."

Saritha leaped into the sky and dived down the sandstone cliff into the Naobian Sea. For a moment, Ithsar held her breath as they plunged into the water. The *sathir* bubble encompassed her, the saddlebags and Thika. This time, she didn't even get her boots wet.

"How did you do that?"

"It takes a little more sathir, *so we'll have to break the surface more often to replenish your air, but we're much faster underwater. I missed the sea life,"* Queen Saritha said.

"So did I," Ithsar answered.

Her sister assassins' faces glowed with wonder as they communed with their sea dragons and took in the beauty of the coral and the stunning multi-colored fish darting out of their way as the wing of dragons swam toward Naobia.

TO NAOBIA

Thut and Lethutle plunged down the cliff and dived into the ocean, a flurry of wings and thrashing tails around them.

"And now?" Thut asked as a shimmering bubble enveloped her so she could breathe.

"We wait." Thut's courageous sea dragon hung back behind the other sea dragons as the women gazed at the wonders in their new underwater world.

Waiting had never been Thut's strong point, but there were plenty of coral formations and fish to look at—if you liked that sort of thing. Thut didn't particularly care.

"Why don't you like Saritha?" she asked.

"I have my reasons," Lethutle replied.

"Where are we going?" Thut asked.

"Somewhere where we can grow strong and powerful, over time, and come back to smite Saritha."

A gleeful shiver raced down Thut's spine. *"I like the sound of that."*

As the other dragons swam toward Naobia, Lethutle slowed, letting the gap between them and the others grow longer, until they looked like a school of tiny fish in the distance.

Lethutle flicked her tail and swam back to the jagged Robandi coast line. They skimmed along sandstone cliffs riddled with dark crevices. Glowing eyes peeked out at them. Occasionally, fanged jaws snapped or a tentacle slithered back into a hole.

"Where did you say we're going, again?" Thut asked, glad she was on this brave dragon, not swimming here alone. Not that she could swim.

Her dragon's grim chuckle resonated in her mind. *"I'm taking you to meet the Scarlett Hand."*

Thut's eyebrows shot up. *"You know the bloodiest pirate captain on the Naobian Sea?"*

"I certainly do. And when we next meet Saritha and her scrawny rider, we'll have our own pirate crew. We'll see how they fare then."

Again, that wild lightning surged through Thut's veins, bucking to be set free.

Lethutle responded, speeding through the water, slashing out with her talons and spearing fish then tossing them aside as they sped along the coastline.

§

The sea dragons and their riders swept through the ocean, riding the currents. Nila gave a shriek as her sea dragon plunged through the water and leapfrogged over a series of coral clusters. Her wild laughter rippled through the sea, bouncing around Ithsar. With a whoop, Nila wrapped her arms around her dragon's spinal ridge and let her body and legs float out behind her. She kicked her legs, leaving a trail of wake, her giggles drifting on the current.

"Nilanna enjoys fun, too," Saritha melded. *"They suit each other."*

Some of the other women laughed, encouraging their dragons to join in. Soon, they were cavorting through the water, diving through coral arches and scaring schools of brightly colored fish that rapidly flitted away to hide in the pink, orange, and purple coral.

A pod of curious dolphins swam over. Bounding around the sea dragons, they chittered and squealed.

"They're always so playful, so excitable, like a wing of newborn sea dragonets," said Saritha.

Ithsar couldn't believe her well-trained, highly-disciplined assassins were exhibiting so much joy and wild abandon—then again, Nila had always had a wild streak. It had just been harnessed under Ashewar's rule.

They passed a huge coral fan with square-shaped bloated yellow fish darting among its lacy fronds. *"Are those fish sick?"* asked Ithsar.

Saritha's chuckle skittered through her mind. *"Those yellow ones with the black spots? That's their natural shape. They're called box fish."*

"They do look like boxes, but with fins, bulging eyes, and fishy lips." Ithsar laughed. *"What about those orange ones with white and black bands?"*

"They're clown fish," Saritha answered. *"They're practical jokers, always pranking the lobsters and hiding among the coral to jump out and scare other fish."*

Indeed, the fish appeared as if they were playing hide and seek, darting in and out of the weeds and red coral, then stilling before they darted off again.

The farther out they got from the shore, the cooler the current and the bluer the ocean.

Misha's dragon swam through some undulating weed, and Ithsar and Saritha followed.

"See that over there? That's a puffer fish. Always so proud and haughty, but not too bad once you get to know them."

The fish was like a brownish spiky ball. *"Do their spines hurt?"*

"Very much so, and puffer fish are poisonous, so even we keep our distance." Saritha's distaste washed over Ithsar.

There were so many new things, so many unusual creatures here. Mind you, Ithsar was riding a sea dragon—and that wasn't exactly your standard camel. They swam past a rocky formation rising from the seabed. A long shape with a glowing luminous stripe along its body slithered out from a crack in the rock. The women gesticulated to each other as their sea dragons swam past.

"I didn't know you had snakes underwater," Ithsar said.

"That's not a snake, it's an electric eel."

"What does electric mean?"

"It jolts you when you touch it." Saritha chuckled. *"I tried to eat one once, but I tell you, after I bit into it, my fangs ached for days."*

A thrill surged through Ithsar's veins. This was all so different, so new, so incredible. *"This is so exciting, Saritha."* Ithsar gazed around at sea turtles drifting among waving kelp. *"It's an amazing world here. I love it."*

To either side, above and below, sea dragons undulated through the water, their jade, blue, and turquoise scales glimmering silver as they passed through shafts of sunlight. Nila whooped again, obviously excited at the beautiful sight.

"Watch this," said Saritha. Her command rippled through Ithsar's mind and the minds of all the sea dragons. *"Be still."*

All of the dragons paused in the water. Some of them dived down to rest against the ocean floor among the rocks and coral. Others were motionless, suspended among weed. Some of the blue and turquoise dragons hung in the current. When they closed their eyes, they almost blended in with the water. Almost, but not quite.

"That's our camouflage trick."

Moments later, the dragons sped off again.

Ithsar's stomach rumbled, almost painfully. *"It's been a long time since breakfast. How do we eat?"*

Saritha gave a command and the dragons rose from the sea in a massive expanse of dripping, glinting wings, like a moving, living carpet over the ocean. Ithsar's bubble of *sathir* popped, and fresh briny air rushed back into her lungs. She turned back to look toward her homeland, but all she could see was a tiny orange strip visible on the distant horizon as if they were suspended above an enormous flowing cloth that stretched on forever.

She swallowed hard. *"How far to Naobia?"*

"A while yet. Reach into the saddlebags and get your food. You must replenish your strength for the long journey ahead." Saritha kept flying.

The women around them were obviously getting the same message from their dragons. They were pulling out fruit, dried meat, and flatbread, miraculously not damp at all. *"This beats traveling by camelback."*

Saritha snorted.

When the women were finished, and the sea dragons dived underwater again, there was an enormous creature with long waving tentacles and a flowing mantle floating through the water, looking like a piece of debris. The creature was as long as a small sea dragon. One of its tendrils snaked out and snatched an enormous silver fish the length of Ithsar's leg. It used those tentacles to stuff the fish inside its mouth, devouring it in two bites.

"That's a giant squid. Sometimes they throw temper tantrums and spill their ink. Hopefully, today this one will behave, because that stuff tastes quite foul." As if the creature had heard them, as the dragons approached, the squid shot off leaving an inky-black, stinky trail in the water.

They sped on toward Naobia, rising above the ocean frequently to refresh their air supply and eat. When it was dark, the dragons flew above the water and the women tied themselves to their dragons' spinal ridges so they didn't fall off. They slept curled over the dragons' backs, and the sea dragons flew on, under a dark velvet sky studded with twinkling diamonds, over the beautiful expanse of rippling moonlit ocean below them.

§

The dragons gathered in the deep sea off the Naobian coast along white cliffs that rose from the ocean floor and towered above the surface. The rocky wall was pockmarked with crevasses and lined with undulating fronds of kelp and sea grass, turning the underwater cliff into a moving, living mass of plant life. Fish darted in and out of the sea grass, and colorful shells encrusted the rock.

After a lifetime in the endless arid sands of the Robandi desert, Ithsar had never imagined so much life and color.

Tired after their long journey, the sea dragons settled on pale patches of sand at the base of the cliff, some flattening sea grass with their haunches.

Ithsar scanned the women, looking for Thut. *"Have you seen her?"* she asked Saritha.

"Not since she imprinted with an old enemy of mine," Saritha replied. *"It's probably best we've lost them."*

Ithsar shrugged, privately relieved.

Saritha's voice rumbled through their minds, *"Ithsar and I will scout the Naobian coast and approach the green guards. The rest of you will wait here."*

Ramisha snarled. *"I won't have my queen go without a guard. It's been years since we've had contact with the green guards. We should be cautious. We don't know what to expect."*

More dragons rumbled in assent, but Saritha's voice was firm. *"You're right, we haven't seen them for years, but if too many of us go, we could provoke an attack."*

Ramisha twitched his tail. *"I refuse to let my new queen go alone. I don't want a third queen within two days."*

Saritha angled her head, observing Misha and her dragon. *"Very well, you may come with me, but the rest of you must wait here. We can't risk inciting fear in the guards. We desperately need them as friends to fight this terrible enemy in the North."* She tensed her haunches and sprang. She and Ithsar ascended through the water, Ramisha and Misha following.

They broke through the surface and flew high up the pale cliffs.

As they crested the hills, Ithsar gasped. *"Everything is so green,"* she said. *"I never imagined anything like this."*

They landed on a grassy meadow on a hilltop speckled with wildflowers and dotted with rocks. Ramisha landed beside Saritha. Ithsar and Misha gazed down across the land.

Northward, a lake glinted, nestled among verdant rolling hills. A sprawling forest lay at the foot of a mountain, but immediately in front of them was a patchwork of green, yellow, and brown fields, and a large rambling town encircled by a city wall. Roads snaked from the town through the fields to smaller villages. And everywhere, everything was green—moss, jade, emerald, lime, olive, sage, mint, and evergreen—all the shades Ithsar could ever imagine.

Orchards of fruit-laden trees sprawled on the edge of the township. People tilled the fields. Strange creatures plodded along roads, pulling wheeled contraptions laden with goods.

"What are those?" Misha asked.

"My father told me about horses and their wagons when I was young," Ithsar answered. "I think that's what they must be."

Saritha rumbled in assent.

"Those creatures look so odd. How in the sun's name do they stay balanced on their legs without a hump?" Misha asked. Saritha turned an eye to her. Misha hastily added, "Not that I mean any disrespect. I mean, I know dragons don't have humps, but…"

Ramisha and Saritha snorted, and Misha blushed.

Ithsar turned to Misha. "Queen Saritha wants you and Ramisha to stay here. She's still concerned that more than one of us approaching may alarm the Naobian green guards. We mustn't make them think we're attacking."

Ramisha clawed at the ground, his talons ripping out chunks of grass and earth, but he and Misha stayed behind on top of the hill. As Saritha flew out over the fields, Ithsar marveled. The sea glinted azure, lapis, and turquoise beneath them. The warm breeze stirred tiny white peaks far out in the deep. The distant hiss of the breakers on the shore was muted by the swish of Saritha's wings.

Ithsar gasped, clasping her hands. *"This is so beautiful. So many different shades of green, so many plants. So much that grows. I'd thought the sea was a wonder with all those creatures and plant life, but this… this is just breathtaking."* The forest was such a deep, dark green, and every field and meadow was a different brilliant green. Some were speckled with flowers. Leafy crops grew in neat rows. Yellow corn stood straight and proud, leaves fluttering in the breeze. *"What are those red things bobbing in the wind?"*

"Those are poppies," Saritha said.

Ahead, waves lapped at a broad expanse of pale sand that formed a bay. At the far end, huge wooden jetties jutted out into the sea. Ships were moored to thick poles along the jetties. People unloaded large barrels, wooden boxes, and trunks onto wagons. As they swooped lower, the bustle of activity and voices carried from the city. The clop of horse hooves on the cobbled roads drifted to them.

Just outside the town, a green dragon leaped from a low hillside, propelling itself into the sky.

"Green guard!" Saritha backwinged, slowing.

The green dragon and rider speared toward them, roaring and shooting a jet of flame.

ATTACKED

Flame lanced through the air, narrowly missing Saritha's tail. She twisted out of reach. *"Sorry, Ithsar, if only I wasn't so tired."* A wave of blistering heat roiled above Ithsar's back. She ducked flat against Saritha's scales as the mighty queen of the sea dragons dived. *"We have no choice but to flee. I don't want to fight,"* Saritha said.

The green guard whirled, his rider low in the saddle, and chased Saritha, blasting more flame.

Thika poked his head out of a saddlebag. "No, Thika, back inside." Ithsar fumbled, shutting the flap.

Saritha ducked and changed course.

Ice skittered through Ithsar's veins. Gods, if that dragon hit them, they'd be nothing but a ball of flame like Queen Aquaria. *"No, Saritha, I can't let that dragon hurt you."* She drew her saber from its sheath and nearly dropped it as Saritha dodged another plume of flame. The pretty green fields spun and blurred as Saritha maneuvered out of the young dragon's reach.

"If we're to secure them as friends, we must be cautious." Saritha shot through the air like an arrow, landing outside the city walls in a meadow fringed on the city side by an orchard.

Snarling, the green dragon landed.

Although Saritha was larger, she prostrated her body upon the ground with her head low.

Ithsar's temper flared, and she waved her saber. *"How dare this beast snarl at you like that. You're the new queen."*

"Not too hasty. We need them as our allies," Saritha said.

"With allies like this, who needs enemies?" Ithsar slid off Saritha, and stomped toward the green dragon.

"No," Saritha called. *"I don't want you to get hurt."* She lashed out with her tail and flicked the saber from Ithsar's hand.

The blade skittered across the grass and thunked against the roots of an enormous tree. The impact knocked ripe golden fruit from the branches to the ground. An overpowering sweet scent filled Ithsar's nostrils.

The green dragon snarled, haunches tensed and mean eyes slitted.

Ithsar stalked forward, a sea breeze whipping her robes about her waist.

A slim, lanky man slid from the dragon's back, his olive skin, lighter than hers, marking him as a Naobian. Taller than her, he gestured with his sword, motioning her to raise her hands.

She complied. She'd best him anyway, with the daggers hidden in her sleeves and boots.

He stopped near her, poised on the balls of his feet, gazing at her, but saying nothing. Tension lined his body.

Ithsar inclined her head. What was he waiting for? Well, if he wasn't going to talk, she would. "Why are you accosting Saritha, queen of the sea dragons?" she asked.

The man waved his sword, motioning her to stand against a tree trunk.

Ithsar backed up until the rough bark was at her back.

Then, his sword at her throat, he patted her down, checking for weapons. A sweet scent overpowered Ithsar as a breeze ruffled her sleeves. "Why do you not talk?" she asked. Had the green guards, too, taken a vow of silence?

His dark eyes glinted as he confiscated the daggers strapped to her arms, two blades from her boots, the knives at her waist and her favorite dagger hidden inside her robes. Still, he hadn't spoken. Ithsar cocked her head. Now that he was closer, he appeared younger than his height suggested. His facial skin was young and unblemished, without stubble. He stepped back, sword still out.

"You can sheathe that thing. We come in peace," she said.

"In peace? If you mean us no harm, why are you carrying an arsenal of blades?"

His voice was young and boyish—no wonder he hadn't wanted to speak. Despite his lanky body, his voice betrayed his age. Ithsar grinned. "You're not much older than me," she said. "Maybe not even as old as me."

He cocked an eyebrow, his sword not wavering. "And how old would that be?"

Ithsar drew herself up to her full height, aware she only came up to his chest. "Old enough to be the new chief prophetess of the Robandi assassins."

"Chief Prophetess?" His jaw dropped. "I always imagined Ashewar taller, more… um…" His eyes flicked over her as if she were a discarded orange rind.

"Yes, she *was* taller." Ithsar's tone was flat.

"Ah." He swallowed, obviously doing mental contortions to figure out that she'd disposed of Ashewar.

Well, let him think that—her or the shark—it was all the same.

"Ah, so now *you're* the chief prophetess? Why are you riding a shadow dragon?" He gestured at Saritha, who was sitting on the grass with her forelegs tucked underneath her and her snout low, while the green dragon prowled around her, a low rumble escaping its throat.

"Don't worry, Ithsar, if things turn bad I can get us out of here." Saritha wrinkled her nose. *"I can still scent the egg shards on this young, freshly-hatched dragonling. He doesn't have much experience and neither does his rider."*

Ithsar believed her. The green was only half Saritha's size.

"Since when do Robandi have shadow dragons?" the boy asked.

"She's hardly a shadow dragon. From what I've heard, they're black."

"Then why are you attacking Naobia?" He flicked his sword toward the ocean. "And where are the rest of your tribe?"

This rider asked more questions than a littling. "Are you hard of hearing?" Ithsar snapped. It had been a long trip—a whole day and night of swimming. Her patience was wearing thin. "I told you, we're here in peace."

"Why should I believe you? You're pretty short and young for a chief prophetess. And I think—"

Ithsar spun, flinging out her foot, and kicked him in the chest.

Unprepared, he crashed to the ground, dropping his sword and her collection of blades.

She snatched up her favorite dagger and leaped onto his chest, pinning him with her legs, her blade at his neck. "Good. Now, we can talk. But I'll ask the questions. How long have you been in the green guards?"

"Two moons." His eyes blazed with indignation.

Only half a moon longer than she'd been Chief Prophetess. "You've attacked Saritha, queen of the sea dragons, and her rider Ithsar, the new chief prophetess of the Robandi assassins. What do you think the leader of the green guards would say about you starting a war with two mighty races?"

His eyes widened, but he said nothing, lying there unmoving. Aware it could be a ruse, Ithsar kept her body taut, ready for action. "Speak."

"Sea dragon? But they only leave the ocean in times of dire need."

Ithsar had never heard that. *"Saritha, is that true?"* Saritha's nod of assent was enough. Ithsar continued, "We are in dire need. Ezaara, the Queen's Rider of Dragons' Realm, sent me a messenger bird. She needs our help and the help of the Naobian green guards." She snorted, pressing the dagger a little more firmly against his neck so he would feel it scratch.

His eyes flew open. "Ezaara asked you? So you've heard of the shadow dragons plaguing the realm?"

Ithsar flashed her teeth in a fierce grin "Yes, and I came here to talk with the Naobian green guards, so we can fight the shadow dragons and prevent Dragons' Realm from becoming a wasteland. Somehow, I'd imagined having this conversation under different circumstances. I suggest you take me to your leader."

"I p-promise not to attack if you l-let me up," he stammered.

Roars split the sky. A wing of green dragons dived toward them, spurting fire.

The boy smirked. "I'd like to see you get out of this."

Standing, he'd be too tall for her blade to even reach his throat. Ithsar slipped off him, her knife still at his neck, and crouched next to his prone body. "Get up." Keeping her blade in position, she grabbed his arm as he clambered to his feet. Then she yanked it behind his back, and pressed her dagger between his shoulder blades.

Saritha rumbled, *"Now we're in trouble."*

Roars rang out from the hilltop. Misha and Ramisha were streaking toward them, talons out and flames blazing. Trailing in their wake were all the sea dragons.

Anger surged through Ithsar. "This is exactly what me and my wise queen were trying to avoid," she barked. "Your foolhardy actions could cause the destruction of both our people and prevent us from helping Dragons' Realm."

The boy licked his lips, eyes darting between the two wings of dragons. "I can ask my dragon to call the green guards off. But if they see you with your blade at my throat, they won't believe me." He shrugged. "It's up to you. It wouldn't be my first battle."

"If one of my people or dragons are harmed, it will be your last," Ithsar snapped.

If she let him free, she had no bargaining power. He could snatch up a weapon and attack her again. Or he could tell those fiery beasts to engage in battle.

The two wings of dragons were nearing each other. In a few heartbeats, their flames would meet.

Saritha sat up, now holding her head high. Talons still tucked beneath her, she nodded at Ithsar. The vision of those evil shadow dragons attacking the northern lands shot through Ithsar's head, and she knew what she had to do.

She had vowed to rule in love and kindness, not in terror. She had to act upon her convictions.

"Very well." Ithsar drew away her blade and stepped aside.

§

Snarls filled the air, and hundreds of wings rustled, creating a breeze that stirred the leaves on the trees.

As Ithsar removed the steel from the boy's back, she put steel into her voice. "One false move, and this dagger will be embedded between your ribs, my friend." He stiffened. She continued, "However, I'd like the opportunity to be your friend and work together to free Dragons' Realm."

The young man turned his head to look her in the eye and thumped his heart. "My name is Stefan and my dragon is Fangora. We will fight for Dragons' Realm." He put his fingers in his mouth and let out a shrill whistle.

As his dragon backed away from Saritha, Stefan called out, "Fangora, did you summon the other green guards?"

Ithsar had never imagined a dragon looking sheepish, but this one managed.

"Now look what you've done! Call them off." Stefan turned to her, face stricken. "I'm sorry. He's young and impatient and didn't know better."

Rather like his rider.

"Fangora says he tried to stop them, but none of them are listening," Stefan cried.

Ithsar snatched up her blades, tucking them into their sheathes as Saritha sprang over. She leaped upon Saritha's back, and her dragon launched herself into the air as Stefan and Fangora took flight.

Flame crackled overhead. Saritha and Fangora surged up into the air between the two wings of dragons. Fangora and Stefan sped off toward flaming green guards, and Saritha and Ithsar wheeled to face the fire of the sea dragons.

Ithsar cringed at the heat. *"Saritha, tell them to stop."*

"I'm trying, but they're all fired up."

Ithsar waved her arms in the Robandi gesture for ceasefire.

Nila waved back, acknowledging her. Instantly, the flame from the sea dragons' maws guttered and died.

"I've mind-melded and told them to land," Saritha said.

Stefan somehow got through to the green guards, who stopped roaring and blasting flame.

"Thank the dracha gods, they listened." Ithsar's breath whooshed out of her. *"I can't believe you were joking at a time like that. 'Fired up' indeed."*

Saritha chuckled. *"Well, they were spurting flame and being rather hotheaded."*

The sea dragons spiraled down to land on the eastern side of the meadow, closest to the cliffs where they'd been hiding. The green guards landed on the other side, nearest the orchard and the city, gouging the ground with their talons. A green dragon's tail lashed a tree, sending fruit flying. That same pungent, sweet aroma filled the air, making Ithsar's belly rumble.

Saritha and Fangora landed side by side between the two wings of dragons. Stefan slid from his saddle and faced the green guards. A tall, seasoned rider with broad shoulders and a face as worn as the Robandi sandstone cliffs dismounted and stalked toward them.

"My fellow green guards and esteemed leader, Goren, please allow me to present Ithsar, the chief prophetess of the Robandi assassins," Stefan said. "She rides Saritha, queen of the sea dragons, and has an important message for us."

"So you're the new chief prophetess." Goren curled his lip, glancing down his nose at her. "I'd expected something... Well, more."

Such rudeness. Aware of her unimpressive height, Ithsar stayed upon Saritha's back. A well-aimed kick in the chest would knock that arrogant man onto his backside in the grass, but Ithsar refrained, looking him up and down. "Oh, so you're the leader of the green guards," she said graciously, refusing to be drawn into a contest of bared teeth and flexed muscles. She had to work with this arrogant man to help Ezaara, not get into a slanging match. So, although her hackles were raised, she smiled sweetly, only baring her teeth a little.

Goren crossed his arms and angled his head, brows furrowed. He gave a weary sigh. "Pleased to meet you." He sounded anything but pleased. "And your message...?"

"Ezaara, the Queen's Rider of Dragons' Realm, is gathering an army to fight Commander Zens," said Ithsar. "I've seen a vision of a terrible war against his shadow dragons and tharuks, a war that could destroy your people, your dragons, and the very land you live on. All will be lost unless we ride to aid Ezaara."

Goren's frown deepened. "Who's paying *you* to fight?" he sneered.

"No one," Ithsar snapped. "We're fighting for the good of the realm, and because Ezaara's my friend."

His eyebrows shot up. "Your friend?"

"Yes." Ithsar met his steely gaze with one of her own. "My closest friend."

He shrugged. "I received a message from Ezaara two days ago. Our troops will be flying north tonight. Ezaara was here only a week and a half ago on her hand-fasting holiday. Rumors from the North do not bode well." He narrowed his eyes. "How much do you know?"

"Not enough. However, we will share what we do know." Saritha lowered her head and Ithsar beckoned Goren to lay his hand upon her dragon's forehead.

Goren stalked over and placed his hand upon the queen's emerald scales. As Saritha shared Ithsar's vision with him, his frown deepened.

When the queen was finished, he swept a hand at the meadow. "You must be tired. Please rest here for the day. You may roam our beautiful city of Naobia as you please." He gave a disparaging glance at their makeshift saddlebags. "We'll provide you with supplies, comfortable saddles, and decent saddlebags. This evening, we'll depart."

"Thank you, that's kind of you." Ithsar inclined her head politely.

"Nothing kind about it," Goren grunted. "If we're going to fight together, it makes good battle sense to fortify your dragons and warriors. If you'd like, our dragons can show yours good hunting grounds for goats and deer."

Saritha wrinkled her nose. *Not more goats.*

Ithsar smiled. Someone had to, and she doubted Goren knew how. "Thanks again, but while we're by the coast, our sea dragons can fish."

"Of course." Goren gave a terse nod, stalked to his dragon, and swung into a finely-crafted saddle Ithsar couldn't help but envy. He pointed at Stefan. "Since you started this mess, I'll leave you to organize the supplies and saddles for our guests."

Within moments, the green guards' wings were stirring Ithsar's robes as they departed and flew back to the city.

Green Guards

The sea dragons were sprawled in the meadow, having a well-deserved rest, their riders leaning against their sides or curled up under their wings, dozing.

Stefan and Ithsar walked through the orchard, discussing what supplies Ithsar's clan would need for their journey. When they were done, Stefan reached up and plucked an enormous piece of fruit from the tree. "Would you like a peach?" he asked. "I don't know if you have them in the Robandi desert."

"This is a peach?" She inhaled the aroma. "It smells different to the dried peaches my mother got from the merchant caravans." No need to mention Ashewar's assassins had slaughtered those very merchants in order to get supplies. She ran her fingertips over the skin. "I didn't know they were fuzzy on the outside." She bit into the peach. Juice ran down her chin. "Oh, this is good." She groaned and took another bite.

"They're delicious, aren't they?" Stefan plucked a few more and sat against a tree trunk. He patted the ground beside him, chewing his own peach. As soon as she was sitting, he handed her more peaches. "Save some for Saritha. Dragons like them too."

Raising an eyebrow, Ithsar replied, "I'm not sharing. These are far too good. Saritha will have to pick her own."

The queen of the sea dragons opened an eyelid and snorted. *"I heard that."* Ithsar threw a peach and Saritha snapped it down. *"Not bad, but I still prefer fish."*

Stefan grinned. "So, what's it like to live in all that endless orange sand?"

Ithsar took another bite and shrugged. "Normal. Dry. Hot. This..." She motioned to the greenery, the trees laden with peaches, the distant mountains. "Um, this is beautiful." She took another bite. "I had no idea peaches were so juicy."

He chuckled. "It'd be hard to tell if you've only ever had them dried. I'll bet there are many things you haven't tried yet. Why don't I show you and a few of your friends around the markets?" He gazed at the sun. "We should have time.

I'll organize the supplies first, and then come back and get you. We can walk. It's not far from here."

From attacking her to hosting her—Stefan certainly was full of surprises—but Ithsar liked his easy, open manner. It was refreshing after growing up under the shadow of Ashewar and Izoldia. She smiled. "I look forward to it."

§

Stefan led Ithsar, Misha, and Nila through the winding alleys of Naobia, the briny tang of sea air wafting through the streets. Ithsar had left Thika back in the orchard with her sisters, but missed his comforting weight on her shoulder. The stone houses were so close, towering three or four stories above them. The streets were narrow and winding, and there was no soft desert sand to mask their footfalls, which echoed loudly off the stone walls like a thousand horses pounding on cobbles.

Ithsar flinched at the rumble of wagon wheels. "Where are you taking us?" Her hand drifted to her hilt, her eyes scanning the mouths of the narrow alleys and lanes that riddled the city.

"To the markets." Stefan grinned as he pressed through the people meandering along the street. "I have some coin. I still feel bad about nearly causing a fight this morning, so I'd like to treat you and your friends."

Nila grinned back, right at home on these narrow, cobbled roads. "Sounds good to me. The more treats, the better." Her dark eyes sparkled in a way Ithsar had seldom seen under Ashewar's rule.

All of them had more space to breathe, to be themselves now—except in this crowded, busy city.

Ithsar sighed. She'd take the wide open spaces of the desert any day. Or maybe one of those pretty meadows, or a house on a hilltop overlooking the fields and sea.

Misha shrugged, her eyes also flitting to the alleys. "Sounds good." Her voice was overly bright, forced.

A man bustled past with a barrow laden with strange vegetables of yellow, orange, red, green, and even deep purple hues. Another wagon rattled along the alley, carrying beautiful bolts of cloth with a lovely sheen—depicting dragons, brightly colored coral, and floral patterns. A tantalizing aroma wafted through the air.

"Oh, that smells good. What is it?" Nila asked eagerly.

"Crum's bakery," Stefan answered. "One of the best. But we're not going there today. I have something better in mind."

"Better than that?" Nila laughed, shaking her dark curls. "I can't wait." They rounded a corner, Nila still laughing, and walked into a piazza.

Ithsar stopped dead in her tracks. Before them was a beautiful fountain—a tangle of sea dragons, glittering in the sun, sparkling water spraying from their maws. Sunshine played across the crystal, making rainbows dance across the scales etched into the dragons' backs. Ithsar approached, running her hand along the smooth tail of a baby sea dragon. Water droplets sprayed her fingers. "This is beautiful. Is it made of glass?"

"That's opaline crystal, from Crystal Lake, two hour's dragon flight north of here," Stefan answered. "Opaline's only found in Naobia. Some say it comes from an extinct volcano that spewed the crystals into the lake, years ago. There's thousands of them up there."

"Sounds beautiful."

"It is." Stefan shrugged. "It's a shame I don't have enough time to take you there. Maybe another time."

Maybe. If they made it back from this war. With a lingering glance at the sea dragon fountain, Ithsar left the piazza and followed Stefan, Misha, and Nila through the hustle and bustle of crowded alleys until they came to a square surrounded by four-story stone buildings with colorful flags and cascading flowers hanging from balconies.

A wave of sights, smells, and sounds crashed into Ithsar's senses. For a moment, she reeled, steadying herself on Misha's arm. The cobbles were filled with people manning stalls, touting their wares. Chickens squawked and vendors shouted. Littlings chased each other, dodging people, laughing and crying out. Voices rose in a babble that would drown out the bray of the loudest camel. And every available space was crammed with people. So many people.

Stefan led them through crowds wearing brightly-colored clothes in all manner of styles, past an old crone selling fragrant herbs, a merchant with fine leather boots, and a jewelry stand.

Ithsar grasped Stefan's arm. "Wait, what are these?" She pointed at earrings shaped like beetles.

"Jewel beetles," he replied. "They live in caves out in the hills. When they die, people collect their shells to make necklaces. Look." He pointed at beetles strung on fine silver chains. Their amber, jade, and turquoise shells were lined with tiny silver and gold veins that winked in the sun. "Would you like one?" Stefan pulled some coin from his pocket and started counting.

Something so dainty in battle? Ithsar shook her head. "No, it's all right, thanks. I was just looking."

Ithsar's mouth watered as they followed Stefan past a boar spit-roasting over an open fire, but it soon stopped watering when she spied a man with a massive cleaver chopping the heads off fish. Mages were selling sticks that shot pretty colored stars into the air. Littlings parted with their coppers with glee, waving the sticks as green and yellow stars exploded from them.

"What are those?" Nila asked. "They look like fun."

"Fire sticks. I loved them as a littling," Stefan replied. His tone made it clear the pretty stars were only for youngsters.

A shame—Ithsar would've liked to try using one.

Minstrels were singing, a flute, shakers, and drums accompanying their pretty voices. After the silence of the oasis, with only the hissing of wind on the desert sands, Ithsar was tempted to block her ears. But she didn't want to seem rude, so she smiled as Stefan pulled her through the throng.

A woman holding a basket of buns jostled her, then a burly man bumped her. "Sorry." He looked down at her. "I didn't see you down there."

True, she was shorter than most of these people, but couldn't they watch where they were going?

Misha nudged her and grimaced.

Nila turned to them, her face radiant. "Oh, isn't it wonderful?" She squeezed their hands. "My father used to bring me here when I was a littling. I loved it. Don't worry, you'll get used to the bustle."

Stefan's eyebrows shot up. "You don't have a market out in the desert?"

Only the type where Ashewar had killed people and helped herself to their wares.

"There is one in the Robandi capital to the south," Nila answered quickly. "But our former chief prophetess only took her personal guard there."

"And none of you were in that guard?" Stefan quirked an eyebrow, staring at Ithsar. "Just how long have you been chief prophetess?" he asked her.

"About as long as you've been a dragon rider," she admitted.

He threw back his head and laughed. "I should've guessed." He flung an arm out at the marketplace. "It must be a shock to see so many people in one place."

"It is a bit," Ithsar admitted.

"Definitely." Misha gave a tight-lipped nod.

He smiled again. "Don't worry, we're nearly there. It'll be worth it, I promise."

Behind his back, Misha rolled her eyes.

"You'd think he was putting you two through torture." Nila giggled. "Come on, enjoy yourselves."

This time, Stefan took Ithsar by the elbow, making sure no one jostled her as he escorted her through the crowd. A delicious aroma danced across Ithsar's tongue, tickling her taste buds and making her mouth water. Something she'd never smelled nor tasted before.

"Come with me." Stefan led her past a table of pretty hand-painted scarves to a stand piled high with little brown and white shapes.

Ithsar flared her nostrils, inhaling. So, this was the source of that mouth-watering aroma.

Stefan raised an eyebrow. "They taste even better than they smell. Your tongue will be in paradise."

Ithsar, Misha, and Nila shot glances at each other, but none of them were brave enough to ask exactly what this stuff was.

Stefan haggled with the woman behind the stall, speaking so rapidly and with such a strong Naobian accent that Ithsar couldn't keep up. He flipped the woman a silver and flashed them yet another smile. "You may each take four pieces of any shape or flavor. This one's the best." He plucked up a brown swirl shaped like a snail's shell and broke it open. A dark gooey substance ran out, revealing a nut in the middle. "It's called chocolate. See, this type has hazelnuts inside." Stefan tossed it into his mouth and licked his fingers.

The aroma hit Ithsar with full force. She couldn't stop salivating, so she picked one up too—a tiny white block with a yellow spiral of lemon rind on top. Ithsar popped the chocolate into her mouth… and couldn't help the groan that escaped her.

"That was lemon," Stefan said. "The rest are just as good, too." He swept his hand in a flourish. "Help yourself."

Misha's eyes flew wide as she tried an orange-flavored one.

Nila squealed as she bit into a dark mint chocolate, then groaned and rolled her eyes. "I'll never be able to eat another thing in my life. I have to move to Naobia and eat these every day."

A ceramic bowl full of chocolates with green leaves caught Ithsar's eye. "What are these like?" she asked shyly.

Stefan's eyes twinkled. "Oh, you'll love those. They're a little different, but you should try one."

When Ithsar bit into the leafy chocolate, her mouth was flooded with juicy sweetness. The inside was succulent, pink, fleshy, and delicious. Her tongue truly was in paradise. "This tastes like fruit, but one I've never had before. What is it?"

"That, my dear Chief Prophetess, is a strawberry ripened under the warm Naobian sun and dipped in chocolate." Stefan bowed. "I promised my treat would be worth putting up with the bustle of the marketplace."

Ithsar laughed, nearly as loud as Nila. "You did. And this is worth it. Do you mind if I have another one?"

He stopped smiling, his eyes serious. "Can you forgive me for my blunder this morning?"

It was Ithsar's turn to grin. "For chocolate, I'd forgive anything."

§

The rustle of wingbeats filled the air as Saritha shot over Naobia, trailed by sea dragons and green guards, on the journey north to join Ezaara and wage war against the shadow dragons. The vibrant, writhing mass of green wings and the pearlescent silver-shot jade and turquoise of the sea dragons merged to create a wild, rippling mosaic that flashed in the sun. Saddles creaked and dragons snorted. The breeze from their wingbeats stirred Ithsar's hair and headscarf. She'd never imagined anything this wondrous. The land was so green, studded with pockets of color—orchards, crops, and tiny settlements of houses. The air swirled with currents and snatches of exotic smells—the briny sea, the tang of fish drying along the coast, freshly turned earth, smoke from hearths, and orchards full of fruit.

The sun dipped, setting the sky on fire. Ithsar gasped as the golden light danced along the dragons' scales, making them look like burnished shimmering gold.

She gave a happy sigh. Everywhere here, people were living in harmony with one another. In the city, she'd seen beggars, but also people giving them coin. And others laughing, being joyous and celebrating their lives with open smiles or friendly hugs.

Her heart ached to feel that same love and acceptance.

"You have me," Saritha hummed. *"And Misha and Nila. And now you have a new friend. It will take time to unlearn the mistrust Ashewar caused in your heart."*

Stefan waved from Fangora's back, then swooped to call out to Nila. The assassin tipped back her head and laughed.

Now loosed from the shackles she'd grown up with, Ithsar knew how Nila felt. Her newfound sense of freedom surged through her veins, making her want to fly harder, faster, higher. But not now, not all at once. Bit by bit, she would forge a new life for her people.

"We certainly will," Saritha replied, *"but first we must fight this war."*

Ithsar's senses reeled as a vision flashed into her mind.

A seething mass of darkness blotted out the sky.

With a start, Ithsar recognized the massive dark dragons as the shadow dragons Ezaara had mentioned in her message.

Plumes of flame shot down onto a village as people fled, screaming. The dark cloud broke up as shadow dragons descended, blasting more flame. Ithsar gasped. There were only four valiant dragons defending this whole settlement against hundreds of shadow dragons.

A beautiful silver dragon with a tall, dark-haired rider shot arrows with a fierce precision that would make any Robandi assassin proud. Her arrows pierced the eyes and skulls of shadow dragons, who plummeted from the sky, shrieking. A sickly dragon with insipid pale-green scales swooped and blasted a horde of tusked furry beasts rampaging through the streets. Tharuks—Ithsar's father had told her about the feral beasts that Commander Zens used to enslave the northerners.

Then she saw Roberto leaping from Erob, the mighty blue dragon Ithsar had met in the oasis. Roberto flew through the air, barreling into Ezaara, knocking her from her gorgeous multi-hued queen. Ezaara and Roberto fought, tumbling toward the ground.

Ithsar's heart pounded as the enormous queen of the dragons dived, her scales flashing with all the colors of the prism-seer, then swooped to grasp Ezaara and Roberto in her talons.

She deposited them on the grass. Roberto straddled Ezaara, but she still fought, bucked and kicked.

And then Ithsar's vision turned cloudy.

Her hands shook. Roberto loved Ezaara. Why would he attack her? And why would her dragon help? *"Saritha, are you able to mind-meld with the green guards and show them this vision? Maybe they'll recognize the village."*

"Yes, I can," Saritha replied.

It seemed like forever before Saritha answered. Meanwhile, the vision flitted over and over through Ithsar's mind.

"*They've told me this is Lush Valley, the former home of Ezaara, she of the golden hair. Wait a moment.*"

Ithsar waited impatiently, her fingers clenching the pommel of her new leather saddle as they rushed through the darkening sky, the landscape slowly swallowed by dusk.

"*The green guards received word five days ago that Lush Valley was under attack last week. The green guards sent reinforcements immediately. Now, the war has moved farther north.*"

"*Where, north? Was Ezaara all right? Why were she and Roberto fighting?*"

Another bone-grinding wait.

"*They don't know, but we'll find out soon enough.*"

"*How long until we get to Lush Valley?*"

"*The green guards say we'll delay our travel by half a day if we go north-east to Lush Valley. We must fly the most direct route, north-west to Dragons' Hold.*"

Ithsar ground her teeth. "*And how long will that take?*"

"*Five days. I know you're impatient to see how Ezaara is, but we're flying our fastest, and we'll need rest if we're to be battle-ready when we arrive.*"

"*Thank you, Saritha. I appreciate your valiant effort.*" There was no point in her being grumpy with Saritha, even though dread gnawed at Ithsar's belly as the dragons flew on through the night.

NORTHWARD

They traveled all night, riders dozing in their saddles, and the next day the enormous mass of green and blue dragons flew on, spreading across the sky, blotting out entire fields with their shadows. Thika's nose twitched as he perched on Saritha's spinal ridge, enjoying the view. Littlings ran outside, laughing and pointing as they passed overhead. The dragons roared, spurting tiny gusts of flame and making the littlings shriek with joy.

Stefan and Fangora swooped and dived.

"Those two seem to like an audience," Saritha commented. *"I'm glad you're more mature. A rider befitting a queen."*

What a shame. Ithsar hesitated, then decided to ask anyway. *"Um, it actually looks like, ah… fun. Are you sure you don't want to try, too?"*

"I thought you'd never ask." Saritha chuckled. *"Hang on."*

Ithsar tucked Thika in her robes and lunged, lying flat against Saritha's back and sliding her arms through the holding straps. Thank the desert sun she now had a good quality Naobian saddle with a harness holding her in.

Saritha plunged, wings furled tightly against her body and her tail whipping up like an arrow. Ithsar's stomach shot right up into her throat. Wind streamed into her face, dragging tears from her eyes. Her headscarf ripped free and her hair flew out behind her.

She couldn't stop grinning. Trees and fields loomed ever closer. When Ithsar could see the needles of the tallest pine, Saritha swooped up and Ithsar's stomach dropped into her boots. Thank the blazing sun she hadn't eaten a heavy breakfast.

"Look at the pretty one. Her scales glimmer silver," an excited littling cried, dancing in the meadow.

"Did you hear that?" Saritha crooned. *"I'm pretty!"*

"Of course you are." Ithsar patted her sleek scales, and they shot back high into the sky.

§

When darkness fell again, the dragons landed in fields of wild grass north of the Naobian forest. The green guards unloaded cauldrons and supplies, and collected wood for a bonfire. Fangora set the wood alight, and while their dragons went off hunting, the assassins and guards set about making soup, throwing in dried vegetables and fresh roots from the nearby forest.

Goren called Stefan over to the cauldrons. "Do your magic, Stefan."

Stefan fetched pouches of herbs and sprinkled them into the soup and tended it until it bubbled for what seemed like forever. Finally, he declared it ready, and ladled soup into mugs for everyone.

Then he came over to Ithsar. "Do you mind if I sit with you?"

She patted the edge of her bedroll and he sat on it, placing two mugs of soup on the ground between them. The firelight danced across his face, making his dark eyes glitter. "You know, because I only imprinted with my dragon a couple of weeks ago, I didn't have time to train properly."

"So you can't fight?" Maybe that's why he was the cook.

Stefan shrugged. "You've seen how good I *wasn't*, the other day."

His comment made Ithsar laugh. "True, you weren't the best at deflecting my attack." She blew on her soup. "And here I was, thinking I'd beaten a mighty warrior."

He chuckled and tilted his head to gaze at the stars. "My whole life, I never thought I'd meet a sea dragon. Or the chief prophetess of the Robandi assassins, let alone have her fight me." He grinned, his teeth flashing.

Ithsar picked up her soup and blew on it. "I never thought I'd meet a sea dragon either. Did you know the former chief prophetess, Ashewar, was my mother?"

"Really?" He said, cocking an eyebrow. "What was she like? Rumors say she was fierce."

Biting her lip, Ithsar met his gaze. She'd been trying not to think about her mother lately. She forced the lump from her throat, trying to swallow, but her voice still came out croaky. "Every bit as fierce as the rumors—and more."

Stefan's smile died. His keen eyes flicked over her face. He nodded, gazing at her and reading her pain. "My parents didn't want me to be a dragon rider," he said at last. "But sometimes we have to make our own lives, despite how they raised us."

Ithsar blinked, fighting her stinging eyes and cradling the warm cup between her hands.

Stefan blew on his soup, waiting before he spoke again, his gaze not leaving her. He motioned at the fire. "See how the flames in the center of the fire burn brightly? But the flames on the edge are the most adventurous, dancing out to test the air and taste everything around them. We're like those flames at the edge of the fire, testing new territory, dancing brightly." He turned back to her, dark eyes earnest. "Dance to your own rhythm, Ithsar, not that of your mother."

Something shifted inside Ithsar. The dark gaping well inside her filled with warmth.

Stefan reached out and took her cup, placing it back on the ground, then squeezed her hand. "I'm your friend. You need not be alone."

She glanced around the fire at the forms of her sister assassins, who were quietly talking, lying in the grass, staring at stars or sitting close to the fire, warming their hands. She shook her head. "I'm not alone."

Stefan smiled, took his hand from hers and passed Ithsar her soup. "Let's eat. We need our strength. Who knows what tomorrow will bring."

Ithsar sipped her soup. A delicious blend of strange herbs danced across her tongue. "Mmm, what's in this?"

"Mint, thyme, tarragon and basil—it's quite a potent mix." He shrugged. "My parents were herbalists. I guess we bring our heritage with us when we become dragon riders."

Ithsar swallowed her soup, warmth trickling into her belly. "It's not as cold here at night as it is in the desert."

"So they say," he replied, "but wait until you get farther north where there's snow on the ground."

"Is it really as chilly as they say?"

Stefan nodded. When they'd finished their soup, he reached into his pocket and pulled out a tiny package wrapped in crumpled waxed cloth. He placed it on the grass and opened it, revealing two of the chocolate delicacies Ithsar had enjoyed at the marketplace.

She sucked in her breath. "For me?"

"Yes, for you."

Ithsar inhaled deeply, already tasting the rich aroma on her tongue. Her mouth watered.

"Go on." He nudged the cloth toward her.

"Is this all you have?" He nodded, so Ithsar took the largest chocolate and broke it, offering him half.

Stefan set the broken chocolate back on the cloth next to the other, and wrapped them and put the package back in his pocket. Then he lay back, sprawled across his bedroll in the grass, his hands tucked behind his head. "Do the stars look different in the Robandi Desert?"

Ithsar leaned back on her elbows and gazed up at the velvet sky studded with twinkling diamonds. Oh, camel dung, the silly things reminded her of her mother's nose studs. "Maybe I can help you learn to fight," she said.

"I'm fine at archery," Stefan replied. "But maybe if we wake early, you can test my sword skills—or lack of them." After a moment, he added, "Thank you."

"You're welcome." Ithsar stared into the fire, the tongues of flame around the edges dancing and reaching for the sky.

§

The next morning, as dawn broke, Ithsar and Stefan finished training.

"You're much better now that you've corrected your balance," Ithsar said, wiping her brow and sheathing her saber.

Stefan rammed his sword into its scabbard and swung his arm in a couple of practice strokes. "I think I've got the hang of those blows, now."

"It didn't take much," Ithsar said as they wandered back to their dragons. "You were already doing a lot right."

Dragons stirred, and the assassins and riders roused themselves from sleep. After a hurried breakfast of bread and fruit, Ithsar and Stefan were repacking their saddlebags as a green dragon landed. A rider staggered from the saddle, his movements sluggish with weariness, and asked after Goren.

After a few hurried words, Goren waved Ithsar over.

The recently-arrived rider nodded. "I have news, Chief Prophetess. The fighting finished in Lush Valley some time ago, but we've spent the last few days patrolling the valley, woods and mountainsides, hunting down tharuks and stray shadow dragons."

Ithsar recounted the vision she'd seen of Ezaara and Roberto fighting in midair until the dragon queen had snatched them in her talons. "Do you have any idea what happened, or is this yet to come?"

The guard nodded gravely. "The folk of Lush Valley said that the enemy turned Ezaara, but that Roberto narrowly prevented her from shooting at her own mother."

"How is that possible? Is she all right now?"

He shrugged. "I'm sorry, I don't know any details. Just that there's still fighting in the North." He turned back to Goren to discuss other business.

Goren gave Ithsar a nod. "Please, get your riders ready. We've a long day's travel ahead. Make sure your women wear the thick cloaks we gave them or they'll freeze further north."

"Thank you." Ithsar went straight back to Saritha, who relayed the message to everyone's sea dragons.

Dracha gods, an enemy that could change a leader's loyalty? She tucked Thika inside her robes to keep him warm, and glanced about at her assassins and Stefan nearby, packing their saddlebags, donning their cloaks and readying for their journey.

She hoped she would never turn on her own friends and sisters.

§

Later that day, they flew over a village. As their shadows fell over the buildings, villagers ran inside, shrieking.

A littling pointed at the sky. "Look."

A man yelled, "They're not shadow dragons, they're green guards."

"Hundreds of them," the littling yelled as her mother herded her inside.

Saritha snorted. *"Hmpff. I never thought I'd be mistaken for a common green guard."*

Ithsar patted her scales. But she couldn't help shudder at the fear the villagers had shown.

KISHA

A large tharuk with a jagged scar down its furry face slammed its tankard on the bar. Saliva dripped down its tusks and its fetid breath washed over Kisha. "Another beer," Scar Face snarled. The tharuk lashed out with its claws, the tattooed 562 flashing on the bald inside of its wrist, and knocked the wooden tankard over, spilling the dregs.

"Just one moment, sir." She took a fresh cloth and wiped the ale off the counter. These brutes seemed to think that their free beer grew on trees; that she could pluck another barrel out of nowhere. With patrons too afraid to enter the tavern after the last brawl with tharuks, she had no income. And the beer was fast running out.

Her grandmother, Anakisha—may she forever fly in peace with departed dragons—would cringe in her grave if she knew tharuks now frequented the Lost King Inn, the oldest inn in Last Stop. Although that hadn't been the name of the inn when her grandmother had been alive. For the thousandth time, Kisha wondered exactly what had happened to Anakisha and Yanir—the ex-Queen's Rider and her consort—and their dragons, when they'd died in battle.

She turned the tap on the barrel and held 562's tankard under it, filling it with the rich golden beer topped with pale foam. This was the last barrel. There'd be mayhem when it was finished and the tharuks learned their precious supply had run out.

A tankard smacked against the other end of the wooden counter and another tharuk snarled as its beer dribbled over the wood.

Cloth in hand, Kisha rushed over to mop the ale up, habitually recalling happy childhood memories to make the soul-destroying job of serving her enemies bearable.

Her favorite was the day she'd discovered she had the gift of prophecy after seeing her dead grandmother in a dream:

Only six years old, she nestled against her mother's lap. Her mother's warm arms enfolded her as she rocked Kisha in front of the fire. "Why couldn't you sleep, my precious blossom?"

"Mama, I saw a lady in my dream. She was wispy, made of clouds, and she had my eyes and the warmest smile I've ever seen."

Ma shot her a sharp look, and then smiled. "Warmer than mine?" she teased, but she'd soon grown serious, asking questions about how the woman looked and what she'd said to Kisha in her dream.

And then Ma had told her something Kisha had never forgotten. "Your grandmother was Anakisha, the last Queen's Rider. She rode upon Queen Zaarusha, the mighty dragon who rules over Dragons' Realm. When Anakisha died, Zaarusha mourned for years and refused to take a new rider." Her mother stroked Kisha's hair from her forehead and kissed her brow. "Your grandmother gave me this, and told me one day you'd be old enough to wear it." She unfastened a fine silver chain from around her neck. At the end of the chain, a pretty jade ring winked in the firelight. "Your grandmother's ring opens a world gate and will take you and a dragon anywhere in Dragons' Realm. To use it, put the ring on, rub it, and say your name, 'Kisha'. Repeat that now."

"Put the ring on, rub it, and say 'Kisha'. That's easy, Mama, because that's my name."

"Yes, we named you after her." As her mother fastened the chain around her neck, Kisha had felt the solid weight of that ring, warm and comforting, against her skin.

Absently, she mopped more beer off the counter and shot a glance at the nearest tharuk. It seemed thirsty. She poured another ale and put the tankard on the bench in front of the beast, keeping her gaze averted. It was a mind-bender. She felt its black eyes probing her as it tried to take over her mind. She slammed a wall around her thoughts.

Her mother had made her practice shielding her thoughts from mind-benders every night before bed—long, boring practices when she'd wished she was outside scampering down the alleys with her friends.

Her tavern, the Lost King, had been named after Yanir, Anakisha's husband and Kisha's grandfather. Her parents had set the tavern up as a place for dragon riders to stay during their arduous journeys across the realm. Now that tharuks frequented the bar, the only dragon rider who'd visited of late was the master healer at Dragons' Hold, Marlies, who'd helped her break up a tharuk brawl two weeks ago. She'd first met Marlies two moons ago when Kisha had given her the—

The door slammed open, jolting Kisha from her reverie. Two more furry beasts entered, their boots thudding dully on her once-finely-polished wooden

EILEEN MUELLER

floors, now marred with mud and gouges. She didn't dare close the inn, or these monsters would probably trash the place. Not that she cared anymore. Things were about to change—not because she had a choice, but because she'd run out of options. She squeezed out the cloth and dunked it into a pail of fresh water.

Kisha forced a polite smile, filled a few more tankards and sat them on the counter. That was the last of the beer. If she didn't get out of here, she'd be ripped to shreds. "I'll get some more food for you, kind sirs."

She stepped into the kitchen and closed the door to the bar. For a moment, she leaned against the door and took a deep breath, then she leaped into action. Kisha took neatly-sliced bacon from the meat safe and threw it, with some eggs, onto the giant skillet on the hearth. She hacked chunks of bread onto an enormous tray, not bothering to arrange everything nicely or garnish it. When the eggs were sputtering and the bacon was sizzling, she slammed the eggs into two giant serving bowls, and the bacon into another. Hopefully this would keep the beasts occupied. But not yet.

First, Kisha had to take care of herself. She'd learned that much tending the bar. She shoveled a few forkfuls of egg into her mouth, straight from the tharuks' bowl—not that it would bother those heinous monsters—and scoffed a rasher of bacon as she dashed around the kitchen. This would be her last hot meal for a while.

Kisha put a waterskin, a sack of dried apples, the last loaf of bread, and a hastily-made sandwich of hot bacon and egg into a rucksack and left it near the back door. As she turned back to the kitchen, the large carving knife caught her eye, so she shoved that into her waistband and stowed an assortment of smaller knives into her rucksack. After a last sweeping glance around the kitchen, Kisha slipped back into the dining room. Stalking between the drinking beasts, she placed the bowls of eggs and bacon, and the tray of bread, onto a long table in the center of the dining area. "Enjoy your meal." She smiled sweetly. As if that would happen.

Tharuks turned from their beer and rushed the table. As the beasts fell on the food, Scar Face snarled, "I eat first. I biggest." The huge monster raked its claws across the head of another tharuk.

The beast fell to its knees, black blood spurting from its cheek and dribbling over its fur.

Another tharuk growled, "I hungry too." Head down, it charged Scar Face and impaled the monster's belly on its tusk.

Scar Face roared and slashed with its claws, but the other tharuk kept running, driving Scar Face against a nearby table. The table flipped, crashed into a wall, and splintered. Shards of wood flew, the bloody beasts brawling amid the debris.

More tharuks jumped in, kicking, slashing, and biting. Blood sprayed across the table and tufts of fur rained over the food. Smaller beasts slunk over to the feast, stuffing their jaws with bloodied eggs, bacon, and bread as the others fought.

Unnoticed by the rampaging beasts, Kisha nipped through the kitchen, donned her rucksack, and threw her cloak over it. She slipped out the back door, across the cobbled courtyard and into the streets, with more than a twinge of guilt and breathing a gusty sigh of relief.

She'd never thought she'd abandon her post at the bar. Had promised her dying mother she wouldn't. She'd even had a vision of Anakisha telling her she was needed here. But now, she had no choice.

Her boots echoed on the cobbles.

A tharuk stepped from the shadow of a nearby building, sizing her up. "Where you going?"

Anywhere but here. In truth, she had nowhere, no one who cared. "I'm taking supplies to my mother on the edge of town," Kisha lied. Somewhere in Last Stop there was a resistance group called Anakisha's Warriors. If only she knew where to find them.

The beast gave her a tusky grin. "Supplies? Let me see."

Kisha undid her cloak and opened her rucksack.

The tharuk bent and reached inside, ripping a chunk of bread off the crusty loaf that would've fed her for days. It stuffed its face, tusks gleaming with saliva. Kisha turned, pretending to fumble with her cloak. She slipped the knife out of her waistband, heart pounding. She'd always wanted to get back at the beasts who'd killed her parents.

As the tharuk bent to snaffle another snack from her rucksack, she plunged her knife at the beast's neck. But the knife glanced off the beast's tough fur. The tharuk spun, bashing her knife away. The blade skittered across the cobbles, out of reach. Kisha was left facing a raging tharuk with a tiny slice in its fur.

Claws sprang from the tharuk's fingertips. It swiped. Kisha ducked. The beast rammed into her, driving her up against the wall of a building. Stone bit into her back as the tharuk grinned, its claws digging into her shoulders, its tattooed number 617 visible on the bald patch inside its wrist.

"Think you could kill me, did you?" 617 smirked, dark saliva dribbling off its tusks.

Dark saliva—by the First Egg, she'd walked straight into a tracker.

"You're dead meat. Tasty meat. Commander Zens say we not eat people. But he's not watching." 617 opened its ugly maw, fangs gleaming in the flickering light of a street lantern. The beast's breath blasted her face, a foul stench wafting over her.

617's dark chuckle made Kisha's spine run cold. Gods, she'd never heard of these monsters eating people. Claws still digging into her shoulder, 617 fastened its other hand around her throat and squeezed.

Kisha thrashed and kicked, but the tharuk's grip tightened. She gurgled, gasping. Stars danced before her eyes. The beast roared in triumph as it squeezed harder. Darkness edged Kisha's vision.

And then 617 slumped against Kisha, its body knocking her to the ground, slamming her elbows and backside onto the cobbles. Rear end throbbing and elbows aching, she struggled out from under the beast.

An arrow was embedded in its back. For a moment, Kisha sat there, stunned, her breath whooshing in and out of her chest in great gulps.

A rope whipped down from a neighboring rooftop. A girl's head appeared over the gutter. "Quick, climb."

Kisha scrambled to her feet, stuffed her knife into her waistband, and threw her rucksack on her back. She grabbed the rope and clambered up the side of the building using her feet against the stones. Panting and arms burning like wildfire, she reached the overhang at the top of the building.

The girl stretched her hand down. "Give me your arm," she hissed, and helped Kisha over the lip of the rooftop onto the tiles.

Kisha slumped, trying to catch her breath.

"No time to rest," the girl snapped. "There could be a tharuk patrol passing at any moment. Follow me." She scrambled nimbly across the rooftop.

Her backside throbbing and head dizzy, Kisha stumbled and slipped on the tiles, then pulled herself upright. There was no point falling to her death, so she followed, more slowly and carefully, trying to ease the pounding of her heart.

A roar shattered the sky, and then more roars. Over the forest, jets of flame lit up the inky night.

Gods, no, shadow dragons were coming to Last Stop.

Anakisha's Warriors

"**D**ragon flame," Saritha murmured, jolting Ithsar awake.

Oh, in the name of the blazing sun, she'd dozed off on dragon-back. No wonder; it was dark already. Ithsar shifted her backside to ease her aching sit bones. They'd been in the saddle most of the day. The glamour of traveling by dragonback was rapidly wearing off.

Far off in the inky night, distant flashes flared in the darkness.

"How far away?" Ithsar asked, snatching Thika from her robes and shoving him into a saddlebag. He clambered out immediately and scampered along Saritha's back. "How am I supposed to keep you safe in battle if you won't stay put?" Ithsar muttered.

"Let me help." Saritha trumpeted and the lizard scurried back into the saddlebags, trembling. Ithsar buckled the straps. If he really wanted, he could probably still sneak out, but hopefully, Saritha's warning would help him stay put.

"So, how far off are we?"

"A couple of thousand wingbeats."

As if that helped. Ithsar checked her weapons, pulled her cloak around her, and peered into the darkness at the distant jets of flame.

§

Kisha dashed over rooftops, glad they weren't leaping over alleys, no matter how narrow they were. Hundreds of pockets of flame lit up the far horizon over Great Spanglewood Forest. A few roiled closer to the far side of town. A huge horde of shadow dragons was coming.

The girl spun to her. "Shadow dragons. We have to hide." She grabbed hold of a rope that was anchored to a chimney top. "Follow me."

What else did that girl think she was going to do, sit on the rooftop and wave? But Kisha didn't say a word. She peered over the edge of the gutter as the girl slipped down the rope and entered an open window halfway down the building. Kisha followed, hands aching and slippery with sweat as she shimmied down the rope and clambered through the window.

In the dim light she could make out a blonde-bearded man, some bedrolls, and a cache of food and waterskins.

The man strode to the windows and pulled the shutters. "I'm Kadran, and this is my daughter Hana." He motioned at the girl who had led her across the rooftops. A door opened and a woman entered with a lantern, placing it on an old rickety table. "And my wife, Katrine."

Hana nodded. "Pleased to meet you."

Katrine approached her, took her rucksack, and placed it against the wall. Then, to Kisha's surprise, she hugged her tightly.

"Hello, Kisha. We've been wanting to reach out to you, but with so many tharuks in the Lost King we haven't had a chance." She held her at arm's distance and looked her over. "It's true, you're Anakisha's granddaughter, aren't you? You have her eyes. Welcome to Last Stop's resistance movement. We call ourselves, Anakisha's Warriors."

Kisha nodded, a lump the size of a dragon egg forming in her throat. So people hadn't forgotten her—or her grandmother.

§

Kadran gestured to a spare bedroll. "You may want to snatch some sleep. We'll be heading out soon to hunt some tharuks, and we may be up fighting all night. Will you join us? Ah, can you fight?"

"My delivery man is Giant John of Great Spanglewood Forest. He trained me."

"You mean *the* Giant John, the best warrior in Dragons' Realm? The one who started our resistance group, Anakisha's Warriors?" Hana asked, eyes round.

"Yes, that Giant John." Kisha sat on the bedroll and unpacked some of her food. "Do you mind if I eat? I'm famished." She unwrapped the waxed cloth to reveal her sandwich and cut it deftly with her dagger, then passed the three of them equal shares. "Giant John still drills me whenever he comes to town. It's been a while, though." Kisha took a bite of her bacon and egg sandwich, glad the tracker hadn't wolfed it down. "I used to train at the back of the inn with some of the locals, but lately there have been too many tharuks around."

Commander Zens' monsters had been frequenting the town for many moons now. Sometimes it felt like they'd always lived under the tharuks' shadow. Ironically, the Lost King had become one of the beasts' favorite haunts.

This week, hundreds of Zens' monsters had flooded the village, taking what they wanted, killing mercilessly, their boots stomping down the alleys, their stench permeating the homes of Last Stop.

Kisha swallowed. "The tavern was running out of ale, and there were too many tharuks for me to fight, so I fled." She turned to Hana. "Thanks for saving my skin. I was a goner back there."

Hana gave her an easy, careless grin. "Anytime."

Kadran patted her shoulder. "You did well to get out. Now get some rest."

Katrine reached out to squeeze her hand. "We're glad to welcome you into Anakisha's Warriors. There are pockets of us throughout Last Stop, fighting Commander Zens and his monsters."

For the first time since her parents had died, Kisha didn't feel alone.

§

Kisha rolled over on the bedroll. Kadran, Katrine, and Hana were already asleep, but she couldn't get comfortable. She tossed and turned, and finally drifted into a fitful sleep.

Anakisha's spirit wisped toward her, those bright blue eyes, the mirror of her own, piercing Kisha to the core.

Kisha was kneeling under a tavern table as tharuks brawled around her. A tankard smashed and its wooden shards skittered under the table, hitting her knees. The boots of furry beasts tromped past her, grinding wood chips into the floor, the way they'd grind her if they caught her. Her hands trembled. Her breath caught in her throat. "Grandmother, I have to abandon the inn. I'm sorry."

"Abandon the inn? No, my littling, you must stay."

A tharuk thudded on top of the table, its arm hanging limply off the edge. Dark blood dribbled off the tabletop , fat black drops hitting the floor. "But the inn's been overtaken by rampaging tharuks."

"You must stay."

"How much longer? What must I do?" A thud overhead. Sharp claws gripped the edge of the table. The tharuk snuffled. Its tusks and snout appeared over the edge. The monster's beady eyes gleamed.

"Follow your heart. You'll know when the time is right."

The tharuk snatched up Kisha and ripped out her throat.

§

Someone grabbed Kisha. Within a heartbeat, she was awake and had palmed her dagger.

Kadran backed away. "I was just shaking you awake. It's all right, Kisha, you're with me, Kadran. And Katrine and Hana—Anakisha's Warriors. We're your friends, remember?"

Heart still bashing against her ribs, Kisha thrust her dagger back in its sheath and grimaced. She'd grown used to sleeping with a dagger under her pillow in case tharuks pummeled down her door. "Sorry, old habits die hard." Gods, what an awful nightmare.

Roars outside made the building shudder. Boots stomped down the streets. How in the name of the First Egg had she slept through that?

Kadran handed Kisha her cloak. "The tharuks are restless tonight and shadow dragons are on the prowl. Want an adventure?" He winked and passed her a bow and quiver.

Katrine placed a hand on Kadran's arm, shooting him a warning glance. "Don't be too eager. I don't want to be responsible for the death of Anakisha's heir."

"We'll take it easy tonight," Kadran said to Katrine. "We won't go for a large troop of tharuks, just pick off some isolated beasts. All over the village, other members of Anakisha's Warriors are doing the same. We'll keep Kisha safe."

Kisha threw on her cloak, bristling and eyes blazing. "I can take care of myself. I've done so for years while hundreds of tharuks visited my tavern." Gods, she'd hoped she'd left that all behind, but now after her dream, she wasn't so sure.

"A fact I don't dispute," Katrine said. "We've been hunting tharuks here for years, too, but I'd hate to face Anakisha in the land of long-departed dragons and tell her I was responsible for her granddaughter's death before she was fully grown."

Kisha bristled again. "I'm nearly fifteen summers."

"Same age as Hana." Kadran clapped her shoulder. "It's all right, Kisha. Katrine and I are just hoping you'll have another twenty summers."

Waiting near the window in her cloak with her bow slung over her back, Hana rolled her eyes. "Come on. She'll be fine; we all will. Let's get going." Hana climbed on to the window sill and headed up the rope.

Katrine followed.

"I'll be right behind you," Kadran said, giving Kisha an encouraging smile.

Cold nipped at Kisha as she clambered up, arms aching by the time she got onto the snowy roof.

"Here." Hana's teeth flashed in a grim smile as she handed Kisha some furs for her boots.

"Good idea." Kisha took them. She didn't want to slip on the snowy tiles and land on the cobbles far below.

They sat on the ridge of the roof and tied the furs around the soles of their boots, then sneaked along the ridge until they came to a gap. The next building was only an arm's length away, but Kisha's heart pounded as she looked at the drop.

"Follow me," Hana whispered and leaped to the next roof without a second thought.

Kisha fastened her gaze upon Hana's face, took a deep breath and jumped over the gap. She landed, tiles barking her knees.

Hana grasped her by the armpits and hauled her to her feet. "That wasn't so bad, was it? You'll get used to this. We've been doing it for ages."

Heart pounding, Kisha nodded as Kadran and Katrine landed on the tiles. They all crept further along the rooftops. Tharuks' boots stomped on the cobbles below. Katrine motioned, and the four of them dropped flat on the rooftop until the beasts had passed. Around a corner, roars and snarls broke out.

"Commander Zens and his troops are up to no good tonight," Kadran muttered.

Well, that was the truth—they'd been up to no good for years. Kisha heard the unmistakable rustle of wingbeats. All four of them snapped their heads up, eyes scanning the dark skies.

"Dragons," hissed Hana.

Many of them, by the sound of those wingbeats.

"Good or evil?" Katrine asked.

Rumors had been rife about the terrible shadow dragons recently plaguing the land. Just last week, the blue guards had killed three shadow dragons outside Last Stop. But a few days ago, things had gone quiet. Then tharuks had flooded the village.

Kisha and her friends readied their bows.

§

The crackle of shadow dragon flame made Ithsar's arm hairs stand on end as they flew toward the village of Last Stop. The wind was chilly, nipping at her through her robes and the heavy archers' cloak that Stefan had given her. Nearby, Fangora skittered and bucked, eager to go into battle.

"*That young one is always so keen to fight.*" Saritha tossed her head. "*One day, he'll get his scales charred and learn a lesson.*"

"*Hopefully, not today.*" It was more likely they'd all be charred. They weren't even at the main battle front, and ahead, the night sky was lighting up like the fire sticks at the Naobian markets. But these were not fire sticks—they were shadow dragons blasting fire and killing innocent people.

Ithsar drew her bow out of the saddlebag and pulled an arrow from her quiver. She nocked her bow as they flew over the town toward the other side where dark beasts were snarling.

"*Remember Ezaara's message and be wary,*" Ithsar said. "*These dragons shoot beams from their eyes that'll slice your skin open.*"

Saritha rumbled.

Although the air was chill, heat roiled toward them as they approached. The dark beasts wheeled in the sky, flapping their ragged wings and shooting spouts of flame onto houses. Screams rang out from the villagers, and stomping echoed from below as furry beasts stalked through the township. Something in Ithsar's bones shuddered. There was something *other* about those dragons— something wrong. Their *sathir* was a roiling dark blanket that coalesced around them, lit up by plumes of flame. Their snarls skittered down her bones.

Saritha rumbled and opened her maw. A shadow dragon wheeled to attack them, its high-pitched screaming splitting through Ithsar's skull. She tensed her jaw and aimed her arrow. The beast swept closer, yellow beams shooting from its eyes, slicing dangerously close to Saritha.

Ithsar loosed her arrow. It punctured the beast's neck. Shrieking, it plummeted onto a rooftop below, splintering the wood and thatched roof and sending the occupants screaming along the streets. The dragon roared and leaped from the ruins of the house, a piece of jagged wood impaled in its hind leg. In midair, the shadow dragon twisted, yanking the wood from its leg with its jaws, and flung it down into the street. The jagged timber hit a man and knocked him to the stone.

Ithsar shot another arrow, missing as the dragon swerved past her. Once again, shrieking filled her head. The next time, she shot the beast right through the eye.

In a flash of green wings, Goren, the green guard leader, speared past Saritha and gave Ithsar an encouraging nod.

That was probably as close to approval as she was going to get, so Ithsar nodded back and smiled. That man's heart was as hard as camel toenails. She nocked her arrow and spun to aim at another feral shadow dragon. Her arrow flew true, hitting the beast in the temple. Golden beams sprang from its eyes and sliced toward her. But Saritha plunged and shot a volley of flame at the beast's belly.

Suddenly, ten beasts were upon them. Stefan whooped as he and Fangora shot forward, flaming a black dragon until it fell from the sky. Nila and Misha wheeled, scales blurring in the flame from shadow dragons' maws as they fought to vanquish their enemy. Saritha roared gusts of flame at anything with ragged dark wings, and Ithsar shot arrow after arrow into their skulls, chests, and eyes.

§

Stefan hunched down over Fangora's neck as they raced over the rooftops. Screams rose from an alley. Two tharuks were chasing a littling through the streets.

Fangora roared. *"That's not playing fair, so many of them chasing a littling. Those filthy stinking beasts reek from way up here. Let's get them."*

"I'm with you." Stefan nocked his arrow and aimed, loosing it. The arrow thwacked into a tharuk's back. It slumped to the cobbles, but the other one kept running. The littling glanced back, screaming, and slipped in a patch of snow.

Stefan flung his bow onto his back, dragged a rope from the saddlebags, and tied it onto Fangora's saddle. *"I'm going down, Fangora. Swoop so I can get between those buildings."*

Fangora descended. Stefan grabbed the rope and jumped. The jolt made his dragon list to one side and nearly yanked Stefan's shoulders from his sockets. *"Sorry."* Arms burning, he lowered himself, hand over hand, down the rope. He swung between the buildings and aimed his boots at the beast chasing the littling. He kicked the tharuk in the head, knocking it to the ground. Stefan dropped to the cobbles and scooped the littling up in his arms.

She sobbed and howled.

Gods, he had to do something to keep her quiet. He reached into his pocket for his chocolate and unwrapped it, shoving it at the girl's mouth. She bit into it, her eyes wide with wonder.

"Now be nice and quiet. We're going to hide from the monster." Stefan spun and dashed off down a side alley, the littling jostling against his side. There was a roar behind him. The tharuk he'd knocked over was already after them. "Where do you live?" Stefan asked.

She shrugged, eyes wide and bottom lip trembling. Gods, oh gods, he was playing nursemaid to a littling in the middle of battle—some great warrior he was. Roars echoing behind him and flame lighting up the sky, Stefan pelted around a corner...

...and smacked into a group of three tharuks.

A beast whirled, claws out, and threw Stefan and the girl against the stone masonry of a decrepit building. Stefan cradled the girl against the impact and hit the stone with his shoulder. He scrambled to his feet and tugged the girl to hers as the monsters advanced. Gods, his shoulder was throbbing.

A burly tharuk with a jagged scar along its snout snarled, "Bought us a littling, have you?" Saliva dribbled off its tusks, splattering onto the cobbles. The three tharuks prowled toward him, claws out.

He thrust the littling behind him, near the wall, and pulled out his knives, one in each hand. "Run," he whispered.

She scampered off around the building.

A small beast swiped at him with its claws, barely missing Stefan's face. He ducked, the swish of air whistling past his cheek, its claws snagging on the end of his hair and ripping out a clump.

"Plenty more where that came from," he muttered, scalp burning. Regaining his footing, he chucked a knife at the beast's chest. But the tharuk dodged and his stupid knife bounced off its shoulder and slid across the cobbles, slamming against the building on the other side of the alley.

Great—one knife against three monsters. If only he hadn't left his sword in his dragon's saddlebag. Who'd have thought he'd need it on dragonback?

Fangora roared, shaking snow from the roof of the building above. A smattering landed on Stefan's hair, but a heavy clump hit the tharuk, distracting it. Stefan lunged and thrust his knife at the beast.

The tharuk swung its arm and sent the weapon flying out of Stefan's hand. The knife ricocheted off the building and clunked to the cobbles.

Stefan swallowed, backing up. Now he had no weapons, only his wits and his dragon. *"Fangora, where are you?"*

"Can you get away from those beasts?"

Before Stefan had a chance to tell Fangora he was cornered, a gust of flame and blistering heat roiled down through the alley. He dived onto the ground as the fire hit a tharuk. It fell screaming to the cobbles. The stench of burned fur and fried meat clogged the narrow alley.

The burnt ends of Stefan's hair stank too. Gods, his dragon was too young, keen and fire-ready. *"Ah, you nearly burned me too,"* Stefan mind-melded. *"I might have to manage this alone."* He scrambled to his feet as the remaining two tharuks got to theirs and lunged for him. They hit Stefan like a wave, slamming him to the ground and pinning him against the cobbles. One tharuk straddled his legs and the other squeezed its furry hands around his throat, its claws piercing his skin. Warm, wet blood trickled down his neck.

"Fangora?" No answer. Oh gods. Stefan swallowed. This was it.

Last Stop

Ithsar hunched low over Saritha as her dragon flamed a bunch of monsters fighting people in the village square. *"It's no good, Saritha. If I fire my arrows, I might hurt the villagers."*

"I'll let you down." Saritha swooped down between the snow-laden buildings into the square and Ithsar slipped from her saddle.

As the queen took to the sky, Ithsar exhaled forcefully, trying to expel the stench of burning fur from her nostrils, and snatched an arrow from her quiver. Misha swooped down on Ramisha. Her dragon snatched up two tharuks in his talons, knocking their heads against each other, and tossed them to the cobbles where they bounced, then lay still. Screams of women and littlings rang from the nearby alleys. Men bellowed, rushing off with their swords ready.

Upon the rooftops, foul shadow beasts breathed fire down at the men rushing to defend their families. Purple rippling stains, so dark they were almost black, wreathed the vicious creatures—the shadow dragons' *sathir*. Ithsar shot a shadow dragon in the eye. It plummeted, shrieking, to the square below, its legs thrashing against the ground. Even in its death throes, a yellow beam bounced from its good eye, slashing at nearby villagers.

"Quick, Saritha, before it hurts anyone else."

Saritha swooped down and burned the beast. Ramisha landed and Misha dismounted.

Ithsar and Misha raced toward the fighting tharuks. Ithsar fired an arrow and hit a tharuk in the thigh. It collapsed onto the cobbles, howling, and swiped its claws across a man's leg. Crimson stained the snow as the man staggered toward another tharuk and drove his sword through its neck. The beast twitched and then lay still. The man spun to meet another beast, his sword striking its breastplate and glancing off. Then he stumbled to one knee while still trying to fight off the monsters.

Ithsar flung her bow over her shoulder and yanked her saber from its sheath, charging into the fray. Her first blow took out a small wiry tharuk that had just killed a littling.

"That horrible beast, picking on small ones." Saritha swooped and plucked up a tharuk, ripping it apart with her talons.

A tharuk whirled, arm flung high to slash a man's throat. Ithsar lunged and drove her saber under its armpit, behind its breastplate. Dark sticky blood spurted from the beast's mouth. Its eyes glazed over and it slumped to the cobbles in an ever-spreading pool of black fluid.

Still more tharuks came. Ramisha flamed a group of tharuks, driving them back from the mouth of an alley to stop them from entering the square. Nila and her dragon, Nilanna, thudded to the square, and Nila raced over. Nilanna shredded a tharuk with her talons and then leaped into the air to fend off a shadow dragon.

Nila and Misha dived in, years of training kicking in as they whirled and spun, slaughtering the beasts with skill and precision that Ithsar hadn't even realized they'd possessed. Ithsar swung her saber beside them, the thrill of the battle singing through her veins. The bodies of the tharuks piled up. Soon, there were only a few left fighting.

A littling burst into the square, screaming about monsters and pointing back down an alley. "Help him," she screamed. "A dragon rider, trapped by tharuks."

The girl's face was covered in chocolate stains. Ithsar's heart sank. *"Saritha, where are Fangora and Stefan?"*

"I don't know," Saritha answered, flinging a tharuk against a building. The beast's body hit the stone and crumpled.

Only two tharuks remained in the square. Ithsar had to find Stefan. "Where's the dragon rider?" Ithsar barked at the littling.

The littling's face crumpled into tears as she pointed back down the alley.

Blood thrumming through her veins, Ithsar ran. She pounded around a corner and stopped, her blood chilling.

Stefan was lying on the ground, an enormous tharuk crouched over him with its claws digging into his throat. Another straddled his legs, pinning him in place. Stefan gurgled and spluttered, blood running from his neck.

On silent feet, Ithsar lunged and drove her saber at the beast on his legs, but as she neared, her shadow danced across Stefan's face. Alerted, the beasts both spun. The larger one barged into Ithsar, slamming her backward onto the cobbles. She rolled through a pile of ice and snow, and bounded to her feet. Then danced in, feinting left. The beast took her ruse, and lunged. She sidestepped and slashed her saber across its neck. Tufts of fur flew through the air and dark blood sprayed as the beast dropped dead.

The other beast bellowed.

Ithsar danced in close, and then sprang through the air, kicking her foot at the beast's chest. It landed in the snow and skidded backward. She landed nimbly, and drove her saber through the monster's throat. Dark blood gushed, spraying her saber and legs. The beast gurgled and was still.

Ithsar pulled her saber from its neck and wiped the blade upon its fur.

"Wow." Stefan sat up. Despite his pale face and the blood trickling down his neck, his eyes were shining. "You were amazing."

She panted, wiped her saber again, and sheathed it. As the hilt smacked the top of the sheath, she gave a grim smile. "Thank you."

"No, thank you." He scrambled to his feet. "You saved my life."

"Are you all right?" Ithsar eyed his neck.

"Nothing but a scratch." He staunched the blood with his hand. "Let's get back to our dragons."

A thundering roar shook the rooftops and snow slid to the ground, splattering into a pool of mush at their feet. Ithsar grabbed Stefan's free hand and they ran back to the square.

The cobbles were littered with charred carcasses of tharuks and shadow dragons. A smoky haze filled the air. Dead villagers lay slumped on the cobbles. Roaring shadow dragons shot overhead. Flames blazed in the distance.

Ithsar ripped a piece of fabric off her robe and wiped his neck. He was right; it wasn't too bad. "You'll need to get that treated by a healer," she said, tearing off another strip and binding his wound. Then she clasped Stefan's arms tightly. "Stay on dragonback. It's safer."

Stefan shook his head. "I had to get down. A littling was in trouble."

Ithsar nodded. "I know. I think she liked your chocolate."

Fangora landed with a thud and nuzzled Stefan. He grinned. Saritha landed, her talons clattering on the cobbles. They climbed onto their dragons and took off toward the distant roars and the flame punching through the night sky.

§

Kisha aimed her arrow and loosed it at a tharuk racing along the alley after a villager. Roars broke out on the far side of town. Snarls and answering roars thundered above and flame lit up the night sky. A wing of shadow dragons flew overhead.

An arrow swished past her cheek as Kadran fired at a tharuk who was slamming a man against the side of a building.

"Quick," hissed Katrine, grabbing her hand.

They scrambled across rooftops, slipping in the snow, as a volley of answering arrows hailed on the roof behind them. Panting, they perched between two chimneys and nocked their bows.

Hana and Kadran shot at shadow dragons wheeling in the air. Katrine and Kisha drew their bows and fired upon tharuks thundering down the street. A blaze of fire lit up the night sky as a shadow dragon shot over the rooftops, claws out, heading for the square.

Despite her thundering heart, Kisha took aim and fired. Her arrow nicked the edge of the dragon's wing, shredding its wingtip. The beast's shrieks of pain echoed through her head as if someone was pounding it with a mallet.

"Look out," Kadran yelled, thrusting Kisha to the rooftop as a volley of flame and blistering heat roiled in the air above them.

"We have to get out of here. It's too dangerous," Kadran said. "Two roofs over, there's another rope. Let's go."

Kisha scrambled to her feet and rushed along the roof after Hana and Katrine. A screech ripped through her head that made her knees buckle. She stumbled on the steep-gabled roof and started sliding. Kadran threw himself to the ridge top and flung out his bow. Kisha grabbed it and scrabbled with her feet as, slowly, he pulled her back up.

"Thank you," Kisha panted.

More roars split the sky as dragons converged over the village. Green and turquoise scales flashed in the light of surges of flame above them. Blue guards? Naobian green guards? But this was so far from Naobia…

Dark leathery wings obscured the stars. Twin beams of light shot through the night from fiery golden eyes. The beams sliced through the bow in Kisha's hands. The weapon shattered into smoldering pieces.

"Hurry," Hana cried from the end of the rooftop.

Still clutching a remnant of her bow, Kisha ran, pounding across the ridge, Kadran close behind. The shadow dragon swept over them again, its scream cutting through Kisha's mind.

"Look out," Katrine screamed, yanking her across the rooftop, nearly pulling her shoulder from its socket. When they reached a massive drop, Katrine didn't stop running. Kisha followed blindly, flying through the air.

She landed on a roof below, jarring her legs through her knees to her hip sockets, and scrambled over so Kadran could land behind her.

Ahead of them, Hana turned and screamed, "No!"

Heat roiled over them. Kisha flung herself onto the tiles. An agonized shriek rang out behind her. The stench of charred fabric and burnt flesh filled her nostrils. Kisha glanced back and her jaw dropped in horror.

Kadran was engulfed in a flaming pyre.

§

Ithsar, Stefan, and Misha sped away from the square, their dragons' wingtips nearly touching as they glided over the roofs. The fighting in this quarter had now been subdued, but on the other side of town, flame lit up the night sky and screeches made Ithsar's nape hair prickle.

"There's something off about those beasts," Saritha grumbled. *"They're strange, unnatural."*

Screeches ripped through Ithsar's head, making her temples pound and her senses reel. She gripped onto the saddle, panting, knuckles clenched tight, and gritted her teeth, trying to withstand it. This was nothing, she told herself, nothing compared to the burns, brands, and beatings Izoldia had given her. They had to save these villagers at all costs.

"Not at all costs, Ithsar," Saritha replied. *"I've only just met you—I don't want to lose you."*

Thika scrambled out of Saritha's saddlebag and across Ithsar's lap. She snatched him up and thrust him back inside as ragged dark wings flapped above them. Saritha shot up, belching a volley of flame at a shadow dragon's belly. The beast shrieked and plummeted through the air, its wings alight. It crashed through a roof, setting the thatch ablaze. A family screamed and raced outside as the dragon's burning body engulfed their house in flame.

"Gods, now we're destroying their homes." Ithsar's throat clenched.

"It's nothing compared to what those beasts are doing," Saritha answered.

In the next alley over, two shadow dragons were flaming thatch. The screams of burning people echoed up through the volley of flames, and the stench of crisped flesh filled the air. Misha and Nila shot in, Ramisha and Nilanna flaming the dark dragons from above. Fangora joined them, setting another dragon's wings alight, as Stefan fired arrows. The shadow dragons plummeted onto the buildings in a spray of cinders and sparks. The flames leaped higher, consuming their bodies.

"I want to save the villagers," Ithsar cried desperately, "not destroy them."

"Here's our chance." Saritha shot toward a shadow dragon chasing a ragged band of people running across rooftops. They slipped and slid, leaving gouges in snow-laden tiles, the dragon's flames nearly upon them. Ithsar and Saritha dived in. As they neared, the shadow dragon extinguished its flames. Yellow beams shot from its eyes, slicing into the flesh of a man at the back of the ragtag group. He stumbled and slipped off the ridge of the roof, leaving bloody red gouges in the snow.

Saritha dived, but before they could reach him, the shadow dragon dived, and his body flared in a burst of fire and fell off the roof near a horde of tharuks. Saritha sped alongside the dark dragon, and Ithsar fired an arrow into its skull. The scream in her head intensified, and then stilled. The beast's body flipped and smacked into the building, scattering roof tiles, and dropping into the street.

Saritha landed on the rooftop.

Ithsar called out, "Come, let us ferry you to a safe place." Although where a safe place was, she didn't quite know. In the dark, it was hard to tell who was winning and who was losing. Bursts of flame illuminated green scales and then black. Yellow beams sliced through the sky. Arrows whooshed. It was chaos. Three people ran back to Ithsar—two girls about her age and a woman.

The woman clambered up behind Ithsar, sobbing, "M-my husband."

"I'm sorry for your loss," Ithsar said. What else could she say? There was nothing that could erase the horror this woman had just experienced.

One of the girls climbed up, but before the other could get upon Saritha's back, a shadow dragon arrowed for them, a green guard on its tail. Saritha tensed and sprang, then swooped over the roof to snatch up the remaining girl. She soared over the village, back to the square, as the harrowing wails of shadow dragons skittered down Ithsar's bones.

THE LOST KING INN

Saritha flew across the rooftops, the snow now scattered with ash and debris, and spiraled down toward the square, the girl still hanging from her talons. Avoiding the dead bodies of shadow dragons, tharuks, and villagers, she deposited the girl on the cobbles, then settled back on her haunches. Ramisha and Nilanna were picking up corpses in their talons and piling them at one end of the square.

Ithsar dismounted and helped the woman and the other girl off Saritha.

"I'm Ithsar," she said, holding out her hand, as was the custom of these northerners.

The old woman shook it. "And I'm Katrine. Thank you for rescuing us from those terrible beasts."

The sky on the far side of the village still blazed with fire, although there now seemed to be more green dragons than dark ones. Despite the shadow dragons' screeches in her head, Ithsar smiled. "Don't thank me. Please thank Saritha." She hesitated. "I'm, um, very sorry about your husband."

"He died fighting to save lives. An honorable death." The woman's eyes were bright with unshed tears and she held her head high. She gestured at the girls. "My daughter, Hana, and this is Kisha, Anakisha's granddaughter."

Ithsar shook the girls' hands too. The girl with the vibrant blue eyes and dark hair was the granddaughter of the legendary Anakisha? Even Ithsar had heard the stories of the bravery and courage of the former Queen's Rider who'd been lost in battle nineteen years ago.

Saritha nudged Ithsar with her snout. *I'd like to meet Anakisha's heir.*

"Kisha, please place your hand on Saritha's forehead. She'd like to introduce herself to you."

"It's you." Kisha stared at Ithsar, those bright blue eyes wide. "I saw you in a vision. I knew you'd come."

"Me?" Ithsar frowned. "You have visions?"

Nodding, the girl touched Saritha's snout.

"You have much in common," Saritha thrummed in Ithsar's mind. *"She has a keen mind, special lineage, and the gift of prophecy, like you."*

Her voice breathy, Kisha murmured, "Jade scales that sparkle silver. Out of all the dragons' scales I've seen growing up, I've never seen any like hers."

"That's because Saritha is a sea dragon," Ithsar said. "I only imprinted with her a moon or two ago. She's queen of the sea dragons and I am the new chief prophetess of the Robandi assassins." It still felt strange to say it aloud.

Kisha's face lit up like the blazing desert sun. "So you see visions too? I've always wanted to meet someone else who could."

"Yes, I do. I had a terrible vision, and then received a message via raven, so I've come north to help Ezaara, the new Queen's Rider."

Kisha nodded. "Good. If you'd like a place to stay, I can offer—"

A tavern door burst open and two brawling tharuks spilled out onto the cobbles, gouging each other's eyes.

"They must've run out of food," Kisha said. "That's my tavern, the Lost King Inn, named after Anakisha's husband, Yanir. In fact, this entire town of Last Stop was the last place Anakisha stopped before they were both lost in battle. If you help me clear out the tharuks, you'll have a place to stay." Her eyes flicked to the dragons. "The riders, at least."

With a roar, one tharuk slit the gut of the other, then surged to its feet, bellowing, and dashed back inside. Crashes and the smash of splintering wood came from the tavern.

Ithsar grinned and held her sword high, issuing the battle cry of the *Sathiri,* "Avanta!"

Misha and Nila flocked to her, and with Kisha, Hana, and Katrine, they surged in through the tavern door.

Ithsar spun, slicing her sword through a tharuk's gut. Another tharuk leaped from the table through the air. Nila lunged, impaling the beast on her sword. The tharuk crashed into her, the impact driving her to her knees, the point of her saber poking through its back.

Nila kicked the tharuk away and sprang onto a table, slashing another's throat. Misha spun her saber, slicing a beast's arm as it lunged toward her. Two enormous beasts lifted a table and threw it across the room at the assassins. For a moment, their reflections glimmered in the dark polished wood as it flew toward them. Ithsar rolled, Misha lunged and Nila ducked. The table crashed into the wall, splinters and shards flying across the tavern. A large chunk of wood impaled itself in a tharuk's eye. It fell to its knees, clutching at its face, screaming, as dark blood sprayed over them.

And then Ithsar saw Thika scurrying across the floor. Oh no! That silly lizard was going to get himself killed.

§

Stefan and Fangora landed in the village square. A window in a tavern shattered as a tharuk was hurled through it into the dirt-strewn snow. More gouges in the snow showed where dragons had been. There was a pile of bodies, and corpses scattered nearby, as if someone had been interrupted while clearing away the dead.

"Saritha, Nilanna, and Ramisha are battling shadow dragons, but they told me their riders are fighting inside that building." Fangora sprang across the square. Stefan slid to the ground and ran toward the tavern.

The door smashed open, ripped off its hinges as an enormous tharuk charged outside.

Stefan was ready. He swung his sword, slashing at the brute and scoring its face. The beast's eyes slitted. Stinking breath and sticky blood washed over Stefan as a fury of claws and fur dived at him. He ducked and swooped in from the side the way Ithsar had taught him, driving his sword through the beast's thick fur. With a crunch of bone he pierced its ribs. An agonized snarl ripped from the beast as it fell to its knees. Stefan drove his sword until the hilt smacked fur, and ducked to avoid the tharuk's flailing claws. The monster twitched and stilled, lifeless.

Pressing his foot on the tharuk's torso, Stefan yanked out his sword, and raced into the Lost King.

Snarls and roars split the air. The tavern was a whirl of orange-robed assassins' swirling cloaks, tufts of flying fur, and pools of dark blood. Dead tharuks were slumped over tables and on the floor, but more were still fighting.

He gasped. A tharuk was chasing Ithsar. She nimbly leaped over a broken chair and swiped her saber at the beast. It slashed and she jumped backward—awesome footwork, but she didn't realize she was about to be cornered.

Stefan sprang onto a tabletop, raced across it, and jumped over a tharuk's sharp, swiping claws. Narrowly missing an assassin's blade, he landed amid smashed crockery and splattered egg and ran.

With rapid swipes of its claws, the tharuk drove Ithsar against the bar. It kicked her saber out of her grip and jammed her neck against the lip of the counter, snarling over her. Ithsar gurgled, eyes wide, and kneed the tharuk's stomach. She palmed a dagger from her sleeve.

Stefan wasn't taking chances. He plunged his sword between the beast's shoulder blades. It slumped over Ithsar and they fell onto the blood-slicked floor. Only black blood, thank the First Egg. Stefan kicked the beast aside and lifted Ithsar in his arms. Gods, she was so tiny. "Are you all right?"

"I'm fine." Her eyes blazed. "I could have got out of that on my own. Now, put me down."

"But—" Stefan choked on his reply and put her on her feet. He scrubbed a hand through his hair. "Oh, sorry for interfering." Like flaming dragon's breath, he was.

Ithsar grinned. "Now we're even. One save each."

He bit back a smile. She'd been teasing him. Stefan snatched his sword out of the dead tharuk's back and spun back to the fight.

KITCHEN BRAWL

One moment, Kisha had been fighting a tharuk next to Katrine, swords flashing. The next, Katrine was chasing the tharuk over a table— and Kisha was facing another beast on her own. The brute whacked her arm, smashing her sword out of her grip. And then, red eyes glinting with malice, it charged.

Kisha dashed past a lanky lad in rider's garb and Ithsar, who were fighting a tharuk near the bar. She threw a tankard at the charging brute's head. The tharuk shrugged it off and kept coming. She ran into the kitchen, scanning the benches for a weapon. Snorting, the tharuk chased her. It thundered past a counter, tusks angled to rip through her body.

Kisha yanked a heavy frying pan from the range and swung. The clang of the tharuk's tusks against metal made her ears ring and her wrists and elbows throb. Kisha swung again, but the tharuk ducked out of the way and snarled at her, its tusks dripping dark saliva.

Another tharuk crashed through the kitchen door, smashing it to pieces. "What we got here?" It grinned—the ugliest smile Kisha had ever seen.

Kisha threw the pan. It glanced off a bench and hit one of the tharuks in the knee. She grabbed the nearest thing she could—a wooden rolling pin—not as heavy as the pan, but easier to wield. As the first tharuk ran at her, she swung the rolling pin and smacked it in the head. The rolling pin shattered in two, the top half flying into a barrel. The tharuk reeled, unsteady on its feet. Kisha leaped onto the kitchen bench and thonked the tharuk on the head with the other half. The monster crashed to the floor.

Snarls ripped through the kitchen. The second tharuk lunged. Pain sliced through her calf as its claws raked her flesh. Oh gods, that *hurt*.

She scrambled over the bench, keeping her head low so she didn't bump the wooden utensil rack hanging by chains from the ceiling. There, if she could get to the empty cauldron on a hook by the hearth, she might have a chance. But the tharuk was faster. It surged over the bench, snatched Kisha up, and sprang to the floor. Roaring, it held her aloft, shaking her body until her teeth clattered.

More tharuks burst through the doorway.

"I got one," the beast roared, shaking Kisha like a rag doll.

Ithsar and her assassins surged, like a sea of orange, across the bodies of broken tharuks on the tavern floor, and through the kitchen doorway. Dodging claws, hacking with their sabers, spinning and slashing. Dark blood sprayed the kitchen. Tharuks fell among the bloody rain.

A slim assassin with dark curly hair launched herself off a bench, caught the utensil rack and, in a spray of wooden spoons, ladles, and roasting forks, swung her feet into the belly of the tharuk holding Kisha. It staggered and fell to one knee, still clutching her.

Women surrounded the beast, their sabers and daggers at its neck, belly and groin.

"Unhand that girl or die." Although Ithsar was tiny, her voice rang with steel.

The assassin with the dark curly hair gave a wicked grin. "Die anyway, brute." She plunged her sword into its neck. It slumped, dropping Kisha on the floor.

"I'm Nila," the curly-haired assassin said. "Is this your inn?"

Kisha nodded and scrambled to her feet, breathing hard. "Yes, it is."

Nila and Ithsar helped her into the taproom. Slain tharuks lay among broken crockery, blood, mashed food, and beer. A table was shattered against a wall with its legs upended. Broken chairs and wood shards littered the tavern, and there was even a tharuk whose head had been impaled with a chair leg. The stench of the beasts was overwhelming.

Kisha's foot slipped in a pool of sticky black blood, but she caught herself before she fell. Aagh, she didn't want to be bathed in the blood of those monsters. It was bad enough smelling them from here—a stench she'd put up with since they'd killed her parents.

Gods, how was she ever going to clean up this mess?

A tall, lanky boy about her age wiped his sword on a tharuk's matted fur and stepped over it. "Hopefully, that's the last of them." He cocked his head. "Must be, there's no more roaring outside."

He was right. After hours of roars, the skies were uncannily silent.

"Hey, Ithsar," he called, "maybe our dragons have slaughtered those shadow dragons too." He grinned at Kisha and held out a hand splattered in black blood. Glancing down at his fingers, he hurriedly wiped his hand on his breeches and offered it again. "I'm Stefan. Nice to meet you."

It was absurd to be fussing over niceties when she was standing ankle deep in debris and dead tharuks, but Kisha shook his hand anyway, then burst out laughing. "And I'm Kisha. Welcome to the Lost King Inn."

"Looks lovely." He wriggled his eyebrows, grinning.

"Ah, Kisha, my sisters and the green guards require a place to stay. If we help you sort out this mess, will you provide us with a roof for the night?" Ithsar asked, as if she hadn't already offered, and winked at Kisha.

The weight of a dragon lifted from Kisha's shoulders, and air rushed back into her lungs. "Oh, thank you. Cleaning up would be rather daunting on my own."

Katrine snatched up a broken chair. "Some of this furniture is beyond repair. I suggest we make a pyre in the courtyard and burn these monsters, too." She quirked an eyebrow at Ithsar. "I'm assuming your dragons wouldn't mind setting these beasts alight."

"I'm sure they'd like nothing better," Ithsar replied.

Stefan chuckled and grabbed up an armful of smashed wood. "I've asked Fangora to bring us more help."

Outside, dragons thudded down into the square. The green guards landed, looking battle-weary and haggard. Orange-robed assassins flooded through the door. Everyone got stuck in, carrying broken furniture outside, dragging tharuks out by their boots and dumping them onto the pile in the corner of the square. They cleared bodies from the rest of the square and shoved the wood from Kisha's broken furniture onto the mound.

Kisha threw some chair shards onto the hearth in the kitchen and boiled up a cauldron of water. Then, she and those valiant women and men scrubbed and cleaned until there was not a drop of tharuk blood left.

When they were finished, she invited all of the green guards, Anakisha's Warriors, and the Robandi Silent Assassins to dine. "Tharuks have devoured all the food in my kitchen, but I don't think they found my secret supplies." Kisha peeled back a rug and lifted the trapdoor that led down to the cellar.

A couple of burly green guards helped her carry up some huge jars of pickles, eggs, a barrel of salted pork, another of flour, and some apple juice. With a few herbs and spices, she soon had a hearty stew in the cauldron and some flatbread toasting over the fire.

Although half the chairs and most of the tables were still intact, there wasn't enough space for everyone to sit, so men and women leaned against walls and sat cross-legged on the floor. They used the inn's entire supply of crockery and cutlery.

Once they'd eaten their fill, Kisha stood. "Thank you so much for ridding the Lost King Inn of tharuks and helping me clean up. My grandmother, Anakisha, the former Queen's Rider, would be proud of you all."

Ithsar stood, too. "I'd like to thank everyone for rising to the challenge of preserving this village. We thank Anakisha's Warriors and mourn their losses." She nodded at Katrine. "We've been lucky that we're not mourning the loss of one of our own tonight. According to reports from Katrine, there are many more shadow dragons in the North. Tomorrow we'll fight again. But tonight, we'll rest and be thankful for the new friendships we're forging." Ithsar's eyes flitted to Stefan and Kisha. "Long may our bonds last after these adventures. Long may we protect Dragons' Realm."

Assassins, warriors, and riders cheered and raised tankards of apple juice.

§

Later that evening, Kisha carried a stray chair leg outside and threw it onto the flaming pyre. The heat was melting the snow on the cobbles, sending rivulets into the gutters on the edge of the square.

Ithsar was moving among small groups of assassins, green guards, and their dragons, as they mended injuries and tidied up the square. Nila was tending her dragon, Nilanna, her slim form bent over its foreleg as the dragon held it up for inspection. Kisha wandered over. A deep slice scored the dragon's flesh. Nila turned to Kisha, eyes bright, and blinked.

It looked as if the brave assassin was trying not to cry.

"Are there any healers in Last Stop?" Nila asked.

"Not anymore. Please, let me see." Kisha bent to examine the wound. The dragon snuffled her shoulder. "It's a clean gash. How did she get it?"

"From one of those yellow beams from a shadow dragon's eye." Nila winced. "She's in a lot of pain."

Ithsar strode over. "Kisha, do you have any of that special healing juice that Ezaara, she of the golden hair, uses?"

Kisha shook her head. "No. Tharuks have destroyed our piaua supplies and destroyed the trees. There's no piaua juice left anywhere." She cocked her head. "However, I am handy with a needle and thread."

"Your dragon is in good hands, then, Nila." Ithsar strode over to talk to a group of assassins who were gesturing at her.

Kisha went into the inn and retrieved a needle, some squirrel gut twine, and another broken chair leg. She gave the chair leg to the dragon to bite down on, and mended her leg with quick, even stitches.

When Kisha was finished, her eyes shot to a red stain blossoming on Nila's orange robes, across her ribs. She was hurt—that's why she'd been blinking back tears and grimacing, not only for her dragon.

"Nilanna wants to thank you." Nila gave a wan smile.

Kisha put her palm against the dragon's warm, leathery scales.

A rumbling voice drifted through her head. *"Thank you, Kisha, but I'm worried. Nila's hiding an injury from me, masking her pain, thinking I can't sense it. Would you tend to her too?"* The dragon's golden eyes blinked and she snuffled Kisha's shoulder.

She nodded. *"I'll tend to her when we're inside the inn, so she doesn't lose face."*

"You have a good heart, young Kisha. A true heart, that of a future dragon rider."

"I've already been for a dragon ride today." Sort of—being clutched in Saritha's talons might not count.

The dragon blinked. *"You know what I mean."*

A sense of awe stole through Kisha. She nodded. *"I do."* She'd always longed to be a dragon rider like her grandmother.

Kisha murmured to Nila, "I'll tend your wound when we get inside. Go upstairs to the second room on the left and wait for me."

Nila's eyes shot to her dragon. "She ratted me out, didn't she? And here I was, trying to fool everyone. What a tattletale."

Nilanna snorted and twitched her tail, flicking the tip at Nila's boot.

Kisha smiled and, together, she and Nila walked back to the inn, leaving the blazing pyre of carcasses and broken furniture crackling in the square.

§

Early the next morning, Kisha assembled a rough and ready breakfast from whatever scraps she could find in the cellar. It was strange, no longer having tharuks in the bar—a huge relief. Just yesterday she would've thought it impossible, now here she was, back in the inn, up at the crack of dawn preparing bread for her guests. She kneaded the dough and formed it into rounds to toast on the hearth.

The assassins and green guards rose and then bustled about, ferrying plates of dried fruit, pickles, jam, and freshly-baked bread to the tables.

Stefan wandered into the kitchen for the tenth time, swiping a dried plum as he picked up a plate. "Hands off, Stefan. You've sneaked enough," Kisha said. "Make sure the food gets into someone's belly other than just your own."

"I'm a growing lad." He winked. "But don't worry, I'm feeling generous, so I'll share." He sauntered back out to the dining room, laden with trays and plates.

As Kisha was washing the dishes, an orange lizard with brown bands scampered across the bench, making her start. "Oh, no, you don't. Not in my kitchen." She caught the little fellow, who was nearly as long as her forearm. She'd never seen anything like it—the lizards in Last Stop were usually green and only the length of her finger.

Ithsar came into the kitchen, stepping between the flour-strewn benches and a half-full barrel of salted pork. "Oh, you've found Thika. That little scamp has been having a great time."

The lizard ran up Kisha's arm and nestled in the crook of her shoulder, rubbing his back against her neck.

Ithsar laughed. "He seems to like you."

"Is he yours?"

"For many years, Thika was my only friend." Ithsar scratched the lizard's throat, then tilted her head. "Visions of destruction have been plaguing me all night. We're heading north to battle shadow dragons. Would you mind looking after him for me? I'm worried that he might get hurt. Last night he kept leaping around Saritha's back in the middle of the fighting. I'd hate to lose him."

"Me?"

Ithsar nodded. "I'd be relieved if you could."

"What does he eat?"

"Bugs, scraps of meat. He usually catches his own beetles or flies but, right now, it's a bit cold for that here."

Kisha fed the lizard a scrap of salted pork, which he gobbled down in a heartbeat. "He's so sweet. I'd love to look after him."

"Thank you." Ithsar hugged her. The assassin's warm, dark eyes regarded Kisha. "And thank you for your hospitality. I appreciate you taking care of Nila, too." Ithsar shook her head. "She's courageous, but headstrong, and takes risks in battle, so I suspect this injury won't be her last."

"I'm happy to help. Thanks for saving my life last night." Kisha dried her hands on a dishtowel. "Are you leaving now?"

Ithsar nodded. "I fear we must hurry north, but I do sense that I'll visit you again."

Kisha swallowed and stroked Thika's chin. Although Ithsar seemed to think she'd be back, any of these assassins or green guards could end up as shadow dragon fodder. Her mother had told her, over and over again, that her grandmother Anakisha's demise had been quick, and no one had expected it. So, instead of pretty, flowery words, Kisha flung her arms around Ithsar and hugged her again.

DRAGONS' HOLD

The sea dragons and the green guards flew north, once again, casting their shadows over the land. But instead of gleeful children greeting them, terrified villagers ran to take cover. Ithsar and Saritha passed over charred farmhouses and ruined farms on the outskirts of settlements. People cowered under the eaves of barns or in copses of trees.

They flew on.

Soon they passed over blackened meadows and came to a village that was nothing but smoking ruins. Tharuks were milling around, hunting through the wreckage.

There were no other signs of life.

Goren swooped on his dragon, Rengar, to fly alongside Saritha and Ithsar. "Do you want to go down?" he called. "We could easily wipe out those monsters."

"Let's fry those beasts," Saritha snarled.

And draw the attention of more shadow dragons that could be lurking nearby, stopping them from heading north.

Images cascaded through Ithsar's mind.

The sky was teeming with shadow dragons. Yellow eye-beams sliced rider and dragon alike. Smoke and flame wreathed the sky, and more dark dragons poured over the horizon, blackening the heavens.

An overwhelming sense of urgency rushed through her. "No," Ithsar called. "We must press north. Time is short."

Goren thrust an arm at the beasts below, calling, "You're wasting an opportunity. We should kill those tharuks."

Although Ithsar's chest ached at the destruction and the loss of lives below, and although anger surged through her veins at those awful beasts, she had to stay true to her vision. They had to help Ezaara save the realm. "These villagers are dead already. The shadow dragons in the North are a threat to everyone's future."

A scowl twisted Goren's face, and Rengar wheeled away.

The further north they flew, the worse the destruction was. Charred orchards, crops laid to waste. Bodies strewn across fields. People camped outside in the snow, in makeshift tents made of blankets, their houses in blackened ruins.

Toward nightfall, Goren wheeled his dragon to fly by Ithsar and Saritha again. "See that haze on the horizon?"

A gray pall hung over a city in the distance. Nestled between two rivers near the edge of a forest that went on forever, the town was the largest Ithsar had ever seen. Bigger than Naobia. Roads snaked into the city with bridges spanning the rivers. Towering spires caught the late evening sun, and stone buildings several stories high sat beneath a backdrop of breathtaking mountains. Even further north, more fierce mountain peaks jutted against the horizon.

The city would have been an amazing sight if not for the gray blanket shrouding its beauty.

Goren pointed east. "That's Great Spanglewood Forest." Then he gestured directly north. "The city is Montanara. We should get there by nightfall. From there, it's only a few hours to Dragons' Hold. I suggest we stop for the night just north of the city so our dragons are well rested for when they face their next battle."

Ithsar didn't voice her fears. Visions had been flitting into her mind all day. If shadow dragons and tharuks had overrun the city, perhaps they wouldn't get out of Montanara to fight the battle in the North. The only thing that mattered now was the urgent need to press on.

They flew on, over the edge of Great Spanglewood Forest. Gaping holes had been smashed in the foliage. Trees were still standing, but some were charred to a crisp, dragon carcasses strewn at their roots.

As they approached, smoke rose from pyres in the surrounding fields, coalescing in a gray cloud over the city.

"They're burning the dead," Saritha said. *"But I can't tell if the corpses are friends or foe."*

The stench of burnt foliage and flesh hung in the air. A building on the outskirts of town had chunks of missing masonry. They swooped over the city. Walls were covered in scorch marks, and there were holes in a few roofs. Other snowy rooftops had gouges where dragons had landed, and some were splattered with black and red blood. Another pyre burnt in the town square, sending a dark smoky plume skyward.

The streets were deserted. The *sathir* that hung over the city was as gray and drab as the smoke that wisped over the rooftops.

Ithsar shuddered at the destruction and desolation.

Fangora flapped up. "The green guards said this is usually a thriving city with a vibrant marketplace," Stefan said.

"Not today," Ithsar muttered.

Saritha mind-melded. *"Something's wrong. This is the territory of the blue guards, so they should be patrolling the area, but we haven't seen a single dragon."*

Had they all been killed? Or fled? Or abandoned this city and its inhabitants to their fate?

Ithsar shielded her dark thoughts from her valiant sea dragon. *"How far to Dragons' Hold?"*

"The green guards say we'll be there in a few hours, but Ithsar..."

"What?"

"The dragons are exhausted. And it's cold here, and there's nowhere to swim. Those stringy goats from Last Stop weren't as fine as a decent feed of fish." Saritha's bone-weariness washed over Ithsar. *"We can't go on. Goren's right. We'll have to stop for the night, and then hunt in the morning, or we won't be fit to fight."*

Ithsar didn't want her sea dragons or the green guards slaughtered because they were too tired to defend themselves, so—despite her dark foreboding that they should push on—she agreed.

§

Ithsar and her wings of sea dragons and green guards spent a restless night under the stars in a freezing cold field north of Montanara. They hadn't dared light a fire in case they were attacked, so the riders huddled on blankets and their dragons draped their wings over them and tucked their snouts underneath, huffing warm breath over them to keep them from freezing.

Ithsar rose early, as usual, to train with Stefan.

After the dragons had hunted, fished in the nearby river, and replenished their strength, they flew up over the mountains behind Montanara and onward, north, toward the fierce peaks of Dragons' Hold. A dark ravine split the wild fields to the east, in a rip that led to the base of mountains that rose like jagged fangs from the plains.

Bitter air nipped at Ithsar. She tugged her cloak tighter.

After hours traversing the plains, the dragons finally ascended the piercing peaks.

Saritha mind-melded, *"Meet Dragon's Teeth, the valiant sentinels that protect Dragons' Hold."*

At last they were here, at the home of Ezaara—she of the golden hair, the Queen's Rider—and the dragons that patrolled Dragons' Realm. Ithsar let out a sigh of relief. They sped up the pristine slopes, their wingbeats thundering off the mountainside.

"Ithsar..." Saritha melded.

Her dragon's tone was ominous. *What is it?*

"I can't see any dragons here. The green guards are saying that the air is usually full of them."

The dragons crested the fierce peaks and glided over a beautiful basin, a silver lake glinting in the sun, nestled among bristling carpets of pines. But that beauty was marred by the carnage below. A stony clearing was strewn with carcasses of dark dragons, colored dragons, and the bodies of tharuks and dragon riders. Wisps of smoke trailed across the basin. The stench of charred flesh rose up to greet them.

Within the peaks of Dragons' Hold, everything was silent, except for the swish of the dragons' wingbeats whispering off the soot-and-blood-stained mountainsides.

Saritha snarled. Fangora, Nilanna, Rengar, and Ramisha answered. Their roars echoed across the basin and bounced off the peaks. Ithsar tugged her heavy cloak again, but the cloak and her thick winter garments did nothing to stop the chill permeating her bones.

They were too late. Dragons' Hold had been devastated.

Ithsar's throat tightened. Were Roberto and Ezaara still alive?

The *sathir* in this basin was stained gray—bleak despair hung over Dragons' Hold, making Ithsar's bones ache. Save the plants and trees, there was nothing here, no one alive, and nothing worth saving.

Misha and Nila turned to her, their faces stark with shock at the torn and bloody carcasses of the dragons below. Corpses of reds, blues, greens, and even orange and purple dragons, lay torn on the blood-congealed stones. Tharuk limbs, bodies, and heads were strewn among them. And shadow dragons, so many shadow dragons. Whoever had killed them had put up a valiant fight.

Ithsar scanned the corpses for the multi-hued dragon she'd seen in her vision, for a Naobian face, or a glimpse of golden hair.

Nothing. Not a sign of her friends.

Even Goren and Stefan's faces were wan. The other assassins and green guards mirrored their grief.

Saritha's usually comforting rumble didn't help Ithsar feel much better.

"*Dragons' Hold was never our destination,*" the queen of the sea dragons said. "*Although this is a shock, think, Ithsar: the vision you showed me was different, over a forest. We just have to find that forest.*"

Ithsar searched her memories. Her vision hadn't been of this pine forest surrounding the lake.

Saritha gained altitude, her mighty wings beating at the frigid air as they sped higher, trailed by dragons. They raced over the lake, searching, the green and blue dragons fanned out behind them, their reflections like tiny dragonets on the lake's silvery surface.

"*Such a beautiful lake, but we will not swim here, not while death taints this basin. Not while we must search for our friends.*" Saritha soared higher. "*Look, Ithsar. What's that?*"

Ithsar gazed over the peaks of Dragon's Teeth. To the south-east, a dark stain hung over Great Spanglewood Forest, shot with tiny pinpoint flashes of light.

Dragon flame.

"*That's our destination.*" Her fist high in the air, Ithsar let out a bloodcurdling cry.

The sea dragons and green guards twisted and backwinged, following Saritha and Ithsar as they surged up over the eastern peaks of Dragon's Teeth. The assassins and dragon riders loosed battle cries that stirred Ithsar's blood. Their dragons bellowed as they crested the peaks, their roars rumbling through Ithsar's bones.

They still had a long, hard flight east before they reached that distant smear of black lit up by bursts of flame.

They swooped down the far side of Dragon's Teeth over Great Spanglewood Forest—an enormous carpet of green bordered by the nearby Northern Alps, and spread for hours of flight, all the way to distant peaks in the east.

"*When I was young, my father wove spellbinding tales of spangles, magical beings that lived in Great Spanglewood Forest.*" Ithsar paused. Gods, how she wished her father had lived to fly on dragonback with her and see this wondrous realm. She'd been so tiny when he'd told those tales, but she'd never forgotten them. Even after he died, she'd lain awake at night, missing him and reciting his stories to keep him alive. Funnily enough, it had worked. Although it was hard to remember his face, his stories lived on inside her. "*Do you know if it's true, Saritha? Is there really magic among the trees?*"

"My mother Queen Aquaria told me spangles exist. We have something similar in the Naobian Sea, tiny glimmering beings of light that shape the currents in the sea."

Dragons beat their wings, racing over the snowy pines. Here and there, Ithsar spied carcasses of shadow dragons among the trees. The northerners must have been fighting these beasts for a while.

Dark visions swirled around Ithsar.

A black swarm of screeching shadow dragons; blinding beams of yellow light slicing open blue dragons and rending limbs from greens; a silver dragon howling with grief; a strange yellow beam streaming from a metal box into the sky; roiling flame and riders screaming; strange mages with identical faces, shooting green balls of fire from the back of dark shadow dragons. Bleak despair shuddered through her bones, making them ache.

Ithsar mind-melded with the queen of the sea dragons. *"Saritha, it's been an honor to fly with you."* She tried to force her vision to show her a glimpse of her future with the queen, but there was nothing. Only emptiness. *"You changed my life."*

"Ithsar," the queen melded. *"We've found the battle, so be of good cheer. Don't give up hope yet."*

Ithsar nodded, throat too tight to speak, mind too tangled with dark visions to feel anything but desolation. She patted Saritha's scaly hide and they flew on, the thunder of her heart drowning out the rustle of hundreds of dragon wings.

§

As they sped across the treetops dusted with snow, another vision drifted through Ithsar's head.

A woman was riding an enormous silver dragon. The shimmering silver sathir around the two nearly blinded Ithsar. This woman had a good heart, a strong heart. Her sathir was pure and vibrant, glimmering in the waning sun.

Silver tendrils snaked out from the woman's sathir and enveloped a man riding a bronze, a young male rider on an orange dragon, and Ezaara riding a multi-hued dragon.

A mage on a shadow dragon blasted mage fire at Ezaara.

There was a flash of silver. The woman screamed and leaped, her dark hair flowing in the wind as her lithe body shot into the path of the roiling mage flame. Within moments, the woman was a pillar of fire.

"Ma! Ma!" Ezaara screamed. "Zaarusha! No, not Ma."

The dragon queen roared, diving after the burning woman. The silver and bronze dragons dived too, nearly colliding in their quest to snatch the burning body.

The towering pillar of green mage fire flared in the sky, and then the woman's silver sathir *and the fire snuffed out. Her ashes swirled in the wind from the dragons' wingbeats.*

The silver dragon stretched her neck skyward and howled, the mournful keening echoing through Ithsar's chest. The bronze joined her and they speared through the mass of shadow dragons, chasing the mage that had killed Ezaara's mother.

The dragon queen's roars shook the sky, making Ithsar gasp. Ezaara screamed and snatched up her bow. Roberto and Erob at her side, Ezaara shot an arrow into the breast of a mage and another at a dark dragon's eye.

As the vision cleared, Ithsar gazed out over the forest at the dark swarm of dragons they were heading for. Had this happened yet? Or was it yet to pass? Perhaps she could prevent it.

"Faster, Saritha, we must save Ezaara's mother." No sooner than she thought the words, there was a brilliant flash of silver and then a blazing green flame lit up that dark cloud, burning as it plummeted, then extinguished completely.

A jolt hit Ithsar's chest, as if she'd been punched, and she knew Ezaara's mother was dead.

MAGE GATE

Straight ahead, Ithsar saw the landscape as she'd seen it in her vision: a winter forest sprawled before her, patches of snow in dark shadows, and grass peeking through in the sunlit clearing. And there was the metal chest she'd seen with the strange yellow beam of light jutting from it. Above it all, spread like a giant awning above an oasis, was a legion of foul beasts spitting fire and shooting yellow beams from their eyes. Mages rode on their backs, lobbing green flame.

There was a flash of multi-hued scales and a cry rang out, "Ithsar!" Blonde hair swirling in the breeze from thousands of wings, Ezaara punched her bow high in the air. She was riding an enormous dragon, the hundreds of hues on its scales rippling in the light as the beast flew.

Thank the *dracha* gods. Ezaara was alive.

"Zaarusha, the dragon queen and fearless leader of Dragons' Realm, welcomes us," Saritha said.

Joy thrummed inside Ithsar's breast, a surging, bucking beast. Moons before, Ezaara—she of the golden hair—had healed her, making her fingers whole, and helped Ithsar discover the power of her *sathir*. And Roberto had restored her faith that kind men like her father still existed. Now, at last, she could repay them.

Ithsar punched her fist into the air, too, shrieking the ancient *Sathiri* battle cry, "Avanta!"

Saritha's jade scales glinted with silver like a brooding sea as the mighty sea dragons and brave assassins surged into the mass of dark dragons. Green guards speared through clusters of dark dragons, breaking groups apart so they could pick them off.

Screeches and howls ripped through Ithsar's mind. Gritting her teeth, she focused on the *sathir* of the shadow dragons—a purple so dark it was almost black, the shadowy stain rippling around the foul creatures.

A huge dragon swooped down toward Saritha, its dark, ragged wings blocking the sunlight. Saritha snarled and shot a jet of flame at the beast. Fangora dived past, chasing another shadow dragon, his flame scorching the foul beast's tail. More shadow dragons blasted flame at dragons of orange, gold, bronze, purple, blue, green, and red.

Saritha dived, spitting fire at a dark dragon who was chasing a blue. Ithsar whipped her bow from her back and an arrow from her quiver, and fired. The arrow plunged into a shadow dragon's neck, but it writhed and bucked. With a swipe of its talons, it freed the arrow and breathed a swathe of flame at the blue dragon, who roared down into the forest and crashed into the trees.

Saritha gave chase. Ithsar fired another arrow, meeting her mark. It pierced the back of the shadow dragon's skull, and in a writhing heap of flaming wings, it let out a piercing shriek, and plummeted into the trees, setting them ablaze.

With a flip of emerald wings, Goren's dragon shot past her, and the green guard leader flashed a grin. Ithsar grinned back. She didn't need his acknowledgment, but it was nice to know he'd noticed.

Heat wafted from the forest below, but they had no time to investigate as Saritha spun to deflect the attack of another shadow dragon. Diving at them, its ragged wings outstretched, it breathed fire. They wheeled, but couldn't shake the dragon off.

The dragon spurted a jet of flame at Saritha. The courageous sea dragon bucked, narrowly avoiding her flank being singed.

A yell cut through the mayhem. Roberto swooped in on Erob—the mighty blue *dracha* Ithsar had met at the oasis. Erob blasted flame at the shadow dragon. It clawed at its flaming wings, trying to extinguish the fire, but the blaze was too great.

Gods, that screaming, always that infernal screaming in her head.

Then a flaming ball of green fire shot across Saritha's head near Ithsar's face. She leaned back, the stench of her own burnt hair jamming itself up her nostrils. Ithsar whipped her head around and loosed an arrow before she was upright. It sailed toward a young female mage with blonde hair riding a shadow dragon and lobbing fireballs at the dragon riders. Behind her another dragon swooped in, an identical mage upon its back.

"A mage fighting her own kind? And two the same? I don't understand."

"Zaarusha says they're evil. Grown from real mages, but unnatural fake mages, made by Commander Zens."

"Strong magic indeed." If he was growing mages, what hope did they have? No matter how many they killed, Zens could grow more. Ithsar loosed an arrow, but one of the mages flung a fireball at it, and the arrow disintegrated in a burst

of green flame. She fired two arrows in rapid succession as Saritha blasted a huge volley of flame. The mages wheeled off after a red dragon.

Ithsar was about to chase them when Fangora shot by. "Look out," Ithsar called as a shadow dragon wheeled for Stefan, opening its maw.

Ithsar fired an arrow into the beast's cavernous mouth. It screamed. Its head jerked back, its flames shooting skyward and missing Stefan. Ithsar followed up with another arrow, piercing the beast's eye ridge, the shaft driving deep into its face. It clawed at its head and plummeted to the forest below.

Face pale with shock, Stefan turned to Ithsar, held up two fingers and pointed at her.

Two saves to her.

Their dragons beat their wings and headed into the towering mass of rolling flame, dark shadows and howling beasts. Saritha breathed fire. Ithsar and Stefan fired arrows. Heat roiled around them as they bucked and twisted, trying to keep out of the paths of the fiery beasts' flames.

§

A shadow dragon charged at Ithsar.

"Let's take this one together," Stefan yelled, swooping at its stomach.

Saritha flamed the dragon's maw, while Fangora fried its wings. Stefan shot an arrow at its belly and Ithsar fired, her arrow punching through the beast's skull.

A cry of triumph rent the sky. "Nice shot," Stefan yelled.

Goren swooped past on his dragon. He punched his fist high in the air and called, "Well done."

Ithsar nearly fell out of her saddle. Knock her down with a vulture feather—Goren had actually praised her! She grinned back and rose in her stirrups to shoot at a snarling dark dragon chasing a blue.

As the dragon dropped, Ithsar cast about. A lull in battle was rare, but soon more dragons would be upon them. A dark cloud of them was rushing in. She grabbed a waterskin and held it up in a toast to Stefan. He grabbed his too, and, together, they swigged down some water, then stowed the skins back in their saddlebags. Nocking an arrow to her bow, Ithsar scanned the battle.

Below, men were battling tharuks among the trees, leaving a swathe of dead and wounded behind them—both tharuks and humans. An enormous barrel-chested man, with two strong fighters beside him, led the warrior troops. They hacked and cut their way through the tharuks, surrounded by brave woman and men fighting those beasts, tooth and nail.

"We can't help there," Ithsar said. "We'll accidentally flame our own."

Saritha rumbled in agreement and shot north over the trees. A towering inferno of green flame ripped through the forest, driving a horde of tharuks toward a river choked with weeds that waved greedy tentacles above the water. Green fireballs shot from the river, killing tharuks. More tharuks plunged into the water, trying to escape the fire. Bolts of green mage fire slammed into some, while tentacles grasped others and dragged them down, gurgling, to their deaths.

Some clever mage must be hiding underwater. But what were those awful tentacles?

As they flew over the inferno, unbearable heat crackled through the air, making Ithsar's skin itch, and then they were behind the green flames. Was that a man down there? *Saritha, get lower.*

The sea dragon queen circled above a young mage—Naobian from the looks of him—extinguishing pockets of fire behind him and funneling the wall of mage flame so it drove the tharuks into that seething river. All that fire, from one man...

"*By the* dracha *gods, he's a powerful mage.*"

"*Indeed. He and the mage in the river have these beasts under control. Our help's not needed here.*" Saritha shot higher.

"*Wait, Saritha. Look.*"

Two tharuks had sneaked around the side of the wall of flames and were creeping up on the mage, about to attack. Ithsar shot an arrow into the front tharuk's head. The other roared and glanced skyward as Saritha blasted it with dragon flame.

Surprised, the mage spun, waved a grateful hand and pressed on, pushing those tharuks with his mage fire into the mages' clever trap.

Saritha flipped her wings and shot up. "*The green guards told me this place is called Mage Gate. Years ago, the mages opened a world gate here and let Commander Zens into Dragons' Realm.*"

"*Stefan said Zens grows those awful tharuks and shadow dragons, as well as those identical mages you told me about,*" Ithsar replied.

"*No one really understands how, but Erob just told me that Roberto and some young mages have destroyed the place in Death Valley where Zens makes them. They say if we can win this battle and kill Zens, the war will be over.*"

"*Now, that would be something to celebrate.*"

Glimmers lit up the leaves in the forest below. The foliage was a surging sea of twinkling lights that swirled as squirrels scampered from branches, down tree trunks, to attack the tharuks. Tiny sparkles of light shot from the trees and wrapped themselves around a young dark-haired boy. He flung out his arms. Foxes crawled out of holes, biting tharuks' legs. Wolves raced through the trees and flung themselves at the monsters. The ground seemed to surge as beetles and rodents swarmed Zens' beasts. Even the trees bowed their branches, thrashing the tharuks.

"Spangles, Saritha! The boy and the spangles are rallying the forest to fight back." Ithsar felt a glimmer of hope. Perhaps they could win this war, after all.

The warriors surged forward, heartened, too.

But a huge tharuk roared, and the tharuk troops rallied, too, slashing through the woodland creatures and hacking them and the men to pieces with their claws.

Saritha dived, but it was hopeless. Ithsar couldn't get a clear shot without hurting the warriors, and Saritha couldn't risk flaming their people. So, they zipped back into the sky to kill shadow dragons.

To the south in a huge clearing, that strange beam of light still streamed from the metal chest she'd seen in her vision, piercing the sky. A dark-haired man with a goatee stood near the chest, with his head back, staring at the beam, his limbs and body frozen. He looked strangely familiar.

Next to the man was an enormous being, with bulbous yellow eyes and dark stubble over his head. Dark shadowy *sathir* wafted around this menacing man, filling Ithsar with a sense of dark foreboding.

Saritha flicked her tail. *"It's no wonder that man gives you a terrible feeling—he's Commander Zens, the one who came through the world gate years ago. He created the tharuks and shadow dragons that are destroying Dragons' Realm."* She angled her head toward the dark-haired man. *"That is the man my mother spoke of, the dragon mage, Master Giddi."*

Now, Ithsar knew where she'd known him from—Queen Aquaria had shown him to her and said, *"This is the dragon mage. Years ago, he saved my life. Aid him in any way you can and send him my greetings. His role in this war is essential, but without your support he will fail and Dragons' Realm will be lost."*

It was unnatural for someone to stand so still. *"Why isn't he moving?"* Oh, by a thousand blazing suns, she hadn't seen *that*. Sickly strands of yellow *sathir* wove from the dragon mage's back toward Commander Zens. *"He's under Zens' control."*

Saritha snarled.

The key to this battle was that metal box with the golden beam streaming from it. Although the *sathir* around the box was neutral, Ithsar was sure it could be used for good or evil—but there was no doubt which course Zens was choosing.

Hordes of tharuks, twenty, thirty, sometimes a hundred deep, surrounded the clearing, protecting their commander. Swarms of shadow dragons circled overhead, staying out of the beam's rays, ready to blast anyone who got near.

"More shadow dragons are coming from the south," Saritha said. *"The blue guards have asked us to fight them."*

A BRIGHT FLAME

Ithsar and Saritha sped southward, flanked by Stefan and Nila, with Misha. Three Naobian green guards flew behind them. They charged across the clearing, avoiding the beam of yellow light that shot into the sky. The day was drawing to a close, but the fighting was not over.

A fake mage, male this time, fired an arrow at a blue dragon, and suddenly, the blue whirled upon a red, biting its wings. The red bit back and the blue slashed out and shredded the red's wing with its sharp talons. As the red plummeted, the blue chased, flaming it.

"By the bleeding First Egg!" Stefan yelled. "What was that?"

Ithsar gaped as the fake mage kept firing arrows, and more blue, orange, green and red dragons turned and attacked each other, tiny trails of sickly-yellow *sathir* issuing from their arrow wounds.

"Zaarusha has told me that these arrows contain methimium implants, yellow crystals that can turn a dragon's loyalty to Zens in a heartbeat. Ezaara was shot when she was battling in Lush Valley and only Roberto's quick action saved her."

"Methimium must be how Zens is controlling Master Giddi, the dragon mage," Ithsar mused. When the fake mage raised his bow again, Ithsar shot him in the back.

They plunged over the foliage, blasting flame down at tharuks. Ithsar let an arrow fly.

A tharuk leader fell, trampled by its own troop's boots as they marched onward, straight over the leader's carcass, their large furry bodies breaking saplings and smashing through underbrush.

"Look out," Stefan yelled. Ithsar spun in the saddle.

A cloud of shadow dragons blotted out the waning sun. Their dragons flapped, speeding through the sky to meet them.

Two shadow dragons broke off from the cloud and charged at Saritha, one on either side. Saritha belched flame, but beams from their eyes sliced toward her. She ducked the beams and shot upward, but the shadow dragons clawed at her wings. She furled her wings and dived, and then ascended again. The two dragons stayed on her tail, flanking her and blasting roiling heat. Their dark purple *sathir* enveloped Saritha and Ithsar. She nocked and fired an arrow. Another of those blonde female mages spun on her shadow dragon's back and blasted a green fireball at Ithsar's arrow. It disintegrated in midair.

She fired another and that, too, burst into flame and fell to the forest. A shadow dragon snarled, lunging for Saritha. Ithsar slung her bow into the crook of her elbow and hung onto Saritha's spinal ridge and her saddle as Saritha reared up in the air, clawing at the dragon's wings with her talons.

Another dragon behind them roared and latched on to Saritha's tail with its fangs. The three dragons twisted and plummeted. Ithsar hung onto the saddle with one hand, snatched her dagger with the other, and flung it down toward Saritha's tail. It plunged into the shadow dragon's neck, but the beast hung on, its jaw clamped tight around Saritha's bleeding tail.

Saritha arched her neck and roared in pain and fury. She flailed as the other shadow dragon locked onto her neck with its jaws.

A purple dragon angled through the air, speeding down, her scales glinting with a tinge of gold in the evening sun. Two young riders were astride her back, both blond; one tall, the other with startling green eyes and wearing a mage cloak. The mage raised his hands and a coil of blistering green flame issued from his palms, licking along the shadow dragon clamped to Saritha's tail. The dark dragon roared, opening its jaws and releasing its grip on Saritha's tail and plunging down to the forest.

Misha and her dragon dived at the dragon clutching Saritha's neck, and the purple dragon and blond rider and mage dived off to help a blue being attacked by another dark dragon.

Zens' mage shot fireballs from the shadow dragon's back. Misha ducked, but the fireball glanced her and set her headscarf alight. Her dragon backwinged from the flailing, fighting dragons as Misha dumped the contents of a waterskin over her head. The air stank of singed hair.

Ithsar threw another dagger, the dragons' screeches ripping through her head, but missed. A waste of a good blade. By the blazing *dracha* gods, if only she could let go of Saritha to use her bow.

Saritha yowled as the shadow dragon bit deeper into her neck. Her wing-beats slowed.

"No, Saritha, no!" A sob burst from Ithsar's chest. "Come on, girl." She tore her saber from its sheath and leaned out over Saritha's neck, trying to slash the dragon, but her arms were too short.

A battle cry sliced through the air.

Stefan fired an arrow into the shadow dragon's neck. And then Fangora was there, golden eyes blazing. He landed on the shadow dragon's back, shredding its wings with his talons and ripping out chunks of flesh with his teeth. Dark blood sprayed Fangora, Stefan, and Saritha. Fangora grasped the mage in his jaws and flung it from the dragon into the forest. Her body was speared on a massive pine and hung, twitching, in the treetops.

Fangora lashed the shadow dragon's limbs with his tail. His strong jaws lunged into the shadow dragons' neck and he crunched through bone. In a spray of blood, the monster's grip on Saritha's throat loosened and it fell away, crashing through the treetops.

A fate they'd soon share if they didn't gain height.

More dark dragons dived. Misha, Nila, and the green guards wheeled to fight them.

Saritha was panting, her neck and tail dripping blood. Ithsar slid her bow out and fired an arrow deep into the belly of a shadow dragon above. And then another, and another. Her dragon's sathir was shimmering, her waves of pain washing over Ithsar. *"We have to get you to a healer."*

"Soon. First, we must fight these beasts," Saritha muttered.

More shadow dragons dived at Saritha, fangs bared and snarling.

A mage shot a green firebolt at Misha, whose dragon shied away. And then Nila lunged in, her dragon attacking the beast with a plume of fire. Nila shot an arrow at the shadow dragon. The arrowhead buried itself deep in its belly. It roared and spun, beating its leathery wings.

Nila grinned. "Come on, you awful coward," she yelled and fired another arrow.

It hit the beast's jaw, but disintegrated in a burst of flame as the shadow dragon shot fire at Nila and knocked her from her saddle in a ball of flame. Nilanna roared and pounced on the beast, shredding it with her talons and letting out a mournful howl that shuddered down Ithsar's spine, rocking her in the saddle.

Nila's bright, vibrant orange *sathir* winked out like an oil lamp snuffed between a great god's fingertips. Her body thudded through the trees and landed in a smoking heap.

Ithsar's chest hollowed. Just like that, Nila's daring, and her wild sense of adventure and fun, were gone. Ithsar's bones ached and her head throbbed. Her throat tightened and a sob burst from her chest.

But there was no time to mourn her friend—a writhing horde of shadow dragons swept at them.

With a cry, Ithsar shot arrows into the beasts' bellies, wings, and skulls. Saritha blasted flame, lashing wings with her tail, clawing beasts with her talons, a snarling mass of vengeance.

Beams from a shadow dragon's eyes sliced at them. They missed, topping a tree.

The green guards, Stefan, and Misha fought, but Saritha's sides were now heaving, her movements slowing.

"Saritha, we must get you to a healer."

"I'm f-fine."

Goren swooped in, waving an arm out over the forest. "Toward the east, there are healers in a clearing. Take Saritha there. That's an order."

Stefan flanked them on Fangora. They headed over the trees, but Saritha lost height rapidly, flying too low, nearly scraping her belly on the treetops. The blood from the fang marks on her throat splattered on strongwoods, turning their snowy foliage pink.

Ithsar swallowed. *"I'm sorry, Saritha. I was too tempestuous. We should've stopped fighting earlier."*

"It doesn't matter," Saritha said, turning her head toward Ithsar, her eyes half-closed and wingbeats slowing.

"It does matter. You matter." Ithsar choked on a sob.

Beside them, Stefan yelled, *"Go, Saritha, we're nearly there. Fly!"*

His cry spurred on the queen of the sea dragons. She swept over the forest and landed with a thud at the edge of the woods.

A pale-faced young boy with lake-blue eyes rushed toward them, bearing a waterskin.

Ithsar slid from the saddle and held up a hand. "No, not water. Do you have any piaua? My *dracha* is badly hurt."

His eyes round, the boy nodded. "Yes, this is piaua."

Saritha's head slumped to the ground. The boy rushed over and tipped pale-green juice from the waterskin, rubbing handfuls of piaua juice into Saritha's gaping neck wounds.

"That burns," Saritha murmured as her eyes slid shut.

Ithsar raced to her head and grasped her snout in her hands. *"Saritha, it's a good burn. This will heal you, just hold on."* A dark hole gaped in Ithsar's belly, threatening to engulf her. By the *dracha* gods, Saritha had to make it. She had to. *"Hold on, Saritha. Please."*

Saritha's eyelids flickered. *"Yes, Ithsar. For you, I will."*

Ithsar bit her lip, unable to tear her gaze from the wounds on Saritha's neck as the boy slowly healed each layer of tissue, the muscle and flesh knitting together before Ithsar's eyes.

Fangora thudded down beside Saritha and nudged her with his snout, huffing warm breath over her and Ithsar. Stefan dismounted and rushed over to the healer, holding out a mug from his saddlebags.

Ithsar bristled. He wanted a drink at a time like this?

"Please, give me some juice so I can heal her tail wound," Stefan panted.

By the *dracha* gods, he'd only been trying to help. "Thank you, Stefan," Ithsar murmured. Nila's bright flare of *sathir* flashed through her mind again, and she was sure her chest would break in two.

Stefan reached into his pocket and pulled out a grubby package. "Here, Ithsar."

As he dashed off to Saritha's tail, she opened it and found a piece of smashed chocolate. Eyes burning, she jammed the package in a pocket of her robes, and tears slid down her cheeks.

Rampaging Tharuks

Ithsar ran her fingers over the new pale scars on Saritha's neck. *"Does it hurt anymore? Are you feeling weak? You lost quite a bit of blood."*

"No, it doesn't hurt. No, I'm not weak, and yes, I'm ready to fight again."

"I didn't ask you that."

"I know, but I'm telling you," Saritha snapped. *"For the sake of everyone we've lost today, and for their dragonets, eggs, and littlings, we must get back into the sky and win this war."* Saritha narrowed her golden eyes. *"Are you afraid?"*

"I don't want you getting hurt again."

"Ithsar, you've seen the visions. We must help."

Sighing, Ithsar nodded.

"I don't like to alarm you, when we're so busy taking care of Saritha, but look." Stefan pointed to the sky.

A dark ring of shadow dragons had surrounded Ezaara's dragons and was growing ever tighter, herding them toward something. "Where are they taking them?" Ithsar asked.

"I think they're being herded toward the clearing to that strange beam of light."

"Then whatever we do, we must avoid that light." Ithsar turned back to Saritha. *"Tell the sea dragons we're ready to fight."*

"I already have."

The healer-boy brought them a quiver of arrows. "Our master healer died, so I'm working here, not fighting. I see you're running low on arrows. Please, take these."

"Thanks." Stefan grabbed a handful and stuffed them in his quiver.

Ithsar took the rest of the arrows from the boy's quiver and put them in her own, tightening the strap across her chest. Wait, there was something familiar about this boy. "Aren't you the one who worked with the spangles against the tharuks?"

"Yes, I am. My name's Taliesin." He bowed. "Pleased to meet you."

"There's no need to bow to me." Ithsar thumped her hand on her heart.

His serious eyes regarded her, their deep blue nearly piercing her. "Yes, there is. I saw you in a vision, and knew you would help us win this battle."

He'd seen her in a vision? Winning? It didn't feel like they were winning, not with Saritha getting injured.

"Besides," he continued, "one of the green guards told me you have visions too, just like me, Lovina, and Ezaara's father, Hans. It's always nice to meet someone else with the gift." He grinned. "And it's also nice to meet a leader who's so young."

She chuckled. "I'm sure it is. Nice to meet you, Taliesin. Thank you for your help."

Their dragons rose from the healers' clearing, leaving the wounded on bedrolls in the muddy snow beneath the trees. Sea dragons joined Saritha and Fangora, forming a spearhead, and rushed over the forest, their wingbeats dislodging snow from the treetops in soft wet clumps.

Tharuks surrounded the clearing in a thick ring, fighting with warriors. Overhead, the wingbeats of hundreds of dragons thundered through the sky—shadow dragons, Dragons' Realm dragons, and those that had been turned with methimium, attacking their own. The screeching shadow dragons made it hard to think.

That metal box's gold beam of light pierced the dusky clouds.

"Where's Ezaara?" Stefan called, pointing at Zaarusha as she ascended from a low hill near the clearing, riderless, with Erob, at her side.

"Roberto's missing too." Ithsar scanned the clearing and surrounding fighters, and caught a glimpse of Ezaara's colorful sathir, wending its way from the bottom of the hill toward the clearing.

Saritha spun to flame a shadow dragon, and Fangora chased it off. By the time Ithsar glanced below again, there was a flaming tunnel of mage fire cutting through the ring of tharuks into the clearing. The huge fighter she'd seen leading the warriors charged through the tunnel with Roberto at his side, warriors pouring through behind them.

Warriors fought and battled to keep that tunnel of flickering green flame open. Ithsar gasped. They couldn't see a swarm of tharuks approaching from the southeast, about to provide reinforcements. She scanned the clearing and could only see Roberto, the barrel-chested man and other warriors. There was a tiny glimmer of multi-hued sathir, but no Ezaara. Worry gnawed at her. *"Saritha, please ask Zaarusha where Ezaara is."*

A heartbeat later, Saritha answered, *"She's down there, wearing an invisibility cloak."*

Ithsar signaled to her assassins and they speared behind her and Stefan toward the swarm of tharuk reinforcements sneaking through the forest with as much stealth as a herd of stampeding camels. Tusks glinted in the last rays of the sun as the furry monsters barged through undergrowth.

Sea dragons wheeled above the forest, trying to blast flame down between towering trunks. Tharuks ducked behind trees and slunk through bushes. Dragon fire surged past foliage, melting snow and making leaves smolder.

"We're going to set the whole forest alight if we're not careful," Ithsar said.

"Our sea dragons could surround them and set the trees on fire to cut off their path," Saritha—not so helpfully—suggested.

This was dragon fire, not mage flame that could be controlled to only burn what was intended. *"If we set the forest on fire, the casualties could be too great."*

Ithsar yanked a rope from her saddlebag and tied it around the saddle, then waved to her Robandi assassins. *"We're going down, Saritha."* Before her dragon could object, she leaped.

Ithsar swung through the trees, to Saritha's mournful howl. *"I don't want to lose you. Be careful."*

Stefan, Misha and countless orange-robed women dropped to the forest floor and ran to attack the tharuks. The assassins spun and slashed, fur flying, dark blood spraying, hewing down tharuks—an orange whirlwind against an endless mass of dark fur, tusks and beady eyes.

Ithsar cried, "Avanta." She plunged her saber into the belly of a wiry brute and kicked its body away, yanking her saber free. Oh, these beasts stank. She wrinkled her nose and spun, hacking through the arm of another tharuk. It crumpled to its knees and she drove her saber through its back and flicked her throwing knife into the neck of another running at her.

As Ithsar retrieved her weapons, Misha slashed a tharuk across the snout, and Stefan parried another's claws. A beast lunged, swiping for Ithsar's head. She ducked, but it sliced her hair and a dark lock fell to the ground.

Stefan whirled in and plunged a dagger up under the beast's chin through its jaw and into its brain. The beast keeled toward him, but he threw it backward. Panting, he bent to grab his weapon, and then grinned and held up three fingers.

She groaned and rolled her eyes.

"Watch out!" Stefan's cry was too late.

The stench of tharuk overpowered her as a beast grabbed Ithsar, its strong furry arms a vice around her ribs.

Stefan's knife glinted. Ithsar flung her head to one side. His blade whistled past her, making a wet thud. The *dracha* gods only knew where it had hit. A spray of dark stinking blood gushed over the back of her neck and the tharuk fell away behind her.

She shook off the slick blood as Stefan held up four fingers. Shaking her head, Ithsar yanked the blade from the monster's neck and threw it to him. "Good shot."

He caught it. "Thanks. That's four to me, only three to you." He gave her another one of his infuriating grins.

Ithsar wiped her hand on her robes and hefted her hilt.

"Incoming tharuks," Misha yelled behind them.

A sword in each hand, Stefan swung them like windmills. The beasts hesitated, following the blades with their eyes.

Ithsar sneaked around behind a bush and slashed her saber across the back of a tharuk's knees as Stefan drove his sword into the eye of the other. Plunging her saber into the tharuk's back, Ithsar finished it off, and straightened.

"Behind you!" Stefan yelled.

A flash of dark fur caught on the edge of Ithsar's vision. She ducked and rolled as a tharuk slashed its sharp claws where she'd just been.

Stefan hacked at the beast. It slashed at him. *Dracha* gods, had it hurt him? He was so coated in dark tharuk blood, it was hard to tell. No, he was swinging again, hacking at the beast's arm, then its belly. It collapsed to its knees, snout open to the sky, roaring. Stefan drove his sword through the monster's maw and out the back of its throat.

He placed his hands on his knees, catching his breath. "Five," he puffed.

§

Stefan grinned, his face and clothes splattered with gore and tharuk blood.

Ithsar knew she didn't look much better.

"Did you see that? Five," he panted. "You only saved me three times—and you're the assassin." He hunched over, his hand clamped onto his side, breathing hard.

"Then we're lucky I drilled you, aren't we?" Ithsar narrowed her eyes.

Red blood was seeping over Stefan's fingers. Within moments, his hand was stained scarlet.

"Let me look at that." Ithsar tried to remove his hand, but Stefan hissed in pain. *"Saritha, come quick. Stefan's hurt."*

Ithsar waited agonizing heartbeats, but there was no answer. *"Saritha?"*

Roars ripped through the forest. Fangora landed on a sapling, crushing it with his talons, his tail lashing the underbrush.

"Sorry, I was telling Fangora." Saritha said, circling the trees.

Stefan leaned heavily on Ithsar's shoulder, still clutching his side. The blood was spreading across his jerkin. Ithsar helped him over to Fangora, who lay as flat as he could against the ground so she could shove Stefan into the saddle. She clambered up behind him.

"Quick, to the healers," she said aloud to Fangora, then mind-melded with Saritha. *"Does he know where to go?"*

"Yes, he remembers and thanks you for letting him transport his rider."

The young green dragon tensed his haunches and leaped above the trees. Teeth gritted, Stefan slumped over the spinal ridge in front of them. Ithsar wriggled forward, arms around him, jamming her short thighs against his long ones, and holding him in place. "Don't you dare let go," she threatened. "Or I'll kill you myself."

Oh gods, had she really just said that? "Just a few moments and we'll be there," she added.

She prayed to the *dracha* gods that her new friend would make it. Her throat suddenly dry, she tried to swallow, but couldn't. So, instead, she hung on to Stefan, willing him to live.

His *sathir* was still green, but shimmering. Nila's had gone out in an instant. She tried to tell herself that this was different, that the healers would fix him, that everything would be all right, but it didn't stop the pounding of her pulse at her throat or the worry that tightened her airways.

Fangora landed gently, backwinging up a storm to slow his descent. This time, a young blonde girl rushed out to meet them, accompanied by a huge warrior with a bandage on his head. The man lifted Stefan from Fangora, as if he were as light as an empty waterskin. Ithsar jumped from the saddle and spread her cloak on the grass next to Fangora. "Please heal him near his dragon."

Fangora huffed warm breath over Stefan's face. The healer lifted Stefan's shredded tunic. Two ugly gaping wounds were ripped in his side.

By the blazing sun, if those claws had gone any deeper...

"Tharuk claws. We've seen a lot of those injuries lately." The healer bit her lip. She was younger than Ithsar—and thin, with red-rimmed eyes. This young girl's *sathir* was the deep blue of mourning. "Usually I'd stitch him, but we don't have time with so many wounded, so he's going to have a scar."

"Better a scar than—" Ithsar swallowed and squeezed Stefan's bloody hand.

"Exactly. Tharuk claws are pretty dirty. Unfortunately, I don't have any clean herb left, so this will have to do." The healer sloshed water over the wound, then patted it dry and dribbled pale-green piaua juice deep into the torn and bloody muscle.

Stefan's eyes were glazed, flitting back and forth, unseeing.

"Hold on, Stefan," Ithsar pleaded. "This will burn like dragon flame, but soon you'll be back on Fangora, ready to fight again."

His eyes cleared and he gazed at her. "Too right," he said, then hissed through gritted teeth as the healer dribbled more piaua juice into his wound.

"You know," he said, "I won. Even at two saves, I won, because I helped save Saritha, queen of the sea dragons. And, without her, you'd be heartbroken."

"Yes," she said, "I would be. You won." She'd never admit that without him, she'd be heartbroken too.

He shuddered, clenching his jaw as the juice burned through him.

Ithsar recalled the burn she'd felt when Ezaara had healed her fingers. Back then, Ezaara had been captive; Izoldia, her jailer; and Ithsar, Ashewar's bullied and tormented servant. She gave Stefan a faint smile. Oh, how her life had changed.

When the deep inner layers of Stefan's muscle had kitted together, the healer dribbled in more juice, progressively healing all the tissue until his skin was whole.

Finally, Stefan's eyes cleared. He sat up and stretched his side. "Thank you." He beamed at the healer. "I didn't catch your name."

"I'm Leah." The healer smiled. "I'm glad to help. Many moons ago, Ezaara healed me, so now I share my gratitude by healing others." She packed up her leather pouch.

Stefan raced back over to Fangora. Saritha landed with an injured warrior on her back. Behind her, more dragons were alighting, bringing injured riders.

Ithsar gently touched the healer's arm. "Have you lost someone you love?"

"Yes," she whispered, eyes pooling with tears. "The Master Healer, Marlies, Ezaara's mother. She taught me, Ezaara, and Taliesin everything we know."

"Do you mind me asking if she rode a silver dragon?"

Leah nodded. "Yes, she did." She went to help the incoming wounded.

So that had been the brilliant flash of silver they'd seen in the sky on the way to Mage Gate.

Ithsar picked up her cloak, now stained with Stefan's fresh blood, and threw it over her shoulders. It was an honor to wear the blood he'd shed in saving her. Then she helped Leah get the wounded warrior off Saritha's back.

As she and Stefan mounted their dragons and sped above the trees on dragonback, that same blinding beam of light cut through the evening sky, but now it was alive, writhing with gold, silver, and black shadowy *sathir*.

WORLD GATE

Shadow dragons lunged through the air at Saritha and Fangora. Ithsar ducked a green fireball, then shot the fake mage before he could fire another. Thank the blazing sun, Taliesin had given her more arrows. Saritha blasted flame at the mage's shadow dragon and it dropped to the clearing, squashing a horde of tharuks. Hopefully, not any warriors.

A silver thread of *sathir* raced from the dragon mage's hands up the yellow beam of light, as a gold thread rushed from a slim crack in the sky down to meet it. Dark shadowy *sathir* swarmed up behind the dragon mage's silver thread, shrouding it. Ithsar knew that if the shadows overtook the silver, all would be lost.

The dragon mage, Giddi, fell to his knees, screaming, "Mazyka!" His desperate cry reverberated through the clearing and echoed through Ithsar's gut, striking a chord deep within her.

The silver thread shot above the clawing shadows and touched the gold. The world exploded in a flash of light.

A rift appeared in the sky and a golden dragon flew through, a woman with flaming red hair upon its back. A mighty battle cry ripped from the woman's throat.

Smaller golden dragons poured through the crack, ridden by mages with blue light springing from their fingers.

"Mazyka," the dragon mage cried.

"Who is she?" Ithsar asked Saritha.

"His wife—the woman who helped the dragon mage break the world and let Commander Zens in," Saritha replied.

Zens thrust his hands up. With a surge, the shadows raced from his hands up the entwined silver and gold threads, and a dark crack opened in the sky. Metal beings glimmered behind it. A shining metal weapon poked through, blasting flame. One of the smaller golden dragons dropped from the sky, dead.

The *sathir* threads grew thicker, twining around one another to form a golden rope threaded with silver. Dark shadows swirled from Zens around

Master Giddi. Head swaying from side to side, the dragon mage held out his hands and roared.

Zens laughed as a metal figure flew through the dark rift, shooting its weapon, felling green, gold, and blue dragons. The legs of more metal beings poked through the rift. Another dropped down. Its metal body gleaming, it fired at a blue dragon, destroying its wing in a burst of flame. The dragon plummeted, roaring in agony.

The metal being chased it, propelled by some unseen magic, blasting more fire.

Goren swooped in. Ithsar, Goren, and Stefan fired at the beings, but their arrows clattered off their metal carapaces.

What manner of powerful beings were these—made of metal and wielding tubes of fire? Fear skittered through Ithsar's bones. They could never withstand an army of these creatures.

Below, Master Giddi ripped off his cloak and shirt, his torso naked. Dark tendrils of mist leaked from methimium arrow wounds in his back, winding around his neck and face.

Zens laughed.

White light burst from a crystal around the dragon mage's neck and swept around the clearing, banishing the shadows. Zens was thrown onto his back. Tharuks and warriors fell to their knees, shielding their eyes.

The light from the crystal on Giddi's chest blazed through the sky, hitting the dark rift. The crack closed, shutting out the metal beings—hopefully forever.

Mazyka's golden dragon swooped upon the remaining metal beings. She blasted them with plumes of blue mage fire. They exploded, metal shards spraying across the forest.

Saritha, Fangora, and Rengar rocked in the air, winging up to dodge the debris. Golden dragons dived and swooped after shadow dragons, mages on their backs shooting blue fireballs from their fingertips at the fake mages upon the dark dragons' backs. Each time a fake mage was hit, it disintegrated into ash. Suddenly, the dark dragons started attacking one another, ripping off each other's limbs and shredding wings.

"What's going on?" Ithsar asked.

"I felt a mental ripple. I think the dragon mage has wrested his control back from Zens and has commanded the shadow dragons to attack one another."

Down in the clearing, Mazyka aimed a metal tube—like the one that had spat fire through the world gate—at Master Giddi, who collapsed.

"She's hurt him!" Ithsar cried out.

"I don't think so. Look again."

Mazyka was cutting the methimium crystals out of Giddi's back, right there in the middle of the field.

Mages on dragonback chased fighting shadow dragons. Ithsar dispatched dark dragons and fake mages with her arrows, the other assassins felling more of the foul beasts. *"It's much easier picking them off when none of them are flaming us. Almost too easy."*

There was a roar, and a blast of heat roiled through the air overhead. Ithsar spun. *"Blue dragon, incoming from above."* The dragon was aiming for Saritha. *"It must have a methimium implant."*

Saritha ducked and dodged but the blue had the advantage of altitude, so Saritha sped off, heading over the forest, flame nearly singeing her wingtips.

By the blazing desert sun, she was a fool for relaxing her guard. If anything happened to Saritha—

Fangora appeared, and the blue dragon screeched and whirled, racing back to the clearing. Stefan held up six fingers and pointed to his chest.

"That was hardly a save," Ithsar yelled, relieved all the same. "Neither of you even fired."

"I can't help it if I'm so fierce and ugly I scare away the most terrible foes," Stefan called.

Ithsar laughed. Stefan was anything but ugly, but she wasn't about to tell him that. Fangora wheeled off to fight another shadow dragon.

Back in the clearing, golden dragons dropped a shadow dragon carcass onto the grass and lured in the methimium-turned dragons to feast.

"Disgusting." Saritha's distaste washed over Ithsar. *"Those were valiant dragons, but Zens has turned them into despicable savages."*

The sight made Ithsar's stomach churn.

Mazyka and a team of warriors shot the turned dragons with metal tubes, and they collapsed, asleep. Mages from the golden dragons clambered over them, digging out their methimium arrowheads.

"Look," Ithsar said. *"Mazyka and her mages are extracting methimium implants from the colored dragons that turned."*

"The battle's not over. Look there, Zaarusha needs help." Saritha shot over the trees toward the river where they'd seen the raging wall of mage flame earlier in the day. That inferno was extinguished now, and the river was choked with

tharuk bodies, the grasping tentacles of feeding plants, and a dying shadow dragon.

On the far bank, Ezaara and Roberto were fighting Commander Zens.

But below them, on this side of the river, Zaarusha was flaming a horde of tharuks that were trying to sneak through the trees. If those beasts broke through Zaarusha's defense, Ezaara and Roberto would have no chance. *"Saritha, those tharuks."*

"I was thinking the same thing."

Her dragon dived as Ithsar nocked her bow and fired at a hulking tharuk leading the troop. Her arrow hit the beast between the eyes, and it crashed to the forest floor. Zaarusha belched a swathe of flame across the front of the troop, and Saritha hit them at the back end, while Ithsar fired arrows into the thick of the horde. Tharuks roared and snarled as arrows struck them in the head, thighs, chest, and neck. They yowled, dragon fire licking over their fur and burning them.

Above Ithsar, the sky roiled with fire. Flashes of green mage flame and streaks of blue stabbed through the flames, incinerating dark dragons. Thick clumps of ash floated down, coating her hair and thighs, but still Ithsar kept firing arrows, and the dragons kept flaming until there were only a few tharuks left.

"Zaarusha has asked us to leave the last few tharuks to her, and to check the forest between here and the clearing in case there are more." Saritha ascended above the forest.

"And Ezaara and Roberto? Should we help them kill Zens?" Ithsar glanced down at the riverbank where Zens lay at Roberto's feet, with Roberto's sword at his throat.

"No. Zaarusha says they want that pleasure themselves."

As Saritha wheeled to head back across the forest, Ithsar glanced back to make sure her friends Ezaara and Roberto were safe. Ezaara stalked up behind Roberto and slashed her sword across Zens' gut, a red stain blooming. Then she drove her sword through his throat.

Even without having seen it, Ithsar would've still known Zens was dead. The *sathir* over the forest lightened, as if a great shadow had lifted from the land—like an awning being rolled back so the blazing desert sun could shine.

After the War

Bonfires crackled high in the clearing at Mage Gate as dragons incinerated piles of tharuks, shadow beasts, and even their own kind, who'd died or been killed after being turned by methimium. Ithsar shook her head at the waste of life—although, as an assassin, she would've been trained specifically to kill, had it not been for her deformed fingers.

The piles of burning, reeking flesh turned her stomach.

Stefan nudged her with his elbow. "It almost makes you want to give up fighting, doesn't it?" He scrubbed his eyes with the back of his hand. "We lost some brave riders today."

Misha nodded. "I've never really enjoyed fighting."

Holding her chin up, Ithsar squeezed Misha's hand and swallowed. Nila's bright flickering flame and her zest for life were no more. It was a sore loss for all of them, but Misha had been Nila's closest friend.

She cast about, looking for Ezaara. In the light of the fire, pockets of assassins and dragon riders were chatting, cleaning their weapons, or making food.

Ithsar paced over to the young dragon rider seated near his purple dragon whose scales glinted gold in the firelight. She inclined her head. "You helped me in battle today when those dragons had Saritha in her clutches. Thank you for killing the one latched to her tail." She clasped his hands, then released them.

"It was nothing," An easy grin lit up his soot-smudged, bloodied face. Blue-gray eyes looked from under from his battle-dirty blonde hair. Eyes that sparkled with fun. "I'm Kierion. Nice to meet you, Ithsar. I've never shaken hands with a chief prophetess before—or an assassin, and lived to tell the tale. Can you predict my future?"

She shook her head, then realized he was teasing her. "No, but one of my assassins may be able to predict your immediate future, or lack of it, if you test their skills with a blade."

He threw back his head and laughed. "Hey, Fenni, come over here."

A tall green-eyed mage with blond hair stalked over and shook Ithsar's hand. "Pleased to meet you. I'm Fenni."

"You're the mage who was riding with Kierion," Ithsar said. "Thanks for your help. Your fireball skills helped save my dragon's life today."

"Did you hear that, Fenni?" Kierion crowed.

Fenni blushed to the tips of his ears. "He's giving me a hard time because fireballs took me ages to master." He grinned. "Seriously, I used to be hopeless."

Ithsar grinned back.

A short Naobian girl raced over and threw her arms around Ithsar, nearly bowling her over. It was strange hugging someone her own size—usually everyone towered over her.

"Hey, Ithsar, I'm Adelina," the girl said. "Thank you for saving my brother." Adelina's voice broke.

Her brother? Ithsar pulled back to gaze at Adelina's olive-back eyes and Naobian complexion. Oh, of course. "I should have realized Roberto was your brother."

Adelina waved a hand. "He's much taller than me, so most people never guess we're related."

It wasn't the height difference as much as their demeanor. Roberto had an air of distrust about him. Adelina was bubbly, her smile bright—they were worlds apart.

Adelina clasped Ithsar's hand. "Ezaara asked me to tell you she had to leave for Dragons' Hold urgently."

Ithsar swallowed a sharp pang of disappointment. So that's where Ezaara was. She'd gone to find out what was left of her shattered people. Ithsar hoped for her sake that her home was still intact. She sighed. Of course, a Queen's Rider would be far too busy to visit with a lowly assassin.

"What do you mean, a lowly assassin?" Saritha growled. *"You're a Queen's Rider too—of the queen of the sea dragons."*

"She said she'd love to see you tomorrow morning at Dragons' Hold to personally thank you for your help." Adelina gave an infectious smile.

"She did?" Ithsar grinned, warmth blossoming her breast.

§

Ithsar and Saritha swooped over the peaks of Dragon's Teeth and into Dragons' Hold. The faint scent of char remained on the breeze, the blackened stones where snow had been melted away, a testament to the bodies that had recently been burned there.

"I see Zaarusha asleep on a ledge on that mountain face," Saritha mind-melded.

The mountainsides above the stony clearing were pockmarked with caves. Some dragons were slumbering on ledges—recovering their strength after the arduous battle—while others flew above the basin, ferrying debris into piles, no doubt for another burning. It took Ithsar a moment to spot Zaarusha. There was space for several dragons on her wide, rocky ledge. An overhang protected the back end, and it was there that Zaarusha was sequestered with her head under her wing. Beside her, Erob was asleep too.

The queen of Dragons' Realm raised her head and looked right at them, tracking Saritha with her eyes as she flew.

"Did you tell her we're coming?" Ithsar's orange robes billowed in the breeze.

"In the sea, we mind-meld when we're visiting another's territory. I thought I'd give Zaarusha the same courtesy. She is another dragon queen, after all."

"Fair enough." Finally, Ithsar would see Ezaara again. Not just a distant glimpse in battle, but a chance to talk to her friend.

Saritha flew in a lazy arc and swooped in to land on the ledge, her talons scrabbling on the rock. *"Zaarusha welcomes you and has told Ezaara you're here. If you don't mind, I'll take a swim later in that beautiful lake."*

"Of course, you can, and please thank Zaarusha." Ithsar leaped off her sea dragon.

"Ithsar!" Ezaara and Roberto appeared at the back of the overhang. Ezaara ran over and they embraced.

"Thank you, Ithsar," Ezaara said. "You changed the tide of the battle. Your sea dragons and the Naobian greens helped us."

"Before I ever met you, I had a vision of us riding into battle together," Ithsar said, her blood thrumming as she remembered. "And then again, when my mother captured you."

Ezaara clasped Ithsar tighter. "I was afraid your mother had killed you because you helped. Gods, I'm glad you're alive."

"Ashewar lives no longer." Sorrow lanced through Ithsar. She would probably always feel this sadness and disappointment, but now she had much more than just a mother who'd hated her. She was the rider of Saritha, and the leader of the Robandi assassins. She'd helped win a war. And she'd found friends who valued her. "I'm now the chief prophetess of the Robandi assassins." She waved her fingers in the air. "And I have fingers that work. Thank you. None of this would've happened without you, Ezaara."

"How in the Egg's name did you become Chief Prophetess? And how did you meet your beautiful dragon?"

"That's a long story," said Ithsar. "And Saritha is hungry and needs time to recover from battle."

"As do you." Ezaara enclosed Ithsar's cool hand in her own warm one. "I suggest Zaarusha takes Saritha hunting and maybe to the lake for a swim, while you and Roberto and I catch up over breakfast."

Roberto laughed and embraced Ithsar. "We'd love to hear your tale."

"That would suit Saritha well. Although she hankers for the sea, she's keen to try your northern lakes." Ithsar grinned. "And I'm famished."

As the dragons flew off together, Ithsar followed them through Zaarusha's den, inside. The Queen's Rider's cavern was more modest than Ithsar had expected—nothing like Ashewar's grand throne room in the Robandi lair under the oasis. There were drawers, a big bed, a beautiful hand-painted wardrobe, a small table, and some chairs. And dragons. Everything was decorated with dragons—the quilt, the rug, the cushions, even the paintings on the wardrobe and the hilts of the two decorative swords mounted on the wall. A dragon tapestry on the far wall had been slashed. Probably by tharuks when they'd overrun the hold.

Ezaara waved a hand. "Sorry, it's a bit of a mess. I'll tidy up eventually, but at the moment, the welfare of my people is more important."

Again, so different to Ashewar.

Roberto pulled three chairs out from the table, and flourished a hand. "Please, take a seat." He sprinkled dried berries from a pouch into three cups, then added water from a waterskin. "I'll ask Erob to heat this brew." He brushed Ezaara's hair with his lips. "Back soon." He wandered out to the ledge as Ithsar and Ezaara sat down.

"It must be nice to have someone care about you like that," Ithsar said.

Ezaara followed him with her gaze, a faint smile on her face. "You know, he wasn't always like this. I positively hated him when we first met. He was so cold and arrogant."

"But he's such a wonderful man now. I could tell that, even back at the oasis."

"Yes, he is. He hid it well." Ezaara gestured at a basket of fruit and some bread. "I'm afraid there's not much else to eat around here. Although we do have a few preserves if you'd like me to fetch some. Tharuks rampaged through the mess cavern and destroyed most of the fresh supplies."

Ithsar bit into a roll of fluffy bread. "I never really had a chance to thank you properly for healing my fingers."

Ezaara laughed. "We were too busy trying to escape a horde of angry assassins. What happened after I left? I was sure Ashewar would be livid."

"Ashewar was. She tried to kill me." Ithsar finished her roll and told Ezaara exactly what had happened.

When she described Stefan's hopeless attack on her, there was a quiet chuckle behind her.

Roberto came over and placed the steaming cups on the table, the fragrant tang of berries wafting toward them.

"What's this?" Ithsar asked.

"Soppleberry tea. One of my favorites." Roberto took a sip. "Luckily." He winked at Ezaara.

"It sounds as if there's a story behind that," Ithsar said.

Roberto's dark eyes, so like her own, were laced with pain. "A while ago, Zens captured and tortured me, then implanted a methimium crystal in my back. When I returned to Dragons' Hold, I was determined to kill Ezaara, but at the last moment, she distracted me with soppleberry tea." He raised his eyebrows, exhaling forcefully. "Even if I hadn't liked soppleberry before, that would be a great reason to make it my favorite."

Ezaara shuddered. "I laced it with woozy weed. He fell asleep within moments. My mother, Marlies..." She bit her lip.

Roberto squeezed her hand and finished for her. "Ezaara and her mother extracted the crystal from my back. Marlies was a great woman, one of the finest healers Dragons' Hold has ever had."

A stray tear on her cheek, Ezaara murmured softly, "It was thanks to my mother that I could fix your fingers."

"She rode a silver dragon, didn't she?" Ithsar asked.

"Yes, she rode Liesar. They'd only been reunited for a few short moons. She sacrificed her life to save me in battle."

"So we've both lost our mothers recently." Ithsar clasped Ezaara's hand and Ezaara squeezed hers back.

"And Roberto lost his father," Ezaara murmured.

"My father sold me to the enemy, who tortured and abused me, and turned me against the ones I loved." Roberto grimaced. "We all have scars. Some of us have done unspeakable things, but now let's make the world a better place."

No matter what their pasts were—despite methimium crystals, murderous mothers, traitorous fathers, and despite the evil monsters that had tried to destroy Dragons' Realm—they could rebuild this realm.

Ezaara put her hand on the table. "Let's make it a place where children may laugh and play in the sun without the fear of being hurt or enslaved."

Ithsar placed her hand on top of Ezaara's. "A place where people may pursue whatever life they want, regardless of where or how they were born."

Roberto placed his hand on top. "A life where mothers and fathers respect and honor their children, and raise them with a sense of dignity and self-worth."

Then Roberto smiled. "Let's start tomorrow. Now, we'll show you around Dragons' Hold."

But Ithsar knew they'd already started rebuilding. From the pride gleaming in Roberto and Ezaara's eyes, they knew it as well.

Reunion

Kisha saw the last of her customers out the door. "Have a lovely evening."

"You too, Kisha, it was a wonderful meal. We're glad you've reopened without those *other* patrons." The gentleman winked, then surreptitiously glanced over his shoulder just to make sure no stray tharuks were listening.

He needn't have feared. The Robandi assassins and green guards had managed to kill most of them and drive the rest away. Hopefully Last Stop would be free of those awful beasts for a while. Kisha walked back to the kitchen, Thika perched upon her shoulder with his tail loosely around her neck, to finish washing the dishes.

She dunked a pan in the tub and scrubbed it. It had been a long day, but a good one. Two days ago, after the Robandi assassins had left the Lost King Inn, Kisha had spread the word around town that she'd be opening to patrons again today. Then she'd rushed back to polish the place until it gleamed. The builder had fixed the front door and the glazier had even managed to replace her window, so even though she had fewer tables and chairs, the inn was in good shape.

She was just putting away the last serving dish when a heavy thud sounded outside the square—an ominous thud, like a shadow dragon landing. Thika's tail coiled tighter as Kisha crept to the window to peek outside.

It wasn't a shadow dragon, but Ithsar on Saritha. Ramisha, Fangora, and Nilanna landed beside her. More sea dragons and green guards wheeled in the air above the town square.

Kisha raced outside as Ithsar dismounted. Ithsar's robes were stained and battle-dirty, but Kisha didn't care. She flung her arms around the chief prophetess. "I'm so glad you're back. I wasn't sure if you'd make it."

Stefan swung out of the saddle and jumped down, his boots thunking on the cobbles. "Thanks to me, she made it." He grinned cheekily. "For a moment there, she was in trouble, but I swooped in and saved her—six times, no less."

Kisha hugged him too, but Ithsar reached past Kisha to slug him on the arm.

Stefan slugged her back.

Kisha glanced around. "Where's Nila?"

Ithsar's smile died.

And Kisha knew. "She didn't make it, did she?" Her throat tightened and her eyes stung.

Nila, gone. Nila, who had laughed as she'd stitched her wound, and told her crazy tales of life in the desert and stories of the underwater world, stoically ignoring the pain in her side—pain that was so bad, she'd been pale and shaking. Nila, who'd swung on the utensil rank in her kitchen to save her from those horrible tharuks.

Nilanna hung back, hunkering down on the edge of the square. She tucked her head under her wing and went to sleep.

Ithsar jerked her head toward the dragon. "It'll take time. For all of us. Nila was a bright star in our lives."

A bright star that had burned out. Had Kisha's grandmother, Anakisha, been like Nila? Although Kisha had never met Anakisha, her mother had told her that she'd been full of life, bold, and not afraid of danger. No one had expected her to be lost in battle.

Kisha forced herself to smile brightly. "Come inside, Ithsar, and call your riders. There's hot stew on the hearth if you'd like some."

"Sounds great." Ithsar forced her own overly-bright smile, and raked a hand through her disheveled hair. Somewhere in battle she must've lost her pretty orange headscarf. Her face was covered in grime and she looked weary.

Thika scrambled from the crook of Kisha's neck, down her forearm and leaped onto Ithsar's arm, racing up to her shoulder. He snuffled her hair and chittered. Ithsar laughed. "Yes, boy, it's good to see you too."

A tiny stab of loss pinged through Kisha. It was fine. Thika was Ithsar's lizard, after all. She'd only been looking after him.

The lizard scampered down the front of Ithsar's robe and burrowed inside, then popped back out, and raced down Ithsar's leg and up Kisha's skirt, onto her forearm again. He perched there, looking back and forth between them both.

Ithsar laughed. "Now that's the funniest thing I've seen in days—apart from Stefan being caught by tharuks down that lane." She waved a hand toward a nearby alley.

"Huh! What about you?" Stefan leaned down and picked up a short end of Ithsar's hair. "You haven't told us yet about how you managed to lose one of your beautiful dark tresses. When exactly did you make the decision to hire a tharuk as a barber?"

Ithsar snorted. "At least my hair's beautiful. When did you decide to wash yours in tharuk blood?"

Misha laughed. "We all decided to do that when we followed you north. Now, will you two stop bickering. Kisha, you mentioned a hearty stew?"

Kisha laughed. "Come inside and tell me everything."

Ithsar groaned. "Don't say that! Stefan will never stop yammering about the six times he saved me."

"There! She admitted it!" Stefan crowed to Misha. "I told you I saved her six times."

Kisha wrinkled her nose. "Well, I'm sorry, but now that I've purged my inn of the stink of tharuk, you're all going to have to take hot baths before dinner."

Ithsar's eyes shone. "Sounds blissful." Her smile was matched by Misha and Stefan's grins.

§

In the end, Kisha didn't have quite enough stew to go around, so Misha and three of the green guards chopped more ingredients and threw them into the cauldron—the same cauldron she'd wanted to hit the tharuk with. They cracked open a few more jars of pickles, and Kisha rustled up some flatbread.

When the food was ready, Kisha bustled out with steaming tureens of stew and baskets of bread, and placed them on the tables.

The Lost King was crammed full of green guards and assassins—many of whom had taken advantage of the bathing facilities upstairs and changed into fresh orange robes or riders' garb. They lounged in chairs, all over the floor, and even stood around the walls as they bit into fresh bread and helped themselves to Kisha's stew.

She sighed. It had been moons and moons since the inn had been this full of anything other than tharuks. She'd only managed to keep the place going so long due to the suppliers who'd taken pity on her and knew she'd be killed if she hadn't kept providing the tharuks with food and ale. Kisha found a quiet corner, ladled herself a bowl of stew, and sat down on the stairs leading up to the bedrooms.

The babble, laughter, and murmuring were like soothing music.

When she'd finished her dinner, Kisha leaned back against the railing on the stairs.

The door opened and Goren, leader of the green guards, stalked in. He wasn't alone.

Kisha's hand flew to her mouth. No, it couldn't be. She looked again. It was. An enormous barrel-chested man filled the doorway, his beard and bushy hair like a dark halo around his friendly face.

He grinned and his voice boomed across the inn. "Kisha, it's great to see you."

Kisha leaped up and propelled herself across the room, racing to meet Giant John. A moment later, she was lifted from the ground as he enfolded her in an enormous bear hug.

"After battling tharuks for days, you're a sight for sore eyes." Giant John placed her back on her feet and grinned. "How are you, girl?"

"It's been interesting." She grinned back. By the First Egg, it was good to see him.

His eyes twinkled in the lamplight. "I like this class of patrons better than the last lot. The sight of those ugly tusky faces guzzling good ale was enough to turn any man's stomach." He slapped a hand against the flat of his stomach, and inhaled deeply. "Something smells good. Mind if we do?"

"Of course. We can't break tradition." Kisha couldn't stop grinning. Her cheeks were already getting sore. "I'm afraid we won't be able to provide your usual seating arrangements." Usually Giant John took two seats or half a bench, but with the scarcity of furniture and the number of dragon riders there tonight, that wouldn't be possible.

He gave a belly laugh. "I don't mind roughing it, as long as I have a soft bed tonight. Got any free rooms? Or have this rowdy lot taken them all?"

"That shouldn't be a problem, as long as you kick a few dragon riders out into the snow."

Giant John flexed his biceps and grinned. "I'll get right onto it."

Goren groaned. "And I thought we were done with fighting. Come on, let's eat."

Kisha went into the kitchen to fry up a few eggs, knowing they were Giant John's favorite.

Giant John followed her in. "I saw tharuk tusk gouges in the tabletops out there. I don't suppose there'd be any bacon left after those brutes have rampaged through the place, would there?"

"No, but I have salted pork. I can fry that for you, if you'd like."

The pork was soon sizzling. Giant John leaned back against a counter and folded his arms. As Kisha reached up for her spatula, he ducked to avoid the utensil rack swinging overhead. Kisha flipped the eggs.

"You look tired. Here, let me do that." Giant John picked Kisha up and sat her on an empty benchtop—something he'd been doing since she was a littling and her parents had run the inn—and then took the spatula and turned the rest of the eggs and pork.

"I have a question," Kisha said, swinging her legs. "Have you seen Marlies? She was here again, about two weeks ago, and helped me sort out a tharuk brawl, but I haven't seen her since."

"Sounds like her." He studied the eggs, avoiding her gaze.

"When Marlies first visited here, two moons ago, I gave her my grandmother's jade ring that controls the realm gate, but last time she was here, she didn't say much about what happened to her."

He gazed at her. "Last time I saw you, I told you how I took her across the flatlands to the foot of the Terramites, hidden in the base of my wagon." Kisha nodded, and he continued, "Well, I found out later that she helped free Zaarusha's orange-scaled son, Maazini, from Zens' clutches, but first, she nearly died when Zens tortured her. Afraid to spill Dragons' Realm's secrets, she took some berries that put her into a deep coma."

"Coma?"

Giant John flipped the pork. The fine aroma wafted to Kisha as the meat sizzled and browned. "She looked like she was dead, barely breathing, barely alive, until her son, Tomaaz, found her and rescued her. Together, they escaped Death Valley using the ring. Now, Tomaaz has returned and freed the slaves."

Kisha gaped. Freed the thousands of slaves in Death Valley? For as long as she'd been alive, Zens had been capturing and enslaving their people. "Death Valley's gone?"

"Well, it's still there, but the slaves are gone. They're at Dragons' Hold. Thanks to a contraption Zens made that held the realm gates open when he used one of those jade rings." Giant John shoveled the eggs onto his plate and moved the pork around the pan with the spatula.

"One of them?"

"Apparently there was another ring too." He tilted his head, grinning at her. "No more slavery. No more tharuks. It's hard to believe, isn't it?"

"So Marlies is responsible for all that? I'd love to see her again."

Giant John turned to her, his eyes full of sorrow. "She didn't make it. She sacrificed her life to save her daughter, Ezaara, the Queen's Rider."

Kisha swallowed. Another bright star had faded. Another person she'd cared about. "How did she die?"

"She leaped from her dragon to save Ezaara from a bolt of mage fire, and died in a blaze of fire that lit up the sky." Giant John shook his head. "The truth is, she was already dying. She never quite recovered from the berries she took in Death Valley."

Kisha swallowed, trying to ease the ache in her throat. It didn't work. "At least Ezaara's alive. I'd like to meet her, some day."

Giant John slid the pork onto his plate and took the pan off the fire. He grabbed a fork and leaned back against the counter, stabbing the eggs with a vengeance. "I'd love to be there when you meet her: the ex-Queen's Rider's granddaughter and the new Queen's Rider. I think you'll like her, Kisha." He put his fork on his plate, and placed his hand on Kisha's shoulder. "Come on. Although we might not feel like it, the revelry out there will probably do us good."

§

Ithsar leaned back in her chair as Stefan entertained half the inn with stories of how brave he and Fangora had been in battle. Even though they'd only known each other a week, Ithsar was going to miss his brash, cheeky smile.

Goren plonked a bowl of stew on the table and sat beside her. "You worked wonders with Stefan's swordsmanship in those few short days. How did you do it?" Eyes on her, he shoveled a spoonful of stew into his mouth.

Ithsar shrugged. "He's a fast learner, but his balance was wrong. Once we corrected that, and I showed him a few simple sword strokes and blocks that suited his build, he was fine."

Goren looked weary, his face lined with grief and his shoulders slumped as he dunked his bread into his stew and bit into it.

"Thanks for bringing Giant John back here to see Kisha," Ithsar said. "He trained her for years, so it means the world to her."

"Anakisha's granddaughter, the bartender to tharuks. I never thought I'd live to see the day. I bet she's glad that's over." Goren took another spoonful of stew. "Ithsar, I, um… you handled yourself well in battle. You're a fine leader."

Ithsar stared, speechless.

Goren grinned. "You led your wing of sea dragons extremely well. Much better than I anticipated. I'm sorry I underestimated you."

She gaped.

Goren chuckled. "Don't look so shocked. I'm not that bad."

Ithsar grinned and they lapsed into companionable silence, watching the bustle and hubbub around them.

Giant John came out of the kitchen with a massive plate of eggs and pork, Kisha at his side. They sat on a step at the bottom of the staircase to the bedrooms. Giant John shoveled eggs and pork into his mouth, gesticulating as he told Kisha wild tales. Every now and then, she answered, and he slapped his thigh, laughter shaking his enormous frame.

As soon as his eggs were gone, Giant John helped himself to a huge bowl of stew, and then another.

Ithsar nudged Goren. "I don't know how he can eat that much…"

Goren grinned, making him look more carefree than Ithsar had ever seen. "It's quite a feat, isn't it? I guess battle makes him hungry."

Just then, Stefan got to the punch line of his latest rescue, and the inn rippled with laughter.

§

The hubbub of the dragon riders perched on chairs, tables, and around the floor of the inn was strangely comforting to Kisha after so many moons of serving tharuks. Stefan was holding the floor, still teasing Ithsar. He hadn't stopped all night. Although the chief prophetess certainly didn't seem to mind, and was giving him back as much as he gave.

"So, here I am, a herbalist who imprinted with the dragon, and I saved the head of the Robandi assassins from a terrible fate." Stefan whacked his thigh, tipped his head back and crowed like a rooster at dawn.

Ithsar groaned and rolled her eyes. "I'm never going to live this down, am I?" She slapped him on the arm, playfully.

He turned to her in mock seriousness, face solemn. "Do that again, and I may not save you next time." And then he burst out laughing again.

The riders laughed too, joining in with tales of how they'd saved each other's hides. Tomorrow, Ithsar had told Kisha, they'd light candles in the square for those who hadn't made it. She'd asked Kisha to invite Katrine, so she could light a candle for Kadran too.

Kisha had seen enough dragon riders and warriors after battle to know that the laughter and camaraderie helped to hide the pain. But with the loss of Nila and the prospect of losing Thika and her new friends again so soon, Kisha needed fresh air. Besides, Nila's dragon was out there, lonely and grieving.

She slipped out into the square with the last of the salted pork on an enormous tray, and tiptoed over to Nila's dragon, Nilanna, who was still sleeping. Kisha laid the tray on the cobbles near her head. Her scales shimmered in the flickering lantern light from the inn's window. She was so beautiful, Kisha was tempted to touch her. She sighed, not wanting to wake her, and carefully stepped away.

The dragon's eyes flicked open. Her nostrils quivered. She angled her head and winked at Kisha.

Winked? Kisha hadn't even realized dragons could wink. And had never expected one to wink at her. She neared and laid her hand upon the creature's forehead.

Nilanna's voice drifted through her mind like a warm summer breeze. *"You have such a big heart, Kisha. Your friends are inside, enjoying each other's company, yet you come outside to care for me, knowing I am lonely and have lost the one I loved."*

"I understand losing the ones you love. It has happened to me too." Kisha's parents' faces swam before her eyes. Ma's lovely brown hair and twinkling blue eyes and Pa's friendly laugh.

"This was your family?"

Kisha nodded.

"Gone?" The sea dragon's voice was like a whisper in a hallowed hall.

"Yes."

"Then you are lonely too?"

Kisha nodded, tears rolling down her cheeks.

The dragon's golden eyes glowed with inner fire. *"Then I claim you as my new rider."*

Warmth washed over Kisha, and she gasped as a tight coil inside her unfurled like a new bud in spring, and blossomed into something warm and vibrant and loving. Sweet music filled her breast, like the melody of the most beautiful songbird. Slowly, the warmth and the music built, until her veins surged with the fire of new adventure.

"Now that we have imprinted, I shall no longer be known as Nilanna, but Kishanna, after you."

This? This beautiful sweet surety that she'd follow this dragon to the ends of the realm was imprinting.

But Anakisha's visions held her in their grip. She didn't dare fly, because, she knew, when she got on that dragon's back, she'd never want to get off again. And she was bound here—by her promise to her dying mother and by her promises to the spirit of her grandmother.

She'd pledged to stay until it was time to leave—and that time was not now. She could feel it in her bones.

Kisha rested her forehead against her dragon's snout as tears rolled down her cheeks.

Follow your heart. You'll know when the time is right.

Her heart was telling her to go, but she knew it wasn't time yet.

Kishanna's sadness washed over her. *"You're a free spirit, Kisha. Yet you remain chained to the past."*

Kisha nodded, sorrow and joy warring in her breast. *"It's my duty. I promised."*

"Then I will wait, and fly without a rider until you're ready."

Kisha flung her arms around Kishanna's scaly neck, and as a thrum built inside the dragon's throat, rumbling through her bones, she knew that this was right, so right. But not now.

With a heavy heart, she traipsed into the Lost King Inn, casting more than one glance back over her shoulder.

A Bizarre Surprise

The next morning, Kisha rose early and popped out into the square before anyone was awake. Kishanna nuzzled Kisha's hand, snuffing warm air over her palms. Kisha laughed and scratched her snout.

"Would you mind scratching my eye ridges?" Kishanna rumbled. *"They get terribly itchy."*

Kisha stretched up her hand and scratched the rough scales above Kishanna's eye. *"It's a shame I can't come with you,"* she said. *"But I sense I still have a purpose here."*

Kishanna blinked. *"You remained here so long, true to the visions from your grandmother, Anakisha. But surely now the war is over, it's no longer necessary."*

The dragon's words were tempting. But a sense of wrongness yawned inside Kisha, so she shook her head. *"Maybe I can follow you some day."* She rubbed a dry scale on Kishanna's jowl. *"But for now, I'll remain here. I've been true to my grandmother for all these years, so I can't sway from that path until it's time."*

There was a flurry of wingbeats above the square. Kisha glanced up, shading her eyes from the early morning sun gleaming off a golden dragon. Two riders were upon its back, a woman with flaming red hair wearing unusual garb, and a dark-haired man wearing a mage cloak. The dragon spiraled down to the square, two long cloth-wrapped packages draped across its haunches.

She swallowed. Surely not. Surely those couldn't be…

The dragon landed. The man smiled and hailed her. "Good morning, Kisha. I have a special message for you from your grandmother."

Her heart caught in her throat. Those bushy eyebrows. That mage cloak.

The man kissed the woman on the cheek and slid from the golden dragon, approaching Kisha. He held out his hand, shaking hers. A trickle of mage power zinged into her palm.

"Are you Master Giddi, the dragon mage?"

He chuckled. "Indeed, I am."

"Then that must be…" But it couldn't be.

"Yes, it is. I'd like you to meet Mazyka, my wife."

Mazyka, who'd opened a world gate with Giddi years before, and let Commander Zens in, and then been locked out when Giddi had closed the gate—along with dozens and dozens of mages.

"We have a special delivery for you. Do have a spare bedroom?"

"The inn is full, but Giant John is leaving today, so you can use his room."

The dragon mage's bushy eyebrows flew up. "Giant John's here?" The mage cupped his hands around his mouth and bellowed, "John! John, we need your help." His voice echoed off the cobbles in the square and rang amongst the buildings, probably waking every resident in Last Stop.

Moments later, the tavern door burst open and Giant John stumbled out in his breeches and nightshirt. "Giddi! You're a sight for sore eyes." He embraced Giddi and Mazyka. "I see you've met my friend, Kisha."

Giddi nodded. "We have a matter of grave importance, something that's puzzled us all for years. I need your help."

Giant John pounded his hand on his heart with a thump that might've knocked a lesser man down.

Mazyka had dismounted and was untying the packages on the dragon's haunches. "Please, John, be careful. These are precious. We must take them inside immediately."

Cradling the smaller of the long parcels as if it would shatter into a million pieces, Giddi lifted one from Mazyka's arms and Giant John carefully eased the other off the dragon's haunches, his eyes full of questions.

Kisha's heart pounded.

Kishanna's gentle voice drifted through her mind. *"Be brave, Kisha. You have a valiant heart. I will always be here if you need me."*

A wave of comfort washed over Kisha. She squared her shoulders and followed Giant John, Master Giddi, and Mazyka inside.

§

Kisha had often wished to see her grandmother, but had never believed it would happen.

Anakisha's body rested on the bed, hands clasped over her breast, and wrinkled face peaceful, as Giddi explained. "Mazyka and I went to Death Valley and found her in Zens' quarters. He was using a strange, peculiar magic to keep her alive."

"It's called science," Mazyka interrupted. "I've told you, Giddi, if we're to teach everyone in Dragons' Realm, we need to be clear. Magic and science are quite different."

Those bushy eyebrows tugged down into a fierce frown. "All right, then. Using science, he kept her alive."

"And this is Yanir?" Her grandfather, the King's Rider, looked much younger than Anakisha, about two thirds her age.

"Yes, he was dead, but Zens pickled him. That's why he looks younger," Giddi said.

Mazyka rolled her eyes and chuckled. "It's called preserving."

"Yes," said Kisha. "I preserve my pickles too."

Mazyka muttered something indecipherable, then laughed. "Come on, let's organize their funerals."

ANAKISHA'S FUNERAL

By mid-morning, most of the citizens of Last Stop had gathered on the outskirts of the village for the funeral of Anakisha and Yanir. Giant John had hastily erected a small dais at one end of a snow-crusted meadow. Mazyka had pulled wondrous bolts of gold cloth from the saddlebags of her golden dragon. And now, Yanir and Anakisha lay on the dais, wrapped in shimmering gold, with only their faces showing under the open, sun-kissed sky.

Birds flitted in and out of the evergreens along the side of the meadow, twittering.

Giant John slung a comforting arm around Kisha's shoulders. Happiness and sorrow warred in her breast. Happiness at finally seeing Anakisha, and sorrow for losing her grandmother.

Giant John squeezed her shoulder, his touch reassuring. "From what Master Giddi says, this will be the first time they've seen the open air in over nineteen years."

Standing on the other side of her, Giddi nodded. "Yes, that's right. Zens kept them both underground in tanks, all that time. The funny thing is, we always referred to Anakisha as being 'lost' in battle. We never said she'd died. But none of us ever dreamed we'd find her." He scratched one of his bushy eyebrows. "You know, she requested that we bring her back here so you could see her, Kisha. She knew you were maintaining a vigil, and listening to her spirit all these years." Master Giddi's eyes were soft.

A lump stuck in Kisha's throat.

Mazyka, red hair flaming like fire in the sun, looked at Giddi with such tenderness, it stole Kisha's breath. "Just as you maintained a vigil for me all these years, Giddi. You never gave up hope."

Giddi kissed her flaming hair. "And you, for me."

Giant John cleared his throat. "Are you two done? Yanir and Anakisha have waited for a decent funeral for over nineteen years. We don't want to keep them waiting any longer."

"Tut, tut, so impatient, John." Giddi winked at Kisha, who laughed. Then the dragon mage pointed northward.

There were specks in the sky above the forest, north of the fields. As they steadily grew larger, the crowd murmured. Dragons—lots of dragons.

Giant John's belly laugh rumbled through Kisha's bones. "You didn't tell me we were expecting guests, Giddi. But of course Anakisha's family would want to be here."

Family? Kisha scarcely dared breathe. Years ago, Anakisha's children had gone into hiding, because they'd been under threat. When Anakisha and Yanir had died, the knowledge of their children's whereabouts had been lost. Her mother had once mentioned that it was possible Kisha might have cousins in far-flung regions.

"Are my long-lost cousins the family you mean?" Kisha asked Giant John. "Or do you mean the large family of dragon riders that loved Anakisha?"

Giant John arched an eyebrow. "Tut, tut, so impatient, Kisha." He winked at Master Giddi and laughed.

Kisha gave him a sharp jab with her elbow, but that just made him laugh harder.

As the dragons neared, the rustle of their wingbeats swished across the meadow, the foliage rippling in the breeze. There were at least forty, of all colors and sizes. Most of them landed near the sea dragons and green guards in the next meadow, but some flew closer and descended to land near Kisha, Giant John, Master Giddi, and Mazyka.

The largest dragon, a multi-hued creature with a regal bearing—Zaarusha, the Dragon Queen—landed nearby and strode toward them, accompanied by an enormous blue.

A tall woman slid from Zaarusha's back, her long blonde hair stirring in the breeze of other dragons' wingbeats as an orange dragon and others dropped down behind Zaarusha.

That pretty rider must be Ezaara.

Kisha wiped her suddenly-sweaty palms on her skirt.

A Naobian with a handsome, hard-edged face dismounted from the mighty blue dragon. He held Ezaara's hand, his smile dissolving those tough edges into tenderness.

Something inside Kisha twanged. All this time, this was what she'd missed, these loving connections.

§

Ezaara strode toward a small band of people assembled near the dais that held the bodies of Anakisha and Yanir. She'd often wondered what Anakisha, the ex-

Queen's Rider, had looked like, and had even been compared to her when she'd first imprinted with Zaarusha. But this chance to see her was something she'd never expected. Such a strange situation. Tomaaz's girl, Lovina, could preserve someone's likeness in a portrait, but Zens had preserved Yanir's *whole body* and kept Anakisha alive with tubes and a… Mazyka had called it a… a ventilator. That was it. She'd never thought she'd live to hear of something so bizarre.

Anakisha's wrinkled blue eyes stared at the sky of her homeland. Beside her, Yanir was younger—even handsome, despite the sallow tinge to his skin. Ezaara strode past the dais, Roberto at her side. There would be time for this later. The living were more important right now.

Giant John had his arm over the shoulders of a young girl, perhaps fourteen or fifteen summers old. From what Ma had told her, this was Kisha. Her hand in Roberto's, Ezaara strode over. She nudged Roberto and mind-melded. *"After you."*

His ebony eyes touched Ezaara's face. *"But you're the Queen's Rider."*

"You're her family."

"No, I really think you should go first as Queen's Rider." He squeezed her hand.

"Very well." Ezaara ignored Master Giddi, Mazyka, and Giant John, and made a beeline for Kisha. "Good morning, Kisha. I'm Ezaara. I believe you met my mother Marlies."

The girl's bright blue eyes were wide. She nodded.

Just saying her mother's name made Ezaara's eyes sting. But Marlies wouldn't have wanted her to cry. "Through your help, my mother helped change the fate of Dragons' Realm." Ezaara pulled the girl into a warm embrace, enfolding her in her arms. She was so tiny, so frail, yet so strong to have held out for all this time on her own. "Ma appreciated your kindness. The ring you gave her was key to her escaping Zens, and she never would've made it across the Flatlands if it weren't for you and Giant John. You've played an important part in this war, and we'll be forever grateful. If you ever need a home, you're welcome at Dragons' Hold." Ezaara stepped back and brushed away the tears that graced her cheeks.

Kisha's eyes were bright with moisture too. She gave a trembling smile. "Thank you. I needed to hear that."

Ezaara swept a hand behind her. "There's someone I'd like you to meet."

Roberto mind-melded, *"She's so dainty."*

"Yet so strong," Ezaara melded. *"She gave Ma the ring that helped her and Tomaaz save Maazini. Without Kisha, I would've lost my family, and we might not be here today."*

"True." Roberto gave a warm smile and clasped Kisha's hands. "Kisha, I'm Roberto, your cousin from Naobia. My mother Lucia was your mother's sister, another of Anakisha's daughters." And then he hugged her.

The joy that lit up Kisha's face was worth all the pain of this war. Worth everything Ezaara had gone through. Zens' torture. Losing Ma. Everything.

"You have a kind and generous heart, Ezaara," Zaarusha rumbled in her mind.

"How could I begrudge anyone this? Look how happy she is."

Adelina raced over and threw her arms around Kisha. "I'm Adelina, Roberto's sister. I always thought that Roberto and I were the only ones left. Welcome to our family."

Ezaara didn't miss the shadow that flitted across Roberto's face. He was thinking of his father, Amato, again. How he'd survived in an underground lake for years, only to throw himself in the path of a tharuk arrow to save Adelina's life.

Her twin, Tomaaz, slid from Maazini, his royal orange-scaled dragon, as Lovina landed with Ajeurina, a royal green, and dismounted. Behind them, Taliesin's red dragon wheeled in and blue guards landed with more people for Kisha to meet.

Tomaaz and Lovina approached Kisha, smiling. Lovina's face was no longer gaunt, and she'd gained new curves since being freed from slavery. That, and her confident smile, had transformed her into a completely different person from the cowering reed-thin slave who'd been drugged on numlock and barely aware of her surroundings in Lush Valley.

Kisha beamed as Lovina said, "I'm your cousin too. Argus was my father, but sadly, the rest of my family died as slaves in Death Valley."

"May I hug you as well?" Tomaaz asked before embracing Kisha. "As Ezaara said, you helped save my life and my mother's by giving Ma Anakisha's ring." He waved a hand behind him. "There's someone else who'd like to meet you."

Maazini strode forward, the tip of his tail leaving a thin trail in the snow. His warm dragon breath huffed over them as he passed Ezaara and snuffled Kisha's hand. Tomaaz scratched his dragon's snout affectionately. "Ma and I rescued Maazini from Death Valley, where Zens kept him captive."

Kisha was weeping openly now, the smile upon her face radiant.

§

Kisha couldn't believe she had a cousin—no, cousins—Roberto, Adelina, *and* Lovina. And the Queen's Rider had thanked her.

Roberto grinned. "Wait, there are more."

More people flooded forward, forming a line. So many, she was never going to keep up with the whirl of faces and names.

A waif-thin boy with dark hair and solemn lake-blue eyes shook her hand. "I'm your cousin, Rhun Taliesin of Waykeep in the Flatlands. You can call me Taliesin," he said. "My pa, Rhun, was Anakisha's son. He died with the rest of my family in Death Valley, but Tomaaz and Marlies helped me to escape. Now, I'm training in prophecy at Dragons' Hold." He beamed. "Thank you for keeping the ring safe or we wouldn't have made it."

All this time alone, tending the bar, mopping up tharuks' spilled beer, staying out of the way when they brawled, and cleaning up the debris, had been worth it. Her loyalty to her grandmother had helped save lives.

Next in line were a woman with her husband and children, not dragon riders by the looks of their clothes. "I'm Esmeralda, your aunt. Meet your uncle Nick and your cousins, Urs, Tom, Greta, Luisa, Markus, and Rona." Urs, the oldest, was way older than Kisha, but the youngest was still a littling. "Until recently, we hailed from Western Settlement in Lush Valley where Nick and I ran the inn."

Tears streamed down Kisha's face as they each hugged her.

A middle-aged woman presented her with a beautiful hand-painted scarf of green and blue sea dragons wheeling above an ocean. "I, too, am your aunt. My name's Ana and this is my husband, Ernst, and my children, Lofty, Mari, Samuel, and Johanna, and Little Ana. We were Ezaara's neighbors in Lush Valley. I also kept a jade ring for Anakisha for many years, until it was needed."

"You did?" Kisha felt an instant sense of kinship with this woman with the kind eyes and warm smile. She wrapped the pretty scarf around her neck. "Thank you."

Kishanna's comforting voice rushed into her mind like a warm breeze. *"Not only do you belong, you are at the very heart of a family that spans Dragons' Realm—from Dragons' Hold to Naobia and all the way across the Flatlands."*

Kisha eyes skimmed over all fifteen cousins and her two aunts and uncles, and she felt as if her skin would explode with joy.

Her family members filed past her grandparents, gently placing their hands over their hearts as they paid their last respects, then stood closest to the dais, near the front of the assembled crowd. The gathered crowd's murmurs died as Kisha faced them, next to Ezaara, Master Giddi, Mazyka, and Giant John.

Zaarusha reared onto her hind legs and roared, then stalked over to Kisha.

"She wants to mind-meld with you," Ezaara said.

As the dragon queen dipped her head, Kisha was struck with awe. Zaarusha's hide glimmered with all the colors of the rainbow. When she laid her hand on the queen's scaly forehead, Zaarusha's memories rushed through her.

Anakisha as a young girl—beautiful, strong-willed, and feisty. Anakisha, the first time Zaarusha had seen her, imprinting. Her meeting Yanir. Snatches of them leading blue dragons into battle. And then the vision that Kisha had seen herself, many times over: Yanir dying and Anakisha trying to save him, but falling off Zaarusha into a swarming mass of tharuks.

"I thank you for being true to the memory of my former rider. As Ezaara said, there will always be a home for you at Dragons' Hold."

The warmth that washed over Kisha settled deep inside her. She belonged.

§

Finally, it was time to start. Kisha waited with bated breath, wondering what she could learn about her grandparents. Ezaara stood before the assembled crowd, her blonde hair shifting in the breeze. Zaarusha roared, quieting the murmurs.

"It's appropriate that we're in Last Stop, the last place Anakisha visited before she was lost in battle. It is with joy and sorrow that we meet here today," Ezaara said, her clear voice rippling through the throng and out across the fields. "Joy that slaves have been freed and families can be reunited. Joy that Zens and his evil monsters have been vanquished. And sorrow that we are mourning many we loved and lost. Today, we celebrate the actions of brave people, who stood up against evil. Alone, none of us could've battled Zens. But together, we managed to triumph. Every one of you can be proud of your actions, no matter how small. Whether you fed a hungry warrior, rode a dragon, flung mage flame, tended to wounded, repaired destruction left by tharuks, or sheltered your family behind closed doors, I thank you."

Despite the watching crowd, Kisha made no move to wipe the tears from her cheeks.

Ezaara swept a hand toward the assembled people. "Today, we're experiencing something that will never happen again. Nineteen years ago, the King Dragon, Syan, Yanir, his rider, and Anakisha, the Queen's Rider, were lost in battle. The world gate was shut and Mazyka and many other mages were locked out of Dragons' Realm. For years, we lived in darkness, with a growing rift between riders and mages that almost spanned a generation. During these dark times, Commander Zens tightened his grasp on the land. None of us suspected his plan went so much deeper. None of us ever dreamed of shadow dragons, of thousands killed in slave camps, or crystals that could turn our loyalty and make us try to kill the ones we love." Tears glimmered on Ezaara's cheeks now, but her voice remained steady. "None of us suspected that Zens had kept Yanir preserved. Or kept Anakisha alive, only to exist as a spirit, trapped in a realm gate, while he nourished her body, imprisoned in a tank." She shuddered. "So, now we'll pay our last respects to Yanir, the King's Rider, and Anakisha, the former Queen's Rider. We'll celebrate their lives, and thank them for their service to Dragons' Realm." Ezaara gestured Master Giddi forward.

Arms gesticulating and his eyebrows shooting up and down to punctuate his stories, Master Giddi recounted anecdote after anecdote of Anakisha's bravery and stubbornness, Yanir's sense of humor and courage, and the way they'd been lost in battle. The crowd was transfixed, laughing as he regaled them with funny stories, moved to tears as he spoke of their bravery and courage, and silent as he finally finished.

So many people spoke of her grandmother and grandfather—Hans, Ezaara and Tomaaz's father; Giant John, who made the crowd laugh as he described some of Anakisha's antics; Lars, the leader of the Council of the Twelve Dragon Masters; and Aidan, the master of battle.

Kisha's tears dried, and her heart filled, and then overflowed. If only Ma could hear these stories.

Finally, Kisha's newfound aunts and uncles spoke, one after the other. And then Ezaara turned to Kisha.

Kisha stood before hundreds of dragons and people, and for the first time since losing her parents, her heart was at peace. She gazed out at people's shining faces, some damp with tears, and others blazing with happiness. And all Kisha could say was, "Thank you for bringing my grandmother and grandfather home."

The ground shook as the dragons roared.

Zaarusha sprang to the dais, accompanied by her offspring, Erob, Maazini, and Ajeurina. The dragons grasped the ends of cords that were bound to the shimmering gold cloth wrapped around Anakisha and Yanir's bodies. Between them, they lifted Kisha's grandparents high into the air, wings flapping valiantly until they were mere shadows against the sun.

The dragons let go.

Moments later, bright twin flames lit the sky, burning like comets, as the dragons chased Anakisha and Yanir, flaming them until they were nothing but ash scattered over the fields.

DANCING

Drums pounded in Last Stop's village square as the melody of flutes and a gittern wound among the flickering torches, conversation, dancing, and laughter. Villagers had pulled tables and chairs into the square, and the dragons had created fire pits for spit-roasted pigs and goats. Fruit, fresh bread, cakes, and cheese adorned the tables, and in the corner was a steaming cauldron of fine sweet potato and lemon-grass soup.

Perched on the rooftops around the square and in the fields surrounding the village, dragons slept with their heads tucked under their wings.

Roberto sat on a bench in a corner with his arm wrapped tightly around Ezaara's waist. Gods, he'd nearly lost her so many times since he'd met her—now, he was never letting go. There'd been attempts on her life and her virtue; the time he'd had to leave her in Zens' hands to be tortured so he could save Adelina—by the First Egg, what a heart-wrenching moment that had been; poisoning; a knife attack; tharuk fights; shadow dragons; and Ashewar, who'd wanted to kill them both. And more.

She turned to him and mind-melded, *"Morbid thoughts?"*

"Just thinking how much I love you."

Her smile was tinged with sadness. It would be for a while. Ezaara had been close to her mother. That wound would take time to heal. He pressed his lips against her hair, inhaling the herbal fragrance of her hair soap. *"Just remember, although many have fallen in battle, we've won the war."*

His thoughts flitted to Tonio, the spymaster who'd died at Mage Gate. Taliesin had told him that Tonio had saved Marlies by taking an arrow for her. Even though the spymaster had borne a grudge against Roberto's father and hated Roberto, in an odd twist of fate, Tonio had bought Marlies enough time to save Ezaara's life. In battle, the actions of many were woven into a complex tapestry.

"I think we should celebrate. How about a dance?" Ezaara asked. *"They're expecting us to."*

"Someone's always going to expect us to do something."

"Well, I am the Queen's Rider."

"*And don't I know it.*" He could still see the terrified waif who'd trembled before the roaring dragons of the dragon council, moons ago, when she'd first arrived at Dragons' Hold. She'd faced down every one of them, despite her fear. And gone on to surprise everyone, time and time again, as she mastered the necessary skills to be the best Queen's Rider she could be. She still surprised him most days.

"Come on," Ezaara said, getting up and pulling him to his feet. "Let's dance."

And as Roberto took Ezaara in his arms, and held her close, he had to admit, it was a great idea.

§

"So, Mazyka's daughter?" Waggling his eyebrows suggestively, Fenni jabbed Jael in the ribs.

Next to Fenni, Gret grinned. "Go on, Jael, tell us all about her." She swung a blonde braid over her shoulder.

Although Jael's cheeks were heating, he ignored their jibes. The sooner he got this over with, the better. Serana would be back at any moment, and he didn't want her embarrassed by his friends' nosiness. "Her name's Serana," he said matter-of-factly. "She happened to heal my gut injury. I've flown on her dragon a few times, just like I fly with Kierion or Tomaaz. That's all there is to it."

Fenni winked. "Yes, we noticed that."

Jael frowned. "What?"

"You, on her dragon." Fenni's grin nearly split his face.

Gret arched an eyebrow, going in for the kill. "We also noticed you were sitting rather close. Closer than most dragon riders and mages sit when they're flying together." She leaned back and snuggled into Fenni, as if to demonstrate how close two people could actually get.

Was it that obvious? Jael snorted, feeling his blush deepen. Thank the First Egg it was dark. Maybe he should slip off and encourage Serana to take him for a flight now. Anything to get away from Fenni and Gret's embarrassing questions.

Oh gods, Serana was making her way over now, two glasses of apple juice in her hands. He couldn't take his eyes off her—the way she moved in those strange clothes from her world, her red hair ablaze with color as it glinted in the firelight. That magical smile. Oh, he was a goner.

Serana approached the table, and Jael took the glasses from her. "Would you like to dance?" he asked.

The smile that lit her face was brighter than any bonfire. "I never thought you'd ask."

He placed his arm around her waist, and glanced over his shoulder at Fenni and Gret, calling, "If you think that was close, then watch this." He led Serana over to the dancers.

"What was that about?" she asked.

He shrugged.

"Go on."

So Jael took a gamble. "They're teasing me for sitting too close when I ride with you on your dragon. It's just idle gossip."

"Is it?" She grinned, eyes blazing. "Let's give them something else to gossip about."

The bonfire crackled, and the drumbeats pulsed through them as Jael took Serana's hand and whirled her among the throng of dancers.

§

Fenni turned to Gret, gesturing at Jael and Serana, who were whirling through the crowd with huge grins on their faces. "That looks like fun. Want to try?"

Gret took his hand, her braid glistening like honey in the torchlight as she led him over to the dancers. She ducked her head shyly. "Do you realize that we haven't danced since Roberto and Ezaara's hand-fasting ceremony?"

Fenni's eyebrows shot up. "We haven't?" He took her warm hands in his. "That's a terrible mistake. We'd better make up for that, tonight."

They swayed and moved in time to the music, getting faster as the crescendo built, and as Gret whirled and spun, her face radiant with joy, Fenni vowed he'd dance with her every day.

Kierion swept past, Adelina in his arms, and winked.

Fenni had to grin. Adelina was so short, she only came up to Kierion's chest. What was Kierion up to now?

His friend lifted Adelina right off the ground as he spun her.

Gret sighed and leaned her head against Fenni's shoulder, making his bones melt.

"You know," she said, "sometimes I wish I was short and petite, like Adelina."

"Really?" Fenni gaped. "Why?"

"I don't know, just because..."

"But you're beautiful the way you are." He slipped his arms around her and let a little mage power trickle through his hands, just enough to keep her warm.

"You're tall and fit and strong, and a great swordswoman, and I'd like to dance with you all night."

"Really?" Her eyes shone.

"Mmm hmm." He nodded. "Every night."

The smile that Gret gave him lit up the night sky.

§

Tomaaz held his arm up as Lovina whirled underneath, then he pulled her close, murmuring in her ear, "So what do you think of your new cousin?"

Lovina smiled, her blue eyes alight with wonder. "I'm just happy to have family again. Happy we freed the slaves. Happy to have you."

Tomaaz grinned. "I feel exactly the same." He twirled her around again.

And again.

And again.

Until Lovina was laughing, her head thrown back and her face radiant with happiness.

§

After all these years, she was in his arms again. A tendril of mage power sizzled from Mazyka's palms through Giddi's shoulder. He laughed. Gods, it was good to have his wife back. "So," he said, "did you dance in that other world?"

"Not once," Mazyka said. "There was no one I wanted to dance with." She grinned and flung her hands above her head. Blue mage flame surged from her fingers, exploding into a shower of blossoms.

Giddi tossed out sparks that turned into green birds, flapping above the heads of the dancers.

Dancing nearby, young Master Jael and Fenni joined in. Fenni's mage lights zipped above the crowd like tiny green fireflies. Jael conjured up green dragonets that flitted between the rooftops.

Mazyka nudged Giddi. "What do you think of those two?" She tilted her head toward Jael, who was dancing with their daughter Serana—a daughter Giddi hadn't even known about until two days ago.

Giddi grinned and pulled Mazyka closer. "I hope they hold each other tightly," he said. "And never let go."

"So do I." Mazyka's dark eyes roamed his face, lit by dancing flames of the bonfire, and Giddi knew they weren't talking about Jael and Serana at all.

§

Giant John waved a haunch of goat toward the dancers, who were silhouetted by the roaring bonfire. "So, what will you do now, Hans?"

Hans shrugged and watched the young ones dance, the way he had danced many times with Marlies when they were young. It was like having an anvil on his chest, this grief—missing her. Her laugh, the quick flick of her turquoise eyes, the sparkle in them whenever she saw him, the warmth of her touch. He'd known this was coming, sooner or later, had been trying to stave off the truth— that she was dying and had been since the piaua berries she'd taken in Death Valley. It was ironic that those berries had been grown in Lush Valley, their home for eighteen years of relative peace. Eighteen years of hiding who they really were. Eighteen years of preparing Ezaara and Tomaaz for the roles they'd just played in saving the realm.

He watched Roberto lead Ezaara from the dance floor to a table in the corner, where Ithsar, the quiet but remarkable orange-robed assassin, was sitting.

Hans knew Ezaara had been down in that clearing with Giddi. He'd sensed her, masked by an invisibility cloak, lending her mental strength and *sathir* to Giddi to open the world gate. Without Ezaara, the whole realm would've been turned into a desolate wasteland.

And so he was glad Marlies had given her life for his daughter. That Ezaara could now dance with Roberto and lead their people in peace.

But it didn't stop the pain. The hurting. The anger at losing his wife.

Or the numbness that sometimes stole over him, deadening everything inside him, so he didn't have to feel anymore.

He considered Giant John's question. What would he do now, without her? "I'm not sure, John, but I'd like it to be something that honors Marlies."

Giant John cocked his head, his goat haunch raised in the air as if he was about to club someone with it, not take a bite. "Did you know that when Taliesin and Leah brought piaua juice back from the brown guards in the North, they also brought seedlings? Hundreds of tiny piaua seedlings."

Hans raised his brows. He hadn't known that. Hadn't really taken much in at all since his wife's death. When Marlies had been injured, the two young ones had gone north in search of the life-giving juice for her. As Master Healer, she'd relied on the juice to heal their wounded riders and dragons. Someone would have to tend to those seedlings, grow and nurture them. "Now that might be worth thinking about," Hans said.

"I think it would," said Giant John, finally taking a bite.

§

Katrine was sitting at a table at the edge of the square, watching Hana and a handsome blue guard dancing.

Kisha made her way past the dancers to Katrine's table. "How are you doing?" she asked.

Katrine shrugged, dabbing at her eyes with a kerchief. "I miss Kadran."

She gestured at Hana and her dance partner. Their gazes were locked upon each other, and their movements were not in time to the music, but to an inner rhythm that no one else could hear. Hana tipped back her head and smiled, then rested her cheek on the blue guard's chest. He stroked her hair and whispered something that made her laugh.

"At least they're happy," Katrine said, dabbing her eyes again.

Kisha squeezed Katrine's hand. "What will you do now?"

"I don't know," Katrine replied. She smiled. "But I'll find something."

Kisha hesitated. Heart pounding, she asked, "How would you like to run the Lost King inn?"

You'll know when the time is right.

Katrine stared at her, gaping. A few heartbeats later, she asked, "What will you do?"

Kisha tilted her head, gazing around the square at the happy, battle-worn faces. "I'm not sure," she said, "but I think it's time for an adventure."

§

After dancing with each of her new family members, her skin nearly exploding with joy, Kisha slipped away from the revelry, down the alley to the courtyard at the back of the Lost King inn. Kishanna was curled up on some hay in a corner outside the stables.

"You're ready for your first flight, now, aren't you?" Her dragon's golden eyes were lit with an inner fire.

Kisha gazed into those beautiful, warm golden eyes. "Yes, I am," she said.

She hadn't thought it was possible for a dragon to raise an eye ridge, but somehow it looked as if Kishanna was doing exactly that. Kisha laughed and flung her arms around her dragon's neck. Kishanna tucked her head over Kisha's shoulder, snuffing warm breath over her. She crooked a hind leg, and Kisha clambered up the smooth scales and rippling muscle onto Kishanna's back. She slid into Nila's old saddle.

"You know, for a long time, I believed that everyone I loved would die. Nila was the last in a long line of people I cared about. Even Kadran, who only helped me for a few hours, was killed. Before that, my parents, my friends..."

"And now?" the dragon rumbled.

"Now, I'm surrounded by people I love or can grow to love."

"Good," Kishanna answered. A wave of love so sweet that Kisha could taste it, washed over her. "Are you ready?"

"I am."

Kishanna tensed her haunches and leaped above the stables and the court-yard, circling over the square. Below, Kisha's family and friends were dancing, the bonfire's flames casting a glow over their wheeling cavorting figures.

The faint rhythm of drumbeats and the high trill of a flute accompanied Kisha and Kishanna as they flew over the village, and out over the fields beyond. Moonlight glinted off Kishanna's scales, making them shimmer with jade, emerald, and silver. Kisha unbound her braid and shook her head, the wind tugging its icy fingers through her hair. But Kisha didn't care about the chilly wind. Inside she was warm and glowing, the fire of new adventure in her veins.

§

Ithsar leaned back in her chair and stretched as the music and heat from the bonfire swirled around her. The *sathir* of the people wended its way among the dancers in a bright tapestry, rich with color. The mages were playful tonight. Tiny birds made of green mage flame zipped between the dancers, chased by green dragonets, and blue blossoms shot above the crowd, with fireflies darting among them. Ithsar hadn't ever seen anything like it.

A voice broke through her thoughts. Someone was mind-melding with her and it wasn't Saritha. "*Ithsar, you did a valiant job.*" It was a rich, deep voice steeped with wisdom.

She cast about, but couldn't tell who was speaking in her head. "*Who are you?*"

"*Look a little further.*"

Her eyes roved across the dancers. Master Giddi, the dragon mage, was watching her, his keen eyes steadfastly upon her as he swayed with his daughter Serana in his arms.

Well, that was a surprise. "*They said you could mind-meld at will, but I wasn't expecting this.*"

He smiled as he danced. *"You did admirably. Although I was trapped with Zens' thrall, I saw the wings of green guards and sea dragons that you brought with you. They turned the tide of the battle. Without you, we would've lost long before I opened the world gate and let Mazyka through. I thank you and honor you."*

His praise was unexpected. A shock. *"I bring you greetings from Queen Aquaria."*

His eyes crinkled as he smiled over Serana's shoulder. *"Give her my greetings too, when you next see her."*

"I'm sorry, she was murdered by an unruly, hateful assassin." Ithsar shared her memory of Izoldia's treachery.

"That saddens me. I met her years ago when she was a dragonet."

"She said you saved her life. She was still grateful."

"As people will be to you, for many years to come."

Serana spoke to the dragon mage and he broke mind-meld, sending a plume of mage flame butterflies into the air to dance around Ithsar.

Next to Ithsar, Roberto's arm around her shoulders, Ezaara grinned. "Let me guess, Master Giddi?"

Ithsar shrugged. "It seems he's happy I came to help."

"As we all are. So, what are your plans?" Roberto asked. "Now that Ashewar is gone, and your women have imprinted, will the sea dragons go with you to live at the oasis? I mean, it's not as if you can live underwater."

Goren put down his ale and cleared his throat. "I've been thinking about that," he said.

Ithsar nearly fell off her chair. "You have?"

He nodded sagely. "The Scarlet Hand and his pirate crews have been raging upon the Naobian Sea for years. We could use your help in keeping the seas a safe place for ships."

Ezaara raised her eyebrows. "That's well worth thinking about." She nudged Roberto. "Tell Ithsar about the time you fought the Scarlet Hand."

Roberto ran a hand through his dark hair. "It wasn't the Scarlet Hand himself, just one of his pirate ships—nonetheless, just as fierce. They attacked us when we were sneaking into Death Valley." He shook his head at Goren. "That's no mean feat you're asking of her, but I'm sure Ithsar and the Robandi assassins are up to the task."

"I'm not sure what we'll do," Ithsar replied. "I'll have to talk to my sisters." She watched the whirling orange robes of her assassins as they danced to the wild, bucking music—a different dance than the dance of the ancient *Sathiri*, but one that suited them just as well. Misha was graceful, her robes swirling around her as she danced with a green guard, her eyes alight.

Stefan appeared, cheeks pink and chest heaving. He bowed and held a hand to Ithsar. "My most revered Chief Prophetess, would you care to dance?"

Ithsar smiled and took his hand. "I would like that, thank you."

Stefan whirled her across the cobbles amongst the throng of joyous, dancing people.

"One moment, I have something to give you." Ithsar pulled him aside and took the wrapped smashed chocolate out of her pocket. She passed it to him.

Stefan opened the wrapping and popped the chocolate in his mouth. He stuffed the cloth back in his pocket and bowed. "And I have something for you." He tugged a cloth, decorated with orange and gold butterflies, out of his jerkin. "For my new best friend."

Ithsar stared at him. "For me?" She opened the cloth to reveal a dragon-shaped chocolate. "Oh, it's too pretty. I couldn't possibly eat it."

"I think you should. It's orange-flavored." He gestured at her robes, then the bonfire. "Besides, if you don't, it'll melt."

Ithsar broke the chocolate in half and grinned. "For my new best friend."

Stefan chuckled and ate his half.

The sweet chocolate and tart orange made Ithsar's taste buds explode.

Stefan grabbed her hand and tugged her into the throng.

The drumbeats throbbed through her feet, her bones, her heart. The flute made her veins sing with magic. Stefan laughed, pulled her close and flung her out to whirl with the dancers. *Sathir* swirled around them, rich and vibrant and full of life. And Ithsar knew the future was bright, and that she and her Robandi assassins would soon be dancing to a different tune. Their own tune.

Riders of Fire

Complete Series Available Now

Ezaara—Book 1

Dragon Hero—Book 2

Dragon Rift—Book 3

Dragon Strike—Book 4

Dragon War—Book 5

Sea Dragon—Book 6

Riders of Fire
Dragon Masters

Coming Soon

Anakisha's Dragon—Book 1

Dragon Mage—Book 2

Dragon Spy —Book 3

Dragon Healer—Book 4

Prequel

Ruby Dragon

To find out how Tonio, the spymaster who saved
Marlies' life, met Antonika, his dragon, read
Ruby Dragon, a Riders of Fire short prequel.

Herbal Lore in Dragons' Realm

Arnica—Small yellow flower with hairy leaves. Reduces pain, swelling and inflammation. The flower and root are used in Marlies' healing salve.

Bear's bane—Pungent oniony numbing salve with bear leek as the primary ingredient.

Bergamot—Citrus fruit with a refreshing scent.

Clean herb—Tangy, pale green leaves with antibacterial properties.

Clear-mind—Orange berries, used to combat numlock. Stronger when dried, but effective when fresh.

Dragon's bane—Clear poison that, when it enters the blood, makes wounds bleed excessively, and then slowly shuts down circulation and breathing.

Dragon's breath—A rare mountain flower that, when shaken, produces a soft glow.

Dragon scale—A gray powder that when swallowed gives the appearance of being numlocked, i.e. gray eyes and fingernails.

Freshweed—A weed that is chewed to mask the user's scent.

Healing salve—A healing paste that contains arnica, piaua juice, peppermint, and clean herb, and promotes healing.

Jasmine—Highly-scented white tubular flowers. Promotes relaxation.

Koromiko—Thin green leaves that, when brewed as a tea, prevent belly gripe.

Lavender—Highly-scented lilac whorled flowers. Relaxant, refreshing.

Limplock—Green sticky paste with an acrid scent used to coat tharuk weapons. Acts on the victim's nervous system, causing slow paralysis, starting with peripheries and making its way to the vital organs.

Limplock remedy—Fine yellow granules that reverse the effect of limplock. Dose: one vial for an adult; three vials for a dragon.

Numlock—Thin gray leaves, ground into a tangy powder. Saps victim's will, determination and coherent thought. Used by Zens and tharuks to keep slaves in submission. Creates a gray sheen over the eyes and fingernails.

Owl-wort—Small leaves that enable sight in the dark.

Peppermint—Dark green leaves with aromatic scent.
Good for circulation, headaches and as a relaxant.

Piaua juice—Pale green juice from succulent piaua leaves.
Heals wounds and knits flesh back together in moments.

Rubaka—Crushed leaves produce a pale green powder
used as a remedy against dragon's bane.

Skarkrak—Bitter gray leaves. A Robandi poison. In mild doses causes sleepiness and vomiting; in strong doses, death.

Swayweed—Fine green tea. Reverses loyalties and allegiances.

Woozy weed—Leaves that causes sleepiness and forgetfulness.

About Eileen

Eileen Mueller is a multiple-award-winning author of heart-pounding fantasy novels that will keep you turning the page. Dive into her worlds, full of magic, love, adventure and dragons! Eileen lives in New Zealand, in a cave, with four dragonets and a shape shifter. She writes action-packed tales for young adults, children and everyone who loves adventure.

Visit her website at www.EileenMuellerAuthor.com for Eileen's FREE books and new releases or to become a Rider of Fire!

Please place a review

I absolutely love reviews! Hear the dragons roar and me squeal with enthusiasm when you post one. Readers are my lifeblood, so I'd love you to pop a line or two on Amazon or Goodreads. Thank you.

Printed in Great Britain
by Amazon